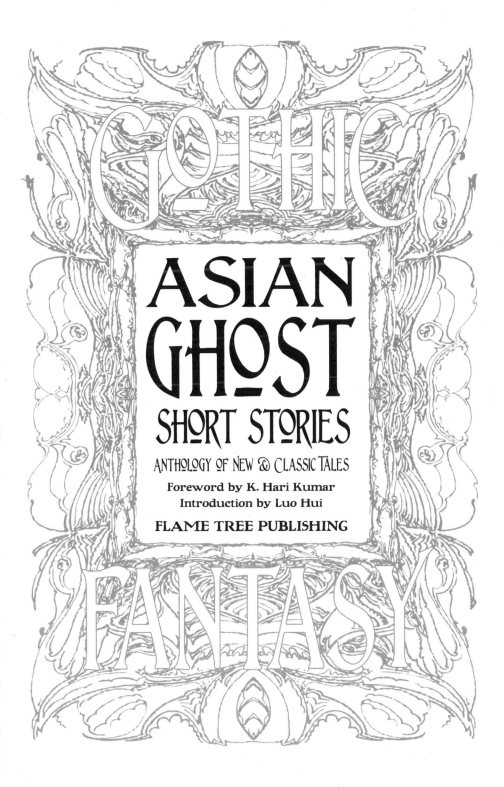

ASIAN GHOST

SHORT STORIES

ANTHOLOGY OF NEW & CLASSIC TALES

Foreword by K. Hari Kumar
Introduction by Luo Hui

FLAME TREE PUBLISHING

This is a FLAME TREE Book

Publisher & Creative Director: Nick Wells
Associate Editor: Lee Murray
Editorial Director: Catherine Taylor
Editorial Board: Catherine Taylor, Gillian Whitaker, Josie Karani and
Taylor Bentley. With special thanks to Tim Leng.

FLAME TREE PUBLISHING
6 Melbray Mews, Fulham,
London SW6 3NS, United Kingdom
www.flametreepublishing.com

First published 2022
Copyright © 2022 Flame Tree Publishing Ltd

24 26 25 23
3 5 7 9 10 8 6 4

ISBN: 978-1-83964-882-3
Special ISBN: 978-1-83964-997-4

The cover image is created by Flame Tree Studio
based on artwork courtesy of Shutterstock.com.

A copy of the CIP data for this book is available from the British Library.

Printed and bound in China

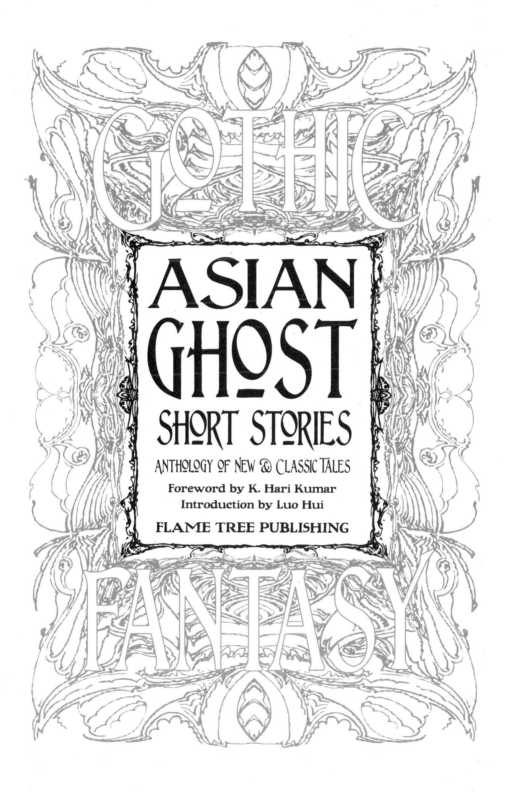

GOTHIC

ASIAN GHOST

SHORT STORIES

ANTHOLOGY OF NEW & CLASSIC TALES

Foreword by K. Hari Kumar
Introduction by Luo Hui

FLAME TREE PUBLISHING

FANTASY

Contents

CONTENTS

CONTENTS

Foreword: Asian Ghost Short Stories

WHO DOESN'T ENJOY a good ghost story, especially in moments of solitude in the rain, or with friends around a campfire? A tale about the supernatural and the macabre can be the perfect form of entertainment. I remember the first time I heard a horror story – it was a South Indian folktale about the *Mohini*, an enchantress who preyed upon unsuspecting men who ventured into the forest at ungodly hours. I was only eight when I heard the story from my grandmother, and that was enough to keep me out of uncharted territories at odd hours until I was in my early twenties. That is the effect and (in most cases) the purpose of such stories. Asia has a rich tradition of horror stories deeply rooted in its myriad folklores and vivid theological beliefs about death, evil and afterlife. Many of these stories have a moral or a life lesson associated with them that aim to stop people from following a hedonistic path in life (if I can put it that way).

Some of these stories vilify ancient 'native' deities, the downtrodden, and free-spirited women. For example, the *Yakshi* of Southern India, *Churel* of Pakistan, *Petni* of Bangladesh, *langsuir* of South East Asia, *Yokai* of Japan, *Nü gui* of China; they can all be generalized as vengeful, blood-sucking female creatures, shifting shapes and preying on men at night. In traditional horror stories, these grudge-bearing vampire-like creatures have emanated from the spirits of women who died in childbirth. It is interesting to note that some of these cultures had an evil tradition of rejecting female babies, which may have paved the way for such legends. 'The Picture of a Dying World', included in this volume, is a beautifully crafted example of how the atrocities faced by a certain section of society at the hands of the living becomes the subject of horror stories for another generation.

Unlike the Western world, which started documenting stories in the written form, in the East it was more common for stories to be shared orally. For centuries, in the absence of books, oral storytelling traditions like the *thekkenpattu*, *burrakatha*, *yakshagana*, *biwa hoshi*, and more, passed old horror stories down, sometimes filtering the more shocking elements for their audience. Eventually, Western writers like the British explorer Richard Burton (1821–90) introduced the *djinns* of Arabian Nights and *Vetaala* of Betaal Pachisi to the English-speaking world, and Lafcadio Hearn (1850–1904) fascinated people with his *Kwaidan*. I remember reading 'The Story of Mimi-nashi Hōichi no Hanashi' a few years back – the Japanese folktale about a blind *biwa hoshi* who has a tryst with the otherworldly. It didn't let me sleep for many nights. In this volume, you will find both Hearn's classic version of the tale and 'Kikinasai', which is an equally fascinating modern adaptation.

In recent times, Asian horror has garnered the spotlight at a global level when Hollywood adapted several popular Japanese movies. Thanks to a new crop of South Asian storytellers, the world has seen the threat posed by the *Kuntilanak*, but Asian horror as we know it still hasn't crossed over in its purest form. In fact, current Western and mainstream awareness is only of the tip of an iceberg that is continuously descending into an endless abyss. There is a lot more to Asian horror than the woman in white with hair falling over her face. It is so vast that even Asians might not be aware of the horror stories told throughout their neighbouring countries. Vast, yet connected at the root. Just like the woman in white, the *brahmarakshas* lore of India is strikingly similar to the Chinese *yi gui* ghosts. Although their corporeal forms may differ, essentially, both are the spirits of humans who committed sins out of lust or greed when they were alive, and have been condemned to suffer in hunger after death.

It goes without saying that a volume of this magnitude does a great service to Asian horror literature, because it will introduce some of the most fascinating horror stories and mythical creatures from this part of the world to the ever-expanding English-speaking universe. Some stories in this anthology will give you sleepless nights, while others will leave you pondering over the atrocities inflicted upon the 'weak'. This takes me back to my grandmother's story about the *Mohini* that preyed on 'unsuspecting' men in the woods because the questions that haunt my mind remain unanswered. *Why did those men venture there in the first place? More importantly … What was their intention?*

K. Hari Kumar

Publisher's Note

FROM ALL MANNER OF VENGEFUL GHOSTS to fox spirits and sparrow hauntings, this collection brings together classic stories and new submissions from across East, South and Southeast Asia. Old tales from authors such as Pu Songling, Rabindranath Tagore, S. Mukerji, Im Bang and Yi Ruk, Lafcadio Hearn and Yei Theodora Ozaki form an influential body of ghostly lore which – notwithstanding the translation and filtering to varying degrees by Western writers and folklorists of the colonial era – represents supernatural concepts and heritage specific to this region.

To redress (to some extent) any cultural misrepresentation occasioned by earlier non-Asian authors and to champion today's Asian writing talent, we consciously sought out new submissions from writers of East, South or Southeast Asian heritage. And what a fabulous response we had, with everything from beautifully lyrical reinterpretations of medieval tales to relatable modern ghost stories weaving in contemporary concerns such as feminism, mental health, homosexuality, heritage and urbanization. The standard of the writing submitted to us has always been impressive and the final selection is always an incredibly hard decision, but ultimately we chose a collection of stories we hope complements the classic tales at the same time as offering the most variety, regionally and thematically.

In addition to the evocative foreword by K. Hari Kumar (a.k.a. 'Horror Kumar') that has just whetted your appetite, this anthology has been further enriched by two key contributors: Luo Hui's fascinating and informative introduction takes you through the historical and literary background and heritage of this genre, including examples of Asian ghosts from different countries, the influences and effects of colonialism, and the cultural legacy witnessed in film and the writing of today's Asian diaspora; while the input and guidance from Lee Murray, a stalwart author-editor and champion of the Asian-diaspora and horror writing community, has been invaluable in the selection of submissions and shaping of the book.

As always, the stories in this book are listed alphabetically in order of author surname (family name). Some readers may initially believe that we have got our alphabet mixed up, but we remind you that some Asian cultures (such as Chinese and Japanese) traditionally present the family name *first* (Pu Songling being one example). We have also left spellings as they are, according to the nationality and era of the author.

Introduction

Why Asian Ghost Stories?

IT IS WIDELY ACCEPTED in many Asian cultures that ghosts remain a part of the human world, whether we see them or not. The ghosts you will encounter in these pages have little to do with the Western image of the ghost, as a pale, passive, posthumous echo of the living. They can be beautiful or grotesque, benevolent or ghastly. They are, above all, fierce, possessing an irrepressible zest for life. They are nothing if not a force of nature.

In 1913, writing in a preface to his *Korean Folk Tales: Imps, Ghosts and Fairies,* James S. Gale (1863–1937) advised that to anyone who would like to look into "the inner soul of the Oriental," ghost stories "will serve as true interpreters." In the same year, George Soulié (1878–1955) echoed this view in his translation of Pu Songling's (1640–1715) *Strange Stories from the Lodge of Leisures* (*Liaozhai zhiyi*; also known as *Strange Stories from a Chinese Studio,* in Herbert A. Giles's translation). Soulié further argued that, in spite of the dominance of the Confucian classics in the Chinese tradition, it is the popular tales about ghosts and spirits that "illustrate in a striking way the idea the Chinese have formed of the other world." We might like to replace 'the Oriental' with the less loaded term 'Asian', but the sentiment that there is something unique and important about the way ghosts are represented in Asian cultures still holds ground.

The first translators of Asian folk tales and ghost stories, like the early European scholars who pioneered the study of 'the Far East', saw this vast body of oral and written literature as a repository of knowledge about the great religious traditions of Asia – Daoism, Buddhism and Confucianism – indigenous beliefs and practices that were markedly different from Christianity. It is not entirely misguided to look for traces of religious influence in these tales. The Buddhist notions of karma, retribution and the cycles of life, the Daoist regard for all sentient beings, and the Confucian rituals of ancestor worship have all left their imprint on the ghost stories in this book.

Yet, it is important to remember that ghosts are the very antithesis of gods, sages and immortals. They emerged from the margins of institutional religion, showing its limitations, blind spots and moral failings. Arthur Wolf, a historian of Chinese religion, has aptly defined ghosts as "other people's ancestors" ('Gods, Ghosts, and Ancestors', 1974). This definition partly explains why many ghosts in the Chinese literary tradition are women who died young or prior to giving birth to a child, thus leaving them unmoored, without status in the kinship system, and without an offspring to care for them in the afterlife. The grief and grievance of the female ghost thus strikes a stark contrast with the Confucian emphasis on patriarchal lineage and ancestor worship.

Ghost stories are not textbook demonstrations of the great teachings of Asian religions. They are best read as a veiled critique, a gentle satire, or a necessary digression from what is considered orthodox. It is this rebellious streak that gave free rein to the ghostly imaginations of ancient Asia. Asian ghost stories defy social and genre conventions. They are spooky, and continue to inspire Asian horror. They can be unapologetically romantic, providing living proof of love beyond life and death. They can be bawdy or erotic. Although some of that eroticism was filtered out in the hands of translators catering to readers in Victorian England, much of it came back with a vengeance in Hong Kong B movies.

In these tales, we get a refreshing sense of fluidity regarding gender and sexuality. We encounter constant disruption of many humanly assumed boundaries, whether biological, social or moral. At the core of this flux and flow of species, identities and habitats, we recognize an ancient and persistent questioning of the place of the human in the world, an abiding skepticism about the Anthropocene, that still resonates in the twenty-first century.

Understanding Asian Ghosts

The Bengali word for ghost, *bhoot*, signifies a broad collection of varied, independent entities from headless ghosts to child-hunters, from flying vampires to *barabhoot*, a ghost that specializes in drowning people. In Bengali, *bhoot* also means 'past'.

In the Chinese imagination, the ghost encompasses a spectrum of spiritual manifestations including ghosts, foxes and fairies, as well as various human, animal and plant spirits. The Chinese character for ghost – *gui* 鬼 – is also a component in various other Chinese characters with spiritual connotations, such as *chi* 魑 *mei* 魅 *wang* 魍 *liang* 魎 (demons, monsters, spectres, goblins) – in other words, ghosts of all kinds. The same character component appears in *hun* 魂 (the heavenly soul) and *po* 魄 (the earthly soul). The Chinese word for ghost also has a homonym, which means 'return'.

The ghost therefore always returns, unexpectedly, from a once-buried past. In Asian ghost stories, ghosts are not merely ideas, or literary devices – they are corporeal, sensual, visceral, and they are best treated not as spectres, but real characters. They are not just a figment of the human imagination – many of them once were, and some of them still want to be, human.

Zhiguai, Chuanqi, and the Chinese Tradition

In contrast with many cultures where ghost stories long remained a part of the oral tradition, Chinese ghost tales were written down early on, first appearing in a genre known as 'records of the strange' (*zhiguai*) in about the fourth century. These terse, unadorned records of strange phenomena, heard, imagined or observed, were recognized as a form of unofficial historiography. Some saw the proliferation of *zhiguai*, and the attendant ghost discourse, as an anxiety-driven response to the spread of Buddhism during a prolonged period of political division and social unrest in China. Whilst Buddhism has left indelible marks on Chinese ghost tales, it has had to contend with a plethora of indigenous Chinese beliefs. The process was never one of passive transmission and reception, but of active engagement and interaction.

The ghost tale eventually branched out to the more embellished and elaborate 'tales of the marvellous' (*chuanqi*) during the Tang Dynasty (AD 618–907). It was in the hands of the Tang poets and scholars that the ghost tale reached its height of complexity and sophistication. The motivations behind the Tang tales also shifted. Although *zhiguai* was still earnestly practised, the Tang literati took an increasingly light-hearted approach to recording the strange. They began to portray the physical beauty of the female ghosts in exquisite detail. The ghosts became not only amorous, but also capable of composing poetry and playing music. The male protagonists, often talented scholars who entered into sexual relationships with the ghosts, were thinly veiled projections of the authors themselves. Thus the ghost tale was transformed from quasi-historical record to literary fiction, and the practice of writing and collecting ghost tales changed from a serious religious discourse to an elegant literati pastime – or as some might call it, a male fantasy.

Zhiguai and *chuanqi* coexisted and continued to be practised alongside each other for centuries. Although there was tension and rivalry between the two, on both literary and ideological fronts, they jointly informed and enriched the subsequent development of the Chinese ghost tale. The two modes found their perfect balance as they intermingled in Pu Songling's *Strange Stories*. Gathering nearly five hundred tales over the course of several decades from the late seventeenth to early eighteenth century, Pu Songling drew from oral traditions (folktales, stories, hearsay), written sources (old books, records, tales), as well as personal experiences (eyewitnesses, dreams, memories). His writing encompasses a broad array of genres and styles, including the short but evocative *zhiguai* and the fanciful *chuanqi*. His themes and subject matter range from ghosts, foxes, and strange flora and fauna of all sorts, to insightful, incisive depictions of human character and social realities.

Pu Songling – Historian of the Strange

No compilation of Chinese ghost stories is complete without a selection from Pu Songling. Popularly known in Chinese as *Liaozhai*, the work has become synonymous with the alluring and yet vaguely ominous image of the female ghost. Although his longer *chuanqi*-style tales are more famous, Pu Songling remained closer in spirit to *zhiguai*. Pu was a self-styled 'Historian of the Strange', collecting and recording anomalies from the peripheries of official history. This position was perhaps reflective of his lifelong struggle as an unsuccessful candidate in the imperial examination system. Unlike other members of the literati who were secure in their scholar-official careers and only dabbled in ghost connoisseurship, Pu Songling was far more personally and emotionally invested in his writing, lending his tales a distinctive poignancy.

Both Franz Kafka and Jorge Luis Borges were Pu Songling fans. Borges distinguishes Pu Songling from Edgar Allan Poe and E.T.A. Hoffman, for "he does not marvel at the marvels he presents," and his satirical tone is closer to Jonathan Swift ('Prologues to *The Library of Babel*', 1985). The Czech scholar Jaroslav Průšek has emphasized Pu's affinity with the common people and the strong note of social criticism in his work, which are seen as an overture to modern literature (*Chinese History and Literature: Collection of Studies*, 1970).

Comparing Pu Songling with Robert Burton, the seventeenth-century English author of *The Anatomy of Melancholy*, John Minford and Tong Man summarize the stylistic affinities between Pu and Burton: the brevity of the narrative, dry, laconic prose, the pregnant use of allusion, the pseudo-historical persona, and the understated pathos of the conclusion ('Whose Strange Stories', 1999).

Korean Ghost Tales and Pan-Asian Connections

Many of these stylistic features that are quintessential to Pu Songling can just as aptly describe the selection of Korean ghost tales by Im Bang and Yi Ryuk. Im lived contemporaneously with Pu, and Yi predated him by two centuries, making any claim of direct lineage or influence untenable. What linked these writers who lived in different countries and eras is an earlier Chinese collection of ghost tales, Qu You's (1341–1427) *New Stories Told While Trimming the Wick (Jiandeng xinhua)*, first published in 1378. Although popular in its time, Qu You's book was eventually banned under the literary inquisition of the late Ming. But, in Korea, as in Japan and Vietnam, Qu's work circulated widely and became something of a 'cult classic' amongst the educated elite. In Korea, an adaptation of this work appeared as *Tales of the Golden Carp (Kumo shinwa)* in the fifteenth century. Thus a collection of Chinese ghost stories became the model for the first novel in classical Korean literature, written in Chinese as it was the custom then.

The cultures of China, Korea and Japan benefited from frequent sharing of literary texts, cultural attitudes and social institutions in the pre-modern period. Yi Ryuk lived in the reign of King Sejo (1455–68) during the Joseon Dynasty, matriculated in 1459, and graduated first in his class in 1464. He would have witnessed the popularity of Qu You's tales like many Korean scholar-officials of his time. Im Bang was born in 1640, the same year as Pu Songling. The difference was, whilst Pu Songling struggled as an obscure examination candidate and took refuge in the writing of his ghost stories, Im Bang enjoyed a highly successful official career, rising to the office of governor of Seoul and secretary of the Cabinet at the age of eighty. However, his life took a dramatic turn when he got swept up in a government power intrigue and died in exile a few years later – something worthy of a tale of the marvellous in its own right!

The fact that a ghost story collection can link up people as different, and as distant, as Qu You, Yi Ryuk, Im Bang and Pu Songling, suggests that, at least in East Asia, the ghost story had long departed from its folk origins and become firmly established as a literary tradition and an ongoing, cross-cultural enterprise. It is therefore not surprising that one of Qu You's stories, 'The Peony Lantern', was transformed into one of the most celebrated Japanese ghost tales, 'Botan Dōrō', and that when Qu You's original book was considered long lost in its native China, it was Japan that provided modern literary historians with the full, authoritative manuscript. And it is not surprising that J.S. Gale based his translation of Yi Ryuk's ghost stories on a reprint of old Korean writings by a Japanese publishing company in 1911. It also explains why Lafcadio Hearn, that indispensable and indefatigable purveyor of Japanese ghostlore, also produced a volume of Chinese ghost tales whilst living in Japan.

Kaidan: Ghosts for Entertainment

Beyond the circulation of classical Chinese sources amongst the elite, Chinese ghosts captured the Japanese imagination more widely during the Edo period (1603–1868), when adaptations of Chinese ghost stories formed an important part of the highly popular ghost genre of the time, known as *kwaidan* (or *kaidan* in modern Japanese). Japanese *kaidan* also began as a form of religious persuasion, based on older Buddhist stories of a didactic nature. However, as *kaidan* became popular through its association with parlour games, the insistence on moral lessons soon gave way to an appetite for stranger and scarier stories that edified as well as entertained.

It was during this period that classical Chinese sources such as Qu You's *Jiandeng xinhua* were reinterpreted and incorporated into the Japanese vernacular. According to Fumiko Jōo (PhD thesis, University of Chicago, 2011), Japanese monks of the early Edo period were still diligently annotating Qu You's ghost tales to convey Buddhist messages. But, by the eighteenth century, 'The Peony Lantern' had already gone through multiple Japanese rewritings, including one by Arakida Reijo, a woman writer who adapted the story with her feminine sensibility.

There are also multiple English renditions of 'The Peony Lantern'. The one that is included in the present volume, entitled 'A Passional Karma', is by Lafcadio Hearn. Another version, retaining the original Chinese title and previously published in *Japanese Myths & Tales* (also from Flame Tree Press), is by F. Hadland Davis. But, according to Davis, his version closely followed the one by Hearn.

Hearn and the Reinvention of Kaidan

Lafcadio Hearn (1850–1904; known as Koizumi Yakumo in Japanese) played an instrumental role in the popularization, and perhaps the modern reinvention, of Japanese *kaidan*. A writer of Greek-Irish origin who spent his early career working for American newspapers, Hearn moved to Japan in 1890, married a Japanese woman and stayed there until his death in 1904. With the help of his wife, who acted as his informant, Hearn collected Japanese ghost stories from traditional sources and rendered them in English, amply embellishing them. He adapted over fifty stories, which are gathered in six collections: *In Ghostly Japan* (1899), *Shadowings* (1900), *A Japanese Miscellany* (1901), *Kottō* (1902), *Kwaidan* (1904) and *The Romance of the Milky Way* (1905).

Not only did Hearn bring Japanese *kaidan* into English, his work of collecting, retelling and thus preserving traditional Japanese ghost stories also deeply influenced the ghost culture of modern Japan. All of Hearn's works were translated into Japanese only a few years after their first publication in English. The collection *Kwaidan* for example, published in English in 1904, appeared in a Japanese 'back-translation' by Takahama Chyōkō in 1910. To Japanese readers, Hearn managed to capture, and augment, that elusive flavour and tone of the Japanese originals. Many stories within the old Japanese collections regained popularity only through Hearn's retelling, and his renditions are considered the golden standard in Japan even today.

India and the Buddhist Effect

Perhaps more than China, India may be considered the true fountainhead of Asian ghostlore. The spread of Buddhism from India to other parts of Asia since the dawn of the first millennium has helped invigorate local and regional religious discourses. The transmission of Mahāyāna Buddhism brought a new moral and spiritual outlook to bear upon the indigenous cultures and belief systems across East Asia. The efforts to comprehend, reconcile and accommodate the multitude of gods, deities, demons and ghosts from different belief systems also led to a shared sense of spirituality that is largely non-sectarian, one that might be best captured in the phrase 'the ghostly'.

This pan-Asian awareness of all things ghostly is already evident in the twelfth-century Japanese compendium, *Anthology of Tales from the Past* (*Konjaku Monogatarishu*). Containing more than a thousand tales organized in three sections – India, China and Japan – the anthology follows the trajectory of the dissemination of Buddhist teachings from country to country whilst picking up local legends, folk tales and ghost stories along the way.

Back in India, Buddhism also has had to contend with both indigenous and foreign influences for dominance in spiritual life. Many Indian ghosts and ghostly beings are of Buddhist, Hindu or Muslim origin. We will sample some of these colourful ghost characters from Lal Behari Dey's (1824–92) *Folk-Tales of Bengal*, published in 1883. A Christian minister turned professor, Dey collected in his native Bengali and wrote in English. But, unlike his British contemporaries who imported ghosts from the Orient, Dey translated from his own culture and exported. It is ironic that Dey, a converted Christian who penned *The Falsity of the Hindu Religion* in his youth, turned to cultural exchange in a totally different direction, perhaps mellower and wiser later in life.

The comic potential of ghosts is most palpably realized in Bengali folk tales. In Dey's stories, ghosts are often friendly, benevolent, with an impish sense of humour. In one story, a man leaves his home to earn his fortune, only to return and find that a ghost has taken his place! In another tale, a poor man tricks a ghost into making him wealthy – a delightful twist on the trope of ghosts playing havoc on humans.

As ghost tales made their way across different social strata, a certain anxiety can be detected in the educated elite who gathered the tales from folk or oral sources – the act of writing them down can seem an act of appropriation, or betrayal. Thus, we have Dey painstakingly recounting his frustrated attempts to source the most authentic tales from the last of the old village grandmothers who were the best ghost-story tellers. This is no different from the most probably apocryphal anecdote of Pu Songling setting up a tea stand in his village, offering a cup to whoever had a ghostly yarn to spin.

Tagore and the Spectre of Colonialism

At the other end of the popular-elite spectrum, we have Rabindranath Tagore (1861-1941), a towering figure in Bengali culture who was keenly interested in ghosts. Whilst Tagore's songs and poems offer philosophical musings on the afterlife, his fiction deals with the subject of the ghost head-on, with equal parts candour, sensitivity and psychological insight. These qualities are on vivid display in Tagore's 'The Skeleton' (*Konkal*), 'In the Dead Of Night' (*Nishithey*) and 'The Hungry Stones' (*Kshudhito Pashan*). Unlike many of the plot-driven tales, Tagore's ghost stories are not easy to pin down. They are strong in atmosphere and must be appreciated for their literary quality.

Tagore lived and wrote in the age of Empire, under the shadow of British colonialism. Colonial influences may have deposited some European elements in his ghost stories, but it is important to not see Tagore's writing as a passive channelling of British colonial tastes or fantasies. Ian Almond has interpreted 'The Hungry Stones', a phantom tale interrupted by an Englishman on a train, as "a recurring Romantic fantasy resurrected against a sterile Enlightenment modernity – the exoticism of past empires set against the banal contemporaneity of a present one" ('The Ghost Story in Mexican, Turkish and Bengali Fiction: Bhut, Fantasma, Hayalet', 2017). This allegorical reading suggests that the critical potential of ghost stories, rooted in the moral and spiritual lacunae of the past, is vast and remains to be fully explored.

South and Southeast Asian Traditions

Apart from a generous selection from the ghostlore of India, China and Japan, this book also provides a healthy balance of ghost tales from the lesser-known traditions in other parts of Asia. The tales from the Himalaya, Sri Lanka and Pakistan would have shared some of the same cultural sources as those of India, but they are included here for their distinctiveness rather than similarity. The Sri Lankan story features a *yaka*, a demonic spirit. Whilst *yaka* can be easily grouped together with *yaksha*, a broad class of nature-spirits in South and Southeast Asian folklore, the Sinhalese *yaka* is quite distinct and the *yaka* mask remains an important feature in Sri Lankan ritual dance and exorcism.

Exorcism also features in the story from Pakistan. Culturally and geographically, Pakistan sits at the gateway between the Buddhist and Islamic worlds. In the Pakistani story, the priest who exorcises the evil spirit is unmistakably Muslim – he presides over the ritual with an open Quran in one hand.

Mixed cultural influences are also a salient feature of the Philippines, which had for centuries stood at the crossroads between East and West. The Filipino stories in this book come to us from *The Filipino Popular Tales* by Dean S. Fansler, an early twentieth-century folklorist from Columbia University. Like Hearn, Fansler collected his tales through local informants and rendered them directly into English. Fansler defends his choice of English ("a foreign medium") and goes to great lengths to explain the method of his fieldwork and to ensure the genuineness of his tales. However, he readily accepts that the boundary between what is 'native' and what is 'derived' or 'imported' is blurry in the Filipino case, pointing to a long history of cultural imports and infiltrations – from the European, Indian and Arab worlds – on the Philippine archipelago.

Orientalism and the Colonial Gaze

One of the joys of reading ghost stories is to immerse ourselves in another time and space, and lose ourselves in another world, or indeed, an otherworld. Yet, we must not forget that these stories reach us through layers of mediation, in the hands of translators, writers, editors and publishers. Most of the classic material in this collection is drawn from the earlier translations of the late nineteenth to early twentieth century. The translators and raconteurs of Asian ghost stories of Victorian England had their biases and limitations, yet their works are the fruits of an important early cultural encounter between East and West. They may be at times deformed, with a bitter aftertaste, or do not keep well, but the obvious enjoyment and hidden lessons that can be derived from these tales begin a crucial process of mutual and self understanding.

Contemporary readers may detect a subtle, or sometimes not-so-subtle, Orientalism that colours some of these early offerings from the late Victorians: Herbert A. Giles, Richard Gordon Smith, Rudyard Kipling. Even a writer as sensitive and sympathetic as Hearn was ultimately constructing his own version of the Orient, with "evocative and occasionally indulgent landscaping of Japan" (Donald Richie, *Lafcadio Hearn's Japan*, 1997).

The inclusion of Kipling in a book of Asian ghost stories may raise a few eyebrows. Kipling writes from a place of privilege, his tone can be condescending, and his ghostly sensibility is vaguely gothic. On the surface, 'The Phantom Rickshaw' has all the appearance of an Edgar Allan Poe tale – the guilt-ridden narrator, the internal monologues bordering on madness, the sense of *it's-all-in-his-head-but-is-it?* Told from the perspective of an Englishman with all the colonial trappings, the story is, significantly, set in India. Even when ensconced in the 'British summer capital' of Simla in the forested ranges of the Himalayas, the facade of English rationalism begins to rupture in the heat of India. The colonial gaze is inverted and redirected on to the conqueror. In the sense that it depicts a once superior and secure position becoming disoriented and destablized through an encounter with 'the Other', Kipling's reckoning with ghostly India is no different in nature to the earlier Confucian encounter with Buddhism, or Japan's encounter with China, or Lal Behari Dey coming to terms with his native Bengal.

The tendency to exoticize is but one effect of the colonial gaze. Victorian prudishness has also meant that much of the sexual candour of the original tales has been lost in translation. Take, for example, Giles's rendition of Pu Songling's 'The Painted Skin' (*Huapi*), about the secret liaison between a scholar and a runaway girl. The original Chinese says, matter-of-factly: "Wang promised her, and went on to have sex with her. He then hid her in a secret chamber for days without telling anyone about it." Giles sanitizes this into: "Wang promised he would not divulge her secret, and so she remained there for some days without anyone knowing anything about it."

Giles's *Strange Stories from a Chinese Studio*, for all its occasional censoriousness, is still believed to have captured something of the unruly heart of Pu Songling. Whilst it is important to understand the cultural positions and preconceptions of our predecessors, it is equally important to be aware of our own biases and limitations. We must also bear in mind that, even in the original Asian contexts, a combination of fascination and unease had always been associated with the very notion of the ghost, and the writing and reading of ghost stories.

Ghosts in the Asian diaspora

That mixture of fascination and unease continues to galvanize new ghost writing from the Asian diaspora. In this book, the contemporary ghost stories are juxtaposed with the classic ones, revealing both threads of continuity and points of departure. The identity crisis of ghosts as 'other people's ancestors' has found particular resonance with the diasporic experience, although contemporary ghosts are born from their own crisis of physical and spiritual dislocation, in a relentlessly mobile and transient world.

The grief and grievance of the female ghost remains at the heart of this contemporary ghost writing, but with strong feminist underpinnings. If, in the traditional stories, the female ghosts emerged like a Freudian slip on the part of the male literati, the female ghosts in contemporary writing are given agency, purpose and pride of place in the narrative – a young woman is stitched to her grandmother's vengeful ghost; an abused daughter returns for her mother's funeral in a house haunted by ghost-victims; a woman sacrifices herself as a ghost bride so that her young niece will survive.

Traditional themes and motifs abound in these contemporary ghost tales. The hungry ghost, the drowned ghost, the *jiangshi*, the *gwishin*, and the fox spirit all return, though they may have come to haunt a Japanese-American household, an earthquake in San Francisco, or a remote shoreline in New Zealand. Some writers have taken on the time-honoured role of the ghost-story translator, reworking a Chinese *zhiguai*, a Japanese *kaidan*, or a Bengali folk tale, with varying degrees of fidelity and inventiveness.

We see an auto-ethnographical turn in these new stories. The earlier Anglophone writers and translators came upon Asian ghost stories as explorers, colonizers, diplomats or folklorists – they discovered ghosts as the Asian other. The current generation of Asian diaspora writers, living in borrowed space, and speaking in borrowed language, is no stranger to ghostly feelings and existences. They use the ghost story as memoir, love letter, autobiography, postcolonial history. They are saying: the ghosts are us.

Ghosts and Asian Horror Cinema

Asian ghost stories have always been intimately connected to popular culture, with their roots in folklore and oral literature, their adaptations into traditional theatre, and finally their modern manifestations on screen. Like many literary classics that have enjoyed a revival of interest amongst modern readers through film adaptations, Asian ghost stories' largest contemporary fanbase might be amongst the cinephiles. Unlike film adaptations of Shakespeare or Austen, which are often met with the smug cliché "the book is always better", Asian horror cinema is exuberantly irreverent towards its literary sources. So a badge of honour, for a Hong Kong ghost movie, might be: "It's so bad that it's good!"

Pu Songling's ghost stories have been adapted into strait-laced scholar-and-beauty romances, slapstick jumping cadaver films, techno-infused horror flicks, and soft porn. They have inspired Japanese manga and Taiwanese comics, and more broadly, the cinematic genre of 'Asian gothic' through a network of intra-Asian connections and influences. Laurence C. Bush provides a hefty entry on Pu Songling in *The Asian Horror Encyclopedia* (2001).

In Japan, the most famous ghost story adaptation may be Masaki Kobayashi's anthology film *Kwaidan* (1964), which won the Special Jury Prize at the 1965 Cannes Film Festival. A sort of adaptation of adaptations, the film is based on four of Lafcadio Hearn's stories: 'The Black hair' (*Kurokami*), adapted from 'The Reconciliation'; 'The Woman of the Snow' (*Yuki-Onna*); 'Hoichi the Earless' (*Mimi-nashi Hōichi no Hanashi*); and 'In a Cup of Tea' (*Chawan no Naka*). The curious reader may sample all four classic stories in this volume, plus an exquisite modern retelling of 'Hoichi the Earless' (Eliza Chan's 'Kikinasai'). And they may want to dig out Kobayashi's film, now almost a sixty-year vintage that has acquired its own ghostly patina.

Contemporary fans of Japanese horror may not have even heard of Hearn, or *Kwaidan*, but the visual connection between 'The Black Hair' and the ghostly image in the 1998 megahit *Ringu* (remade as *The Ring* by Hollywood in 2002) would not be lost on them. Those who are willing to dig further might see a link between the film's trope of a videotape that kills whoever watches it and Hearn's 'Furisodé', a story about a cursed kimono that kills anyone who wears it.

If Asian ghost stories contributed to the shaping of Asian cinema, the new medium of cinema also contributed to shaping the ghost figure in contemporary popular culture. There is something about ghosts that make them particularly suited to the film medium. Both ghost and film exist in a sort of twilight zone, between image and idea, visibility and invisibility, belief and disbelief. Both are ephemeral, yet both recurring.

The Asian Ghost Sensibility

Patrick Galloway, author of *Asia Shock* (2006), talks of a grounded quality in Asian horror – "these are ancient cultures that have seen it all"; yet at the same time, Galloway acknowledges the ghost's continued relevance in contemporary societies such as China, where "ghosts are still very much a going concern" (horrornews.net). What is it that makes the Asian ghost story both timeless and urgent?

Mikhail Bakhtin famously stated that "every genre has its own orientation in life" (*The Formal Method in Literary Scholarship*, 1985). The ghost story takes a certain human narcissism and turns it into an altruism towards the Other. The ghost, the ultimate Other, is initially a projection of human fear, but that catharsis of fear also marks the beginning of a difficult ghost-human relationship.

The history of the ghost story is also a history of taming. From the first act of collecting and writing it down to the practice of ghost connoisseurship, from the gender dominance of the male literati to the 'civilizing' effects of the colonial powers, the ghost figure has gone through a long process of domestication and control. Contemporary audiences, desensitized to graphic depictions of violence and death, may find even the scariest ancient tale now somewhat tame. But every now and then, there comes a new Asian ghost story, a new translation, retelling or film adaptation that reawakens in us that primordial sense of fear. And that is a good thing. To admit fear is to recognize the power of the ghost, and in overcoming fear, human beings can hope to reach a better understanding of ghosts and of themselves.

Dr. Luo Hui
Victoria University of Wellington

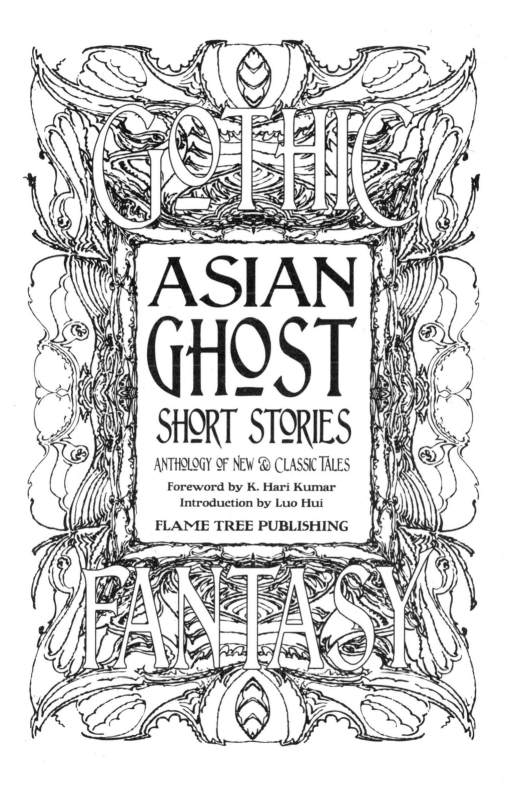

GOTHIC

ASIAN GHOST

SHORT STORIES

ANTHOLOGY OF NEW & CLASSIC TALES

Foreword by K. Hari Kumar
Introduction by Luo Hui

FLAME TREE PUBLISHING

FANTASY

Juramentado

Joshua Bartolome

ON NOVEMBER 14th, *1907, a platoon of soldiers led by Lieutenant John Brooder entered Cotabato's hinterlands. They never returned. Thirty-eight years later, during the Second World War, his journal was discovered after the liberation of Mindanao from the Japanese Imperial Forces.*

* * *

My Dearest Lisa,

This will be my final letter.

Our situation in Mindanao is dire, and I see no hope of coming home alive. We have been defeated. That, I cannot deny. But it was not for lack of skill or courage that my men were slain, and our forces scattered, overcome by an enemy that cannot be touched by steel or gunpowder.

I do not have much time. As best as possible, I will try to recount the circumstances that brought us to this juncture. On August 30, 1907, we received calls for aid from the soldiers stationed at our garrison along the benighted forests of Cotabato. They were under constant, nightly attack and had lost almost half of their troop strength. In a message addressed to Major General Leonard Wood, Lieutenant David Billings of the 6th Infantry Regiment wrote about nighttime chanting coming from the woods, accompanied by the wild beating of drums and other, less fathomable noises. These rituals, reminiscent of the Ghost Dances performed by the Lakota tribesmen, preceded vicious midnight assaults that whittled down the garrison's defenses.

The Major General ordered us to relieve Lieutenant Billings, who seemed on the verge of lunacy after half-a-year of guarding the Tampakan encampment. We were tasked to hold the position and quell any signs of rebellion among the populace. The platoon of soldiers under my command, totaling forty-five in strength, was composed of veterans from the Battle of Wounded Knee. Two capable commanders assisted me in this mission: Sergeant Caleb Mossworth and Sergeant Thomas Gillman. Each of us led three squads of fifteen men personally handpicked from a choice selection of specialists. Regardless of their backgrounds, my soldiers all had one thing in common:

They knew how to hunt Indians.

During our march to Tampakan, the annual monsoon made the unpaved dirt roads arduous to cross. We trudged through pathways caked with mud that had the consistency of quicksand. Our platoon would not have been able to navigate these treacherous trails teeming with snakes, leeches, and other hidden dangers if our companion, a Christian native named Pablo, did not guide us.

Upon arriving, we found the garrison in a severe state of disrepair. The soldiers looked as if they hadn't slept in weeks, their eyes glazed and anxious. Lieutenant Billings himself had the hollow stare of a man suffering from shell shock. Although he expressed relief at seeing fellow Americans, Billings was also more than eager to leave that accursed place.

In our debriefing, the Lieutenant described tales of lunatic singing that rose above the trees at night. Afterward, the natives would swarm out from the forest, armed with spears, bows, and arrows. Billings and his men managed to repel the savages time and again, but when morning came, they found no corpses, no signs of attack. The nightly raids continued for six months, causing mounting losses. Billings claimed that he saw silhouettes of giant, nameless things skulking in the forest, their eyes glowing red as rubies in the midnight gloom. I blamed these feverish testimonies on fatigue, hallucinations caused by restless nights, hunger, and disease.

After Billings and his remaining men left for the relative safety and comfort of Manila, we spent weeks waiting for word from the Major General. During this time, my thoughts were filled with memories of you, my Lisa. In moments of idleness, I would close my eyes and recall the first time we met in your father's ballroom, how you danced so gracefully with a jonquil tucked in your hair. Such fleeting visions kept me from losing my nerve, especially after sunset.

That was when the chanting started.

First came the drumbeats, a faint, percussive thumping that grew with intensity, soon joined by the shrill notes of reed pipes playing a discordant and utterly alien melody. To call this cacophony 'music' would be blasphemous, for it held nothing in common with symphonies of Bach or Mozart. Blessedly, however, no attacks transpired during or after this unsettling ritual. It seemed that the savages befouling the woodland with their grotesque ceremonies and heathen witchcraft only wanted to fluster our spirits and weaken our resolve.

* * *

"We have to act," Caleb Mossworth said as we sat around an open fire in the garrison's courtyard at midnight. Thomas Gillman nodded his assent while our guide, Pablo, remained unspeaking. A pot of boiling Batangueno coffee lifted our downcast spirits somewhat, but the unceasing howls and shrieks of joy coming from the forest kept our dispositions morose.

"What do you suggest?" I asked.

"It's only a matter of time before they attack. We can hold out for two or three days. But after that...." Thomas trailed off. I knew exactly what he implied. With our dwindling supplies, we would have to eventually hunt and forage for food in the woodland.

"So we strike now, take the initiative," Caleb replied.

"You know these lands better than us, Pablo," I said. "What say you?"

"I think we should call for reinforcements, Senor Brooder," Pablo replied.

"Why?"

"The tribesmen in those hills aren't like the ones in Bud Dajo. Blades cannot cut them. Bullets will not stop them. They charge into battle wielding curved swords, wearing nothing but curses tattooed on their skins. The Peninsulares called them the Juramentado. Oath-Keepers."

"You believe this horseshit, John?" Caleb asked, scoffing.

Pablo's eyes flared, but he held his tongue.

"Tell me more about them, these Oath-Keepers," I told Pablo, amused.

"The Juramentado have lived in these woods before Datu Sikatuna swore a blood oath with Miguel Lopez de Legaspi. They are an old, old people, their lineage stretching back to the witch cults of ancient and fabled Srivijaya. Legend has it that they pledged allegiance to a terrible god that dwells beneath Mount Matutum, selling their souls in exchange for immortality."

"What sort of god?" I asked. "Are they not Muslim?"

"Oh, no. Not at all," Pablo replied. "The Juramentado pray to a giant woman whose face is so horrifying, to look upon it would mean certain death. I cannot speak her name. She lives in a dark house under the earth with her thousands of children, whom she nurses with poisonous milk dripping from her leprous breasts. There, in the corpse-city of Gimokodan, they wait and breed until the time comes when the stars are right. Only then will they rise and reclaim what's theirs."

"Reclaim what, exactly?" Thomas asked.

"Why, this land, of course. And everything in it."

Caleb and Thomas began to laugh. Pablo, however, did not protest. He didn't even seem embarrassed by the mockery he received from my adjutants. Pablo merely stared at them.

"Pablo, this nation and its citizens are now under the United States of America's protection," I said calmly, without spite or ridicule. "I cannot allow such pagan barbarism to fester unchecked, or else it will inspire rebellion in the hearts of our little brown brothers."

Pablo looked away from us and toward the forest's direction, where the maddening cries and rapturous shrieks of the Juramentado continued unabated. "Very well, Senor Brooder," he replied. "But we had best move at daybreak. The forest can be murderous come nightfall."

At dawn, we set off southward in the direction of Mount Matutum. The sky had an ashen pallor, while pregnant clouds hung heavy above us, threatening to unleash a downpour of biting rain. As a precaution, we left ten soldiers to guard the garrison, with instructions to report back to the Major General if our mission went awry. Twenty riflemen and five cavalry riders marched with us, along with two carriages bearing armaments, ammunition, and other provisions. I did not expect us to spend more than three days afield, but we carried enough supplies to last a week.

Soon enough, the storm came, and with it, bitter winds seeped through the soaked fabric of our uniforms, chilling us to the bone. It felt as if the earth itself fought to stifle our pace as we trudged through the weald's loose and muddy soil. Nara trees festooned with ancient moss and fungi hemmed us from all sides. Shivering and exhausted, we pressed on.

Pablo claimed that the Juramentado dwelled in villages hidden in the forest, where ancient menhirs sculpted from solid basalt stood like silent sentinels. Despite our slow but consistent progress, we could find no trace of our quarry. When the storm abated, it was already five o'clock. With evening almost upon us, I commanded the men to stop and make camp.

Though resting in the middle of enemy territory made me uneasy, we had little choice. Our troop had traveled a considerable distance, and I couldn't in good conscience order the soldiers to march back in the dead of night. Although no one spoke, I could sense their apprehension as we constructed a makeshift encampment. To keep the perimeter secure, five men would keep watch for four hours each, to be relieved by newly-rested guards once their shifts had passed. God willing, I thought, the Juramentado wouldn't attack while we caught a much-needed respite.

Crackling, thunderous gunshots and frantic shouting roused me from an uneasy sleep. By the time I managed to catch my bearings, bedlam had erupted. The Juramentado emerged from the forest, swift as shadows, flitting in and out of sight. I tried to rally the troops, but a few savages would close the distance with alarming speed. Gouts of blood erupted as they drove sharp, rippled blades into the bodies of a few hapless soldiers, cutting and slicing flesh wherever they could.

Screaming, I ordered the others to gather around the supply carriages. While blocking out the agonized shrieking of the wounded and the dying, I shouted at the men to open fire and repay those impudent brutes with gunpowder and lead. The piercing retort of Winchester rifles restored a semblance of order among the disoriented soldiers. Slowly, gradually, we gathered in formation, emptying our rifles into the darkness. The smell of sulfur hung heavy in the midnight air. After a full minute of consistent firing, I raised my hand and ordered the others to cease. We stood our ground, guns at the ready, waiting for the enemy to spring forth and assail our ranks once more.

They didn't.

We lost several men that night. During the chaos, most of our horses had also been slain. Those tribesmen crippled our only means of transportation, leaving behind only one horse-drawn carriage to ferry our supplies. Without another spare bronco, we couldn't send a rider back to the garrison for aid. Thomas counted only four savages among the dead, a disheartening exchange.

At daylight, I said a short prayer for our dead.

We had no time to bury those men since we needed to clear the area by nightfall. Pablo proposed a tactical retreat, which I refused to consider. Thomas and Caleb agreed to go deeper into the forest and find the village of the Juramentado. We would show them no mercy, no quarter.

* * *

On the next day, some of our men developed a fever. At first, I believed it to be nothing more than the after-effects of our long march through the rain. But when I started feeling nauseous and light-headed, we had to take frequent stops to rest. Once more, we found ourselves unable to progress further at day's end. All of us felt unusually feeble. Some of our soldiers couldn't take a single step without throwing up. I had an inkling of what caused this sudden and inexplicable malaise: we had filled our canteens with water from a river during our march. Fearing that it might have been contaminated in some manner, I ordered the men to empty their flasks and told them never to drink from any stream. Instead, we would rely solely on rainfall to slake our thirst.

While we were at our most vulnerable, the Juramentado attacked. Though enfeebled, I gathered the soldiers and cobbled a defensive position, shielding the others who lay helpless. The savages came from nowhere, ambushing us with a ferocity that rivalled the warriors of Sitting Elk. It was impossible to keep track of their numbers by the bonfire's glow. They sniped at us with their bows from the trees. Occasionally, a half-naked warrior would leap from the undergrowth and rush toward our line. It took two full clips to bring one of these berserkers down. Time seemed to crawl as if the world had been submerged underwater. I could do nothing but rally the men into a tight circle as the Juramentado closed in, chanting oaths in their strange, sibilant tongue.

Then, bizarrely, the attacks stopped.

A ghastly howl reverberated through the trees, sending nesting birds fleeing from the branches. It did not sound like the cry of an earthly animal. We watched in stunned silence as the Juramentado slinked back into the brush like cowed dogs.

The battle was a lopsided slaughter. By morning light, we counted the dead. My troop lost eight men, bringing our strength down to fifteen soldiers, most of whom couldn't fight back. Our enemy, on the other hand, suffered only three casualties. Begrudgingly, I had to call a retreat. We were in no condition to press on. To do so would be disastrous.

I understood, too late, that we were fighting an enemy unlike any we had faced before. My worst fears were realized sometime later when we came across the carcass of a water buffalo lying on the banks of a river, bloated and infested with flies and maggots.

Those heathens had poisoned their own water supply to infect us with dysentery.

Delirious, we stumbled through unfamiliar, weed-choked paths. The topography had shifted through some devilry, and the landmarks once registered on our map no longer existed.

We found ourselves traveling down uncharted routes only to circle back to locations our scouts had explored. Tempers flared. Twice, Caleb intervened when a group of soldiers almost engaged in fisticuffs. As we staggered along, a faint whispering noise seemed to come from the undergrowth. One of the men cried out and said that he saw a face leering at him from the trees.

Night, darker than a crow's wings, descended upon the treetops, and with it came the fearful expectation that the Juramentado would ambush us again, this time to finish us all off. No matter how bone-weary we all felt, we did not rest. To stop for even one second would court death. The men themselves did not object. We all shared an unspoken sense of impending catastrophe, a fear of the encroaching darkness that drove us on despite our condition.

Something was coming. But what, we didn't know.

Until it finally found us.

* * *

Oh, God forgive me. We should never have entered the forest.

I smelled the thing, the creature, even before I saw it.

The beast stank of wet soil and manure, and the trees groaned as it pushed them aside. Chittering, it undulated toward us, a cloud of black flies swarming around its skull. The men screamed, but I remained frozen. Though crawling, it was easily ten or twelve feet tall, more sizable than a bear or any land animal that I had ever seen. Multiple limbs protruded out of the creature's pale, serpentine body, a monstrous centipede with human arms for legs. Segmented feelers extended from its eyeless face while a sickly green substance dripped from its curved mandibles.

I must have gone mad in that instant.

There was nothing I could do as the creature shrieked and then pounced on our vanguard. It picked up a soldier using one of its many hands and then slammed him repeatedly on the ground, sending bits of gristle and broken bone flying in every direction.

"Lieutenant!" A voice screamed. "John!"

Someone grabbed my shoulder.

It was Thomas.

"We have to move!"

Raising my rifle, I fired two shots at the beast. The creature merely flinched before tossing the battered corpse of its victim into a mob of soldiers, scattering them like a row of tenpins.

Afterward, I yelled at the men behind me to close ranks and form a line. Our training took over. In unison, we fired our weapons at the creature, hoping to slow down its rampage. Caleb and Thomas gathered the sick and the wounded and tried to usher them away safely. Five other riflemen and I provided covering fire, backing off inch by inch, unloading a hailstorm of lead.

"Fall back!" I cried out.

Bleeding from superficial wounds on its inhumanly thick hide, the beast slithered forward and slew two more men, snapping them like twigs. Then, the chimera reared itself up like a snake about to strike before unleashing a stream of putrid, rancid-smelling liquid from its mouth, spraying a soldier standing beside me. He didn't even have time to scream as the acid liquified his body almost instantly, turning the poor man's flesh and bones into smoking puddles of pinkish soup that lay steaming on the ground. Hissing, the creature charged at us again. I didn't have enough time to dodge. Fortunately, a rifleman shoved me aside, only for him to be caught directly in the nameless demon's mandibles. I heard the man howling as serrated jaws dug deep into his torso. The world became a blur of soil and sky, soil and sky, as I rolled downhill, stopping only after hitting the side of a protruding balete root. My midsection throbbed with white-hot agony.

Around me, men screamed and died, and I could do nothing.

The last thoughts that crossed my mind were of you, dearest Lisa. You stood at the doorway of our cottage, waiting for me. Then, I sank into the cold and the dark, and I kept on sinking.

* * *

When I awoke, it was already daybreak.

"Senor Brooder?" Pablo whispered. I couldn't see him clearly. My vision swam as I struggled to sit up. The pain in my ribs had lessened somewhat, although every breath felt like inhaling powdered glass. I leaned against a tree while Pablo tended to my wounds.

"You're lucky to be alive," he said. Pablo applied a greenish paste to the throbbing bruise on my left side. Although the ointment did not completely banish the ache, it provided a cool, soothing sensation that made my broken ribs slightly tolerable.

"Where are the others?"

"I don't know," Pablo replied. "I pulled you away as fast as I could, and we hid behind a fallen trunk. Thank God you didn't wake up. That thing, that demon, it – it was eating them."

My soul had already tasted enough horror. I should have wept. Should have broken down, sobbing, like a lost child. Instead, all I felt was a suffocating weariness and a desire to close my eyes and not think, not feel anything. "What was that creature?" I asked Pablo at length.

"It is the child of the mountain-woman," Pablo replied. "This is what happens when one of the Juramentado comes of age. They embark on a pilgrimage to the underground rivers of Gimokodan, where they feast on black rice and drink the poisonous milk of their ancient mother. Those who survive the horrible transformation become demons. Like that beast."

"There are more of those fiends?"

"Thousands."

"We have to send word back to the Major General," I said, wincing in pain. "If they ever crawl out of their holes, we won't be able to repel them. They would easily overwhelm us."

"Lieutenant," Pablo said, "they want nothing to do with you."

I stared at him, confused.

"If the mountain-woman wanted you dead, then your armies would have been destroyed the moment they stepped on Mindanao. She cares not for the affairs of mortal men, and neither do her children. One of them may traverse the surface from time-to-time to feel the warmth of the sun and the touch of rain, but always they return to Gimokodan. They only wish to be left alone."

"You knew what would happen if we entered the forest."

Pablo didn't reply.

"Why didn't you tell me?" I asked.

A smile, bereft of humour and laced with bitterness, crossed Pablo's face.

"You Americans were never good listeners. Especially to your little brown brothers."

Once Pablo was finished treating my injuries, he then tore his shirt sleeve and wrapped it around my midsection. "This land is theirs," he said. "It has always been. It always will be."

* * *

Dusk descended on our fourth night in the forest, and with it came fresh horrors.

The awful chanting that had haunted us ever since we arrived in Tampakan passed through the trees. Although Pablo and I skulked away from the source of the noise, it seemed as if the sound drew us even closer. Soon, we came across a curious sight: a circle of bonfires flickering wildly at the base of Mount Matutum. Cautiously, we approached. Using the undergrowth to conceal ourselves, Pablo and I arrived at the periphery of a clearing. The earth seemed to throb from the pounding of buffalo-skin drums joined by the high notes of reed flutes.

An old race, Pablo called them, proud, ancient, and cruel.

Thick plumes of smoke curled upward into the night like ghostly fingers, obscuring our vision but also hiding us from the revelers congregating in the grove. In the clearing stood a sizeable upright tablet hewn from solid basalt. By my estimation, this monolith towered at least fifty meters from the ground. Slowly, my eyes grew accustomed to the smoky air. Epigraphs that looked like ancient Sanskrit were chiseled on the monolith, along with figures of beings that looked damnably human but had the proportions and features of other indescribable entities.

It was, however, the central effigy that held my gaze. The figure had a woman's body, or what appeared to be a woman's form, with a distended belly and large, ponderous breasts that dangled above its waist. This, I thought, must be the mountain-woman, the great mother whom the Juramentado worshipped during their midnight revels. Long, flowing locks of hair covered the goddess's shoulders. Two bulbous eyes stared at the throng of twisted, dancing abominations cavorting at her feet, while her mouth grinned fiendishly, exposing rows of sharp, jagged fangs.

"Dios mio," Pablo whispered.

Along the basalt menhir's base gathered a throng of female natives, young and old. Each held an instrument, ranging from reed pipes to two-stringed bamboo lutes and leather drums. In the center of the congregation stood an old woman garbed in a red and yellow cloak with strange circular patterns. In her right hand, she brandished a dagger that had a serpentine, wave-like design.

With mounting horror, I realized what the crone intended to do. On a stone altar, lying motionless as if drugged, lay Caleb Mossworth, my second-in-command. They had stripped him naked, exposing his body to the mountain-woman's baleful gaze. Though frozen, Caleb's eyes remained open, glancing around wildly. The crone approached him with slow, deliberate steps, holding the knife in one hand while simultaneously chanting a hymn in an alien, fricative tongue. Upon seeing the old woman raise the dagger high above Caleb's stomach, I rose from my position, gun in hand, ready to strike. Pablo, however, grabbed my arm and pulled me backward.

"Senor, please," Pablo said. "Don't."

"They're gonna kill him."

"And they'll kill us too," Pablo replied, eyes wide, fearful. "I have a family. They're waiting for me. Don't you want to see yours again? Por favor. I just want to come home."

Pablo's words quelled the fury burning in my gut. I didn't have the right to put his life in danger any further, not when I had failed so miserably to keep the other men in my company safe.

"We have to go," Pablo tugged at my arm. At first, I hesitated. I couldn't just leave Caleb to suffer alone, so far from hearth and home, from his wife and children and all that he loved. Biting my lower lip hard enough to draw blood, I forced myself to look away.

As Pablo and I slinked off into the night, the triumphant chanting of the savage women rose to a feverish pitch. I prayed that they would grant Caleb an ounce of mercy and end his suffering quickly. This futile hope was dashed, however, when Caleb's sharp cries of agony flickered in the dark like embers drifting from a dying bonfire. He cried out for his wife. He cried out for his mother. He cried out for me. Ashamed, I kept on moving and never looked back.

* * *

I promised myself that I would never return to this accursed land seething with dark magic and nameless demons. Our ignorance and hubris had blinded us to the foul truth: kingdoms and principalities far older than our fledgling republic exist in the unexplored corners of the earth, ruled by sleeping gods whose mere presence poisons the land with malevolence and barbarity.

No sooner had we traversed a few meters away from the grove when the familiar stench of dung and autumnal rot assailed my senses. An uncanny howl rippled through the frigid midnight air, ear-piercing and inhuman, the war-cry of the monster that had torn my men into pieces and devoured them. The sound of trees and bushes being trampled spurred Pablo and me to scamper away like a pair of frightened stags. A resounding roar that seemed to rend the air, accompanied by the viscous slithering of an immense, unseen creature, bore down upon us. I dared not look back. I knew exactly what pursued us. To see the mountain-woman's offspring once more would have crushed the crumbling remnants of my sanity like brittle limestone.

Just when I thought that the rampaging beast would crush us both beneath its gargantuan mass, Pablo's yelp of pain made me glance backward for a brief second. Our most trustworthy guide – the man who saved my life as I lay unconscious and injured – had tripped on an upturned root. Crying in desperation, Pablo stretched out a hand and begged for help. I stopped and ran toward him, but it was too late. From out of the forest, the beast emerged, clicking and hissing in obscene and ravenous delight. It pounced on Pablo and sank its mandibles into his neck.

The sight became too much for my frayed mind to bear.

Screaming in delirious panic, I ran like a coward, no longer the proud soldier. I do not know how long I've been roaming these hills. The paths I've crossed have become twisted, unfamiliar, riddled with shadowy, uncanny forms that slither and hiss with malevolent delight. Occasionally, I can hear the wingbeat of some enormous, bat-like animal passing through the trees above, but I am too terrified to look up and see. I will not look. I dare not look.

I write these words now in case the Major General sends reinforcements to see what became of my platoon. Please, if anyone finds this, tell my wife that I love her and that I miss her, and that I am so dreadfully sorry. To Lisa, the light of my life, know that my last thoughts were of you, of our cottage on the prairie, and your hair that smells like freshly baked bread.

I must stop now. Footsteps. In the distance.

It's them. I can hear their singing.

Oh, God, oh, Lord of Mercy, I beg you.

Help me.

* * *

The loss of the Tampakan garrison dealt a heavy blow to the American settlement of Mindanao. In 1910, another force created by Brigadier General John 'Black Jack' Pershing tried to retake the lost territory, to no avail. During the advent of the Second World War, an expeditionary force commissioned by General Tomoyuki Yamashita searched for treasure in Cotabato's forests. Only one soldier survived, carrying the lost diary of Lieutenant Brooder.

In 1946, after the Japanese occupation ended, the Treaty of Manila was bilaterally signed by the United States Government and the Filipino Commonwealth. President Harry S. Truman then issued Proclamation 2695, recognizing the birth of an independent Philippine Republic.

The Pious Woman

Translated by Cecil Henry Bompas

THERE WAS ONCE a very pious woman and her special virtue was that she would not eat or drink on any day until she had first given alms to a beggar. One day no beggar came to her house, so by noon she got tired of waiting, and, tying in her cloth some parched rice, she went to the place where the women drew water. When she got there she saw a Jugi coming towards her, she greeted him and said that she had brought dried rice for him. He said that omens had bidden him come to her and that he came to grant her a boon: she might ask one favour and it would be given her. The woman said: "Grant me this boon – to know where our souls go after death, and to see at the time of death how they escape, whether through the nose or the mouth, and where they go to; and tell me when I shall die and where my soul will go to; this I ask and no more." Then the Jugi answered, "Your prayer is granted, but you must tell no one; if you do, the power will depart from you." So saying he took from his bag something like a feather and brushed her eyes with it and washed them with water. Then the woman's eyes were opened and she saw spirits – bongas, bhuts, dains, churins, and the souls of dead men; and the Jugi told her not to be afraid, but not to speak to them lest men should think her mad; then he took his leave, and she returned home.

Now in the village lived a poor man and his wife and they were much liked because they were industrious and obedient; shortly afterwards this poor man died and the pious woman saw men come with a palankin and take away the poor man's soul with great ceremony. She was pleased at the sight and thought that the souls of all men were taken away like this. But shortly afterwards her father-in-law died. He had been a rich man, but harsh, and while the family were mourning the pious woman saw four sipahis armed with iron-shod staves and of fierce countenance come to the house and two entered and took the father-in-law by the neck and thrust him forth; they bound him and beat him, they knocked him down and as he could not walk they dragged him away by his legs. The woman followed him to the end of the garden and when she saw him being dragged away, she screamed. When her husband's relatives saw her screaming and crying they were angry and said that she must have killed her father-in-law by witchcraft, for she did not sit by the corpse and cry but went to the end of the garden. So after the body had been burnt they held a council and questioned her and told her that they would hold her to be a witch, if she could not explain. So she told them of the power which the Jugi had conferred on her and of what she had seen, and they believed her and acquitted her of the charge of witchcraft; but from that time she lost her power and saw no more spirits.

Kikinasai

Eliza Chan

A FLY BANGED ERRATICALLY into the light bulb, looking for a way into that enticing honeydew elixir, unaware that it was nothing more than white hot filament. Its drone was the melody of a gypsy song, the percussion supplied by the instrument buzzing in the tattoo artist's hand.

The artist thrust a worn photocopy into his face. She pointed. "This one?"

Kazuya nodded, pulling his hat down over his eyes. He had not really looked. It didn't matter which one he chose. Dark roses and laughing skulls tacked to the walls blurred together. The tones of skin and ink swirled like an oil slick. He winced as the needle cut under the skin of his back. It had been nearly two years since his first tattoo. A tattoo he had not even wanted, but had needed.

* * *

The noise pounded through the walls of the tiny venue; clapping and stamping. The crowd was going to go home happy. Their crowds always did.

"Did you see the two in the front? I'd take either of them home," Taichi said.

Kazuya shook his head, caressing his guitar and adjusting one string until it sounded just right. "Don't give a shit about girls. Were any of the journalists we invited here? I gave guest passes to half a dozen bloggers as well."

Yosuke offered Kazuya the joint. "We can't rush these things, Kazu. It was a good gig. We nearly sold the place out."

"To teenagers who know nothing about music!" Kazuya argued, shaking his head to the weed.

Taichi had dropped out of the conversation, crooning the opening chords to their encore song, a background track to the discussion.

"It pays the bills." Yosuke shrugged. "Maybe think about lowering those expectations a bit."

"Fuck off," Kazuya said, "*I'm* going to be someone. We all are."

Yosuke smiled and took a drag from the joint. Kazuya looked down at his guitar, picking his frustrations out in the encore's chords, matching Taichi's melody. Something ran through his head like a forgotten promise, pressing at his attention until he acknowledged it. There, *there*; he caught it. If he changed the key on that chord it sounded like something familiar, an old song his father had taught him on the biwa perhaps. He strummed it on his guitar and it was changing, his fingers altering the melody into something else. It flew from his hands without conscious thought, mutating in the space between his nails and the steel strings.

"Kazu, time!" Taichi yelled him back into reality as they stood to go. Kazuya nodded but still his hands were at his guitar, finger-picking the haunting melody. He didn't want to stop. It was like muscle memory of a tune he knew, its name just catching in his throat. If he kept playing, he would remember it. But now the band would force him back on stage to go through the motions, play the worn covers that would predictably get a bigger reaction than their own material, and the tune would be gone. He'd be the same nobody he'd always been. Mediocre as he had always feared. Kazuya looked up, knowing he had to refuse and yet not knowing what words could suffice.

He used his foot to kick open the door that was closing in their wake.

"Guys, I—" Kazuya stopped. An empty white corridor greeted him. Silence. The smell of cigarettes and sweat had gone. And where were the cables, the precarious boxes of toilet rolls and mop bucket that reeked of stale beer, the staff rotas stuffed in dog-eared plastic wallets, the crowd, the people, the band? The corridor wasn't just silent, it was still. A reverential art gallery air. He realized that his fingers were still strumming, but they made no noise; not even the unplugged metallic twang.

He sensed movement and saw that a figure had appeared in the corridor, although he was certain no door had opened. In the white jōe robes of a Shinto priest, it moved like a sheet of paper drifting in the wake of a gust, slip-sliding until it was almost upon him.

"Master musician, Kazuya Hoichi! We've heard of your skills! Your talent. We want to hear you play." The voice possessed neither gender nor accent. Its words, Kazuya noted, were ancient Japanese, stiff-backed as the cherry wood baton the figure pointed at him.

Kazuya looked at his hands and saw he no longer held his guitar, but a stunning carved shamisen with tiger claw tuning pegs. His fingers held a fat fan-shaped plectrum carved like a diving fish with ivory teeth. The figure turned and walked quickly, so fast that it was soon a speck far along the white hall and Kazuya had neither the time nor voice to call out.

He followed on, feeling the firm ground beneath each step but losing the sense of where the walls met ceiling and floor. The robed figure bobbed at the limit of his vision. Or was that just a twitch of his eye? Kazuya couldn't tell. He blinked and he couldn't see. He dare not reach out to touch the corridor walls for fear that the contact would make him lose that song that now played beneath his skin; silent to his ears but within his fingers and inside his head, a rhythm more than a melody, a series of erratic numbers and movements. He walked on, blind. Bodiless voices, blaring, screeching, droning like musical instruments, spoke to him from all around, blowing air around his ears and brushing past his face like an itch, buffeting him playfully with their sounds.

Play, play, wonderful music, rare and precious, the voices whispered, pushing at his hands with their cajoling words, caressing his ego and clamouring round him until he stopped walking. The shamisen, so silent up until now, started mid-refrain. Music flamed unbidden from his fingers and changed. The muscles in his arms tightened. Sound flew from taut strings. He felt the strain across his range and his fingertips grew inflamed and then numb as the music swept through him.

Chords poured out of him instinctively, as effortless as drawing breath. The song was forceful, waves of sound spilling from the strings. Two countermelodies twisted together in a duel. One engulfed the other, gaining tempo and reaching a crescendo as it twisted bodily around its opponent.

The song crashed to a close like waves battering their heads against a rocky shore. The last note reverberated and there wasn't even an exhale as the adrenaline drained rapidly from Kazuya's body. He was devastated. Slowly, he crumpled to the floor, his eyes squeezed as he sought the comfort of darkness.

"I knew," he said. "I always knew I had the talent."

"Beautiful music," a voice said with sincerity. "Our ancient arts live through masters such as you. Play for us. Stay and entertain us for a week. Everywhere you go, music will follow. You will receive the acclaim you have always coveted. And then, your reward."

"Yes," Kazuya said, his voice soaring as his eyes flashed open, "I want it." I *deserve it*, his mind whispered. He let the unspoken words sink in.

"Then tomorrow, we will meet again tomorrow…"

Kazuya clutched the shamisen until his knuckles shook. He had the drive, the ability. His mind filled with the rich possibilities. The light drained from the corridor as he contemplated, turning the world to dusk and then on to night.

* * *

A pinprick of colour reached Kazuya's eyes as if from the end of a telescope. It grew suddenly, a riot of shades spilling over him; sound and smells, too, overpowering his senses. Then, flashes of movement and hundreds of faces were screaming at him. Awareness came back with the sound of the bass and drums, the people in the front row and the lights blinding him.

Someone was jamming out an insane guitar solo. Intense finger-picking staccatoed with body-slapping rolls and taps. It wasn't the band's normal style but it was sending feedback through the sound system and the crowd into a frenzy. Kazuya looked down. It was him. His hands were making those delirious sounds. His fingers were like claws at the strings and the rest of the band were struggling to keep up. Yosuke had just stopped playing and stared.

With an abrupt off-key slide, Kazuya's hands slipped off the guitar strings and fell limp to his sides. It didn't matter. The crowd were in a dazed state and the drummer had the sense to wrap it up nicely in a flourish of cymbals and rolls.

Kazuya's hands ached like he'd been clenching his fists for years. He examined his fingers; the calluses, hardened since he was a teenager, were bleeding. The music rang through the noise. No, the music was the noise: the applause, the shouts and whistles, Taichi's under-the-breath swearing, the buzz of the amp behind him and the erratic dripping of sweat down the back of his neck. It was his. All his.

That night, the music flowed through him even as he slept. Tossed between the buffers of melody and rhythm, he woke to find his toes twitching out the beat and his voice crooning softly to itself. He grabbed handfuls of sheet music and let his pencil fall over them, salting the pages with notes and then lines, guitar chords and vocal melodies.

* * *

They came for him that night, and every night after. He opened his bedroom door and found the same white corridor, the same robed figure beckoning him. The questions he had prepared dissipated into the blinding silence. He played again, played songs he had never even learnt. He played the koto zither, the biwa lute and even drew a bow across the kokyu. He played to fill in the gaps when he was not speaking or eating because the hunger would never be sated. Only once did he dare pause, to ask if he could play the guitar for them instead. But the voices hissed in the harmony of sho pipes. Nothing new.

It was like being possessed, he thought as he headed for the Shibuya subway. It started to rain and all he could hear were those rain drops falling on car roofs, a thousand tempered taps on a taiko drum. A woman shook her closed umbrella free of rain and the scattered water trickled through bamboo flutes in a forest.

On the subway the hiss of the doors opening made his hand roll and slap against his leg. He clicked his tongue in time as he sat down next to a sleeping salary man.

"Is that him?" he heard someone whisper in excitement. A group of high school kids peered over a phone screen then looked up at Kazuya. The one with the phone grinned, brandishing his screen in Kazuya's direction. "It is you, isn't it?"

Kazuya had seen the first video clip from the gig already. It had half a million hits when he last checked. He had not seen this clip though. It was him alright, the day before at a ramen stand with Taichi, making percussion sounds on his beer glass and rim of the noodle bowl as they argued about their set list. As he watched, the viewing number increased by another one.

"Yes, that's me."

His neighbour was startled awake as everyone reached for their phones in bags and pockets, sending a rustle of anticipation down the length of the carriage. Kazuya laughed as he cracked his fingers and stood up. His audience awaited.

* * *

Near the end of the week, he was in the coffee shop where they had already nicknamed him Drummer Boy. They had taken a selfie with him to put on the wall, and his drinks were constantly being paid for by other customers. The waitress brought him an empty glass and plate with his coffee and loitered by the table with a grin on her face. Kazuya grabbed chopsticks from the container on the table and played a percussion sequence on the crockery, alternating beats with the table top and the back of a metal chair. The beat slid him to the counter top, the improvised drumsticks travelling down its long edge and onto to leather sofas at the end. He played on the tray of change, making the coins dance. He tapped on the teapot and sent the forks rattling towards each other. Drum-rolling on a plastic tray, Kazuya rang the service bell as he spun and let the chopsticks fall to the floor in a flourish. Someone was already uploading the video on the internet. Which reminded him, he hadn't had time to respond to the emails for interviews yet. Or return Yosuke's call about record labels. A young woman sitting with her boyfriend, caught his eye and blushed. Kazuya held her gaze and stood up a bit taller. This was it. The cover songs, the shitty day jobs, the lacklustre applause and crowds that talked through their sets. They would stand up and listen now. Others clapped as he swaggered back to his booth, grin broad across his face.

"You, are very loud."

Kazuya winced at the grating edge of the voice. There was someone sat at his table. One tattooed hand circled Kazuya's coffee cup, the other hand, the whole left arm, was missing entirely. A baseball cap and beard obscured the stranger's face. "Makes it really easy to find you." Kazuya sucked in air through his teeth, the discordant music emanating from the stranger like sweat, pulsing feedback off a loudspeaker. He looked around but the other people seemed oblivious.

"Sorry, do I know you?" Kazuya said.

"No. But tell me, do you know *Heike Monogatari*?"

"Children know what *monogatari* means: a story, a tale. What the heck is the *Heike* and why should I care?"

"It's classic literature! You know it, you've been chanting it under your breath the whole time I've been watching you." The man's voice cracked and slipped off-key.

Heike Monogatari was the song, the unknown song he had performed for *them*, Kazuya realized. He knew the story. A tale of warring clans that had traditionally been recited by travelling monks. The balance. The proud fell and the humble rose. "What do you want?"

The stranger took off his cap and Kazuya found himself slipping from the seat in fright. The cacophony grew with his alarm. "I always get that reaction," the other man said with a wry smile. "You've played for them, haven't you? You have the look of a blind man enjoying the music of a truck horn as it careers towards him. They liked my drumming, so they took my arm as a souvenir." He waved his stumped left arm across his chest. "But you! Your smug sense of self-worth is loud and brash. They can hear you a mile off. You can't hold onto what you have forever. Everything is in decay."

Kazuya couldn't take his eyes off the man's skin. Every inch of exposed skin was inked. Tattooed. Faces winked at him from the stranger's cheeks. And the beautiful melodies which had followed him around jarred in broken strings and mistimed beats. Kazuya could not bear it any longer. He pressed his fingers against his ears.

"I, need to go…" Kazuya said as he edged towards the door.

"You need to hide. A fool wants everything now and pays for it all in one sharp fall of the katana. I learnt the hard way. Before I hid they took my arm. So I ran. And never stopped running. Until five days ago, when it all stopped. They stopped haunting me because they found you."

* * *

The tattoo artist passed him a hand-mirror so thick in fingerprints that it had acquired an opaque quality. Kazuya shook his head and pushed it away as he had done the day before. He never looked.

The music still ran through him. But he ran ahead of it. It always came back, assailing Kazuya and begging to be heard. Weakness made him give in. Scratch out the song on a busker's guitar or write down chords on the back of receipts before the itch consumed all of his concentration. At other times it simply simmered. Low level elevator music or someone else's headphones on the train. But always it came back.

He would get to a new town, seek out a tattoo parlour and pay, beg or lie to get this strange manuscript, his camouflage, painted one square at a time across the canvas of his skin. He had started on his chest and radiated outwards in ripples towards his neck and down his limbs by the end of his first year. Then, like a carefully wrapped parcel, it started to envelope him, tattooing around his sides and back inwards so that the last space of clear skin was at the centre. His back. This was the final piece.

The tattoo artist was clearing up her accessories. The fan whirled behind them, sending the posters of tattoos fluttering briefly in its wake. It was quiet. Kazuya slipped his hand into his jeans' pocket and felt the smooth surface of the one-way train ticket he had bought the day before. That would take him to the next town in two days time. Reverently he pushed it further down into his pocket.

"There's a live night over at Zepp tonight," the woman said, leaning back in her chair to tear a flyer from the corkboard behind. She handed it to Kazuya as he tucked his ears carefully beneath his beanie hat. "Up and coming bands. Reckon it's your scene."

Scanning the line-up, Kazuya was struck by the name of the third band. He remembered his old band with fond nostalgia. He could still strum their familiar set list. But none of it poured music into his ears. None of it sent him on a percussion trip across the room. The music simmered quietly in whispered breaths.

For the first time in almost two years, Kazuya smiled.

* * *

At the door, the guy collecting money did a double-take. Kazuya was used to it. Used to the stares, the nervous laughter and slowly retreating feet. Most people took at least a minute before they even thought to feign indifference. But it wasn't just the tattoos this time. Kazuya found himself man-handled from his place slouching against the wall near the bar. Taiko drums rumbled gently as he was marched backstage and thrown into a back room. The music died and before he could see the occupants, someone had spat in his face. Kazuya blinked through the wet phlegm. Taichi was glaring at him.

"Well look who returns! If it isn't Jack White himself!"

Taichi's hair had grown in the last two years. Age had sketched lines over his face but he still wore the same glam rock leather jacket. Just a little more worn now, as they all were.

"Shit man, did you get mixed up with the yakuza?" Yosuke asked, throwing Kazuya a hand towel to wipe down his face.

Kazuya took a moment before he answered, noticing the other two in the room, new band members who looked bewildered. "Something like that."

"Well it had better be something like that, Kazu," Taichi said, "for fuck's sake we were in talks with a record label on the back of that night! And then, you bastard, you just walked out!"

"You seem to be doing alright," Kazuya commented.

"This is not alright! We've been playing in tiny bars against high school bands who only know four chords. The Tokyo Budokan! That's where we should be right now. That's where we were headed!"

Yosuke moved between them, his hands held out placatingly. Taichi groaned and sat down, a scowl lingering on his brow. He pulled out a cigarette.

"Kazu, just, tell us what happened? Nerves? We all get it. But an email, a message you know, would've been nice." Yosuke said. He patted Kazuya on this shoulder awkwardly. The noise reminded Kazuya of the wooden naruko clappers that dancers raised in the air during festival performances. Kazuya pushed it back, zipping the music beneath his jacket. It quietened.

"It, it wasn't safe. I need protection," he said. Fans. Colourful fans waved across his vision, twisting to the rhythm of the drumming. Kazuya rubbed his eyes and the colours faded. The sound subsided to a dull headache.

"How does this shit protect you? Can't believe my cousin even recognized you under all this crap," Taichi said, grabbing his hand and turning it over and over like he was looking for a secret door. Kazuya rolled down the sleeves of his shirt rather than answering.

"QR codes," the new drummer said, "like the ones you can scan on your mobile phone to get to a website."

"A website?"

"You don't know what a website is, Tai?" Kazuya said.

"Fuck off, I know what a website is."

"Hey, it works!" Yosuke mused, his phone aligned with a QR code on Kazuya's neck. "Japanese Medical Association Journal?"

"This one is the BBC website," the drummer commented. In mutual agreement they all had their phones out now, checking the exposed squares of Kazuya's skin.

"The National Geographic"

"The Human Genome Project."

"University of Tokyo … what are you, a university research project?"

"It's, hard to explain," Kazuya said quietly. The smiling tattoos of celebrities and politicians all across the man's face and neck still gave Kazuya nightmares to this day. But he heeded the warning. He had to. It wasn't merely his words, it was the noise that wafted from the one-armed stranger: the antithesis of harmony. At the first tattoo parlour, Kazuya had grabbed his phone, looking for something that was modern, something they would dislike. He had blanked. His mind so filled with musicality that everything else was being pushed to the very edges. Finally he had tapped the phone itself, told the man to tattoo it across his chest, for want of inspiration. The music had engulfed him, leaving him senseless to anything until the tattoo artist had shaken his shoulder and pointed down. A 2D barcode the size of a CD cover centred on Kazuya's sternum. The image had been on his phone's screen, a link to a news article his sister had sent him. It had evolved from there.

Yosuke yanked the knitted hat from Kazuya's head. "You idiot, you missed out your ears," he said, flicking Kazuya's right lobe with a finger.

Kazuya ducked and batted his friend's hand away. Grabbing the hat back, he pulled it firmly over his head. "I didn't forget, no-one is getting near my fucking ears with a needle! My life wouldn't be worth shit without my hearing."

"But you let them ink your dick? Then you are a fucking idiot!" Yosuke said.

"Piss off," Kazuya said.

"So where've you been then? The last couple of years?" Taichi cut in.

"I couldn't stay anywhere for a week. I just had to keep moving," Kazuya said.

"And now?" Taichi asked. He had lost his anger, always as quick to forget as he was to get pissed off.

"Now things have changed," Kazuya said, rubbing the dressing on his back. "I can... well I can do anything."

"*We* can do anything," Yosuke said. He looked at Taichi who nodded. "We'll do the circuits, get our name back out there, make a demo, send it out. Busk in Yayogi Park if we need to".

"Screw that," Taichi said, "Kazuya here was an internet sensation. All we need is to upload a couple of new videos and the record labels will be phoning us. We deserve a break!"

Yosuke, Taichi, even the other two were looking at him expectantly. Kazuya listened. The music remained tranquil. Kazuya nodded, slowly.

Yosuke handed him a glass and poured out a large measure of whiskey. The golden liquid trickled and flowed, swirling around the glass's surfaces and swaying from side to side as Kazuya looked. It was him that was moving, not the glass. His hand was shaking. The squares of black that covered his skin blurred together in a dark mass.

"Kazu?" Yosuke asked. The band had all raised their drinks. They were waiting.

Kazuya forced himself to be still. He listened. It was still quiet. So what if he felt sick tomorrow, he could sleep in, take his time. He was safe, cloaked from them. The possibilities unfurled before him: rejoin the band, make a new one, sell the scribbles he had written over the past two years, get what he deserved. He felt cheek muscles tighten and a smile breaking across his mouth.

"To new beginnings," he said.

* * *

Taichi's floor smelt like weed and stale beer. Opening his eyes, Kazuya found his head next to a pile of mildewed music magazines and half a bottle of shochu. He didn't dare sit up, knowing the inevitable headache was looming. Music played in another room and he could hear the bass line rattling low and unobtrusive. It was a warm towel pressed against the throbbing of his temples. He had been catching up with Taichi and Yosuke for days now. And catching up mostly meant drinking.

Kazuya used the toilet and went to wash his face, startled to see his own reflection. For once, he forced himself to look. It was as if a child had drawn across his face with black markers, rendering his features indistinct. The code was a chequerboard of squares within squares. His eyes stared back at him, wide and bloodshot.

Reverently he peeled off his shirt and twisted to see his back. The tattoo still looked shiny, the skin an angry red around the pixelated squares. Peering over his shoulder his eyes roved the mirror, looking for gaps. It was seamless. The joins from tattoo to tattoo were unperceivable. A patchwork quilt made by over a hundred artists.

His mobile vibrated from his back pocket and he answered the call, still staring into the mirror.

"Yeah?"

"Even Taichi showed up on time. You were supposed to be here twenty minutes ago," Yosuke said.

"Chill, I just woke up. You can't rush talent."

"We've been waiting for two years already."

"Then thirty more minutes won't hurt."

"For pity's sake, just get here already," Yosuke said, his voice tense with annoyance, "I can't keep stalling. And put on a clean shirt or something. They are going to freak out as it is with your face. Throw us out as yakuza."

"Not when they hear me play."

"Well you have to be here for that," Yosuke said as he hung up the phone.

Kazuya smiled at his reflection, put his shirt back on, looking for his hat before he headed out. He thought about taking a shower, breezing in an hour late and blowing those industry snobs off their feet. But he pitied Yosuke. The bass player needed a break and Kazuya was feeling generous enough to share his.

The music, barely registering on his conscience up until now, had grown louder. Like a glitching track on a loop, the same few bars played over and over. It was a peculiar song, ethereal and full of choral voices singing dazzling upward spirals against a lackadaisical beat. Kazuya didn't recognize it. Probably a local DJ. He walked back through to the main room and saw a stereo-shape under half empty bottles of green tea. The black box was retro, the buttons markings completely worn off. But it wasn't on. It wasn't even plugged in. Through in Taichi's bedroom there was a mixing deck, currently an expensive clothes horse, hooked up to a laptop. It was on standby.

He opened the window, letting the cool air sweep around him and listened, straining his ears to identify the source of the music. It wasn't out on street level. His bare feet padding on the tatami mat flooring like additional bass beats to the crescendo of sound.

The music grew louder still, waves emanating, ripples so loud they were almost visible as they poured over him. It was coming from the front door. Kazuya walked towards it, fumbling for the spare key hanging on the same hook as a dog-earred calendar. He didn't have to look. It had been a week and he had not run.

Kazuya threw open the front door and the music stopped. Voices muted. The silence was so sudden that he found himself clutching onto the door handle for support. The robed figure walked in slow measured steps of certainty down the corridor. Kazuya didn't dare breathe. He stood as still as his panicking mind would let him.

"Hoichi! Kazuya Hoichi!" the voice rumbled.

He didn't reply. Kazuya shut his eyes so tight that they began to twitch. He covered his ears with his hands, trying to block out the voices.

"How terrible, the great musician Hoichi has gone. Gone and left only his ears behind? We gave him the gift and he must pay for it."

Kazuya's eyes snapped open. The robed figure reached. Ice sank through Kazuya's hands, through his hat, to pinch at both ear lobes.

"He will receive his reward," the voice said. The flat tone of the clipped words gave him warning. But not enough.

The hands ripped and twisted with equal force. Kazuya felt his ears being pulled, stretched around tightening tuning pegs. With an audible tear, the strings broke. Pain speared through his skull. His eyes closed again, trying to deny the pain, contain the scream that ripped through him and demanded to be voiced. He would not let them rip out his tongue also. The liquid warmth of his own blood trickled down his neck and dripped from his forearms, a steady rhythm at odds with the pulse at his temples. But he couldn't hear it.

It was just noise.

Kyuzaemon's Ghostly Visitor

*Adapted by F. Hadland Davis from a story
collected by Richard Gordon Smith*

KYUZAEMON, A POOR FARMER, had closed the shutters of his humble dwelling and retired to rest. Shortly before midnight he was awakened by loud tapping. Going to the door, he exclaimed: "Who are you? What do you want?"

The strange visitor made no attempt to answer these questions, but persistently begged for food and shelter. The cautious Kyuzaemon refused to allow the visitor to enter, and, having seen that his dwelling was secure, he was about to retire to bed again, when he saw standing beside him a woman in white flowing garments, her hair falling over her shoulders.

"Where did you leave your *geta*?" demanded the frightened farmer.

The white woman informed him that she was the visitor who had tapped upon his door. "I need no *geta*," she said, "for I have no feet! I fly over the snow-capped trees, and should have proceeded to the next village, but the wind was blowing strongly against me, and I desired to rest awhile."

The farmer expressed his fear of spirits, whereupon the woman inquired if her host had a *butsudan* (a family altar). Finding that he had, she bade him open the *butsudan* and light a lamp. When this was done the woman prayed before the ancestral tablets, not forgetting to add a prayer for the still much-agitated Kyuzaemon.

Having paid her respects at the *butsudan*, she informed the farmer that her name was Oyasu, and that she had lived with her parents and her husband, Isaburo. When she died her husband left her parents, and it was her intention to try to persuade him to go back again and support the old people.

Kyuzaemon began to understand as he murmured to himself: "Oyasu perished in the snow, and this is her spirit I see before me." However, in spite of this recollection he still felt much afraid. He sought the family altar with trembling footsteps, repeating over and over again: "Namu Amida Butsu!" ("Hail, Omnipotent Buddha!")

At last the farmer went to bed and fell asleep. Once he woke up to hear the white creature murmur farewell; but before he could make answer she had disappeared.

The following day Kyuzaemon went to the next village, and called upon Isaburo, whom he now found living with his father-in-law again. Isaburo informed him that he had received numerous visits from the spirit of his wife in the guise of Yuki-Onna. After carefully considering the matter Kyuzaemon found that this Lady of the Snow had appeared before Isaburo almost immediately after she had paid him such a mysterious visit. On that occasion Isaburo had promised to fulfil her wish, and neither he nor Kyuzaemon were again troubled with her who travels in the sky when the snow is falling fast.

The Ghost-Brahman

Lal Behari Dey

ONCE ON A TIME there lived a poor Brahman, who not being a *Kulin*, found it the hardest thing in the world to get married. He went to rich people and begged of them to give him money that he might marry a wife. And a large sum of money was needed, not so much for the expenses of the wedding, as for giving to the parents of the bride. He begged from door to door, flattered many rich folk, and at last succeeded in scraping together the sum needed. The wedding took place in due time; and he brought home his wife to his mother. After a short time he said to his mother – "Mother, I have no means to support you and my wife; I must therefore go to distant countries to get money somehow or other. I may be away for years, for I won't return till I get a good sum. In the meantime I'll give you what I have; you make the best of it, and take care of my wife." The Brahman receiving his mother's blessing set out on his travels.

In the evening of that very day, a ghost assuming the exact appearance of the Brahman came into the house. The newly married woman, thinking it was her husband, said to him – "How is it that you have returned so soon? You said you might be away for years; why have you changed your mind?" The ghost said – "To-day is not a lucky day, I have therefore returned home; besides, I have already got some money." The mother did not doubt but that it was her son. So the ghost lived in the house as if he was its owner, and as if he was the son of the old woman and the husband of the young woman. As the ghost and the Brahman were exactly like each other in everything, like two peas, the people in the neighbourhood all thought that the ghost was the real Brahman. After some years the Brahman returned from his travels; and what was his surprise when he found another like him in the house. The ghost said to the Brahman – "Who are you? what business have you to come to my house?"

"Who am I?" replied the Brahman, "let me ask who you are. This is my house; that is my mother, and this is my wife." The ghost said – "Why herein is a strange thing. Every one knows that this is my house, that is my wife, and yonder is my mother; and I have lived here for years. And you pretend this is your house, and that woman is your wife. Your head must have got turned, Brahman." So saying the ghost drove away the Brahman from his house. The Brahman became mute with wonder. He did not know what to do. At last he bethought himself of going to the king and of laying his case before him. The king saw the ghost-Brahman as well as the Brahman, and the one was the picture of the other; so he was in a fix, and did not know how to decide the quarrel. Day after day the Brahman went to the king and besought him to give him back his house, his wife, and his mother; and the king, not knowing what to say every time, put him off to the following day. Every day the king tells him to – "Come to-morrow"; and every day the Brahman goes away from the palace weeping and striking his forehead with the palm of his hand, and saying – "What a wicked world this is! I am driven from my own house, and another fellow has taken possession of my house and of my wife! And what a king this is! He does not do justice."

Now, it came to pass that as the Brahman went away every day from the court outside the town, he passed a spot at which a great many cowboys used to play. They let the cows graze on the meadow, while they themselves met together under a large tree to play. And they played at royalty. One cowboy was elected king; another, prime minister or vizier; another, *kotwal*, or prefect of the police; and others, constables. Every day for several days together they saw the Brahman passing by weeping. One day the cowboy king asked his vizier whether he knew why the Brahman wept every day. On the vizier not being able to answer the question, the cowboy king ordered one of his constables to bring the Brahman to him. One of them went and said to the Brahman – "The king requires your immediate attendance." The Brahman replied – "What for? I have just come from the king, and he put me off till to-morrow. Why does he want me again?"

"It is our king that wants you – our neat-herd king," rejoined the constable.

"Who is neat-herd king?" asked the Brahman.

"Come and see," was the reply.

The neat-herd king then asked the Brahman why he every day went away weeping. The Brahman then told him his sad story. The neat-herd king, after hearing the whole, said, "I understand your case; I will give you again all your rights. Only go to the king and ask his permission for me to decide your case." The Brahman went back to the king of the country, and begged his Majesty to send his case to the neat-herd king, who had offered to decide it. The king, whom the case had greatly puzzled, granted the permission sought. The following morning was fixed for the trial. The neat-herd king, who saw through the whole, brought with him next day a phial with a narrow neck. The Brahman and the ghost-Brahman both appeared at the bar. After a great deal of examination of witnesses and of speech-making, the neat-herd king said – "Well, I have heard enough. I'll decide the case at once. Here is this phial. Whichever of you will enter into it shall be declared by the court to be the rightful owner of the house the title of which is in dispute. Now, let me see, which of you will enter."

The Brahman said – "You are a neat-herd, and your intellect is that of a neat-herd. What man can enter into such a small phial?"

"If you cannot enter," said the neat-herd king, "then you are not the rightful owner. What do you say, sir, to this?" turning to the ghost-Brahman and addressing him. "If you can enter into the phial, then the house and the wife and the mother become yours."

"Of course I will enter," said the ghost. And true to his word, to the wonder of all, he made himself into a small creature like an insect, and entered into the phial. The neat-herd king forthwith corked up the phial, and the ghost could not get out. Then, addressing the Brahman, the neat-herd king said, "Throw this phial into the bottom of the sea, and take possession of your house, wife, and mother." The Brahman did so, and lived happily for many years and begat sons and daughters.

A Ghostly Wife

Lal Behari Dey

ONCE ON A TIME there lived a Brahman who had married a wife, and who lived in the same house with his mother. Near his house was a tank, on the embankment of which stood a tree, on the boughs of which lived a ghost of the kind called *Sankchinni*. One night the Brahman's wife had occasion to go to the tank, and as she went she brushed by a *Sankchinni* who stood near; on which the she-ghost got very angry with the woman, seized her by the throat, climbed into her tree, and thrust her into a hole in the trunk. There the woman lay almost dead with fear. The ghost put on the clothes of the woman and went into the house of the Brahman. Neither the Brahman nor his mother had any inkling of the change. The Brahman thought his wife returned from the tank, and the mother thought that it was her daughter-in-law.

Next morning the mother-in-law discovered some change in her daughter-in-law. Her daughter-in-law, she knew, was constitutionally weak and languid, and took a long time to do the work of the house. But she had apparently become quite a different person. All of a sudden she had become very active. She now did the work of the house in an incredibly short time. Suspecting nothing, the old woman said nothing either to her son or to her daughter-in-law; on the contrary, she only rejoiced that her daughter-in-law had turned over a new leaf. But her surprise became every day greater and greater. The cooking of the household was done in much less time than before. When the mother-in-law wanted the daughter-in-law to bring anything from the next room, it was brought in much less time than was required in walking from one room to the other. The ghost, instead of going inside the next room, would stretch a long arm – for ghosts can lengthen or shorten any limb of their bodies – from the door and get the thing. One day the old woman observed the ghost doing this. She ordered her to bring a vessel from some distance, and the ghost unconsciously stretched her hand to several yards' distance, and brought it in a trice. The old woman was struck with wonder at the sight. She said nothing to her, but spoke to her son.

Both mother and son began to watch the ghost more narrowly. One day the old woman knew that there was no fire in the house, and she knew also that her daughter-in-law had not gone out of doors to get it; and yet, strange to say, the hearth in the kitchen-room was quite in a blaze. She went in, and, to her infinite surprise, found that her daughter-in-law was not using any fuel for cooking, but had thrust into the oven her foot, which was blazing brightly. The old mother told her son what she had seen, and they both concluded that the young woman in the house was not his real wife but a she-ghost. The son witnessed those very acts of the ghost which his mother had seen. An *Ojha* was therefore sent for.

The exorcist came, and wanted in the first instance to ascertain whether the woman was a real woman or a ghost. For this purpose he lighted a piece of turmeric and set it below the nose of the supposed woman. Now this was an infallible test, as no ghost, whether male or female, can put up with the smell of burnt turmeric. The moment the lighted turmeric was taken near her, she screamed aloud and ran away from the room. It was now plain that she was either a ghost or a woman possessed by a ghost. The woman was caught hold of by main force and asked who she was. At first she refused to make any disclosures, on which the *Ojha* took up his slippers and began belabouring her with them. Then the ghost said with a strong nasal accent – for all ghosts speak through the nose – that she was a

Sankchinni, that she lived on a tree by the side of the tank, that she had seized the young Brahmani and put her in the hollow of her tree because one night she had touched her, and that if any person went to the hole the woman would be found. The woman was brought from the tree almost dead; the ghost was again shoebeaten, after which process, on her declaring solemnly that she would not again do any harm to the Brahman and his family, she was released from the spell of the *Ojha* and sent away; and the wife of the Brahman recovered slowly. After which the Brahman and his wife lived many years happily together and begat many sons and daughters.

The Ghost Who Was Afraid of Being Bagged

Lal Behari Dey

ONCE ON A TIME there lived a barber who had a wife. They did not live happily together, as the wife always complained that she had not enough to eat. Many were the curtain lectures which were inflicted upon the poor barber. The wife used often to say to her mate, "If you had not the means to support a wife, why did you marry me? People who have not means ought not to indulge in the luxury of a wife. When I was in my father's house I had plenty to eat, but it seems that I have come to your house to fast. Widows only fast; I have become a widow in your lifetime."

She was not content with mere words; she got very angry one day and struck her husband with the broomstick of the house. Stung with shame, and abhorring himself on account of his wife's reproach and beating, he left his house, with the implements of his craft, and vowed never to return and see his wife's face again till he had become rich. He went from village to village, and towards nightfall came to the outskirts of a forest. He laid himself down at the foot of a tree, and spent many a sad hour in bemoaning his hard lot.

It so chanced that the tree, at the foot of which the barber was lying down, was dwelt in by a ghost. The ghost seeing a human being at the foot of the tree naturally thought of destroying him. With this intention the ghost alighted from the tree, and, with outspread arms and a gaping mouth, stood like a tall palmyra tree before the barber, and said, "Now, barber, I am going to destroy you. Who will protect you?" The barber, though quaking in every limb through fear, and his hair standing erect, did not lose his presence of mind, but, with that promptitude and shrewdness which are characteristic of his fraternity, replied, "O spirit, you will destroy me! Wait a bit and I'll show you how many ghosts I have captured this very night and put into my bag; and right glad am I to find you here, as I shall have one more ghost in my bag."

So saying the barber produced from his bag a small looking-glass, which he always carried about with him along with his razors, his whet-stone, his strop and other utensils, to enable his customers to see whether their beards had been well shaved or not. He stood up, placed the looking-glass right against the face of the ghost, and said, "Here you see one ghost which I have seized and bagged; I am going to put you also in the bag to keep this ghost company."

The ghost, seeing his own face in the looking-glass, was convinced of the truth of what the barber had said, and was filled with fear. He said to the barber, "O, sir barber, I'll do whatever you bid me, only do not put me into your bag. I'll give you whatever you want." The barber said, "You ghosts are a faithless set, there is no trusting you. You will promise, and not give what you promise."

"O, sir," replied the ghost, "be merciful to me; I'll bring to you whatever you order; and if I do not bring it, then put me into your bag."

"Very well," said the barber, "bring me just now one thousand gold mohurs; and by to-morrow night you must raise a granary in my house, and fill it with paddy. Go and get the gold mohurs immediately: and if you fail to do my bidding you will certainly be put into my bag."

The ghost gladly consented to the conditions. He went away, and in the course of a short time returned with a bag containing a thousand gold mohurs. The barber was delighted beyond measure at the sight of the gold mohurs. He then told the ghost to see to it that by the following night a granary was erected in his house and filled with paddy.

It was during the small hours of the morning that the barber, loaded with the heavy treasure, knocked at the door of his house. His wife, who reproached herself for having in a fit of rage struck her husband with a broomstick, got out of bed and unbolted the door. Her surprise was great when she saw her husband pour out of the bag a glittering heap of gold mohurs.

The next night the poor devil, through fear of being bagged, raised a large granary in the barber's house, and spent the live-long night in carrying on his back large packages of paddy till the granary was filled up to the brim. The uncle of this terrified ghost, seeing his worthy nephew carrying on his back loads of paddy, asked what the matter was. The ghost related what had happened. The uncle-ghost then said, "You fool, you think the barber can bag you! The barber is a cunning fellow; he has cheated you, like a simpleton as you are."

"You doubt," said the nephew-ghost, "the power of the barber! come and see." The uncle-ghost then went to the barber's house, and peeped into it through a window. The barber, perceiving from the blast of wind which the arrival of the ghost had produced that a ghost was at the window, placed full before it the self-same looking-glass, saying, "Come now, I'll put you also into the bag." The uncle-ghost, seeing his own face in the looking-glass, got quite frightened, and promised that very night to raise another granary and to fill it, not this time with paddy, but with rice. So in two nights the barber became a rich man, and lived happily with his wife begetting sons and daughters.

The Story of a Brahmadaitya

Lal Behari Dey

ONCE ON A TIME there lived a poor Brahman who had a wife. As he had no means of livelihood, he used every day to beg from door to door, and thus got some rice which they boiled and ate, together with some greens which they gleaned from the fields. After some time it chanced that the village changed its owner, and the Brahman bethought himself of asking some boon of the new laird. So one morning the Brahman went to the laird's house to pay him court. It so happened that at that time the laird was making inquiries of his servants about the village and its various parts. The laird was told that a certain banyan-tree in the outskirts of the village was haunted by a number of ghosts; and that no man had ever the boldness to go to that tree at night. In bygone days some rash fellows went to the tree at night, but the necks of them all were wrung, and they all died. Since that time no man had ventured to go to the tree at night, though in the day some neat-herds took their cows to the spot. The new laird on hearing this said, that if any one would go at night to the tree, cut one of its branches and bring it to him, he would make him a present of a hundred *bighas* of rent-free land. None of the servants of the laird accepted the challenge, as they were sure they would be throttled by the ghosts. The Brahman, who was sitting there, thought within himself thus – "I am almost starved to death now, as I never get my bellyful. If I go to the tree at night and succeed in cutting off one of its branches I shall get one hundred *bighas* of rent-free land, and become independent for life. If the ghosts kill me, my case will not be worse, for to die of hunger is no better than to be killed by ghosts." He then offered to go to the tree and cut off a branch that night. The laird renewed his promise, and said to the Brahman that if he succeeded in bringing one of the branches of that haunted tree at night he would certainly give him one hundred *bighas* of rent-free land.

In the course of the day when the people of the village heard of the laird's promise and of the Brahman's offer, they all pitied the poor man. They blamed him for his foolhardiness, as they were sure the ghosts would kill him, as they had killed so many before. His wife tried to dissuade him from the rash undertaking; but in vain. He said he would die in any case; but there was some chance of his escaping, and of thus becoming independent for life. Accordingly, one hour after sundown, the Brahman set out. He went to the outskirts of the village without the slightest fear as far as a certain *vakula*-tree, from which the haunted tree was about one rope distant. But under the *vakula*-tree the Brahman's heart misgave him. He began to quake with fear, and the heaving of his heart was like the upward and downward motion of the paddy-husking pedal. The *vakula*-tree was the haunt of a Brahmadaitya, who, seeing the Brahman stop under the tree, spoke to him, and said, "Are you afraid, Brahman? Tell me what you wish to do, and I'll help you. I am a Brahmadaitya." The Brahman replied, "O blessed spirit, I wish to go to yonder banyan-tree, and cut off one of its branches for the zemindar, who has promised to give me one hundred *bighas* of rent-free land for it. But my courage is failing me. I shall thank you very much for helping me." The Brahmadaitya answered, "Certainly I'll help you, Brahman. Go on towards the tree, and I'll come with you." The Brahman, relying on the supernatural strength of his invisible patron, who is the object of the fear and reverence of common ghosts, fearlessly walked towards the haunted tree, on reaching which he began to cut a branch with the bill which was in his hand. But the moment the first stroke was given, a great many ghosts rushed towards the Brahman, who would have been torn to pieces but for the interference of the Brahmadaitya. The Brahmadaitya said in a commanding tone, "Ghosts, listen. This is a poor Brahman. He wishes to get a branch of this tree which will be of great use to him. It is my will that you let him cut a branch." The ghosts, hearing the voice of the Brahmadaitya, replied, "Be it according to thy will, lord. At thy bidding we are ready to do anything. Let not the Brahman take the trouble of cutting; we ourselves will cut a branch for him." So saying, in the twinkling of an eye, the ghosts put into the hands of the Brahman a branch of the tree, with which he went as fast as his legs could carry him to the house of the zemindar. The zemindar and his people were not a little surprised to see the branch; but he said, "Well, I must see to-morrow whether this branch is a branch of the haunted tree or not; if it be, you will get the promised reward."

Next morning the zemindar himself went along with his servants to the haunted tree, and found to their infinite surprise that the branch in their hands was really a branch of that tree, as they saw the part from which it had been cut off. Being thus satisfied, the zemindar ordered a deed to be drawn up, by which he gave to the Brahman for ever one hundred *bighas* of rent-free land. Thus in one night the Brahman became a rich man.

It so happened that the fields, of which the Brahman became the owner, were covered with ripe paddy, ready for the sickle. But the Brahman had not the means to reap the golden harvest. He had not a pice in his pocket for paying the wages of the reapers. What was the Brahman to do? He went to his spirit-friend the Brahmadaitya, and said, "Oh, Brahmadaitya, I am in great distress. Through your kindness I got the rent-free land all covered with ripe paddy. But I have not the means of cutting the paddy, as I am a poor man. What shall I do?" The kind Brahmadaitya answered, "Oh, Brahman, don't be troubled in your mind about the matter. I'll see to it that the paddy is not only cut, but that the corn is threshed and stored up in granaries, and the straw piled up in ricks. Only you do one thing. Borrow from men in the village one hundred sickles, and put them all at the foot of this tree at night. Prepare also the exact spot on which the grain and the straw are to be stored up."

The joy of the Brahman knew no bounds. He easily got a hundred sickles, as the husbandmen of the village, knowing that he had become rich, readily lent him what he wanted. At sunset he took the hundred sickles and put them beneath the *vakula*-tree. He also selected a spot of ground near his hut for his magazine of paddy and for his ricks of straw; and washed the spot with a solution of cow-dung and water. After making these preparations he went to sleep.

In the meantime, soon after nightfall, when the villagers had all retired to their houses, the Brahmadaitya called to him the ghosts of the haunted tree, who were one hundred in number, and said to them, "You must to-night do some work for the poor Brahman whom I am befriending. The hundred *bighas* of land which he has got from the zemindar are all covered with standing ripe corn. He has not the means to reap it. This night you all must do the work for him. Here are, you see, a hundred sickles; let each of you take a sickle in hand and come to the field I shall show him. There are a hundred of you. Let each ghost cut the paddy of one *bigha*, bring the sheaves on his back to the Brahman's house, thresh the corn, put the corn in one large granary, and pile up the straw in separate ricks. Now, don't lose time. You must do it all this very night." The hundred ghosts at once said to the Brahmadaitya, "We are ready to do whatever your lordship commands us." The Brahmadaitya showed the ghosts the Brahman's house, and the spot prepared for receiving the grain and the straw, and then took them to the Brahman's fields, all waving with the golden harvest. The ghosts at once fell to it. A ghost harvest-reaper is different from a human harvest-reaper. What a man cuts in a whole day, a ghost cuts in a minute. *Mash, mash, mash*, the sickles went round, and the long stalks of paddy fell to the ground. The reaping over, the ghosts took up the sheaves on their huge backs and carried them all to the Brahman's house. The ghosts then separated the grain from the straw, stored up the grain in one huge store-house, and piled up the straw in many a fantastic rick. It was full two hours before sunrise when the ghosts finished their work and retired to rest on their tree. No words can tell either the joy of the Brahman and his wife when early next morning they opened the door of their hut, or the surprise of the villagers, when they saw the huge granary and the fantastic ricks of straw. The villagers did not understand it. They at once ascribed it to the gods.

A few days after this the Brahman went to the *vakula*-tree and said to the Brahmadaitya, "I have one more favour to ask of you, Brahmadaitya. As the gods have been very gracious to me, I wish to feed one thousand Brahmans; and I shall thank you for providing me with the materials of the feast." "With the greatest pleasure," said the polite Brahmadaitya; "I'll supply you with the requirements of a feast for a thousand Brahmans; only show me the cellars in which the provisions are to be stored away." The Brahman improvised a store-room. The day before the feast the store-room was overflowing with provisions. There were one hundred jars of *ghi* (clarified butter), one hill of flour, one hundred jars of sugar, one hundred jars of milk, curds, and congealed milk, and the other thousand and one things required in a great Brahmanical feast. The next morning one hundred Brahman pastrycooks were employed; the thousand Brahmans ate their fill; but the host, the Brahman of the story, did not eat. He thought he would eat with the Brahmadaitya. But the Brahmadaitya, who was present there though unseen, told him that he could not gratify him on that point, as by befriending the Brahman the Brahmadaitya's allotted period had come to an end, and the *pushpaka* chariot had been sent to him from heaven. The Brahmadaitya, being released from his ghostly life, was taken up into heaven; and the Brahman lived happily for many years, begetting sons and grandsons.

The Bunniah's Ghost

Collected by Alice Elizabeth Dracott

FAR AWAY IN A VALLEY in the Himalayan mountains lies a little village, where once lived a good man who had his home beside a field in which grew a beautiful mulberry tree – so big and so beautiful that it was the wonder of the country round.

Hundreds of people were wont to gather together beneath it, and the poor carried away basket loads of its fruit. Thus it became a meeting place where a *mela*, or fair, was held when the fruit season was on.

Now the fame of it reached a certain Rajah who had rented out the land, and one day he came with all his retinue to see it.

"There is no such tree in the Royal Gardens," said the Grand Vizier.

"It is not meet that a subject should possess what the Rajah hath not," added the Prime Minister.

The Rajah replied not a word, for his heart was filled with envy; and that night, before going to bed, he gave orders that, on a certain day, in the early dawn, before anybody was astir, a party of armed men should take their axes to the village, and fell the mulberry tree even with the ground. But ill dreams disturbed the Rajah's rest, and he could not sleep.

Could it be fancy, or did he really see a strange man standing before him?

The strange man spoke: "O king, live for ever! I am the spirit of a Bunniah (or merchant) who died in yonder village many years ago. During my lifetime I defrauded the people. I gave them short measure and adulterated their food.

"When I died and passed into the Land of Unhappy Spirits, the gods, who are just, O king! decreed that I should give back what I had stolen. My soul therefore went into a mulberry tree, where year after year the people gather fruit, and regain their losses.

"In one year more they will be repaid to the uttermost *cowrie*; but you mean to destroy the tree and drive my soul I know not whither. Wherefore have I come to plead with you to spare it this once, for when a year is past it will die of itself and my soul find its way to that Land of Shadows which is the abode of the gods – where it will find peace."

So the Rajah listened, and the strange man went away.

For one year longer the people sat as before under the cool shadow of the mulberry tree, and then it died. And was that all?

No: when they cut it down there was found deep in the earth one living root, and that they left, for who can destroy the soul?

A Legend of Sardana

Collected by Alice Elizabeth Dracott

IN A CITY CALLED SARDANA there once lived a man whose name was Simru. This man had great riches and lands, and also owned a place of worship.

He married a lady of Sardana, who was called Begum.

After a few years of married life Simru died, and his wealthy widow gave alms and much money to the poor.

In the same city lived an oil dealer who also died, and the angels took him to Heaven and presented him before the Almighty.

"Who have you brought?" asked the Creator. "This man's days upon earth are not yet completed: take him back before his body is buried, and let his spirit re-possess his body; but in the city of Sardana you will find another man of the same name: bring him to me."

On leaving the Court of God, some former creditor of the oil dealer's, who had preceded him into the Unseen, recognized him, and laying hold of him, demanded the sum of five *rupees* which he had owed him during his lifetime.

The poor man being unable to pay this debt, the angels once more took him before the Almighty, who asked why they had returned.

The angels replied: "O God, there is a man here to whom this oil dealer owes five *rupees*, and he will not let us return until the debt is paid."

The Almighty enquired if this was true, and the oil dealer replied: "Yes, but I am a poor man, and not able to repay it."

Then the Almighty said: "In the city of Sardana lives a rich Begum; do you know her?"

"Yes, O king."

"Well, the Begum's treasury is here, and I will advance you five *rupees* out of it, if, when you return to earth, you promise faithfully to give it back to the Begum."

So the oil dealer gratefully took the loan, paid his debt, and returned with the angels to earth, where he arrived just too late to re-enter his body, which his friends had already taken away to prepare for burial. Watching his opportunity, he waited till they were otherwise engaged, and at once re-entered it; but when he sat up, and began to speak, his terrified friends and relations fled, thinking it was his ghost.

On this the oil dealer called out: "Do not fear, I am not a spirit; but God has released me, as my days upon earth are not yet fulfilled. The man who ought to have died is Kungra, the vegetable man; go and see whether he is dead or alive."

The friends, on going to the house of Kungra, found that he had just fallen from a wall and been killed on the spot; all his relations were wailing and lamenting his sudden end.

Thus everybody knew that the words of the old oil dealer were correct.

In the meantime, the oil dealer called his son, and said: "Son, when I went to Heaven I there met a man to whom I owed five *rupees*, and he caught me and would not let me return before I paid it, so the Almighty advanced me the money from the Begum's treasury in Heaven, and bade me give her back that amount on my return to earth. Therefore do I entreat you, my son, to come with me, and together we will visit the Begum, and give her five *rupees*."

So they took the money and went to the Begum's house.

"Who are you?" asked she.

The oil dealer then told her the whole story, ending with: "And now I come to return you the five *rupees*."

The Begum was very pleased, and, taking the money, she called her servants and ordered a further sum of one hundred *rupees* to be added to it. This money she spent on sweets, which were distributed amongst the poor.

Many years afterwards the good Begum of Sardana died, but her houses and lands are still in existence; nor does anybody living in that town forget the story of the oilman who died and lived again.

The Manglalabas

Dean S. Fansler

ONCE UPON A TIME, in the small town of Balubad, there was a big house. It was inhabited by a rich family. When the head of the family died, the house was gloomy and dark. The family wore black clothes, and was sad.

Three days after the death of the father, the family began to be troubled at night by a manglalabas. He threw stones at the house, broke the water-jars, and moved the beds. Some pillows were even found in the kitchen the next day. The second night, Manglalabas visited the house again. He pinched the widow; but when she woke up, she could not see anything. Manglalabas also emptied all the water-jars. Accordingly the family decided to abandon the house.

A band of brave men in that town assembled, and went to the house. At midnight the spirit came again, but the brave men said they were ready to fight it. Manglalabas made a great deal of noise in the house. He poured out all the water, kicked the doors, and asked the men who they were. They answered, "We are fellows who are going to kill you." But when the spirit approached them, and they saw that it was a ghost, they fled away. From that time on, nobody was willing to pass a night in that house.

In a certain *barrio* of Balubad there lived two queer men. One was called Bulag, because he was blind; and the other, Cuba, because he was hunchbacked. One day these two arranged to go to Balubad to beg. Before they set out, they agreed that the blind man should carry the hunchback on his shoulder to the town. So they set out. After they had crossed the Balubad River, Cuba said, "Stop a minute, Bulag! here is a hatchet." Cuba got down and picked it up. Then they proceeded again. A second time Cuba got off the blind man's shoulder, for he saw an old gun by the roadside. He picked this up also, and took it along with him.

When they reached the town, they begged at many of the houses, and finally they came to the large abandoned house. They did not know that this place was haunted by a spirit. Cuba said, "Maybe no one is living in this house;" and Bulag replied, "I think we had better stay here for the night."

As they were afraid that somebody might come, they went up into the ceiling. At midnight they were awakened by Manglalabas making a great noise and shouting, "I believe that there are some new persons in my house!" Cuba, frightened, fired the gun. The ghost thought that the noise of the gun was some one crying. So he said, "If you are truly a big man, give me some proofs."

Then Cuba took the handle out of the hatchet and threw the head down at the ghost. Manglalabas thought that this was one of the teeth of his visitor, and, convinced that the intruder was a powerful person, he said, "I have a buried treasure near the barn. I wish you to dig it up. The reason I come here every night is on account of this treasure. If you will only dig it up, I will not come here any more."

The next night Bulag and Cuba dug in the ground near the barn. There they found many gold and silver pieces. When they were dividing the riches, Cuba kept three-fourths of the treasure for himself. Bulag said, "Let me see if you have divided fairly," and, placing his hands on the two piles, he found that Cuba's was much larger.

Angry at the discovery, Cuba struck Bulag in the eyes, and they were opened. When Bulag could see, he kicked Cuba in the back, and straightaway his deformity disappeared. Therefore they became friends again, divided the money equally, and owned the big house between them.

Mabait and the Duende

Dean S. Fansler

MENGUITA, A KING OF CEBU, had two slaves – Mabait and Masama. Mabait was honest and industrious, while Masama was envious and lazy. Mabait did nearly all of the hard work in the palace, so he was admired very much by the king. Masama, who was addicted to gambling, envied Mabait.

One night, while Mabait was asleep, a duende awakened him, and said, "I have seen how you labour here patiently and honestly. I want to be your friend."

Mabait was amazed and frightened. He looked at the duende carefully, and saw that it resembled a very small man with long hair and a white beard. It was about a foot high. It had on a red shirt, a pair of green trousers, a golden cap, and a pair of black shoes. At last Mabait answered in a trembling voice, "I don't want to be a friend of an evil spirit."

"I am not evil, I am a duende."

"I don't know what duendes are, so I don't want to be your friend."

"Duendes are wealthy and powerful spirits. They can perform magic. If you are the friend of one of them, you will be a most fortunate man."

"How did you come into the world?" said Mabait.

"Listen! When Lucifer was an angel, a contest in creating animals arose between him and God. He and his followers were defeated and thrown into hell. Many angels in that contest belonged neither to God's side nor to Lucifer's. They were dropped on the earth. Those that fell in the forests became tigbalangs, ikis, and mananangals; those in the seas became mermaids and mermen; and those in the cities became duendes."

"Ah, yes! I know now what duendes are."

"Now let our friendship last forever," said the duende. "I am ready at any time to help you in your undertakings."

From that time on Mabait and the duende were good friends. The duende gave Mabait two or three isabels every day, and by the end of the month he had saved much money. He bought a fine hat and a pair of wooden shoes.

Masama wondered how Mabait, who was very poor, could buy so many things. At last he asked, "Where do you get money? Do you steal it?"

"No, my friend gives it to me."

"Who is your friend?"

"A duende."

Masama, in great envy, went to the king, and said, "Master, Mabait, your favourite slave, has a friend. This friend is a duende, which will be injurious to us if you let it live here. As Mabait said, it will be the means of his acquiring all of your wealth and taking your daughter for his wife."

The king, in great rage, summoned Mabait, and punished him severely by beating his palms with a piece of leather. Then he ordered his servants to find the duende and kill it. The duende hid in a small jar. Masama saw it, and covered the mouth of the jar with a saint's dress. The duende was afraid of the dress, and dared not come out. "Open the jar, and I will give you ten isabels," said the little man.

"Give me the money first."

After Masama received the money, he went away to the cockpit without opening the jar. On his way there he lost his money. He went back to the duende, and said, "Friend, give me ten isabels more, and I will open the jar."

"I know that you will cheat me," answered the duende. "Just let me come out of the jar, and I promise that you shall have the princess here for your wife."

"What! Will the princess be my wife?"

"Yes."

"How can you make her love me?"

"I will enter the princess's abdomen. I will talk, laugh, and do everything to make her afraid. I will not leave her for anybody but you."

"Good, good!" Masama opened the jar, and the duende, flew away to the princess's tower.

Only a few weeks after that time a proclamation of the king was read in public. It was as follows: "The princess, my daughter, has something in her abdomen. It speaks and laughs. No one knows what it is, and no one can force it to come out. Whoever can cure my daughter shall be my heir and son-in-law; but he who tries and fails shall lose his head."

When Masama heard this, he said to Mabait, "Why don't you cure the princess? You are the only one who can cure her."

"Don't flatter me!" answered Mabait.

"I'm not flattering you. It is the duende, your friend, who is in her abdomen, and no one can persuade it to come out but you. So go now, for fortune is waiting for you."

Mabait was at last persuaded, and so he departed. Before going to the king, he first went to a church, and there he prayed Bathala that he might be successful in his undertakings. When Mabait was gone, Masama said to himself, "It is not fortune, but it is death, that is waiting for him. When he is dead, I shall not have anybody to envy."

After sitting for about a half-hour, Masama also set out for the princess's tower, but he reached the palace before Mabait. There he told the king that he could cure his daughter. He was conducted into the princess's room. He touched her abdomen, and said, "Who are you?"

"I am the duende."

"Why are you there?"

"Because I want to be here."

"Go away!"

"No, I won't."

"Don't you know me?"

"Yes, I know you. You are Masama, who cheated me once. Give your head to the king." So the executioner cut Masama's head off.

Then Mabait came, and told the king that he could cure the princess. After he was given permission to try, he said to the duende, "Who are you?"

"I am the duende, your friend."

"Will you please come out of the princess's abdomen?"

"Yes, I will, for the sake of our friendship."

Mabait was married to the princess, was crowned king, and lived happily with his friend the duende.

The Wicked Woman's Reward

Dean S. Fansler

ONCE THERE LIVED a certain king. He had concubines, five in number. Two of them he loved more than the others, for they were to bear him children. He said that the one who should give birth to a male baby he would marry. Soon one of them bore a child, but it was a girl, and shortly afterward the other bore a handsome boy. The one which had given birth to the baby girl was restless: she wished that she might have the boy. In order to satisfy her wish, she thought of an ingenious plan whereby she might get possession of the boy.

One midnight, when all were sound asleep, she killed her own baby and secretly buried it. Then she quietly crept to her rival's bed and stole her boy, putting in his place a newborn cat. Early in the morning the king went to the room of his concubine who had borne the boy, and was surprised to find a cat by her side instead of a human child. He was so enraged, that he immediately ordered her to be drowned in the river. His order was at once executed. Then he went into the room of the wicked woman. The moment he saw the boy baby, he was filled with great joy, and he smothered the child with kisses. As he had promised, he married the woman. After the marriage the king sent away all his other concubines, and he harboured a deep love for his deceitful wife.

Soon afterwards there was a great confusion throughout the kingdom. Everybody wondered why it was that the river smelled so fragrant, and the people were very anxious to find out the cause of the sweet odour. It was not many days before the townspeople along the river-bank found the corpse of the drowned woman floating in the water; and this was the source of the sweetness that was causing their restlessness. It was full of many different kinds of flowers which had been gathered by the birds. When the people attempted to remove the corpse from the water, the birds pecked them, and would not let the body be taken away.

At last the news of the miracle was brought to the ears of the king. He himself went to the river to see the wonderful corpse. As soon as he saw the figure of the drowned woman, he was tortured with remorse. Then, to his great surprise and fear, the corpse suddenly stood up out of the water, and said to him in sorrowful tones, "O king! as you see, my body has been floating on the water. The birds would have buried me, but I wanted you to know that you ordered me to be killed without any investigation of my fault. Your wife stole my boy, and, as you saw, she put a cat by my side." The ghost vanished, and the king saw the body float away again down the river. The king at once ordered the body of his favourite to be taken out of the water and brought to the palace; and he himself was driven back to the town, violent with rage and remorse. There he seized his treacherous wife and hurled her out of the window of the palace, and he even ordered her body to be hanged.

Having gotten rid of this evil woman, the king ordered the body of the innocent woman to be buried among the noble dead. The corpse was placed in a magnificent tomb, and was borne in a procession with pompous funeral ceremonies. He himself dressed entirely in black as a sign of his genuine grief for her; yet, in spite of his sorrow for his true wife, he took comfort in her son, who grew to be a handsome boy. As time went on, the prince developed into a brave youth, who was able to perform the duties of his father the king: so, as his father became old, no longer able to bear the responsibilities of regal power, the prince succeeded to the throne, and ruled the kingdom well. He proved himself to be the son of the good woman by his wise and just rule over his subjects.

Returning My Sister's Face

Eugie Foster

MY EARLIEST MEMORIES are of Oiwa in the sunlight, brushing her magnificent hair. Unbound, it trailed to the floor, a waterfall of shimmering black, the same color as a raven's wing. It was Oiwa who picked me up from the dirt with words of comfort and wisdom when my pony threw me off for shouting in his ear.

"Yasuo, do not cry, silly boy," she said as she dried my tears with the hem of her kimono. "And you should not rage at your pony either, but thank him for only tossing you from his back. If you had shouted in my ear like that, I would have bitten you besides."

And it was Oiwa's proud smile I looked for when I won the praise of my sword master. I remember how small she looked, kneeling in her kimono with her hands folded in her lap. But she was always my big sister, even when I towered over her in my samurai armor.

Our father died when I was a boy, felled by the sword of a barbarian from the west. He was a brave warlord. I barely remember him. Oiwa told me how he laughed when he swung me in his arms, proud of how fearless I was as a babe.

With his death, our prosperity ended. Mother grew sick, and people turned away from us, loathe to help those who had so obviously been touched by bad luck, as though it might be contagious. We would have become thieves or beggars if not for Shigekazu – the lord of Yotsuya. He took pity on us and took me in, gave me a swordsman's education, and let us stay in our ancestral home.

To repay him, when I earned my warrior's katana, I became his most loyal captain. I patrolled his borders and kept bandits from abusing his farmers and tradesmen.

It was the start of plum blossom season during my seventeenth year when Iyemon arrived. The white and fuchsia petals shed their heavy perfume, and there was anticipation of the upcoming Ume Matsuri festival. Iyemon rode to Lord Shigekazu's gate, a masterless samurai, shining in his fine michiyuki overcoat, astride a golden stallion. He brought with him his katana and his servant, Kohei, and nothing else.

He went to Shigekazu and petitioned to be allowed to join his guard. In turn, my lord Shigekazu asked me to look after him.

It was strange for me, as Iyemon was a well-grown man, ten years my senior. Yet, I was in the teacher's position. Even so, Iyemon was gracious. He did not chafe when I instructed him as to how we set our watches and shifts, nor did he sneer to spar at bamboo canes with me. Indeed he laughed when I bested him in our first bout, and was as genial in triumph in our second.

He had no kin in the area and no hearth, so I invited him to dinner.

Oiwa was surprised to see three men – Iyemon, Kohei, and myself – walking up the path, but she was sweetly courteous, as I knew she would be. She ran to put more water on for tea and returned with a basin of scented water for us to splash upon our hands and faces.

If I try, I can still remember the flavors from that dinner. Hot soup with tangy seaweed, sticky rice that melted on my tongue, tart umeboshi from the plum trees, and sweet bean cakes that could have been clouds of nectar fallen from the heavens.

After the meal, Kohei washed the pots and bowls while Oiwa went to tend our mother. Iyemon and I sat on tatami mats and smoked pipes, awash in tranquil harmony.

With the blue smoke wreathing his face, Iyemon cast his eyes down. "Tell me, Yasuo," he said. "Why is your beautiful sister without a husband?"

I was surprised at how forthright he was on this matter of delicacy, but then he was new to Yotsuya and did not know our family's story.

"None will take her," I said. "For though Oiwa is noble, she can bring no dowry to a marriage. Our father died with his riches plundered. What household wealth we had we spent on medicine and doctors for our mother, who languishes with a wasting disease."

"But you have this fine house in the country—"

"We owe all to Lord Shigekazu. Without his mercy and generosity, we would be penniless, cast out into the streets."

"Still, your sister is sweet of face and graceful of temperament. Surely there are men who would take her to wife?"

"She is considered a bad luck woman," I admitted. "She has no suitors."

"Outrageous!" Iyemon declared. Of course, I was not going to disagree.

When Oiwa came from our mother's room, Iyemon rose to his feet and bowed low to her. A soft blush, like the new glow of camellia blossoms on a white bough, filled her face, and she hid behind her fan.

"Lady Oiwa," Iyemon said, "I would be honored if you would walk with me at the Ume Matsuri festival. May I call upon you tomorrow?"

My sister's blush deepened, turning the enchanting hue of sunset clouds at midsummer. "I will look forward to it."

The Ume Matsuri festival was the traditional start of spring. The plum trees displayed their five-petalled blooms during the month of YaYohi, while beneath them, maidens and youths strolled together. The maidens wore kimonos to rival the flowers – violet silk embroidered with golden bamboo shoots, apricot sleeves with scarlet chrysanthemum, sea foam brocade with glowing koi painted on them. And the young men wore the maidens like banners upon their arms.

Oiwa did not have much finery, as we had sold her most lavish kimonos long ago. But she had kept one kimono, our great-great grandmother's good luck silk. It was peacock blue brocade with silver pine trees and malachite maple leaves woven through the cloth. With her hair piled high on her head and wooden geta sandals on her feet, Oiwa looked like a princess.

Iyemon's eyes widened when he saw her. He bore with him a perfect white plum blossom for her hair, and she let him affix it in her gleaming locks. They walked arm-and-arm together among the plum trees.

Iyemon became a frequent caller, and as the first cherry blossoms began to bud, they announced their Yui-no betrothal. Since there was but meager wealth on both sides, the gifts they exchanged were, of necessity, modest. Iyemon gave my sister a white obi to use as a belt on her wedding kimono. It was fine silk, embroidered with snow-white phoenixes. In return, Oiwa gave her husband-to-be a black hakama she had sewn with her own hands, every stitch a prayer of loyalty and fidelity.

At the wedding ceremony, Oiwa was radiant as the dawn star as she glided through the humble Shinto shrine of our ancestors. We had hired a maid from town to dress her hair with rented kanzashi combs and to help her don the traditional shiro-maku kimono.

Iyemon was composed, an expression of serenity on his face as he spoke the commitment vows. He looked like a king in his newly made hakama robe. Oiwa's hand was steady, without a whisper of tremor, when she lit the customary lamps.

But barely had the taste of the wedding sake faded when trouble visited. Our mother, too weak even to attend the ceremony, worsened. We thought death was ready to harvest her, yet she clung with grim tenacity to this world. The newlyweds' month of sweetness was cut short, barely begun.

Then Lord Shigekazu received word that Lady Uma, his granddaughter, would be traveling from the city of Edo to visit him on her quest to find a husband. As he had not seen the daughter of his daughter in many years, he was jubilant at the news. He asked me to take a regiment of men to meet her at his border. For the first time, I was loathe to do his bidding.

"Please, Lord Shigekazu," I said. "My mother is very ill. I would prefer to stay near. Will you give me leave to decline this obligation?"

"Obligation?" Lord Shigekazu demanded. "Is it not basic courtesy that the captain I have raised as a grandson should feel honorbound to protect the safety of my only granddaughter? What if there are bandits on the road? Come, Yasuo, your mother has had many a bad turn, surely she will last a fortnight longer?"

"Please, my lord, it is my least desire to defy you, but I also owe duty to she who bore me."

Lord Shigekazu might have said harsher words then, ones that would have made me lose face if I did not bow to his wishes, but Iyemon intervened.

"If my lord would be willing to indulge one so new to his service," he said. "I would be greatly privileged if I could take my brother's place as escort for the Lady Uma."

Lord Shigekazu's brow still creased with darkness, but he allowed the substitution as Iyemon was now my kin, and to refuse him would disgrace both of us. And so the next morning, Iyemon took his golden stallion and a regiment of my most trusted men to the Yotsuya borders.

There was a great storm that night. Rain clattered against the wooden shutters and the fierce wind tipped and twirled the lanterns so their light cast stark shadows and dancing silhouettes. Oiwa and I kneeled by our mother's tatami mat, holding her hand and taking turns fanning her brow. She complained of a burning thirst, but her throat was too ragged to swallow the weak tea Oiwa brewed.

Mother's mind flitted like a bird between this world and the next. She rarely knew us, babbling instead as though we were spirits and ancestors long dead. I knew she would leave us soon. They say if someone sees their ancestors in a fever dream, it is not long before they will go to join them.

Oiwa continued to fight against the inexorable. "Mama," she whispered. "Mama, try to drink a little of this green tea. It will cool you."

Mother sat bolt upright and stared at Oiwa. "Where is your face?" she cried.

Oiwa reached a hand to her cheek. "I – It is at the front of my head, where it always is."

"No, only half of it," Mother replied. She glared at me. "I pledge you to return the other half of your sister's face. Swear it, Yasuo!"

Oiwa and I exchanged troubled looks. I do not swear oaths lightly, so I hesitated to promise to some fantasy of fever. But our mother was insistent.

"Swear it, or I will haunt you after I die! Swear!"

Oiwa leaned to me. "There is no harm in giving your word to something that requires no deed. Do not let her final words be a curse."

So I bowed my head over our mother's hand and promised to return Oiwa's missing half-face. I was uneasy, but truthfully, what harm was there in such a promise?

The next thunderbolt brought a sudden gale into the room, crashing open the shutter and blowing out the oil lamp. When we had relit it, our mother was gone, extinguished with the lamp, and unlike it, forever dark.

My sister's ragged sobs filled the room as she clutched our mother's body to her breast. I bowed my head.

* * *

Lord Shigekazu's anger with me was somewhat assuaged by the news of Mother's death. Still, I knew he harbored resentment. After her cremation ceremony, he insisted I return to the soldier's barracks.

Though Oiwa was pale and weak with grief, she urged me to go.

"We must not lose Shigekazu's favor," she said. "We owe him a debt we will never be able to repay."

I knew in a mere fortnight Iyemon would return, so I packed my saddlebags and kissed her farewell.

I dined at home when I could escape for an evening so Oiwa would not be alone. She was always glad to see me, but grief haunted her eyes, and where once her cheeks were blushing peaches, they had begun to sink and grow sallow. I saw a strand of white in her lustrous hair, and it saddened me. Oiwa had spent her youth tending our mother. Now her joy had flown with Mother's death. I prayed that Iyemon's devoted attentions would be able to restore her joy, if not her youth.

As though in answer to my prayers, the gods delivered Iyemon at last. And like a sunrise, with him came the Lady Uma. Having spent time in the royal courts, she was like a jeweled butterfly among moths. She wore layers of fine, silk kimonos, twelve of them together, with the sleeve cuffs and collars cut to display each distinctive color – lilac, damson, azure, indigo, emerald, topaz, citrine, garnet, peach, scarlet, magenta, and finally at the last, creamy white – and each one embroidered with a different design in gold thread.

It seemed all the unmarried men in Yotsuya found themselves captivated by the flashing hems of Lady Uma's kimonos and the elusive perfume she wore – jasmine and crushed lily. I, along with half my men, wrote sonnets of love and admiration to her.

But then, more misfortune. Word came of raiders from the west, great men with shaggy faces and beastly apparel, plundering the countryside. I was assigned the duty of quashing their incursion before it became an invasion.

It was with a mournful heart that I left Lady Uma's presence, but I did not dare to protest. I was already a low man.

The barbarians were vicious and tenacious. They had set up a rude fortification on the edge of Yotsuya. I knew if I did not disperse them, they would foray deeper in, burning villages and razing fertile farmlands. I organized my men for a siege.

The month of rice planting, UTzuki, passed, then the month of rice sprouting, SaTsuki. Summer lapsed in a blur of sun and waiting. My soldiers took turns fishing the waters and hunting the forest for our meals. We cooked upwind of the barbarians to torment them with the smell of fresh fish and sweet rice while they were reduced to hard loaves and dry meat.

It was my turn with net and rod. The water laved cool around my knees and I grew lost in thoughts of the perfection of Lady Uma's face with its dusting of rice powder. A great tug on my line nearly pulled me over. I called my men to help bring in the grandfather fish.

We soon saw it was not a fish tangled in my line. It was a most terrible article I had caught – two bodies, nailed to either side of a black door, the prescribed punishment for convicted adulterers. They were purple and bloated. Her face in particular was most terrible to look upon. Half of it seemed to have melted away as though it were wax beside a fire.

I swept away the debris of riverweed from the grisly plank. The woman was wrapped in a peacock blue kimono, the silk ruined by the water. I could make out the memory of silver pine trees and dark green maple leaves outlined on the brocade.

It was Oiwa's festival kimono. Oh, my sister! And sharing her door of disgrace was Iyemon's servant, Kohei. I recognized his face and the yukata robe he wore.

I do not know what I screamed then – a curse on my sister, or on the gods, or on myself. I bolted from that place, flung myself upon my stallion, and galloped away.

I rode through rain and sun and night until my steed collapsed beneath me. Then I ran. When my armor and helmet weighed me down, I tossed them aside. I kept only the clothes on my back and my katana, for I would need it to spill the cursed blood from my veins at the altar of my ancestors.

* * *

It was night when I stumbled through the gardens of my ancestral home and up the steps of our shrine. I ignited four sticks of incense and lit four candles, the number for death and misfortune. Around me, the icons of the most revered ancestors of my lineage – dukes and warlords and virtuous ladies – watched as I removed my soiled and tattered shirt. I felt their eyes as I knelt and drew my katana.

"Yasuo, do not cry, silly boy." Oiwa stood in the shadow of a bamboo screen, holding a fan over her face. I leaped to my feet, ready to embrace her. But when she came closer, I saw by the light of the four candles that Oiwa had no legs. Where in the darkness I had thought them concealed by night, in the circle of candleshine, I saw she trailed away to a wisp of translucence.

"Oiwa," I whispered, "what has befallen you?"

"Remember the oath you made to our mother?"

"Y – yes."

"I call upon you to honor it." She dropped her fan. What had been dreadful on her poor body, on her visage as a yurei, an angry ghost, was even more terrible. One side of her face was sweet and whole, the other melted away. One eye rolled in its socket, yellow and diseased. A crust of tears tracked from it down her sagging cheek. Her once-opulent hair was lank and thin, dirty strands hanging from her torn scalp. Half her mouth was curled down, black and putrid, a wad of spittle hovering at the edge. And the skin on that cheek and that side of her brow was gray and curdled.

I shrieked in horror, and there was only blackness.

* * *

I woke in the shrine, the four candles burned away, and the cloying scent of incense hovering in a cloud. Iyemon supported me, dragged me to my feet.

"I thought the voices in the garden were cats fighting or the shriek of night birds," he said. "If I had known you had returned, my brother, I would have run to your side."

"I was fishing," I mumbled, on the edge of delirium. "There was a door. Oiwa and Kohei." I remembered terrible images of Oiwa, her face dripping and her blackened mouth, but no, that was how I saw her on the door, surely?

"That is not how I would have had you learn of it. Come inside. I will tell the sorry tale."

Within, Iyemon poured me a bowl of plum wine which I drank in two gulps. He poured another that I clutched in trembling fingers.

"It was my fault," Iyemon said. "If I had not volunteered to escort Lady Uma to her grandfather's house, perhaps Oiwa would not have gone mad with loneliness."

"What are you saying?"

"I found them together. Oiwa drank poison, some mixture of the garden – suicide. I treated Kohei to the blade of my katana."

"My sister was an honorable woman!"

"I would not have revealed their sin, truly, but—"

"Liar!" I shrieked. "Get out of my house!"

His face, so beseeching a moment before, hardened. "Yasuo, this is now my house. Your mother bequeathed it to Oiwa, and as her husband, I am her beneficiary."

The half-full bowl of wine shattered on the floor. "You are throwing me out?"

Immediately, he was the picture of solicitude. "No, no. Never. I do not blame you for your sister's wantonness. But you must face the truth."

I sank to my knees, sobbing like a child, calling to Oiwa. Iyemon left me alone to preserve what little honor I could still lay claim to.

In the subsequent days, I refused to leave the house, and Iyemon let me brood and weep as I would. He also left me casks of plum wine and bags of opium to ease my grief. Welcoming the blunting of memory, I drank and smoked my days away.

It was during one of these opium-muddled twilights that Oiwa returned.

The peacock blue silk of her kimono was stained by river water, but she protected me from the worst of her terrible appearance. She held a paper fan across the sinister half of her face.

"My face is still half missing," she said.

I scrambled away, cowering in a corner of the room. "What face do you want to recover?" I whimpered. "Your honor or your beauty?"

"Ah, little brother, you have come to the crux of it. Know this, while you have sunk yourself in wine and opium, the nuptial plans rush forward. I will return on their wedding night. Look for me then. See to it my face is restored that night, or I will haunt you forever."

"Oiwa, I'm so sorry."

Her voice softened. "Do not cry, little brother. I have shed enough tears for us both."

Then she was gone, and all the opium cobwebs swept from my mind with her.

It was dark, the sun long fled beneath the horizon. I crept from my chambers, disheveled and bleary. Voices drifted from the sitting room, two men at dinner. I clung to the shadows and listened.

"It was a fortuitous day when you came to Yotsuya." It was Lord Shigekazu.

"I am honored that you say it, my lord," Iyemon replied.

"Come now, surely you can call me 'grandfather'?"

"I would not wish for unseemly haste."

"Tut. Your Yui-no to my granddaughter can be announced soon enough. It is well you discovered your wife, that slattern's betrayal, and dealt with her and your servant so decisively. Otherwise the smear on your reputation—"

I did not breathe while I struggled to make sense of their words. Shigekazu as Iyemon's grandfather? Iyemon engaged to Lady Uma?

It was the first revelation. The second came after their words penetrated further. Shigekazu had said dealt with her, meaning Oiwa. Iyemon had told me my sister had taken poison – dishonorable suicide. But now it seemed more likely Iyemon had dispatched her himself.

A lie. It is well known that falsehoods come in threes. This was the second lie, the first being that Oiwa had been unfaithful. But the third lie I did not yet know.

I slunk back to my chambers. While I poured the last of the wine onto the thirsty rocks outside (for I did not wish to be tempted by the seduction of euphoric forgetfulness), I mused over the question. I was about to scatter the opium to the winds when I paused.

I put on fresh clothing – a short haori jacket and hakama pants – as befitting a lowly servant. Stealing Iyemon's golden stallion from the stable, I rode to Lord Shigekazu's pavilion.

There, I slipped through the watch corridors and guard niches I knew so well from my time as Shigekazu's captain, until I came to Lady Uma's chambers.

By the light of a muted lamp, I set a porcelain plate by her head and set fire to the opium until a deep, sweet smoke filled the room. In order to keep my own head clear, I wrapped my face with the silk sleeve of one of Uma's kimonos. It also muffled my mouth and thereby my voice, which further served my purposes.

When I was sure she was deep in the opium's thrall, I spoke.

"Uma, Uma," I intoned. "This is your ancestral kami, your family's spirit of fertility. If you wish to bear sons, you must honor me."

Uma mumbled and stirred.

"Speak up, Uma, I cannot hear you," I sang.

"What do you want?" Her speech was sluggish. "Let me sleep."

"If you wish for your union to Iyemon to be blessed with sons, you must answer my questions so I can cast your horoscope."

This seemed to pique her interest. "How many sons will I have?" she murmured.

"As many sons as the fortnights of your courtship."

"That is good. We will have many sons."

"Was your courtship so long?"

She laughed, her throat sultry. "He courted me as soon as he saw me on my palfrey, on the very border of Yotsuya."

"As your escort?"

"Even then."

"Was he not married?"

"I suppose so, but it is common knowledge in the Emperor's court that wives are but a passing inconvenience."

Such a place of depravity the Emperor's house must be. "Did you plot with Iyemon to loosen this 'inconvenience?'"

"A noblewoman does not dirty herself with such details. But when his wife and his servant were found forming the double-backed demon, well, I was hardly surprised."

It was enough. I had discovered the third lie. It was Uma herself. Where Oiwa had been pure and innocent, Uma was corrupt and evil. My fingers trembled to wrap around her traitorous throat. I loomed over her, but then I felt an icy touch at my shoulder.

I glanced back, almost upsetting the lamp when I saw Oiwa's yurei. Thankfully, she continued to shield her face with her fan, although her single clear eye was baleful.

"In order to bear sons," she said, in imitation of my kami voice, "you must marry Iyemon tomorrow."

"We have only just announced our intention to marry to Grandfather today."

"Regardless, you must marry tomorrow or you will be barren forever."

I stared at Oiwa. What was she about?

"Do you understand me, Uma?" she demanded. "You must marry tomorrow!"

"I will, kami. I will."

"Do not forget." This last she directed at me, but Uma, with her eyes shut, did not notice the difference.

Oiwa's fan fluttered, an unspoken threat, and she dissolved into the night.

Trembling like a wind-wracked pine tree, I smothered the still-smoldering opium and blew it cool before pouring ashes and plate into the pocket of my haori jacket. I made sure to light incense to mask the scent as I skulked out of Uma's room. Making as much haste as I dared, I darted to where I had stashed Iyemon's stallion, and rode him full out, all the way back.

I had him re-stabled, my clean clothes shucked, and the ashes of the opium smeared in my hair while Iyemon and Shigekazu lingered over sake. After Shigekazu returned to his pavilion, Iyemon came to my quarters with a jar of wine, which I dutifully drank.

* * *

The next morning, Iyemon trotted me out. A man from the town came to shave and dress us. Through this purification, Iyemon continued to ply me with wine. I drank enough to keep my hand steady and my resolve strong, but poured two bowls out for every one I drank.

Iyemon dressed in the black hakama Oiwa had given him, a travesty of my sister's devotion.

"Why the finery?" I asked, speaking the words as though through half-numbed lips.

"I am to become engaged to the Lady Uma," Iyemon replied. "As you are my brother, I think you should know before the public announcement. I would prefer to stay single, for my heart lies yet with Oiwa, but Lord Shigekazu insisted. He thought good fortune could be restored to his house by a prosperous match."

The lies tripped so easily off his tongue. "I don't begrudge you happiness, my brother." I giggled like a courtesan, high-pitched and merry, and pretended not to see the look of disgust on my 'brother's' face.

When the guests arrived, I played the drunkard for them all, spilling tea and sake, and tripping over my own feet.

Shigekazu, especially, was revolted by me. After I groped one of Uma's maidens, he grabbed me and dragged me from the house. It was what I had hoped he would do.

Dropping my dissembling act, I bowed low.

"My lord, I hope you will forgive my display. I needed to speak to you in private."

He was surprised at my sudden lucid speech, but he was not inclined to hear me. He twisted away.

"Wait! My ancestors have warned me. They have given me two things to share with you. If you recognize the signs, will you humor me?"

He turned back, suspicion and distaste marking lines in his brow.

I handed him the plate from his granddaughter's room.

"Why, this is the expensive plate I gave Uma when she arrived. How did you – ?"

"Lady Uma will insist that the wedding be held today," I said. "She will not be swayed. This too my ancestors divulged to me. Will you hear me?"

"If Uma insists upon marrying Iyemon today, which I know she will not, then yes, I will."

* * *

How Shigekazu's eyes bulged when Uma announced she wished to go to the temple that very day to wed Iyemon. No words could change her mind, and so their Yui-no engagement became their wedding party.

And that is how I pressed lord Shigekazu into accompanying me in hiding behind a bamboo screen in their wedding chambers. His patience with me was at its limits, though. It was the height of impropriety for us to be there, but when the bride in her tsuno kakushi veil stepped into the room, her face concealed, he was as silent as I could have wished.

Behind her, Iyemon followed, and together they lit the ceremonial lamps.

"Why such haste, my blossom?" Iyemon said. "It goes against the plan we made and looks improper."

"Do you not burn for me after all, my husband?" Through the veil, Uma's voice was muffled and strange. My blood turned chill and slow. It was not Uma's voice at all. I had heard that cadence, that tone every day as a boy, singing and talking and shouting. I would know it in my sleep. It was Oiwa.

My plan had been to force a confession from Iyemon and Uma at blade-point, witnessed by Shigekazu. My sister's yurei had other intentions.

Iyemon wrapped his arms around his bride. "How could you ask such a thing?"

"I just wonder if you truly wished to marry me. Were your words of promise lies? Did you instead plan to stay with your wife, Oiwa?"

"Oiwa? That bad luck slut?" Iyemon stepped back. "How could you think that?"

"Perhaps you did not intend for Oiwa to betray you, and were put out by it?"

He caught one of her lily hands. "Come, if it will make you believe my love for you, I will tell you the truth of Oiwa's fate.

"Oiwa did not betray me. She was utterly devoted to me, the simpering cow. You were jealous of her face, you said. She was so sickly after the death of her mother. It was easy to pour poison into her tea. I did it while she watched, calling it medicine. She took it from my hands with such trust. Didn't you hear how the poison I chose disfigured her? Would I have delivered such a caustic potion to anyone I loved?"

"Tell me the symptoms of the poison." Her voice turned harsh. Could Iyemon not hear it?

"It made her ugly, for your enjoyment, my love. It made her hair fall out in great clumps."

The figure of Uma reached under the tsuno kakushi and shed a handful of long, black hair with dried blood at their roots.

"What else?"

"Uma, what – ?"

"What else!"

"H – her face, one eye grew swollen and infected, weeping pus and tears, while the skin puckered, rotting from within."

"She must have been in great pain."

"She screamed for hours."

Lord Shigekazu looked like the gods themselves had touched him, and they had used a heavy hand.

"It must have felt like a lifetime of suffering," the bride continued.

"Better her lifetime than mine. Come, let us lie together, my beautiful blossom."

He lifted his hands to the tsuno kakushi. The thin, white silk slid to the floor. Beneath it, as I had known, was not Uma's pretty face, but Oiwa's terrible one. The white rice powder did not conceal the crust of seeping yellow that oozed from her eye. Nor did it cover the bleak decay of her skin as it sloughed off.

"Come, my husband, kiss me." Oiwa held her arms out to Iyemon. "Embrace me."

Iyemon shrieked and pulled his katana from its sheath. With a single slice, he swept the head off her shoulders. It rolled to where Shigekazu and I spied from behind the bamboo screen.

But it was not Oiwa's face on that severed head, but Uma's.

Shigekazu and I scrambled from cover, away from the grisly remains. Iyemon screamed when he saw us, a cry of rage and madness. He charged at us with his katana upraised. I freed my blade, parried aside his wild strike, and Shigekazu tangled his legs from behind. I knocked his katana from his hand, and together, Shigekazu and I bound him. He gibbered all the while, raving that he saw Oiwa's face in the lantern, her yurei in the corner, her shadow behind the bamboo screen. When I glanced at these places, all I saw were lantern, corner, and screen.

* * *

Shigekazu sent for the magistrate and told them the whole story, clearing Oiwa of any sin. The magistrate sentenced Iyemon to death for his crimes.

In the days before his execution, Iyemon continued to screech and wail in his tiny cell, mad with terror. His eyes rolled in his head, following unseen specters, unknown horrors, all with Oiwa's face. In the end, the headman's sword was a mercy.

That night, I prayed before the altar of my ancestors.

"Oiwa, my part in restoring your honor is done. Are you pleased?"

There was no sound but the wind.

I did not see her again that night, or any other. Although I have heard stories in the village of a beautiful maiden wearing a peacock blue kimono, walking among the plum trees, singing. They say her face is exquisite, but her song sad.

Furisodé

Lafcadio Hearn

RECENTLY, WHILE PASSING THROUGH a little street tenanted chiefly by dealers in old wares, I noticed a *furisodé*, or long-sleeved robe, of the rich purple tint called *murasaki*, hanging before one of the shops. It was a robe such as might have been worn by a lady of rank in the time of the Tokugawa. I stopped to look at the five crests upon it; and in the same moment there came to my recollection this legend of a similar robe said to have once caused the destruction of Yedo.

Nearly two hundred and fifty years ago, the daughter of a rich merchant of the city of the Shōguns, while attending some temple-festival, perceived in the crowd a young *samurai* of remarkable beauty, and immediately fell in love with him. Unhappily for her, he disappeared in the press before she could learn through her attendants who he was or whence he had come. But his image remained vivid in her memory – even to the least detail of his costume. The holiday attire then worn by *samurai* youths was scarcely less brilliant than that of young girls; and the upper dress of this handsome stranger had seemed wonderfully beautiful to the enamoured maiden. She fancied that by wearing a robe of like quality and colour, bearing the same crest, she might be able to attract his notice on some future occasion.

Accordingly she had such a robe made, with very long sleeves, according to the fashion of the period; and she prized it greatly. She wore it whenever she went out; and when at home she would suspend it in her room, and try to imagine the form of her unknown beloved within it. Sometimes she would pass hours before it – dreaming and weeping by turns. And she would pray to the gods and the Buddhas that she might win the young man's affection – often repeating the invocation of the Nichiren sect: *Namu myō hō rengé kyō*!

But she never saw the youth again; and she pined with longing for him, and sickened, and died, and was buried. After her burial, the long-sleeved robe that she had so much prized was given to the Buddhist temple of which her family were parishioners. It is an old custom to thus dispose of the garments of the dead.

The priest was able to sell the robe at a good price; for it was a costly silk, and bore no trace of the tears that had fallen upon it. It was bought by a girl of about the same age as the dead lady. She wore it only one day. Then she fell sick, and began to act strangely – crying out that she was haunted by the vision of a beautiful young man, and that for love of him she was going to die. And within a little while she died; and the long-sleeved robe was a second time presented to the temple.

Again the priest sold it; and again it became the property of a young girl, who wore it only once. Then she also sickened, and talked of a beautiful shadow, and died, and was buried. And the robe was given a third time to the temple; and the priest wondered and doubted.

Nevertheless he ventured to sell the luckless garment once more. Once more it was purchased by a girl and once more worn; and the wearer pined and died. And the robe was given a fourth time to the temple.

Then the priest felt sure that there was some evil influence at work; and he told his acolytes to make a fire in the temple-court, and to burn the robe.

So they made a fire, into which the robe was thrown. But as the silk began to burn, there suddenly appeared upon it dazzling characters of flame – the characters of the invocation, *Namu myō hō rengé kyō* – and these, one by one, leaped like great sparks to the temple roof; and the temple took fire.

Embers from the burning temple presently dropped upon neighbouring roofs; and the whole street was soon ablaze. Then a sea-wind, rising, blew destruction into further streets; and the conflagration spread from street to street, and from district into district, till nearly the whole of the city was consumed. And this calamity, which occurred upon the eighteenth day of the first month of the first year of Meiréki (1655), is still remembered in Tōkyō as the *Furisodé-Kwaji* – the Great Fire of the Long-sleeved Robe.

According to a story-book called *Kibun-Daijin*, the name of the girl who caused the robe to be made was O-Samé; and she was the daughter of Hikoyemon, a wine-merchant of Hyakushō-machi, in the district of Azabu. Because of her beauty she was also called Azabu-Komachi, or the Komachi of Azabu. The same book says that the temple of the tradition was a Nichiren temple called Hon-myoji, in the district of Hongo; and that the crest upon the robe was a *kikyō*-flower. But there are many different versions of the story; and I distrust the *Kibun-Daijin* because it asserts that the beautiful *samurai* was not really a man, but a transformed dragon, or water-serpent, that used to inhabit the lake at Uyéno – Shinobazu-no-Iké.

A Passional Karma

Lafcadio Hearn

I

THERE ONCE LIVED in the district of Ushigomé, in Yedo, a *hatamoto* called Iijima Heizayémon, whose only daughter, Tsuyu, was beautiful as her name, which signifies 'Morning Dew'. Iijima took a second wife when his daughter was about sixteen; and, finding that O-Tsuyu could not be happy with her mother-in-law, he had a pretty villa built for the girl at Yanagijima, as a separate residence, and gave her an excellent maidservant, called O-Yoné, to wait upon her.

O-Tsuyu lived happily enough in her new home until one day when the family physician, Yamamoto Shijō, paid her a visit in company with a young *samurai* named Hagiwara Shinzaburō, who resided in the Nedzu quarter. Shinzaburō was an unusually handsome lad, and very gentle; and the two young people fell in love with each other at sight. Even before the brief visit was over, they contrived, – unheard by the old doctor, – to pledge themselves to each other for life. And, at parting, O-Tsuyu whispered to the youth, – *"Remember! If you do not come to see me again, I shall certainly die!"*

Shinzaburō never forgot those words; and he was only too eager to see more of O-Tsuyu. But etiquette forbade him to make the visit alone: he was obliged to wait for some other chance to accompany the doctor, who had promised to take him to the villa a second time. Unfortunately the old man did not keep this promise. He had perceived the sudden affection of O-Tsuyu; and he feared that her father would hold him responsible for any serious results. Iijima Heizayémon had a reputation for cutting off heads. And the more Shijō thought about the possible consequences of his introduction of Shinzaburō at the Iijima villa, the more he became afraid. Therefore he purposely abstained from calling upon his young friend.

Months passed; and O-Tsuyu, little imagining the true cause of Shinzaburō's neglect, believed that her love had been scorned. Then she pined away, and died. Soon afterwards, the faithful servant O-Yoné also died, through grief at the loss of her mistress; and the two were buried side by side in the cemetery of Shin-Banzui-In, – a temple which still stands in the neighbourhood of Dango-Zaka, where the famous chrysanthemum-shows are yearly held.

II

Shinzaburō knew nothing of what had happened; but his disappointment and his anxiety had resulted in a prolonged illness. He was slowly recovering, but still very weak, when he unexpectedly received another visit from Yamamoto Shijō. The old man made a number of plausible excuses for his apparent neglect. Shinzaburō said to him: "I have been sick ever since the beginning of spring; – even now I cannot eat anything.... Was it not rather unkind of you never to call? I thought that we were to make another visit together to the house of the Lady Iijima; and I wanted to take to her some little present as a return for our kind reception. Of course I could not go by myself."

Shijō gravely responded, – "I am very sorry to tell you that the young lady is dead!"

"Dead!" repeated Shinzaburō, turning white, – "did you say that she is dead?"

The doctor remained silent for a moment, as if collecting himself: then he resumed, in the quick light tone of a man resolved not to take trouble seriously:

"My great mistake was in having introduced you to her; for it seems that she fell in love with you at once. I am afraid that you must have said something to encourage this affection – when you were in that little room together. At all events, I saw how she felt towards you; and then I became uneasy, – fearing that her father might come to hear of the matter, and lay the whole blame upon me. So – to be quite frank with you, – I decided that it would be better not to call upon you; and I purposely stayed away for a long time. But, only a few days ago, happening to visit Iijima's house, I heard, to my great surprise, that his daughter had died, and that her servant O-Yoné had also died. Then, remembering all that had taken place, I knew that the young lady must have died of love for you.... [*Laughing*] Ah, you are really a sinful fellow! Yes, you are! [*Laughing*] Isn't it a sin to have been born so handsome that the girls die for love of you? [*Seriously*] Well, we must leave the dead to the dead. It is no use to talk further about the matter; – all that you now can do for her is to repeat the Nembutsu.... Good-bye."

And the old man retired hastily, – anxious to avoid further converse about the painful event for which he felt himself to have been unwittingly responsible.

III

Shinzaburō long remained stupefied with grief by the news of O-Tsuyu's death. But as soon as he found himself again able to think clearly, he inscribed the dead girl's name upon a mortuary tablet, and placed the tablet in the Buddhist shrine of his house, and set offerings before it, and recited prayers. Every day thereafter he presented offerings, and repeated the *Nembutsu*; and the memory of O-Tsuyu was never absent from his thought.

Nothing occurred to change the monotony of his solitude before the time of the Bon, – the great Festival of the Dead, – which begins upon the thirteenth day of the seventh month. Then he decorated his house, and prepared everything for the festival; – hanging out the lanterns that guide the returning spirits, and setting the food of ghosts on the *shōryōdana*, or Shelf of Souls. And on the first evening of the Bon, after sun-down, he kindled a small lamp before the tablet of O-Tsuyu, and lighted the lanterns.

The night was clear, with a great moon, – and windless, and very warm. Shinzaburō sought the coolness of his verandah. Clad only in a light summer-robe, he sat there thinking, dreaming, sorrowing; – sometimes fanning himself; sometimes making a little smoke to drive the mosquitoes away. Everything was quiet. It was a lonesome neighbourhood, and there were few passers-by. He could hear only the soft rushing of a neighbouring stream, and the shrilling of night-insects.

But all at once this stillness was broken by a sound of women's *geta* approaching – *kara-kon, kara-kon*; – and the sound drew nearer and nearer, quickly, till it reached the live-hedge surrounding the garden. Then Shinzaburō, feeling curious, stood on tiptoe, so as to look over the hedge; and he saw two women passing. One, who was carrying a beautiful lantern decorated with peony-flowers, appeared to be a servant; – the other was a slender girl of about seventeen, wearing a long-sleeved robe embroidered with designs of autumn-blossoms. Almost at the same instant both women turned their faces toward Shinzaburō; – and to his utter astonishment, he recognized O-Tsuyu and her servant O-Yoné.

They stopped immediately; and the girl cried out, – "Oh, how strange!... Hagiwara Sama!"

Shinzaburō simultaneously called to the maid: "O-Yoné! Ah, you are O-Yoné! – I remember you very well."

"Hagiwara Sama!" exclaimed O-Yoné in a tone of supreme amazement. "Never could I have believed it possible!... Sir, we were told that you had died."

"How extraordinary!" cried Shinzaburō. "Why, I was told that both of you were dead!"

"Ah, what a hateful story!" returned O-Yoné. "Why repeat such unlucky words?... Who told you?"

"Please to come in," said Shinzaburō; – "here we can talk better. The garden-gate is open."

So they entered, and exchanged greeting; and when Shinzaburō had made them comfortable, he said:

"I trust that you will pardon my discourtesy in not having called upon you for so long a time. But Shijō, the doctor, about a month ago, told me that you had both died."

"So it was he who told you?" exclaimed O-Yoné. "It was very wicked of him to say such a thing. Well, it was also Shijō who told us that *you* were dead. I think that he wanted to deceive you, – which was not a difficult thing to do, because you are so confiding and trustful. Possibly my mistress betrayed her liking for you in some words which found their way to her father's ears; and, in that case, O-Kuni – the new wife – might have planned to make the doctor tell you that we were dead, so as to bring about a separation. Anyhow, when my mistress heard that you had died, she wanted to cut off her hair immediately, and to become a nun. But I was able to prevent her from cutting off her hair; and I persuaded her at last to become a nun only in her heart. Afterwards her father wished her to marry a certain young man; and she refused. Then there was a great deal of trouble, – chiefly caused by O-Kuni; – and we went away from the villa, and found a very small house in Yanaka-no-Sasaki. There we are now just barely able to live, by doing a little private work.... My mistress has been constantly repeating the *Nembutsu* for your sake. To-day, being the first day of the Bon, we went to visit the temples; and we were on our way home – thus late – when this strange meeting happened."

"Oh, how extraordinary!" cried Shinzaburō. "Can it be true? – or is it only a dream? Here I, too, have been constantly reciting the *Nembutsu* before a tablet with her name upon it! Look!" And he showed them O-Tsuyu's tablet in its place upon the Shelf of Souls.

"We are more than grateful for your kind remembrance," returned O-Yoné, smiling.... "Now as for my mistress," – she continued, turning towards O-Tsuyu, who had all the while remained demure and silent, half-hiding her face with her sleeve, – "as for my mistress, she actually says that she would not mind being disowned by her father for the time of seven existences, or even being killed by him, for your sake! Come! will you not allow her to stay here to-night?"

Shinzaburō turned pale for joy. He answered in a voice trembling with emotion:

"Please remain; but do not speak loud – because there is a troublesome fellow living close by, – a *ninsomi* called Hakuōdō Yusai, who tells peoples fortunes by looking at their faces. He is inclined to be curious; and it is better that he should not know."

The two women remained that night in the house of the young *samurai*, and returned to their own home a little before daybreak. And after that night they came every night for seven nights, – whether the weather were foul or fair – always at the same hour. And Shinzaburō became more and more attached to the girl; and the twain were fettered, each to each, by that bond of illusion which is stronger than bands of iron.

IV

Now there was a man called Tomozō, who lived in a small cottage adjoining Shinzaburō's residence. Tomozō and his wife O-Miné were both employed by Shinzaburō as servants. Both seemed to be devoted to their young master; and by his help they were able to live in comparative comfort.

One night, at a very late hour, Tomozō heard the voice of a woman in his master's apartment; and this made him uneasy. He feared that Shinzaburō, being very gentle and affectionate, might be made the dupe of some cunning wanton, – in which event the domestics would be the first to suffer. He therefore resolved to watch; and on the following night he stole on tiptoe to Shinzaburō's dwelling, and looked through a chink in one of the sliding shutters. By the glow of a night-lantern within the sleeping-room, he was able to perceive that his master and a strange woman were talking together under the mosquito-net. At first he could not see the woman distinctly. Her back was turned to him; – he only observed that she was very slim, and that she appeared to be very young, – judging from the fashion of her dress and hair. Putting his ear to the chink, he could hear the conversation plainly. The woman said:

"And if I should be disowned by my father, would you then let me come and live with you?"

Shinzaburō answered:

"Most assuredly I would – nay, I should be glad of the chance. But there is no reason to fear that you will ever be disowned by your father; for you are his only daughter, and he loves you very much. What I do fear is that some day we shall be cruelly separated."

She responded softly:

"Never, never could I even think of accepting any other man for my husband. Even if our secret were to become known, and my father were to kill me for what I have done, still – after death itself – I could never cease to think of you. And I am now quite sure that you yourself would not be able to live very long without me." ... Then clinging closely to him, with her lips at his neck, she caressed him; and he returned her caresses.

Tomozō wondered as he listened, – because the language of the woman was not the language of a common woman, but the language of a lady of rank. Then he determined at all hazards to get one glimpse of her face; and he crept round the house, backwards and forwards, peering through every crack and chink. And at last he was able to see; – but therewith an icy trembling seized him; and the hair of his head stood up.

For the face was the face of a woman long dead, – and the fingers caressing were fingers of naked bone, – and of the body below the waist there was not anything: it melted off into thinnest trailing shadow. Where the eyes of the lover deluded saw youth and grace and beauty, there appeared to the eyes of the watcher horror only, and the emptiness of death. Simultaneously another woman's figure, and a weirder, rose up from within the chamber, and swiftly made toward the watcher, as if discerning his presence. Then, in uttermost terror, he fled to the dwelling of Hakuōdō Yusai, and, knocking frantically at the doors, succeeded in arousing him.

V

Hakuōdō Yusai, the *ninsomi*, was a very old man; but in his time he had travelled much, and he had heard and seen so many things that he could not be easily surprised. Yet the story of the terrified Tomozō both alarmed and amazed him. He had read in ancient Chinese books of love between the living and the dead; but he had never believed it possible. Now, however, he felt convinced that the statement of Tomozō was not a falsehood, and that something very strange was really going on in the house of Hagiwara. Should the truth prove to be what Tomozō imagined, then the young *samurai* was a doomed man.

"If the woman be a ghost," – said Yusai to the frightened servant, "—if the woman be a ghost, your master must die very soon, – unless something extraordinary can be done to save him. And if the woman be a ghost, the signs of death will appear upon his face. For the spirit of the living is *yōki*, and pure; – the spirit of the dead is *inki*, and unclean: the one is Positive, the other Negative. He whose bride is a ghost cannot live. Even though in his blood there existed the force of a life of one hundred years, that force must quickly perish.... Still, I shall do all that I can to save Hagiwara Sama. And in the meantime, Tomozō, say nothing to any other person, – not even to your wife, – about this matter. At sunrise I shall call upon your master."

VI

When questioned next morning by Yusai, Shinzaburō at first attempted to deny that any women had been visiting the house; but finding this artless policy of no avail, and perceiving that the old man's purpose was altogether unselfish, he was finally persuaded to acknowledge what had really occurred, and to give his reasons for wishing to keep the matter a secret. As for the lady Iijima, he intended, he said, to make her his wife as soon as possible.

"Oh, madness!" cried Yusai, – losing all patience in the intensity of his alarm. "Know, sir, that the people who have been coming here, night after night, are dead! Some frightful delusion is upon you!… Why, the simple fact that you long supposed O-Tsuyu to be dead, and repeated the *Nembutsu* for her, and made offerings before her tablet, is itself the proof!… The lips of the dead have touched you! – the hands of the dead have caressed you!… Even at this moment I see in your face the signs of death – and you will not believe!… Listen to me now, sir, – I beg of you, – if you wish to save yourself: otherwise you have less than twenty days to live. They told you – those people – that they were residing in the district of Shitaya, in Yanaka-no-Sasaki. Did you ever visit them at that place? No! – of course you did not! Then go to-day, – as soon as you can, – to Yanaka-no-Sasaki, and try to find their home!…"

And having uttered this counsel with the most vehement earnestness, Hakuōdō Yusai abruptly took his departure.

Shinzaburō, startled though not convinced, resolved after a moment's reflection to follow the advice of the *ninsomi*, and to go to Shitaya. It was yet early in the morning when he reached the quarter of Yanaka-no-Sasaki, and began his search for the dwelling of O-Tsuyu. He went through every street and side-street, read all the names inscribed at the various entrances, and made inquiries whenever an opportunity presented itself. But he could not find anything resembling the little house mentioned by O-Yoné; and none of the people whom he questioned knew of any house in the quarter inhabited by two single women. Feeling at last certain that further research would be useless, he turned homeward by the shortest way, which happened to lead through the grounds of the temple Shin-Banzui-In.

Suddenly his attention was attracted by two new tombs, placed side by side, at the rear of the temple. One was a common tomb, such as might have been erected for a person of humble rank: the other was a large and handsome monument; and hanging before it was a beautiful peony-lantern, which had probably been left there at the time of the Festival of the Dead. Shinzaburō remembered that the peony-lantern carried by O-Yoné was exactly similar; and the coincidence impressed him as strange. He looked again at the tombs; but the tombs explained nothing. Neither bore any personal name, – only the Buddhist *kaimyō*, or posthumous appellation. Then he determined to seek information at the temple. An acolyte stated, in reply to his questions, that the large tomb had been recently erected for the daughter of Iijima Heizayémon, the *hatamoto* of Ushigomé; and that the small tomb next to it was that of her servant O-Yoné, who had died of grief soon after the young lady's funeral.

Immediately to Shinzaburō's memory there recurred, with another and sinister meaning, the words of O-Yoné: "*We went away, and found a very small house in Yanaka-no-Sasaki. There we are now just barely able to live – by doing a little private work….*" Here was indeed the very small house, – and in Yanaka-no-Sasaki. But the little *private work*…?

Terror-stricken, the *samurai* hastened with all speed to the house of Yusai, and begged for his counsel and assistance. But Yusai declared himself unable to be of any aid in such a case. All that he could do was to send Shinzaburō to the high-priest Ryōseki, of Shin-Banzui-In, with a letter praying for immediate religious help.

VII

The high-priest Ryōseki was a learned and a holy man. By spiritual vision he was able to know the secret of any sorrow, and the nature of the karma that had caused it. He heard unmoved the story of Shinzaburō, and said to him:

"A very great danger now threatens you, because of an error committed in one of your former states of existence. The karma that binds you to the dead is very strong; but if I tried to explain its character, you would not be able to understand. I shall therefore tell you only this, – that the dead person has no desire to injure you out of hate, feels no enmity towards you: she is influenced, on the contrary, by the most passionate affection for you. Probably the girl has been in love with you from a time long preceding your present life, – from a time of not less than three or four past existences; and it would seem that, although necessarily changing her form and condition at each succeeding birth, she has not been able to cease from following after you. Therefore it will not be an easy thing to escape from her influence.... But now I am going to lend you this powerful *mamori*. It is a pure gold image of that Buddha called the Sea-Sounding Tathâgata – *Kai-On-Nyōrai*, – because his preaching of the Law sounds through the world like the sound of the sea. And this little image is especially a *shiryō-yoké*, – which protects the living from the dead. This you must wear, in its covering, next to your body – under the girdle.... Besides, I shall presently perform in the temple, a segaki-service for the repose of the troubled spirit.... And here is a holy sutra, called *Ubō-Darani-Kyō*, or 'Treasure-Raining Sûtra' you must be careful to recite it every night in your house – without fail.... Furthermore I shall give you this package of *o-fuda*; – you must paste one of them over every opening of your house, – no matter how small. If you do this, the power of the holy texts will prevent the dead from entering. But – whatever may happen – do not fail to recite the sutra."

Shinzaburō humbly thanked the high-priest; and then, taking with him the image, the sutra, and the bundle of sacred texts, he made all haste to reach his home before the hour of sunset.

VIII

With Yusai's advice and help, Shinzaburō was able before dark to fix the holy texts over all the apertures of his dwelling. Then the *ninsomi* returned to his own house – leaving the youth alone.

Night came, warm and clear. Shinzaburō made fast the doors, bound the precious amulet about his waist, entered his mosquito-net, and by the glow of a night-lantern began to recite the *Ubō-Darani-Kyō*. For a long time he chanted the words, comprehending little of their meaning; – then he tried to obtain some rest. But his mind was still too much disturbed by the strange events of the day. Midnight passed; and no sleep came to him. At last he heard the boom of the great temple-bell of Dentsu-In announcing the eighth hour.

It ceased; and Shinzaburō suddenly heard the sound of *geta* approaching from the old direction, – but this time more slowly: *karan-koron, karan-koron*! At once a cold sweat broke over his forehead. Opening the sutra hastily, with trembling hand, he began again to recite it aloud. The steps came nearer and nearer, – reached the live hedge, – stopped! Then, strange to say, Shinzaburō felt unable to remain under his mosquito-net: something stronger even than his fear impelled him to look; and, instead of continuing to recite the *Ubō-Darani-Kyō*, he foolishly approached the shutters, and through a chink peered out into the night. Before the house he saw O-Tsuyu standing, and O-Yoné with the peony-lantern; and both of them were gazing at the Buddhist texts pasted above the entrance. Never before – not even in what time she lived – had O-Tsuyu appeared so beautiful; and Shinzaburō felt his heart drawn towards her with a power almost resistless. But the terror of death and the terror of the unknown restrained; and there went on within him such a struggle between his love and his fear that he became as one suffering in the body the pains of the Shō-netsu hell.

Presently he heard the voice of the maid-servant, saying:

"My dear mistress, there is no way to enter. The heart of Hagiwara Sama must have changed. For the promise that he made last night has been broken; and the doors have been made fast to keep us out.... We cannot go in to-night.... It will be wiser for you to make up your mind not to think any more about him, because his feeling towards you has certainly changed. It is evident that he does not want to see you. So it will be better not to give yourself any more trouble for the sake of a man whose heart is so unkind."

But the girl answered, weeping:

"Oh, to think that this could happen after the pledges which we made to each other!... Often I was told that the heart of a man changes as quickly as the sky of autumn; – yet surely the heart of Hagiwara Sama cannot be so cruel that he should really intend to exclude me in this way!... Dear Yone, please find some means of taking me to him.... Unless you do, I will never, never go home again."

Thus she continued to plead, veiling her face with her long sleeves, – and very beautiful she looked, and very touching; but the fear of death was strong upon her lover.

O-Yoné at last made answer, – "My dear young lady, why will you trouble your mind about a man who seems to be so cruel?... Well, let us see if there be no way to enter at the back of the house: come with me!"

And taking O-Tsuyu by the hand, she led her away toward the rear of the dwelling; and there the two disappeared as suddenly as the light disappears when the flame of a lamp is blown out.

IX

Night after night the shadows came at the Hour of the Ox; and nightly Shinzaburō heard the weeping of O-Tsuyu. Yet he believed himself saved, – little imagining that his doom had already been decided by the character of his dependents.

Tomozō had promised Yusai never to speak to any other person – not even to O-Miné – of the strange events that were taking place. But Tomozō was not long suffered by the haunters to rest in peace. Night after night O-Yoné entered into his dwelling, and roused him from his sleep, and asked him to remove the *o-fuda* placed over one very small window at the back of his master's house. And Tomozō, out of fear, as often promised her to take away the *o-fuda* before the next sundown; but never by day could he make up his mind to remove it, – believing that evil was intended to Shinzaburō. At last, in a night of storm, O-Yoné startled him from slumber with a cry of reproach, and stooped above his pillow, and said to him: "Have a care how you trifle with us! If, by to-morrow night, you do not take away that text, you shall learn how I can hate!" And she made her face so frightful as she spoke that Tomozō nearly died of terror.

O-Miné, the wife of Tomozō, had never till then known of these visits: even to her husband they had seemed like bad dreams. But on this particular night it chanced that, waking suddenly, she heard the voice of a woman talking to Tomozō. Almost in the same moment the talk-ing ceased; and when O-Miné looked about her, she saw, by the light of the night-lamp, only her husband, – shuddering and white with fear. The stranger was gone; the doors were fast: it seemed impossible that anybody could have entered. Nevertheless the jealousy of the wife had been aroused; and she began to chide and to question Tomozō in such a manner that he thought himself obliged to betray the secret, and to explain the terrible dilemma in which he had been placed.

Then the passion of O-Miné yielded to wonder and alarm; but she was a subtle woman, and she devised immediately a plan to save her husband by the sacrifice of her master. And she gave Tomozō a cunning counsel, – telling him to make conditions with the dead.

They came again on the following night at the Hour of the Ox; and O-Miné hid herself on hearing the sound of their coming, – *karan-koron, karan-koron!* But Tomozō went out to meet them in the dark, and even found courage to say to them what his wife had told him to say:

"It is true that I deserve your blame; – but I had no wish to cause you anger. The reason that the *o-fuda* has not been taken away is that my wife and I are able to live only by the help of Hagiwara Sama, and that we cannot expose him to any danger without bringing misfortune upon ourselves. But if we could obtain the sum of a hundred *ryō* in gold, we should be able to please you, because we should then need no help from anybody. Therefore if you will give us a hundred *ryō*, I can take the *o-fuda* away without being afraid of losing our only means of support."

When he had uttered these words, O-Yoné and O-Tsuyu looked at each other in silence for a moment. Then O-Yoné said:

"Mistress, I told you that it was not right to trouble this man, – as we have no just cause of ill will against him. But it is certainly useless to fret yourself about Hagiwara Sama, because his heart has changed towards you. Now once again, my dear young lady, let me beg you not to think any more about him!"

But O-Tsuyu, weeping, made answer:

"Dear Yone, whatever may happen, I cannot possibly keep myself from thinking about him! You know that you can get a hundred *ryō* to have the *o-fuda* taken off.... Only once more, I pray, dear Yone! – only once more bring me face to face with Hagiwara Sama, – I beseech you!" And hiding her face with her sleeve, she thus continued to plead.

"Oh! why will you ask me to do these things?" responded O-Yoné. "You know very well that I have no money. But since you will persist in this whim of yours, in spite of all that I can say, I suppose that I must try to find the money somehow, and to bring it here to-morrow night...." Then, turning to the faithless Tomozō, she said: "Tomozō, I must tell you that Hagiwara Sama now wears upon his body a *mamori* called by the name of *Kai-On-Nyōrai*, and that so long as he wears it we cannot approach him. So you will have to get that *mamori* away from him, by some means or other, as well as to remove the *o-fuda*."

Tomozō feebly made answer:

"That also I can do, if you will promise to bring me the hundred *ryō*."

"Well, mistress," said O-Yoné, "you will wait, – will you not, – until to-morrow night?"

"Oh, dear Yoné!" sobbed the other,—"have we to go back to-night again without seeing Hagiwara Sama? Ah! it is cruel!"

And the shadow of the mistress, weeping, was led away by the shadow of the maid.

X

Another day went, and another night came, and the dead came with it. But this time no lamentation was heard without the house of Hagiwara; for the faithless servant found his reward at the Hour of the Ox, and removed the *o-fuda*. Moreover he had been able, while his master was at the bath, to steal from its case the golden *mamori*, and to substitute for it an image of copper; and he had buried the *Kai-On-Nyōrai* in a desolate field. So the visitants found nothing to oppose their entering. Veiling their faces with their sleeves they rose and passed, like a streaming of vapour, into the little window from over which the holy text had been torn away. But what happened thereafter within the house Tomozō never knew.

The sun was high before he ventured again to approach his master's dwelling, and to knock upon the sliding-doors. For the first time in years he obtained no response; and the silence made him afraid. Repeatedly he called, and received no answer. Then, aided by O-Miné, he succeeded in effecting an entrance and making his way alone to the sleeping-room, where he called again in vain. He rolled back the rumbling shutters to admit the light; but still within the house there was no stir. At last he dared to lift a corner of the mosquito-net. But no sooner had he looked beneath than he fled from the house, with a cry of horror.

Shinzaburō was dead – hideously dead; – and his face was the face of a man who had died in the uttermost agony of fear; – and lying beside him in the bed were the bones of a woman! And the bones of the arms, and the bones of the hands, clung fast about his neck.

XI

Hakuōdō Yusai, the fortune-teller, went to view the corpse at the prayer of the faithless Tomozō. The old man was terrified and astonished at the spectacle, but looked about him with a keen eye. He soon perceived that the *o-fuda* had been taken from the little window at the back of the house; and on searching the body of Shinzaburō, he discovered that the golden *mamori* had been taken from its wrapping, and a copper image of Fudō put in place of it. He suspected Tomozō of the theft; but the whole occurrence was so very extraordinary that he thought it prudent to consult with the priest Ryōseki before taking further action. Therefore, after having made a careful examination of the premises, he betook himself to the temple Shin-Banzui-In, as quickly as his aged limbs could bear him.

Ryōseki, without waiting to hear the purpose of the old man's visit, at once invited him into a private apartment.

"You know that you are always welcome here," said Ryōseki. "Please seat yourself at ease.... Well, I am sorry to tell you that Hagiwara Sama is dead."

Yusai wonderingly exclaimed: "Yes, he is dead; – but how did you learn of it?"

The priest responded:

"Hagiwara Sama was suffering from the results of an evil karma; and his attendant was a bad man. What happened to Hagiwara Sama was unavoidable, – his destiny had been determined from a time long before his last birth. It will be better for you not to let your mind be troubled by this event."

Yusai said:

"I have heard that a priest of pure life may gain power to see into the future for a hundred years; but truly this is the first time in my existence that I have had proof of such power.... Still, there is another matter about which I am very anxious...."

"You mean," interrupted Ryōseki, "the stealing of the holy *mamori*, the *Kai-On-Nyōrai*. But you must not give yourself any concern about that. The image has been buried in a field; and it will be found there and returned to me during the eighth month of the coming year. So please do not be anxious about it."

More and more amazed, the old *ninsomi* ventured to observe:

"I have studied the *In-Yō*, and the science of divination; and I make my living by telling peoples' fortunes; – but I cannot possibly understand how you know these things."

Ryōseki answered gravely:

"Never mind how I happen to know them.... I now want to speak to you about Hagiwara's funeral. The House of Hagiwara has its own family-cemetery, of course; but to bury him there would not be proper. He must be buried beside O-Tsuyu, the Lady Iijima; for his karma-relation to her was a very deep one. And it is but right that you should erect a tomb for him at your own cost, because you have been indebted to him for many favours."

Thus it came to pass that Shinzaburō was buried beside O-Tsuyu, in the cemetery of Shin-Banzui-In, in Yanaka-no-Sasaki.

Ingwa-banashi

Lafcadio Hearn

THE DAIMYO'S WIFE was dying, and knew that she was dying. She had not been able to leave her bed since the early autumn of the tenth Bunsei. It was now the fourth month of the twelfth Bunsei, – the year 1829 by Western counting; and the cherry-trees were blossoming. She thought of the cherry-trees in her garden, and of the gladness of spring. She thought of her children. She thought of her husband's various concubines, – especially the Lady Yukiko, nineteen years old.

"My dear wife," said the *daimyo*, "you have suffered very much for three long years. We have done all that we could to get you well, – watching beside you night and day, praying for you, and often fasting for your sake, But in spite of our loving care, and in spite of the skill of our best physicians, it would now seem that the end of your life is not far off. Probably we shall sorrow more than you will sorrow because of your having to leave what the Buddha so truly termed 'this burning-house of the world'. I shall order to be performed – no matter what the cost – every religious rite that can serve you in regard to your next rebirth; and all of us will pray without ceasing for you, that you may not have to wander in the Black Space, but may quickly enter Paradise, and attain to Buddha-hood."

He spoke with the utmost tenderness, pressing her the while. Then, with eyelids closed, she answered him in a voice thin as the voice of in insect:

"I am grateful – most grateful – for your kind words.... Yes, it is true, as you say, that I have been sick for three long years, and that I have been treated with all possible care and affection.... Why, indeed, should I turn away from the one true Path at the very moment of my death?... Perhaps to think of worldly matters at such a time is not right; – but I have one last request to make, – only one.... Call here to me the Lady Yukiko; – you know that I love her like a sister. I want to speak to her about the affairs of this household."

Yukiko came at the summons of the lord, and, in obedience to a sign from him, knelt down beside the couch. The *daimyo*'s wife opened her eyes, and looked at Yukiko, and spoke: "Ah, here is Yukiko!... I am so pleased to see you, Yukiko!... Come a little closer, – so that you can hear me well: I am not able to speak loud.... Yukiko, I am going to die. I hope that you will be faithful in all things to our dear lord; – for I want you to take my place when I am gone.... I hope that you will always be loved by him, – yes, even a hundred times more than I have been, – and that you will very soon be promoted to a higher rank, and become his honoured wife.... And I beg of you always to cherish our dear lord: never allow another woman to rob you of his affection.... This is what I wanted to say to you, dear Yukiko.... Have you been able to understand?"

"Oh, my dear Lady," protested Yukiko, "do not, I entreat you, say such strange things to me! You well know that I am of poor and mean condition: how could I ever dare to aspire to become the wife of our lord!"

"Nay, nay!" returned the wife, huskily, – "this is not a time for words of ceremony: let us speak only the truth to each other. After my death, you will certainly be promoted to a higher place; and I now assure you again that I wish you to become the wife of our lord – yes, I wish this, Yukiko, even more than I wish to become a Buddha!... Ah, I had almost forgotten! – I want you to do something for me, Yukiko. You know that in the garden there is a *yaë-zakura*, which was brought here, the year before last, from

Mount Yoshino in Yamato. I have been told that it is now in full bloom; – and I wanted so much to see it in flower! In a little while I shall be dead; – I must see that tree before I die. Now I wish you to carry me into the garden – at once, Yukiko, – so that I can see it…. Yes, upon your back, Yukiko; – take me upon your back…."

While thus asking, her voice had gradually become clear and strong, – as if the intensity of the wish had given her new force: then she suddenly burst into tears. Yukiko knelt motionless, not knowing what to do; but the lord nodded assent.

"It is her last wish in this world," he said. "She always loved cherry-flowers; and I know that she wanted very much to see that Yamato-tree in blossom. Come, my dear Yukiko, let her have her will."

As a nurse turns her back to a child, that the child may cling to it, Yukiko offered her shoulders to the wife, and said:

"Lady, I am ready: please tell me how I best can help you."

"Why, this way!" – responded the dying woman, lifting herself with an almost superhuman effort by clinging to Yukiko's shoulders. But as she stood erect, she quickly slipped her thin hands down over the shoulders, under the robe, and clutched the breasts of the girl, and burst into a wicked laugh.

"I have my wish!" she cried – "I have my wish for the cherry-bloom, – but not the cherry-bloom of the garden!… I could not die before I got my wish. Now I have it! – oh, what a delight!"

And with these words she fell forward upon the crouching girl, and died.

The attendants at once attempted to lift the body from Yukiko's shoulders, and to lay it upon the bed. But – strange to say! – this seemingly easy thing could not be done. The cold hands had attached themselves in some unaccountable way to the breasts of the girl, – appeared to have grown into the quick flesh. Yukiko became senseless with fear and pain.

Physicians were called. They could not understand what had taken place. By no ordinary methods could the hands of the dead woman be unfastened from the body of her victim; – they so clung that any effort to remove them brought blood. This was not because the fingers held: it was because the flesh of the palms had united itself in some inexplicable manner to the flesh of the breasts!

At that time the most skilful physician in Yedo was a foreigner, – a Dutch surgeon. It was decided to summon him. After a careful examination he said that he could not understand the case, and that for the immediate relief of Yukiko there was nothing to be done except to cut the hands from the corpse. He declared that it would be dangerous to attempt to detach them from the breasts. His advice was accepted; and the hands' were amputated at the wrists. But they remained clinging to the breasts; and there they soon darkened and dried up, – like the hands of a person long dead.

Yet this was only the beginning of the horror.

Withered and bloodless though they seemed, those hands were not dead. At intervals they would stir – stealthily, like great grey spiders. And nightly thereafter, – beginning always at the Hour of the Ox, – they would clutch and compress and torture. Only at the Hour of the Tiger the pain would cease.

Yukiko cut off her hair, and became a mendicant-nun, – taking the religious name of Dassetsu. She had an *ihai* (mortuary tablet) made, bearing the *kaimyō* of her dead mistress, – 'Myō-Kō-In-Den Chizan-Ryō-Fu Daishi'; – and this she carried about with her in all her wanderings; and every day before it she humbly besought the dead for pardon, and performed a Buddhist service in order that the jealous spirit might find rest. But the evil karma that had rendered such an affliction possible could not soon be exhausted. Every night at the Hour of the Ox, the hands never failed to torture her, during more than seventeen years, – according to the testimony of those persons to whom she last told her story, when she stopped for one evening at the house of Noguchi Dengozayémon, in the village of Tanaka in the district of Kawachi in the province of Shimotsuké. This was in the third year of Kōkwa (1846). Thereafter nothing more was ever heard of her.

Jiu-roku-zakura

Lafcadio Hearn

IN WAKEGORI, a district of the province of Iyo, there is a very ancient and famous cherry-tree, called Jiu-roku-zakura, or 'the Cherry-tree of the Sixteenth Day', because it blooms every year upon the sixteenth day of the first month (by the old lunar calendar), – and only upon that day. Thus the time of its flowering is the Period of Great Cold, – though the natural habit of a cherry-tree is to wait for the spring season before venturing to blossom. But the Jiu-roku-zakura blossoms with a life that is not – or, at least, that was not originally – its own. There is the ghost of a man in that tree.

He was a *samurai* of Iyo; and the tree grew in his garden; and it used to flower at the usual time, – that is to say, about the end of March or the beginning of April. He had played under that tree when he was a child; and his parents and grandparents and ancestors had hung to its blossoming branches, season after season for more than a hundred years, bright strips of coloured paper inscribed with poems of praise. He himself became very old, – outliving all his children; and there was nothing in the world left for him to live except that tree. And lo! in the summer of a certain year, the tree withered and died!

Exceedingly the old man sorrowed for his tree. Then kind neighbours found for him a young and beautiful cherry-tree, and planted it in his garden, – hoping thus to comfort him. And he thanked them, and pretended to be glad. But really his heart was full of pain; for he had loved the old tree so well that nothing could have consoled him for the loss of it.

At last there came to him a happy thought: he remembered a way by which the perishing tree might be saved. (It was the sixteenth day of the first month.) Along he went into his garden, and bowed down before the withered tree, and spoke to it, saying: "Now deign, I beseech you, once more to bloom, – because I am going to die in your stead." (For it is believed that one can really give away one's life to another person, or to a creature or even to a tree, by the favour of the gods; – and thus to transfer one's life is expressed by the term *migawari ni tatsu*, 'to act as a substitute'.) Then under that tree he spread a white cloth, and divers coverings, and sat down upon the coverings, and performed hara-kiri after the fashion of a *samurai*. And the ghost of him went into the tree, and made it blossom in that same hour.

And every year it still blooms on the sixteenth day of the first month, in the season of snow.

Yuki-Onna

Lafcadio Hearn

IN A VILLAGE of Musashi Province, there lived two woodcutters: Mosaku and Minokichi. At the time of which I am speaking, Mosaku was an old man; and Minokichi, his apprentice, was a lad of eighteen years. Every day they went together to a forest situated about five miles from their village. On the way to that forest there is a wide river to cross; and there is a ferry-boat. Several times a bridge was built where the ferry is; but the bridge was each time carried away by a flood. No common bridge can resist the current there when the river rises.

Mosaku and Minokichi were on their way home, one very cold evening, when a great snowstorm overtook them. They reached the ferry; and they found that the boatman had gone away, leaving his boat on the other side of the river. It was no day for swimming; and the woodcutters took shelter in the ferryman's hut, – thinking themselves lucky to find any shelter at all. There was no brazier in the hut, nor any place in which to make a fire: it was only a two-mat hut, with a single door, but no window. Mosaku and Minokichi fastened the door, and lay down to rest, with their straw rain-coats over them. At first they did not feel very cold; and they thought that the storm would soon be over.

The old man almost immediately fell asleep; but the boy, Minokichi, lay awake a long time, listening to the awful wind, and the continual slashing of the snow against the door. The river was roaring; and the hut swayed and creaked like a junk at sea. It was a terrible storm; and the air was every moment becoming colder; and Minokichi shivered under his rain-coat. But at last, in spite of the cold, he too fell asleep.

He was awakened by a showering of snow in his face. The door of the hut had been forced open; and, by the snow-light (*yuki-akari*), he saw a woman in the room, – a woman all in white. She was bending above Mosaku, and blowing her breath upon him; – and her breath was like a bright white smoke. Almost in the same moment she turned to Minokichi, and stooped over him. He tried to cry out, but found that he could not utter any sound. The white woman bent down over him, lower and lower, until her face almost touched him; and he saw that she was very beautiful, – though her eyes made him afraid. For a little time she continued to look at him; – then she smiled, and she whispered: "I intended to treat you like the other man. But I cannot help feeling some pity for you, – because you are so young.... You are a pretty boy, Minokichi; and I will not hurt you now. But, if you ever tell anybody – even your own mother – about what you have seen this night, I shall know it; and then I will kill you.... Remember what I say!"

With these words, she turned from him, and passed through the doorway. Then he found himself able to move; and he sprang up, and looked out. But the woman was nowhere to be seen; and the snow was driving furiously into the hut. Minokichi closed the door, and secured it by fixing several billets of wood against it. He wondered if the wind had blown it open; – he thought that he might have been only dreaming, and might have mistaken the gleam of the snow-light in the doorway for the figure of a white woman: but he could not be sure. He called to Mosaku, and was frightened because the old man did not answer. He put out his hand in the dark, and touched Mosaku's face, and found that it was ice! Mosaku was stark and dead...

By dawn the storm was over; and when the ferryman returned to his station, a little after sunrise, he found Minokichi lying senseless beside the frozen body of Mosaku. Minokichi was promptly cared for, and soon came to himself; but he remained a long time ill from the effects of the cold of that terrible night. He had been greatly frightened also by the old man's death; but he said nothing about the vision of the woman in white. As soon as he got well again, he returned to his calling, – going alone every morning to the forest, and coming back at nightfall with his bundles of wood, which his mother helped him to sell.

One evening, in the winter of the following year, as he was on his way home, he overtook a girl who happened to be travelling by the same road. She was a tall, slim girl, very good-looking; and she answered Minokichi's greeting in a voice as pleasant to the ear as the voice of a song-bird. Then he walked beside her; and they began to talk. The girl said that her name was O-Yuki; that she had lately lost both of her parents; and that she was going to Yedo, where she happened to have some poor relations, who might help her to find a situation as a servant. Minokichi soon felt charmed by this strange girl; and the more that he looked at her, the handsomer she appeared to be. He asked her whether she was yet betrothed; and she answered, laughingly, that she was free. Then, in her turn, she asked Minokichi whether he was married, or pledged to marry; and he told her that, although he had only a widowed mother to support, the question of an 'honourable daughter-in-law' had not yet been considered, as he was very young.... After these confidences, they walked on for a long while without speaking; but, as the proverb declares, *Ki ga areba, me mo kuchi hodo ni mono wo iu*: "When the wish is there, the eyes can say as much as the mouth." By the time they reached the village, they had become very much pleased with each other; and then Minokichi asked O-Yuki to rest awhile at his house. After some shy hesitation, she went there with him; and his mother made her welcome, and prepared a warm meal for her. O-Yuki behaved so nicely that Minokichi's mother took a sudden fancy to her, and persuaded her to delay her journey to Yedo. And the natural end of the matter was that Yuki never went to Yedo at all. She remained in the house, as an 'honourable daughter-in-law'.

O-Yuki proved a very good daughter-in-law. When Minokichi's mother came to die, – some five years later, – her last words were words of affection and praise for the wife of her son. And O-Yuki bore Minokichi ten children, boys and girls, – handsome children all of them, and very fair of skin.

The country-folk thought O-Yuki a wonderful person, by nature different from themselves. Most of the peasant-women age early; but O-Yuki, even after having become the mother of ten children, looked as young and fresh as on the day when she had first come to the village.

One night, after the children had gone to sleep, O-Yuki was sewing by the light of a paper lamp; and Minokichi, watching her, said:

"To see you sewing there, with the light on your face, makes me think of a strange thing that happened when I was a lad of eighteen. I then saw somebody as beautiful and white as you are now – indeed, she was very like you...."

Without lifting her eyes from her work, O-Yuki responded:

"Tell me about her.... Where did you see her?"

Then Minokichi told her about the terrible night in the ferryman's hut, – and about the White Woman that had stooped above him, smiling and whispering, – and about the silent death of old Mosaku. And he said:

"Asleep or awake, that was the only time that I saw a being as beautiful as you. Of course, she was not a human being; and I was afraid of her, – very much afraid, – but she was so white!... Indeed, I have never been sure whether it was a dream that I saw, or the Woman of the Snow...."

O-Yuki flung down her sewing, and arose, and bowed above Minokichi where he sat, and shrieked into his face:

"It was I – I – I! Yuki it was! And I told you then that I would kill you if you ever said one word about it!… But for those children asleep there, I would kill you this moment! And now you had better take very, very good care of them; for if ever they have reason to complain of you, I will treat you as you deserve!…"

Even as she screamed, her voice became thin, like a crying of wind; – then she melted into a bright white mist that spired to the roof-beams, and shuddered away through the smoke-hole.… Never again was she seen.

Hoichi the Earless
(Mimi-nashi Hōichi no Hanashi)

Lafcadio Hearn

MORE THAN SEVEN HUNDRED YEARS AGO, at Dan-no-ura, in the Straits of Shimonoseki, was fought the last battle of the long contest between the Heiké, or Taira clan, and the Genji, or Minamoto clan. There the Heiké perished utterly, with their women and children, and their infant emperor likewise – now remembered as Antoku Tenno. And that sea and shore have been haunted for seven hundred years.... Elsewhere I told you about the strange crabs found there, called Heiké crabs, which have human faces on their backs, and are said to be the spirits of the Heiké warriors. But there are many strange things to be seen and heard along that coast. On dark nights thousands of ghostly fires hover about the beach, or flit above the waves, – pale lights which the fishermen call *Oni-bi*, or demon-fires; and, whenever the winds are up, a sound of great shouting comes from that sea, like a clamour of battle.

In former years the Heiké were much more restless than they now are. They would rise about ships passing in the night, and try to sink them; and at all times they would watch for swimmers, to pull them down. It was in order to appease those dead that the Buddhist temple, Amidaji, was built at Akamagaseki. A cemetery also was made close by, near the beach; and within it were set up monuments inscribed with the names of the drowned emperor and of his great vassals; and Buddhist services were regularly performed there, on behalf of the spirits of them. After the temple had been built, and the tombs erected, the Heiké gave less trouble than before; but they continued to do queer things at intervals, – proving that they had not found the perfect peace.

Some centuries ago there lived at Akamagaseki a blind man named Hoichi, who was famed for his skill in recitation and in playing upon the *biwa*. From childhood he had been trained to recite and to play; and while yet a lad he had surpassed his teachers. As a professional *biwa-hoshi* he became famous chiefly by his recitations of the history of the Heiké and the Genji; and it is said that when he sang the song of the battle of Dan-no-ura "even the goblins [kijin] could not refrain from tears."

At the outset of his career, Hoichi was very poor; but he found a good friend to help him. The priest of the Amidaji was fond of poetry and music; and he often invited Hoichi to the temple, to play and recite. Afterwards, being much impressed by the wonderful skill of the lad, the priest proposed that Hoichi should make the temple his home; and this offer was gratefully accepted. Hoichi was given a room in the temple-building; and, in return for food and lodging, he was required only to gratify the priest with a musical performance on certain evenings, when otherwise disengaged.

One summer night the priest was called away, to perform a Buddhist service at the house of a dead parishioner; and he went there with his acolyte, leaving Hoichi alone in the temple. It was a hot night; and the blind man sought to cool himself on the verandah before his sleeping-room. The verandah overlooked a small garden in the rear of the Amidaji. There Hoichi waited for the priest's return, and tried to relieve his solitude by practicing upon his *biwa*. Midnight passed; and the priest did not appear. But the atmosphere was still too warm for comfort within doors; and Hoichi remained outside. At last he heard steps approaching from the back gate. Somebody crossed the garden, advanced to the verandah, and halted directly in front of him – but it was not the priest. A deep voice called the blind man's name – abruptly and unceremoniously, in the manner of a *samurai* summoning an inferior:

"Hoichi!"

Hoichi was too much startled, for the moment, to respond; and the voice called again, in a tone of harsh command, –

"Hoichi!"

"*Hai!*" answered the blind man, frightened by the menace in the voice, – "I am blind! – I cannot know who calls!"

"There is nothing to fear," the stranger exclaimed, speaking more gently. "I am stopping near this temple, and have been sent to you with a message. My present lord, a person of exceedingly high rank, is now staying in Akamagaseki, with many noble attendants. He wished to view the scene of the battle of Dan-no-ura; and to-day he visited that place. Having heard of your skill in reciting the story of the battle, he now desires to hear your performance: so you will take your *biwa* and come with me at once to the house where the august assembly is waiting."

In those times, the order of a *samurai* was not to be lightly disobeyed. Hoichi donned his sandals, took his *biwa*, and went away with the stranger, who guided him deftly, but obliged him to walk very fast. The hand that guided was iron; and the clank of the warrior's stride proved him fully armed, – probably some palace-guard on duty. Hoichi's first alarm was over: he began to imagine himself in good luck; – for, remembering the retainer's assurance about a "person of exceedingly high rank," he thought that the lord who wished to hear the recitation could not be less than a *daimyo* of the first class. Presently the *samurai* halted; and Hoichi became aware that they had arrived at a large gateway; – and he wondered, for he could not remember any large gate in that part of the town, except the main gate of the Amidaji. "*Kaimon!*" the *samurai* called, – and there was a sound of unbarring; and the twain passed on. They traversed a space of garden, and halted again before some entrance; and the retainer cried in a loud voice, "Within there! I have brought Hoichi." Then came sounds of feet hurrying, and screens sliding, and rain-doors opening, and voices of women in converse. By the language of the women Hoichi knew them to be domestics in some noble household; but he could not imagine to what place he had been conducted. Little time was allowed him for conjecture. After he had been helped to mount several stone steps, upon the last of which he was told to leave his sandals, a woman's hand guided him along interminable reaches of polished planking, and round pillared angles too many to remember, and over widths amazing of matted floor, – into the middle of some vast apartment. There he thought that many great people were assembled: the sound of the rustling of silk was like the sound of leaves in a forest. He heard also a great humming of voices, – talking in undertones; and the speech was the speech of courts.

Hoichi was told to put himself at ease, and he found a kneeling-cushion ready for him. After having taken his place upon it, and tuned his instrument, the voice of a woman – whom he divined to be the *Rojo*, or matron in charge of the female service – addressed him, saying, –

"It is now required that the history of the Heiké be recited, to the accompaniment of the *biwa*."

Now the entire recital would have required a time of many nights: therefore Hoichi ventured a question:

"As the whole of the story is not soon told, what portion is it augustly desired that I now recite?"

The woman's voice made answer:

"Recite the story of the battle at Dan-no-ura, – for the pity of it is the most deep."

Then Hoichi lifted up his voice, and chanted the chant of the fight on the bitter sea, – wonderfully making his *biwa* to sound like the straining of oars and the rushing of ships, the whirr and the hissing of arrows, the shouting and trampling of men, the crashing of steel upon helmets, the plunging of slain in the flood. And to left and right of him, in the pauses of his playing, he could hear voices murmuring praise: "How marvellous an artist!" – "Never in our own province was playing heard like this!" – "Not in all the empire is there another singer like Hoichi!" Then fresh courage came to him, and he played and sang yet better than before; and a hush of wonder deepened about him. But when at last he came to tell the fate of the fair and helpless, – the piteous perishing of the women and children, – and the death-leap of Nii-no-Ama, with the imperial infant in her arms, – then all the listeners uttered together one long, long shuddering cry of anguish; and thereafter they wept and wailed so loudly and so wildly that the blind man was frightened by the violence and grief that he had made. For much time the sobbing and the wailing continued. But gradually the sounds of lamentation died away; and again, in the great stillness that followed, Hoichi heard the voice of the woman whom he supposed to be the *Rojo*.

She said:

"Although we had been assured that you were a very skillful player upon the *biwa*, and without an equal in recitative, we did not know that any one could be so skillful as you have proved yourself to-night. Our lord has been pleased to say that he intends to bestow upon you a fitting reward. But he desires that you shall perform before him once every night for the next six nights – after which time he will probably make his august return-journey. To-morrow night, therefore, you are to come here at the same hour. The retainer who to-night conducted you will be sent for you.… There is another matter about which I have been ordered to inform you. It is required that you shall speak to no one of your visits here, during the time of our lord's august sojourn at Akamagaseki. As he is traveling incognito, he commands that no mention of these things be made.… You are now free to go back to your temple."

After Hoichi had duly expressed his thanks, a woman's hand conducted him to the entrance of the house, where the same retainer, who had before guided him, was waiting to take him home. The retainer led him to the verandah at the rear of the temple, and there bade him farewell.

It was almost dawn when Hoichi returned; but his absence from the temple had not been observed, – as the priest, coming back at a very late hour, had supposed him asleep. During the day Hoichi was able to take some rest; and he said nothing about his strange adventure. In the middle of the following night the *samurai* again came for him, and led him to the august assembly, where he gave another recitation with the same success that had attended his previous performance. But during this second visit his absence from the temple was accidentally discovered; and after his return in the morning he was summoned to the presence of the priest, who said to him, in a tone of kindly reproach: -

"We have been very anxious about you, friend Hoichi. To go out, blind and alone, at so late an hour, is dangerous. Why did you go without telling us? I could have ordered a servant to accompany you. And where have you been?"

Hoichi answered, evasively, –

"Pardon me kind friend! I had to attend to some private business; and I could not arrange the matter at any other hour."

The priest was surprised, rather than pained, by Hoichi's reticence: he felt it to be unnatural, and suspected something wrong. He feared that the blind lad had been bewitched or deluded by some evil spirits. He did not ask any more questions; but he privately instructed the men-servants of the temple to keep watch upon Hoichi's movements, and to follow him in case that he should again leave the temple after dark.

On the very next night, Hoichi was seen to leave the temple; and the servants immediately lighted their lanterns, and followed after him. But it was a rainy night, and very dark; and before the temple-folks could get to the roadway, Hoichi had disappeared. Evidently he had walked very fast, – a strange thing, considering his blindness; for the road was in a bad condition. The men hurried through the streets, making inquiries at every house which Hoichi was accustomed to visit; but nobody could give them any news of him. At last, as they were returning to the temple by way of the shore, they were startled by the sound of a *biwa*, furiously played, in the cemetery of the Amidaji. Except for some ghostly fires – such as usually flitted there on dark nights – all was blackness in that direction. But the men at once hastened to the cemetery; and there, by the help of their lanterns, they discovered Hoichi, – sitting alone in the rain before the memorial tomb of Antoku Tenno, making his *biwa* resound, and loudly chanting the chant of the battle of Dan-no-ura. And behind him, and about him, and everywhere above the tombs, the fires of the dead were burning, like candles. Never before had so great a host of *Oni-bi* appeared in the sight of mortal man....

"Hoichi San! – Hoichi San!" the servants cried, – "you are bewitched!... Hoichi San!"

But the blind man did not seem to hear. Strenuously he made his *biwa* to rattle and ring and clang; – more and more wildly he chanted the chant of the battle of Dan-no-ura. They caught hold of him; – they shouted into his ear, –

"Hoichi San! – Hoichi San! – come home with us at once!"

Reprovingly he spoke to them:

"To interrupt me in such a manner, before this august assembly, will not be tolerated."

Whereat, in spite of the weirdness of the thing, the servants could not help laughing. Sure that he had been bewitched, they now seized him, and pulled him up on his feet, and by main force hurried him back to the temple, – where he was immediately relieved of his wet clothes, by order of the priest. Then the priest insisted upon a full explanation of his friend's astonishing behaviour.

Hoichi long hesitated to speak. But at last, finding that his conduct had really alarmed and angered the good priest, he decided to abandon his reserve; and he related everything that had happened from the time of first visit of the *samurai*.

The priest said:

"Hoichi, my poor friend, you are now in great danger! How unfortunate that you did not tell me all this before! Your wonderful skill in music has indeed brought you into strange trouble. By this time you must be aware that you have not been visiting any house whatever, but have been passing your nights in the cemetery, among the tombs of the Heiké; – and it was before the memorial-tomb of Antoku Tenno that our people to-night found you, sitting in the rain. All that you have been imagining was illusion – except the calling of the dead. By once obeying them, you have put yourself in their power. If you obey them again, after what has already occurred, they will tear you in pieces. But they would have destroyed you, sooner or later, in any event.... Now I shall not be able to remain with you to-night: I am called away to perform another service. But, before I go, it will be necessary to protect your body by writing holy texts upon it."

Before sundown the priest and his acolyte stripped Hoichi: then, with their writing-brushes, they traced upon his breast and back, head and face and neck, limbs and hands and feet, – even upon the soles of his feet, and upon all parts of his body, – the text of the holy sutra called *Hannya-Shin-Kyo*. When this had been done, the priest instructed Hoichi, saying:

"To-night, as soon as I go away, you must seat yourself on the verandah, and wait. You will be called. But, whatever may happen, do not answer, and do not move. Say nothing and sit still – as if meditating. If you stir, or make any noise, you will be torn asunder. Do not get frightened; and do not think of calling for help – because no help could save you. If you do exactly as I tell you, the danger will pass, and you will have nothing more to fear."

After dark the priest and the acolyte went away; and Hoichi seated himself on the verandah, according to the instructions given him. He laid his *biwa* on the planking beside him, and, assuming the attitude of meditation, remained quite still, – taking care not to cough, or to breathe audibly. For hours he stayed thus.

Then, from the roadway, he heard the steps coming. They passed the gate, crossed the garden, approached the verandah, stopped – directly in front of him.

"Hoichi!" the deep voice called. But the blind man held his breath, and sat motionless.

"Hoichi!" grimly called the voice a second time. Then a third time – savagely:

"Hoichi!"

Hoichi remained as still as a stone, – and the voice grumbled:

"No answer! – that won't do!… Must see where the fellow is.…"

There was a noise of heavy feet mounting upon the verandah. The feet approached deliberately, – halted beside him. Then, for long minutes, – during which Hoichi felt his whole body shake to the beating of his heart, – there was dead silence.

At last the gruff voice muttered close to him:

"Here is the *biwa*; but of the *biwa*-player I see – only two ears!… So that explains why he did not answer: he had no mouth to answer with – there is nothing left of him but his ears.… Now to my lord those ears I will take – in proof that the august commands have been obeyed, so far as was possible.…"

At that instant Hoichi felt his ears gripped by fingers of iron, and torn off! Great as the pain was, he gave no cry. The heavy footfalls receded along the verandah, – descended into the garden, – passed out to the roadway, – ceased. From either side of his head, the blind man felt a thick warm trickling; but he dared not lift his hands…

Before sunrise the priest came back. He hastened at once to the verandah in the rear, stepped and slipped upon something clammy, and uttered a cry of horror; – for he saw, by the light of his lantern, that the clamminess was blood. But he perceived Hoichi sitting there, in the attitude of meditation – with the blood still oozing from his wounds.

"My poor Hoichi!" cried the startled priest, – "what is this?… You have been hurt?"

At the sound of his friend's voice, the blind man felt safe. He burst out sobbing, and tearfully told his adventure of the night.

"Poor, poor Hoichi!" the priest exclaimed, – "all my fault! – my very grievous fault!… Everywhere upon your body the holy texts had been written – except upon your ears! I trusted my acolyte to do that part of the work; and it was very, very wrong of me not to have made sure that he had done it!… Well, the matter cannot now be helped; – we can only try to heal your hurts as soon as possible.… Cheer up, friend! – the danger is now well over. You will never again be troubled by those visitors."

With the aid of a good doctor, Hoichi soon recovered from his injuries. The story of his strange adventure spread far and wide, and soon made him famous. Many noble persons went to Akamagaseki to hear him recite; and large presents of money were given to him, – so that he became a wealthy man.… But from the time of his adventure, he was known only by the appellation of Mimi-nashi-Hoichi: 'Hoichi-the-Earless'.

In a Cup of Tea

Lafcadio Hearn

HAVE YOU EVER attempted to mount some old tower stairway, spiring up through darkness, and in the heart of that darkness found yourself at the cobwebbed edge of nothing? Or have you followed some coast path, cut along the face of a cliff, only to discover yourself, at a turn, on the jagged verge of a break? The emotional worth of such experience – from a literary point of view – is proved by the force of the sensations aroused, and by the vividness with which they are remembered.

Now there have been curiously preserved, in old Japanese story-books, certain fragments of fiction that produce an almost similar emotional experience.... Perhaps the writer was lazy; perhaps he had a quarrel with the publisher; perhaps he was suddenly called away from his little table, and never came back; perhaps death stopped the writing-brush in the very middle of a sentence. But no mortal man can ever tell us exactly why these things were left unfinished.... I select a typical example.

On the fourth day of the first month of the third *Tenwa*, – that is to say, about two hundred and twenty years ago, – the lord Nakagawa Sado, while on his way to make a New Year's visit, halted with his train at a tea-house in Hakusan, in the Hongō district of Yedo. While the party were resting there, one of the lord's attendants, – a *wakatō* named Sekinai, – feeling very thirsty, filled for himself a large water-cup with tea. He was raising the cup to his lips when he suddenly perceived, in the transparent yellow infusion, the image or reflection of a face that was not his own. Startled, he looked around, but could see no one near him. The face in the tea appeared, from the coiffure, to be the face of a young *samurai*: it was strangely distinct, and very handsome, – delicate as the face of a girl. And it seemed the reflection of a living face; for the eyes and the lips were moving. Bewildered by this mysterious apparition, Sekinai threw away the tea, and carefully examined the cup. It proved to be a very cheap water-cup, with no artistic devices of any sort. He found and filled another cup; and again the face appeared in the tea. He then ordered fresh tea, and refilled the cup; and once more the strange face appeared, – this time with a mocking smile. But Sekinai did not allow himself to be frightened. "Whoever you are," he muttered, "you shall delude me no further!" – then he swallowed the tea, face and all, and went his way, wondering whether he had swallowed a ghost.

Late in the evening of the same day, while on watch in the palace of the lord Nakagawa, Sekinai was surprised by the soundless coming of a stranger into the apartment. This stranger, a richly dressed young *samurai*, seated himself directly in front of Sekinai, and, saluting the *wakatō* with a slight bow, observed:

"I am Shikibu Heinai – met you to-day for the first time.... You do not seem to recognize me."

He spoke in a very low, but penetrating voice. And Sekinai was astonished to find before him the same sinister, handsome face of which he had seen, and swallowed, the apparition in a cup of tea. It was smiling now, as the phantom had smiled; but the steady gaze of the eyes, above the smiling lips, was at once a challenge and an insult.

"No, I do not recognize you," returned Sekinai, angry but cool; – "and perhaps you will now be good enough to inform me how you obtained admission to this house?"

[In feudal times the residence of a lord was strictly guarded at all hours; and no one could enter unannounced, except through some unpardonable negligence on the part of the armed watch.]

"Ah, you do not recognize me!" exclaimed the visitor, in a tone of irony, drawing a little nearer as he spoke. "No, you do not recognize me! Yet you took upon yourself this morning to do me a deadly injury!…"

Sekinai instantly seized the *tantō* at his girdle, and made a fierce thrust at the throat of the man. But the blade seemed to touch no substance. Simultaneously and soundlessly the intruder leaped sideward to the chamber-wall, and through it! … The wall showed no trace of his exit. He had traversed it only as the light of a candle passes through lantern-paper.

When Sekinai made report of the incident, his recital astonished and puzzled the retainers. No stranger had been seen either to enter or to leave the palace at the hour of the occurrence; and no one in the service of the lord Nakagawa had ever heard of the name 'Shikibu Heinai'.

On the following night Sekinai was off duty, and remained at home with his parents. At a rather late hour he was informed that some strangers had called at the house, and desired to speak with him for a moment. Taking his sword, he went to the entrance, and there found three armed men, – apparently retainers, – waiting in front of the doorstep. The three bowed respectfully to Sekinai; and one of them said:

"Our names are Matsuoka Bungō, Tsuchibashi Bungō, and Okamura Heiroku. We are retainers of the noble Shikibu Heinai. When our master last night deigned to pay you a visit, you struck him with a sword. He was much hurt, and has been obliged to go to the hot springs, where his wound is now being treated. But on the sixteenth day of the coming month he will return; and he will then fitly repay you for the injury done him…."

Without waiting to hear more, Sekinai leaped out, sword in hand, and slashed right and left, at the strangers. But the three men sprang to the wall of the adjoining building, and flitted up the wall like shadows, and…

Here the old narrative breaks off; the rest of the story existed only in some brain that has been dust for a century.

I am able to imagine several possible endings; but none of them would satisfy an Occidental imagination. I prefer to let the reader attempt to decide for himself the probable consequence of swallowing a Soul.

The Ghost of O-Kiku
from 'The Banchō Sarayashiki'
or 'The Lady of the Plates'

Excerpt from 'In a Japanese Garden'

Lafcadio Hearn

THERE IS ONE PLACE in Japan where it is thought unlucky to cultivate chrysanthemums, for reasons which shall presently appear; and that place is in the pretty little city of Himeji, in the province of Harima. Himeji contains the ruins of a great castle of thirty turrets; and a *daimyo* used to dwell therein whose revenue was one hundred and fifty-six thousand *koku* of rice. Now, in the house of one of that *daimyo*'s chief retainers there was a maid-servant, of good family, whose name was O-Kiku; and the name 'Kiku' signifies a chrysanthemum flower. Many precious things were intrusted to her charge, and among others ten costly dishes of gold. One of these was suddenly missed, and could not be found; and the girl, being responsible therefor, and knowing not how otherwise to prove her innocence, drowned herself in a well. But ever thereafter her ghost, returning nightly, could be heard counting the dishes slowly, with sobs:

Ichi-mai, Yo-mai, Shichi-mai,
Ni-mai, Go-mai, Hachi-mai,
San-mai, Roku-mai, Ku-mai—

Then would be heard a despairing cry and a loud burst of weeping; and again the girl's voice counting the dishes plaintively: "One – two – three – four – five – six – seven – eight – nine—"

Her spirit passed into the body of a strange little insect, whose head faintly resembles that of a ghost with long dishevelled hair; and it is called O-Kiku-mushi, or 'the fly of O-Kiku'; and it is found, they say, nowhere save in Himeji. A famous play was written about O-Kiku, which is still acted in all the popular theatres, entitled *Banshu-O-Kiku-no-Sara-yashiki*; or, 'The Manor of the Dish of O-Kiku of Banshu'.

Some declare that Banshu is only the corruption of the name of an ancient quarter of Tokyo (*Yedo*), where the story should have been laid. But the people of Himeji say that part of their city now called Go-Ken-Yashiki is identical with the site of the ancient manor. What is certainly true is that to cultivate chrysanthemum flowers in the part of Himeji called Go-Ken-Yashiki is deemed unlucky, because the name of O-Kiku signifies 'Chrysanthemum'. Therefore, nobody, I am told, ever cultivates chrysanthemums there.

Of Ghosts and Goblins

Lafcadio Hearn

I

THERE WAS A BUDDHA, according to the *Hokkekyo* who "even assumed the shape of a goblin to preach to such as were to be converted by a goblin." And in the same Sutra may be found this promise of the Teacher: *"While he is dwelling lonely in the wilderness, I will send thither goblins in great number to keep him company."* The appalling character of this promise is indeed somewhat modified by the assurance that gods also are to be sent. But if ever I become a holy man, I shall take heed not to dwell in the wilderness, because I have seen Japanese goblins, and I do not like them.

Kinjuro showed them to me last night. They had come to town for the *matsuri* of our own *ujigami*, or parish-temple; and, as there were many curious things to be seen at the night festival, we started for the temple after dark, Kinjuro carrying a paper lantern painted with my crest.

It had snowed heavily in the morning; but now the sky and the sharp still air were clear as diamond; and the crisp snow made a pleasant crunching sound under our feet as we walked; and it occurred to me to say: "O Kinjuro, is there a God of Snow?"

"I cannot tell," replied Kinjuro. "There be many gods I do not know; and there is not any man who knows the names of all the gods. But there is the Yuki-Onna, the Woman of the Snow."

"And what is the Yuki-Onna?"

"She is the White One that makes the Faces in the snow. She does not any harm, only makes afraid. By day she lifts only her head, and frightens those who journey alone. But at night she rises up sometimes, taller than the trees, and looks about a little while, and then falls back in a shower of snow."

"What is her face like?"

"It is all white, white. It is an enormous face. And it is a *lonesome* face."

[The word Kinjuro used was *samushii*. Its common meaning is 'lonesome'; but he used it, I think, in the sense of 'weird'.]

"Did you ever see her, Kinjuro?"

"Master, I never saw her. But my father told me that once when he was a child, he wanted to go to a neighbour's house through the snow to play with another little boy; and that on the way he saw a great white face rise up from the snow and look lonesomely about, so that he cried for fear and ran back. Then his people all went out and looked; but there was only snow; and then they knew that he had seen the Yuki-Onna."

"And in these days, Kinjuro, do people ever see her?"

"Yes. Those who make the pilgrimage to Yabumura, in the period called *Dai-Kan*, which is the Time of the Greatest Cold, they sometimes see her."

"What is there at Yabumura, Kinjuro?"

"There is the Yabu-jinja, which is an ancient and famous temple of Yabu-no-Tenno-San – the God of Colds, Kaze-no-Kami. It is high upon a hill, nearly nine *ri* from Matsue. And the great *matsuri* of that temple is held upon the tenth and eleventh days of the Second Month. And on those days strange things may be seen. For one who gets a very bad cold prays to the deity of Yabu-jinja to cure it, and takes a vow to make a pilgrimage naked to the temple at the time of the matsuri."

"Naked?"

"Yes: the pilgrims wear only *waraji*, and a little cloth round their loins. And a great many men and women go naked through the snow to the temple, though the snow is deep at that time. And each man carries a bunch of *gohei* and a naked sword as gifts to the temple; and each woman carries a metal mirror. And at the temple, the priests receive them, performing curious rites. For the priests then, according to ancient custom, attire themselves like sick men, and lie down and groan, and drink, potions made of herbs, prepared after the Chinese manner."

"But do not some of the pilgrims die of cold, Kinjuro?"

"No: our Izumo peasants are hardy. Besides, they run swiftly, so that they reach the temple all warm. And before returning they put on thick warm robes. But sometimes, upon the way, they see the Yuki-Onna."

II

Each side of the street leading to the *miya* was illuminated with a line of paper lanterns bearing holy symbols; and the immense court of the temple had been transformed into a town of booths, and shops, and temporary theatres. In spite of the cold, the crowd was prodigious. There seemed to be all the usual attractions of a *matsuri*, and a number of unusual ones. Among the familiar lures, I missed at this festival only the maiden wearing an *obi* of living snakes; probably it had become too cold for the snakes. There were several fortune-tellers and jugglers; there were acrobats and dancers; there was a man making pictures out of sand; and there was a menagerie containing an emu from Australia, and a couple of enormous bats from the Loo Choo Islands – bats trained to do several things. I did reverence to the gods, and bought some extraordinary toys; and then we went to look for the goblins. They were domiciled in a large permanent structure, rented to showmen on special occasions.

Gigantic characters signifying 'IKI-NINGYO', painted upon the signboard at the entrance, partly hinted the nature of the exhibition. *Iki-ningyo* ('living images') somewhat correspond to our occidental 'wax figures'; but the equally realistic Japanese creations are made of much cheaper material. Having bought two wooden tickets for one *sen* each, we entered, and passed behind a curtain to find ourselves in a long corridor lined with booths, or rather matted compartments, about the size of small rooms. Each space, decorated with scenery appropriate to the subject, was occupied by a group of life-size figures. The group nearest the entrance, representing two men playing *samisen* and two *geisha* dancing, seemed to me without excuse for being, until Kinjuro had translated a little placard before it, announcing that one of the figures was a living person. We watched in vain for a wink or palpitation. Suddenly one of the musicians laughed aloud, shook his head, and began to play and sing. The deception was perfect.

The remaining groups, twenty-four in number, were powerfully impressive in their peculiar way, representing mostly famous popular traditions or sacred myths. Feudal heroisms, the memory of which stirs every Japanese heart; legends of filial piety; Buddhist miracles, and stories of emperors were among the subjects. Sometimes, however, the realism was brutal, as in one scene representing the body of a woman lying in a pool of blood, with brains scattered by a sword stroke. Nor was this unpleasantness altogether atoned for by her miraculous resuscitation in the adjoining compartment, where she reappeared returning thanks in a Nichiren temple, and converting her slaughterer, who happened, by some extraordinary accident, to go there at the same time.

At the termination of the corridor there hung a black curtain behind which screams could be heard. And above the black curtain was a placard inscribed with the promise of a gift to anybody able to traverse the mysteries beyond without being frightened.

"Master," said Kinjuro, "the goblins are inside."

We lifted the veil, and found ourselves in a sort of lane between hedges, and behind the hedges we saw tombs; we were in a graveyard. There were real weeds and trees, and *sotoba* and *haka*, and the effect was quite natural. Moreover, as the roof was very lofty, and kept invisible by a clever arrangement of lights, all seemed darkness only; and this gave one a sense of being out under the night, a feeling accentuated by the chill of the air. And here and there we could discern sinister shapes, mostly of superhuman stature, some seeming to wait in dim places, others floating above the graves. Quite near us, towering above the hedge on our right, was a Buddhist priest, with his back turned to us.

"A *yamabushi*, an exorciser?" I queried of Kinjuro.

"No," said Kinjuro; "see how tall he is. I think that must be a Tanuki-Bozu."

The Tanuki-Bozu is the priestly form assumed by the goblin-badger (tanuki) for the purpose of decoying belated travellers to destruction. We went on, and looked up into his face. It was a nightmare – his face.

"In truth a Tanuki-Bozu," said Kinjuro. "What does the Master honourably think concerning it?"

Instead of replying, I jumped back; for the monstrous thing had suddenly reached over the hedge and clutched at me, with a moan. Then it fell back, swaying and creaking. It was moved by invisible strings.

"I think, Kinjuro, that it is a nasty, horrid thing…. But I shall not claim the present."

We laughed, and proceeded to consider a Three-Eyed Friar (Mitsu-me Nyudo). The Three-Eyed Friar also watches for the unwary at night. His face is soft and smiling as the face of a Buddha, but he has a hideous eye in the summit of his shaven pate, which can only be seen when seeing it does no good. The Mitsu-me-Nyudo made a grab at Kinjuro, and startled him almost as much as the Tanuki-Bozu had startled me.

Then we looked at the Yama-Uba – the 'Mountain Nurse'. She catches little children and nurses them for a while, and then devours them. In her face she has no mouth; but she has a mouth in the top of her head, under her hair. The Yama-Uba did not clutch at us, because her hands were occupied with a nice little boy, whom she was just going to eat. The child had been made wonderfully pretty to heighten the effect.

Then I saw the spectre of a woman hovering in the air above a tomb at some distance, so that I felt safer in observing it. It had no eyes; its long hair hung loose; its white robe floated light as smoke. I thought of a statement in a composition by one of my pupils about ghosts: "*Their greatest Peculiarity is that They have no feet.*" Then I jumped again, for the thing, quite soundlessly but very swiftly, made through the air at me.

And the rest of our journey among the graves was little more than a succession of like experiences; but it was made amusing by the screams of women, and bursts of laughter from people who lingered only to watch the effect upon others of what had scared themselves.

III

Forsaking the goblins, we visited a little open-air theatre to see two girls dance. After they had danced awhile, one girl produced a sword and cut off the other girl's head, and put it upon a table, where it opened its mouth and began to sing. All this was very prettily done; but my mind was still haunted by the goblins. So I questioned Kinjuro:

"Kinjuro, those goblins of which we the ningyo have seen – do folk believe in the reality, thereof?'

"Not any more," answered Kinjuro – "not at least among the people of the city. Perhaps in the country it may not be so. We believe in the Lord Buddha; we believe in the ancient gods; and there be many who believe the dead sometimes return to avenge a cruelty or to compel an act of justice. But we do not now believe all that was believed in ancient time.... Master," he added, as we reached another queer exhibition, "it is only one *sen* to go to hell, if the Master would like to go—"

"Very good, Kinjuro," I made reply. "Pay two *sen* that we may both go to hell."

IV

And we passed behind a curtain into a big room full of curious clicking and squeaking noises. These noises were made by unseen wheels and pulleys moving a multitude of *ningyo* upon a broad shelf about breast-high, which surrounded the apartment upon three sides. These *ningyo* were not *ikiningyo*, but very small images – puppets. They represented all things in the Under-World.

The first I saw was Sozu-Baba, the Old Woman of the River of Ghosts, who takes away the garments of Souls. The garments were hanging upon a tree behind her. She was tall; she rolled her green eyes and gnashed her long teeth, while the shivering of the little white souls before her was as a trembling of butterflies. Farther on appeared Emma Dai-O, great King of Hell, nodding grimly. At his right hand, upon their tripod, the heads of Kaguhana and Mirume, the Witnesses, whirled as upon a wheel. At his left, a devil was busy sawing a Soul in two; and I noticed that he used his saw like a Japanese carpenter – pulling it towards him instead of pushing it. And then various exhibitions of the tortures of the damned. A liar bound to a post was having his tongue pulled out by a devil – slowly, with artistic jerks; it was already longer than the owner's body. Another devil was pounding another Soul in a mortar so vigorously that the sound of the braying could be heard above all the din of the machinery. A little farther on was a man being eaten alive by two serpents having women's faces; one serpent was white, the other blue. The white had been his wife, the blue his concubine. All the tortures known to medieval Japan were being elsewhere deftly practiced by swarms of devils. After reviewing them, we visited the Sai-no-Kawara, and saw Jizo with a child in his arms, and a circle of other children running swiftly around him, to escape from demons who brandished their clubs and ground their teeth.

Hell proved, however, to be extremely cold; and while meditating on the partial inappropriateness of the atmosphere, it occurred to me that in the common Buddhist picture-books of the Jigoku I had never noticed any illustrations of torment by cold. Indian Buddhism, indeed, teaches the existence of cold hells. There is one, for instance, where people's lips are frozen so that they can say only "Ah-ta-ta!" – wherefore that hell is called Atata. And there is the hell where tongues are frozen, and where people say only "Ah-baba!" for which reason it is called Ababa. And there is the Pundarika, or Great White-Lotus hell, where the spectacle of the bones laid bare by the cold is 'like a blossoming of white lotus-flowers'. Kinjuro thinks there are cold hells according to Japanese Buddhism; but he is not sure. And I am not sure that the idea of cold could be made very terrible to the Japanese. They confess a general liking for cold, and compose Chinese poems about the loveliness of ice and snow.

V

Out of hell, we found our way to a magic-lantern show being given in a larger and even much colder structure. A Japanese magic-lantern show is nearly always interesting in more particulars than one, but perhaps especially as evidencing the native genius for adapting Western inventions to Eastern tastes. A Japanese magic-lantern show is essentially dramatic. It is a play of which the dialogue is uttered by invisible personages, the actors and the scenery being only luminous shadows. Wherefore it is peculiarly well suited to goblinries and weirdnesses of all kinds; and plays in which ghosts figure are the favourite subjects. As the hall was bitterly cold, I waited only long enough to see one performance – of which the following is an epitome:

SCENE I. – A beautiful peasant girl and her aged mother, squatting together at home. Mother weeps violently, gesticulates agonizingly. From her frantic speech, broken by wild sobs, we learn that the girl must be sent as a victim to the Kami-Sama of some lonesome temple in the mountains. That god is a bad god. Once a year he shoots an arrow into the thatch of some farmer's house as a sign that he wants a girl – to eat! Unless the girl be sent to him at once, he destroys the crops and the cows. Exit mother, weeping and shrieking, and pulling out her grey hair. Exit girl, with downcast head, and air of sweet resignation.

SCENE II. – Before a wayside inn; cherry-trees in blossom. Enter coolies carrying, like a palanquin, a large box, in which the girl is supposed to be. Deposit box; enter to eat; tell story to loquacious landlord. Enter noble *samurai*, with two swords. Asks about box. Hears the story of the coolies repeated by loquacious landlord. Exhibits fierce indignation; vows that the Kami-Sama are good – do not eat girls. Declares that so-called Kami-Sama to be a devil. Observes that devils must be killed. Orders box opened. Sends girl home. Gets into box himself, and commands coolies under pain of death to bear him right quickly to that temple.

SCENE III. – Enter coolies, approaching temple through forest at night. Coolies afraid. Drop box and run. Exeunt coolies. Box alone in the dark. Enter veiled figure, all white. Figure moans unpleasantly; utters horrid cries. Box remains impassive. Figure removes veil, showing Its face – a skull with phosphoric eyes. [*Audience unanimously utter the sound 'Aaaaaa!'*] Figure displays Its hands – monstrous and apish, with claws. [*Audience utter a second 'Aaaaaa!'*] Figure approaches the box, touches the box, opens the box! Up leaps noble *samurai*. A wrestle; drums sound the roll of battle. Noble *samurai* practices successfully noble art of ju-jutsu. Casts demon down, tramples upon him triumphantly, cuts off his head. Head suddenly enlarges, grows to the size of a house, tries to bite off head of *samurai*. *Samurai* slashes it with his sword. Head rolls backward, spitting fire, and vanishes. Finis. *Exeunt omnes*.

VI

The vision of the *samurai* and the goblin reminded Kinjuro of a queer tale, which he began to tell me as soon as the shadow-play was over. Ghastly stories are apt to fall flat after such an exhibition; but Kinjuro's stories are always peculiar enough to justify the telling under almost any circumstances. Wherefore I listened eagerly, in spite of the cold:

"A long time ago, in the days when Fox-women and goblins haunted this land, there came to the capital with her parents a *samurai* girl, so beautiful that all men who saw her fell enamoured of her. And hundreds of young *samurai* desired and hoped to marry her, and made their desire known to her parents. For it has ever been the custom in Japan that marriages should be arranged by parents. But there are exceptions to all customs, and the case of this maiden was such an exception. Her parents declared that they intended to allow their daughter to choose her own husband, and that all who wished to win her would be free to woo her.

"Many men of high rank and of great wealth were admitted to the house as suitors; and each one courted her as he best knew how – with gifts, and with fair words, and with poems written in her honour, and with promises of eternal love. And to each one she spoke sweetly and hopefully; but she made strange conditions. For every suitor she obliged to bind himself by his word of honour as a *samurai* to submit to a test of his love for her, and never to divulge to living person what that test might be. And to this all agreed.

"But even the most confident suitors suddenly ceased their importunities after having been put to the test; and all of them appeared to have been greatly terrified by something. Indeed, not a few even fled away from the city, and could not be persuaded by their friends to return. But no one ever so much as hinted why. Therefore it was whispered by those who knew nothing of the mystery, that the beautiful girl must be either a Fox-woman or a goblin.

"Now, when all the wooers of high rank had abandoned their suit, there came a *samurai* who had no wealth but his sword. He was a good man and true, and of pleasing presence; and the girl seemed to like him. But she made him take the same pledge which the others had taken; and after he had taken it, she told him to return upon a certain evening.

"When that evening came, he was received at the house by none but the girl herself. With her own hands she set before him the repast of hospitality, and waited upon him, after which she told him that she wished him to go out with her at a late hour. To this he consented gladly, and inquired to what place she desired to go. But she replied nothing to his question, and all at once became very silent, and strange in her manner. And after a while she retired from the apartment, leaving him alone.

"Only long after midnight she returned, robed all in white – like a Soul – and, without uttering a word, signed to him to follow her. Out of the house they hastened while all the city slept. It was what is called an *oborozuki-yo* – 'moon-clouded night'. Always upon such a night, 'tis said, do ghosts wander. She swiftly led the way; and the dogs howled as she flitted by; and she passed beyond the confines of the city to a place of knolls shadowed by enormous trees, where an ancient cemetery was. Into it she glided – a white shadow into blackness. He followed, wondering, his hand upon his sword. Then his eyes became accustomed to the gloom; and he saw.

"By a new-made grave she paused and signed to him to wait. The tools of the grave-maker were still lying there. Seizing one, she began to dig furiously, with strange haste and strength. At last her spade smote a coffin-lid and made it boom: another moment and the fresh white wood of the kwan was bare. She tore off the lid, revealing a corpse within – the corpse of a child. With goblin gestures she wrung an arm from the body, wrenched it in twain, and, squatting down, began to devour the upper half. Then, flinging to her lover the other half, she cried to him, *'Eat, if thou lovest me! this is what I eat!'*

"Not even for a single instant did he hesitate. He squatted down upon the other side of the grave, and ate the half of the arm, and said, *'Kekko degozarimasu! mo sukoshi chodai.'* For that arm was made of the best *kwashi* that Saikyo could produce.

"Then the girl sprang to her feet with a burst of laughter, and cried: 'You only, of all my brave suitors, did not run away! And I wanted a husband: who could not fear. I will marry you; I can love you: you are a *man!*'"

VII

"O Kinjuro," I said, as we took our way home, "I have heard and I have read many Japanese stories of the returning of the dead. Likewise you yourself have told me it is still believed the dead return, and why. But according both to that which I have read and that which you have told me, the coming back of the dead is never a thing to be desired. They return because of hate, or because of envy, or because they cannot rest for sorrow. But of any who return for that which is not evil – where is it written? Surely the common history of them is like that which we have this night seen: much that is horrible and much that is wicked and nothing of that which is beautiful or true."

Now this I said that I might tempt him. And he made even the answer I desired, by uttering the story which is hereafter set down:

"Long ago, in the days of a *daimyo* whose name has been forgotten, there lived in this old city a young man and a maid who loved each other very much. Their names are not remembered, but their story remains. From infancy they had been betrothed; and as children they played together, for their parents were neighbours. And as they grew up, they became always fonder of each other.

"Before the youth had become a man, his parents died. But he was able to enter the service of a rich *samurai*, an officer of high rank, who had been a friend of his people. And his protector soon took him into great favour, seeing him to be courteous, intelligent, and apt at arms. So the young man hoped to find himself shortly in a position that would make it possible for him to marry his betrothed. But war broke out in the north and east; and he was summoned suddenly to follow his master to the field. Before departing, however, he was able to see the girl; and they exchanged pledges in the presence of her parents; and he promised, should he remain alive, to return within a year from that day to marry his betrothed.

"After his going much time passed without news of him, for there was no post in that time as now; and the girl grieved so much for thinking of the chances of war that she became all white and thin and weak. Then at last she heard of him through a messenger sent from the army to bear news to the *daimyo* and once again a letter was brought to her by another messenger. And thereafter there came no word. Long is a year to one who waits. And the year passed, and he did not return.

"Other seasons passed, and still he did not come; and she thought him dead; and she sickened and lay down, and died, and was buried. Then her old parents, who had no other child, grieved unspeakably, and came to hate their home for the lonesomeness of it. After a time they resolved to sell all they had, and to set out upon a *sengaji* – the great pilgrimage to the Thousand Temples of the Nichiren-Shu, which requires many years to perform. So they sold their small house with all that it contained, excepting the ancestral tablets, and the holy things which must never be sold, and the *ihai* of their buried daughter, which were placed, according to the custom of those about to leave their native place, in the family temple. Now the family was of the Nichiren-Shu; and their temple was Myokoji.

"They had been gone only four days when the young man who had been betrothed to their daughter returned to the city. He had attempted, with the permission of his master, to fulfil his promise. But the provinces upon his way were full of war, and the roads and passes were guarded by troops, and he had been long delayed by many difficulties. And when he heard of his misfortune he sickened for grief, and many days remained without knowledge of anything, like one about to die.

"But when he began to recover his strength, all the pain of memory came back again; and he regretted that he had not died. Then he resolved to kill himself upon the grave of his betrothed; and, as soon as he was able to go out unobserved, he took his sword and went to the cemetery where the girl was buried: it is a lonesome place – the cemetery of Myokoji. There he found her tomb, and knelt before it, and prayed and wept, and whispered to her that which he was about to do. And suddenly he heard her voice cry to him: 'Anata!' and felt her hand upon his hand; and he turned, and saw her kneeling beside him, smiling, and beautiful as he remembered her, only a little pale. Then his heart leaped so that he could not speak for the wonder and the doubt and the joy of that moment. But she said: 'Do not doubt: it is really I. I am not dead. It was all a mistake. I was buried, because my people thought me dead – buried too soon. And my own parents thought me dead, and went upon a pilgrimage. Yet you see, I am not dead – not a ghost. It is I: do not doubt it! And I have seen your heart, and that was worth all the waiting, and the pain…. But now let us go away at once to another city, so that people may not know this thing and trouble us; for all still believe me dead.'

"And they went away, no one observing them. And they went even to the village of Minobu, which is in the province of Kai. For there is a famous temple of the Nichiren-Shu in that place; and the girl had said: 'I know that in the course of their pilgrimage my parents will surely visit Minobu: so that if we dwell there, they will find us, and we shall be all again together.' And when they came to Minobu, she said: 'Let us open a little shop.' And they opened a little food-shop, on the wide way leading to the holy place; and there they sold cakes for children, and toys, and food for pilgrims. For two years they so lived and prospered; and there was a son born to them.

"Now when the child was a year and two months old, the parents of the wife came in the course of their pilgrimage to Minobu; and they stopped at the little shop to buy food. And seeing their daughter's betrothed, they cried out and wept and asked questions. Then he made them enter, and bowed down before them, and astonished them, saying: 'Truly as I speak it, your daughter is not dead; and she is my wife; and we have a son. And she is even now within the farther room, lying down with the child. I pray you go in at once and gladden her, for her heart longs for the moment of seeing you again.'

"So while he busied himself in making all things ready for their comfort, they entered the inner, room very softly – the mother first.

"They found the child asleep; but the mother they did not find. She seemed to have gone out for a little while only: her pillow was still warm. They waited long for her: then they began to seek her. But never was she seen again.

"And they understood only when they found beneath the coverings which had covered the mother and child, something which they remembered having left years before in the temple of Myokoji – a little mortuary tablet, the *ihai* of their buried daughter."

I suppose I must have looked thoughtful after this tale; for the old man said:

"Perhaps the Master honourably thinks concerning the story that it is foolish?"

"Nay, Kinjuro, the story is in my heart."

The Reconciliation

Lafcadio Hearn

THERE WAS A YOUNG Samurai of Kyōto who had been reduced to poverty by the ruin of his lord, and found himself obliged to leave his home, and to take service with the Governor of a distant province. Before quitting the capital, this Samurai divorced his wife, – a good and beautiful woman, – under the belief that he could better obtain promotion by another alliance. He then married the daughter of a family of some distinction, and took her with him to the district whither he had been called.

But it was in the time of the thoughtlessness of youth, and the sharp experience of want, that the Samurai could not understand the worth of the affection so lightly cast away. His second marriage did not prove a happy one; the character of his new wife was hard and selfish; and he soon found every cause to think with regret of Kyōto days. Then he discovered that he still loved his first wife – loved her more than he could ever love the second; and he began to feel how unjust and how thankless he had been. Gradually his repentance deepened into a remorse that left him no peace of mind. Memories of the woman he had wronged – her gentle speech, her smiles, her dainty, pretty ways, her faultless patience – continually haunted him. Sometimes in dreams he saw her at her loom, weaving as when she toiled night and day to help him during the years of their distress: more often he saw her kneeling alone in the desolate little room where he had left her, veiling her tears with her poor worn sleeve. Even in the hours of official duty, his thoughts would wander back to her: then he would ask himself how she was living, what she was doing. Something in his heart assured him that she could not accept another husband, and that she never would refuse to pardon him. And he secretly resolved to seek her out as soon as he could return to Kyōto, – then to beg her forgiveness, to take her back, to do everything that a man could do to make atonement. But the years went by.

At last the Governor's official term expired, and the Samurai was free. "Now I will go back to my dear one," he vowed to himself. "Ah, what a cruelty, – what a folly to have divorced her!" He sent his second wife to her own people (she had given him no children); and hurrying to Kyōto, he went at once to seek his former companion, – not allowing himself even the time to change his travelling-garb.

When he reached the street where she used to live, it was late in the night, – the night of the tenth day of the ninth month; – and the city was silent as a cemetery. But a bright moon made everything visible; and he found the house without difficulty. It had a deserted look: tall weeds were growing on the roof. He knocked at the sliding-doors, and no one answered. Then, finding that the doors had not been fastened from within, he pushed them open, and entered. The front room was matless and empty: a chilly wind was blowing through crevices in the planking; and the moon shone through a ragged break in the wall of the alcove. Other rooms presented a like forlorn condition. The house, to all seeming, was unoccupied. Nevertheless, the Samurai determined to visit one other apartment at the further end of the dwelling, – a very small room that had been his wife's favourite resting-place. Approaching the sliding-screen that closed it, he was startled to perceive a glow within. He pushed the screen aside, and uttered a cry of joy; for he saw her there, – sewing by the light of a paper-lamp. Her eyes at the same instant met his own; and with a happy smile she greeted him, – asking only: "When did you come back to Kyōto? How did you find your way here to me, through all those black rooms?" The years had not changed her. Still she seemed as fair and young as in his fondest memory of her; – but sweeter than any memory there came to him the music of her voice, with its trembling of pleased wonder.

Then joyfully he took his place beside her, and told her all: how deeply he repented his selfishness, – how wretched he had been without her, – how constantly he had regretted her, – how long he had hoped and planned to make amends; – caressing her the while, and asking her forgiveness over and over again. She answered him, with loving gentleness, according to his heart's desire, – entreating him to cease all self-reproach. It was wrong, she said, that he should have allowed himself to suffer on her account: she had always felt that she was not worthy to be his wife. She knew that he had separated from her, notwithstanding, only because of poverty; and while he lived with her, he had always been kind; and she had never ceased to pray for his happiness. But even if there had been a reason for speaking of amends, this honourable visit would be ample amends; – what greater happiness than thus to see him again, though it were only for a moment? "Only for a moment!" he answered, with a glad laugh, – "say, rather, for the time of seven existences! My loved one, unless you forbid, I am coming back to live with you always – always – always! Nothing shall ever separate us again. Now I have means and friends: we need not fear poverty. To-morrow my goods will be brought here; and my servants will come to wait upon you; and we shall make this house beautiful.... To-night," he added, apologetically, "I came thus late – without even changing my dress – only because of the longing I had to see you, and to tell you this." She seemed greatly pleased by these words; and in her turn she told him about all that had happened in Kyōto since the time of his departure, – excepting her own sorrows, of which she sweetly refused to speak. They chatted far into the night: then she conducted him to a warmer room, facing south, – a room that had been their bridal chamber in former time. "Have you no one in the house to help you?" he asked, as she began to prepare the couch for him. "No," she answered, laughing cheerfully: "I could not afford a servant; – so I have been living all alone."

"You will have plenty of servants to-morrow," he said, – "good servants, – and everything else that you need." They lay down to rest, – not to sleep: they had too much to tell each other; – and they talked of the past and the present and the future, until the dawn was grey. Then, involuntarily, the Samurai closed his eyes, and slept.

When he awoke, the daylight was streaming through the chinks of the sliding-shutters; and he found himself, to his utter amazement, lying upon the naked boards of a mouldering floor.... Had he only dreamed a dream? No: she was there; – she slept.... He bent above her, – and looked, – and shrieked; – for the sleeper had no face!... Before him, wrapped in its grave-sheet only, lay the corpse of a woman, – a corpse so wasted that little remained save the bones, and the long black tangled hair.

Slowly, – as he stood shuddering and sickening in the sun, – the icy horror yielded to a despair so intolerable, a pain so atrocious, that he clutched at the mocking shadow of a doubt. Feigning ignorance of the neighbourhood, he ventured to ask his way to the house in which his wife had lived.

"There is no one in that house," said the person questioned. "It used to belong to the wife of a Samurai who left the city several years ago. He divorced her in order to marry another woman before he went away; and she fretted a great deal, and so became sick. She had no relatives in Kyōto, and nobody to care for her; and she died in the autumn of the same year, – on the tenth day of the ninth month...."

The Corpse-Rider

Lafcadio Hearn

THE BODY was cold as ice; the heart had long ceased to beat: yet there were no other signs of death. Nobody even spoke of burying the woman. She had died of grief and anger at having been divorced. It would have been useless to bury her, – because the last undying wish of a dying person for vengeance can burst asunder any tomb and rift the heaviest graveyard stone. People who lived near the house in which she was lying fled from their homes. They knew that she was only waiting for the return of the man who had divorced her.

At the time of her death he was on a journey. When he came back and was told what had happened, terror seized him. "If I can find no help before dark," he thought to himself, "she will tear me to pieces." It was yet only the Hour of the Dragon; but he knew that he had no time to lose.

He went at once to an *inyōshi* and begged for succour. The *inyōshi* knew the story of the dead woman; and he had seen the body. He said to the supplicant: "A very great danger threatens you. I will try to save you. But you must promise to do whatever I shall tell you to do. There is only one way by which you can be saved. It is a fearful way. But unless you find the courage to attempt it, she will tear you limb from limb. If you can be brave, come to me again in the evening before sunset." The man shuddered; but he promised to do whatever should be required of him.

At sunset the *inyōshi* went with him to the house where the body was lying. The *inyōshi* pushed open the sliding-doors, and told his client to enter. It was rapidly growing dark. "I dare not!" gasped the man, quaking from head to foot; – "I dare not even look at her!"

"You will have to do much more than look at her," declared the *inyōshi*; – "and you promised to obey. Go in!" He forced the trembler into the house and led him to the side of the corpse.

The dead woman was lying on her face. "Now you must get astride upon her," said the *inyōshi*, "and sit firmly on her back, as if you were riding a horse.... Come! – you must do it!" The man shivered so that the *inyōshi* had to support him – shivered horribly; but he obeyed. "Now take her hair in your hands," commanded the *inyōshi*, – "half in the right hand, half in the left.... So!... You must grip it like a bridle. Twist your hands in it – both hands – tightly. That is the way!... Listen to me! You must stay like that till morning. You will have reason to be afraid in the night – plenty of reason. But whatever may happen, never let go of her hair. If you let go – even for one second – she will tear you into gobbets!"

The *inyōshi* then whispered some mysterious words into the ear of the body, and said to its rider: "Now, for my own sake, I must leave you alone with her.... Remain as you are!... Above all things, remember that you must not let go of her hair." And he went away, closing the doors behind him.

Hour after hour the man sat upon the corpse in black fear; – and the hush of the night deepened and deepened about him till he screamed to break it. Instantly the body sprang beneath him, as to cast him off; and the dead woman cried out loudly, "Oh, how heavy it is! Yet I shall bring that fellow here now!"

Then tall she rose, and leaped to the doors, and flung them open, and rushed into the night – always bearing the weight of the man. But he, shutting his eyes, kept his hands twisted in her long hair – tightly, tightly – though fearing with such a fear that he could not even moan. How far she went, he never knew. He saw nothing: he heard only the sound of her naked feet in the dark – *picha-picha, picha-picha* – and the hiss of her breathing as she ran.

At last she turned, and ran back into the house, and lay down upon the floor exactly as at first. Under the man she panted and moaned till the cocks began to crow. Thereafter she lay still.

But the man, with chattering teeth, sat upon her until the *inyōshi* came at sunrise. "So you did not let go of her hair!" – observed the *inyōshi*, greatly pleased. "That is well … Now you can stand up." He whispered again into the ear of the corpse, and then said to the man: "You must have passed a fearful night; but nothing else could have saved you. Hereafter you may feel secure from her vengeance."

Nightmare-Touch

Lafcadio Hearn

I

WHAT IS THE FEAR OF GHOSTS among those who believe in ghosts?

All fear is the result of experience – experience of the individual or of the race – experience either of the present life or of lives forgotten. Even the fear of the unknown can have no other origin. And the fear of ghosts must be a product of past pain.

Probably the fear of ghosts, as well as the belief in them, had its beginning in dreams. It is a peculiar fear. No other fear is so intense; yet none is so vague. Feelings thus voluminous and dim are super-individual mostly – feelings inherited – feelings made within us by the experience of the dead.

What experience?

Nowhere do I remember reading a plain statement of the reason why ghosts are feared. Ask any ten intelligent persons of your acquaintance, who remember having once been afraid of ghosts, to tell you exactly why they were afraid – to define the fancy behind the fear; – and I doubt whether even one will be able to answer the question. The literature of folk-lore – oral and written – throws no clear light upon the subject. We find, indeed, various legends of men torn asunder by phantoms; but such gross imaginings could not explain the peculiar quality of ghostly fear. It is not a fear of bodily violence. It is not even a reasoning fear – not a fear that can readily explain itself – which would not be the case if it were founded upon definite ideas of physical danger. Furthermore, although primitive ghosts may have been imagined as capable of tearing and devouring, the common idea of a ghost is certainly that of a being intangible and imponderable.

Now I venture to state boldly that the common fear of ghosts is *the fear of being touched by ghosts* – or, in other words, that the imagined Supernatural is dreaded mainly because of its imagined power to touch. Only to *touch*, remember! – not to wound or to kill.

But this dread of the touch would itself be the result of experience – chiefly, I think, of prenatal experience stored up in the individual by inheritance, like the child's fear of darkness. And who can ever have had the sensation of being touched by ghosts? The answer is simple: *Everybody who has been seized by phantoms in a dream.*

Elements of primeval fears – fears older than humanity – doubtless enter into the child-terror of darkness. But the more definite fear of ghosts may very possibly be composed with inherited results of dream-pain – ancestral experience of nightmare. And the intuitive terror of supernatural touch can thus be evolutionally explained.

Let me now try to illustrate my theory by relating some typical experiences.

II

When about five years old I was condemned to sleep by myself in a certain isolated room, thereafter always called the Child's Room. (At that time I was scarcely ever mentioned by name, but only referred to as 'the Child'.) The room was narrow, but very high, and, in spite of one tall window, very gloomy.

It contained a fire-place wherein no fire was ever kindled; and the Child suspected that the chimney was haunted.

A law was made that no light should be left in the Child's Room at night – simply because the Child was afraid of the dark. His fear of the dark was judged to be a mental disorder requiring severe treatment. But the treatment aggravated the disorder. Previously I had been accustomed to sleep in a well-lighted room, with a nurse to take care of me. I thought that I should die of fright when sentenced to lie alone in the dark, and – what seemed to me then abominably cruel – actually *locked* into my room, the most dismal room of the house. Night after night when I had been warmly tucked into bed, the lamp was removed; the key clicked in the lock; the protecting light and the footsteps of my guardian receded together. Then an agony of fear would come upon me. Something in the black air would seem to gather and grow – (I thought that I could even *hear* it grow) – till I had to scream. Screaming regularly brought punishment; but it also brought back the light, which more than consoled for the punishment. This fact being at last found out, orders were given to pay no further heed to the screams of the Child.

* * *

Why was I thus insanely afraid? Partly because the dark had always been peopled for me with shapes of terror. So far back as memory extended, I had suffered from ugly dreams; and when aroused from them I could always see the forms dreamed of, lurking in the shadows of the room. They would soon fade out; but for several moments they would appear like tangible realities. And they were always the same figures.... Sometimes, without any preface of dreams, I used to see them at twilight-time – following me about from room to room, or reaching long dim hands after me, from story to story, up through the interspaces of the deep stairways.

I had complained of these haunters only to be told that I must never speak of them, and that they did not exist. I had complained to everybody in the house; and everybody in the house had told me the very same thing. But there was the evidence of my eyes! The denial of that evidence I could explain only in two ways: Either the shapes were afraid of big people, and showed themselves to me alone, because I was little and weak; or else the entire household had agreed, for some ghastly reason, to say what was not true. This latter theory seemed to me the more probable one, because I had several times perceived the shapes when I was not unattended; – and the consequent appearance of secrecy frightened me scarcely less than the visions did. Why was I forbidden to talk about what I saw, and even heard – on creaking stairways, – behind wavering curtains?

"Nothing will hurt you," – this was the merciless answer to all my pleadings not to be left alone at night. But the haunters *did* hurt me. Only – they would wait until after I had fallen asleep, and so into their power – for they possessed occult means of preventing me from rising or moving or crying out.

Needless to comment upon the policy of locking me up alone with these fears in a black room. Unutterably was I tormented in that room – for years! Therefore I felt relatively happy when sent away at last to a children's boarding-school, where the haunters very seldom ventured to show themselves.

* * *

They were not like any people that I had ever known. They were shadowy dark-robed figures, capable of atrocious self-distortion – capable, for instance, of growing up to the ceiling, and then across it, and then lengthening themselves, head-downwards, along the opposite wall. Only their faces were distinct; and I tried not to look at their faces. I tried also in my dreams – or thought that I tried – to awaken myself from the sight of them by pulling at my eyelids with my fingers; but the eyelids would remain closed, as if sealed.... Many years afterwards, the frightful plates in Orfila's *Traité des Exhumés*, beheld for the first time, recalled to me with a sickening start the dream-terrors of childhood. But to understand the Child's experience, you must imagine Orfila's drawings intensely alive, and continually elongating or distorting, as in some monstrous anamorphosis.

Nevertheless the mere sight of those nightmare-faces was not the worst of the experiences in the Child's Room. The dreams always began with a suspicion, or sensation of something heavy in the air – slowly quenching will, slowly numbing my power to move. At such times I usually found myself alone in a large unlighted apartment; and, almost simultaneously with the first sensation of fear, the atmosphere of the room would become suffused, half-way to the ceiling, with a sombre-yellowish glow, making objects dimly visible – though the ceiling itself remained pitch-black. This was not a true appearance of light: rather it seemed as if the black air were changing colour from beneath.... Certain terrible aspects of sunset, on the eve of storm, offer like effects of sinister colour.... Forthwith I would try to escape – feeling at every step a sensation as of *wading* – and would sometimes succeed in struggling half-way across the room; but there I would always find myself brought to a standstill, paralyzed by some innominable opposition. Happy voices I could hear in the next room; I could see light through the transom over the door that I had vainly endeavoured to reach; I knew that one loud cry would save me. But not even by the most frantic effort could I raise my voice above a whisper.... And all this signified only that the Nameless was coming – was nearing – was mounting the stairs. I could hear the step – booming like the sound of a muffled drum – and I wondered why nobody else heard it. A long, long time the haunter would take to come – malevolently pausing after each ghastly footfall. Then, without a creak, the bolted door would open – slowly, slowly – and the thing would enter, gibbering soundlessly, and put out hands, and clutch me, and toss me to the black ceiling – and catch me descending to toss me up again, and again, and again.... In those moments the feeling was not fear: fear itself had been torpified by the first seizure. It was a sensation that has no name in the language of the living. For every touch brought a shock of something infinitely worse than pain – something that thrilled into the innermost secret being of me – a sort of abominable electricity, discovering unimagined capacities of suffering in totally unfamiliar regions of sentiency.... This was commonly the work of a single tormentor; but I can also remember having been caught by a group, and tossed from one to another – seemingly for a time of many minutes.

III

Whence the fancy of those shapes? I do not know. Possibly from some impression of fear in earliest infancy; possibly from some experience of fear in other lives than mine. That mystery is forever insoluble. But the mystery of the shock of the touch admits of a definite hypothesis.

First, allow me to observe that the experience of the sensation itself cannot be dismissed as 'mere imagination'. Imagination means cerebral activity: its pains and its pleasures are alike inseparable from nervous operation, and their physical importance is sufficiently proved by their physiological effects. Dream-fear may kill as well as other fear; and no emotion thus powerful can be reasonably deemed undeserving of study.

One remarkable fact in the problem to be considered is that the sensation of seizure in dreams differs totally from all sensations familiar to ordinary waking life. Why this differentiation? How interpret the extraordinary massiveness and depth of the thrill?

I have already suggested that the dreamer's fear is most probably not a reflection of relative experience, but represents the incalculable total of ancestral experience of dream-fear. If the sum of the experience of active life be transmitted by inheritance, so must likewise be transmitted the summed experience of the life of sleep. And in normal heredity either class of transmissions would probably remain distinct.

Now, granting this hypothesis, the sensation of dream-seizure would have had its beginnings in the earliest phases of dream-consciousness – long prior to the apparition of man. The first creatures capable of thought and fear must often have dreamed of being caught by their natural enemies. There could not have been much imagining of pain in these primal dreams. But higher nervous development in later forms of being would have been accompanied with larger susceptibility to dream-pain. Still later, with the growth of reasoning-power, ideas of the supernatural would have changed and intensified the character of dream-fear. Furthermore, through all the course of evolution, heredity would have been accumulating the experience of such feeling. Under those forms of imaginative pain evolved through reaction of religious beliefs, there would persist some dim survival of savage primitive fears, and again, under this, a dimmer but incomparably deeper substratum of ancient animal-terrors. In the dreams of the modern child all these latencies might quicken – one below another – unfathomably – with the coming and the growing of nightmare.

It may be doubted whether the phantasms of any particular nightmare have a history older than the brain in which they move. But the shock of the touch would seem to indicate *some point of dream-contact with the total race-experience of shadowy seizure*. It may be that profundities of Self – abysses never reached by any ray from the life of sun – are strangely stirred in slumber, and that out of their blackness immediately responds a shuddering of memory, measureless even by millions of years.

Notes on a Haunted Patient

T.M. Hurree

EKTA PACES BACK AND FORTH outside Mary's home, trying to glimpse a friendly face through the windows. Her ghosts trail dutifully behind, twisting in the frigid night air. Ekta shivers beneath her greatcoat. The cold nibbles at her tiny brown fingers. Mary's music is loud enough to hear from the street – a poppy, synthetic beat fit for dancing. There will be laughter and conversation inside. Drinking, smoking, perhaps even flirting.

It's not too late for Ekta to flee. No one has seen her pacing outside yet. She could scurry back to the tube station, text Mary to apologise: *Sorry! So sorry! I'm not feeling well tonight, but I hope you have an awesome birthday!* Mary probably doesn't like Ekta anyway, because why would anyone like the shy, haunted girl cowering at the back of their pathology lectures? No, Mary only invited Ekta to be polite, and if Ekta actually goes inside she'll just embarrass Mary in front of all her cool friends, because Ekta ruins everything, absolutely everything, and then Mary will hate her just like everyone else, and –

Stop. Breathe. Ekta's mind has an unfortunate tendency to tumble out of control, too fast for her to keep up. Dr Chandrasekar says that when this happens, she should stop, breathe, and ask herself whether her response is reasonably warranted by the situation. Ekta makes a mental list:

REASONS TO BE SCARED OF A BIRTHDAY PARTY

1. What if I don't know anyone there, and I have no one to talk to? People will think I'm weird if I spend the whole night in the corner with my ghosts.

2. What if I get food poisoning from that leftover biryani? My tummy's already cramping a little. People will think I'm disgusting if I spend the whole night in the bathroom with my ghosts.

3. What if everyone there secretly hates me, and they only invited me as a joke? "Mary, wouldn't it be so funny if you invite that haunted freak from pathology?" People will think I'm stupid if I actually fall for it.

Dr Chandrasekar would probably say there are no rational reasons to be afraid of a birthday party. He would say Ekta should attend, because forming friendships with peers can hasten recovery. He would encourage her to destigmatise her stressors.

Grandfather's ghost floats towards Mary's window. He can see alcohol inside, technicolour bottles lined up on the counter – whiskey, rum, vodka, gin. He had a monstrous thirst in life, and still thirsts in death, despite lacking a tongue to taste and a stomach to fill.

Ekta takes a deep breath. She is going to do it. She is going to march up those steps and push the doorbell. She is going to smile, and laugh, and chat, and dance and pretend to be a normal person. She is going to –

"Excuse me, are you looking for Mary's place?"

Ekta turns. The speaker is a young man, with dark, curly hair and round glasses which frame his face in a dreadfully pleasant manner. It's too bad. He surely saw Ekta pacing outside, and he'll think she's a freak, and he'll tell everyone inside the party, and –

Ekta makes a rash decision. "I don't know who that is."

"Oh. Sorry. I must have mistaken you for someone else."

The boy frowns. Does he recognise her from their anatomy tutorials? Is he trying to figure out why anyone would lie about something so simple? Ekta scurries away before he can ask another uncomfortable question. The ghosts follow, forced to watch her squander the many gifts of life. She cannot escape them. They are her constant audience, judging Ekta's every failing – and she has so very many failings. On the train back to East London, Ekta considers texting Mary to apologise, but decides against it. She's already bothered the poor girl enough for one lifetime.

* * *

The first ghost belongs to Ekta's Grandfather, Mahindra. He appears hunched beneath the weight of his years, with yellow jaundiced eyes set deep in sunken sockets. Mahindra emigrated in his early twenties, seeking a better future for his family. During the day, he drove taxis. During the night, he swept the floors of a clock factory. At the age of thirty-four, while driving on three hours sleep, Mahindra swerved into oncoming traffic. He survived the crash, though his broken leg never fully healed. Unable to afford expensive painkillers, he turned to alcohol. Mahindra spoke five languages, though most people remember him as a miserable, violent drunk. His daughter chose not to visit him, as he lay dying of liver failure at the age of sixty-six. His favourite place in London is the Brixton Arms, where the beer flows free and cheap.

* * *

Ekta shuts the front door as quietly as she can, which is not quiet enough. Perhaps Mama hears the slight jangle of her keys? Perhaps the groaning hinges? Either way, Mama hears. Mama always hears.

"Ekta! Get up here!"

Ekta must have done a bad thing. She's always doing bad things. It often feels like she's incapable of doing anything right. The house is dark, lit only by pale ghost-light. Ekta creeps up the stairs, as silent as the spirits that haunt her.

"Don't you ignore me, girl! Come here right now!"

Mama sits at the kitchen table, hunched over the landline. Her long hair is streaked with grey and beginning to thin. Her dark face is pinched into a glare. She holds the phone as though she wants to crush it in her fist, smash it against the wall, drop it from the window.

"A doctor called for you," she says, "Dr Chandrasekar."

Ekta cannot look Mama in the eye. "He's one of my lecturers. He wanted to congratulate me on my mid-semester marks."

"I looked him up online. He's not a lecturer. He's a psychiatrist."

Ekta knows she's been caught, but like a fly struggling in a web, she persists. "He lectures part time. He's been helping with our psychiatry module."

"Don't lie to me, girl."

The ghosts grow restless. They also loathe Ekta. Grandfather trembles with rage. The ghost of Great-Uncle Ajay shakes his rotting head, spraying the kitchen with spectral seawater.

"There's something wrong with me, Mama. I don't feel well."

"Because you're letting quacks like him play with your head!" Mama doesn't believe in psychiatrists, and never has. If she could manage without one, why can't everyone else? "He just wants to make money off you, stupid girl! What have you got to be upset about? I *wish* I was lucky enough to have your life, Ekta. I'd have *killed* for the chances you have."

Ekta tries to explain, but the words lodge in her throat. Breathe, breathe, but she cannot. She is choking on her despair. Drowning, just like Great-Uncle Ajay.

"This will haunt you, Ekta, like an evil spirit. Every time you apply for a job, they'll ask. Every time. And you'll have to tell them. Every time. *Yes, I can't handle a bit of stress. I'm weak and my brain doesn't work properly.*"

Ekta coughs up a word, lumpy and malformed. "Sorry."

"It's too late to be sorry, stupid girl. You could have had a brilliant career. You could have been the best neurosurgeon in Britain!" Mama stands, shaking her head. She pushes past, but cannot leave without one final barb. "Do you even know what was sacrificed to bring you here? Do you even care how we suffered, to give you the opportunities you've just squandered?"

Mama goes to bed, but Ekta finds she cannot move. She is frozen, staring out the window as the first snow begins to fall. The ghosts watch from every angle, and all is silent, except for Ekta's sobs, and the clack-clacking of spectral crabs scuttling across the floorboards.

* * *

The second ghost belongs to Ekta's Great-Uncle, Ajay. His body is sodden, dripping seawater wherever he floats. Phantom crabs crawl across his carcase, and a phantom eel peeks from his empty eye socket. Ajay tried to emigrate at the age of eighteen, following the advice of his elder brother, Mahindra. Ajay's boat was less lucky. There was a storm off the Cape of Good Hope, and his body sunk to the seabed. Ajay's favourite part of London is the docks, where he once hoped to take the first step in his new life.

* * *

Ekta's room is filthy. Clothes lie strewn across the floor. Her bedside table is piled high with old coffee mugs, some with fuzzy grey mould spilling over their brims. Textbooks lie open on her desk, alongside stacks and stacks of poorly scribbled notes. Ekta's been meaning to tidy for some time, but the very notion is exhausting. Mama suggests starting small – dusting her desk, ordering her bookcase – but why start something she'll never finish? They've had many arguments over Ekta's squalor.

Ekta flops down at her desk. She's utterly drained, but there isn't time to rest. She's already wasted an hour being upset, standing in the kitchen, struggling to breathe. There's a big exam next Friday, for which she must learn every disease of the kidney: tumours and infections, atrophies, hypertrophies and obstructions, acute kidney injury and chronic kidney failure – their causes, their treatments, their prognoses. There's still so much to learn, and Ekta must learn it all, *she must*, because she'll fail if she doesn't, and her scholarship will be revoked, and she'll be forced to drop out, and Mama will hate her even more, and—

Breathe. Breathe. Breathe.

How is Ekta supposed to concentrate, with her mind spiralling out of control at the slightest provocation? The ghosts circle above – vultures, circling dying meat. Ekta tried to outrun them once, dashing through the frozen streets, skidding along the black ice, but she wasn't fast enough. Not even close. *Do you even know what was sacrificed to bring you here?* Of course she does. How could Ekta possibly forget?

A cockroach crawls from Ekta's old coffee mug, and scurries across her rushed sketch of the renal capsule. The ghost of Great-Great-Great Grandfather Nirav tries to squash it, his phantom hand passing harmlessly through the desk. In life, Nirav was no stranger to slaughter. In his final days, he killed six Germans at the Somme. He was brave and noble and strong, everything Ekta is not. Ekta makes a mental list of her many failings:

REASONS I AM A TERRIBLE PERSON:
1. I am ungrateful.
2. I am a coward.
3. I am a liar.
4. I am selfish.
Et cetera, et cetera.

Ekta could continue, but she wouldn't be finished by the big exam in a week's time. The cockroach scuttles across her notes, long antennae twitching. Cockroaches surely lead simple lives: hunt for food scraps, hide from foes. Repeat until dead. They are not haunted by the efforts of their ancestors. They have no ghosts to disappoint.

Ekta traps the cockroach beneath her coffee mug, and gently deposits it on the windowsill. Mama leaves poison in the pantry, and Ekta doesn't want to wake and find a six-legged corpse twitching on the kitchen tiles.

5. I am no better than a roach.

Ekta returns to her study, struggling through a lengthy passage about glomerulonephritis. The ghosts circle above. Watching. Judging.

* * *

The third ghost belongs to Ekta's great-great-great grandfather, Nirav. He still wears his uniform, dotted with bloodstains like poppies blooming on a barren battlefield. Nirav joined the Second Indian Cavalry Division because, like so many of his countrymen, he believed the British would reward their valour with a crumb of autonomy. Over one million Indians sailed the globe, to defend a country they did not love, against men they did not hate. An eternal optimist, Nirav's smile weathered the mud and guts and razor wire, the rats and mortars and machine gun fire. He fell on the 9th July 1916, still clutching the dream of a better future in his bloodied hands. The British never recognised his sacrifice with medals, or equality, or home-rule, but in 2002 the London City Council did approve a memorial to all the black and brown soldiers who died defending the empire that enslaved them. The Memorial Gates at Constitution Hill were officially inaugurated just eighty years after the Treaty of Versailles was signed. This is Nirav's favourite place in London, for obvious reasons.

* * *

Ekta spends Sunday working, working, working. There is always more to know, and Ekta must learn it all, or she'll lose everything. There is no in-between. She reads till her eyes burn and her head is pounding. She reads till the letters dissolve into inky gibberish. *Phaeochromocytoma? Adenocarcinoma? Glomerulonephritis?* These cannot be real words. They're just squiggles on the page, as meaningless to Ekta as the language of her great-great-great-great-great grandmother.

Ekta doesn't leave her desk to shower, or brush her teeth. She nibbles at a biscuit for breakfast, eats nothing for lunch. When the bad thoughts rise, she calms herself with classical music – Chopin, Vivaldi, Liszt. As a young girl, Ekta dreamt of joining an orchestra, touring the world, bringing joy to strangers. She still has her old violin, buried somewhere beneath a mound of dirty laundry, but her ancestors did not cross the globe so she could become a penniless musician.

Mama says money protects. Money preserves. Money keeps a roof over their head, and food in the pantry. Without a good job, Ekta will freeze, and starve, and waste away just like her great-great-great-great-great grandmother, Parvati. The old lady's ghost floats by the window, listless and gaunt, twisted fingers dangling uselessly. Her grim visage makes Ekta's heart beat faster with guilt.

Ekta flicks through page after page of disease. So many have obvious lesions: in Addison's disease, the adrenal glands shrivel and atrophy; in pyelonephritis, the kidney swells with blood and pus. Ekta wishes there was some way to scan her mind, to produce indisputable proof of the bad thoughts flitting about. Then she could show Mama. *See! I'm not making it up! See! It is a real disease! This is the reason I need help!*

For dinner, the two share the last dregs of leftover biryani. Ekta forces down a cold, congealed spoonful, trying not to think about all the awful toxins that grow in old rice…

"This is really nice, Mama," she says.

Mama nods, but says nothing. She is focused on her own slop.

Ekta tries again. "We're learning about kidneys at the moment." She waits. "It's pretty interesting, but I don't think I could ever be a nephrologist."

"You'll be lucky to get any job now," sighs Mama.

"Why? What do you mean?" Ekta knows what she means. It was a mistake to ask.

"Why would anyone trust a doctor who crumbles under the slightest pressure?"

Ekta blinks. "I'm trying to get better, Mama."

"You were never sick in the first place, stupid girl. Everyone gets upset sometimes. You just had to take the easy option."

"You think this is easy?"

"Did Tati Nirav run crying to a psychiatrist, when his friends were being gunned down all around? Did Nani Parvati, when they smashed her fingers? Did I?" Mama shakes her head.

Ekta stops trying to make conversation. She pushes a spoonful of slop around her plate, eyes burning. Really, this is Dr Chandrasekar's fault. She told him all about Mama. Why did he have to call Ekta's home phone? Why couldn't he just call her mobile? Ekta wants to scream at him, hit him, snap his stupid glasses—

"I might get back to work." Ekta chokes on her words.

"Do whatever you want," hisses Mama. "That's what you always do, anyway."

Ekta staggers to her room. The walls darken around her, pressing in. The floor shifts treacherously beneath her feet. Breathe. Breathe! She can't manage more than an urgent rasp. She's being strangled by phantom hands. Ekta flings open her window, gasping at the cold night air. Snow speckles her face, settling in her greasy black hair.

A small brown ghost scuttles along the windowsill. The cockroach is lying where Ekta left it, legs stiff and frozen. Of course it's dead. It's the middle of winter. Why didn't Ekta think of that? Why does she ruin everything? If Ekta can't be trusted to keep one cockroach alive, how can she ever be trusted with patients? Mama's right. She'll never get a job, and she'll be forced onto the streets, and she'll freeze to death just like that poor little roach, and—

Ekta flops back on her bed, sweaty, wheezing. The ghosts peer down at her, pale faces twisted in scorn. They hate Ekta. Why shouldn't they? She is pathetic. She is less than pathetic. She is nothing. Great Uncle Ajay trembles with rage, sprinkling seawater across her duvet. Old Parvati tears at her hair with twisted fingers.

"I'm sorry," sobs Ekta. She isn't strong like them. She wouldn't have survived the trenches, or the Raj, or the open ocean. She can barely survive the good life they gave her. "I'm so sorry."

The ghosts do not accept her apology, growing more restless. They wrap their pale arms around her, smothering her. Crushing her. Trying to choke the life from her useless flesh. Ekta shuts her eyes.

Breathe. She can't continue like this. She wants to get better. She really does. Breathe. She wants to make the ghosts proud. She doesn't want Mama to hate her.

Breathe.

Dr Chandrasekar says that recovery does not end in a glorious final battle. It is a war, a dreadful slog, with a thousand little skirmishes fought every day. Today, Ekta will open her eyes, and face the world, and that will be enough. Breathe. Ekta looks at her clock. Forty minutes have passed. Forty minutes she has wasted.

Breathe.

Ekta's next appointment isn't for another two weeks. She doesn't know how she'll survive till then.

* * *

The fourth ghost belongs to Ekta's great-great-great-great-great grandmother, Parvati. Her fingers are broken and bloodied, but her silks are the finest in the afterlife. Before the British invaded, she was considered the best seamstress in the known world. Her silks were worn by Muslim Caliphs, Chinese Emperors, European Princes. When she was fifty-seven, the redcoats arrived, hoping to reduce competition for their own inferior products. They smashed Parvati's fingers and burnt her stocks. Popular retellings suggest that The Great Seamstress Parvati starved to death because she could no longer earn a living. Like many stories to emerge from the Raj, this is a fundamental misconception. Parvati had plenty of children to support her. She could afford to eat. What she lacked was the will. Parvati had been robbed of her greatest joy in life – the ability to create. Inconsolable, she wasted away and died of a broken heart. Parvati hates every inch of this miserable city, because why the hell wouldn't she?

* * *

Ekta doesn't want to attend class on Monday, but Dr Chandrasekar would insist. Besides, Mama will only be even angrier if she stays home. The lecture theatre is already packed when Ekta arrives. Mary sits in the front row, chatting to the handsome boy with dark, curly hair and glasses. She must have spotted someone standing directly behind Ekta, because Mary smiles, waves, and gestures frantically to an empty seat close by the conversation.

Ekta pretends not to notice, and scampers out of Mary's way. She doesn't want to be looked at – with her dirty clothes and cheap trainers and dark skin. She doesn't belong there, with the children of politicians, lawyers, businessmen. She is an imposter, and everyone in the room knows it. Ekta sits in the back row, close by the fire exit. Her ghosts settle in the five empty seats nearby.

Today's lecture is about kidney transplants, and the various conditions that warrant them. As the professor explains the difference between dysuria (painful urination) and haematuria (bloody urine), Ekta feels an urgent pressure building in her pelvis. She *knows* her kidneys are fine. She knows her bladder is empty – but that knowledge doesn't make the need any less real.

According to the clock on the far wall, Ekta's only been there ten minutes. She crosses her legs, rocks back and forth. This always happens. Every time. During the dermatology module, Ekta's every freckle became a malignant melanoma, invading deeper into her flesh, seeding her organs with vile metastases. During the respiratory module, Ekta's common cold was really tuberculosis, black lung, Spanish flu. After her eighth appointment in three months, Ekta's GP began to suspect something psychological. Ekta glances at her watch. Fourteen minutes.

Everyone is staring at Ekta. She can feel their eyes boring through to her shrivelled black soul. She could flee. Run and hide in the bathroom. Ekta needs to pee anyway, except no she doesn't, she went right before class started. Lots of renal diseases can cause frequency (increased urination), but Ekta *knows* there will barely be a trickle. And it won't be bloody, or cloudy, or musty, or anything even mildly suggestive of disease. She won't successfully diagnose herself. She'll just make her classmates wonder why she can never sit still through an entire class.

Ekta closes her eyes. This is just her latest skirmish. She's going to sit in that lecture theatre for the full hour, and even if she doesn't jot down a single note, she's going to be proud of herself for it. Ekta opens her eyes. Apart from the ghosts, no one is staring at her. No one is sniggering, or pointing. No one thinks she's a freak.

Ekta can do it. She can get better, *will* get better, with or without Mama's help. Ekta turns to the fifth ghost, father's ghost. She cannot read the expression on his sunken face.

* * *

The final ghost belongs to Ekta's father, Manu. He died of a stroke, just two months before she was born. In their cardiovascular module, medical students learn that the risk factors for stroke include advanced age, obesity, diabetes and smoking. Manu was a healthy thirty-one year old, who despised cigarettes and those who smoked them, but sometimes disease does not obey human rules. Some diseases strike seemingly at random, careless and callous. Like the other ghosts, Manu does not care if Ekta becomes rich, or renowned. They just want her to be happy. Why else would anyone fight across France, sail the Atlantic, endure the Raj? Manu misses the screech of Ekta's violin – not because she was very good, but because she was never sad with her bow in hand. He wishes Ekta had joined an orchestra, followed her dreams. It's been too long since he last saw her smile. Manu's favourite place in London is St. James' Hospital, specifically the maternity ward, where his little angel took her first ever breath.

* * *

The professor ends his lecture with an anecdote about a young boy, suffering from congenital kidney failure. He might have lived with a transplant, but his parents refused to consent on religious grounds.

"They weren't evil people," said the misty eyed professor, "They sincerely believed they were acting in their child's best interests, but that is the tragedy of modern medicine. You will always know more than the patient in front of you, and think you know better. Our role is not to command. We can only educate, facilitate and obey. We are powerless, against a patient who does not want our help."

As her cohort shuffles outside into the snow and sleet, Ekta runs, runs, to catch up with Mary. "I'm sorry I missed your birthday." She forces herself to meet Mary's gaze.

The other girl does not scowl, or snigger, or jeer. She smiles. "Not a problem, friendo. We can catch up some other time. How about coffee on Friday, after the big exam?"

Ekta copies Mary's smile. It's difficult to say for sure, but the ghosts might be smiling too. Nirav nods so hard, his head falls off. A phantom clownfish peeks through the gaps in Great Uncle Ajay's teeth.

"I'd like that. Friendo." Ekta takes a deep breath. It's still hard – harder than it should be – but it's a little easier every time.

Picture of a Dying World

Nur Nasreen Ibrahim

THE MORNING A TREE APPEARED outside my window, I received a phone call informing me my mother was dying. Mashal amma's voice was muffled and the signal kept breaking. Red flowers dotting the sumbal tree that had crept in from my father's farm in Punjab, flashed like a warning. The tree shook in the cold mountain wind.

Somehow the tree had made it past the convent gates in the beginning of summer, settled on the slope under my office which overlooked the hill station, the pines, the marketplace with its dwindling stream of tourists, the high grey walls around St. Mary's, the creaking swings that hosted a girl or two.

"Asiya bibi," Mashal amma whispered. "Sahiba is very sick, and sahib refuses to take her to the doctor."

"Can you put her in the car and get Ashfaq to drive her to the army hospital?"

"Bibi, sahib has taken the keys. I think he is drunk."

I did not ask Sister Isabelle for leave at first, hesitant to depart the high stone walls of the convent, which for so many years had been a sanctuary for me. As stories reached us over crackling mobile phone connections of strange occurrences down south, I could not leave my cold, but comforting, grey bedroom with a tin roof that rattled under continuous hailstorms.

I taught literature to Class Eleven, a group old enough to understand subtext beyond the government approved curriculum, yet young enough to refuse its importance. These days, with loo winds extending into the winter, daisies emerging in the snow, everything was text.

Mashal amma called me again, two days later, when I finally decided to return home. "Asiya bibi, your mother is with Allah now."

* * *

I fell asleep watching the pine trees race pass the dusty window of our school van, lit up by the golden sunset of the mountains and awoke in the oppressive heat of the plains. I arrived late in the evening and our fields were covered by darkness so absolute, I had to turn on the flashlight from my cell phone. Not a star in the sky, the moon completely shrouded with a veil of thick black. The van had to stop every few feet just to make sure we were still on the dirt road.

As I disembarked, a rush of air dampened my cheeks. The wind came from the river many miles away, but the sound of water felt so near, right around my ankles, as if it was preparing to rise up and submerge me.

A few candles lit the front porch. My mother was hunched over a pile of pine nuts, her stubby nails digging into their black shells which fell at her feet. The wooden floor was dark from days of nut casings or perhaps just from the lack of light.

"Mama," I tried to say. But she was not paying attention and when I turned back to the verandah after dropping my bags in the hallway, she and the pine nut casings were gone.

All the bulbs in the house had stopped working. A heavy smell of old paint, plastic and dirt hung over every room. My mother's body was on her bed, wrapped in a white shroud, surrounded by gas lanterns.

A few women from the village had gathered, waiting for me to help wash the body. Mashal amma held my face in her shaking hands, her eyes shining with tears against the candlelight.

I had never noticed this in Mashal amma when I was a child, or it is more accurate to say I never looked closely. Now with years of bitterness behind me, dislocation from my mother, and a near-permanent estrangement from my father, I saw her. Like the melting candles lining our hallways, Mashal amma too had sunk into the floor of this house, so permanent was her bondage. Her once sharp nose dipped over loosened lips that also were turned downward at the edges. Her mahogany complexion had darkened even further because of the lines that had deepened in her cheeks, around her bright sparrow eyes so much like shining obsidian. She seemed so tired.

"Asiya baby, we worried you would be too late."

"I didn't want to be. I am sorry, Mashal amma."

"We called you many days ago about her illness. Why did it take so long?"

Her white hair hung like a shock of lightning around her thin face.

I stared back in silence and Mashal amma muttered, "You children think that by leaving you can forget all your responsibilities. You aren't better than us because you left."

I had spent the last decade avoiding this place, relying only on occasional phone calls from my mother who sighed about the way things had been, who believed so fervently that my return would correct the balance of this earth as it was spinning off its axis. She was a specter in this old house, even before her illness, clinging onto Mashal amma, letting moths get into her treasured chests of clothes and shawls, filling them with holes.

The villagers' weariness clung to me like an illness. They were all old, and there were no young people left here to hold their hands on the way to their graves.

My mother's body had shrunk, as if all water and fluids had been drained out of it. Her skin was a sickly yellow that hung loose against her bones, her wide lips and full cheeks had sunk into her skull. She had somehow, in just a few years, aged by twenty years.

I rubbed water and soap over her face with a washcloth and Mashal amma began to brush and braid the grey hair tinged with orange from henna.

Someone had forgotten to take out the tiny diamond piercing on her right nostril. I tugged it and with a click, the diamond stud fell into my hand. The pin holding the stud in was stuck in the nostril. I half hoped she would suddenly breathe in and it would get caught up her nose. I tried sticking my finger inside the nostril, large like mine with hair that tended to grow too far out if she didn't trim it. Mashal amma coughed, and I pulled my finger out of my dead mother's nose. I wiped it surreptitiously on my shalwar.

I woke the next morning to find two uprooted trees and a tractor fallen over outside my window. I imagined my mother breathed overnight, and overturned everything.

* * *

The tractor lay on its side, wheels slowly turning, propelled by a wind that seemed to have no direction. The world outside shifted as if the earth turned on its axle around our house. I awoke expecting to see verdant green farmlands, the long dirt road below my window stretching into the distance, surrounded by tall stalks of sugarcane, mustard, and thin tributaries of water gleaming at the edges of the horizon. Instead, the river had moved closer to our house, cutting through the sugarcane, tearing a purple and red line through the yellow mustard field, a gush of blood with no intention of receding.

A heavy gust of wind blew open my window with a loud crack, one pane shattered, and the net outside tore. A number of books above my desk had toppled over.

As a child, I spent many nights on the roof of the house, tossing broken pieces of brick over the edge of the banister, aiming for the bushes of the queen of the night. As the sun set over the fields, the flowers would open up to the moonlight, exuding a sweet fragrance that I still remember to this day. When my father was not home, ruling with an iron fist, my mother and I would collect those flowers by the handful, and leave them around the house overnight. By morning, every room smelled like the garden.

We were to take her body around the broken limbs of the trees blocking our driveway, around the river bend, past the dead stalks of sugarcane, to the graveyard where she would be laid to rest. I thought of the silver stud back quietly resting in her nose. As her body disintegrated many feet below ground, the stud would still live amongst the tightly packed dirt, with the earthworms, stained by soil that could no longer sustain the world above.

Mashal amma had opened the French windows leading to our verandah, and faint remnants of the floral smell mixed with camphor from my mother's body. She – it – lay wrapped in white in the middle of the floor, surrounded by mourning women, their heads covered and bent over prayer beads. Some rocked backwards and forwards as they muttered, like pale stalks of wheat being brushed by the stale wind coming through the door. Someone had scattered rose petals and crushed the queen of the night around her.

The day she married my father, my mother wore those flowers on her wrists and in her hair. Before my father locked himself away in his study, before there was too little water for their fields, and then suddenly too much, before there were no more queens populating the garden at night and their shimmering white faces faded into dark. Before our house was uprooted by the wind and rain, and her precious bushes drowned, my mother's flowers were her pride and joy.

* * *

Even when I thought of my father after I left for the convent, I only saw him in fragments, a thick beard and mustache, a firm belly that would soften with excess, and a dark eye that twitched.

I still see my father's back to me that evening in my childhood, as he faced my mother and Mashal amma in the garden, as clearly as if it were happening today. It was a powerful back, swathed in a cool white kameez and flecked with damp spots between its shoulder blades, and a wider sea of sweat growing beneath the armpits, sweat that made the cloth cling to him, revealing dark brown skin beneath.

Seeing the shape of him under wet cloth felt more intimate than seeing him naked.

My memory outfitted my mother in similarly pale yellow and white, a kurta pajama with a dupatta that appeared to ripple with the wind and blur amongst the flowers. But this could be me painting a picture pulled from romantic films, it was too idyllic to be real.

"Take her inside," my father was instructing Mashal amma, who glanced at my mother for confirmation.

"No, she should see this," my mother was saying. She lay down on her stomach, her shalwar spread out around her legs, and she was running her hands over the grass, grasping it and pulling it out by the handful.

The queen of the night had just been planted that year, they had all grown into thick white buds against bushes of bright green leaves that darkened as the sun set.

"Are you seeing these, Zia?" she was saying to my father. "Asiya baby," she sat up on her elbows and turned to me. "Do you know that in Japan, the queen of the night blooms for only one night in the year?"

My eyes widened, and I stared at the buds.

My father's back heaved, as if he was sighing, and he swatted away the mosquitoes that began to swirl like a tornado above his head. "For once do something useful with your time," I heard him say. "You are obsessed with this garden, while this house is falling apart!"

My mother would sing gently to herself most days, but today she lay there singing loudly at the top of her lungs. She sang about moonlit nights, about the lover's hair, the end of innocence. The more my father spoke, the louder she sang.

Even then I knew the signs that awakened the sleeping beast inside him, and my mother knew how to goad him. He was shaking and the wet kept pooling in his crevices, my mother laughed, and Mashal amma and I cowered.

I still see my father's foot before I see his face, because that foot struck my mother on the hip that afternoon, with its brown leather sandal, the sturdy flat toes with overgrown nails. It left a grey mark on her white shalwar, grey that disappeared among the grass stains that spread as she rolled over and laughed until she hiccuped.

The darkness gathered, and I ignored the scene unfolding around me, waiting only for the petals of the queen of the night. Did the flower twitch? Did one petal separate from the others?

But someone grabbed me around the waist and the breath was knocked out of me as my father's thick arms hoisted me up. I screamed and clawed at his shoulder.

I smelled his musty breath, and heard the door slamming behind us. My mother lay curled on her side in the grass, her laughter giving way to quiet sobbing, and I did not get to see the flowers bloom that night.

* * *

A thin buzzing grew louder and louder outside the open window of our living room and the mosquitoes gathering above each bush swarmed inside. The mourning women jumped up, waving their arms and swatting into the air. I sidestepped the frantic activity and turned to the front door, where a tall figure with a thin shawl wrapped around her shoulders beckoned me.

She looked like my mother, but younger. She stared at me as if I was a book she wanted to peruse for a long time.

"I am sorry for your loss. May Allah grant her the highest place in jannah," she said.

"Thank you. Did you know my mother?" I asked.

"Yes. She took care of my children."

"How many children? Are they here?"

"Too many," she smiled. "But this village has no more children."

We looked out at the edges of the fields where for the first time I noticed a curious fog hanging low over browned and withered stalks. I turned, begging my leave of this strange woman, but she had vanished.

It was still midday, but the queen of the night was awake. To my shock, I saw three, four, and then ten white faces gleaming at me from the bushes around the house. These bushes had been uprooted and destroyed in last night's wind, but the flowers shone as if they had just been freshly watered. I held the door frame tightly.

The sound of porcelain shattering made its way through the door of my father's study. He had knocked over another teacup.

Many years ago, after I left home and moved to the convent, I received a frantic phone call from him.

"Have you read anything about the dolphins with legs that have been eating crops?" he said abruptly. This was how most of our rare conversations began.

"The dolphins? I thought they died," I said.

"Something has been eating our crops and Mukhtar says he saw something that looked like the river dolphin except it was crawling. On land."

"Abbu, Mukhtar is senile."

"Strange things keep happening here. The other day your mother swore she saw the trees move from one corner of the garden to the other. It was dark then, but in the morning the tree had definitely moved."

"I don't know what to say," I was easily exasperated back then. "You both need to get your eyes checked. When was the last time you went to the doctor?"

I refused to listen to them then, even after I heard from Mashal amma how the land was revolting against its own nature. My mother's accelerated aging, her body turning her once tall frame into a withered, shrunken, dried up root, I explained away by the stress of my father's drinking. My father's sudden return to drinking I explained as the habit of an addict, unable to forget the moments of forgetfulness.

I explained away many things growing up on that land. I explained away the late nights and the early mornings where women materialized from my father's study, covering their heads, muttering about being asked to help him with something, wiping away tears, adjusting their shalwar, hiding the bruises on their cheeks. I could explain Mashal amma's miscarriages, her constant illnesses, the babies who emerged out of the woodwork. As an overeducated college student, I could blame it all on the uneducated, backward villagers who refused to learn about contraception, didn't understand our country was bursting to the brim with babies.

But the queen of the night opening its eyes in the morning, the moving trees, the tractor quietly appearing overnight, the shifting water, I could not explain.

* * *

The women took over carrying my mother's body to the gravesite. After the men's feeble protests, and my father's inability to protest, they placed her gently on the charpayee. Two women held the front legs, while a number of villagers gathered underneath the charpayee, its knotted ropes tangling with their scarves. I took up the back, propping one corner of the charpayee on my shoulder, clasping the leg, and dragging my feet as the villagers traversed our weed-covered lawn.

A group of men, mostly farmers, stood outside. At first I thought they would stop us, seeing all these women bearing the body of the lady of the house, but they quietly stood aside. They had laid their tools down for many days, maybe even months. The colors in the fields were muted and washed over many times by a coat of dirty yellow, and the brown sky began to fade into dull grey and purple clouds giving the morning an evening glow. Most of the men followed us. The cloth wrapped around my mother's face rose and fell and I imagined she sat up suddenly, awoken by the gentle rocking of her favorite charpayee.

Dust gathered around our feet, as our procession made its way down the narrow path. The newly formed river undulated beside us, a wet breathing body with mysterious dark shapes floating in its depths. A myna bird hopped alongside us. It opened its beak and a crow's screech emerged from its little throat.

A long line of almond trees used to shade the graves. We often drove past them, and I would admire their proud stances, the gentle bounce in their branches that angled to fly away from the earth. Now the earth lay flat and still, without the trees, as if they had never existed. No one commented on their disappearance, no one seemed to notice that browning blossoms from the almond branches were still scattered on the graves like the trees had left them as a parting gift and walked off.

The graveyard had once belonged only to the farmers; our family burials took place in the city. But my father's isolation and my late arrival meant my mother would be buried with the people her husband controlled with an iron grip.

Mashal amma held my hand as the women lowered the charpayee to the ground where a deep hole had been dug. The grass around her had dried, the once white headstones were grey or black. One woman started praying loudly and everyone adjusted their scarves and held up their hands.

A distant wind from the mountains brought the smell of pines, shaking the grass around us, and I shivered in surprise.

As my mother was lowered into her grave with unexpected speed and strength, one woman began covering her up with mud, her wrinkled hands grasping a shovel and with little effort tossed chunks of soil onto the white shroud.

"Why have you returned?" I heard my mother's voice next to me as I watched her body sink deeper and deeper into the earth.

"To say goodbye."

"Not to me." I heard her laugh. "You said goodbye to me long ago when you ran away. You came to say goodbye to this place."

"This place is still here," I said aloud.

"No it is not. It died a long time ago. You are standing on its corpse."

That night, the women cooked large pots of food from the last of the chickens and the cattle. They brought the last buffalo to the center of our garden and sacrificed it. I watched as they ran a long knife against the neck of the barely struggling creature, its eyes rolled back into its head, the tongue lolled out, and its blood ran into the scattered bushes, some of it splattering the white face of the queen of the night.

Mashal amma looked happier, calmer, her tears long dried.

Everyone feasted on heavy meat and bread, licking our fingers and gulping down large tumblers of milk. I was on the front steps of the verandah, listening to the unusual sound of laughter and activity in the kitchen, when Mashal amma sat down next to me bearing a full plate. She nudged it toward me.

"Baby, will you eat?"

"I don't feel like it," I said.

She nodded, and looked past me at the darkened fields.

"How did you do it?" I turned to her, and saw her white eyebrows rise. "How did you put up with her? Put up with *him*?"

"Did I have a choice, baba? Where could I go?" she sighed. "None of us have prospects anywhere else."

I felt the barb. I had indeed left, and found a world away from here.

"Don't think that way." Her hand reached for mine, "Someone had to leave, I suppose it could have only been you." Even she didn't try to mask the bitterness.

The house was ravenous, sucking in mourners and their smells and the food they brought with them. Light from gas lanterns and candles filled our hallways, the deep red carpets and old portraits moved with renewed activity.

My father's round figure moved on the edges where light could not reach, shuffling away from the putrid smell that emerged from his den, pulled by the noise and movement like a hungry beast prowling or a lesser god hiding in the quiet and dark places untouched by human hands.

* * *

In another world, death happened and the stars kept shining, the sun rose and set, the rain fell at the designated time, and dried soon after. Anything out of the ordinary was just that, an aberration that must be shoved under the carpet. But my mother's death was different; the world had cracked open with us.

The next day the river had come to us, or we had shifted closer to the river. I woke to the soft sound of lapping water, splashing against the side of our house. Spray from the river found its way through the window netting and onto my face. I woke up with a start, tears finally springing to my eyes as I realized the bed was wet.

Something like shame bubbled up within me.

I was not sure if this was a dream, but I found myself in front of the house.

The disappeared children of the village were seated on our front steps. The soil around them shifted softly, gently, and their eyes, my father's eyes stared back at me, their stubby hands, so like his, their heavy gait, some older than others with his low paunch. Some were still small, impishly grinning, like he once did.

But their mothers had not left. Mashal amma had not left.

The smells, lights, groomed garden, everything had returned to its former ruin.

The door to my father's study was open, and his shadow filled the doorframe. I heard the muffled grunts that always seemed to emanate from there, the heavy creaking, the slamming of a door, a book against a wall, a glass rolling against the floor, his dragging heavy unmistakably distinctive gait, the lighter pitter patter of mysterious feet that seemed to run around the room before they were stopped with a loud hush.

A rush of last night's food filled my mouth and I wanted to revive the buffalo, remove all remnants of my father's property from myself. I wanted this rotating new world to spin faster, this river to submerge us, these dying trees to take over, and my father to die with his farm.

* * *

I once introduced my students to poems written after our bloodiest war. The poems were about guilt, guilt in silence, guilt in comfort, guilt in sitting behind large brick walls as the world around us transformed. The nuns reprimanded me; we were not to talk about a century-old war, when our army needs our support today. They had been so focused on protecting us from violent actors, from unruly politicians, from our unruly selves, they did not know how to protect us from unruly nature that slowly crept into their barracks, destroyed their weaponry, flooded their tanks, struck down their jets from the sky. They could not surround and contain the infection that wormed its way through window sills, into water, into the deep recesses of the mind where everything I saw twisted into strange shapes, where past and present and future seemed to be one, and the dead and living existed in tandem, and the world I once escaped from had always been following me, keeping me in check.

The destruction of my house was slow and deliberate at first, and then violent and rushed. The women started with the interior, throwing out our settees and sofas, stripping the carpet from the floor and then breaking the tiles with hammers and shovels. One woman tore down the paintings and drapery on the walls, smashed the vases with dried and dead flowers, another broke the glass in the French windows. They cascaded onto the tiles like a waterfall, and revealed a dark sky filled with clouds that seemed to anticipate the inevitable end. The river had moved closer, the sounds of water crashing and receding in a rush of air that burst into the living room in spurts.

They moved to my father's study. I stayed outside in the hope that I would not have to look into his eyes and see my own staring back at me. I heard the crashing, I heard shuffling, I heard a loud grunt. But when they emerged, I could still hear some ghostly weeping from behind the door, distant and faint.

They took my mother's jewelry and her dusty, moth-eaten box filled with her trousseau. Two women carried the box outside, her earrings, shaped like large flowers with little pearls hanging off the bottom, necklaces of kundan and emerald, and gold bracelets that she once wore from elbow to wrist, were distributed. Some pieces were broken apart with tongs, some diamonds were gouged out of their golden shells, some pearls were piled onto a shawl and women grabbed them by the handful. When everyone received a portion, one diamond necklace from my mother's bridal set remained.

I pushed it into Mashal amma's hands.

"I will not take it, my child," she said. She tried closing my fingers around it.

"I don't want anything he bought," I said. "I have my own money."

"How long will that last?" She said. "What will I do with all this money?"

"Find your children, go to the city. They are all out there somewhere."

"They are strangers to me. Your father made sure of that. I have nothing, and I will leave with nothing. Don't give me her blood jewels," she said with a sudden vehemence that I pulled back and dropped the necklace onto the ground where someone may have grabbed it or it was forgotten.

"You can come with us, or stay here," she said. "I will get you out of here, and after that is up to you. But this place is dying and soon the river will take care of the rest."

The river had crept up slowly to our feet, silt and sediment seeped into the grass, the clouds had grown darker and I heard a low moaning through the fog settling above the lapping waves. Even though the wind had just picked up speed, the waves were already smashing into the fields and flooding the landscape, and the sky looked tired and bruised, groaning to burst open and deluge us with its contents.

In the distance I noticed that the villagers had gathered and lined up a collection of rafts and boats. The tractor from our garden creaked and toppled over again in a gust of wind. The moan grew louder, this time coming from the house where we had left my father.

They took my hand and led me to the boats and with each step I felt the waves rising behind us, the purple sky sinking over us and I turned around to look once again at my home. My father stood under the door frame, his face in shadow, his arms held forward trying to shield him from the buffeting wind. A bush of the queen of the night flew across the doorway, scattering flowers at his feet. From this distance, I saw his past, present and future, I saw the door slam into him and the house sank in the rising water.

The Story of Chang To-Ryong

Im Bang; translated by James S. Gale

IN THE DAYS of King Chung-jong (AD 1507–26) there lived a beggar in Seoul, whose face was extremely ugly and always dirty. He was forty years of age or so, but still wore his hair down his back like an unmarried boy. He carried a bag over his shoulder, and went about the streets begging. During the day he went from one part of the city to the other, visiting each section, and when night came on he would huddle up beside some one's gate and go to sleep. He was frequently seen in *Chong-no* (Bell Street) in company with the servants and underlings of the rich. They were great friends, he and they, joking and bantering as they met. He used to say that his name was Chang, and so they called him Chang To-ryong, *To-ryong* meaning an unmarried boy, son of the gentry. At that time the magician Chon U-chi, who was far-famed for his pride and arrogance, whenever he met Chang, in passing along the street, would dismount and prostrate himself most humbly. Not only did he bow, but he seemed to regard Chang with the greatest of fear, so that he dared not look him in the face. Chang, sometimes, without even inclining his head, would say, "Well, how goes it with you, eh?" Chon, with his hands in his sleeves, most respectfully would reply, "Very well, sir, thank you, very well." He had fear written on all his features when he faced Chang.

Sometimes, too, when Chon would bow, Chang would refuse to notice him at all, and go by without a word. Those who saw it were astonished, and asked Chon the reason. Chon said in reply, "There are only three spirit-men at present in *Cho-sen*, of whom the greatest is Chang To-ryong; the second is Cheung Puk-chang; and the third is Yun Se-pyong. People of the world do not know it, but I do. Such being the case, should I not bow before him and show him reverence?"

Those who heard this explanation, knowing that Chon himself was a strange being, paid no attention to it.

At that time in Seoul there was a certain literary undergraduate in office whose house joined hard on the street. This man used to see Chang frequently going about begging, and one day he called him and asked who he was, and why he begged. Chang made answer, "I was originally of a cultured family of Chulla Province, but my parents died of typhus fever, and I had no brothers or relations left to share my lot. I alone remained of all my clan, and having no home of my own I have gone about begging, and have at last reached Seoul. As I am not skilled in any handicraft, and do not know Chinese letters, what else can I do?" The undergraduate, hearing that he was a scholar, felt very sorry for him, gave him food and drink, and refreshed him.

From this time on, whenever there was any special celebration at his home, he used to call Chang in and have him share it.

On a certain day when the master was on his way to office, he saw a dead body being carried on a stretcher off toward the Water Gate. Looking at it closely from the horse on which he rode, he recognized it as the corpse of Chang To-ryong. He felt so sad that he turned back to his house and cried over it, saying, "There are lots of miserable people on earth, but who ever saw one as miserable as poor Chang? As I reckon the time over on my fingers, he has been begging in Bell Street for fifteen years, and now he passes out of the city a dead body."

Twenty years and more afterwards the master had to make a journey through South Chulla Province. As he was passing Chi-i Mountain, he lost his way and got into a maze among the hills. The day began to wane, and he could neither return nor go forward. He saw a narrow footpath, such as woodmen take, and turned into it to see if it led to any habitation. As he went along there were rocks and deep ravines. Little by little, as he advanced farther, the scene changed and seemed to become strangely transfigured. The farther he went the more wonderful it became. After he had gone some miles he discovered himself to be in another world entirely, no longer a world of earth and dust. He saw some one coming toward him dressed in ethereal green, mounted and carrying a shade, with servants accompanying. He seemed to sweep toward him with swiftness and without effort. He thought to himself, "Here is some high lord or other coming to meet me, but," he added, "how among these deeps and solitudes could a gentleman come riding so?" He led his horse aside and tried to withdraw into one of the groves by the side of the way, but before he could think to turn the man had reached him. The mysterious stranger lifted his two hands in salutation and inquired respectfully as to how he had been all this time. The master was speechless, and so astonished that he could make no reply. But the stranger smilingly said, "My house is quite near here; come with me and rest."

He turned, and leading the way seemed to glide and not to walk, while the master followed. At last they reached the place indicated. He suddenly saw before him great palace halls filling whole squares of space. Beautiful buildings they were, richly ornamented. Before the door attendants in official robes awaited them. They bowed to the master and led him into the hall. After passing a number of gorgeous, palace-like rooms, he arrived at a special one and ascended to the upper storey, where he met a very wonderful person. He was dressed in shining garments, and the servants that waited on him were exceedingly fair. There were, too, children about, so exquisitely beautiful that it seemed none other than a celestial palace. The master, alarmed at finding himself in such a place, hurried forward and made a low obeisance, not daring to lift his eyes. But the host smiled upon him, raised his hands and asked, "Do you not know me? Look now." Lifting his eyes, he then saw that it was the same person who had come riding out to meet him, but he could not tell who he was. "I see you," said he, "but as to who you are I cannot tell."

The kingly host then said, "I am Chang To-ryong. Do you not know me?" Then as the master looked more closely at him he could see the same features. The outlines of the face were there, but all the imperfections had gone, and only beauty remained. So wonderful was it that he was quite overcome.

A great feast was prepared, and the honoured guest was entertained. Such food, too, was placed before him as was never seen on earth. Angelic beings played on beautiful instruments and danced as no mortal eye ever looked upon. Their faces, too, were like pearls and precious stones.

Chang To-ryong said to his guest, "There are four famous mountains in Korea in which the genii reside. This hill is one. In days gone by, for a fault of mine, I was exiled to earth, and in the time of my exile you treated me with marked kindness, a favour that I have never forgotten. When you saw my dead body your pity went out to me; this, too, I remember. I was not dead then, it was simply that my days of exile were ended and I was returning home. I knew that you were passing this hill, and I desired to meet you and to thank you for all your kindness. Your treatment of me in another world is sufficient to bring about our meeting in this one." And so they met and feasted in joy and great delight.

When night came he was escorted to a special pavilion, where he was to sleep. The windows were made of jade and precious stones, and soft lights came streaming through them, so that there was no night. "My body was so rested and my soul so refreshed," said he, "that I felt no need of sleep."

When the day dawned a new feast was spread, and then farewells were spoken. Chang said, "This is not a place for you to stay long in; you must go. The ways differ of we genii and you men of the world. It will be difficult for us ever to meet again. Take good care of yourself and go in peace." He then called a servant to accompany him and show the way. The master made a low bow and withdrew. When he had gone but a short distance he suddenly found himself in the old world with its dusty accompaniments.

The path by which he came out was not the way by which he had entered. In order to mark the entrance he planted a stake, and then the servant withdrew and disappeared.

The year following the master went again and tried to find the citadel of the genii, but there were only mountain peaks and impassable ravines, and where it was he never could discover.

As the years went by the master seemed to grow younger in spirit, and at last at the age of ninety he passed away without suffering. "When Chang was here on earth and I saw him for fifteen years," said the master, "I remember but one peculiarity about him, namely, that his face never grew older nor did his dirty clothing ever wear out. He never changed his garb, and yet it never varied in appearance in all the fifteen years. This alone would have marked him as a strange being, but our fleshly eyes did not recognize it."

The Grateful Ghost

Im Bang; translated by James S. Gale

IT IS OFTEN TOLD that in the days of the Koryo Dynasty (AD 918–1392), when an examination was to be held, a certain scholar came from a far-distant part of the country to take part. Once on his journey the day was drawing to a close, and he found himself among the mountains. Suddenly he heard a sneezing from among the creepers and bushes by the roadside, but could see no one. Thinking it strange, he dismounted from his horse, went into the brake and listened. He heard it again, and it seemed to come from the roots of the creeper close beside him, so he ordered his servant to dig round it and see. He dug and found a dead man's skull. It was full of earth, and the roots of the creeper had passed through the nostrils. The sneezing was caused by the annoyance felt by the spirit from having the nose so discommoded.

The candidate felt sorry, washed the skull in clean water, wrapped it in paper and reburied it in its former place on the hill-side. He also brought a table of food and offered sacrifice, and said a prayer.

That night, in a dream, a scholar came to him, an old man with white hair, who bowed, thanked him, and said, "On account of sin committed in a former life, I died out of season before I had fulfilled my days. My posterity, too, were all destroyed, my body crumbled back into the dust, my skull alone remaining, and that is what you found below the creeper. On account of the root passing through it the annoyance was great, and I could not help but sneeze. By good luck you and your kind heart, blessed of Heaven, took pity on me, buried me in a clean place and gave me food. Your kindness is greater than the mountains, and like the blessing that first brought me into life. Though my soul is by no means perfect, yet I long for some way by which to requite your favour, and so I have exercised my powers in your behalf. Your present journey is for the purpose of trying the official Examination, so I shall tell you beforehand what the form is to be, and the subject. It is to be of character groups of fives, in couplets; the rhyme sound is 'pong', and the subject 'Peaks and Spires of the Summer Clouds'. I have already composed one for you, which, if you care to use it, will undoubtedly win you the first place. It is this—

> *'The white sun rode high up in the heavens,*
> *And the floating clouds formed a lofty peak;*
> *The priest who saw them asked if there was a temple there,*
> *And the crane lamented the fact that no pines were visible;*
> *But the lightnings from the cloud were the flashings of the woodman's axe,*
> *And the muffled thunders were the bell calls of the holy temple.*
> *Will any say that the hills do not move?*
> *On the sunset breezes they sailed away.'"*

After thus stating it, he bowed and took his departure.

The man, in wonder, awakened from his dream, came up to Seoul; and behold, the subject was as foretold by the spirit. He wrote what had been given him, and became first in the honours of the occasion.

An Encounter with a Hobgoblin

Im Bang; translated by James S. Gale

I GOT MYSELF INTO TROUBLE in the year *Pyong-sin*, and was locked up; a military man by the name of Choi Won-so, who was captain of the guard, was involved in it and locked up as well. We often met in prison and whiled away the hours talking together. On a certain day the talk turned on goblins, when Captain Choi said, "When I was young I met with a hobgoblin, which, by the fraction of a hair, almost cost me my life. A strange case indeed!"

I asked him to tell me of it, when he replied, "I had originally no home in Seoul, but hearing of a vacant place in Belt Town, I made application and got it. We went there, my father and the rest of the family occupying the inner quarters, while I lived in the front room.

"One night, late, when I was half asleep, the door suddenly opened, and a woman came in and stood just before the lamp. I saw her clearly, and knew that she was from the home of a scholar friend, for I had seen her before and had been greatly attracted by her beauty, but had never had a chance to meet her. Now, seeing her enter the room thus, I greeted her gladly, but she made no reply. I arose to take her by the hand, when she began walking backwards, so that my hand never reached her. I rushed towards her, but she hastened her backward pace, so that she eluded me. We reached the gate, which she opened with a rear kick, and I followed on after, till she suddenly disappeared. I searched on all sides, but not a trace was there of her. I thought she had merely hidden herself, and never dreamed of anything else.

"On the next night she came again and stood before the lamp just as she had done the night previous. I got up and again tried to take hold of her, but again she began her peculiar pace backwards, till she passed out at the gate and disappeared just as she had done the day before. I was once more surprised and disappointed, but did not think of her being a hobgoblin.

"A few days later, at night, I had lain down, when suddenly there was a sound of crackling paper overhead from above the ceiling. A forbidding, creepy sound it seemed in the midnight. A moment later a curtain was let down that divided the room into two parts. Again, later, a large fire of coals descended right in front of me, while an immense heat filled the place. Where I was seemed all on fire, with no way of escape possible. In terror for my life, I knew not what to do. On the first cock-crow of morning the noise ceased, the curtain went up, and the fire of coals was gone. The place was as though swept with a broom, so clean from every trace of what had happened.

"The following night I was again alone, but had not yet undressed or lain down, when a great stout man suddenly opened the door and came in. He had on his head a soldier's felt hat, and on his body a blue tunic like one of the underlings of the yamen. He took hold of me and tried to drag me out. I was then young and vigorous, and had no intention of yielding to him, so we entered on a tussle. The moon was bright and the night clear, but I, unable to hold my own, was pulled out into the court. He lifted me up and swung me round and round, then went up to the highest terrace and threw me down, so that I was terribly stunned. He stood in front of me and kept me a prisoner. There was a garden to the rear of the house, and a wall round it. I looked, and within the wall were a dozen or so of people. They were all dressed in military hats and coats, and they kept shouting out, 'Don't hurt him, don't hurt him.'

"The man that mishandled me, however, said in reply, 'It's none of your business, none of your business'; but they still kept up the cry, 'Don't hurt him, don't hurt him'; and he, on the other hand, cried, 'Never you mind; none of your business.' They shouted, 'The man is a gentleman of the military class; do not hurt him.'

"The fellow merely said in reply, 'Even though he is, it's none of your business'; so he took me by the two hands and flung me up into the air, till I went half-way and more to heaven. Then in my fall I went shooting past Kyong-keui Province, past Choong-chong, and at last fell to the ground in Chulla. In my flight through space I saw all the county towns of the three provinces as clear as day. Again in Chulla he tossed me up once more. Again I went shooting up into the sky and falling northward, till I found myself at home, lying stupefied below the verandah terrace. Once more I could hear the voices of the group in the garden shouting, 'Don't hurt him – hurt him.' But the man said, 'None of your business – your business.'

"He took me up once more and flung me up again, and away I went speeding off to Chulla, and back I came again, two or three times in all.

"Then one of the group in the garden came forward, took my tormentor by the hand and led him away. They all met for a little to talk and laugh over the matter, and then scattered and were gone, so that they were not seen again.

"I lay motionless at the foot of the terrace till the following morning, when my father found me and had me taken in hand and cared for, so that I came to, and we all left the haunted house, never to go back."

A Visit From the Shades

Im Bang; translated by James S. Gale

THERE WAS A MINISTER in olden days who once, when he was Palace Secretary, was getting ready for office in the morning. He had on his ceremonial dress. It was rather early, and as he leaned on his arm-rest for a moment, sleep overcame him. He dreamt, and in the dream he thought he was mounted and on his journey. He was crossing the bridge at the entrance to East Palace Street, when suddenly he saw his mother coming towards him on foot. He at once dismounted, bowed, and said, "Why do you come thus, mother, not in a chair, but on foot?"

She replied, "I have already left the world, and things are not where I am as they are where you are, and so I walk."

The secretary asked, "Where are you going, please?"

She replied, "We have a servant living at Yong-san, and they are having a witches' prayer service there just now, so I am going to partake of the sacrifice."

"But," said the secretary, "we have sacrificial days, many of them, at our own home, those of the four seasons, also on the first and fifteenth of each month. Why do you go to a servant's house and not to mine?"

The mother replied, "Your sacrifices are of no interest to me, I like the prayers of the witches. If there is no medium we spirits find no satisfaction. I am in a hurry," said she, "and cannot wait longer," so she spoke her farewell and was gone.

The secretary awoke with a start, but felt that he had actually seen what had come to pass.

He then called a servant and told him to go at once to So-and-So's house in Yong-san, and tell a certain servant to come that night without fail. "Go quickly," said the secretary, "so that you can be back before I enter the Palace." Then he sat down to meditate over it.

In a little the servant had gone and come again. It was not yet broad daylight, and because it was cold the servant did not enter straight, but went first into the kitchen to warm his hands before the fire. There was a fellow-servant there who asked him, "Have you had something to drink?"

He replied, "They are having a big witch business on at Yong-san, and while the *mutang* (witch) was performing, she said that the spirit that possessed her was the mother of the master here. On my appearance she called out my name and said, 'This is a servant from our house.' Then she called me and gave me a big glass of spirit. She added further, 'On my way here I met my son going into the Palace.'"

The secretary, overhearing this talk from the room where he was waiting, broke down and began to cry. He called in the servant and made fuller inquiry, and more than ever he felt assured that his mother's spirit had really gone that morning to share in the *koot* (witches' sacrificial ceremony). He then called the *mutang*, and in behalf of the spirit of his mother made her a great offering. Ever afterwards he sacrificed to her four times a year at each returning season.

Hong's Experiences in Hades

Im Bang; translated by James S. Gale

HONG NAI-POM was a military graduate who was born in the year AD 1561, and lived in the city of Pyeng-yang. He passed his examination in the year 1603, and in the year 1637 attained to the Third Degree. He was eighty-two in the year 1643, and his son Sonn memorialized the king asking that his father be given rank appropriate to his age. At that time a certain Han Hong-kil was chief of the Royal Secretaries, and he refused to pass on the request to his Majesty; but in the year 1644, when the Crown Prince was returning from his exile in China, he came by way of Pyeng-yang. Sonn took advantage of this to present the same request to the Crown Prince. His Highness received it, and had it brought to the notice of the king. In consequence, Hong received the rank of Second Degree.

On receiving it he said, "This year I shall die," and a little later he died.

In the year 1594, Hong fell ill of typhus fever, and after ten days of suffering, died. They prepared his body for burial, and placed it in a coffin. Then the friends and relatives left, and his wife remained alone in charge. Of a sudden the body turned itself and fell with a thud to the ground. The woman, frightened, fainted away, and the other members of the family came rushing to her help. From this time on the body resumed its functions, and Hong lived.

Said he, "In my dream I went to a certain region, a place of great fear where many persons were standing around, and awful ogres, some of them wearing bulls' heads, and some with faces of wild beasts. They crowded about and jumped and pounced toward me in all directions. A scribe robed in black sat on a platform and addressed me, saying, 'There are three religions on earth, Confucianism, Buddhism and Taoism. According to Buddhism, you know that heaven and hell are places that decide between man's good and evil deeds. You have ever been a blasphemer of the Buddha, and a denier of a future life, acting always as though you knew everything, blustering and storming. You are now to be sent to hell, and ten thousand *kalpas* will not see you out of it.'

"Then two or three constables carrying spears came and took me off. I screamed, 'You are wrong, I am innocently condemned.' Just at that moment a certain Buddha, with a face of shining gold, came smiling toward me, and said, 'There is truly a mistake somewhere; this man must attain to the age of eighty-three and become an officer of the Second Degree ere he dies.' Then addressing me he asked, 'How is it that you have come here? The order was that a certain Hong of Chon-ju be arrested and brought, not you; but now that you have come, look about the place before you go, and tell the world afterwards of what you have seen.'

"The guards, on hearing this, took me in hand and brought me first to a prison-house, where a sign was posted up, marked, 'Stirrers up of Strife'. I saw in this prison a great brazier-shaped pit, built of stones and filled with fire. Flames arose and forked tongues. The stirrers up of strife were taken and made to sit close before it. I then saw one infernal guard take a long rod of iron, heat it red-hot, and put out the eyes of the guilty ones. I saw also that the offenders were hung up like dried fish. The guides who accompanied me, said, 'While these were on earth they did not love their brethren, but looked at others as enemies. They scoffed at the laws of God and sought only selfish gain, so they are punished.'

"The next hell was marked, 'Liars'. In that hell I saw an iron pillar of several yards in height, and great stones placed before it. The offenders were called up, and made to kneel before the pillar. Then I saw an executioner take a knife and drive a hole through the tongues of the offenders, pass an iron chain through each, and hang them to the pillar so that they dangled by their tongues several feet from the ground. A stone was then taken and tied to each culprit's feet. The stones thus bearing down, and the chains being fast to the pillar, their tongues were pulled out a foot or more, and their eyes rolled in their sockets. Their agonies were appalling. The guides again said, 'These offenders when on earth used their tongues skilfully to tell lies and to separate friend from friend, and so they are punished.'

"The next hell had inscribed on it, 'Deceivers'. I saw in it many scores of people. There were ogres that cut the flesh from their bodies, and fed it to starving demons. These ate and ate, and the flesh was cut and cut till only the bones remained. When the winds of hell blew, flesh returned to them; then metal snakes and copper dogs crowded in to bite them and suck their blood. Their screams of pain made the earth to tremble. The guides said to me, 'When these offenders were on earth they held high office, and while they pretended to be true and good they received bribes in secret and were doers of all evil. As Ministers of State they ate the fat of the land and sucked the blood of the people, and yet advertised themselves as benefactors and were highly applauded. While in reality they lived as thieves, they pretended to be holy, as Confucius and Mencius are holy. They were deceivers of the world, and robbers, and so are punished thus.'

"The guides then said, 'It is not necessary that you see all the hells.' They said to one another, 'Let's take him yonder and show him'; so they went some distance to the south-east. There was a great house with a sign painted thus, 'The Home of the Blessed'. As I looked, there were beautiful haloes encircling it, and clouds of glory. There were hundreds of priests in cassock and surplice. Some carried fresh-blown lotus flowers; some were seated like the Buddha; some were reading prayers.

"The guides said, 'These when on earth kept the faith, and with undivided hearts served the Buddha, and so have escaped the Eight Sorrows and the Ten Punishments, and are now in the home of the happy, which is called heaven.' When we had seen all these things we returned.

"The golden-faced Buddha said to me, 'Not many on earth believe in the Buddha, and few know of heaven and hell. What do you think of it?'

"I bowed low and thanked him.

"Then the black-coated scribe said, 'I am sending this man away; see him safely off.' The spirit soldiers took me with them, and while on the way I awakened with a start, and found that I had been dead for four days."

Hong's mind was filled with pride on this account, and he frequently boasted of it. His age and Second Degree of rank came about just as the Buddha had predicted.

His experience, alas! was used as a means to deceive people, for the Superior Man does not talk of these strange and wonderful things.

Yi Tan, a Chinaman of the Song Kingdom, used to say, "If there is no heaven, there is no heaven, but if there is one, the Superior Man alone can attain to it. If there is no hell, there is no hell, but if there is one the bad man must inherit it."

If we examine Hong's story, while it looks like a yarn to deceive the world, it really is a story to arouse one to right action. I, Im Bang, have recorded it like Toi-chi, saying, "Don't find fault with the story, but learn its lesson."

Haunted Houses

Im Bang; translated by James S. Gale

THERE ONCE LIVED a man in Seoul called Yi Chang, who frequently told as an experience of his own the following story: He was poor and had no home of his own, so he lived much in quarters loaned him by others. When hard pressed he even went into haunted houses and lived there. Once, after failing to find a place, he heard of one such house in Ink Town (one of the wards of Seoul), at the foot of South Mountain, which had been haunted for generations and was now left vacant. Chang investigated the matter, and finally decided to take possession.

First, to find whether it was really haunted or not, he called his elder brothers, Hugh and Haw, and five or six of his relatives, and had them help clean it out and sleep there. The house had one upper room that was fast locked. Looking through a chink, there was seen to be in the room a tablet chair and a stand for it; also there was an old harp without any strings, a pair of worn shoes, and some sticks and bits of wood. Nothing else was in the room. Dust lay thick, as though it had gathered through long years of time.

The company, after drinking wine, sat round the table and played at games, watching the night through. When it was late, towards midnight, they suddenly heard the sound of harps and a great multitude of voices, though the words were mixed and unintelligible. It was as though many people were gathered and carousing at a feast. The company then consulted as to what they should do. One drew a sword and struck a hole through the partition that looked into the tower. Instantly there appeared from the other side a sharp blade thrust out towards them. It was blue in colour. In fear and consternation they desisted from further interference with the place. But the sound of the harp and the revelry kept up till the morning. The company broke up at daylight, withdrew from the place, and never again dared to enter.

In the South Ward there was another haunted house, of which Chang desired possession, so he called his friends and brothers once more to make the experiment and see whether it was really haunted or not. On entering, they found two dogs within the enclosure, one black and one tan, lying upon the open verandah, one at each end. Their eyes were fiery red, and though the company shouted at them they did not move. They neither barked nor bit. But when midnight came these two animals got up and went down into the court, and began baying at the inky sky in a way most ominous. They went jumping back and forth. At that time, too, there came some one round the corner of the house dressed in ceremonial robes. The two dogs met him with great delight, jumping up before and behind in their joy at his coming. He ascended to the verandah, and sat down. Immediately five or six multi-coloured demons appeared and bowed before him, in front of the open space. The man then led the demons and the dogs two or three times round the house. They rushed up into the verandah and jumped down again into the court; backwards and forwards they came and went, till at last all of them mysteriously disappeared. The devils went into a hole underneath the floor, while the dogs went up to their quarters and lay down.

The company from the inner room had seen this. When daylight came they examined the place, looked through the chinks of the floor, but saw only an old, worn-out sieve and a few discarded brooms. They went behind the house and found another old broom poked into the chimney. They ordered a servant to gather them up and have them burned. The dogs lay as they were all day long, and neither ate nor moved. Some of the party wished to kill the brutes, but were afraid, so fearsome was their appearance.

This night again they remained, desiring to see if the same phenomena would appear. Again at midnight the two dogs got down into the court and began barking up at the sky. The man in ceremonial robes again came, and the devils, just as the day before.

The company, in fear and disgust, left the following morning, and did not try it again.

A friend, hearing this of Chang, went and asked about it from Hugh and Haw, and they confirmed the story.

There is still another tale of a graduate who was out of house and home and went into a haunted dwelling in Ink Town, which was said to have had the tower where the mysterious sounds were heard. They opened the door, broke out the window, took out the old harp, the spirit chair, the shoes and sticks, and had them burned. Before the fire had finished its work, one of the servants fell down and died. The graduate, seeing this, in fear and dismay put out the fire, restored the things and left the house.

Again there was another homeless man who tried it. In the night a woman in a blue skirt came down from the loft, and acted in a peculiar and uncanny way. The man, seeing this, picked up his belongings and left.

Again, in South Kettle Town, there were a number of woodmen who in the early morning were passing behind the haunted house, when they found an old woman sitting weeping under a tree. They thinking her an evil bogey, one man came up behind and gave her a thrust with his sickle. The witch rushed off into the house, her height appearing to be only about one cubit and a span.

Qian Xian

Frances Lu-Pai Ippolito

I stood as silent as I could in the gap between my Aunt Xiao-Lin's and Aunt Joyce's chairs, watching them sip tea and write Chinese characters onto a piece of my construction paper. Glancing down, I couldn't read most of the characters scrawled across the paper, but I recognized the word for 'no', 'yes', and 'love'. One Chinese character, 'home', was printed larger than the rest and held the spot in the center of a red circle drawn in the middle of the page. In that circle, Aunt Xiao-Lin, placed a quarter, head side up.

"Is this a good idea?" Xiao-Lin asked the others.

"It's just a game," Joyce said, giving an easy grin while grabbing a fortune cookie from a filled cardboard box at our family's Chinese restaurant, The Moon Gate Inn. She used her teeth to rip the plastic wrapper and pulled a cookie out. "Maybe it'll help you get a husband finally." She smirked and offered Xiao-Lin a cookie.

A joke between the sisters, Joyce and Xiao-Lin were the 'shengnu' or leftover ladies, spinsters, of the family. With Joyce married to an American, Xiao-Lin was now the only single sister left. She rolled her eyes, but didn't seem bothered by the joke-turned-jab, accepting the cookie after sticking out her tongue at Joyce. Joyce snorted, choking on her tea and Xiao-Lin snickered as she broke the crescent cookie shell in half. She popped a piece into her mouth, and crunched without bothering to read the slip of paper inside.

"Alright, *ladies*," my mother said as she eyed both of them over the rim of her glasses. The oldest of the three, I knew she wasn't really scolding them like children, even though she'd half-raised them when Poh-Poh died. Mainly, she was glad to be all together – the first time since Joyce moved to Tampa five months ago.

"Ruyi, please throw these away for me?" Xiao-Lin said, handing me the spent wrappers and paper. I nodded, but stuffed everything into my back pocket with the gum wrapper and other garbage I'd cached there until the pocket got too full. I felt my mother's glare, but pretended not to see it.

"Let's start." Joyce said, clapping her hands with excitement.

"Ruyi, go play somewhere else," my mother said.

"Please, can I watch?" I pleaded. "Is it like Mah-Jong? I can play that." I wanted to be included with my family's women so badly, especially because there weren't any other children around.

"Too young, only twelve," she answered, shooing me away.

"It's ok," Xiao-Lin said quickly, beckoning to me. "Stand by me."

At thirty-three, she was the youngest and my favorite – the fun one who played pretend and gave me candy. I hopped over to her side of the table and quietly watched as each woman placed a single fingertip on the edge of the quarter and began to chant, "Spirit, Spirit, please come out."

A minute or two passed but nothing happened while they chanted and pressed their fingers to the quarter. Bored, I wandered away to a booth of cold burgundy leather. At my table and on the layer of Plexiglas covering a coarse red tablecloth, I poured driblets of soy sauce into clean tea cups. I picked up the bamboo chopsticks from where they lay on the Chinese Zodiac placemat, cracked and split them apart, using the tips to swirl the black liquid at the bottom of the cups. A little hungry, I popped the chopstick tip in my mouth and sucked on the saltiness.

"AHH!" The women suddenly gasped, their arms lurching in an imperfect circle around their table. That's strange, I thought, watching them move like the insides of a washing machine where clothes were dragged along by the twisting and turning of agitators, except these clothes had people in them.

I wandered over and stood behind Xiao-Lin's chair, peering over her shoulder at the fingertips crowded together on the quarter's face. It slid in halting spirals over my construction paper, taking the fingers of the women with it. Abruptly, it stopped in front of Xiao-Lin and me. Her jaw clenched and I noticed her pulse bounding under her neck skin, pulsating faster and faster. This close to her, I could not help but admire her delicate features, pale skin and long silky black hair. She was so pretty and I wanted to be like her when I grew up.

"Alright, who's pushing it? My back is sore," my mother complained through pinched breath. Her seat was farthest from Xiao-Lin, which forced her to lean across the table to maintain the contact between the coin and her fingertip. Her mouth was nearly kissing the tabletop and her glasses were slipping down the bridge of her nose.

"A ghost!" Joyce giggled gleefully, wiggling in her chair. "Now we ask questions!"

A chill ran down my spine. *A ghost? Was she joking?*

"Go ahead. Ask a question," my mother urged Xiao-Lin.

But she hesitated, little worry lines constellating her forehead. After dry swallowing, she said, "Umm, are you a ghost?"

The quarter skated across the paper, roaming to the edges and corners before gliding back to sit over a character. Yes.

"I'm scared," Xiao-Lin murmured. She seemed paler than just moments ago. With her free hand, my mother placed her index finger over her own lips to hush my aunt.

"Did you die here?" My mother asked, taking over.

Yes.

"Man or woman?" She asked next. The quarter circled again and the room was silent except for the 'shooshing' noise of metal running over the surface of paper fibers.

Man.

"Will my sister get married soon? She's getting a bit stale like stinky tofu." Joyce grinned widely at Xiao-Lin.

"Seriously?" Xiao-Lin frowned at Joyce.

"I'm helping you." Joyce wagged her brows. "You're the only one left. I don't want you to be old and alone."

In response, the quarter darted between the two women before circling to stop on 'Yes'.

"See," Joyce said triumphantly, tapping her fingers on the table. "I'm sussing it out for you. Spirit, when?"

The quarter passed and stopped over two characters. Tonight.

Xiao-Lin's shoulders stiffened. "That's not funny, Joyce. Stop pushing it."

"I'm not moving it." Joyce was no longer grinning and her eyes had narrowed.

Though there wasn't a question, the quarter passed over several characters, forming a sentence. I don't like you. It stopped in front of Joyce.

"Very funny, Xiao-Lin," Joyce said with no laughter in her eyes. Her lips pursed.

"How old are you?" My mother asked, probably trying to ease the tension.

The coin passed over the written numbers, one through one hundred, before stopping on thirty-five.

"Did you have a wife or children?" Xiao-Lin asked this time.

No.

Joyce, always so fearless, asked, "How did you die?"

Murder.

My mother's brow furrowed. "This is not good," she said, "a vengeful spirit is never truthful. We should ask it to leave."

Though there was no question, the quarter moved to cover the word 'No'.

My mother flinched and pushed so hard against the quarter that her fingertip turned white under the nail. "We need to stop," she said.

Again, the quarter moved without a question, circling before returning to 'No'.

Xiao-Lin squirmed in her chair and her arm sagged.

"Keep your finger on!" Joyce hissed. "Bad luck to take it off before the Spirit leaves." Xiao-Lin bowed her head, staring straight at the floor.

"I want to stop," Xiao-Lin said in a strained whisper.

The quarter moved again. No.

"We are sorry for your death. We will burn paper money to help bring you peace." Though my mother's words were conciliatory, her tone was sharp, angry. I knew she meant paper offerings in the form of paper money, houses, clothes, food, and other things that, once burned, were believed to turn into usable things for spirits in the afterlife.

The quarter moved. No.

"Is there something you need help with? Unfinished business?" Joyce offered.

Yes.

"We may not be able to help you. But we can, at least, hear your request," my mother spoke slowly, like she was carefully choosing and measuring out each word – afraid to bargain.

The quarter passed over several words – the leftover is mine. It stopped in front of Xiao-Lin.

"Joyce, that's enough. This is NOT funny," Xiao-Lin said, her face ashen, shoulders shaking.

But both Joyce's eyes and mouth were wide with shock. "I swear, I'm not doing anything. I'm not moving it."

"Then, you," Xiao-Lin gave my mother a hurt look.

My mother shook her head.

The quarter moved again.

Xiao-Lin whispered, "Ghost bride. Oh god, it really wants me." Her free hand clenched and twisted her shirt tail under the table.

The quarter moved twice. Yes. Mine.

"You can't have her." As soon as my mother spoke, I felt the temperature in the room drop until goosebumps covered my arms and neck, prickling against the fabric of my long sleeved turtleneck.

The quarter moved to several characters.

"The other one? We're already married," Joyce said, flipping her hand to show her ring.

The quarter repeated: The other one. And right then, all eyes turned to me.

I felt my heart seize. "Are … are you talking about me?" I stammered.

The quarter answered me three times, the same way. Mine. Mine. Mine.

"She's a child!" My mother shouted, furious. Her cheeks suddenly red, nose flaring.

At that, Joyce leapt up, took her finger off the quarter, and yanked the sheet of paper out from under the other women. She began tearing into the paper, shredding it into smaller pieces before crumpling each one in her fist.

Xiao-Lin and my mother gaped at her in horror. "Joyce, you said—" Xiao-Lin began.

Joyce interrupted, "I know what I said, but it's just a game. We'll burn lots of joss paper for the dead, every day for a whole month. It'll be fine." The women continued to watch Joyce, but I saw movement above us. The red silk lanterns tied to the ceiling were swaying though there wasn't any wind inside our building.

As if a switch had been flipped, the adults scrambled to toss out the paper remnants and the quarter was dropped into a 'Feed the Children' donation box sitting by the cash register. Almost by conspiracy, the adults refused to talk about the qian xian board.

"Mommy, what's a ghost bride?" I asked her as she tied an oil splotched black apron around her waist.

"Don't meddle in things you don't understand. Go into the office. We have work to do." My mother nudged me towards the office at the back of the kitchen and shut the door after scooting me inside.

* * *

At ten pm, I heard shouting and sobbing from the kitchen on the other side of the office. I peeked through a small opening in the door. Joyce sat on the tile floor by the deep fryer, tears streaming down her face with one hand cradling her forearm.

My mother rushed over, dropping to her knees beside her.

"What happened?"

"I was going to change out the oil. But it was hot and splattered on my arm. It hurts so much." Joyce said through gritted teeth and closed eyes.

"Get me some ice and a cloth napkin!" My mother yelled frantically at a busboy who nearly dropped his tray of washed dishes.

From the other-side of the kitchen, I watched Xiao-Lin walk slowly toward Aunt Joyce, so slowly that it felt intentionally done with the opposite speed of urgency. When she finally reached her, she stood straight as a pencil, staring down at her collapsed body.

"Didn't you turn it off?!" My mother asked Xiao-Lin.

"Don't I usually?" Xiao-Lin replied softly.

My mother didn't notice her vague response, all her attention on tying the corners of the napkin to hold the ice cubes. She tried to be gentle, but Joyce still screamed and arched against the wall when my mother placed the makeshift ice pack on her burnt arm. With each scream, a smile grew wider over Xiao-Lin's lips. Then she looked at me and when our eyes met, she winked.

"Xiao-Lin, you have to take her to the hospital."

Xiao-Lin shook her head. "I think you'd better go. Your English is better and they'll ask about her husband's insurance."

"But—," my mother looked uncertain and called, "—Ruyi!" I hurried to her, almost there when Xiao-Lin's arm snaked out, intercepting and pulling me to her side.

"Ruyi can stay with me tonight." Xiao-Lin patted my mother's shoulder. "I'll take real good care of this one." Xiao-Lin grinned at me, showing her teeth.

"Are you sure?" My mother glanced at me and then at Joyce crying on the floor.

"We'll have fun." Xiao-Lin's grip tightened around my waist.

Nodding, my mother said to me, "Aunty needs to see a doctor. Listen to Aunty Xiao-Lin. I'll come get you in the morning." I wiggled out of Xiao-Lin's hold and wrapped my arms around my mother's waist. Her skin smelled of comfort – five-spice, garlic, and fried meat – making me want to go with her, but I knew I would only be in the way.

"Will she be ok?" I asked, scared.

"She'll be fine." My mother squeezed me once and let go.

"Xiao-Lin. I'll call you later." My mother grabbed her purse and keys from the office and helped Joyce up.

When my mother left the kitchen, Xiao-Lin stepped closer to me. She reached for my head and stroked my bobbed hair. "You're growing up so fast." Her hand slid down to my face, closing around my chin. Then, she tugged my head up. "I'm sure you'll be pretty."

"Uh, thanks." I turned my head away.

She smirked and leaned to purr into my ear. "We'll have fun tonight, won't we?"

I nodded, but the way she continued to study me was creepy and unsettling in its intensity.

"Good night, Xiao-Lin, Ruyi! I hope Joyce is ok! See you tomorrow." We heard the busboy shout his goodbyes from the front door.

"Bye, George," she said, but her eyes were on me.

"Can we go home?" I asked, shrinking back a few steps. "Please, Aunty?"

She didn't answer and her eyes stayed fixed on where I had been standing moments earlier. I shuffled to the side, but her gaze remained unchanged. "Aunty?" I shook her gently.

She inhaled deeply, blinking rapidly. "Oh, Ruyi? What were we saying?" Confusion filled her face.

"You're taking me home? Mom took Aunty Joyce to the hospital."

"Take you home. That's right," her voice trailed off.

"Aunty, are you alright?"

She smiled wanly. "Probably tired. Let's go home."

In the parking lot, Xiao-Lin and I climbed into her Pontiac hatchback. She buckled me into the passenger seat and I was relieved that she was acting more like herself now. Just tired, I thought. *It's been a long week with Joyce visiting. That's all it is. I'm tired too.*

"That's odd," she said and turned on the overhead car light. She dug into her unzipped pink purse, taking out her checkbook, eyeglass holder, and a stick of fresh gum.

"What's wrong?"

"I must have left the apartment keys inside. I only have the car and restaurant keys with me." She held up two sets of keys in the palm of her hand. "I'll have to go back to find them."

I yawned and began unbuckling myself. She placed her hand over mine.

"You stay here. Lock the doors and don't go outside. I'll just be a couple of minutes."

I nodded and reclined my backrest. Xiao-Lin opened the car door and checked that each one was locked before turning off the overhead light and closing the driver's side door.

With only the signal light at the intersection to illuminate the night, I watched the darkness swallow her bit by bit as she strode back toward the restaurant doors. As she reached the doors, I saw a light flash across one of the windows on the opposite side of where she was standing. It was there only for a moment and I rubbed my eyes, dismissing it as the reflection of headlights on the glass.

About ten minutes later, I was startled by loud screaming – sharp and piercing. I pressed my face to the windshield, scanning in the direction of where I thought the scream came from. This late at night, the streets were completely empty without a single car in any direction. The gas station and convenience store across the street were closed. My heart raced in its cage as I realized that I was completely alone in the only car parked in the restaurant lot.

Lights suddenly flickered on and then off through the restaurant windows. *Aunty must have tried to turn the lights on, but got hurt or fell. I have to help her,* I decided but my fingers quivered as I lifted the lock latch. A brisk biting wind buffeted my face when I finally opened the door. I tucked my chin, wrapped my arms around myself, and sprinted across the parking lot to the red lacquered double doors at the restaurant entrance. As soon as I touched the doorknob, both doors swung open. I walked a couple of steps into the foyer to escape the wind, but struggled to find my way in the dark.

My hands groped ahead as I moved carefully toward where I thought the order counter would be. If I could reach the control box there, I'd be able to turn on the lights in the main dining room. But just as I took a step, I heard a noise on my right – a soft panting coming from the deep recesses of the room. It was too dark for me to see beyond the silhouettes of chairs stacked on top of tables, but the room felt occupied by another presence, something alive and breathing. Maybe watching me. The hairs on my neck rose and I jumped as a gust of wind slammed the doors shut.

"Aunty? Is that you?" I whispered in the direction of the panting. There was no answer.

I inhaled slowly and forced myself to continue walking for where I thought the counter was. When my fingers touched the edge, I grabbed at it and pulled myself behind the counter, feeling for the top drawer, opening it for the dials, slides, and switches of the main dining room's control panel. Unable to read any of the labels, I flipped on all the switches with the meaty part of my hand. Instantly, light from the chandeliers flooded the room and Tiffany's 'I Think We're Alone Now' blasted at maximum volume. I hurried to turn off the radio and lessen the brightness.

The room was almost the same as when we left it. On all but one table, the chairs were stacked on top, leaving the carpet clear. However, unlike the rest, the raised banquet table in the back corner had all eight chairs neatly placed around it. By design, even under normal conditions, this table was different. Used for celebrations, like weddings, this dais table placed the bride and groom on display before their guests.

Feeling braver in the familiar room, I skirted past the rows of tables and clambered up the platform. The banquet table was set for two – a pair of plates, rice bowls, soup spoons, chopsticks, and teacups. A teapot and large platters of raw foods weighed down the lazy susan, making it slow and sluggish when I attempted to rotate it. As it circled, I made a mental count of the bleeding ball of ground meat, a whole unscaled fish, a raw chicken with the head and feet intact, and twitching lobsters and crabs taken live from the tanks. Laying beside the teacups was a Hello Kitty ring of keys. My aunt's missing keys.

I turned, hearing the kitchen doors swing open. A figure about the shape and size of Xiao-Lin moved through the doors. Below the waist, I recognized her jeans and white Keds. But her entire upper body was covered in a red tablecloth draped over her head like an opaque crimson veil of a Chinese bride.

"Aunty? Are you ok?"

"How nice of your family to join us for the wedding," a man's voice, decidedly not my aunt's, came out from under the red fabric. My breath hitched and I stumbled back as light bounced off the metal cleaver in her hand. She lifted it from beneath the corners of the tablecloth hanging down her sides.

"There's plenty to eat."

My eyes followed the kitchen cleaver as my aunt walked through the rows of tables and stepped up to the platform. The red cloth shrouded her face, but her path was perfect as if her eyes were open and uncovered.

"Sit," the voice commanded and the cleaver was raised in my direction.

I sat down stonily in one of the chairs. She sat as well, in the chair across the table from me. I stared at her, at the lumpy shapes poking through the tablecloth where a face would be.

"Do you want to see what's underneath?" The voice asked and my aunt's shoulders seemed to shudder as a whimpering noise emitted from cloth like suppressed laughter or sobbing. "She's prettier now that I've fixed her up. My future wife." I hadn't noticed before, but patches of the red cloth appeared a darker shade than the rest. The darker parts were spreading, like water or some other wetness.

"Aunty, what's going on?" I managed to breathe out, barely audible to my own ears.

Her body slouched against the chair and a loud, hoarse laugh erupted out of the slumped form. "Won't marry me. But—," the voice paused and my aunt's body suddenly straightened to attention, "—you can take her place. I've always liked them young."

My mouth went dry and an invisible band tightened around my chest. "Aunty, you're scaring me," I whispered, but fixed my eyes on the plate in front of me.

"Come closer. Pour the tea." Her hand, the one with the cleaver, gestured to the metal teapot.

I bit down on my tongue, creating pain to stifle screams. Everything inside me recoiled at getting closer to whatever was underneath that cloth.

"Come closer!" The voice shouted this time, startling me. Not knowing what else to do, I turned the lazy susan and picked up the teapot. My hands shook as I poured cold tea into two tea cups.

"Serve me."

I held my breath and tried to keep my hand steady, but the tea spilled when I fumbled the cup in front of my aunt. Her hand shot out from under the red cloth and grabbed my wrist.

"Tsk, tsk," the voice said. "Let me teach you how to serve your husband properly." My aunt's hand tightened on my wrist as she raised the cleaver high above her head in her other hand. The intended aim of the blade unmistakably my wrist.

"You can still serve tea with only one hand." The voice laughed.

"Don't hurt her."

I looked up with relief upon hearing the sweet, soft voice of my aunt. Her real voice that spoke from under the cloth.

"You'll marry me, then?" The man's voice came through the cloth again.

"Yes. Let her go."

"For now. Ha! Ha! Ha!" The man laughed, almost uncontrollably, and even though I was scared, I hated the way he found amusement in our pain. When the laughter finally died down, my aunt's gentle voice urged, "Ruyi, kuai pao."

"Yes! Run! But, when I'm bored with your aunt, I'll come for you." The man roared with laughter as the hold on my hand released. "She better satisfy me."

I wanted to run, as far away as I could, but I didn't want to abandon my aunt to this man or whatever it was. "Aunty, come with me," I begged, not sure how she could leave behind something that had her already.

"Kuai pao," she repeated as her hand fisted around the tail of the raw fish and brought the entire fish under the cloth. As I turned to leave, I heard her teeth ripping into scales and wet flesh.

"Don't worry, we'll come visit you soon. Very soon," I heard the voice call after me.

Climbing into the car, I scrambled to the floor of the backseat and hid under the reclined passenger seat. I cried, but kept quiet in case he changed his mind and came for me after all. For hours, I stayed there compressed on folded knees until the rising sun swept layers of reds and oranges over the sky.

My mother found me in the morning, when the police had to break the glass of the car windows to pull me out. At first, she hadn't even known I was there, too concerned by the unlocked restaurant, ransacked cash register, and the possibility of a burglar lurking inside. They did not find my aunt.

"Missing person, but no evidence of foul play," the Police Report read.

But I knew better.

That's why, now, every night, I wear my red wedding dress. He's coming, you see? Drape the red sheet over my head. Sit on the edge of the bed, waiting. And sometimes I reread that slip of paper from the fortune cookie. The one that none of us read before playing the qian xian board. The one that I didn't throw away.

"Do not walk into the darkness alone."

We should have listened.

The Strange Story of the Golden Comb

Grace James

IN ANCIENT DAYS two *samurai* dwelt in Sendai of the North. They were friends and brothers in arms.

Hasunuma one was named, and the other Saito. Now it happened that a daughter was born to the house of Hasunuma, and upon the selfsame day, and in the selfsame hour, there was born to the house of Saito a son. The boy child they called Konojo, and the girl they called Aiko, which means the Child of Love.

Or ever a year had passed over their innocent heads the children were betrothed to one another. And as a token the wife of Saito gave a golden comb to the wife of Hasunuma, saying: "For the child's hair when she shall be old enough." Aiko's mother wrapped the comb in a handkerchief, and laid it away in her chest. It was of gold lacquer, very fine work, adorned with golden dragon-flies.

This was very well; but before long misfortune came upon Saito and his house, for, by sad mischance, he aroused the ire of his feudal lord, and he was fain to fly from Sendai by night, and his wife was with him, and the child. No man knew where they went, or had any news of them, nor of how they fared, and for long, long years Hasunuma heard not one word of them.

The child Aiko grew to be the loveliest lady in Sendai. She had longer hair than any maiden in the city, and she was the most graceful dancer ever seen. She moved as a wave of the sea, or a cloud of the sky, or the wild bamboo grass in the wind. She had a sister eleven moons younger than she, who was called Aiyamé, or the Water Iris; and she was the second loveliest lady in Sendai. Aiko was white, but Aiyamé was brown, quick, and light, and laughing. When they went abroad in the streets of Sendai, folk said, "There go the moon and the south wind."

Upon an idle summer day when all the air was languid, and the cicala sang ceaselessly as he swung on the pomegranate bough, the maidens rested on the cool white mats of their lady mother's bower. Their dark locks were loose, and their slender feet were bare. They had between them an ancient chest of red lacquer, a Bride Box of their lady mother's, and in the chest they searched and rummaged for treasure.

"See, sister," said Aiyamé, "here are scarlet thongs, the very thing for my sandals … and what is this? A crystal rosary, I declare! How beautiful!"

Aiko said, "My mother, I pray you give me this length of violet silk, it will make me very fine undersleeves to my new grey gown; and, mother, let me have the crimson for a petticoat; and surely, mother, you do not need this little bit of brocade?"

"And what an *obi*," cried Aiyamé, as she dragged it from the chest, "grass green and silver!" Springing lightly up, she wound the length about her slender body. "Now behold me for the finest lady in all Sendai. Very envious shall be the daughter of the rich Hachiman, when she sees this wonder *obi*; but I shall be calm and careless, and say, looking down thus humbly, 'Your pardon, noble lady, that I wear this foolish trifling obi, unmeet for your great presence!' Mother, mother, give me the *obi*."

"Arah! Arah! Little pirates!" said the mother, and smiled.

Aiko thrust her hand to the bottom of the chest. "Here is something hard," she murmured, "a little casket wrapped in a silken handkerchief. How it smells of orris and ancient spices! – now what may it be?" So saying, she unwound the kerchief and opened the casket. "A golden comb!" she said, and laid it on her knee.

"Give it here, child," cried the mother quickly; "it is not for your eyes."

But the maiden sat quite still, her eyes upon the golden comb. It was of gold lacquer, very fine work, adorned with golden dragon-flies.

For a time the maiden said not a word, nor did her mother, though she was troubled; and even the light Lady of the South Wind seemed stricken into silence, and drew the scarlet sandal thongs through and through her fingers.

"Mother, what of this golden comb?" said Aiko at last.

"My sweet, it is the love-token between you and Konojo, the son of Saito, for you two were betrothed in your cradles. But now it is full fifteen years since Saito went from Sendai in the night, he and all his house, and left no trace behind."

"Is my love dead?" said Aiko.

"Nay, that I know not – but he will never come; so, I beseech you, think no more of him, my pretty bird. There, get you your fan, and dance for me and for your sister."

Aiko first set the golden comb in her hair. Then she flung open her fan to dance. She moved like a wave of the sea, or a cloud of the sky, or the wild bamboo grass in the wind. She had not danced long before she dropped the fan, with a long cry, and she herself fell her length upon the ground. From that hour she was in a piteous way, and lay in her bed sighing, like a maid lovelorn and forsaken. She could not eat nor sleep; she had no pleasure in life. The sunrise and the sound of rain at night were nothing to her any more. Not her father, nor her mother, nor her sister, the Lady of the South Wind, were able to give her any ease.

Presently she turned her face to the wall. "It is more than I can understand," she said, and so died.

When they had prepared the poor young maid for her grave, her mother came, crying, to look at her for the last time. And she set the golden comb in the maid's hair, saying:

"My own dear little child, I pray that in other lives you may know happiness. Therefore take your golden token with you; you will have need of it when you meet the wraith of your lover." For she believed that Konojo was dead.

But, alas, for Karma that is so pitiless, one short moon had the maid been in her grave when the brave young man, her betrothed, came to claim her at her father's house.

"Alas and alack, Konojo, the son of Saito, alas, my brave young man, too late you have come! Your joy is turned to mourning, for your bride lies under the green grass, and her sister goes weeping in the moonlight to pour the water of the dead." Thus spoke Hasunuma the *samurai*.

"Lord," said the brave young man, "there are three ways left, the sword, the strong girdle, and the river. These are the short roads to Yomi. Farewell."

But Hasunuma held the young man by the arm. "Nay, then, thou son of Saito," he said, "but hear the fourth way, which is far better. The road to Yomi is short, but it is very dark; moreover, from the confines of that country few return. Therefore stay with me, Konojo, and comfort me in my old age, for I have no sons."

So Konojo entered the household of Hasunuma the *samurai*, and dwelt in the garden house by the gate.

Now in the third month Hasunuma and his wife and the daughter that was left them arose early and dressed them in garments of ceremony, and presently were borne away in *kago*, for to the temple they were bound, and to their ancestral tombs, where they offered prayers and incense the live-long day.

It was bright starlight when they returned, and cold the night was, still and frosty. Konojo stood and waited at the garden gate. He waited for their home-coming, as was meet. He drew his cloak about him and gave ear to the noises of the evening. He heard the sound of the blind man's whistle, and the blind man's staff upon the stones. Far off he heard a child laugh twice; then he heard men singing in chorus, as men who sing to cheer themselves in their labour, and in the pauses of song he heard the creak, creak of swinging *kago* that the men bore upon their shoulders, and he said, "They come."

> *"I go to the house of the Beloved,*
> *Her plum tree stands by the eaves;*
> *It is full of blossom.*
> *The dew lies in the heart of the flowers,*
> *So they are the drinking-cups of the sparrows.*
> *How do you go to your love's house?*
> *Even upon the wings of the night wind.*
> *Which road leads to your love's house?*
> *All the roads in the world."*

This was the song of the *kago* men. First the *kago* of Hasunuma the *samurai* turned in at the garden gate, then followed his lady; last came Aiyamé of the South Wind. Upon the roof of her *kago* there lay a blossoming bough.

"Rest well, lady," said Konojo, as she passed, and had no answer back. Howbeit it seemed that some light thing dropped from the *kago*, and fell with a little noise to the ground. He stooped and picked up a woman's comb. It was of gold lacquer, very fine work, adorned with golden dragon-flies. Smooth and warm it lay in the hand of Konojo. And he went his way to the garden house. At the hour of the rat the young *samurai* threw down his book of verse, laid himself upon his bed, and blew out his light. And the selfsame moment he heard a wandering step without.

"And who may it be that visits the garden house by night?" said Konojo, and he wondered. About and about went the wandering feet till at length they stayed, and the door was touched with an uncertain hand.

"Konojo! Konojo!"

"What is it?" said the *samurai*.

"Open, open; I am afraid."

"Who are you, and why are you afraid?"

"I am afraid of the night. I am the daughter of Hasunuma the *samurai*.... Open to me for the love of the gods."

Konojo undid the latch and slid back the door of the garden house to find a slender and drooping lady upon the threshold. He could not see her face, for she held her long sleeve so as to hide it from him; but she swayed and trembled, and her frail shoulders shook with sobbing.

"Let me in," she moaned, and forthwith entered the garden house.

Half smiling and much perplexed, Konojo asked her:

"Are you Aiyamé, whom they call the Lady of the South Wind?"

"I am she."

"Lady, you do me much honour."

"The comb!" she said, "the golden comb!"

As she said this, she threw the veil from her face, and taking the robe of Konojo in both her little hands, she looked into his eyes as though she would draw forth his very soul. The lady was brown and quick and light. Her eyes and her lips were made for laughing, and passing strange she looked in the guise that she wore then.

"The comb!" she said, "the golden comb!"

"I have it here," said Konojo; "only let go my robe, and I will fetch it you."

At this the lady cast herself down upon the white mats in a passion of bitter tears, and Konojo, poor unfortunate, pressed his hands together, quite beside himself.

"What to do?" he said; "what to do?"

At last he raised the lady in his arms, and stroked her little hand to comfort her.

"Lord," she said, as simply as a child, "lord, do you love me?"

And he answered her in a moment, "I love you more than many lives, O Lady of the South Wind."

"Lord," she said, "will you come with me then?"

He answered her, "Even to the land of Yomi," and took her hand.

Forth they went into the night, and they took the road together. By river-side they went, and over plains of flowers; they went by rocky ways, or through the whispering pines, and when they had wandered far enough, of the green bamboos they built them a little house to dwell in. And they were there for a year of happy days and nights.

Now upon a morning of the third month Konojo beheld men with *kago* come swinging through the bamboo grove. And he said:

"What have they to do with us, these men and their *kago*?"

"Lord," said Aiyamé, "they come to bear us to my father's house."

He cried, "What is this foolishness? We will not go."

"Indeed, and we must go," said the lady.

"Go you, then," said Konojo; "as for me, I stay here where I am happy."

"Ah, lord," she said, "ah, my dear, do you then love me less, who vowed to go with me, even to the Land of Yomi?"

Then he did all that she would. And he broke a blossoming bough from a tree that grew near by and laid it upon the roof of her *kago*.

Swiftly, swiftly they were borne, and the *kago* men sang as they went, a song to make labour light.

> *"I go to the house of the Beloved,*
> *Her plum tree stands by the eaves;*
> *It is full of blossom.*
> *The dew lies in the heart of the flowers,*
> *So they are the drinking-cups of the sparrows.*
> *How do you go to your love's house?*
> *Even upon the wings of the night wind.*
> *Which road leads to your love's house?*
> *All the roads in the world."*

This was the song of the *kago* men.

About nightfall they came to the house of Hasunuma the *samurai*.

"Go you in, my dear lord," said the Lady of the South Wind. "I will wait without; if my father is very wroth with you, only show him the golden comb." And with that she took it from her hair and gave it him. Smooth and warm it lay in his hand. Then Konojo went into the house.

"Welcome, welcome home, Konojo, son of Saito!" cried Hasunuma. "How has it fared with your knightly adventure?"

"Knightly adventure!" said Konojo, and blushed.

"It is a year since your sudden departure, and we supposed that you had gone upon a quest, or in the expiation of some vow laid upon your soul."

"Alas, my good lord," said Konojo, "I have sinned against you and against your house." And he told Hasunuma what he had done.

When he had made an end of his tale:

"Boy," said the *samurai*, "you jest, but your merry jest is ill-timed. Know that my child lies even as one dead. For a year she has neither risen nor spoken nor smiled. She is visited by a heavy sickness and none can heal her."

"Sir," said Konojo, "your child, the Lady of the South Wind, waits in a *kago* without your garden wall. I will fetch her in presently."

Forth they went together, the young man and the *samurai*, but they found no *kago* without the garden wall, no *kago*-bearers and no lady. Only a broken bough of withered blossom lay upon the ground.

"Indeed, indeed, she was here but now!" cried Konojo. "She gave me her comb – her golden comb. See, my lord, here it is."

"What comb is this, Konojo? Where got you this comb that was set in a dead maid's hair, and buried with her beneath the green grass? Where got you the comb of Aiko, the Lady of the Moon, that died for love? Speak, Konojo, son of Saito. This is a strange thing."

Now whilst Konojo stood amazed, and leaned silent and bewildered against the garden wall, a lady came lightly through the trees. She moved as a wave of the sea, or a cloud of the sky, or the wild bamboo grass in the wind.

"Aiyamé," cried the *samurai*, "how are you able to leave your bed?"

The young man said nothing, but fell on his knees beside the garden wall. There the lady came to him and bent so that her hair and her garments overshadowed him, and her eyes held his.

"Lord," she said, "I am the spirit of Aiko your love. I went with a broken heart to dwell with the shades of Yomi. The very dead took pity on my tears. I was permitted to return, and for one short year to inhabit the sweet body of my sister. And now my time is come. I go my ways to the grey country. I shall be the happiest soul in Yomi – I have known you, beloved. Now take me in your arms, for I grow very faint."

With that she sank to the ground, and Konojo put his arms about her and laid her head against his heart. His tears fell upon her forehead.

"Promise me," she said, "that you will take to wife Aiyamé, my sister, the Lady of the South Wind."

"Ah," he cried, "my lady and my love!"

"Promise, promise," she said.

Then he promised.

After a little she stirred in his arms.

"What is it?" he said.

So soft her voice that it did not break the silence but floated upon it.

"The comb," she murmured, "the golden comb."

And Konojo set it in her hair.

A burden, pale but breathing, Konojo carried into the house of Hasunuma and laid upon the white mats and silken cushions. And after three hours a young maid sat up and rubbed her sleepy eyes. She was brown and quick and light and laughing. Her hair was tumbled about her rosy cheeks, unconfined by any braid or comb. She stared first at her father, and then at the young man that was in her bower. She smiled, then flushed, and put her little hands before her face.

"Greeting, O Lady of the South Wind," said Konojo.

On the Jiangshi and Other Returns

Ji Yun; Translated by Yi Izzy Yu and John Yu Branscum

1. Exhumation

SOMETIMES, when a Taoist is exhumed or digs himself out of the grave, he has no skin. It has rotted away. However, the organs are still plump and whole, and everything else beneath the skin as if fresh. This is because these individuals have cultivated the three treasures of essence, breath, and spirit so well that they can slow their respiration and the beating of their hearts to less than whispers, and thus enter a coma in which they can remain for years, even if buried – as well preserved as if submerged in a coffin full of mercury. This is what is said.

2. Treason

I have not been a direct witness to this Taoist miracle of inner alchemy. However, my friend Dong Qujiang told me that just as the bodies of saints may be preserved so may the bodies of their opposites: criminals.

For example, his neighbor saw the body of the writer Lü Liuliang dragged from his grave fifty years after his death in Zhejiang so that his bones might be incinerated – the result of a posthumous sentence passed against him for inspiring, through his books, treasonous talk about returning the Chinese empire to Ming rule.

However, when Lü Liuliang's body was pulled from the ground, it was not that of a dead man, but fresh and lifelike – as if the gods had refused his admission to the yin realms. Thus the emperor's men decided against consigning him to the flames right away. Instead, their knives went to work on his flesh.

Blood soon oozed and trickled from his lacerated body, giving the impression that Lü Liuliang were somehow still alive – and feeling everything although unable to move.

3. Imbalance

Neither of these preservations is particularly dangerous. The Taoists mean no ill will. Criminals, imprisoned in their own bodies, can do none.

There are other cases, however, that concern far more vicious beings. Those creatures of the night known as jiangshi (僵尸), for example.

Jiangshi are living corpses who feed on the qi of living things, and sometimes their blood and flesh too.

There are two main types. The weak type occurs when a freshly dead body, one that hasn't had the necessary burial rites performed, temporarily reanimates and becomes violent. Like a guttering flame, these creatures are easily subdued and generally turn quite dead once placed in their coffins.

The strong type of jiangshi is far more dangerous. They are corpses that have been dead long enough to be buried in their coffins but then have become reanimated by an outside agent (a spell, lightning, a pregnant cat walking across their grave).

However, the deceased are not what they were. While in the grave, their emotions have soured, their thoughts gone feral, and their rank bodies have fermented and stiffened into more monstrous possibilities. If freed of the dirt, these fiends will spread terror in the night – killing, infecting, feeding, and leaving the dry husks of their victims in their wake.

As depraved as they are, there is a complexity to these creatures. Sometimes, a lingering attraction to family and friends remains – albeit in a perverted form.

In his *Tales Forbidden by the Master*, for example, the zhiguai writer Yuan Mei tells of a government official who encountered a deceased friend while on a stroll at night.

The official, following his Confucian training, kept his emotions steady and registered neither surprise nor fear – as if it were the most natural thing to come across the dead in the midnight hours. His formerly stoic friend though manically cycled through several extreme emotions: chattiness, gratitude, and finally a deep sadness – a state from which he suddenly emerged with ferocious energy to launch himself at the official – snarling and clacking his teeth as he tried to sink them into his former friend.

4. Hun and Po

Many have shared stories of such things with me. It is difficult to make sense of them.

In the normal course of life, a person's spiritual essence leaves after death, just as smoke drifts from a fire that has gone out. Therefore, how could a body be active enough to attack and strangle?

Then there is the even more perplexing question of why a person, who for the entirety of their life was virtuous, should suddenly turn evil after death – so twisted that they'll attack their sons and daughters, or mothers and fathers.

Yuan Mei explains such accounts through the possession of two souls by human beings: the bestial po, which drives the body and its appetites; and the heavenly hun, which is responsible for our more refined thoughts and emotions.

During life, the hun controls the po, moderating its primal impulses. When a person dies, however, the hun goes onto the nether realms to reincarnate or to explore other heavenly states of being. The po at this time is supposed to sink into the earth and dissolve.

But sometimes, it refuses. Instead, it witlessly clings to the body and uses it to rage, rampage, and steal life from others so that it can linger. Such abominations, Yuan Mei maintains, are nearly unkillable because they're already dead and can only be defeated by the spells and rituals of the most powerful magicians.

This theory has bits and pieces of truth in it. Certainly, jiangshi show that stray memories and habits from a body's former inhabitant remain accessible – even if rotting. But in the end, I find myself more persuaded by the view that it is not the po that animates the corpse at all, but rather the case that the deceased body has been opportunely possessed by a nonhuman force or wandering spirit that has snatched it up like a thug might snatch up a club.

5. The Mysterious Dr. Hu

When I was around six or seven, my father had an acquaintance named Hu Gongshan.

Dr. Hu was reserved about his past. So, many rumors circulated. One of the most popular held that he served in Wu Sangui's rebel army under the family name of Jin, and that upon Wu Sangui's defeat, he changed his family name to Hu to escape punishment.

No one offered proof of this, and Dr. Hu neither confirmed nor denied it. However, he was an extremely skilled martial artist and would have been a valuable member of an army. Even when he was in his eighties, he remained limber – with hands and feet as quick as a macaque's. Once, some bandits tried to seize control of his sailing vessel, expecting a helpless old man. But he snatched up a long-stemmed smoking pipe and whipped it around like a fishing pole to fight them off, jabbing its tail-end up into their nostrils and eyes repeatedly.

Dr. Hu was brave when it came to fighting men. But he wasn't entirely fearless. As soon as the sun set and the moon rose, he'd tremble like a child at the wind's moans and flinch at the flickering of shadows.

And on those nights where he had no one to keep him company, he would lock himself inside his house and refuse to come out until the sun was back.

When I first became aware of Dr. Hu's dramatic change in behavior toward evening, I couldn't understand why someone with his skills would act afraid of the dark. But then he shared two episodes from his past.

6. Two Episodes to Consider

Jiangshi, Dr. Hu said, were not just monsters made up to frighten children. They were actual creatures. At least, he had encountered two entities in his long life that corresponded to jiangshi legends.

The first attacked him in the dark of the woods one evening when he was a young man. As with the villains in the boat, he fought back. He could barely see what he was fighting, other than that it was person-shaped and oddly stiff and spastic in its movements – as if missing half its joints. Still, he felt hopeful because he was so good at fighting men. But this time his martial skills meant nothing.

Although he punched and smashed his knuckles against the figure, Dr. Hu might as well have been punching a wooden door or a rock wall. At last, he rushed to a tree to scramble as high as he could on its swaying branches. He was sure the creature would follow, but it turned out that its weirdly rigid body was no good at climbing – although he could hear it trying like a bird beating itself against a window.

The creature tried to reach Dr. Hu all night. Its dumb, stubborn arms hugged the tree stiffly, as it circled it in broken little skips, trying to gain the momentum to launch itself upward.

Exhausted and terrified, Dr. Hu clung to his perch until morning came, bringing with it the yang light of the sun. At this point, the figure's movements slowed until it stopped moving altogether – as if it had abruptly died while holding the tree and now adhered there like a cicada shell.

Despite the apparent death of the creature, Dr. Hu remained afraid to move until he heard jangling sounds. They belonged to a procession of belled camels and their owners. The numbers of the travelling group gave him the courage to scramble down from his sanctuary.

On the ground, Dr. Hu got his first close look at what tried to kill him. Man-shaped, yes, but not a man, although it looked like it might have been at one time. Covered with a snowy something resembling fur or mold, and possessing blood-colored eyes, talon-like hands, and pointed teeth so long that they jutted past the lips, the deep wrongness of the creature – which managed to be both aesthetic and moral – disturbed Dr. Hu to his core.

* ✝ *

As bad as this first encounter was, Dr. Hu's second proved worse. It happened at a guest house in a remote spot in the mountains. He was sound asleep when a movement beneath his sheets woke him.

Thinking a rat or a snake had found its way into his bed, Dr. Hu refrained from sudden motion to avoid getting bitten, and lay still to watch the progress of whatever it was, at least until it poked its head out of the sheets and could easily be caught by the neck.

However, before his widened eyes, the thing beneath the sheets began to impossibly swell until it was the size of a human head, and then the sheets inflated further as the rough form of a body formed around that. When the thing did poke out of the sheets, it was indeed a head, a woman's, and it stretched its way onto his pillow as its owner's naked body turned to him, feverishly warm.

Despite the woman-thing's beauty and the silky heat of her flesh, Dr. Hu felt no lust. But he was so paralyzed with fear that he did not fight her either when her impossibly long arms wound around him and crushed him close. Nor did he fight when she forced her stinking mouth against his in a kiss so pungent with decay and blood that he gagged and passed out. He was unconscious during what happened after that.

His blackout would have been a mercy except for one thing. He couldn't be roused from it when he was discovered later. In fact, he would have likely died without ever opening his eyes again if a physician hadn't been found with the good sense to treat Dr. Hu with anti-toxins and reversal agents. These were massaged down his gullet until he regained consciousness. It was after this that the dark began to make Dr. Hu tremble because he knew it was not empty.

One Extra at a Wedding

Ji Yun; Translated by Yi Izzy Yu and John Yu Branscum

MY MOTHER'S FAMILY had a nanny with yin-yang eyes. Thus dirt roads that appeared empty to others sometimes looked crowded to her, and she observed many other unusual things.

One day, my grandmother asked this woman about the saddest ghost she'd ever seen. This is what she said:

"To protect the reputations of the people involved, I won't tell you their names. I won't give you any other personal details either. But I will tell you this. The family was a good one. And the ghost belonged to a man who died when he was around twenty-seven.

"I was close friends with the young widow. So, on the one hundred-day anniversary of her husband's death, she asked me to visit to cheer her up.

"We sat inside the widow's house, along with her baby boy and ill-tempered sister-in-law, and talked. No matter the topic, every so often she broke down sobbing. Each time, like a small ripple coming from a bigger one, her boy cried too. A while into my visit, I looked up and saw *him* through the window – the husband's ghost. He gazed mournfully at us from the shadows of a cluster of clove trees in the courtyard.

"The ghost kept a fair distance. Ghosts, being yin in nature, become confused when too close to the yang heat of living creatures. This is especially true of new ones. Nevertheless, he was keenly aware of the emotions of his family. Whenever his widow and the baby boy cried, he winced. Not wanting to upset my friend, I told her none of this.

"About a year later, my friend's family persuaded her to find a new husband. A matchmaker visited. I came over too to lend my support. By this time, the ghost could bear the heat of the living well enough to enter the widow's house – although he still pressed against the walls. This is where he was when he realized what was being discussed.

"The idea of the widow remarrying threw him into a frenzy. He thrashed about for a long time, as if in the jaws of something, and kept reaching for the widow. But he could no longer touch her.

"In the weeks that followed, amidst discussions of potential matches, the winnowing down to a final selection, and then subsequent preparations, the ghost remained in a state of barely-controlled panic. He took turns desperately following everyone around as if he could convince them to plead his case. His only deviation from these pitiful displays was whenever there was a snag in the matrimonial negotiations. At such times, a smile cracked his face.

"But then the traditional wedding gifts from the groom arrived. And the ghost realized that a dead man has no power to stop anything. Anguished, he fled to the shadows of the clove trees, his usual refuge, and bawled there a long time. After he was done, he came back inside. From that moment forward his sad eyes refused to leave his wife.

"On the night before the wedding, the widow rushed around, wrapping up this to take and throwing away that. The ghost paced wildly along the wrap-around porch outside as if rhyming her busy movements, which he watched through the open doors and windows with great alarm. Even when the widow went to bed, he kept up his spectral pacing – except for those times when he slumped against the porch columns in a defeated way, or when he heard a sharp cough or some other noise come from the widow's room. This prompted him to rush in that direction until he realized that she was not trying to communicate.

"It was hard to see the spirit suffer so, but his selfish clinging angered me too. When I was sure that the widow was asleep, I whispered to the air: 'Begone! It's time to let her go.'

"But he stayed.

"The next morning, the groom – carrying a torch to light the early morning darkness for the wedding party – arrived. The whole group, now including the bride's family and myself, marched toward the groom's residence for the ceremony.

"The ghost should have stayed behind, but the stubborn thing did not. It struggled after us, step by step, although it must have been painful to brave the brightening day and bear the wounding proximity of the living.

"Soon, we reached the groom's home. That was nearly the end of the ghost's journey.

"The groom had nailed a magical sigil, depicting two armored door guards, to the front doorway. The thought-forms the sigil conjured, invisible to everyone except the ghost and myself, blocked his path so that he could not trespass. However, the ghost must have begged so pitifully that he convinced the guardians to let him inside. Because a little while later, I saw him slip into the garden. He chose a shady spot to stand and watch the ceremony and the banquet afterwards.

"During the ceremony and the banquet, the ghost stayed as still as a stone, at least until the evening had grown so late that the newlyweds retreated – amidst laughter, applause, and scattered jokes – to the special matrimonial bed.

"This is when the ghost acted up again. Lewdly, it positioned itself outside the bedroom window, its face ugly with weeping, as if it had decided to watch the new couple become each other's mates – from start to finish. But maybe it thought it could paralyze them with its gaze, thus preventing the marriage's consummation. Or maybe it even thought my friend might change her mind at the last moment.

"Whatever the case, the sigil guardians appeared and chased it off.

"After that night, the new bride did not return to her old residence. Her little boy though stayed there with her sister-in-law so that the newlyweds could have time alone. This was hard on her son. Every day, he cried for his mother. Knowing he was fond of me, my friend asked me to go to her old house and spend time with him.

"As I played with the boy, I observed the dead husband's ghost. It was much diminished – more a disturbance in the air than a man. Numbly, it drifted, misting hands sliding over the places its wife had touched. The only time it seemed to come alive was whenever the little boy periodically broke down into tears to plead for his mother. Then the ghost would lurch toward him as if to offer comfort.

"Eventually, the aunt grew irritated with the little boy's crying. The next time he shrieked for his mother, just as the ghost moved in his direction, she slapped the boy.

"This was too much for the ghost – to see its son hurting but be unable to console him, to see the sister-in-law attack the boy but be unable to stop her. And so it broke down into a violent fit.

"Shaking.

"Clacking its teeth.

"Beating wildly at its chest and face.

"Unable to bear the sight of such pain, I made excuses and left.

"I never returned to that house. I have no idea what became of the ghost. However later, I told my friend everything. She clenched her teeth to keep from crying and fell into a despondent state.

"Not long after that, the story of her husband's misery made its way to another widow who was thinking of remarrying. The story changed her mind."

* * *

It's commonly assumed that the bonds of love dissolve upon death. This is not true. The connection remains. So too do the feelings of the dead. How could anyone not be moved when considering what they suffer? As for what we owe the dead, I think we know deep in our hearts what decisions and rites must be made in each individual case. And our natures will guide us in this – just as they determine how compassionately or treacherously we deal with the living.

Of course, some Confucians argue the dead feel nothing and that ghosts aren't real. They dismiss the existence of spirits because deluded or dishonest people say untrue things.

I am not that sort of Confucian. After all, every good law that exists was either delivered by a spiritual entity or articulated by a spiritual influence inside us. And it is just as lazy and foolish to believe nothing one hears about ghosts as it is to believe everything. Personally, I believe ghosts are real enough to hurt us and for us to hurt them.

Besides, in the final analysis, I find that the nanny's story contains more wisdom and heart than what its naysayers can offer.

The Phantom 'Rickshaw

Rudyard Kipling

May no ill dreams disturb my rest,
Nor Powers of Darkness me molest.
– Evening Hymn.

ONE OF THE FEW ADVANTAGES that India has over England is a great Knowability. After five years' service a man is directly or indirectly acquainted with the two or three hundred Civilians in his Province, all the Messes of ten or twelve Regiments and Batteries, and some fifteen hundred other people of the non-official caste. In ten years his knowledge should be doubled, and at the end of twenty he knows, or knows something about, every Englishman in the Empire, and may travel anywhere and everywhere without paying hotel-bills.

Globe-trotters who expect entertainment as a right, have, even within my memory, blunted this open-heartedness, but none the less to-day, if you belong to the Inner Circle and are neither a Bear nor a Black Sheep, all houses are open to you, and our small world is very, very kind and helpful.

Rickett of Kamartha stayed with Polder of Kumaon some fifteen years ago. He meant to stay two nights, but was knocked down by rheumatic fever, and for six weeks disorganized Polder's establishment, stopped Polder's work, and nearly died in Polder's bedroom. Polder behaves as though he had been placed under eternal obligation by Rickett, and yearly sends the little Ricketts a box of presents and toys. It is the same everywhere. The men who do not take the trouble to conceal from you their opinion that you are an incompetent ass, and the women who blacken your character and misunderstand your wife's amusements, will work themselves to the bone in your behalf if you fall sick or into serious trouble.

Heatherlegh, the Doctor, kept, in addition to his regular practice, a hospital on his private account – an arrangement of loose boxes for Incurables, his friend called it – but it was really a sort of fitting-up shed for craft that had been damaged by stress of weather. The weather in India is often sultry, and since the tale of bricks is always a fixed quantity, and the only liberty allowed is permission to work overtime and get no thanks, men occasionally break down and become as mixed as the metaphors in this sentence.

Heatherlegh is the dearest doctor that ever was, and his invariable prescription to all his patients is, "lie low, go slow, and keep cool." He says that more men are killed by overwork than the importance of this world justifies. He maintains that overwork slew Pansay, who died under his hands about three years ago. He has, of course, the right to speak authoritatively, and he laughs at my theory that there was a crack in Pansay's head and a little bit of the Dark World came through and pressed him to death. "Pansay went off the handle," says Heatherlegh, "after the stimulus of long leave at Home. He may or he may not have behaved like a blackguard to Mrs. Keith-Wessington. My notion is that the work of the Katabundi Settlement ran him off his legs, and that he took to brooding and making much of an ordinary P.&O. flirtation. He certainly was engaged to Miss Mannering, and she certainly broke off the engagement. Then he took a feverish chill and all that nonsense about ghosts developed. Overwork started his illness, kept it alight, and killed him poor devil. Write him off to the System – one man to take the work of two and a half men."

I do not believe this. I used to sit up with Pansay sometimes when Heatherlegh was called out to patients, and I happened to be within claim. The man would make me most unhappy by describing in a low, even voice, the procession that was always passing at the bottom of his bed. He had a sick man's command of language. When he recovered I suggested that he should write out the whole affair from beginning to end, knowing that ink might assist him to ease his mind. When little boys have learned a new bad word they are never happy till they have chalked it up on a door. And this also is Literature.

He was in a high fever while he was writing, and the blood-and-thunder Magazine diction he adopted did not calm him. Two months afterward he was reported fit for duty, but, in spite of the fact that he was urgently needed to help an undermanned Commission stagger through a deficit, he preferred to die; vowing at the last that he was hag-ridden. I got his manuscript before he died, and this is his version of the affair, dated 1885:

My doctor tells me that I need rest and change of air. It is not improbable that I shall get both ere long – rest that neither the red-coated messenger nor the midday gun can break, and change of air far beyond that which any homeward-bound steamer can give me. In the meantime I am resolved to stay where I am; and, in flat defiance of my doctor's orders, to take all the world into my confidence. You shall learn for yourselves the precise nature of my malady; and shall, too, judge for yourselves whether any man born of woman on this weary earth was ever so tormented as I.

Speaking now as a condemned criminal might speak ere the drop-bolts are drawn, my story, wild and hideously improbable as it may appear, demands at least attention. That it will ever receive credence I utterly disbelieve. Two months ago I should have scouted as mad or drunk the man who had dared tell me the like. Two months ago I was the happiest man in India. Today, from Peshawur to the sea, there is no one more wretched. My doctor and I are the only two who know this. His explanation is, that my brain, digestion, and eyesight are all slightly affected; giving rise to my frequent and persistent 'delusions'. Delusions, indeed! I call him a fool; but he attends me still with the same unwearied smile, the same bland professional manner, the same neatly trimmed red whiskers, till I begin to suspect that I am an ungrateful, evil-tempered invalid. But you shall judge for your-selves.

Three years ago it was my fortune – my great misfortune – to sail from Gravesend to Bombay, on return from long leave, with one Agnes Keith-Wessington, wife of an officer on the Bombay side. It does not in the least concern you to know what manner of woman she was. Be content with the knowledge that, ere the voyage had ended, both she and I were desperately and unreasoningly in love with one another. Heaven knows that I can make the admission now without one particle of vanity. In matters of this sort there is always one who gives and another who accepts. From the first day of our ill-omened attachment, I was conscious that Agnes's passion was a stronger, a more dominant, and – if I may use the expression – a purer sentiment than mine. Whether she recognized the fact then, I do not know. Afterward it was bitterly plain to both of us.

Arrived at Bombay in the spring of the year, we went our respective ways, to meet no more for the next three or four months, when my leave and her love took us both to Simla. There we spent the season together; and there my fire of straw burned itself out to a pitiful end with the closing year. I attempt no excuse. I make no apology. Mrs. Wessington had given up much for my sake, and was prepared to give up all. From my own lips, in August, 1882, she learned that I was sick of her presence, tired of her company, and weary of the sound of her voice. Ninety-nine women out of a hundred would have wearied of me as I wearied of them, seventy-five of that number would have promptly avenged themselves by active and obtrusive flirtation with other men. Mrs. Wessington was the hundredth. On her neither my openly expressed aversion nor the cutting brutalities with which I garnished our interviews had the least effect.

"Jack, darling!" was her one eternal cuckoo cry: "I'm sure it's all a mistake – a hideous mistake; and we'll be good friends again some day. *Please* forgive me, Jack, dear."

I was the offender, and I knew it. That knowledge transformed my pity into passive endurance, and, eventually, into blind hate – the same instinct, I suppose, which prompts a man to savagely stamp on the spider he has but half killed. And with this hate in my bosom the season of 1882 came to an end.

Next year we met again at Simla – she with her monotonous face and timid attempts at reconciliation, and I with loathing of her in every fibre of my frame. Several times I could not avoid meeting her alone; and on each occasion her words were identically the same. Still the unreasoning wail that it was all a "mistake"; and still the hope of eventually "making friends." I might have seen had I cared to look, that that hope only was keeping her alive. She grew more wan and thin month by month. You will agree with me, at least, that such conduct would have driven any one to despair. It was uncalled for; childish; unwomanly. I maintain that she was much to blame. And again, sometimes, in the black, fever-stricken night-watches, I have begun to think that I might have been a little kinder to her. But that really is a 'delusion'. I could not have continued pretending to love her when I didn't; could I? It would have been unfair to us both.

Last year we met again – on the same terms as before. The same weary appeal, and the same curt answers from my lips. At least I would make her see how wholly wrong and hopeless were her attempts at resuming the old relationship. As the season wore on, we fell apart – that is to say, she found it difficult to meet me, for I had other and more absorbing interests to attend to. When I think it over quietly in my sick-room, the season of 1884 seems a confused nightmare wherein light and shade were fantastically intermingled – my courtship of little Kitty Mannering; my hopes, doubts, and fears; our long rides together; my trembling avowal of attachment; her reply; and now and again a vision of a white face flitting by in the 'rickshaw with the black and white liveries I once watched for so earnestly; the wave of Mrs. Wessington's gloved hand; and, when she met me alone, which was but seldom, the irksome monotony of her appeal. I loved Kitty Mannering; honestly, heartily loved her, and with my love for her grew my hatred for Agnes. In August Kitty and I were engaged. The next day I met those accursed 'magpie' *jhampanies* at the back of Jakko, and, moved by some passing sentiment of pity, stopped to tell Mrs. Wessington everything. She knew it already.

"So I hear you're engaged, Jack dear." Then, without a moment's pause: "I'm sure it's all a mistake – a hideous mistake. We shall be as good friends some day, Jack, as we ever were."

My answer might have made even a man wince. It cut the dying woman before me like the blow of a whip. "Please forgive me, Jack; I didn't mean to make you angry; but it's true, it's true!"

And Mrs. Wessington broke down completely. I turned away and left her to finish her journey in peace, feeling, but only for a moment or two, that I had been an unutterably mean hound. I looked back, and saw that she had turned her 'rickshaw with the idea, I suppose, of overtaking me.

The scene and its surroundings were photographed on my memory. The rain-swept sky (we were at the end of the wet weather), the sodden, dingy pines, the muddy road, and the black powder-riven cliffs formed a gloomy background against which the black and white liveries of the *jhampanies*, the yellow-panelled 'rickshaw and Mrs. Wessington's down-bowed golden head stood out clearly. She was holding her handkerchief in her left hand and was leaning back exhausted against the 'rickshaw cushions. I turned my horse up a bypath near the Sanjowlie Reservoir and literally ran away. Once I fancied I heard a faint call of "Jack!" This may have been imagination. I never stopped to verify it. Ten minutes later I came across Kitty on horseback; and, in the delight of a long ride with her, forgot all about the interview.

A week later Mrs. Wessington died, and the inexpressible burden of her existence was removed from my life. I went Plainsward perfectly happy. Before three months were over I had forgotten all about her, except that at times the discovery of some of her old letters reminded me unpleasantly of our bygone relationship. By January I had disinterred what was left of our correspondence from among my scattered belongings and had burned it. At the beginning of April of this year, 1885, I was at Simla – semi-deserted

Simla – once more, and was deep in lover's talks and walks with Kitty. It was decided that we should be married at the end of June. You will understand, therefore, that, loving Kitty as I did, I am not saying too much when I pronounce myself to have been, at that time, the happiest man in India.

Fourteen delightful days passed almost before I noticed their flight. Then, aroused to the sense of what was proper among mortals circumstanced as we were, I pointed out to Kitty that an engagement ring was the outward and visible sign of her dignity as an engaged girl; and that she must forthwith come to Hamilton's to be measured for one. Up to that moment, I give you my word, we had completely forgotten so trivial a matter. To Hamilton's we accordingly went on the 15th of April, 1885. Remember that – whatever my doctor may say to the contrary – I was then in perfect health, enjoying a well-balanced mind and an absolute tranquil spirit. Kitty and I entered Hamilton's shop together, and there, regardless of the order of affairs, I measured Kitty for the ring in the presence of the amused assistant. The ring was a sapphire with two diamonds. We then rode out down the slope that leads to the Combermere Bridge and Peliti's shop.

While my Waler was cautiously feeling his way over the loose shale, and Kitty was laughing and chattering at my side – while all Simla, that is to say as much of it as had then come from the Plains, was grouped round the Reading-room and Peliti's verandah, – I was aware that some one, apparently at a vast distance, was calling me by my Christian name. It struck me that I had heard the voice before, but when and where I could not at once determine. In the short space it took to cover the road between the path from Hamilton's shop and the first plank of the Combermere Bridge I had thought over half a dozen people who might have committed such a solecism, and had eventually decided that it must have been singing in my ears. Immediately opposite Peliti's shop my eye was arrested by the sight of four *jhampanies* in 'magpie' livery, pulling a yellow-panelled, cheap, bazar 'rickshaw. In a moment my mind flew back to the previous season and Mrs. Wessington with a sense of irritation and disgust. Was it not enough that the woman was dead and done with, without her black and white servitors reappearing to spoil the day's happiness? Whoever employed them now I thought I would call upon, and ask as a personal favour to change her *jhampanies'* livery. I would hire the men myself, and, if necessary, buy their coats from off their backs. It is impossible to say here what a flood of undesirable memories their presence evoked.

"Kitty," I cried, "there are poor Mrs. Wessington's *jhampanies* turned up again! I wonder who has them now?"

Kitty had known Mrs. Wessington slightly last season, and had always been interested in the sickly woman.

"What? Where?" she asked. "I can't see them anywhere."

Even as she spoke her horse, swerving from a laden mule, threw himself directly in front of the advancing 'rickshaw. I had scarcely time to utter a word of warning when, to my unutterable horror, horse and rider passed through men and carriage as if they had been thin air.

"What's the matter?" cried Kitty; "what made you call out so foolishly, Jack? If I am engaged I don't want all creation to know about it. There was lots of space between the mule and the verandah; and, if you think I can't ride – There!"

Whereupon wilful Kitty set off, her dainty little head in the air, at a hand-gallop in the direction of the Bandstand; fully expecting, as she herself afterward told me, that I should follow her. What was the matter? Nothing indeed. Either that I was mad or drunk, or that Simla was haunted with devils. I reined in my impatient cob, and turned round. The 'rickshaw had turned too, and now stood immediately facing me, near the left railing of the Combermere Bridge.

"Jack! Jack, darling!" (There was no mistake about the words this time: they rang through my brain as if they had been shouted in my ear.) "It's some hideous mistake, I'm sure. *Please* forgive me, Jack, and let's be friends again."

The 'rickshaw-hood had fallen back, and inside, as I hope and pray daily for the death I dread by night, sat Mrs. Keith-Wessington, handkerchief in hand, and golden head bowed on her breast.

How long I stared motionless I do not know. Finally, I was aroused by my syce taking the Waler's bridle and asking whether I was ill. From the horrible to the commonplace is but a step. I tumbled off my horse and dashed, half fainting, into Peliti's for a glass of cherry-brandy. There two or three couples were gathered round the coffee-tables discussing the gossip of the day. Their trivialities were more comforting to me just then than the consolations of religion could have been. I plunged into the midst of the conversation at once; chatted, laughed, and jested with a face (when I caught a glimpse of it in a mirror) as white and drawn as that of a corpse. Three or four men noticed my condition; and, evidently setting it down to the results of over-many pegs, charitably endeavoured to draw me apart from the rest of the loungers. But I refused to be led away. I wanted the company of my kind – as a child rushes into the midst of the dinner-party after a fright in the dark. I must have talked for about ten minutes or so, though it seemed an eternity to me, when I heard Kitty's clear voice outside inquiring for me. In another minute she had entered the shop, prepared to roundly upbraid me for failing so signally in my duties. Something in my face stopped her.

"Why, Jack," she cried, "what *have* you been doing? What has happened? Are you ill?" Thus driven into a direct lie, I said that the sun had been a little too much for me. It was close upon five o'clock of a cloudy April afternoon, and the sun had been hidden all day. I saw my mistake as soon as the words were out of my mouth: attempted to recover it; blundered hopelessly and followed Kitty in a regal rage, out of doors, amid the smiles of my acquaintances. I made some excuse (I have forgotten what) on the score of my feeling faint; and cantered away to my hotel, leaving Kitty to finish the ride by herself.

In my room I sat down and tried calmly to reason out the matter. Here was I, Theobald Jack Pansay, a well-educated Bengal Civilian in the year of grace, 1885, presumably sane, certainly healthy, driven in terror from my sweetheart's side by the apparition of a woman who had been dead and buried eight months ago. These were facts that I could not blink. Nothing was further from my thought than any memory of Mrs. Wessington when Kitty and I left Hamilton's shop. Nothing was more utterly commonplace than the stretch of wall opposite Peliti's. It was broad daylight. The road was full of people; and yet here, look you, in defiance of every law of probability, in direct outrage of Nature's ordinance, there had appeared to me a face from the grave.

Kitty's Arab had gone *through* the 'rickshaw: so that my first hope that some woman marvellously like Mrs. Wessington had hired the carriage and the coolies with their old livery was lost. Again and again I went round this treadmill of thought; and again and again gave up baffled and in despair. The voice was as inexplicable as the apparition. I had originally some wild notion of confiding it all to Kitty; of begging her to marry me at once; and in her arms defying the ghostly occupant of the 'rickshaw. "After all," I argued, "the presence of the 'rickshaw is in itself enough to prove the existence of a spectral illusion. One may see ghosts of men and women, but surely never of coolies and carriages. The whole thing is absurd. Fancy the ghost of a hillman!"

Next morning I sent a penitent note to Kitty, imploring her to overlook my strange conduct of the previous afternoon. My Divinity was still very wroth, and a personal apology was necessary. I explained, with a fluency born of night-long pondering over a falsehood, that I had been attacked with sudden palpitation of the heart – the result of indigestion. This eminently practical solution had its effect; and Kitty and I rode out that afternoon with the shadow of my first lie dividing us.

Nothing would please her save a canter round Jakko. With my nerves still unstrung from the previous night I feebly protested against the notion, suggesting Observatory Hill, Jutogh, the Boileaugunge road – anything rather than the Jakko round. Kitty was angry and a little hurt: so I yielded from fear of provoking further misunderstanding, and we set out together toward Chota Simla. We walked a greater part of the way, and, according to our custom, cantered from a mile or so below the Convent to the stretch of level road by the Sanjowlie Reservoir. The wretched horses appeared to fly, and my heart beat quicker and quicker as we neared the crest of the ascent. My mind had been full of Mrs. Wessington all the afternoon; and every inch of the Jakko road bore witness to our oldtime walks and talks. The bowlders were full of it; the pines sang it aloud overhead; the rain-fed torrents giggled and chuckled unseen over the shameful story; and the wind in my ears chanted the iniquity aloud.

As a fitting climax, in the middle of the level men call the Ladies' Mile the Horror was awaiting me. No other 'rickshaw was in sight – only the four black and white *jhampanies*, the yellow-panelled carriage, and the golden head of the woman within – all apparently just as I had left them eight months and one fortnight ago! For an instant I fancied that Kitty must see what I saw – we were so marvellously sympathetic in all things. Her next words undeceived me – "Not a soul in sight! Come along, Jack, and I'll race you to the Reservoir buildings!" Her wiry little Arab was off like a bird, my Waler following close behind, and in this order we dashed under the cliffs. Half a minute brought us within fifty yards of the 'rickshaw. I pulled my Waler and fell back a little. The 'rickshaw was directly in the middle of the road; and once more the Arab passed through it, my horse following. "Jack! Jack dear! *Please* forgive me," rang with a wail in my ears, and, after an interval: "It's a mistake, a hideous mistake!"

I spurred my horse like a man possessed. When I turned my head at the Reservoir works, the black and white liveries were still waiting – patiently waiting – under the grey hillside, and the wind brought me a mocking echo of the words I had just heard. Kitty bantered me a good deal on my silence throughout the remainder of the ride. I had been talking up till then wildly and at random. To save my life I could not speak afterward naturally, and from Sanjowlie to the Church wisely held my tongue.

I was to dine with the Mannerings that night, and had barely time to canter home to dress. On the road to Elysium Hill I overheard two men talking together in the dusk. – "It's a curious thing," said one, "how completely all trace of it disappeared. You know my wife was insanely fond of the woman (never could see anything in her myself), and wanted me to pick up her old 'rickshaw and coolies if they were to be got for love or money. Morbid sort of fancy I call it; but I've got to do what the *Memsahib* tells me. Would you believe that the man she hired it from tells me that all four of the men – they were brothers – died of cholera on the way to Hardwar, poor devils, and the 'rickshaw has been broken up by the man himself. Told me he never used a dead *Memsahib*'s 'rickshaw. Spoiled his luck. Queer notion, wasn't it? Fancy poor little Mrs. Wessington spoiling any one's luck except her own!" I laughed aloud at this point; and my laugh jarred on me as I uttered it. So there were ghosts of 'rickshaw after all, and ghostly employments in the other world! How much did Mrs. Wessington give her men? What were their hours? Where did they go?

And for visible answer to my last question I saw the infernal Thing blocking my path in the twilight. The dead travel fast, and by short cuts unknown to ordinary coolies. I laughed aloud a second time and checked my laughter suddenly, for I was afraid I was going mad. Mad to a certain extent I must have been, for I recollect that I reined in my horse at the head of the 'rickshaw, and politely wished Mrs. Wessington "Good-evening." Her answer was one I knew only too well. I listened to the end; and replied that I had heard it all before, but should be delighted if she had anything further to say. Some malignant devil stronger than I must have entered into me that evening, for I have a dim recollection of talking the commonplaces of the day for five minutes to the Thing in front of me.

"Mad as a hatter, poor devil – or drunk. Max, try and get him to come home."

Surely *that* was not Mrs. Wessington's voice! The two men had overheard me speaking to the empty air, and had returned to look after me. They were very kind and considerate, and from their words evidently gathered that I was extremely drunk. I thanked them confusedly and cantered away to my hotel, there changed, and arrived at the Mannerings' ten minutes late. I pleaded the darkness of the night as an excuse; was rebuked by Kitty for my unlover-like tardiness; and sat down.

The conversation had already become general; and under cover of it, I was addressing some tender small talk to my sweetheart when I was aware that at the further end of the table a short red-whiskered man was describing, with much broidery, his encounter with a mad unknown that evening.

A few sentences convinced me that he was repeating the incident of half an hour ago. In the middle of the story he looked round for applause, as professional story-tellers do, caught my eye, and straightway collapsed. There was a moment's awkward silence, and the red-whiskered man muttered something to the effect that he had "forgotten the rest," thereby sacrificing a reputation as a good story-teller which he had built up for six seasons past. I blessed him from the bottom of my heart, and – went on with my fish.

In the fulness of time that dinner came to an end; and with genuine regret I tore myself away from Kitty – as certain as I was of my own existence that It would be waiting for me outside the door. The red-whiskered man, who had been introduced to me as Doctor Heatherlegh, of Simla, volunteered to bear me company as far as our roads lay together. I accepted his offer with gratitude.

My instinct had not deceived me. It lay in readiness in the Mall, and, in what seemed devilish mockery of our ways, with a lighted head-lamp. The red-whiskered man went to the point at once, in a manner that showed he had been thinking over it all dinner time.

"I say, Pansay, what the deuce was the matter with you this evening on the Elysium road?" The suddenness of the question wrenched an answer from me before I was aware.

"That!" said I, pointing to It.

"*That* may be either D.T. or Eyes for aught I know. Now you don't liquor. I saw as much at dinner, so it can't be D.T. There's nothing whatever where you're pointing, though you're sweating and trembling with fright like a scared pony. Therefore, I conclude that it's Eyes. And I ought to understand all about them. Come along home with me. I'm on the Blessington lower road."

To my intense delight the 'rickshaw instead of waiting for us kept about twenty yards ahead – and this, too whether we walked, trotted, or cantered. In the course of that long night ride I had told my companion almost as much as I have told you here.

"Well, you've spoiled one of the best tales I've ever laid tongue to," said he, "but I'll forgive you for the sake of what you've gone through. Now come home and do what I tell you; and when I've cured you, young man, let this be a lesson to you to steer clear of women and indigestible food till the day of your death."

The 'rickshaw kept steady in front; and my red-whiskered friend seemed to derive great pleasure from my account of its exact whereabouts.

"Eyes, Pansay – all Eyes, Brain, and Stomach. And the greatest of these three is Stomach. You've too much conceited Brain, too little Stomach, and thoroughly unhealthy Eyes. Get your Stomach straight and the rest follows. And all that's French for a liver pill. I'll take sole medical charge of you from this hour! for you're too interesting a phenomenon to be passed over."

By this time we were deep in the shadow of the Blessington lower road and the 'rickshaw came to a dead stop under a pine-clad, over-hanging shale cliff. Instinctively I halted too, giving my reason. Heatherlegh rapped out an oath.

"Now, if you think I'm going to spend a cold night on the hillside for the sake of a stomach-*cum*-Brain-*cum*-Eye illusion.... Lord, ha' mercy! What's that?"

There was a muffled report, a blinding smother of dust just in front of us, a crack, the noise of rent boughs, and about ten yards of the cliff-side – pines, undergrowth, and all – slid down into the road below, completely blocking it up. The uprooted trees swayed and tottered for a moment like drunken giants in the gloom, and then fell prone among their fellows with a thunderous crash. Our two horses stood motionless and sweating with fear. As soon as the rattle of falling earth and stone had subsided, my companion muttered: "Man, if we'd gone forward we should have been ten feet deep in our graves by now. 'There are more things in heaven and earth.' ... Come home, Pansay, and thank God. I want a peg badly."

We retraced our way over the Church Ridge, and I arrived at Dr. Heatherlegh's house shortly after midnight.

His attempts toward my cure commenced almost immediately, and for a week I never left his sight. Many a time in the course of that week did I bless the good-fortune which had thrown me in contact with Simla's best and kindest doctor. Day by day my spirits grew lighter and more equable. Day by day, too, I became more and more inclined to fall in with Heatherlegh's 'spectral illusion' theory, implicating eyes, brain, and stomach. I wrote to Kitty, telling her that a slight sprain caused by a fall from my horse kept me indoors for a few days; and that I should be recovered before she had time to regret my absence.

Heatherlegh's treatment was simple to a degree. It consisted of liver pills, cold-water baths, and strong exercise, taken in the dusk or at early dawn – for, as he sagely observed: "A man with a sprained ankle doesn't walk a dozen miles a day, and your young woman might be wondering if she saw you."

At the end of the week, after much examination of pupil and pulse, and strict injunctions as to diet and pedestrianism, Heatherlegh dismissed me as brusquely as he had taken charge of me. Here is his parting benediction: "Man, I can certify to your mental cure, and that's as much as to say I've cured most of your bodily ailments. Now, get your traps out of this as soon as you can; and be off to make love to Miss Kitty."

I was endeavouring to express my thanks for his kindness. He cut me short.

"Don't think I did this because I like you. I gather that you've behaved like a blackguard all through. But, all the same, you're a phenomenon, and as queer a phenomenon as you are a blackguard. No!" – checking me a second time – "not a rupee, please. Go out and see if you can find the eyes-brain-and-stomach business again. I'll give you a *lakh* for each time you see it."

Half an hour later I was in the Mannerings' drawing-room with Kitty – drunk with the intoxication of present happiness and the fore-knowledge that I should never more be troubled with Its hideous presence. Strong in the sense of my new-found security, I proposed a ride at once; and, by preference, a canter round Jakko.

Never had I felt so well, so overladen with vitality and mere animal spirits, as I did on the afternoon of the 30th of April. Kitty was delighted at the change in my appearance, and complimented me on it in her delightfully frank and outspoken manner. We left the Mannerings' house together, laughing and talking, and cantered along the Chota Simla road as of old.

I was in haste to reach the Sanjowlie Reservoir and there make my assurance doubly sure. The horses did their best, but seemed all too slow to my impatient mind. Kitty was astonished at my boisterousness. "Why, Jack!" she cried at last, "you are behaving like a child. What are you doing?"

We were just below the Convent, and from sheer wantonness I was making my Waler plunge and curvet across the road as I tickled it with the loop of my riding-whip.

"Doing?" I answered; "nothing, dear. That's just it. If you'd been doing nothing for a week except lie up, you'd be as riotous as I."

> "*Singing and murmuring in your feastful mirth,*
> *Joying to feel yourself alive;*
> *Lord over Nature, Lord of the visible Earth,*
> *Lord of the senses five.*"

My quotation was hardly out of my lips before we had rounded the corner above the Convent; and a few yards further on could see across to Sanjowlie. In the centre of the level road stood the black and white liveries, the yellow-panelled 'rickshaw, and Mrs. Keith-Wessington. I pulled up, looked, rubbed my eyes, and, I believe must have said something. The next thing I knew was that I was lying face downward on the road with Kitty kneeling above me in tears.

"Has it gone, child!" I gasped. Kitty only wept more bitterly.

"Has what gone, Jack dear? what does it all mean? There must be a mistake somewhere, Jack. A hideous mistake." Her last words brought me to my feet – mad – raving for the time being.

"Yes, there *is* a mistake somewhere," I repeated, "a hideous mistake. Come and look at It."

I have an indistinct idea that I dragged Kitty by the wrist along the road up to where It stood, and implored her for pity's sake to speak to It; to tell It that we were betrothed; that neither Death nor Hell could break the tie between us; and Kitty only knows how much more to the same effect. Now and again I appealed passionately to the Terror in the 'rickshaw to bear witness to all I had said, and to release me from a torture that was killing me. As I talked I suppose I must have told Kitty of my old relations with Mrs. Wessington, for I saw her listen intently with white face and blazing eyes.

"Thank you, Mr. Pansay," she said, "that's *quite* enough. *Syce ghora lao.*"

The syces, impassive as Orientals always are, had come up with the recaptured horses; and as Kitty sprang into her saddle I caught hold of the bridle, entreating her to hear me out and forgive. My answer was the cut of her riding-whip across my face from mouth to eye, and a word or two of farewell that even now I cannot write down. So I judged, and judged rightly, that Kitty knew all; and I staggered back to the side of the 'rickshaw. My face was cut and bleeding, and the blow of the riding-whip had raised a livid blue wheal on it. I had no self-respect. Just then, Heatherlegh, who must have been following Kitty and me at a distance, cantered up.

"Doctor," I said, pointing to my face, "here's Miss Mannering's signature to my order of dismissal and... I'll thank you for that *lakh* as soon as convenient."

Heatherlegh's face, even in my abject misery, moved me to laughter.

"I'll stake my professional reputation" – he began.

"Don't be a fool," I whispered. "I've lost my life's happiness and you'd better take me home."

As I spoke the 'rickshaw was gone. Then I lost all knowledge of what was passing. The crest of Jakko seemed to heave and roll like the crest of a cloud and fall in upon me.

Seven days later (on the 7th of May, that is to say) I was aware that I was lying in Heatherlegh's room as weak as a little child. Heatherlegh was watching me intently from behind the papers on his writing-table. His first words were not encouraging; but I was too far spent to be much moved by them.

"Here's Miss Kitty has sent back your letters. You corresponded a good deal, you young people. Here's a packet that looks like a ring, and a cheerful sort of a note from Mannering Papa, which I've taken the liberty of reading and burning. The old gentleman's not pleased with you."

"And Kitty?" I asked, dully.

"Rather more drawn than her father from what she says. By the same token you must have been letting out any number of queer reminiscences just before I met you. Says that a man who would have behaved to a woman as you did to Mrs. Wessington ought to kill himself out of sheer pity for his kind. She's a hot-headed little virago, your mash. Will have it too that you were suffering from D.T. when that row on the Jakko road turned up. Says she'll die before she ever speaks to you again."

I groaned and turned over to the other side.

"Now you've got your choice, my friend. This engagement has to be broken off; and the Mannerings don't want to be too hard on you. Was it broken through D. T. or epileptic fits? Sorry I can't offer you a better exchange unless you'd prefer hereditary insanity. Say the word and I'll tell 'em it's fits. All Simla knows about that scene on the Ladies' Mile. Come! I'll give you five minutes to think over it."

During those five minutes I believe that I explored thoroughly the lowest circles of the Inferno which it is permitted man to tread on earth. And at the same time I myself was watching myself faltering through the dark labyrinths of doubt, misery, and utter despair. I wondered, as Heatherlegh in his chair might have wondered, which dreadful alternative I should adopt. Presently I heard myself answering in a voice that I hardly recognized, –

"They're confoundedly particular about morality in these parts. Give 'em fits, Heatherlegh, and my love. Now let me sleep a bit longer."

Then my two selves joined, and it was only I (half crazed, devil-driven I) that tossed in my bed, tracing step by step the history of the past month.

"But I am in Simla," I kept repeating to myself. "I, Jack Pansay, am in Simla and there are no ghosts here. It's unreasonable of that woman to pretend there are. Why couldn't Agnes have left me alone? I never did her any harm. It might just as well have been me as Agnes. Only I'd never have come back on purpose to kill *her*. Why can't I be left alone – left alone and happy?"

It was high noon when I first awoke: and the sun was low in the sky before I slept – slept as the tortured criminal sleeps on his rack, too worn to feel further pain.

Next day I could not leave my bed. Heatherlegh told me in the morning that he had received an answer from Mr. Mannering, and that, thanks to his (Heatherlegh's) friendly offices, the story of my affliction had travelled through the length and breadth of Simla, where I was on all sides much pitied.

"And that's rather more than you deserve," he concluded, pleasantly, "though the Lord knows you've been going through a pretty severe mill. Never mind; we'll cure you yet, you perverse phenomenon."

I declined firmly to be cured. "You've been much too good to me already, old man," said I; "but I don't think I need trouble you further."

In my heart I knew that nothing Heatherlegh could do would lighten the burden that had been laid upon me.

With that knowledge came also a sense of hopeless, impotent rebellion against the unreasonableness of it all. There were scores of men no better than I whose punishments had at least been reserved for another world; and I felt that it was bitterly, cruelly unfair that I alone should have been singled out for so hideous a fate. This mood would in time give place to another where it seemed that the 'rickshaw and I were the only realities in a world of shadows; that Kitty was a ghost; that Mannering, Heatherlegh, and all the other men and women I knew were all ghosts; and the great, grey hills themselves but vain shadows devised to torture me. From mood to mood I tossed backward and forward for seven weary days; my body growing daily stronger and stronger, until the bedroom looking-glass told me that I had returned to everyday life, and was as other men once more. Curiously enough my face showed no signs of the struggle I had gone through. It was pale indeed, but as expression-less and commonplace as ever. I had expected some permanent alteration – visible evidence of the disease that was eating me away. I found nothing.

On the 15th of May, I left Heatherlegh's house at eleven o'clock in the morning; and the instinct of the bachelor drove me to the Club. There I found that every man knew my story as told by Heatherlegh, and was, in clumsy fashion, abnormally kind and attentive. Nevertheless I recognized that for the rest of my natural life I should be among but not of my fellows; and I envied very bitterly indeed the laughing coolies on the Mall below. I lunched at the Club, and at four o'clock wandered aimlessly down the Mall in the vague hope of meeting Kitty. Close to the Band-stand the black and white liveries joined me; and I heard Mrs. Wessington's old appeal at my side. I had been expecting this ever since I came out; and was only surprised at her delay. The phantom 'rickshaw and I went side by side along the Chota Simla road in silence. Close to the bazar, Kitty and a man on horseback overtook and passed us. For any sign she gave I might have been a dog in the road. She did not even pay me the compliment of quickening her pace; though the rainy afternoon had served for an excuse.

So Kitty and her companion, and I and my ghostly Light-o'-Love, crept round Jakko in couples. The road was streaming with water; the pines dripped like roof-pipes on the rocks below, and the air was full of fine, driving rain. Two or three times I found myself saying to myself almost aloud: "I'm Jack Pansay on leave at Simla – at *Simla*! Everyday, ordinary Simla. I mustn't forget that – I mustn't forget that." Then I would try to recollect some of the gossip I had heard at the Club: the prices of So-and-So's horses – anything, in fact, that related to the workaday Anglo-Indian world I knew so well. I even repeated the multiplication-table rapidly to myself, to make quite sure that I was not taking leave of my senses. It gave me much comfort; and must have prevented my hearing Mrs. Wessington for a time.

Once more I wearily climbed the Convent slope and entered the level road. Here Kitty and the man started off at a canter, and I was left alone with Mrs. Wessington. "Agnes," said I, "will you put back your hood and tell me what it all means?" The hood dropped noiselessly, and I was face to face with my dead and buried mistress. She was wearing the dress in which I had last seen her alive; carried the same tiny handkerchief in her right hand; and the same cardcase in her left. (A woman eight months dead with a cardcase!) I had to pin myself down to the multiplication-table, and to set both hands on the stone parapet of the road, to assure myself that that at least was real.

"Agnes," I repeated, "for pity's sake tell me what it all means." Mrs. Wessington leaned forward, with that odd, quick turn of the head I used to know so well, and spoke.

If my story had not already so madly overleaped the bounds of all human belief I should apologize to you now. As I know that no one – no, not even Kitty, for whom it is written as some sort of justification of my conduct – will believe me, I will go on. Mrs. Wessington spoke and I walked with her from the Sanjowlie road to the turning below the Commander-in-Chief's house as I might walk by the side of any living woman's 'rickshaw, deep in conversation. The second and most tormenting of my moods of sickness had suddenly laid hold upon me, and like the prince in Tennyson's poem, "I seemed to move amid a world of ghosts." There had been a garden-party at the Commander-in-Chief's, and we two joined the crowd of homeward-bound folk. As I saw them then it seemed that *they* were the shadows – impalpable, fantastic shadows – that divided for Mrs. Wessington's 'rickshaw to pass through. What we said during the course of that weird interview I cannot – indeed, I dare not – tell. Heatherlegh's comment would have been a short laugh and a remark that I had been "mashing a brain-eye-and-stomach chimera." It was a ghastly and yet in some indefinable way a marvellously dear experience. Could it be possible, I wondered, that I was in this life to woo a second time the woman I had killed by my own neglect and cruelty?

I met Kitty on the homeward road – a shadow among shadows.

If I were to describe all the incidents of the next fortnight in their order, my story would never come to an end; and your patience would be exhausted. Morning after morning and evening after evening the ghostly 'rickshaw and I used to wander through Simla together. Wherever I went there the four black and white liveries followed me and bore me company to and from my hotel. At the Theatre I found them amid the crowd or yelling *jhampanies*; outside the Club verandah, after a long evening of whist; at the Birthday Ball, waiting patiently for my reappearance; and in broad daylight when I went calling. Save that it cast no shadow, the 'rickshaw was in every respect as real to look upon as one of wood and iron. More than once, indeed, I have had to check myself from warning some hard-riding friend against cantering over it. More than once I have walked down the Mall deep in conversation with Mrs. Wessington to the unspeakable amazement of the passers-by.

Before I had been out and about a week I learned that the 'fit' theory had been discarded in favour of insanity. However, I made no change in my mode of life. I called, rode, and dined out as freely as ever. I had a passion for the society of my kind which I had never felt before; I hungered to be among the realities of life; and at the same time I felt vaguely unhappy when I had been separated too long from my ghostly companion. It would be almost impossible to describe my varying moods from the 15th of May up to to-day.

The presence of the 'rickshaw filled me by turns with horror, blind fear, a dim sort of pleasure, and utter despair. I dared not leave Simla; and I knew that my stay there was killing me. I knew, moreover, that it was my destiny to die slowly and a little every day. My only anxiety was to get the penance over as quietly as might be. Alternately I hungered for a sight of Kitty and watched her outrageous flirtations with my successor – to speak more accurately, my successors – with amused interest. She was as much out of my life as I was out of hers. By day I wandered with Mrs. Wessington almost content. By night I implored Heaven to let me return to the world as I used to know it. Above all these varying moods lay the sensation of dull, numbing wonder that the Seen and the Unseen should mingle so strangely on this earth to hound one poor soul to its grave.

August 27. – Heatherlegh has been indefatigable in his attendance on me; and only yesterday told me that I ought to send in an application for sick leave. An application to escape the company of a phantom! A request that the Government would graciously permit me to get rid of five ghosts and an airy 'rickshaw by going to England. Heatherlegh's proposition moved me to almost hysterical laughter. I told him that I should await the end quietly at Simla; and I am sure that the end is not far off. Believe me that I dread its advent more than any word can say; and I torture myself nightly with a thousand speculations as to the manner of my death.

Shall I die in my bed decently and as an English gentleman should die; or, in one last walk on the Mall, will my soul be wrenched from me to take its place forever and ever by the side of that ghastly phantasm? Shall I return to my old lost allegiance in the next world, or shall I meet Agnes loathing her and bound to her side through all eternity? Shall we two hover over the scene of our lives till the end of Time? As the day of my death draws nearer, the intense horror that all living flesh feels toward escaped spirits from beyond the grave grows more and more powerful. It is an awful thing to go down quick among the dead with scarcely one-half of your life completed. It is a thousand times more awful to wait as I do in your midst, for I know not what unimaginable terror. Pity me, at least on the score of my 'delusion', for I know you will never believe what I have written here. Yet as surely as ever a man was done to death by the Powers of Darkness I am that man.

In justice, too, pity her. For as surely as ever woman was killed by man, I killed Mrs. Wessington. And the last portion of my punishment is ever now upon me.

My Own True Ghost Story

Rudyard Kipling

As I came through the Desert thus it was –
As I came through the Desert.
– The City of Dreadful Night.

SOMEWHERE IN THE OTHER WORLD, where there are books and pictures and plays and shop windows to look at, and thousands of men who spend their lives in building up all four, lives a gentleman who writes real stories about the real insides of people; and his name is Mr. Walter Besant. But he will insist upon treating his ghosts – he has published half a workshopful of them – with levity. He makes his ghost-seers talk familiarly, and, in some cases, flirt outrageously, with the phantoms. You may treat anything, from a Viceroy to a Vernacular Paper, with levity; but you must behave reverently toward a ghost, and particularly an Indian one.

There are, in this land, ghosts who take the form of fat, cold, pobby corpses, and hide in trees near the roadside till a traveller passes. Then they drop upon his neck and remain. There are also terrible ghosts of women who have died in child-bed. These wander along the pathways at dusk, or hide in the crops near a village, and call seductively. But to answer their call is death in this world and the next. Their feet are turned backward that all sober men may recognize them. There are ghosts of little children who have been thrown into wells. These haunt well curbs and the fringes of jungles, and wail under the stars, or catch women by the wrist and beg to be taken up and carried. These and the corpse ghosts, however, are only vernacular articles and do not attack Sahibs. No native ghost has yet been authentically reported to have frightened an Englishman; but many English ghosts have scared the life out of both white and black.

Nearly every other Station owns a ghost. There are said to be two at Simla, not counting the woman who blows the bellows at Syree dâk-bungalow on the Old Road; Mussoorie has a house haunted of a very lively Thing; a White Lady is supposed to do night-watchman round a house in Lahore; Dalhousie says that one of her houses 'repeats' on autumn evenings all the incidents of a horrible horse-and-precipice accident; Murree has a merry ghost, and, now that she has been swept by cholera, will have room for a sorrowful one; there are Officers' Quarters in Mian Mir whose doors open without reason, and whose furniture is guaranteed to creak, not with the heat of June but with the weight of Invisibles who come to lounge in the chairs; Peshawur possesses houses that none will willingly rent; and there is something – not fever – wrong with a big bungalow in Allahabad. The older Provinces simply bristle with haunted houses, and march phantom armies along their main thoroughfares.

Some of the dâk-bungalows on the Grand Trunk Road have handy little cemeteries in their compound – witnesses to the 'changes and chances of this mortal life' in the days when men drove from Calcutta to the Northwest. These bungalows are objectionable places to put up in. They are generally very old, always dirty, while the *khansamah* is as ancient as the bungalow. He either chatters senilely, or falls into the long trances of age. In both moods he is useless. If you get angry with him, he refers to some Sahib dead and buried these thirty years, and says that when he was in that Sahib's service not a *khansamah* in the province could touch him. Then he jabbers and mows and trembles and fidgets among the dishes, and you repent of your irritation.

In these dâk-bungalows, ghosts are most likely to be found, and when found, they should be made a note of. Not long ago it was my business to live in dâk-bungalows. I never inhabited the same house for three nights running, and grew to be learned in the breed. I lived in Government-built ones with red brick walls and rail ceilings, an inventory of the furniture posted in every room, and an excited snake at the threshold to give welcome. I lived in 'converted' ones – old houses officiating as dâk-bungalows – where nothing was in its proper place and there wasn't even a fowl for dinner. I lived in second-hand palaces where the wind blew through open-work marble tracery just as uncomfortably as through a broken pane. I lived in dâk-bungalows where the last entry in the visitors' book was fifteen months old, and where they slashed off the curry-kid's head with a sword. It was my good luck to meet all sorts of men, from sober traveling missionaries and deserters flying from British Regiments, to drunken loafers who threw whisky bottles at all who passed; and my still greater good fortune just to escape a maternity case. Seeing that a fair proportion of the tragedy of our lives out here acted itself in dâk-bungalows, I wondered that I had met no ghosts. A ghost that would voluntarily hang about a dâk-bungalow would be mad of course; but so many men have died mad in dâk-bungalows that there must be a fair percentage of lunatic ghosts.

In due time I found my ghost, or ghosts rather, for there were two of them. Up till that hour I had sympathized with Mr. Besant's method of handling them, as shown in *The Strange Case of Mr. Lucraft and Other Stories*. I am now in the Opposition.

We will call the bungalow Katmal dâk-bungalow. But THAT was the smallest part of the horror. A man with a sensitive hide has no right to sleep in dâk-bungalows. He should marry. Katmal dâk-bungalow was old and rotten and unrepaired. The floor was of worn brick, the walls were filthy, and the windows were nearly black with grime. It stood on a bypath largely used by native Sub-Deputy Assistants of all kinds, from Finance to Forests; but real Sahibs were rare. The *khansamah*, who was nearly bent double with old age, said so.

When I arrived, there was a fitful, undecided rain on the face of the land, accompanied by a restless wind, and every gust made a noise like the rattling of dry bones in the stiff toddy palms outside. The *khansamah* completely lost his head on my arrival. He had served a Sahib once. Did I know that Sahib? He gave me the name of a well-known man who has been buried for more than a quarter of a century, and showed me an ancient daguerreotype of that man in his prehistoric youth. I had seen a steel engraving of him at the head of a double volume of Memoirs a month before, and I felt ancient beyond telling.

The day shut in and the *khansamah* went to get me food. He did not go through the pretense of calling it '*khana*' – man's victuals. He said '*ratub*', and that means, among other things, 'grub' – dog's rations. There was no insult in his choice of the term. He had forgotten the other word, I suppose.

While he was cutting up the dead bodies of animals, I settled myself down, after exploring the dâk-bungalow. There were three rooms, beside my own, which was a corner kennel, each giving into the other through dingy white doors fastened with long iron bars. The bungalow was a very solid one, but the partition walls of the rooms were almost jerry-built in their flimsiness. Every step or bang of a trunk echoed from my room down the other three, and every footfall came back tremulously from the far walls. For this reason I shut the door. There were no lamps – only candles in long glass shades. An oil wick was set in the bathroom.

For bleak, unadulterated misery that dâk-bungalow was the worst of the many that I had ever set foot in. There was no fireplace, and the windows would not open; so a brazier of charcoal would have been useless. The rain and the wind splashed and gurgled and moaned round the house, and the toddy palms rattled and roared. Half a dozen jackals went through the compound singing, and a hyena stood afar off and mocked them. A hyena would convince a Sadducee of the Resurrection of the Dead – the worst sort of Dead. Then came the *ratub* – a curious meal, half native and half English in composition – with the old *khansamab* babbling behind my chair about dead and gone English people, and the wind-blown candles playing shadow-bo-peep with the bed and the mosquito-curtains. It was just the sort of dinner and evening to make a man think of every single one of his past sins, and of all the others that he intended to commit if he lived.

Sleep, for several hundred reasons, was not easy. The lamp in the bath-room threw the most absurd shadows into the room, and the wind was beginning to talk nonsense.

Just when the reasons were drowsy with blood-sucking I heard the regular – "Let-us-take-and-heave-him-over" grunt of doolie-bearers in the compound. First one doolie came in, then a second, and then a third. I heard the doolies dumped on the ground, and the shutter in front of my door shook. "That's some one trying to come in," I said. But no one spoke, and I persuaded myself that it was the gusty wind. The shutter of the room next to mine was attacked, flung back, and the inner door opened. "That's some Sub-Deputy Assistant," I said, "and he has brought his friends with him. Now they'll talk and spit and smoke for an hour."

But there were no voices and no footsteps. No one was putting his luggage into the next room. The door shut, and I thanked Providence that I was to be left in peace. But I was curious to know where the doolies had gone. I got out of bed and looked into the darkness. There was never a sign of a doolie. Just as I was getting into bed again, I heard, in the next room, the sound that no man in his senses can possibly mistake – the whir of a billiard ball down the length of the slates when the striker is stringing for break. No other sound is like it. A minute afterwards there was another whir, and I got into bed. I was not frightened – indeed I was not. I was very curious to know what had become of the doolies. I jumped into bed for that reason.

Next minute I heard the double click of a cannon and my hair sat up. It is a mistake to say that hair stands up. The skin of the head tightens and you can feel a faint, prickly, bristling all over the scalp. That is the hair sitting up.

There was a whir and a click, and both sounds could only have been made by one thing – a billiard ball. I argued the matter out at great length with myself; and the more I argued the less probable it seemed that one bed, one table, and two chairs – all the furniture of the room next to mine – could so exactly duplicate the sounds of a game of billiards. After another cannon, a three-cushion one to judge by the whir, I argued no more. I had found my ghost and would have given worlds to have escaped from that dâk-bungalow. I listened, and with each listen the game grew clearer. There was whir on whir and click on click. Sometimes there was a double click and a whir and another click. Beyond any sort of doubt, people were playing billiards in the next room. And the next room was not big enough to hold a billiard table!

Between the pauses of the wind I heard the game go forward – stroke after stroke. I tried to believe that I could not hear voices; but that attempt was a failure.

Do you know what fear is? Not ordinary fear of insult, injury or death, but abject, quivering dread of something that you cannot see – fear that dries the inside of the mouth and half of the throat – fear that makes you sweat on the palms of the hands, and gulp in order to keep the uvula at work? This is a fine Fear – a great cowardice, and must be felt to be appreciated. The very improbability of billiards in a dâk-bungalow proved the reality of the thing. No man – drunk or sober – could imagine a game at billiards, or invent the spitting crack of a 'screw-cannon'.

A severe course of dâk-bungalows has this disadvantage – it breeds infinite credulity. If a man said to a confirmed dâk-bungalow-haunter: "There is a corpse in the next room, and there's a mad girl in the next but one, and the woman and man on that camel have just eloped from a place sixty miles away," the hearer would not disbelieve because he would know that nothing is too wild, grotesque, or horrible to happen in a dâk-bungalow.

This credulity, unfortunately, extends to ghosts. A rational person fresh from his own house would have turned on his side and slept. I did not. So surely as I was given up as a bad carcass by the scores of things in the bed because the bulk of my blood was in my heart, so surely did I hear every stroke of a long game at billiards played in the echoing room behind the iron-barred door. My dominant fear was that the players might want a marker. It was an absurd fear; because creatures who could play in the dark would be above such superfluities. I only know that that was my terror; and it was real.

After a long, long while the game stopped, and the door banged. I slept because I was dead tired. Otherwise I should have preferred to have kept awake. Not for everything in Asia would I have dropped the door-bar and peered into the dark of the next room.

When the morning came, I considered that I had done well and wisely, and inquired for the means of departure.

"By the way, *khansamah*," I said, "what were those three doolies doing in my compound in the night?"

"There were no doolies," said the *khansamah*.

I went into the next room and the daylight streamed through the open door. I was immensely brave. I would, at that hour, have played Black Pool with the owner of the big Black Pool down below.

"Has this place always been a dâk-bungalow?" I asked.

"No," said the *khansamah*. "Ten or twenty years ago, I have forgotten how long, it was a billiard room."

"A how much?"

"A billiard room for the Sahibs who built the Railway. I was *khansamah* then in the big house where all the Railway-Sahibs lived, and I used to come across with brandy-shrab. These three rooms were all one, and they held a big table on which the Sahibs played every evening. But the Sahibs are all dead now, and the Railway runs, you say, nearly to Kabul."

"Do you remember anything about the Sahibs?"

"It is long ago, but I remember that one Sahib, a fat man and always angry, was playing here one night, and he said to me: 'Mangal Khan, brandy-*pani* do', and I filled the glass, and he bent over the table to strike, and his head fell lower and lower till it hit the table, and his spectacles came off, and when we – the Sahibs and I myself – ran to lift him. He was dead. I helped to carry him out. Aha, he was a strong Sahib! But he is dead and I, old Mangal Khan, am still living, by your favour."

That was more than enough! I had my ghost – a firsthand, authenticated article. I would write to the Society for Psychical Research – I would paralyze the Empire with the news! But I would, first of all, put eighty miles of assessed crop land between myself and that dâk-bungalow before nightfall. The Society might send their regular agent to investigate later on.

I went into my own room and prepared to pack after noting down the facts of the case. As I smoked I heard the game begin again, – with a miss in balk this time, for the whir was a short one.

The door was open and I could see into the room. *Click – click!* That was a cannon. I entered the room without fear, for there was sunlight within and a fresh breeze without. The unseen game was going on at a tremendous rate. And well it might, when a restless little rat was running to and fro inside the dingy ceiling-cloth, and a piece of loose window-sash was making fifty breaks off the window-bolt as it shook in the breeze!

Impossible to mistake the sound of billiard balls! Impossible to mistake the whir of a ball over the slate! But I was to be excused. Even when I shut my enlightened eyes the sound was marvellously like that of a fast game.

Entered angrily the faithful partner of my sorrows, Kadir Baksh.

"This bungalow is very bad and low-caste! No wonder the Presence was disturbed and is speckled. Three sets of doolie-bearers came to the bungalow late last night when I was sleeping outside, and said that it was their custom to rest in the rooms set apart for the English people! What honour has the *khansamah?* They tried to enter, but I told them to go. No wonder, if these *Oorias* have been here, that the Presence is sorely spotted. It is shame, and the work of a dirty man!"

Kadir Baksh did not say that he had taken from each gang two *anna*s for rent in advance, and then, beyond my earshot, had beaten them with the big green umbrella whose use I could never before divine. But Kadir Baksh has no notions of morality.

There was an interview with the *khansamah*, but as he promptly lost his head, wrath gave place to pity, and pity led to a long conversation, in the course of which he put the fat Engineer-Sahib's tragic death in three separate stations – two of them fifty miles away. The third shift was to Calcutta, and there the Sahib died while driving a dogcart.

If I had encouraged him the *khansamah* would have wandered all through Bengal with his corpse.

I did not go away as soon as I intended. I stayed for the night, while the wind and the rat and the sash and the window-bolt played a ding-dong 'hundred and fifty up'. Then the wind ran out and the billiards stopped, and I felt that I had ruined my one genuine, hall-marked ghost story.

Had I only stopped at the proper time, I could have made anything out of it.

That was the bitterest thought of all!

The Pavilion of Far-Reaching Fragrance

K.P. Kulski

MISDEEDS ARE A STENCH that clings to the descendants of the malefactor. Sins that furrow into bone marrow, generation after generation. *Gwishin* are born of these things. The living become vehicles for their battered ghostly rage, the burning heat of their never-ending rotting revenge. Until my eventual death, we will be together, *her* and I. She will press her terrible end upon me, push her fire crisped flesh into mine until the pain, the fury, and the flames become mine too.

Some places are haunted, sometimes objects, but a family can be too. For me, for us, those who are born with the bones of *Yi* clan and can draw a direct line, all the way to the sinner, we will carry her with us forever.

I have told this story before, to believers and unbelievers. To people lustful for confirmation of their beliefs and others who stood at the ready to disprove me. They are both voyeurs, desperate to make what they believe true. How they love to force me to undress the experience, the hell, so that they may gawk. So you see, you are neither the first or the last that will come to hear my tale. And like them, you will gawk, then when you are finished, you will gather your things and leave me, yet again, alone … with *her*.

You are uncomfortable, I can see your unease as you fumble for a notebook and pen, apologize for your disorganization. There was a time I would have tried to make you comfortable in my presence, no more. I am too tired for that, instead I simply wait and watch. Once you know the whole story, you will look at this small apartment with a new layer of apprehension, perhaps even terror. Then you will look at me and will feel *her* looking back at you.

My name is Lusi Douglas and am thirty-two years old. My mother, and I by default, are descendants of the ancient nobility of the *Yi* clan. My occupation – nurse. But I am one no longer…

* * *

Lusi

  "A mouse in an earthen jar"

When I was a child, my mother took me from our home in Baltimore, Maryland, to visit the place of her birth, the place known as the 'Land of the Morning Calm', South Korea. There we went to visit the great *Joseon* palace complex, *Gyeongbokgung*. Within, I found the most beautiful world, a captive fairytale, a royal pavilion built on a tiny island within a manmade lake. To reach it, visitors must cross an ornate wooden bridge over water so inundated with blooming lotus that one floats upon a cloud of fragrance.

There are times I wish that I could pull this memory up and find comfort in its beauty, but I cannot, because with that beauty is the first memory I have of darkness. You see, as my mother led me back across the bridge, I happened to look back to the pavilion and for the first time I saw the *gwishin* – her long black hair like a veil over her face, skin kissed by fire, peeling and red, white robes criss-crossed with the stains of blood. She reached for me, a single arm outstretched, a call to my future, and as I stared at her, I knew it would not be the last time she would come to me.

* * *

I've seen my share of the dying, mostly those with lengthy illnesses. But some are startling in their suddenness, leaving the living in an especially uncomfortable awareness of their own mortality. I have gone to their hospital rooms to insert IVs, give medicine, and even sometimes, simply to hold hands.

On a usual night of rounds, I was told a new patient had been admitted to room 440. Described simply as 'an older woman'. Imagine my surprise at finding my mother as the occupant of that bed. A million ominous possibilities rushed through me all at once. "*Omma*, what are you doing here? What happened?"

"I am alright, Lusi," she said, her voice weary. "For the moment, at least."

"My god. When were you admitted?"

"Just a few hours ago." Her usually prim permed iron gray hair looked like a deflated balloon. I moved to her, noting the circles under her eyes, her pallor. Worried, I picked up her hand, checking capillary refill, despite the good oxygen readout.

"Are you going to tell me why, or do I have to look at your chart?" I raised an eyebrow at her.

"You should've read the chart before you walked in."

Pursing my lips, I scowled.

"Fine. I've been sick," she said.

"Not helpful. You do realize you're in a hospital?"

At this she lifted her chin with wounded pride. "It's this," she said finally, pointing to the back of her neck.

She let me check her, where, just as she said, a lump the size of a persimmon had formed, it was red and angry looking. "How long have you had this?"

"Four months."

"Jesus, *omma*, why didn't you tell me?"

I thought I saw tears, but she turned her face away before I could be sure and fixed her stare on the wall.

"*Omma*?" Waves of cold washed through me, a knowing that something was terribly wrong.

"Because," she hesitated, "you'd know soon enough."

* * *

My shift ended with the summer sunrise. As I made my way to the parking lot, I felt as if I swam not only from the hazy humidity, but also with the jumble of worries on my mind. Clearly, my mother would have to move into my little apartment, so I could care for her. While I took an accounting of that decision, I had a sensation of someone staring at me. That would be the second time I saw *her*. Across the lot, where the sun already nursed waves of heat on the newly tarred blacktop. The *gwishin* was much like she was before in my childhood memory. But this time, as she stretched out her arm, I had the distinct awareness that it would not be long before I would know the clutch of her despair.

* * *

Within six months of my mother moving in, *omma* went into her tiny bedroom, set out her scant valuables, and died.

Near the end, all she talked about were *gwishin*. Said she saw ghosts all around me, a busy circus of the dead. "Lusi," she'd say, "I see *halmoni* next to you" or "I see a friend from my young-time." It frightened me, of course. She'd shake her head, all the while rubbing her neck where the cancerous lesion continued to grow.

She told me that our family bones hold the memory of a horrible death. Something I did not understand then – I understand all too well now. This is the when the dreams started, of a place and time far away. For a long while, I was sure, those dreams were more real than me.

* * *

Korea 1895

Gyeongbokgung Palace does not supplicate itself. Doesn't seek to make excuses for its immense existence among the hovels. It's unrelenting white-washed walls are an announcement of the authority of the *Joseon* Dynasty. Built from the heart of many hardwood trees, the gates are painted red, with doors that are reinforced with iron, thick and heavy enough to have taken many horses to place them upon their great hinges. Any enemy wishing to breach the walls would be like eggs smashing against the immovable might of the Korean Empire.

But there are many ways to breach a kingdom, many ways to break it. Many ways to make those walls yield.

The soft rhythmic knocks at the gate are expected, four-two-break, four-one-one-stop. His stomach drops. The time is neigh. He still owns the power to refuse, at this eleventh hour. He doesn't have to be part of this and truth be told, he doesn't want a foreign power in Korea. But immediate needs always trump the needs of the future. That's what the queen has always been good at, planning and seeing into the future, seeing what was coming. She feared this very moment, tried to stop it. The merciless trajectory begun long before her ascent. Yet she will be the one who will pay for it.

He doesn't hate her. He doesn't love her either. Admire at times, yes. But it isn't enough to stop this and if not him, there will be another guard who will take the money of the assassins. Better it is him that gets the money. Better that he can use that money to keep his family safe.

The knock comes again, this time impatient, insistent. He breathes in, gathering himself, unbars the palace gate. It opens with a low groan.

His heart flutters, there are so many shrouded figures, mere shadows in the darkness. They writhe like demon spirits, ready to commit the most unspeakable of things. He knows in an instant the depth of his sin, his betrayal. A coin filled pouch drops into his hand and those shadows stream past soundlessly on their way to the queen's pavilion.

* * *

Lusi

"They scatter like baby spiders"

Omma did and said many strange things near the end. She knew, tried to tell me in her own way. But each time, the *gwishin* appeared, I found a way to disbelieve my own senses. To discredit my eyes and mind. Too tired, too stressed, too something.

Historical K-Dramas were *omma*'s favorite. The woman could watch them all day and talk as if she had become an expert historian.

"You do realize they are fiction?" I asked.

She shook her head. "Lusi, they are windows. Sometimes foggy but still give us a glimpse of something we wouldn't have seen if we didn't look out of them."

I probably smiled at this, she always had a special way of seeing the world. That night I brought dinner to her, trying to coax her to eat. When she turned to me, there were tears in her eyes.

"What's wrong? Was it a sad part in the show?"

"Very sad," she whispered. "Very sad end."

"Here," I urged, adjusting the food tray over her lap. "At least it was just a story, *omma*. Please try to eat something, ok?"

Her withered hand shot out suddenly, throwing a butter knife from the tray. It clattered to the floor, her face seemed a painted twisted thing, eyes wild. She suppressed a groan in her throat.

"*Omma*! Why'd you do that?" I said with aggravation as I immediately turned to retrieve the butter knife.

"Don't," she begged. "you shouldn't see. Not yet."

"What are you talking about?" Of course, I had ignored her request, dismissed it as ridiculous, couldn't hear the warning. I picked up the knife, it's glossy surface glinting in the lamp light. As I brought it up, I saw the blurry lines of my mother's gray head. Only for a moment, a flash, there was something else ... something perching upon her shoulders, a figure straddling her neck, legs dangling like a shawl. Snapping up, I looked at her with alarm and confusion.

My mother's face pinched with worry. "Once I am gone, she will be your burden too."

* * *

Korea 1895

The shadows disappear into the darkness, melting and reappearing beside *Okhoru* Pavilion. Women's screams shred the night, even the wind ceases, the dry leaves of the autumn trees go silent in shock. The pouch of coins grow heavier tucked against his chest, no doubt the metal has grown warm with his body heat, becoming part of him. Soon the coins would be transformed into goods and food, consumed and made part of him, just as the crime would be. The currency of evil and cruelty.

The assassins heave the women out, they stumble over the pavilion platform, trying desperately to run. Their robes and hair tumble about them in disarray. Hatred falls off the assassins in waves. He wants to tell them to stop, to yell that these ladies are attendants to the queen and should be treated with respect.

But he caused this, didn't he? The one who agreed to betray the queen. All for a pouch of coins.

* * *

Lusi

"A widower knows a widow's sorrow"

You ask me how I am able to go on living here in the same place where my mother died? I do it because this apartment doesn't matter. If I went somewhere else, the *gwishin* would follow. The only way I can manage is to try not to think too much about *her*.

I've fixed things so that there are no mirrors, nothing that can cause a reflection. You see how the windows are covered with paper. I eat with plastic forks and knives, cover and dismantle anything that would allow me to see *her*.

Only the television remains, but as you can also see, I keep it on at all times. Right on *omma*'s favorite channel. I've come to realize that the shows mesmerize the *gwishin*. I think they stir memories of her life long ago. But I cannot be sure. I only know that the pain and pressure lessens when these shows are played.

I have a small hope, that since I have no children of my own, the *gwishin* will cease to haunt our family. It is the one solace I have, the possibility that she may not be passed along to another. It is startling, when I began to research the cause of deaths in my family tree, there is a straight line like a dart, all dying from the same lesion.

* * *

Korea 1895

The queen is the last to be flung from the pavilion, down the flag stones and onto packed dirt. Her night robe and hair in the same disarray as her maids. Her face is different however, where they wear wild expressions of fear, she keeps from shouting out, raising her head in a final defiance.

"I am not afraid of you," she says to the shadow spirits. All the while, around her, the maids are beaten, falling like rain from ripe persimmon trees. She is iron. Her eyes fall upon the out of place gate guard and he can see that she ascertains his betrayal.

"Captain *Yi*," she mouths, an affirmation.

"You will know fear and when you do your screams will only end when your life ends," an assassin tells her, his voice thick with hatred. And then the shadow spirits descend upon her. It is not long until the queen does scream and those screams go long into the night.

* * *

Lusi

"Ignorance is medicine and knowledge is sickness"

Four weeks after my mother's death, I discovered she had placed out a single *mun* coin, an old currency used in *Joseon* Korea. I recognized it immediately from my dreams, knew it as the very last of the blood money, the one piece remained unspent.

At this point, I had been overwhelmed with the financial burdens of the remaining medical bills and finally, her burial. Of course, I dared not even attempt to pawn the coin or even venture to discover it's worth in today's antique market. Out of the necessity to pay these bills, I did as most Americans do in such times – overworked myself. I picked up as many additional shifts as I could almost right away. I had little time to grieve or to think about anything for that matter.

After weeks of bone-aching endless shifts, I allowed myself a single weekend off and truly the luxury of it was so appreciated at the time. The first thing I did was to take a long shower, so hot that I stepped out of the tub completely pink all over.

Wiping at the fogged mirror, my own haggard face peered back. I looked puffy, as if I'd been eating too much salt. Honestly, thoughts of the coin plagued me, I thought perhaps I should bury it or leave in an alms bucket at some church. As if these things could placate the cloud that pressed toward me.

Suddenly, the shower curtain's blurry form swayed as if clutched and released. Alarmed, I twirled. Was it my eyes? Was it moving again? My mind hammered sirens of urgency.

With one motion, I turned and swiped open the curtain with enough force that I almost ripped the thing off its rings. But nothing was there, only water beads on the tiles.

I remember drawing a long shaky breath. Already telling myself those lies again … overactive imagination, overworked, over tired.

Back to the mirror, my hand pushed again at the steam, leaving behind a streak of a figure in the tub. Black hair falling in long tangles, charred flesh peeling to reveal red meat beneath, her white *hanbok* a tattered and scorched thing. Unable to move, an awful knowing crawled from the pit of my stomach upwards, stabbing like a regurgitated barb. My chest heaved, lungs desperately sucking at the air.

She lifted her head, the hair parting, seared lids left her eyes more whites than iris, tears of blood trickled down dead cheeks. Her mouth opened so wide I cannot perceive a jaw. Blood gushed out, an ocean of red joining the tears. Then all I could think was finally, she was here for me.

Like the other times I had seen the *gwishin*, she lifted an arm, reaching out for me. At last my brain and body finally synchronized and I made a panicked move to escape. A foot slipped across a puddle of condensation. I stumbled and flailed like a fish out of water.

Yet, somehow I was able to get myself together and back on to my feet. But in the mirror, I saw that she was already upon me. A single hand clutched at my shoulder, then the other, blood fell into my hair like a baptism. I moaned but could not move. Rough charred fingers clawed, pressure building on my shoulders. I realized she was climbing me like a tree. One charred leg dangled over a shoulder, I began to shake, the world shimmered in my vision like a mirage. Then her other leg was there too over my other shoulder. I forced myself to raise my eyes, to look at what I already knew would be there.

Her unblinking face loomed over my head, her hair slapping my cheeks as she slowly wrapped her peeling arms around me in a loving embrace.

* * *

Korea 1895

The assassins have done what they came to do. As they pour gasoline over the mutilated bodies of the queen and her maids, a chill passes over Captain Yi. The queen saw him, knew him. The coins against his chest go cold and he begins to shake. As the flames lick forward and burst into a roar, the Captain feels the curse. Yet at that moment, all he can think is how odd it is – that he can neither smell gasoline or even burning flesh.

He can only smell the scent of the lotus flowers in full bloom.

* * *

Lusi

"It is dark under the lamp"

Before you left in a hurry, unease creasing your face like slices of a knife, I asked you a simple question and gave you a simple warning.

Do you see her? She's grinning at you with that terrible mouth of blood. She sees you and maybe one day, you too will see her, or your very own *gwishin*. Go check your family stories and pray that when you do, you find no great and horrible misdeeds committed by *your* ancestors.

I continue to sit in the half-broken recliner that my mother favored. The tumor on my neck has broken open into a weeping sore. The familiar creak and chime of a broken spring reminds me of her, in fact the chair still smells like her. I feel the fabric arms and close my eyes. For a moment, I pretend to be part of one of her K-Dramas. I am the one sitting on a throne. Officials look to me, asking for my permission, my ideas. I hold my head high and straight listening to their supplication.

Little Bone Collector

Monte Lin

IN THE CHINA HOLD, Li-hao can't sleep, for the voices beg him for their own rest. It could be the endless rocking of the ship or the stale air of the hold. It could be the endless protestations of the wood as the wind and water slams and squeezes the hull. It could be the moans and groans from the men of Tang in the hold, similarly unable to sleep or feverish or fearful the sickness will spread like an untended fire.

Li-hao wishes for the steady, marshy grounds of his home, the warm breeze of Kwangchow, or the food in the carts and stalls: fish fresh or pickled, duck and chicken, pork, pickled radish, bao. He hopes for a safe journey across the ocean. He wishes he had bought a more expensive ticket, but it would have meant having to wait for a steamship, and he didn't have the nerve to wait. An irony perhaps; if he had taken the steamship, he would have crossed the ocean faster.

Li-hao had also not paid for access to the deck, unlike the British and American passengers, to save money. The men of Tang whisper of banquets, dish upon dish upon long tables stretching from bow to stern. Those passengers dance nightly in flowing dresses, adorned in jewels and gold, glinting from the flame and wax.

"There isn't enough room up there for banquets," Li-hao says. "And why would they take gold back to the land of gold?"

"That's what the rich do. Gold drops from their fingertips."

Gold, avarice, is base and vulgar, Li-hao's father had once said, while clutching an ever-empty purse. *Gold is the color and metal of emperors. Money shouldn't be the concern of the educated.* But then, is Li-bak, his brother, not wandering the wastes of Giu Gimsan for money? Is Li-hao not on this ship, carrying this empty bone box, on the way to Giu Gimsan because of money, the money he left wrapped in paper for his mother, right now?

Gold, the men of Tang whisper. *Gold.*

This is why you all die in Giu Gimsan, Li-hao thinks when he sits up and slides out of his hammock. But then, home has seen so much death too. Out of nervous habit, he checks to make sure the bone box remains tied up in his sack by the hammock. Normally, a bone box gets built overseas in Giu Gimsan or Bilu or Lhin Gimsan, storing the bones of the lost for shipment back home. This family, however, wanted to make sure their lost would have a comfortable and homemade trip, carving the name on the top and lacquering the wood. Li-hao didn't have the heart to tell them the box was too small, not even large enough to fit a skull.

The soft breathing of sleepers (with the occasional snort or snore) melds with the soft creaking of this ship. Perhaps they had all been swallowed by a beast during the night that only sounds like a ship. Best check to make sure.

On bare feet, Li-hao carefully steps past the hammocks toward the stairs up onto the upper decks. He shouldn't go there. He hasn't paid the money for the right, but the sweet salt air and the bright blue sky or deep black with stars would be a reminder that they were alive and not swallowed.

"Ah Toi," a voice whispers.

Li-hao freezes. This voice does not come from half-remembered dreams but from a hammock nearby.

"Where are you going, Ah Toi?" the boy asks. The boy, as Li-hao likes to think of him, despite being a few years older, has only basic knowledge, a *peasant's* education.

"Stop calling me that."

"You walk like you're rich."

This can't be true. He steps carefully and quietly like a mouse. Being quiet and unseen has always been his strength. "Go back to sleep."

"Go back to your palace."

The educated do not fight, his father had said, years after picking up his spear to follow men to war. So Li-hao unclenches his fist and buries the wound deep. "I do not live in a palace."

"You talk like an emperor, though," the boy, Kiang-san, says, sliding out of the hammock, his own feet landing heavy on the wood. Contempt flows both ways; the flame of ire from Kiang-san, strong, steady, relentless, and flickering against a stream of pity from Li-hao, a cool exhalation in a sneer, a steady hiss as he inhales.

"Your father fought for the emperor, didn't he?" Kiang-san says. "How many uncles of mine did yours kill?"

Li-hao bites his tongue. *His father killed no one*! But he did follow imperial soldiers against the rebels. His spear may have even tasted blood. Instead, Li-hao speaks an intact truth though not the full truth. "He found men, brought their bones back to their families. My brother does the same in Giu Gimsan. And I am doing the same as he."

"A bone gatherer? You?"

"My father brought starving bones back to their families. He taught me and my brother." This, Li-hao believes, despite veiling the truth, and his voice must have carried that faith, since Kiang-san stops in his tracks.

"How do you find the bones?"

"The dead speak. You have to listen in perfect silence. They whisper so softly, you could mistake them for the wind."

At that moment, the ship creaks, a groan begging for relief. Kiang-san inhales, water winning out over fire, becoming light and carefree. Well, not carefree. The pall continues to weigh the air.

"We should sleep," Li-hao says, his limbs and heart heavy. His own fire spent. "Maybe tomorrow the geilau will allow us to fish."

Kiang-san nods and grunts in agreement. He slips into his hammock and slips into dreams just as easily. Li-hao lies back in his own, but the memories refuse to allow him his own thoughts.

* * *

The morning comes with more muttering voices, but corporeal ones from the hold. In the light, Li-hao sees the cluster of men around the communal bucket, where each passenger gives a portion of their daily share of water for bathing. Boys no younger than Li-hao himself to men almost already grandfathers all sit equal in status in the eyes of the sailors, but the men of Tang have already established a hierarchy of Uncles, then elders, then men, then children.

The muttering circles like carrion birds onto a singular topic: bone gathering.

"He's so young."

"His youth means he's gifted."

"His family are all bone collectors."

"Perhaps he has heard them in the night."

Those words leave pinpricks on Li-hao's skin. But he goes about his own routine, bathing and washing his hair, and carefully combing and tying it into the queue.

"Ah Toi."

Kiang-san squats onto his heels to keep him level with Li-hao, who still kneels over the wash bucket. "Ah Toi, the Uncles have something to ask from you."

His reverent tone, despite the sneering nickname, also leaves pinpricks on Li-hao's skin. He nods as austerely as he can muster, carefully puts on his jacket and shoes and walks over to the cluster of Uncles.

Everyone on this boat is a Big Brother, Uncle, Nephew, Little Brother, a few Grandpas. The council of Uncles speaks with the sailors above, gathers consensus below, and organizes the water and food rationing. Li-hao was too nephew to join in the council.

"Ah Feng. Ah Tou. Ah Bo," Li-hao says. "Kiang-san said you needed me?"

They gesture for him to sit next to them and offer breakfast: rice porridge stewed with some old, dried pork for flavor, some pickled vegetables, and tea. One brings out his pipe to pack tobacco. Li-hao hides his grimace, masking with disinterested politeness. It reminds him of one of his older brothers, smoking incessantly in Kwangchow, shrouded by vapors, his spirit also as ephemeral.

"Nephew said you can speak to bones."

"Uh…" Li-hao takes a drink from his teacup to clear his mind and throat. "My father found the lost during the war. My brother searches for the lost in Giu Gimsan. I plan on joining him."

The Uncles all chatter. "So only in training."

"Following in his family's footsteps."

"Maybe inexperienced, but must have talent. Look at his face."

More stories, tales, no more true than the books his father had him study. Just as useless too. The world was changing. Rumors say the imperial court is ending, taking the country down with them, leaving nothing but stories. What story did Li-hao belong to?

Ah Feng shushes the rest of the Uncles. "Can you stop the voices, little bone collector?"

Li-hao's mouth almost drops open and he barely avoids spitting out, "You can hear them?!"

The Uncles all grunt in grim unison. Ah Tou takes a puff of his pipe, smoke swirling around him, a chimney fire.

Ah Bo coughs. "You stink. And your pipe too."

Ah Tou only grunts, but takes a deeper breath and exhales a thicker cloud of smoke in Ah Bo's direction. Ah Feng shakes his head. "We can feel something is wrong. We have heard of other ships, worse ones, those that don't go to Giu Gimsan. Places where there is no gold."

"Ships of death," Ah Bo says, waving away the smoke. "They go to Bilu."

"They dig for shit! Literal shit!" Ah Tou interrupts. "And then they die in the shit!"

Ah Feng waves away the Uncle's words with a pained expression on his face. "That's not the point! We're the ones being haunted. The men of Tang have died on these ships, to Bilu, to Giu Gimsan, to elsewhere, and they are thrown overboard instead of taken home."

"They are forgotten and lost," Li-hao finally realizes. "They have no family to take care of them."

"Can you help them, little bone collector?"

"But if they are in the bottom of the ocean, there are no bones to collect."

"Yes, that's what we're afraid of…"

Ah Bo says, "There must be something you can do. Your father must have taught you something."

Li-hao tries to express thoughtfulness in his expression to hide his lack of knowledge. He was too young at the time. His father had taken only Li-bak out to hunt for the lost. By the time Li-hao was old enough, his father had only the energy for stories, and Li-bak sought fortunes elsewhere, across the ocean.

Thus his father had always been old to Li-hao. Father sat in his chair, hands on his knees staring off not into the distance where the war was, but to the ground, to the dust underneath his feet, to home. Sometimes he'd see his children or his wife and his hands would reach out, eyes searching. Usually, that person would take his hand and sit with him for a while. Once in a while, however, no one would, and his father's hand would drift back down onto his lap like a flower petal and he reverted to his stony visage.

Li-bak once mentioned that their father had been vibrant, a warrior, glancing at the broken spear in the corner of the plaza. "The blade is still intact," Li-bak said, "it just needs a new shaft to make it whole again." Even Li-hao understood this metaphor, and why his brother took the spear blade with him to Giu Gimsan.

"My father once couldn't find the bones," Li-hao recalls. "He found the battlefield, but other than a broken spear or sword, a bit of cloth, no remains. So he built a spirit box and invited the lost to rest in it. The man's family buried the box in the family plot."

The Uncles nod. "Can you do this?"

"I … I never learned how to use a spirit box." This truth, Li-hao hopes, should cover the previous lie. The Uncles already think of him as an apprentice, not yet a master.

Kiang-san interjects, "You already have a box! I saw it with your stuff."

"No! That one is for someone else. His family carved it themselves. It's for the wrong person."

"Can't you study it? Figure out how it works? See if you can make a new one?" Ah Feng leans forward. "You have to try, little bone collector. An old man like me needs his sleep, you see."

Li-hao nods out of habit, satisfying the Uncles.

* * *

Li-hao doesn't know how to be a bone collector. He is a liar, of a sort, but definitely a coward with no nerve. He had listened to his father's stories, asked his brother questions, even written letters that have not been answered. He has stories of being a bone collector but not the knowledge. He doesn't even know how to prepare bones for the bone box. He wants to know, but for whatever reason, he has not been taught. Instead, his purpose was to become a scholar for a dynasty in decay.

The yearning to be taught drove him to lie. Being called 'little bone collector', he feels a connection to his family. Before he was merely a shadow, a shadow of his older brother overseas, and a shadow of a living shadow, his father wan and frail in person, vibrantly alive only in stories. To be living this lie, his family feels solid and real.

He sits in an isolated spot (no such thing) in the hold, legs crossed and hands pressed together, knees bumping into things and other people. He had seen monks sit like this once when they visited a village after the wars. He closes his eyes and waits.

The voices don't come, not dead ones. He can hear whispers, prayers to Tin How for a safe journey across the sea, prayers to loved ones left behind, and whispers about Li-hao and if he can or can't silence the voices.

Li-hao sleeps. He didn't intend to, but sitting still, the ship rocking back and forth, and the absolute boredom of being in the hold lures him to the easy escape of dreams. He sees his brother hold the hand of Tin How, dressed in her usual regal finery. In his other, Li-bak holds the spearhead, the broken shaft cut and dressed in leather wrapping to form a makeshift sword. They step off the boat onto the dock of a busy city that looks very much like Kwangchow except all in shining gold. A crowd of people all come to greet them, and Li-hao quickly realizes they are the dead of Giu Gimsan, all of the dead, thousands all crushed by gold, drowned by gold, smothered by gold. The dead slowly climb the gangplank up into the ship to be carried back home.

"Ah Toi."

The voice doesn't wake him. The rough shaking does, enough so for his head to smack against the hull.

"Ahh…" Li-hao rubs the back of his head, looking at Kiang-san looking back at him.

"You fell asleep."

While he dreamt of the Goddess of the Sea and his brother, everyone else dreamt of death and doom, forever haunting the hills of Giu Gimsan, forever carrying massive blocks of gold on their backs. Their feet bloodied and worn down to the bones, their backs bent at right angles, their skin desiccated and papery.

Li-hao looks at Kiang-san's feet, the soles split and bleeding. He notices the boy's face so sunken and thin, he can see his skull.

"Please help us."

* * *

"Tell me about the men who were lost in the ocean," Li-hao says to the Uncles.

He remembered something his brother told him about bone collecting. Li-bak and their father had to learn about the men they were looking for: their families, their history, their temperament. By knowing who they were, you could retrace their steps.

Once, they had been out for half a month longer than they should have. They found the battlefield the lost had supposedly died in, but couldn't find the bones. Their father decided to push on to a village, in order to rest someplace dry and find something to eat. There they discovered the lost was not dead but a deserter, had ran away to this village. They followed the trail of cowardice, the desperation to not be found, the foolishness as he left civilization to go deeper into the woods.

They found his bones in a den of a wild animal.

The Uncles look about, puzzled. Ah Feng says, "We don't know. They were thrown overboard on other ships."

Ah Tou smokes. "We all know someone who is missing. They might be at Giu Gimsan, alive and rich, bellies full and ready to come home. Or they might be dead, buried in alien soil, nothing but their bones. They might be in the ocean, lost forever."

Ah Bo grabs Ah Tou's pipe. "Shut up! That is not helping!"

Ah Feng lets the two Uncles argue, but turns to Li-hao. "How can we remember the lost if we don't even know who they are?"

The days stretch long. The Uncles carefully ration out the food and water, but the voices weigh heavy on everyone's heads. They become languid, sleeping for hours, food not filling, water not slaking. Locked in the hold, each day is exactly the same as the next. Talk of the hold being a wooden tomb spreads across all of the men of Tang. The Uncles say they have heard this happen on these long trips. Being treated like cargo turns a man into cargo.

Li-hao sifts through his memory, of his father's stories, of his brother's stories, hoping for a clue. The malaise affects him too; he finds himself without appetite and unaware of his dry, slightly swollen tongue. The Uncles, though affected, bring a cup of tea to him and nudge him to drink.

In truth, he feels he has failed them. At first, his chest welled with pride to be called a 'little bone collector', a worthy successor of his father's profession. Bone collectors aren't exactly given due respect. They do deal with the dead and dig in the dirt. They are odd interveners in other family affairs, but without them, families would remain unwhole.

The lack of food makes him dizzy, and he finds himself talking to no one, speaking his father's and brother's stories out loud. Sometimes an Uncle listens, sometimes it's Kiang-san. There was the story of a battlefield littered with bones. How the crows and animals had dug around for human food, scattering the bodies about, as if making a puzzle.

Li-hao prays. He claps his hands together once and realizes a truth:

His father never wanted to become a bone collector. Family is supposed to take care of the bones, not a stranger. Bone collectors dig in the dirt, like farmers, and his father had sworn never to go back to that life. "Bone collectors are haunted by the dead they find," Li-hao's mother had said. "There must be some other way to make money."

The imperial officials had paid his father a stipend only to accompany their soldiers, to be a guide in the province and to identity which villages were rebels and which were loyal. He had never fought. And they had never intended to promote him to an official position, much less a magistrate. Was he naive to believe this, or desperate?

"Bone collectors unite families," Li-hao's father had reasoned, but the real reason was money, and he already had a reputation of finding the lost.

Li-hao realizes that Kiang-san is kneeling next to him, also praying. They clap their hands together a second time:

Li-hao tells the story of him arguing with his mother, trying to explain how him going to Giu Gimsan with the box, delivering it to Li-bak, would save money instead of his brother having to travel all the way back home first. This was not an argument he won; he was not too old to receive a switch to the butt.

Sneaking away, he saw his father, leaning against the doorway, arms shaking, legs shaking from standing too long, in his nightgown. Li-hao should have gone back inside to help him back into bed. Instead he fled, knowing his own father was too frail to stop him. Now in this haunted hold, Li-hao wonders if he has done the wrong thing. He should have stayed home to help his family, even if it was only to watch over his brothers and sisters while his mother did work.

He convinced himself that he was running away to help. His middle brother was supposed to find work in Kwangchow, but fell to the city's vices. It was up to Li-hao to be the man of the house, but really, he wanted to go and prove himself, to show he could brave the uncivilized lands of Giu Gimsan.

Li-hao doesn't realize that he almost fell over, propped up only by Kiang-san. He claps his hands together the last time:

He tells the story of his brother deciding to go out on his own. Their father's injury had become too painful even to leave the bed. Li-hao remembers feeling a terrible dread that something had changed and he would never see his brother again. This was not true, and within the month, his brother had returned, a little taller, it seemed, a little more confident, ready to go to Giu Gimsan, the spear point tied to his hip. The Six Companies in Giu Gimsan were willing to pay well for an expert to come and find the lost workers. Easy work, but long work. By the time he'd come back, Li-hao would be a man, maybe even married.

Li-hao's eyes open in shock. "I heard a name!"

The Uncles and several others, those who hadn't completely succumbed to the malaise, gather around him. Kiang-san holds on to the little bone collector brother.

"They heard me!" It wasn't a whisper Li-hao heard, more of a certainty.

Ah Feng says, "What do we do, little bone collector?"

"They *want* to stay in a spirit box and come home." Li-hao looks at the empty bone box. "It doesn't matter what it is. As long as they can be carried home."

The men of Tang gather small things: a cracked bowl, a broken teacup, and small box that once held some sweet pickled plums, a cardboard packet of tobacco.

"Is that all you have?"

"We didn't bring much."

"That isn't enough. There are too many names."

Li-hao's mind races. How can he choose which to save and which to leave in the bottom of the ocean? They need more containers. Perhaps they could sacrifice all of their dishware? Eat out of their hands?

His gaze goes to the floor, the walls, and the ceiling. "The ship can be the spirit box!"

Kiang-san's eyes bug out. "But they'll haunt here!"

"At least until someone can take them home."

The Uncles grunt gravely, but in agreement. At least here, in the ship, the lost can be sated, appeased, fed.

Li-hao grabs an errant rusty nail and makes a fist with it, the point through his fingers. He presses his ear to the hull and the hold goes silent. Another boy opens his mouth to speak and his father pinches his nose. They all feel the boat rock back and forth and the wood groans.

"Lam Siu-fu," Li-hao whispers. He carefully scratches the name on the wooden hull of the ship, a faint, ghostly outline. He slides down to the next blank spot and presses his ear against the wood.

"Leng Yot."

More names trace a web of humanity tenuous and invisible, but present and deeper than the scratches in the wood. The nameless voices now have wooden flesh, carved voices, written history. Several dozen names on a dozen ribs of the ship, as if swallowed by a wooden whale.

"This is good, Little Bone Collector," Ah Feng says, his heavy, calloused hand on Li-hao's shoulder. "Your father would be proud."

Li-hao beams, the weight on his shoulder familiar, warm, enveloping. The feeling melts away as fast as it came. Too early for congratulations.

With the rusty iron nail, Li-hao begins his work deepening the names. It might take him the rest of the journey to carve them all out, but at least he and the others can sleep well for the first time since leaving home.

The Fortune of Sparrows

Usman T. Malik

THE COURTYARD of the orphanage was haunted by birds.

Songbirds, sparrows, gray hornbills, yellow-footed green pigeons, starlings, crows – every species ever glimpsed in Lahore. Twice or thrice a week they came in doles and murders and murmurations, swooping down and carpeting the roof and the walls. To this day I've not figured out where they came from in such large numbers or why they gravitated to the orphanage at peculiar intervals. Unsatisfactory theories involving magnetism and satisfactory gossip about corpses buried beneath the old housing were flung about, but no one could explain why on arrival these birds were so quiet – why they would neither cheep nor caw; nor a warbler warble. Hushed, they clung to the courtyard trees, congregated on high wires running parallel to the enclosure walls from one electric pylon to another. It was a sight that gave many a twilight visitor pause when they first glimpsed these silent sentinels. At least until the muezzin called the maghrib prayer and, suddenly, the courtyard came alive with the sound of bird music, the notes of the melodies in harmony with bird colors. The warbler, the cuckoo, the bulbul, the mynah – how they would sing!

For a long time now I have been afraid of birds.

But, then, living in the orphanage with my sisters, playing Ice Water when it drizzled, listening to the gurgle of water sluicing off rain gutters into the courtyard's red earth, I was not. I liked them. All us girls did. We picked their feathers off the ground and made garlands out of them. We looked for bird nests in the courtyard trees and giggled when Mano stalked them, his mangled tail bristling, and, from hidden corners, sprang at the crows, parrots, and pigeons, making the creatures explode skyward in a flurry of black, blue, and green. The color specks circled the enclosure until night crept up from the horizon and took the birds with it.

Mano the wedding cat belonged to Bibi Soraiya who managed the orphanage's affairs. Mano was old and two-colored. Neha used to say that was why prescience boiled in his blood, that he was a creature fleshed from opposites and could glimpse things we could not. Angels, jinns, and the ghosts of martyrs walk among us and every one knows spirits are fond of cats. Who knew what they whispered in his ear when they floated past him or brushed his fur?

And when Mano settled down by the orphanage gate, licking his fur and purring, we knew the Rishtay Wali Aunty was to come for us that day or night.

The wedding cat was never wrong about the matchmaker's arrival.

My sisters and I were fond of Mano – we fed him from our plate – but sometimes, when the wedding cat's eyes gleamed in the darkness and he slid across the courtyard, back arched, the sounds from his throat indistinguishable from the rumble of a motor engine outside the orphanage door or the passage of something large and ponderous high above the clouds, we weren't so fond of him.

Sometimes we wished Mano would run away and not come back.

* * *

The orphanage was a house of many doors.

A long time ago during the British Raj, we were told, it was a hospital with two wings that flanked the courtyard. The east wing was the smaller building with limited rooms for dying or contagious patients, as if they were the same. It had a long corridor that ran parallel to the courtyard and formed a semicircle connecting it with the west wing, where the rest of the patients were housed.

These rooms were ours now and we loved playing in them. Most of us had mirrors above the washbasin and we pretended that people from the past still stayed within our rooms, that the change of morning and afternoon light in the mirrors meant they were stirring and moving about and such cohabitation made us all a big family. The lives of our family spanned centuries.

I remember one afternoon when we were playing Ice Water. Barefoot, we rushed at the fleeing team, trying to touch theirs arms or torsos, to pretend-petrify them into captivity. The escapees would circle back and try to tap the captives 'awake'. Half of my sisters were already statues frozen by the chasing team, but Neha cheated by hiding, which wasn't allowed.

It had rained the night before. The ground was marked with footprints. The trees whispered in the courtyard and the mirrors in our rooms rippled when we ran past the open doors, and I thought I heard Neha giggle and dive into one of the rooms at the end of the east corridor. I sprinted across the courtyard, shouting her name. She giggled again and waved a spindly arm from the doorway. I reached the corridor and went in after her.

No one was in the room. A large wet crow with a broken wing perched on the edge of the skylight. It watched me with red beady eyes and shook raindrops off its feathers.

I whirled, taking in each corner. I remember feeling a sense of loss. Daylight was waning, and when I turned again it wasn't the room I'd entered. Instead of the sparse wooden charpoy there was a finely made bed with pillows and brocaded quilts, a sandalwood footstool placed at its end. A body-length mirror gleamed beside the bed. The walls were hung with canted paintings whose beauty, strangely, could not be admired: the moment I leaned in for a closer look, the pictures blurred.

I turned to look at the mirror. It was a fabulous piece of workmanship, its edges carved in mahogany with sparrows in flight. The girl in the mirror looked back at me with wide, black eyes. She couldn't have been more than my age. Her eyelids were swollen, her lips red, shaped like leaves felled by autumn rain. A bruise flowered from the root of her left ear, all the way up her scalp. She looked neither happy nor unhappy. A passing ghost, I thought, gone forever the moment I departed from this strange new room.

As I watched, the girl in the mirror leaned back, pointed at me, and began to laugh. The sound filled the room, a cacophony of maddened birdsong. She laughed and laughed and the air heated with her laughter and the skylight darkened with night. A whoosh of blistering air, my nostrils filling up with a bitter smell like charred flesh or feathers, and the girl in the mirror was smoking. Coils of gray-black rose from her hair like braids. Smoke ringed her eyes, now orange-blue. She flapped her skinny, crinkling arms, and I cried out and turned, knocking over the footstool, and fled from the room.

Later, after I was calmed by Sangeeta Apa and Bibi Soraiya with hot tea and a thin slice of buttered bread, I told them about the room and its fiery inhabitant. Sangeeta Apa and Bibi glanced at each other.

"Was there a stove in the room?" Bibi Soraiya asked.

"I didn't see one," I said.

She nodded. "Go to your room, *bachey*. Shut the door and get some sleep. I'll tell your sisters not to bother you."

Neha came to my bed that night. We were roommates, three of us, but our third was sick and they'd put her up in the east wing. "What happened?" Neha asked, draping an arm across my body.

I told her. When I got to the part about following her into the room, her eyes widened, like the girl-in-the-mirror's had and she began to breathe irregularly – an exacerbation of her asthma. We had to rush her to Mayo Hospital where the doctors made her spend that night and the night after.

To this day she insists that girl with the spindly arm wasn't her. Neha was hiding atop one of the courtyard trees and showed me fresh scratches from the branches on her left arm. I believed her. I have always believed her.

That was the first time I saw a ghost in the orphanage. There were two more instances.

Both on the night before Sangeeta Apa's wedding dinner.

* * *

In story hour on a Friday, Sangeeta Apa told us the tale of the mythical bird Huma. Persian legend holds, she said, that the Huma never rests. It circles ceaselessly high above the earth forever, invisible to prisoners of earthly time; impervious.

Furthermore, they say (said Sangeeta Apa):

It eats bones. The female lays her eggs in the air. As the egg drops, the hatchling squirms out and escapes before the shell hits the earth. It is a bridge between the heavens and earth. It's a bird of fortune. The shadow of the Huma falling on a man bequeaths royalty on his person. The Huma once declined to travel to the far ends of the earth, for wherever its shadow fell the masses would become kings and the Huma is very particular. Like the phoenix, it is old and deathless. In an alternate form, it has seen the destruction of the world three times over

and

it cannot be taken alive. Whosoever captures it will die in forty days.

It is a story I have thought about many times since.

* * *

We were all in love with the bird man. Who wouldn't be?

Every evening he came cycling down Multan Road, trilling the bell on his bicycle which was laden with bird cages and wicker baskets. The baskets brimmed with candles, lice combs, fans, attar bottles, incense, and other household items. He was a short, thin man, and very clumsy – I can't tell you how many times we helped him pick up dropped merchandise, cages, even his turban. The turban was large and sequined with a starched turra at the top. Many times we saw him in clothes with holes in them – once he even circled the neighborhood bare-foot – but we never saw that turra unstarched, even if his awkwardness meant we frequently glimpsed his long beautiful well-oiled hair, which would have suited our own heads so well, we thought.

The bird man would stop under a peepal tree near the entrance of the orphanage. Grinning, he'd get off the bicycle and spread a wool shawl on the ground. He'd set his cages down and begin twittering. He could whistle, warble, chirrup, cheep and caw as well as any bird he carried, startling new customers and delighting old.

He followed this musical prologue with a show displaying his birds' impeccable training in divination.

The bird man sold all manner of bird: parrots, pigeons, bank mynahs, Australian lovebirds (his hottest item), but there were two he wouldn't part with – a pair of green rose-necked parakeets. These parakeets had mastered the art of soothsaying. They fluttered impatiently in a painted blue wooden cage, while the bird man fanned out a stack of white envelopes on the shawl. The envelopes had gilded borders, and soaring birds, dulled by time and use, were embossed in the corners.

Curious customers, many of them prematurely aged women, would come up and look. Shy at first, they would slowly gather courage, put out their hands for examination, and pose their questions:

Will I ever get married? Will my firstborn be a boy? Will that please my husband? My mother-in-law wants more dowry and loathes me. What should I do?

and

Should I stay away from the gas stove in the kitchen?

We girls would gather around the bird man as he frowned and took their hands. His fingernails were long and manicured, and softly they traced the lines on the women's palms. He had a comforting smell about him, like earth, or bird, or the way my hands smelled after rolling dough peras on the nights it was my turn to bake roti. He spoke gently to the women, whispering, calming their nerves.

Only then would he lift the door of the blue cage, letting one of the parakeets hop out.

The bird would pace back and forth across the envelopes. It nipped and pecked at them, its small head darting, until finally it gripped an envelope's edge. It would lift it in its beak and prop it against its emerald body. The bird man would take the envelope, extract the piece of paper inside, pop a tablet of sweet choori into the parakeet's beak, and read the prophecy to the wide-eyed customer.

He was never wrong, the women said. So many before him were charlatans, they said. Their eyes glowed when they said it and the bird man's admirers grew and grew.

My sisters and I were his admirers as well. Sangeeta Apa would watch him from the entrance, the end of her cotton dopatta caught between her teeth. He would laugh with us and tell us our fortunes for free. Sometimes he teased Apa, "Whoever you marry will become a king among men." Often he would give us gifts: bird-shaped candles he'd designed, vials of cheap attar, bottles of scented rubbing oil. He was a good man, we thought. Wise and ageless.

Sometimes after the Rishtay Wali Aunty had been by, we would ask him to tell us the would-be bride's future. Always he refused.

"Palm lines and the paths of heavenly bodies are malleable. Hard work, prayer, love – they can reshape them," he would say. "Take care of your families and all will be well."

We wanted to believe him and sometimes we did, but, even at that age, we knew better. The orphanage was our father and mother. Beyond its walls, who knew?

* * *

The walls of the orphanage were dun-colored.

I remember this even if I have forgotten other things – the face of the old pastor who came tottering down the courtyard on Sundays; the smell of trees that lined the courtyard (which trees? I remember orange and red mulberry, but which one at the courtyard's end by Sangeeta Apa's room that cast a long, shocked shadow); the color of the bird man's turban the sequins of which flared red as he pedaled his bicycle down Multan road at dusk. Strange how we drown in recollection at the least propitious of times but cannot pluck memories from the past's branches when we need them.

Sangeeta Apa.

No end or beginning to some tales, but middles are always there. She was the middle of all our stories, the center sitting still and somber when everyone around her rode, quickly or sluggishly, the tide of time in the orphanage. Days and weeks and months and years – the Rishtay Wali Aunty's arrival marked them and whittled them away. Thirty-six girls of all ages. So many marriages and migrations. So many of my sisters came and went, yet Sangeeta Apa remained, braiding our hair, peeling mangoes, husking peas and walnuts, dyeing Bibi Soraiya's hair with henna (the smell of that henna, rich and secret, like a sunset glimpsed from a crevice under the canal bridges); and as we giggled and ran around the courtyard, singing songs

We are a flock of sparrows, Father
One day we will fly away

Sangeeta Apa would shake her head and laugh, the sound ringing out loud and shrill and mysterious, until its final notes couldn't be told from the twilight bird song.

It was a very long time before the Rishtay Wali Aunty came for her. By then Apa was in her forties, half her head silvered with age.

I remember the day well because Mano was sick, he had been puking all morning. Red and black feathers glistened in the wedding cat's vomit. Bibi Soraiya fretted over him and fetched him digestive sherbet from the animal doctor in the alley three streets down, but Mano wouldn't touch it. Nor would he eat anything else. He just crawled across the courtyard and lay next to the entrance, waiting.

The Rishtay Wali Aunty arrived in a green-backed rickshaw. We were in class in the north corridor and from the window I saw her dismount. A squat woman with one droopy eye and features hardened by time and sun, she waddled to the entrance and rang the bell. Bibi Soraiya appeared and opened the door. Together, they stepped over Mano, crossed the courtyard, and disappeared behind the thick line of trees in the direction of Bibi's quarters.

A good match had been found for Sangeeta Apa, we would discover.

"The boy is fifty-one and very pious," Bibi Soraiya told us the next day when we assembled in the courtyard to sing the national anthem. "He lives in Gujranwala and owns a dairy shop. Your Apa is really lucky. His dowry demands are so reasonable."

We whooped and cheered and congratulated Apa. She stood there, still as a lake, her gaze on the wedding cat, who was feeling better and kept walking between her legs, mewling. The hem of Apa's dopatta crept into her mouth and the din we made startled a host of sparrows that escaped, cheeping, into the sky.

That night I saw my second and third ghosts.

I was returning from the cigarette stall – Bibi Soraiya had a fondness for hookah and gave me a bar of Jubilee chocolate each time I fetched her tobacco. A clear night with a blue moon full as a houri's lips shining above the orphanage, and Mano was by the entrance, his tail twitching. I bent to scratch his chin. He slipped away, turned, and watched me, eyes glinting like coins in the dark beneath the trees.

"You hungry? Want some milk, Mano-billi?" I said, patting my pocket to make sure the roll of tobacco hadn't fallen out.

The wedding cat purred. He arched his back, twisted, and started for the east corridor. He circled a (maple?) trunk, stopped, looked back at me.

"What is it? Not feeling better?"

Mano gazed at me. Night dilated around us. The cat shivered and hissed, his tail puffing up, and lunged toward the trees. I would have left him to whatever mischief he was up to and gone my way but Mano had been acting odd all day. I called, then dashed after him.

He was a blur in the blackness and sometimes he was a sound. I followed him to the edge of the east corridor where he waited, ears pinned back, pawing the ground before one of the rooms. He saw me and blinked.

The wedding cat went inside the room.

I glanced down the unlit corridor. Nothing moved through its length. No sounds. Not one rectangle of light stretching from open doorways, which seemed more numerous and narrower than I had ever seen.

I looked at the room Mano had entered. A peculiar effect of light and dark turned the framework of its door pale blue, as if a thin coating of paint had been applied to the wood. The doorway was wedged between Sangeeta Apa's room and another girl's whose name escapes me. Inside, silver light flickered. Shadows moved beyond a curtain of mist or smoke.

I mothed to the strange light and entered the room.

* * *

By this time I had been at the orphanage for a number of years and watched half a dozen of my sisters get married. Their ages ranged from thirteen to thirty. Out of the six, we escorted three to the train station and one to the bus. One disappeared, nobody knew where, and one was married to an elderly clerk in the local municipality office who was, happily, receptive to bribes from the needful. This man had thrived and could afford a lavish wedding in a real wedding hall – Lala's Shadi House near Data Darbar. My sisters and I, therefore, had occasion to put on our best dresses, and we danced and sang at the baaraat party to our heart's content. It remains one of my fondest memories.

The wedding hall I was in now made the other seem like a shanty.

It was the grandest room I had ever seen or would see. Pentagonal in shape, flanked by pillared archways, it was strewn with rose petals at the entrance and the far end. Motia and bright feather wreaths decked the walls, as did colorful mosaics and tapestries (these blurred when I passed them so I could never make out the images). Persian rugs were arranged in geometric patterns on the floor and spiraling crystal chandeliers sparkled and glimmered overhead. Candelabras lined the walls and threw a chiaroscuro of light and shadow such that the rugs (so fine they felt like extensions of my skin) seemed to shift beneath my passage.

My memory of the room is perfect, so vivid that it still lives behind my eyelids. I can shut my eyes now and see everything in profuse detail.

At the far end of the room was a cage on a raised platform. A bridegroom and his bride sat cross-legged on an embellished takht inside it.

I walked forward. The groom wore a sherwani glittering with sequins, and garlands of red flowers and rupee notes around his neck. His face was covered with a veil of charred feathers. The woman wore a gold-red wedding dress and was laden with jewelry from head to toe. Wherever her skin was exposed it was painted with henna. She was breathtaking.

Now I noticed other cages secreted away in arched recesses on either side of me. Silent men and women in colorful shalwar kurtas and saris sat inside on wooden perches and swings. Their eyes followed me as I moved down the hall. Their lips were parted. From each mouth protruded what I first thought were albino tongues. A second look dismissed the idea. The objects were pale and card-shaped.

Soundless, the doors of all cages slid up. The inmates rose and stepped outside.

I was surrounded by the wedding procession now. My nostrils filled with a smell as organic as it was old.

In a flurry of blue and green and black we marched to the couple's cage. Their door swung open, revealing a three-step deck carpeted with red feathers and fall leaves. The crowd surged forward, elbow to elbow, carrying me on its breast. Their footfall was perfectly silent. I couldn't even hear their breathing.

We halted before the stage.

Two men in raven black swept across the hall, up the stair deck, into the cage. They held a bowl of milk. The bridegroom swung his veil of burnt feathers aside and sipped. The raven men presented the bowl to the bride. She dipped her head coyly (but not before I saw that her eyes were large and different-colored) and drank until the man gently removed the bowl from her lips and placed it on the step deck.

Mano the wedding cat appeared from behind the stage. He sauntered up the steps and began to lap up the remaining milk. Come to me, Mano, I tried to say, but the words wouldn't leave my lips. Satiated, Mano yawned, licked his haunches, and started circling the wedding cage.

A woman in all white with a birthmark beneath her left eye was beside me. She was built like a briefcase, short and squat and business-like. She gazed at me for a moment and pointed at the ceiling.

I looked up.

The hall's ceiling was covered in the fresco of a giant bird. The bird was perfectly captured in mid-flight, its golden dark serrated wings scything a blue sky. It had a rainbow plumage, black horns, and a peacock tail. Glinting feathers, like embers, showered from its underbelly. In the flickering light, the painting appeared to cast a vast shadow over the proceedings.

I lowered my gaze and the woman was gone. In her place was one of the raven men. Gray sparrows sat on his shoulders and pecked at his hair. He held out an enamel basin in front of him. Liquid sloshed inside. Its vapors made my eyes water.

The raven man bowed and began walking to the wedding cage.

Now rose excited chittering as the guests removed the card-like objects from their mouths and showered the wedding couple with them. Prayers, cheers, shouts, and the wailing of women overcome by the prospect of a daughter's separation mounted, until you couldn't tell if the procession were celebrating or mourning.

Mubarak! Mubarak! Be blessed in your husband's house.

May you never have cause to leave that home. May you never be short of dowry.

May your firstborns be healthy baby boys.

May your mother-in-law never hate you.

May you never return to your parents. Should you return, come only as a dead body

and

May you stay safe from the stove, the stove, the stove!

Now burst the wedding songs from a hundred throats, ancient, powerful, loving, imprisoning, humiliating; and yet the raven man walked, he walked toward the bride with the basin of slopping liquid that gave off fumes.

She sat in her cage, placid as a sea, ageless like a vow unfulfilled. Only when the man reached her and doused her in the vaporous liquid did she stir. Her jewels slid and chinked. The tapestries on the walls darkened. The groom's veil of charred feathers dropped from his head and the red of the bride's dress deepened until it turned a perfect black.

The procession rejoiced.

May you stay safe from the stove!

Mano was between my legs. The wedding cat flicked his tail and tripped me. I flailed my arms, stumbled, and when I looked up, the wedding hall was gone. The cages, the guests, the beautiful bride with her splendid mismatched eyes (which I have seen in dream many times since), the elegant ornamentation – all vanished.

Just an orphan's room, empty of poise and promise.

I was afraid. I wasn't afraid. I went back to the courtyard and looked at the sky. So many stars that night, and the blue moon, it watched the world as it always had. A bulbous bird staked to the heavens, it spread its vast gaze over all our affairs. Its eye was filled with something deep and raw. Now when I close my eyes and imagine that moon, I think what I saw was mystery and memory and a longing so old it makes me shudder.

My cheeks were wet. I went to deliver the tobacco (still in my pocket) and as I passed Sangeeta Apa's door, the sounds of hushed conversation came as did soothing odors of incense, earth, and rubbing oil. When I returned from Bibi Soraiya's quarters, the door was ajar. Leaves rustled. I glanced up to see a figure, bulky, as if with a thick garment, clinging to the tree (which tree?) outside her room.

The moon fled behind a cloud. When it returned, the ghostly figure was gone.

* * *

The wedding dinner was short and sweet. There was biryani, sweet lassi, mangoes, and lychees (it was summer). Rumors of silver-papered firni-in-jotas from Gawal Mandi floated for a while before Bibi Soraiya dismissed them.

The groom was a looming, forbidding man who bowed his head again and again and made squeezing gestures with his fists when too many of my sisters crowded him. Sangeeta Apa and he wore matching wedding outfits. She wouldn't look at him, but peeked from behind her ghoongat, smiling, when Neha and I tried to steal his brown leather shoes – Joota Chupai is an accepted custom. Bibi Soraiya yelled at us and we reluctantly returned them.

They left for Gujranwala the next day by train.

I have not seen nor heard of my Sangeeta Apa since. If she called or wrote letters, Bibi Soraiya didn't tell us, which was strange because my others sisters stayed in touch – for a few years, at least, before life overtook them. The unsettling shadow of Apa's absence grew, but even after I was all grown up, if I asked about her, Bibi's eyes would change. With age, Bibi developed a tremor in her face and limbs and mere mention of Apa would send her shaking to bed.

It got so bad that I stopped asking.

In ensuing years, Neha and many of my other sisters were married off. Sorted out, arranged, and packed away. Bus stops with their tang of sweat and diesel on your tongue. Train stations odorous with dust and cheap perfume and the ashy smell of sparks from rail tracks. Young girls appeared and replaced my sisters – a ceaseless commotion of laughs and shouts and dopattas flying in the courtyard wind. I loved them all but, bless my memory, I remember few. Sometimes when I peered at their faces, it seemed as if their features blurred and ran together and one familiar mask emerged, winter breath rising from its lips like smoke. When that happened, I would get up and walk to the entrance of the orphanage. I would stand there and watch the world beyond those walls, an unfettered landscape stretching away beyond the limits of my vision. Somewhere out there, I thought, you didn't need to be wedded to resignation or despair. There was stuff in between. Hearths instead of stoves. If you got too warm, you could step away. You could leave. You didn't have to leave. You didn't have to fear leaving, or falling, or ceaselessly circling and not ever coming to rest. You didn't have to fear remembering.

You could travel to the ends of the earth.

By then I was busy helping Bibi run the orphanage. I had to put such thoughts out of my head. Still, I sometimes dreamed. Of discomfiting things that became grainy, wispy echoes in the morning. Crossroads with signs askew pointing this way and that; graveyards planted next to wedding halls; windows that shuttered open and closed; doorways that seemed to lead to more doorway, their gaping mouths atremble with flickering light; and in the distance, always, the flutter of dark wings. I would wake from these dreams with my fists darkened by sweat and dust, the taste of smoke already fading from my tongue.

The bird man still visited. He crouched on his shawl and twittered and chirped and spread the gilded envelopes, waiting for his parakeets to tell his admirers' fortunes. Maybe I was getting older or he, but his bird music seemed duller to me, as if his voice had aged. Once he came inside the orphanage to talk to Bibi Soraiya about something and my sisters gathered around him. I sat and watched him play to the girls. He turned his head from side to side. His turban fell off. I picked it up and handed it to him.

"Thank you," he said, dusting it with his large earthy hand. "Sometimes I wonder if it's time to take this off for good."

"Why?"

"Vanity be damned, it's just an old turban, you know." He laughed, a loud, booming sound that startled me. "One can dream, but that won't change it to a crown." His eyes looked a little feverish. He said, "You know sparrows are a delicacy in Gujranwala. They trap dozens in nets and roast them slow on large stoves. My father used to go eat with friends once in a while, but my mother would get angry. She said the poor things had no meat on them at all and it was a sin to take so many tiny lives for nothing."

I must have frowned or my face lost color, for he changed the subject. Shortly after, he left.

The oddest thing I remember after Apa's departure?

Exactly forty days after Bibi took her to the train station, all the birds, the silent birds, the soaring splendid birds that came to us from every corner of Lahore, stopped visiting. The courtyard trees grew heavy with unpecked fruit, the electric poles became forlorn. Long after they vanished, the courtyard remained filled with the rich, old smell of bird. (These days, the odor makes me break out in a sweat.)

And in our rooms the mirrors rippled and moonlight changed and people from the past walked restlessly back and forth between places of some one else's making.

Devil on the Night Train

Samuel Marzioli

A BROILING SUMMER DAY had turned the house into a sauna. For hours, Maja and her grandfather Esidro rested on the front porch, waiting for a touch of cold that only night would bring. While she read, he soaked his old bones in the quiet, gobs of smoke spewing from the fat cigar trapped between his lips – a smell like earth and wood and spices.

"I finished another scary book yesterday," Maja said when the light began to fail. She crimped a page to mark her place and set her book aside.

"Oh?" Esidro said, tapping an inch of ash into his ashtray.

"Yeah. This one was about a clown who lives in the sewers and feeds off the fears of children."

"Clowns aren't scary. What did he do? Pop a balloon and make the children cry?"

Maja had to lean in close to understand him. Not because of his accent which broke syllables into separate words. It was the way he sometimes let his voice lapse, a thin sound that wavered with a tired flourish.

"Oh Grandpa," she said, when she finally caught his meaning. "I guess you'd have to read it to understand." And then, "Do you have any stories for me today?"

"Ghost stories?"

"Of course."

"Maybe. Did I ever tell you about Ongloc, who hunts bad children and turns them into coconuts?"

"And eats the coconuts with his razor-sharp teeth whenever he's hungry? Yeah."

"What about the aswang, who can transform into an animal and suck a baby right out of their mother's stomach?"

"The shape-shifting, blood-sucking, human-eating ghoul? Yeah, that too."

"Then maybe it's time you heard about the Devil Man."

"Who's that?"

"There are many versions of the story, but the one I know is this: they say he drives a train around on the darkest nights, searching for a victim. Once he finds one, he kills them, trapping their souls within his passenger cars forever."

Maja pursed her lips, sucking on the taste of indecision. "I guess that's kind of creepy."

Esidro humphed. "You guess?" he asked and diverted his attention to the sky.

Maja followed his gaze. The sun had dragged the clouds along its westward path, leaving a full moon and ample stars, their soft light glinting in the smear of gray above them. Night had come, and – Maja knew – so had bedtime.

As if Esidro read her mind, he said, "It's getting late. You should go to bed."

"How about one more story. Please?"

"No."

"Fine," said Maja. "But you should know I won this round. My story is definitely scarier."

She waited by the doorway for a hug, but Esidro didn't rise, didn't say goodnight, didn't even turn to face her. When his sulking mood persisted minutes longer, she sighed and strolled inside, letting the front door bang shut behind her.

* * *

Maja barely slept that night. A black train invaded her dreams, its polished dome cover glinting in the moonlight, its endless cars grinding, clacking, squealing on phantom rails. The dead pressed up against the windows as they hurtled down her street, staring through the open curtains of her bedroom, to her dream-self sleeping oblivious within. Worse, she realized her grandfather had been a passenger. Huddled in his chair, his expression wasn't simply sad, but lost, defeated.

That image of her grandfather stayed with her long after she woke. The diversion of a school day helped, but it was never far outside her mind and filled her with thoughts of death and pain and misery. Only six years had passed since she'd lost her parents, but her memories of them were too distant to be real. The idea of losing her grandfather – the only family she had left – made her feel sick, a profound ache beyond the reach of any words she could muster.

She did her best to cheer herself up during the bus ride home and as she whittled the day away playing on her computer. She pictured the Devil Man's train painted the colors of a rainbow, spewing cotton-candy clouds, with zoo animals sitting in the passenger cars like humans. The idea made her smile, but wasn't strong enough to calm her. By the time she and her grandfather went outside, to enjoy the final dregs of light, she could no longer hold it in.

"Grandpa. Remember what you said about the Devil Man last night?"

"Yes."

"That wasn't real, right? It can't be."

"What makes you say that?"

"Because it doesn't make any sense. How would a devil get a train or know how to drive it? Also, trains aren't exactly quiet. Why couldn't someone hear it coming from a mile away and run in the opposite direction?"

Esidro knocked cigar ash against his shoe, watching the swirling nimbus of gray smoke suspended above him. "I don't know."

"So it was just a story!"

"I didn't say that. While growing up in the Philippines, I saw and heard many strange things, but none as peculiar as the Devil Man. Do you remember when I told you about my experiences during World War Two?"

She shrugged. "Kind of."

"I only shared part of what happened. Never this. After the Japanese attacked the Philippines, I had nightmares of a shadow man piloting a plane over my home, the symbol of the rising sun emblazoned on its wings. When the Japanese occupation forces arrived, I had nightmares of that same phantom pilot. Only now he drove a tank that cruised the city streets, the barrel of its gun pointed at buildings and the helpless citizens cowering within.

"Once I came to the United States, his tank became a boat. I traveled across the continent, from New York to Oregon, and the boat became a train. So no, I don't know how he gets these things, or whether they're real or some kind of illusion. But I believe them to be the Devil Man's way of taking my greatest joys and deepest fears and using them against me. Does that make sense?"

Not wanting to upset him by admitting it did not, she nodded and then changed the subject. "I noticed you have two cigars tonight. Is one meant for me?"

He answered her grin with a patient smile. "As it so happens, almost fifty years have passed since the liberation of the Philippines." He lifted the second cigar from his shirt pocket and exposed its chipped and peeling wrapper. "Sad as it is, this one means a great deal to me. I'm saving it, for when the mood for celebration strikes."

Tonight his smoke smelled sweet, with just a hint of nuts and pepper. She satisfied herself by taking gulps of air into her mouth, hoping she could collect enough smoke to blow rings like he did. He in turn humphed and held the trail of his smoke as far from her as possible.

Maja yawned. "I'm going to bed."

"Sweet dreams."

"Goodnight Grandpa."

They hugged and she went inside, leaving him lost beneath an ample cloud of smoke and reverie.

* * *

Maja had another night of troubled sleep. In her dreams, she crawled out of bed in a stupor, crouched by her window as a black train chuffed into the small confines of her front yard. Three figures staggered down the steps from the murk of the first passenger car. They lined up side by side on the low grass, their limbs held stiff, bodies swaying with intoxication – or so she thought, before the interior of the train flared and the truth revealed itself more clearly.

They weren't drunk, they were dead. Light threaded through their wounds, accentuating every opening with a sickly yellow glow. The man on the left watched her from a pale crater in his forehead. The man in the middle smiled from the broad glimmer of his throat. The man on the right beckoned to her, his finger framed between the puckered flesh that was his headless neck. She gasped. As if triggered by the sound, the light blinked off, smothering the men again in darkness.

Maja sunk below the window frame. Only the chattering of her teeth alerted her that she wasn't sleeping anymore. So then, what part of what she'd seen had been real? She couldn't bring herself to guess, didn't dare peek up over the windowsill to find out for herself, merely pushed in closer to the wall and waited.

An answer came sooner than she expected. It started with a rapping on the front door. She heard a tap coming from the window of her grandfather's room, followed by a bang against the bathroom's outer wall, and then a voice flitted in from some unknown distance, attended by the steady drum of footsteps. Waves of cold enfolded her, sunk like needles into her skin. Whatever ounce of courage her uncertainty had offered vanished.

"Esidro. Nasaan ka, Esidro?" said a man's voice, his gravel baritone sweetened by the honey of its timbre.

"Esidro, nandito ang mga kaibigan mo. Lumabas ka at kausapin mo sila. Naaalala ka nila."

She knew the language was Tagalog, but she'd never learned, couldn't recognize a word apart from her grandfather's name. At first the voice veered away, but then it scuttled closer, as if its owner had circled the house and was now rounding back on her position. She swallowed hard, the wet grinding of her throat exploding in her ears.

"Perhaps you'll only answer if I speak English? It tastes like burning charcoal on my tongue, but I'll use it if I must."

The footsteps and voice converged on her. Her window screen crackled, followed by a deep, harsh sniffing mere inches from her head.

"I can smell you Esidro, can smell the stink of flesh rotting on your bones. Why hide? Why make this difficult when you're so close to death already?"

Maja had to run, had to get help, but her legs were slender lengths of rope that couldn't possibly support her. Her only chance was to wait it out. Maybe if she didn't move, didn't make a sound, he wouldn't notice her. Wouldn't know that she was—

"Little girl?"

She held her breath.

The voice, now stern, continued. "Little girl. Didn't your grandfather teach you manners? When the Devil speaks, you answer."

The cry that escaped her throat endured long after the Devil Man left and her grandfather stormed the room, accompanied by the modest reassurance of the lights. When white spots twinkled in her vision, and her lungs reversed from want of air, she settled into a whimper. Her grandfather held her for an hour. But nothing, not even his crushing hugs and his promise of "It's okay," could restore her to her senses.

Esidro fell asleep on her bed. For the remainder of the night, she cuddled close to him. Weariness clawed at her, dragged her eyelids down. But she didn't bother going back to sleep. As far as she was concerned, she'd never sleep again.

* * *

Maja dressed and caught the morning school bus. Usually her grandfather accompanied her to the bus stop, but he'd looked so frail in his exhaustion she couldn't bear to wake him. At school, she kept to herself, barely listening when her friends or teachers spoke. She prayed the Devil Man was only a dream. But her mind rebelled against such a convenient notion, piling memories into a wall of evidence before her. At recess, she sat beneath the shade of the breezeway, rocking back and forth. So many thoughts about the night before crowded in her mind she had no room left for new ones.

After school, her grandfather met her in the entryway. She could tell something had upset him. His eyes, normally so calm and passive, darted inside the thin cover of their lids, as if searching the house for latent signs of danger.

"Are you ready to talk?" he asked.

"Yes."

"Good. Follow me."

He led her outside. As they passed through their neighborhood, it bothered her how complacent everything appeared. Children gamboled through the streets and adults worked in their garages, or wrangled with the chaos of front lawns. She couldn't find a trace of wayward shadow or a crack in reality's veneer, just a bright, suburban stretch that knew its limits and didn't as much as creep an inch out of place. It wasn't right, wasn't fair. A devil had violated her sense of what was normal and now nothing had a right to feel sane.

Once they reached the corner park, they found an isolated bench and sat. The stifling heat made her armpits damp and her face drip sweat, but she didn't care, barely noticed.

"A long-dead friend visited me last night," he said, wiping his forehead with the back of his hand. "I could hear him calling through my window. 'Come outside Esidro. Let's talk beneath the stars like we used to.' Judging by your screams, I take it someone visited you as well?"

She nodded.

"Which means he has come back."

She nodded again.

"I thought he'd forgotten me. I'm sorry, Maja. I didn't mean to get you involved."

"But why? What did you do to make him hate you so much?"

He humphed, hands purple from the strain of his clenching fingers. "You say that like this is one of your books or movies. As if I'd robbed a grave or broke a Bulul statue and am now being punished for my sins."

"I'm sorry," she said, brushing his arm. "I didn't mean to blame you. But what did happen, Grandpa? I need to know."

His apprehension made him stiffen. The momentary flexing of his muscles filled his sagging clothes so that he seemed much younger, much stronger than before. But he sighed, shrunk down again, as if the burden of her question or the memories it summoned had deflated him, aging him back into himself.

"I'll tell you what I can remember."

* * *

This was after the initial blitz, when Japanese war planes ripped into our cities, killing many of my friends and family, including my mother. It was after invasion forces landed on our shores and the evacuation of our cities and towns to the hope of someplace safer. It was also after the Bataan Death March where ten thousand prisoners of war, including my father, were killed during a sixty-mile trek into captivity.

I was a teenager, not yet a man, when my little sister and I returned home to meet the inevitability of an occupation. We quickly learned to live with our enemies, adapting to their rules, their curfews, their violence. To be honest, it wasn't hard. To disobey meant death. We wanted to live so we simply didn't disobey.

Beyond that, the Japanese meant to turn the Philippines into a proper possession and made allowances, to keep the civil peace. During that time, they let us grow gardens, clear roads, and repair damaged buildings. Weekly swap meets were instituted where we could trade for food and clothes. They even let us gather and play games, albeit under their unwavering vigilance.

My friends and I never cared for sports. Instead, we took the opportunity to smoke cigars, mostly the ones left in my father's private collection. The four of us would meet by the edge of town. There we would speak nonsense, tell stories, or make crude jokes that only young boys would find amusing.

The Japanese didn't care what we did so long as we didn't appear to be colluding. We also shared cigars with them from time to time, a goodwill gesture meant to win us more freedoms. Because of this, we thought nothing when a stranger appeared in our midst, asking if he could have a cigar. A wide-brim straw hat threw a deep shadow across his face. We assumed from his strange accent that he was a Japanese soldier, though he didn't wear a uniform or carry a gun.

From that day forward, he visited every time we met. He never showed his face and never spoke, only puffed on his cigar and listened. Were it up to me, we would have put up with his unwelcome presence for as long as it lasted. We were nobodies, meant nothing, and it wouldn't have taken much for someone to convince the men in charge to shoot us. But Lorenzo, the boldest of my friends, soon grew annoyed by the stranger's constant beggaring.

"We don't have any more cigars to give. Maybe you can ask your Japanese friends if they will share their cigarettes."

The stranger shook his head. "No. I only want Filipino leaf, not that Japanese poison."

"I'm sorry. What little we have is ours."

Lorenzo turned his back on him. The rest of us began to do the same when the stranger made a disgruntled noise, something like a growl. He snatched his hat from off his head and for the first time we saw what was hiding beneath the shadow of the brim. His face was smooth and white. Though he had no eyes, he tracked us all the same, sneering from a little crumpled hole that passed for a mouth. We were wrong before. He wasn't Japanese, Filipino, or even a man. He was a devil.

"You think war is hell?" the devil said. "This is only a taste of what is waiting on the other side." He put his hat on, this time turning his back on us. "We'll meet again, when the time is right. Maybe then you will realize a cigar is a small price to pay for my good favor."

He left. We were too stunned to speak, to make sense of what we'd seen or heard, so we left too, each to our separate houses. The devil's words began to work its curse that very night. We discovered Lorenzo the next day, lying by his front door with his throat slit. Soon after, the Japanese took my friend

Manual and his family and beheaded them for suspicions of collaborating with the resistance. Lastly, an officer shot Aurelio because "he didn't bow to a superior like he was supposed to."

Once soldiers kidnapped my sister and forced her to work as a prostitute in a comfort station, I had no reason left to stay. Home wasn't home without my friends and family. I waited for the cover of darkness, gathered as much as I could cram into my pockets, and fled into the jungle. Eventually, I was found and taken in by a group of Filipino guerrillas.

The war truly started for me then. I had no time to worry about devils or curses any longer. For a time, I even managed to convince myself that he was a figment of my imagination, created to explain all the pain and death and suffering around me. But I heard stories – on long days waiting for the raids at night, or long nights waiting for sleep to find me – and they were always the same: refuse to give the devil-man a smoke and he'll drag you down to hell.

When General MacArthur returned and helped liberate the Philippines, I left my country behind, thinking I could escape my curse by hiding far away. It seemed to work. Despite bad dreams and omens, the passing years made the devil's words feel like empty threats. But I was wrong again; there is no escape. The Devil Man has found me and he won't stop until he has collected my body and my soul, just like my friends before me.

* * *

Dinner was a solemn hour. Maja's fear inhabited the house like a living thing, its presence filling up the rooms, threatening to suck the air out. Every so often, an unexpected noise presented itself – the yowling of a cat or the scuffling of a branch against the windowpane – and she would tense, waiting for the intrusion to succumb to the greater pull of silence. Esidro was of a different mind. He eventually flipped on the TV and watched a sitcom while they ate, his rasping titters dwarfed by a chorus of the show's canned laughter.

Maja was astonished by his composure. With sunlight fading, it wouldn't be long before shadows spawned and broke into the silhouettes of dead men and a monster. The first time had been a warning, meant to frighten them – of that, she had no doubt. So, what would happen the next time the Devil Man appeared?

She pushed food into her mouth, let the scrap roll across her tongue. It was the only thing she could do to keep herself from crying.

* * *

The goodnights Maja traded with her grandfather felt more like goodbyes. Before he closed his door, he begged her to stay inside the house, to promise that she wouldn't interfere no matter what she saw and heard. She promised, but she regretted her decision as soon as she cut her bedroom lights.

Her only option now was to stay awake, to support her grandfather with nothing but good thoughts and best wishes. A sense of disconnect pervaded her while she lay in bed, as if she were in two places at once, the real her watching with frustration from the corner of the room.

She tried to pass the time by praying. But as her vigil lurched into the dark of early morning, Heaven's only answer was a stubborn disregard. She fell asleep still muttering at her ceiling and the vast expanse of stars she imagined far above it.

She only snapped awake again when the front door groaned and the wall shuddered at its closing.

"Oh God," she said, throwing herself from bed.

Through the window, she saw her grandfather standing in the modest strip of their front yard, still wearing a long, white t-shirt and jeans. He stuffed something into the waistband at the small of his back that she couldn't see in the insufficient moonlight. The world faltered. In the stillness that followed, the black train appeared, a blur gliding through the muted streets, the vagueness of its details clarifying with every forward thrust. Once it eased onto the outer edge of their front lawn, the Devil Man descended from the engine.

"Esidro," he said, arms held wide as if intending to embrace him. "I thought I'd find you hiding beneath your covers or cowering behind your granddaughter again. I thought it'd take at least a dozen more visits before you met me face to face. But here you are, the very second I arrive. Could it be you missed me as much as I missed you?"

"Don't talk to me like that," said Esidro. "I'm not here to make friends, but to end this."

"I agree. The time is finally right. Take your place inside my train, among your friends, and this will finally be over."

Esidro humphed. "It won't be that easy. First agree to leave my granddaughter alone. Promise me you won't hurt her or let her come to harm and maybe I'll go with you."

The Devil Man laughed. "Don't forget your place, old man. I came out of respect for our history together, but if I had wanted to I could have coaxed a thief to cut your neck while you slept, or a drunk to take a detour through your bedroom. The choice isn't if you'll come, but when."

He motioned, a subtle nod in Maja's direction.

Maja heard a noise behind her, like the parting of wet lips, and swiveled around to find the dead men standing in her bedroom. At first they stared, inanimate like statues, like a company of marionettes left slumped against their strings. But then they twitched, energized, imbued with life.

"Grandpa!"

Despite the swollen volume of her scream, she could still hear the Devil Man's gloating.

"Your friends are meeting your granddaughter. Better hurry. It won't be long before they rip her flesh apart."

The dead men trudged forward in synchronous strides. Maja threw herself against the window screen, knocking it loose. But with a sudden burst of speed, they encircled her, seizing her in the shackles of their hands, fingers pressing purple bruises into her skin.

She snarled in savage fury, twisted to free herself. "Grandpa, help!"

"Board the train," said the Devil Man, "and I promise this will all be over."

"No!" Esidro shouted.

He reached into the waistband at the small of his back and pulled the hidden object out. It was a pistol, its blue steel finish reflecting specks and streaks of light. With his hands wrapped around its grip, he let his eyes drift along the barrel and fired twice at the Devil Man.

"You should be ashamed of yourself," the Devil Man said, shaking his head. "Fifty years and this is the best you could come up with? You can't kill what never lived."

As if Esidro hadn't heard, he spun around, rushed toward Maja's bedroom and ripped the dangling screen from off its perch. Maja did the best she could to sag and cup her ears. Her grandfather squeezed off three more rounds. The bullets slammed into the dead men, knocking them aside, loosening their grip enough for Maja to wrench free.

"Run!" Esidro yelled.

Maja did as commanded, retreated from her room, scrambled down the hallway, almost overcome by the raw terror sloshing through her insides. But once she reached the back door, a memory barreled through her mind and she froze in place. It was the image of her grandfather from her nightmares. He was seated on the Devil Man's train, his ashen face stricken of all its joy. If she left now, the Devil Man would take him. Her nightmares would become true and she would have no one left. She loved him, needed him, too much to ever let that happen.

"Please," she whispered to the sky beyond the empty room. "Help me save him."

At once her thoughts returned to the stories her grandfather told her. If she'd learned anything, it was that Filipino monsters always had a weakness: raw rice to ward off the manananggal, salt to burn the aswang, a split coconut to trap Ongloc. Could it be the Devil Man had a weakness too? It seemed ridiculous to consider, more Dumbo's Magic Feather than a stake through a vampire's heart, but it was all she had.

An inkling of a plan blossomed inside her. She raced to the bookcase in the living room, tipped up the lid of her grandfather's humidor. To her relief, the chipped and peeling cigar he'd shown her lay inside. First she cut the cap off and then waved a butane lighter beneath its foot – like she'd seen her grandfather do a hundred times before. Vague suspicions of its provenance seeded her with hope, but she didn't dare even think about them for fear of jinxing it.

By the time she ran outside, the Devil Man led Esidro by the hand, all three dead men men flanking them on both sides.

"Wait!"

Esidro turned to her, shivering, his cheeks streaked with tears. "I'm sorry, Maja, but I have to go with them. It's the only way to save you."

"But—"

"Remember your promise. Go inside. I don't want you to see what happens next."

She held the cigar out, letting the red eye of its burning tip peer into the distance. "I brought something for the Devil Man."

The Devil Man chuckled, but then sniffed the air and his earnest strides slowed into an amble. "It can't be. That's impossible."

Throwing Esidro's hand aside, he bounded straight for Maja. The urge to flee roiled up inside her, but she couldn't move, felt like an animal trapped in the hypnotic lull of headlights. He plucked the cigar from her hands and her skin began to twinge, as if desperately trying to peel away from the spot where his fingers had made contact. But that was nothing compared to when he removed his hat. At the sight of his round and swollen face, she thought of seeping wounds, of the pale borders of deep gashes and the white rims of ulcerations. She almost vomited, but turned away in time to keep the sick from rising up.

"Ah, vintage Filipino leaf," he said. "Brings back memories." He took a deep puff, held it in for minutes before releasing the smoke in a long, contented sigh. "Was that so hard, Esidro? You could learn a thing or two from your granddaughter."

Maja swallowed, barely daring to look up. "I gave you what you wanted. Now will you leave my grandpa alone?"

The Devil Man stepped closer, the threat of his proximity nearly shoving her back. He studied her. Something like a smile pulled the muscles of his cheeks before he set his hat upon his head, shrouding his face again in darkness.

"As I said to your grandfather before, a cigar is a small price to pay for my good favor. Keep him if you want him. A bag of skin and bones would make a sad addition to my collection anyway."

He took another earnest puff and withdrew back to his train, ascending to the engine. The dead men trailed after him, boarding just as a whistle blew a harsh, enduring, suffocating note. With that, the black train plunged into the ground, dragging the stiff segments of its passenger cars like a snake sliding into its burrow.

Esidro staggered over to Maja and latched onto her shoulder, his profound exhaustion matched only by his stupefied expression. "How did you know that would work?"

"I didn't, but I hoped," she said.

Together, they scanned the space the black train had occupied, half expecting it to reverse, for the Devil Man to return and claim his prize. But as if to prove the world had resumed its proper course, a police siren wailed, announcing its approach, winds blew and trees began to sway again. Whatever had occurred was finally over.

"Do you think he'll keep his word?" asked Maja.

"Who can say for sure? But let's act as if he will and trust in God to make it so."

"Grandpa."

"Yes?"

"I'm sorry."

"For what?" he said, cradling her face, brushing the hair out of her eyes. "After all you've done, what could you possibly have to be sorry for?"

"You won. You were right before. The Devil Man is definitely scarier."

Esidro grinned and wrapped his arms around her. Maja cried, remembering that image from her nightmares and realizing she'd never expected to see him smile again. With a squeal of brakes and throbbing lights, the police arrived. Soon they would ask their questions about gunfire, and screams over dead men and a monster that had left no evidence behind. But Maja couldn't find the strength to care. She hugged her grandfather close, pressing hard against his chest, too numb to feel anything but the stinging of her tears and the solace of his living, breathing, still-warm body.

Jaded Winds

Rena Mason

MING LI WOKE to the sounds of a skeleton in motion, flat percussions reminding him of primitive bamboo wind chimes. The clacking came from the bed mat behind him. Last week, on their third wedding anniversary, he'd strangled his wife to death as she slept there.

They married in Chinatown the first week of April in 1903, and she still hadn't borne him any sons. He had to get rid of her before he could get a new wife, one who would fulfill her duty. *Ridiculous Western laws*. Ming dumped the body in the Oakland side of San Francisco Bay. Now her *gu nu* bone demon returned for his soul.

Never one to fear a woman, supernatural or not, Ming turned over and opened his eyes. Face to face with Xi, he marveled at the way her long, black hair undulated in the air above as if under water. Her porcelain skin glowed and rippled in the moonlight. Stark eyes squinted at him, but Ming felt no remorse for what he'd done.

"Come closer," she whispered in a soft voice, a timid expression on her face. Xi parted her robe, exposing flawless breasts.

A pinch of excitement tweaked his groin. Then he rolled away from her. "Go, now."

"Not until you have me one last time."

With his back to Xi, Ming reached for a wooden box on the floor.

"No. Please don't," she said.

He struck a match, lit a candle, then turned toward her and held up the light. Xi's mouth opened wide, and she screamed, her jaws unhinging until half her face became a howling orifice. Her cries grew louder as her flesh melted, leaving nothing but animated skeletal remains. She reached for him, but he moved the flame closer, forcing her back. Xi's bones clacked once more before falling away and disappearing.

Ming smiled, blew out the candle, and slept deeply.

* * *

Packed within a throng of other Chinese immigrants in black robes and beanies, many with queue braids swinging behind them, Lew Hong spotted his business partner Ming. They acknowledged one another with a nod, wove around people, and met in the middle. Together they shuffled to their small ironworks on Sacramento Street. Morning mist from the San Francisco Bay clung to the sides of brick buildings, vaporous specters defying the sun.

The men jostled forward in rhythmic surges with the crowd. Lew listened as Ming spoke in Cantonese. "The Dragon Boat Festival is only two months away. Are you certain ours will be ready?"

"Yes, of course. The men work hard to keep us on schedule. They know it's important."

"Will you be going straight to Oakland this morning?"

Lew paused before answering. "I planned to but shouldn't. Yu is due any time."

"May the heavens bless you with another son. Yes, they will. This is your year, year of the horse," Ming said.

Lew smiled and nodded. He'd thought the same thing when he left his wife sleeping. She nearly bled to death on the floor of their cramped living quarters after the premature birth of their first child. He'd made a vow then to work harder and give her a more comfortable living.

Images of a bigger house and a better life for his family occupied every moment of his days for the last decade. After the success of their small ironworks, they'd started a fishing boat manufacturing business, and he couldn't be happier with how well production moved along.

Lew's good fortune made him feel somewhat guilty after Ming's wife had recently run away and left him.

"I'll go," Ming said.

"You're a good friend and business partner." Lew patted Ming's shoulder.

* * *

After Lew entered their factory, Ming turned down Stockton Street. He despised walking alone outside of Chinatown where Chinese often became targets for prejudiced cruelty. Mechanical sounds thundered behind him as he crossed Kearny. He quickened his pace, stepped into a small crowd of Westerners and tried to blend in. Someone shouted, "Chinaman, stop."

Every muscle tensed, he scowled and clenched his fists. People scattered with shocked looks of disgust. A covered motorcar pulled up alongside him. The metal demon twitched and sputtered. The driver ignored Ming's presence, kept focused on the road ahead. Dark curtains over the windows concealed everything inside.

A door opened. A familiar voice came from within. "Need a ride?"

Ming scanned the area then got in.

"Shut the door," said Carl Worthington.

Ming did, and then the car rumbled forward.

"You headed to the docks?"

"Yes."

"Take the long way, Sam," Carl said.

The man up front nodded.

"Well Mr. Li, have you talked to your partner?"

"No. Not yet, but—"

"You're not trying to get out of our little agreement are you?"

"I need more time. My partner's wife is about to have a baby."

"No one on the city council cares. We made a deal didn't we?"

"Yes."

"So?"

"Very soon. I promise."

"Soon isn't good enough Mr. Li. If you want payment and more acreage around your boat business in Oakland then you need to be faster. You people aren't in short supply, if you know what I mean."

"No." Ming shook his head. He didn't understand, but even with the language barrier, the Westerner made his air of superiority clear.

"My goodness, your kind are slow in the head." Carl pointed to his temple. "I mean someone else will take my offer of money and land to move Chinatown across the bay if you don't want it – other Chinese. I bet you understand now."

The driver laughed.

White devil! "Yes," Ming said.

"Next week, then. Sam and I will find you. Make sure you have the signed papers."

Ming nodded.

"Good. Now get out."

The motor car stopped and Ming had barely stepped down when the car sped off again.

Anger roiled his insides on the ferry ride to Oakland harbor. He walked up to the bow's railing, looked over, and vomited morning tea. It stirred the dark water below. A pale white, familiar face floated up to the surface. Xi! It couldn't be. He'd weighted the body.

The prow moved through her and into a thick fog bank. Damp, frigid air embraced him and squeezed the breath from his lungs.

Ming looked up and imagined a fleet of his boats fishing the waters. Dealing with the Westerner had its downside but not for long. Ming planned to outsmart them all. Once Lew signed over the ironworks everything would be his. Why should he care if the white devils reclaimed Chinatown in San Francisco? Better success awaited them across the bay in Oakland. Lew would eventually see it and be forever grateful. Or join Xi at the bottom of the bay.

New business, a wife, wealth, and many sons would soon be his. He'd build his own Nob Hill to entice the other rising entrepreneurial Chinese.

Soft coughing came from nearby.

He looked over his shoulder. White, silky air stirred to his right. A petite shadow emerged from the fog in a slow twirl. The most beautiful woman Ming had ever seen. She stopped with one foot forward and bowed.

"Jiu wei," she said.

"Jiu ... wei?" He gasped. *The Fox Demon?*

Bright red lips exposed an impish smirk across her perfect face. She nodded, and he backed away.

"I know what you want, demon. Go away."

"I can be your new wife. Give you many sons." Jiu danced toward him. Pink lotus petals flowed from her imperial robes to cushion every step she made.

"You will take all my money."

"And your soul." Two fans appeared in her hands. She flicked them open and continued to dance. After a slow pirouette she held them up side by side. "Look."

Watercolor scenes moved across the folds. A blurred image rode atop ocean waves toward Chinatown, to the ironworks building, and at the end, Ming's body lay in a widening pool of crimson.

"I know your tricks, demon!"

Jiu giggled. "Marry me, and I'll save you."

"Never."

Childish whimpers came from behind the fan to echo through the fog, but Ming couldn't look away. The blood from his body in the pictures spread, spilled off the sides, and trickled down Jiu's hands and arms.

"As you wish," she said.

The fans closed, spurting blood in all directions, forcing Ming to close his eyes. When he opened them again, a blast of seawater sprayed him. Jiu and all her vibrant colors vanished. Overcast skies hung low as far as he could see.

The ferry bumped the slip several times before docking. He used a sleeve to wipe his face and smiled. A good life must be in store if the Fox Demon chose to visit him. The old legends said she sought the riches and protection of men by seducing kings and emperors. Indeed, he would soon be the royalty of a new Chinatown – in Oakland.

* * *

Lew kept busy inspecting the work and safety of the employees. The factory specialized in working iron anchors and link chains. Generations of his family had a formula and techniques Lew brought with him from mainland China. With population increases forcing San Francisco to become a large port city, their small business quickly grew.

He always believed *too busy* paralleled good fortune and less time to squander. The workers seemed to appreciate their jobs and never complained about toiling too hard and past their time to keep up with demands. He felt they wanted the factory to be as successful as he did, and this gave him a great sense of pride – of family.

Chen stood atop a high ladder against a water-cooling vat shouting orders to men working pulleys below. A large anchor moved overhead, inching toward the foreman as he yelled directions and climbed down. The workers slowly lowered the warm iron. Steam billowed up to the ceiling as a soft burble and hiss came from the vat.

"Nice work," Lew shouted. He walked over to his dear friend. "You make it look easy."

"It is." Both men laughed.

"Where's Ming?" Chen said.

"I told him I didn't want to be far from home. He offered to check the Oakland factory."

Chen looked away, stared at the evaporating steam. "He spends a lot of time there."

His foreman had never been the kind of a man to speak lightly of anything bothering him, which made the muscles between Lew's shoulders tense. "Someone has to monitor the progress … what do you mean exactly?"

"Every chance he gets, like when you go home for lunch to spend time with Yu, Ming leaves and doesn't always return."

"Maybe it upsets him that I go home to my wife when his left him only a short time ago."

"Even before that."

"I've known him a long time. We're like brothers, and I trust him. So unless you have some evidence he's been up to something, I think you should keep quiet about this."

Chen lowered his eyes and looked at Lew. "I'm sorry. It's just that—"

"Enough. I'll be in the office." He walked away, conflicting thoughts chasing each other in circles around his head like too many fish in a pond.

Lew rounded a corner and saw Ming running and shouting toward him. His partner came up then hunched over to catch his breath.

"What is it?" Lew said.

"On my way back…" Ming gasped for air. "It's Yu."

Lew put his hand on Ming's shoulder. "Is she all right?"

Ming nodded. "Yes, yes, I'm sure she's fine. A neighbor of yours asked if you would come see her before your usual lunch time."

"Ah, I should probably go then."

"First, please sign some important papers for the Oakland factory."

"Okay, but let's do it now, so I can go to Yu."

Both men stepped into the office. While Ming went to his desk and rifled through papers, Lew went over to his and picked up a pen.

"What are these?" Lew said.

"Dock rental agreement."

"But—"

"Just sign. I'll take care of the rest. Your neighbor seemed a little upset when she told me Yu sent for you."

"You should have said that before." Lew signed the papers and then rushed out of the office.

As he sprinted the two blocks to his home, he prayed for everything to be all right. The concerned looks on the neighbors' faces who'd gathered outside his house only made his anxiety worse. Lew barreled through the door and saw Yu lying on their bed mat, her sweaty face twisted in a grimace of pain. A Chinese apothecary from across the street sat beside her. The man stood up and shook his head when he saw Lew.

"You must take her to the Western hospital. Something isn't right."

He looked at his wife. "How will we get there?" Lew said.

"My son will pull her in the rickshaw we use for deliveries. Don't worry, he's young and fast, but you'll have to meet them there."

"No. Please, don't leave," Yu said. She reached out to him.

Lew took her hand and knelt on the edge of the mat. Blood seeped from underneath her onto his knee. He fought back a wave of panic and spoke in a calm voice. "I must go now, but I'll be there soon, or maybe even before you." He forced a smile.

She nodded.

"You know I can run fast," Lew said

"Yes. Run with dragon's breath behind you."

He kissed her hand then released it and looked up at the apothecary.

"Go now," the man said. "My son will be back any minute."

"Please, take care of—"

"Just leave," the apothecary yelled.

Lew bolted out the door.

Crowds blurred as he flew past Portsmouth Plaza, his long braid tapped his back in rhythmic thumps. Yu's words carried him. He prayed a dragon followed close behind and blew strong winds.

* * *

Lew had waited near the hospital's reception desk for over an hour when he saw a Chinese man pushing Yu in a wheelchair toward him. A Western doctor wearing a white coat walked alongside them.

"She's your wife?" he said.

The Chinese man translated the Westerner's words.

Lew nodded. He understood English better than he could speak it, but having the translator made things easier.

"She needs to see a specialist south of here. We've done what we can for now, but if you don't leave soon it could be too late."

"South of here?" Lew scratched his head. "How far?"

"Several hours away."

His heart sank when the doctor told him. "But how will we get there?"

The Westerner shrugged his shoulders and left.

"I know a way." The Chinese man spoke up.

"Please, tell me. I'll do anything."

"You know the Tongs," he whispered.

"No. I, I can't. They're criminals. It's too dangerous to ask."

"Then your wife and baby will die."

Lew thought for a moment. "What do I have to do?"

"I know a Westerner who's a soldier from the Bo Sin Seer Tong group that owns a motorcar. You will have to pay him a lot. You have any sycee? He likes to collect our things."

Yu gripped the sides of the wheelchair and groaned.

"Yes, I have one. A gold one saved for—"

The man's eyes lit up. "He'll want it before."

"Just get him here."

"Meet us out front in an hour. I'll keep your wife safe until you get back."

Lew nodded and ran for home. *What had he done to deserve this?* He and Yu had survived the plague that killed so many in Chinatown. He thought for sure this meant they should live. Not once did he ever think he'd have anything to do with the Tong gangs, and now he'd made a deal with the devils. With no other choices, perhaps he should feel lucky the translator had a connection to someone with a motorcar. Yes. It had been fortunate. "Thank you," he said aloud.

Yu's pale face haunted his vision as he hurried down streets. On his return, the small sycee boat of gold with a dragon carved on the side, all his earned savings, weighed heavily on his mind as well as in his hand. Lew's other treasure, his first son, Bao, lightened his heart as he pulled the three-year-old along with his other hand.

* * *

Ming got up and closed the door after Lew left. He separated the signed papers from the dock receipts he'd had on his desk and slid them inside his robe pocket. Maybe he should go find Worthington. No. *It's better to make him wait.* Feeling satisfied, he walked over to Lew's desk, sat back in the chair and put his feet up.

Chen walked up and peered in through a window. His eyes opened wide, and then he came around and entered the office. "Hey, what are you doing? So disrespectful to put those there." He tsked and pointed to Ming's dirty shoes.

"Get back to work and mind your own business."

The foreman scowled.

"You know, you're right," Ming said. "I've had a long day and should have my feet up at home. I'm certain you'll keep that watchful eye of yours on the factory while I'm gone." He got up and bumped Chen on his way out.

Dreaming of riches, Ming napped for an hour until clapping sounds woke him. He sat up and patted his robe for the signed papers. Although he wanted to make the Westerner wait, unease and restlessness nibbled the edges of his confidence. His decision to bring the contract to Worthington after opening the factory tomorrow morning gave him relief.

More claps came from outside. After putting his slippers on, Ming went to the door, opened it and looked out. Low clouds on the horizon glowed soft pinks above the setting sun. They reminded him of the beautiful Fox Demon. He stepped down and walked to the front of his apartment building.

Twilight faded to darkness as Ming stood and gazed out. Peripheral movement made him turn to the right. He gasped. A woman who could have been his wife's twin sat in a chair.

"Who are you?"

The woman smiled, raised her hands, and clapped three times. Her head fell off and landed into her open palms.

Ming's eyes widened. She flicked her wrists, and the head flew at him.

"Headless demon!" he said.

It circled him several times in the air chomping its teeth while lunging for his face.

"Why are you afraid?" she said. "You are the one who called me here."

"I did not."

"You killed your wife, and the bugs come. I'm here to eat them." She cackled then darted at him again.

He waved his arms to keep the gnashing maw away. The head landed on the pavement in front of him with a wet smack, eyes focused on the ground. An elongated, pointy tongue stretched out of its mouth and lapped at a trail of ants, inching the disembodied head forward with every swallow.

Ming ran back to his apartment and bolted the door. That hungry thing out there and the rest of the headless demon would leave when the ant supply ran out. Plenty of bigger bugs could be found elsewhere. He'd cleaned up good after strangling Xi. Ming had always taken pride in keeping a tidy abode. Still, little sleep would be had until it left. He lay back on his mat and listened to the moist, sticky sounds outside.

After several hours tossing and turning, Ming got up and washed his face. He didn't remember when the noises had stopped. Not that long ago he guessed, but his body needed the hour of sleep it got when the Fei Tou Bie finally left. These supernatural visits had to end. He'd find a shaman to cleanse the way and lessen the demons' dark natures after he handed the papers over to the Westerner.

The sun wouldn't rise for a couple hours, but Ming couldn't wait. Outside, a fog had rolled in. The demon's body no longer sat patiently waiting for its head. Even the chair had disappeared. Wary, Ming watched his steps until he felt the familiar sidewalk underfoot.

Chen showed up fifteen minutes after Ming opened the factory doors. Ming wondered if the foreman had followed him in. He walked over to secure a pulley and then went into the office. Moments later Chen yelled to Ming.

"What is this?" he shouted.

Ming looked through the office windows and saw Chen holding up papers. He patted his jacket and felt nothing. They must have fallen out! He opened the door and ran to Chen.

"Give them to me!"

Chen held the papers out of Ming's reach. Ming lunged at him, and the men fell to the floor, wrestling for the contract. Ming landed two hard punches to Chen's chest. The foreman let go. While Chen gasped for air, Ming grabbed the papers and climbed to his feet.

"Traitor!" Chen said.

Ming turned as Chen rose, a determined look on his face. Before he could fully regain his balance, Ming rushed Chen, pushing him hard. The foreman stumbled and then let out a choked cry as the point of an unfinished anchor tore through his chest from the back. Blood dripped off shredded flesh that hung from the curved barb.

"Traitor," he muttered once more, blood running from his mouth. Then his eyes closed.

A loud crack sounded, and the floor between them split open. The deceased Chen, the anchor, worktable and its vice fell into the widening fissure. Everything rumbled, shook and swayed. Ming lost his footing and fell. With his free hand, he clawed at the floor and rolled over.

An ancient warrior dressed in full Chinese armor stood at Ming's feet. Maggots filled the sockets of the decayed warrior's head, giving him writhing, white eyes. The foul worms wriggled across his face in a pulsing trail.

"General Lang!" Ming said. Every muscle in his body trembled.

The warrior raised a massive sword engraved with a long list of names on both sides. A forged dragon decorated the hilt and part of the blade; one of its ruby eyes twinkled. Ming watched as his name appeared on the blade. He knew the names carved there had been traitors of the Chinese people.

Ming lay paralyzed on the factory floor. Lightning bolted from the tip of the general's blade and blasted through the ceiling. Burning pieces of the roof crashed down. Ming's body buckled, and he screamed as falling debris landed on top of his body. He gasped for air, but his breath became blood. It seeped out around the brick pile that now covered him into a widening pool of crimson.

Pinned to the ground, he could do nothing but watch as General Chi Lang drifted upward, his vengeance done. Ming looked away. His hand caught on fire. The skin bubbled and melted off the bones – bones that clutched an unharmed contract. A deal he never should have made with the white devils.

That morning, sunrise brought no light to Chinatown. Thick layers of smoke darkened the skies and black clouds massed overhead, circling into vortices of soot and ash that dropped toward Ming. Behind them, two dragons breathed fire.

* * *

The Western Tong soldier slid the sycee into his coat pocket and glanced at Yu.

"Let's get," the Westerner said, hurrying them into his motorcar.

The man raced south in silence, looking back occasionally with concerned expressions. Bao leaned against Lew's right arm and slept. Yu held his left hand and wrenched it when she felt pain. Several hours had passed since his upper extremities went numb. The Tong soldier dropped them off at the hospital entrance, nodded once to Lew, and then sped away as the sun set. His wife gave birth to their second son Feng soon after. She didn't return from surgery for several hours. The Western doctors had stopped the bleeding but had to remove her womb.

Lew struggled with mixed feelings of loss and gratefulness until he saw Feng. One look at his son, and he'd never been so thankful. He watched over his family as they rested, and then he fell asleep in a chair.

Thunder rolled through and woke him. He stood and quietly left the room. Outside, dawn never came. Black clouds hung low in the sky. Lew thought he saw dragons behind them. He yawned and rubbed his eyes.

* * *

Lew left his family in safety and headed back to Chinatown. It took two weeks for him to get through the carnage. He crawled over bricks and twisted metal that filled the streets ten feet deep in some areas. Thick, dirty air choked his every breath. Decaying bodies lay strewn among layers of rubble across miles of wasteland.

The entrance and one side wall of the ironworks remained erect. Lew had passed the collapsed building several times without recognition. He spent countless days moving debris, his hands raw and bleeding.

He climbed toward folded white papers jutting from a mound. Bricks slid underneath him as he scrabbled up. They fell away and left him looking down at charred remains. Skeletal fingers clutched the papers. Lew tugged on them, and the tiny bones fell apart. He sat back, read the papers, and wept with joy and sorrow.

* * *

Lew Hong sat on a bench in a small garden, burning the contract he'd found in Ming's hand. A funerary honor for his business partner, despite the story they told. Ming's deception saved his family from the great earthquake that had demolished San Francisco.

At their Oakland fishing boat warehouse, which hadn't been damaged, Lew provided housing and care to survivors. He'd been a part of the Chinese Six Companies that helped plan and propose rebuilding a new Chinatown to which the Westerners might agree.

After three years of keeping the scorched bones of his business partner in an urn, Lew had arranged for them to be exhumed and ground to ash. With a large, private donation, he handed the remains over to the caretaker at the Chapel of the Chimes, ensuring Ming received the eternity of golden splendor he deserved after all.

How an Evil Spirit Was Exorcised

Major J.F.A. McNair and Thomas Lambert Barlow

ONCE UPON A TIME there lived in the city of Peshawar, not very long ago, an old Priest who had obtained a reputation for the power he possessed over malignant spirits. This Priest usually had under his tuition two or three boys who were 'Jinns', and to whom as it pleased him from time to time he communicated the knowledge he possessed of the black art.

This old Priest came to dwell in the village of Haji Shah, and took up his abode near to the Mahomedan mosque there. This mosque was in close proximity to the quarters of the '*Chuprassies*', who you know, are employed by the Sirkar or Government in the suppression of salt smuggling.

The Chief of these '*Chuprassies*' had in his household a man of the name of Gopee, whose brother Shivedas was one of the '*Chuprassies*', and lived with the others in the quarters provided for them.

Shivedas was occasionally seized with violent fits, and when under their influence would rave like a maniac. All kinds of medicine had been tried to relieve him of the disorder, but it was all in vain; so at last his friends left him to himself, and only sought to prevent his doing any injury to himself when the fits came upon him.

One day when Shivedas was returning to his quarters he was again attacked by his old malady, and so violent was he on this occasion that it took four men to hold him down on his '*charpai*', or bed. His brother Gopee was at once sent for, and he found him in one of the severest fits he had ever had. On reaching his bedside, Shivedas cried out, "Save me, Gopee; save me!"

Those round the bed, and the four holding him, said, "Why do you not do something for your brother?" He replied, "I have done all I can, but there is no cure for his disease." They said, "Then why do you not send for the Priest here, who would soon expel this evil spirit, which comes now and again to torment him?" Now Gopee did not believe in the power of the Priest. At last one of the '*Chuprassies*' went to their European Chief's house, and begged him to come up to the quarters to see what could be done. When he arrived there and saw the state that Shivedas was in, and Gopee, his brother, in such great distress, he said, "What can be done to relieve this man?" They all said, "Send for the Priest, the old Peshawar man, and he will soon put him right." The Chief said, "Well, do so if you like." They replied, "He will not come for us, for he is a grumpy old man; but he will come for you." So the Chief, to relieve the sufferer, and perhaps to satisfy his own curiosity, sent to ask the Priest to come.

In a short time he made his appearance, just when Shivedas was in one of his worse struggles, and looking at him for some time, he all of a sudden seemed to make up his mind, and drawing his Quran from his pocket went close to the bedside and called out, "Are you going to leave this man, or not?" And a voice came from Shivedas, "No! I will not." Now, many present heard the voice, but it was not the voice of Shivedas.

The Priest then asked for some rag, and many ran to get a piece of an old '*Chudder*', or cloth, but he said, "No! this will not do; it must be blue rag." And in very quick time someone ran and brought a piece from the Bazaar.

When the Priest took it into his hand he called for a light, and then proceeded to burn it in the flame. Then, again advancing to the bedside, with the burning rag in one hand and the open Quran in the other, he called out in a louder tone than before, "Are you going to leave this man, or are you not? If not

I will burn you out and all your generation." The same voice then uttered the words, "I will not leave him; and who are you?"

The old Priest then placed the smouldering rag to the nose of Shivedas, and again threatened the evil spirit; and then, to the astonishment of all, the voice said, "I will go away this time if you will not trouble nor worry me."

After this Shivedas became still and tranquil, and went off into a profound sleep.

Some hours afterwards, when he awoke, and was questioned as to what had occurred, he could call nothing to his remembrance.

The '*Chuprassies*' believed that the evil spirit had been exorcised by the Priest, and it is certainly true that Shivedas had no return of his fits; and I tell you this tale, for it is believed by many of us to this day.

His Dead Wife's Photograph

S. Mukerji

THIS STORY CREATED A SENSATION when it was first told. It appeared in the papers and many big Physicists and Natural Philosophers were, at least so they thought, able to explain the phenomenon. I shall narrate the event and also tell the reader what explanation was given, and let him draw his own conclusions.

This was what happened.

A friend of mine, a clerk in the same office as myself, was an amateur photographer; let us call him Jones.

Jones had a half plate Sanderson camera with a Ross lens and a Thornton Picard behind lens shutter, with pneumatic release. The plate in question was a Wrattens ordinary, developed with Ilford Pyro Soda developer prepared at home. All these particulars I give for the benefit of the more technical reader.

Mr Smith, another clerk in our office, invited Mr. Jones to take a likeness of his wife and sister-in-law.

This sister-in-law was the wife of Mr. Smith's elder brother, who was also a Government servant, then on leave. The idea of the photograph was of the sister-in-law.

Jones was a keen photographer himself. He had photographed every body in the office including the peons and sweepers, and had even supplied every sitter of his with copies of his handiwork. So he most willingly consented, and anxiously waited for the Sunday on which the photograph was to be taken.

Early on Sunday morning, Jones went to the Smiths'. The arrangement of light in the verandah was such that a photograph could only be taken after midday; and so he stayed there to breakfast.

At about one in the afternoon all arrangements were complete and the two ladies, Mrs. Smiths, were made to sit in two cane chairs and after long and careful focussing, and moving the camera about for an hour, Jones was satisfied at last and an exposure was made. Mr. Jones was sure that the plate was all right; and so, a second plate was not exposed although in the usual course of things this should have been done.

He wrapped up his things and went home promising to develop the plate the same night and bring a copy of the photograph the next day to the office.

The next day, which was a Monday, Jones came to the office very early, and I was the first person to meet him.

"Well, Mr. Photographer," I asked "what success?"

"I got the picture all right," said Jones, unwrapping an unmounted picture and handing it over to me "most funny, don't you think so?"

"No, I don't … I think it is all right, at any rate I did not expect anything better from you …", I said.

"No," said Jones "the funny thing is that only two ladies sat …"

"Quite right," I said "the third stood in the middle."

"There was no third lady at all there …", said Jones.

"Then you imagined she was there, and there we find her …"

"I tell you, there were only two ladies there when I exposed" insisted Jones. He was looking awfully worried.

"Do you want me to believe that there were only two persons when the plate was exposed and three when it was developed?" I asked. "That is exactly what has happened," said Jones.

"Then it must be the most wonderful developer you used, or was it that this was the second exposure given to the same plate?"

"The developer is the one which I have been using for the last three years, and the plate, the one I charged on Saturday night out of a new box that I had purchased only on Saturday afternoon."

A number of other clerks had come up in the meantime, and were taking great interest in the picture and in Jones' statement.

It is only right that a description of the picture be given here for the benefit of the reader. I wish I could reproduce the original picture too, but that for certain reasons is impossible.

When the plate was actually exposed there were only two ladies, both of whom were sitting in cane chairs. When the plate was developed it was found that there was in the picture a figure, that of a lady, standing in the middle. She wore a broad-edged *dhoti* (the reader should not forget that all the characters are Indians), only the upper half of her body being visible, the lower being covered up by the low backs of the cane chairs. She was distinctly behind the chairs, and consequently slightly out of focus. Still everything was quite clear. Even her long necklace was visible through the little opening in the *dhoti* near the right shoulder. She was resting her hands on the backs of the chairs and the fingers were nearly totally out of focus, but a ring on the right ring-finger was clearly visible. She looked like a handsome young woman of twenty-two, short and thin. One of the ear-rings was also clearly visible, although the face itself was slightly out of focus. One thing, and probably the funniest thing, that we overlooked then but observed afterwards, was that immediately behind the three ladies was a barred window. The two ladies, who were one on each side, covered up the bars to a certain height from the bottom with their bodies, but the lady in the middle was partly transparent because the bars of the window were very faintly visible through her. This fact, however, as I have said already, we did not observe then. We only laughed at Jones and tried to assure him that he was either drunk or asleep. At this moment Smith of our office walked in, removing the trouser clips from his legs.

Smith took the unmounted photograph, looked at it for a minute, turned red and blue and green and finally very pale. Of course, we asked him what the matter was and this was what he said:

"The third lady in the middle was my first wife, who has been dead these eight years. Before her death she asked me a number of times to have her photograph taken. She used to say that she had a presentiment that she might die early. I did not believe in her presentiment myself, but I did not object to the photograph. So one day I ordered the carriage and asked her to dress up. We intended to go to a good professional. She dressed up and the carriage was ready, but as we were going to start news reached us that her mother was dangerously ill. So we went to see her mother instead. The mother was very ill, and I had to leave her there. Immediately afterwards I was sent away on duty to another station and so could not bring her back. It was in fact after full three months and a half that I returned and then though her mother was all right, my wife was not. Within fifteen days of my return she died of puerperal fever after child-birth and the child died too. A photograph of her was never taken. When she dressed up for the last time on the day that she left my home she had the necklace and the ear-rings on, as you see her wearing in the photograph. My present wife has them now but she does not generally put them on."

This was too big a pill for me to swallow. So I at once took French leave from my office, bagged the photograph and rushed out on my bicycle. I went to Mr. Smith's house and looked Mrs. Smith up. Of course, she was much astonished to see a third lady in the picture but could not guess who she was. This I had expected, as supposing Smith's story to be true, this lady had never seen her husband's first wife. The elder brother's wife, however, recognized the likeness at once and she virtually repeated the story which Smith had told me earlier that day. She even brought out the necklace and the ear-rings for my inspection and conviction. They were the same as those in the photograph.

All the principal newspapers of that time got hold of the fact and within a week there was any number of applications for the ghostly photograph. But Mr. Jones refused to supply copies of it to anybody for various reasons, the principal being that Smith would not allow it. I am, however, the fortunate possessor of a copy which, for obvious reasons, I am not allowed to show to anybody. One copy of the picture was sent to America and another to England. I do not now remember exactly to whom. My own copy I showed to the Rev. Father —— M.A., D.SC., B.D., etc., and asked him to find out a scientific explanation of the phenomenon. The following explanation was given by the gentleman. (I am afraid I shall not be able to reproduce the learned Father's exact words, but this is what he meant or at least what I understood him to mean).

"The girl in question was dressed in this particular way on an occasion, say ten years ago. Her image was cast *on space* and the reflection was projected from one luminous body (one planet) on another till it made a circuit of millions and millions of miles in space and then came back to earth at the exact moment when our friend, Mr. Jones, was going to make the exposure.

"Take for instance the case of a man who is taking the photograph of a mirage. He is photographing place X from place Y, when X and Y are, say, two hundred miles apart, and it may be that his camera is facing east while place X is actually towards the west of place Y."

In school I had read a little of Science and Chemistry and could make a dry analysis of a salt; but this was an item too big for my limited comprehension.

The fact, however, remains and I believe it, that Smith's first wife did come back to this terrestrial globe of ours over eight years after her death to give a sitting for a photograph in a form which, though it did not affect the retina of our eye, did impress a sensitized plate; in a form that did not affect the retina of the eye, I say, because Jones must have been looking at his sitters at the time when he was pressing the bulb of the pneumatic release of his time and instantaneous shutter.

The story is most wonderful but this is exactly what happened. Smith says this is the first time he has ever seen, or heard from, his dead wife. It is popularly believed in India that a dead wife gives a lot of trouble, if she ever revisits this earth, but this is, thank God, not the experience of my friend, Mr. Smith.

It is now over seven years since the event mentioned above happened; and the dead girl has never appeared again. I would very much like to have a photograph of the two ladies taken once more; but I have never ventured to approach Smith with the proposal. In fact, I learnt photography myself with a view to take the photograph of the two ladies, but as I have said, I have never been able to speak to Smith about my intention, and probably never shall. The ten pounds, that I spent on my cheap photographic outfit may be a waste. But I have learnt an art which though rather costly for my limited means is nevertheless an art worth learning.

The Major's Lease

S. Mukerji

A CURIOUS LITTLE STORY was told the other day in a certain Civil Court in British India.

A certain military officer, let us call him Major Brown, rented a house in one of the big Cantonment stations where he had been recently transferred with his regiment.

This gentleman had just arrived from England with his wife. He was the son of a rich man at home and so he could afford to have a large house. This was the first time he had come out to India and was consequently rather unacquainted with the manners and customs of this country.

Major Brown took this house on a long lease and thought he had made a bargain. The house was large and stood in the centre of a very spacious compound. There was a garden which appeared to have been carefully laid out once, but as the house had no tenant for a long time the garden looked more like a wilderness. There were two very well kept lawn tennis courts and these were a great attraction to the Major, who was very keen on tennis. The stablings and out-houses were commodious and the Major, who was thinking of keeping a few polo ponies, found the whole thing very satisfactory. Over and above everything he found the landlord very obliging. He had heard on board the steamer on his way out that Indian landlords were the worst class of human beings one could come across on the face of this earth (and that is very true), but this particular landlord looked like an exception to the general rule.

He consented to make at his own expense all the alterations that the Major wanted him to do, and these alterations were carried out to Major and Mrs. Brown's entire satisfaction.

On his arrival in this station Major Brown had put up at an hotel and after some alterations had been made he ordered the house to be furnished. This was done in three or four days and then he moved in.

Annexed is a rough sketch of the house in question. The house was a very large one and there was a number of rooms, but we have nothing to do with all of them. The spots marked 'C' and 'E' represent the doors.

Dressing room	Bedroom E			
Dressing room	Bedroom G C	Corridor		
Spare room	Dining room		Drawing room	Spare room
	Front verandah			

Now what happened in court was this:

After he had occupied the house for not over three weeks the Major and his wife cleared out and took shelter again in the hotel from which they had come. The landlord demanded rent for the entire period stipulated for in the lease and the Major refused to pay. The matter went to court. The presiding Judge, who was an Indian gentleman, was one of the cleverest men in the service, and he thought it was a very simple case.

When the case was called on the plaintiff's pleader said that he would begin by proving the lease. Major Brown, the defendant, who appeared in person, said that he would admit it. The Judge who was a very kind hearted gentleman asked the defendant why he had vacated the house.

"I could not stay," said the Major "I had every intention of living in the house, I got it furnished and spent two thousand *rupees* over it, I was laying out a garden...."

"But what do you mean by saying that you could not stay?"

"If your Honour passed a night in that house, you would understand what I meant," said the Major.

"You take the oath and make a statement," said the Judge. Major Brown then made the following statement on oath in open court.

"When I came to the station I saw the house and my wife liked it. We asked the landlord whether he would make a few alterations and he consented. After the alterations had been carried out I executed the lease and ordered the house to be furnished. A week after the execution of the lease we moved in. The house is very large."

Here followed a description of the building; but to make matters clear and short I have copied out the rough pencil sketch which is still on the record of the case and marked the doors and rooms, as the Major had done, with letters.

"I do not dine at the mess. I have an early dinner at home with my wife and retire early. My wife and I sleep in the same bedroom (the room marked 'G' in the plan), and we are generally in bed at about eleven o'clock at night. The servants all go away to the out-houses which are at a distance of about forty yards from the main building, only one *Jamadar* (porter) remains in the front verandah. This *Jamadar* also keeps an eye on the whole main building, besides I have got a good, faithful watch dog which I brought out from home. He stays outside with the *Jamadar*.

"For the first fifteen days we were quite comfortable, then the trouble began.

"One night before dinner my wife was reading a story, a detective story, of a particularly interesting nature. There were only a few more pages left and so we thought that she would finish them before we put out the reading lamp. We were in the bedroom. But it took her much longer than she had expected it would, and so it was actually half an hour after midnight when we put out the big sixteen candle power reading lamp which stood on a teapoy near the head of the beds. Only a small bedroom lamp remained.

"But though we put out the light we did not fall asleep. We were discussing the cleverness of the detective and the folly of the thief who had left a clue behind, and it was actually two o'clock when we pulled our rugs up to our necks and closed our eyes.

"At that moment we heard the footsteps of a number of persons walking along the corridor. The corridor runs the whole length of the house as will appear from the rough sketch. This corridor was well carpeted still we heard the tread of a number of feet. We looked at the door 'C'. This door was closed but not bolted from inside. Slowly it was pushed open, and, horror of horrors, three shadowy forms walked into the room. One was distinctly the form of a white man in European night attire, another the form of a white woman, also in night attire, and the third was the form of a black woman, probably an Indian nurse or *ayah*.

"We remained dumb with horror, as we could see clearly that these unwelcome visitors were not of this world. We could not move.

"The three figures passed right round the beds as if searching for something. They looked into every nook and corner of the bed-room and then passed into the dressing room. Within half a minute they returned and passed out into the corridor in the same order in which they had come in, namely, the man first, the white woman next, and the black woman last of all.

"We lay as if dead. We could hear them in the corridor and in the bedroom adjoining, with the door 'E', and in the dressing room attached to that bedroom. They again returned and passed into the corridor … and then we could hear them no more.

"It must have taken me at least five minutes to collect my senses and to bring my limbs under control. When I got up I found that my wife had fainted. I hurried out of the room, rushed along the corridor, opened the front door and called the servants. The servants were all approaching the house across the land which separated the servants' quarters from the main building. Then I went into the dining room, and procuring some brandy, gave it to my wife. It was with some difficulty that I could make her swallow it, but it revived her and she looked at me with a bewildered smile on her face.

"The servants had in the meantime arrived and were in the corridor. Their presence had the effect of giving us some courage. Leaving my wife in bed I went out and related to the servants what I had seen. The *Chaukidar* (the night watchman) who was an old resident of the compound (in fact he had been in charge of the house when it was vacant, before I rented it) gave me the history of the ghost, which my *Jamadar* interpreted to me. I have brought the *Chaukidar* and shall produce him as my witness."

This was the statement of the Major. Then there was the statement of Jokhi Passi, *Chaukidar*, defendant's witness.

The statement of this witness as recorded was as follows:

"My age is sixty years. At the time of the Indian Mutiny I was a full-grown young man. This house was built at that time. I mean two or three years after the Mutiny. I have always been in charge. After the Mutiny one Judge came to live in the house. He was called Judge Parson (probably Pearson). The Judge had to try a young Muhammadan charged with murder and he sentenced the youth to death. The aged parents of the young man vowed vengeance against the good Judge. On the night following the morning on which the execution took place it appeared that certain undesirable characters were prowling about the compound. I was then the watchman in charge as I am now. I woke up the Indian nurse who slept with the Judge's baby in a bed-room adjoining the one in which the Judge himself slept. On waking up she found that the baby was not in its cot. She rushed out of the bed-room and informed the Judge and his wife. Then a feverish search began for the baby, but it was never found. The police were communicated with and they arrived at about four in the morning. The police enquiry lasted for about half an hour and then the officers went away promising to come again. At last the Judge, his wife, and nurse all retired to their respective beds where they were found lying dead later in the morning. Another police enquiry took place, and it was found that death was due to snake-bite. There were two small punctures on one of the legs of each victim. How a snake got in and killed each victim in turn, especially when two slept in one room and the third in another, and finally got out, has remained a mystery. But the Judge, his wife, and the nurse are still seen on every Friday night looking for the missing baby. One rainy season the servants' quarters were being re-roofed. I had then an occasion to sleep in the corridor; and thus I saw the ghosts. At that time I was as afraid as the Major Saheb is to-day, but then I soon found out that the ghosts were quite harmless."

This was the story as recorded in court. The Judge was a very sensible man (I had the pleasure and honour of being introduced to him about twenty years after this incident), and with a number of people, he decided to pass one Friday night in the haunted house. He did so. What he saw does not appear from the record; for he left no inspection notes and probably he never made any. He delivered judgment on Monday following. It is a very short judgment.

After reciting the facts the judgment proceeds: "I have recorded the statements of the defendant and a witness produced by him. I have also made a local inspection. I find that the landlord, (the plaintiff) knew that for certain reasons the house was practically uninhabitable, and he concealed that fact from his tenant. He, therefore, could not recover. The suit is dismissed with costs."

The haunted house remained untenanted for a long time. The proprietor subsequently made a gift of it to a charitable institution. The founders of this institution, who were Hindus and firm believers in charms and exorcisms, had some religious ceremony performed on the premises. Afterwards the house was pulled down and on its site now stands one of the grandest buildings in the station, that cost fully ten thousand pounds. Only this morning I received a visit from a gentleman who lives in the building, referred to above, but evidently he has not even heard of the ghosts of the Judge, his wife, and his Indian *ayah*.

It is now nearly fifty years; but the missing baby has not been heard of. If it is alive it has grown into a fully developed man. But does he know the fate of his parents and his nurse?

In this connection it will not be out of place to mention a fact that appeared in the papers some years ago.

A certain European gentleman was posted to a district in the Madras Presidency as a Government servant in the Financial Department.

When this gentleman reached the station to which he had been posted he put up at the Club, as they usually do, and began to look out for a house, when he was informed that there was a haunted house in the neighbourhood. Being rather sceptical he decided to take this house, ghost or no ghost. He was given to understand by the members of the Club that this house was a bit out of the way and was infested at night with thieves and robbers who came to divide their booty in that house; and to guard against its being occupied by a tenant it had been given a bad reputation. The proprietor being a wealthy old native of the old school did not care to investigate. So our friend, whom we shall, for the purposes of this story, call Mr. Hunter, took the house at a fair rent.

The house was in charge of a *Chaukidar* (care-taker, porter or watchman) when it was vacant. Mr. Hunter engaged the same man as a night watchman for this house. This *Chaukidar* informed Mr. Hunter that the ghost appeared only one day in the year, namely, the 21st of September, and added that if Mr. Hunter kept out of the house on that night there would be no trouble.

"I always keep away on the night of the 21st September," said the watchman.

"And what kind of ghost is it?" asked Mr. Hunter.

"It is a European lady dressed in white," said the man.

"What does she do?" asked Mr. Hunter.

"Oh! she comes out of the room and calls you and asks you to follow her," said the man.

"Has anybody ever followed her?"

"Nobody that I know of, Sir," said the man. "The man who was here before me saw her and died from fear."

"Most wonderful! But why do not people follow her in a body?" asked Mr. Hunter.

"It is very easy to say that, Sir, but when you see her you will not like to follow her yourself. I have been in this house for over twenty years, lots of times European soldiers have passed the night of the 21st of September, intending to follow her but when she actually comes nobody has ever ventured."

"Most wonderful! I shall follow her this time," said Mr. Hunter.

"As you please Sir," said the man and retired.

It was one of the duties of Mr. Hunter to distribute the pensions of all retired Government servants.

In this connection Mr. Hunter used to come in contact with a number of very old men in the station who attended his office to receive their pensions from him.

By questioning them Mr. Hunter got so far that the house had at one time been occupied by a European officer.

This officer had a young wife who fell in love with a certain Captain Leslie. One night when the husband was out on tour (and not expected to return within a week) his wife was entertaining Captain Leslie. The gentleman returned unexpectedly and found his wife in the arms of the Captain.

He lost his self-control and attacked the couple with a meat chopper – the first weapon that came handy.

Captain Leslie moved away and then cleared out leaving the unfortunate wife at the mercy of the infuriated husband. He aimed a blow at her head which she warded off with her hand. But so severe was the blow that the hand was cut off and the woman fell down on the ground quite unconscious. The sight of blood made the husband mad. Subsequently the servants came up and called a doctor, but by the time the doctor arrived the woman was dead.

The unfortunate husband who had become raving mad was sent to a lunatic asylum and thence taken away to England. The body of the woman was in the local cemetery; but what had become of the severed hand was not known. The missing limb had never been found. All this was fifty years ago, that is, immediately after the Indian Mutiny.

This was what Mr. Hunter gathered.

The 21st September was not very far off. Mr. Hunter decided to meet the ghost.

The night in question arrived, and Mr. Hunter sat in his bed-room with his magazine. The lamp was burning brightly.

The servants had all retired, and Mr. Hunter knew that if he called for help nobody would hear him, and even if anybody did hear, he too would not come.

He was, however, a very bold man and sat there awaiting developments.

At one in the morning he heard footsteps approaching the bed-room from the direction of the dining-room.

He could distinctly hear the rustle of the skirts. Gradually the door between the two rooms began to open wide. Then the curtain began to move. Mr. Hunter sat with straining eyes and beating heart.

At last she came in. The Englishwoman in flowing white robes. Mr. Hunter sat panting unable to move. She looked at him for about a minute and beckoned him to follow her. It was then that Mr. Hunter observed that she had only one hand.

He got up and followed her. She went back to the dining-room and he followed her there. There was no light in the dining-room but he could see her faintly in the dark. She went right across the dining-room to the door on the other side which opened on the verandah. Mr. Hunter could not see what she was doing at the door, but he knew she was opening it.

When the door opened she passed out and Mr. Hunter followed. Then she walked across the verandah down the steps and stood upon the lawn. Mr. Hunter was on the lawn in a moment. His fears had now completely vanished. She next proceeded along the lawn in the direction of a hedge. Mr. Hunter also reached the hedge and found that under the hedge were concealed two spades. The gardener must have been working with them and left them there after the day's work.

The lady made a sign to him and he took up one of the spades. Then again she proceeded and he followed.

They had reached some distance in the garden when the lady with her foot indicated a spot and Mr. Hunter inferred that she wanted him to dig there. Of course, Mr. Hunter knew that he was not going to discover a treasure-trove, but he was sure he was going to find something very interesting. So he began digging with all his vigour. Only about eighteen inches below the surface the blade struck against some hard substance. Mr. Hunter looked up.

The apparition had vanished. Mr. Hunter dug on and discovered that the hard substance was a human hand with the fingers and everything intact. Of course, the flesh had gone, only the bones remained. Mr. Hunter picked up the bones and knew exactly what to do.

He returned to the house, dressed himself up in his cycling costume and rode away with the bones and the spade to the cemetery. He waked the night watchman, got the gate opened, found out the tomb of the murdered woman and close to it interred the bones, that he had found in such a mysterious fashion, reciting as much of the service as he could remember. Then he paid some *buksheesh* (reward) to the night watchman and came home.

He put back the spade in its old place and retired. A few days after he paid a visit to the cemetery in the day-time and found that grass had grown on the spot which he had dug up. The bones had evidently not been disturbed.

The next year on the 21st September Mr. Hunter kept up the whole night, but he had no visit from the ghostly lady.

The house is now in the occupation of another European gentleman who took it after Mr. Hunter's transfer from the station and this new tenant had no visit from the ghost either. Let us hope that 'she' now rests in peace.

The following extract from a Bengal newspaper that appeared in September 1913, is very interesting and instructive.

"The following extraordinary phenomenon took place at the Hooghly Police Club Building, Chinsurah, at about midnight on last Saturday.

"At this late hour of the night some peculiar sounds of agony on the roof of the house aroused the resident members of the Club, who at once proceeded to the roof with lamps and found to their entire surprise a lady clad in white jumping from the roof to the ground (about a hundred feet in height) followed by a man with a dagger in his hands. But eventually no trace of it could be found on the ground. This is not the first occasion that such beings are found to visit this house and it is heard from a reliable source that long ago a woman committed suicide by hanging and it is believed that her spirit loiters round the building. As these incidents have made a deep impression upon the members, they have decided to remove the Club from the said buildings."

What Uncle Saw

S. Mukerji

UNCLE WAS A VERY STRONG and powerful man and used to boast a good deal of his strength. He was employed in a Government Office in Calcutta. He used to come to his village home during the holidays. He was a widower with one or two children, who stayed with his brother's family in the village.

Uncle has had no bed-room of his own since his wife's death. Whenever he paid us a visit one of us used to place his bed-room at uncle's disposal. It is a custom in Bengal to sleep with one's wife and children in the same bed-room. So whenever Uncle turned up I used to give my bed-room to him as I was the only person without children. On such occasions I slept in one of the *'Baithaks'* (drawing-rooms). A *Baithak* is a drawing-room and guest-room combined.

In rich Bengal families of the orthodox style the *'Baithak'* or *'Baithak khana'* is a very large room generally devoid of all furniture, having a thick rich carpet on the floor with a clean sheet upon it and big *takias* (pillows) all around the wall. The elderly people would sit on the ground and lean against the *takias*; while we, the younger lot, sat upon the *takias* and leaned against the wall which in the case of the particular room in our house was covered with some kind of yellow paint which did not come off on the clothes.

Sometimes a *takia* would burst and the cotton stuffing inside would come out; and then the old servant (his status is that of an English butler, his duty to prepare the hookah for the master) would give us a chase with a *lathi* (stick) and the offender would run away, and not return until all incriminating evidence had been removed and the old servant's wrath had subsided.

Well, when Uncle used to come I slept in the *'Baithak'* and my wife slept somewhere in the *zenana*, I never inquired where.

On this particular occasion Uncle missed the train by which he usually came. It was the month of October and he should have arrived at eight p.m. My bed had been made in the *Baithak*. But the eight p.m. train came and stopped and passed on and Uncle did not turn up.

So we thought he had been detained for the night. It was the Durgapooja season and some presents for the children at home had to be purchased and, we thought, that was what was detaining him. And so at about ten p.m. we all retired to bed. The bed that had been made for me in the *'Baithak'* remained there for Uncle in case he turned up by the eleven p.m. train. As a matter of fact we did not expect him till the next morning.

But as misfortune would have it Uncle did arrive by the eleven o'clock train.

All the house-hold had retired, and though the old servant suggested that I should be waked up, Uncle would not hear of it. He would sleep in the bed originally made for me, he said.

The bed was in the central *Baithak* or hall. My Uncle was very fond of sleeping in side-rooms. I do not know why. Anyhow he ordered the servant to remove his bed to one of the side-rooms. Accordingly the bed was taken to one of them. One side of that room had two windows opening on the garden. The garden was more a park-like place, rather neglected, but still well wooded abounding in jack fruit trees. It used to be quite shady and dark during the day there. On this particular night it must have been very dark. I do not remember now whether there was a moon or not.

Well, Uncle went to sleep and so did the servants. It was about eight o'clock the next morning, when we thought that Uncle had slept long enough, that we went to wake him up.

The door connecting the side-room with the main *Baithak* was closed, but not bolted from inside; so we pushed the door open and went in.

Uncle lay in bed panting. He stared at us with eyes that saw but did not perceive. We at once knew that something was wrong. On touching his body we found that he had high fever. We opened the windows, and it was then that Uncle spoke "Don't open or it would come in—"

"What would come in Uncle – what?" we asked.

But uncle had fainted.

The doctor was called in. He arrived at about ten in the morning. He said it was high fever – due to what he could not say. All the same he prescribed a medicine.

The medicine had the effect of reducing the temperature, and at about six in the evening consciousness returned. Still he was in a very weak condition. Some medicine was given to induce sleep and he passed the night well. We nursed him by turns at night. The next morning we had all the satisfaction of seeing him all right. He walked from the bed-room, though still very weak and came to the Central *Baithak* where he had tea with us. It was then that we asked what he had seen and what he had meant by "It would come in."

Oh how we wish, we had never asked him the question, at least then.

This was what he said:

"After I had gone to bed I found that there were a few mosquitoes and so I could not sleep well. It was about midnight when they gradually disappeared and then I began to fall asleep. But just as I was dozing off I heard somebody strike the bars of the windows thrice. It was like three distinct strokes with a cane on the gratings outside. 'Who is there?' I asked; but no reply. The striking stopped. Again I closed my eyes and again the same strokes were repeated. This time I nearly lost my temper; I thought it was some urchin of the neighbourhood in a mischievous mood. 'Who is there?' I again shouted – again no reply. The striking however stopped. But after a time it commenced afresh. This time I lost my temper completely and opened the window, determined to thrash anybody whom I found there – forgetting that the windows were barred and fully six feet above the ground. Well in the darkness I saw, I saw—"

Here uncle had a fit of shivering and panting, and within a minute he lost all consciousness. The fever was again high. The doctor was summoned but this time his medicines did no good. Uncle never regained consciousness. In fact after twenty-four hours he died of heart failure the next morning, leaving his story unfinished and without in any way giving us an idea of what that terrible thing was which he had seen beyond the window. The whole thing remains a deep mystery and unfortunately the mystery will never be solved.

Nobody has ventured to pass a night in the side-room since then. If I had not been a married man with a very young wife I might have tried.

One thing however remains and it is this that though uncle got all the fright in the world in that room, he neither came out of that room nor called for help.

One cry for help and the whole house-hold would have been awake. In fact there was a servant within thirty yards of the window which uncle had opened; and this man says he heard uncle open the window and close and bolt it again, though he had not heard uncle's shouts of "Who is there?"

Only this morning I read this funny advertisement in the *Morning Post*.

"*Haunted Houses*. – Man and wife, cultured and travelled, gentle people – having lost fortune ready to act as care-takers and to investigate in view of removing trouble—"

Well – in a haunted house these gentle people expect to see something. Let us hope they will not see what our Uncle saw or what the Major saw.

This advertisement clearly shows that even in countries like England haunted houses do exist, or at least houses exist which are believed to be haunted.

If what we see really depends on what we think or what we believe, no wonder that there are so many more haunted houses in India than in England. This reminds me of a very old incident of my early school days. A boy was really caught by a ghost and then there was trouble. We shall not forget the thrashing we received from our teacher in the school; and the fellow who was actually caught by the ghost – if ghost it was, will never say in future that ghosts don't exist.

In this connection it may not be out of place to narrate another incident, though it does not fall within the same category with the main story that heads this chapter. The only reason why I do so is that the facts tally in one respect, though in one respect only, and that is that the person who knew would tell nothing.

This was a friend of mine who was a widower. We were in the same office together and he occupied a chair and a table next but one to mine. This gentleman was in our office for only six months after narrating the story. If he had stayed longer we might have got out his secret, but unfortunately he went away; he has gone so far from us that probably we shall not meet again for the next ten years.

It was in connection with the 'Smith's dead wife's photograph' controversy that one day one of my fellow clerks told me that a visit from a dead wife was nothing very wonderful, as our friend Haralal could testify.

I always took of a lot of interest in ghosts and their stories. So I was generally at Haralal's desk cross-examining him about this affair; at first the gentleman was very uncommunicative but when he saw I would give him no rest he made a statement which I have every reason to believe is true. This is more or less what he says.

"It was about ten years ago that I joined this office. I have been a widower ever since I left college – in fact I married the daughter of a neighbour when I was at college and she died about three years afterwards, when I was just thinking of beginning life in right earnest. She has been dead these ten years and I shall never marry again, (a young widower in good circumstances, in Bengal, is as rare as a blue rose).

"I have a suite of bachelor rooms in Calcutta, but I go to my suburban home on every Saturday afternoon and stay there till Monday morning, that is, I pass my Saturday night and the whole of Sunday in my village home every week.

"On this particular occasion nearly eight years ago, that is, about a year and a half after the death of my young wife I went home by an evening train. There is any number of trains in the evening and there is no certainty by which train I go, so if I am late, generally everybody goes to bed with the exception of my mother.

"On this particular night I reached home rather late. It was the month of September and there had been a heavy shower in the town and all tram-car services had been suspended.

"When I reached the railway station I found that the trains were not running to time either. I was given to understand that a tree had been blown down against the telegraph wire, and so the signals were not going through; and as it was rather dark the trains were only running on the report of a motor trolly that the line was clear. Thus I reached home at about eleven instead of eight in the evening.

"I found my father also sitting up for me though he had had his dinner. He wanted to learn the particulars of the storm at Calcutta.

"Within ten minutes of my arrival he went to bed and within an hour I finished my dinner and retired for the night.

"It was rather stuffy and the bed was damp as I was perspiring freely; and consequently I was not feeling inclined to sleep.

"A little after midnight I felt that there was somebody else in the room.

"I looked at the closed door – yes there was no mistake about it, it was my wife, my wife who had been dead these eighteen months.

"At first I was – well you can guess my feeling – then she spoke:

"'There is a cool bed-mat under the bedstead; it is rather dusty, but it will make you comfortable.'

"I got up and looked under the bedstead – yes the cool bed-mat was there right enough and it was dusty too. I took it outside and I cleaned it by giving it a few jerks. Yes, I had to pass through the door at which she was standing within six inches of her, – don't put any questions; Let me tell you as much as I like; you will get nothing out of me if you interrupt – yes, I passed a comfortable night. She was in that room for a long time, telling me lots of things. The next morning my mother enquired with whom I was talking and I told her a lie. I said I was reading my novel aloud. They all know it at home now. She comes and passes two nights with me in the week when I am at home. She does not come to Calcutta. She talks about various matters and she is happy – don't ask me how I know that. I shall not tell you whether I have touched her body because that will give rise to further questions.

"Everybody at home has seen her, and they all know what I have told you, but nobody has spoken to her. They all respect and love her – nobody is afraid. In fact she never comes except on Saturday and Sunday evenings and that when I am at home."

No amount of cross-examination, coaxing or inducement made my friend Haralal say anything further.

This story in itself would not probably have been believed; but after the incident of 'His dead wife's picture' nobody disbelieved it, and there is no reason why anybody should. Haralal is not a man who would tell yarns, and then I have made enquiries at Haralal's village where several persons know this much; that his dead wife pays him a visit twice every week.

Now that Haralal is five hundred miles from his village home I do not know how things stand; but I am told that this story reached the ears of the Bara Saheb and he asked Haralal if he would object to a transfer and Haralal told him that he would not.

I shall leave the reader to draw his own conclusions.

The Bridal Party

S. Mukerji

IN BENARES, the sacred city of the Hindus, situated in the United Provinces of Agra and Oudh, there is a house which is famed pretty far and wide. It is said that the house is haunted and that no human being can pass a night in that house.

Once there was a large Bridal party.

In India the custom is that the bridegroom goes to the house of the bride with great pomp and show with a number of friends and followers and the ceremony of '*Kanya Dan*' (giving away the girl) takes place at the bride's house.

The number of the people who go with the bridegroom depends largely upon the means of the bride's party, because the guests who come with the groom are to be fed and entertained in right regal style. It is this feeding and entertaining the guests that makes a daughter's marriage so costly in India, to a certain extent.

If the bride and the bridegroom live in the same town or village then the bridegroom's party goes to the bride's house in the evening, the marriage is performed at night and they all come away the same night or early the next morning. If, however, the places of residence of the bride and the bridegroom are say five hundred miles apart as is generally the case, the bridegroom with his party goes a day or two earlier and stays a day or two after the marriage. The bride's people have to find accommodation, food and entertainment for the whole period, which in the case of rich people extends over a week.

Now I had the pleasure of joining such a bridal party as mentioned last, going to Benares.

We were about thirty young men, besides a number of elderly people.

Since the young men could not be merry in the presence of their elders the bride's father, who was a very rich man, had made arrangements to put up the thirty of us in a separate house.

This house was within a few yards of the famed haunted house.

We reached Benares at about ten in the morning and it was about three in the afternoon that we were informed that the celebrated haunted house was close by. Naturally some of us decided that we should occupy that house rather than the one in which we were. I myself was not very keen on shifting but a few others were. Our host protested but we insisted, and so the host had to give way.

The house was empty and the owner was a local gentleman, a resident of Benares.

To procure his permission and the key was the work of a few minutes and we took actual possession of the house at about six in the evening. It was a very large house with big rooms and halls (rather poorly furnished) but some furniture was brought in from the house which we had occupied on our arrival.

There was a very big and well-ventilated hall and in this we decided to sleep. Carpet upon carpet was piled on the floor and there we decided to sleep (on the ground) in right Oriental style. Lamps were brought and the house was lighted up.

At about nine p.m. our dinner was announced. The Oriental dinner is conducted as follows:

The guests all sit on the floor and a big plate of metal (say twenty inches in diameter) is placed in front of each guest. Then the service commences and the plates are filled with dainties. Each guest generally gets thrice as much as he can eat. Then the host who does not himself join stands with joined hands and requests the guests to do full justice, and the dinner begins. Very little is eaten in fact, and whatever is left goes to the poor. That is probably the only consolation. Now on this particular occasion the bride's father, who was our host and who was an elderly gentleman had withdrawn, leaving two of his sons to look after us. He himself, we understood, was looking after his more elderly guests who had been lodged in a different house.

The hall in which we sat down to dine was a large one and very well lighted.

Adjoining it was the hall in which our beds had been made. The sons of *mine host* with a number of others were serving. I always was rather unconventional. So I asked my fellow guests whether I could fall to, and without waiting for permission I commenced eating, a very good thing I did, as would appear hereafter.

In about twenty minutes the serving was over and we were asked to begin. As a matter of fact I was nearly half through at that time. And then the trouble began.

With a click all the lights went out and the whole house was in total darkness.

Of course, the reader can guess what followed.

"Who has put out the lights?" shouted Jagat, who was sitting next but one to me on the left.

"The ghost" shouted another in reply.

"I shall kill him if I can catch him" shouted Jagat.

The whole place was in darkness, we could not see anything but we could hear that Jagat was trying to get up.

Then he received what was a stunning blow on his back. We could hear the thump.

"Oh" shouted Jagat "who is that?"

He sat down again and gave the man on his right a blow like the one he had received. The man on the right protested. Then Jagat turned to the man on his left. The man on Jagat's left evidently resisted and Jagat had the worst of it.

Then Narain, another one of us shouted out.

"What is the matter with you?" asked his neighbour.

"Why did you pull my hair" shouted Narain.

"I did not pull" shouted the neighbour.

Then a servant was seen approaching with a lamp and things became quiet.

But the servant did not reach the hall. He stumbled against something and fell headlong on the ground, the lamp went out, and our trouble began again.

One of the party received a slap on the back of his head which sent his cap rolling and in his attempt to recover it he upset a glass of water that was near his right hand.

Matters went on in this fashion till a lamp came. The whole thing must have taken about four minutes. When the lamp came we found that all the dishes were clean.

The eatables had mysteriously disappeared.

The sons of *mine host* looked stupidly at us and we looked stupidly at them and at each other. But there it was, there was not a particle of solid food left.

We had therefore no alternative but to adjourn to the nearest confectioner's shop and eat some sweets there. That the night would not pass in peace we were sure, but nobody dared suggest that we should not pass the night in the haunted house. Once having defied the ghost we had to stand to our guns for one night at least.

It was well after eleven o'clock at night when we came back and went to bed. We went to bed but not to sleep.

The room in which we all slept was a big one as I have said already, and there were two wall lamps in it. We lowered the lamps and—

Then the lamps went out, and we began to anticipate trouble. Our hosts had all gone home leaving us to the tender mercies of the ghost.

Shortly afterwards we began to feel as if we were lying on a public road and horses passing along the road within a yard of us. We also imagined we could hear men passing close to us whispering. Sleeping was impossible. We all remained awake talking about different things, till a horse came very near. And thus the night passed away. At about four in the morning one of us got up and wanted to go out.

We shouted for the servant called Kallu and within a minute Kallu came with a lantern. One of our fellow guests got up and went out of the room followed by Kallu.

We could hear him going along the dining hall to the head of the stairs. Then we heard him shriek. We all rushed out. The lighted lantern was there at the head of the stairs and our fellow guest at the bottom. Kallu had vanished.

We rushed down, picked up our friend and carried him upstairs. He said that Kallu had given him a push and he had fallen down. Fortunately he was not hurt. We called the servants and they all came, Kallu among them. He denied having come with a lantern or having pushed our friend down the stairs. The other servants corroborated his statement. They assured us that Kallu had never left the room in which they all were.

We were satisfied that this was also a ghostly trick.

At about seven in the morning when our hosts came we were glad to bid good-bye to the haunted house with our bones whole.

The funniest thing was that only those of my fellow guests had the worst of it who had denied the existence of ghosts. Those of us who had kept respectfully silent had not been touched.

Those who had received a blow or two averred that the blows could not have been given by invisible hands inasmuch as the blows were too substantial. But all of us were certain that it was no trick played by a human being.

The passing horses and the whispering passers-by had given us a queer creepy sensation.

* * *

In this connection may be mentioned a few haunted houses in other parts of India. There are one or two very well-known haunted houses in Calcutta.

The 'Hastings House' is one of them. It is situated at Alipore in the Southern suburb of Calcutta. This is a big palatial building now owned by the Government of Bengal. At one time it was the private residence of the Governor-General of India whose name it bears. At present it is used as the 'State Guest House' in which the Indian Chiefs are put up when they come to pay official visits to His Excellency in Calcutta. It appears that in a lane not very far from this house was fought the celebrated duel between Warren Hastings, the first Governor-General of India and Sir Philip Francis, a Member of his Council and the reputed author of the 'Letters of Junius'.

While living in this house Warren Hastings married Baroness Imhoff sometime during the first fortnight of August about one hundred and forty years ago. "The event was celebrated by great festivities"; and, as expected, the bride came home in a splendid equipage. It is said that this scene is re-enacted on the anniversary of the wedding by supernatural agency and a ghostly carriage duly enters the gate in the evening once every year. The clatter of hoofs and the rattle of iron-tyred wheels are distinctly heard advancing up to the portico; then there is the sound of the opening and closing of the carriage door, and lastly the carriage proceeds onwards, but it does not come out from under the porch. It vanishes mysteriously.

To-day is the 15th of August and this famous equipage must have glided in and out to the utter bewilderment of watchful eyes and ears within the last fortnight.

* * *

There is another well-known ghostly house in Calcutta in which the only trouble is that its windows in the first floor bedrooms open at night spontaneously.

People have slept at night for a reward in this house closing the windows with their own hands and have waked up at night shivering with cold to find all the windows open.

Once a body of soldiers went to pass a night in this house with a view to solve the mystery. They all sat in a room fully determined not to sleep but see what happened; and thus went on chatting till it was about midnight. There was a big lamp burning on a table around which they were seated. All of a sudden there was a loud click – the lamp went out and all the windows opened simultaneously. The next minute the lamp was alight again. The occupants of the room looked at their watches; it was about one a.m. The next night they sat up again and one of them with a revolver. At about one in the morning this particular individual pointed his revolver at one of the windows. As soon as the lamp went out this man pulled the trigger five times and there were five reports. The windows, however, opened and the lamp was alight again as on the previous night. They all rushed to the window to see if any damage had been done by the bullets.

The five bullets were found in the room but from their appearance it seemed as if they had struck nothing, evidently the bullets would have been changed in shape if they had impinged upon any hard substance. But then this was another enigma. How did the bullets come back? No man could have put the bullets there from before, (for they were still hot when discovered) or could have guessed the bore of the revolver that was going to be used.

On the third night to make assurance doubly sure, these soldiers were again present in the room, but on this occasion they had loaded their revolver with marked bullets.

As it neared one o'clock, one of them pointed the revolver at the window. He had decided to pull the trigger as soon as the lamp would go out. But he could not. As soon as the lamp went out this soldier received a sharp cut on his wrist with a cane and the revolver fell clattering on the floor. The invisible hand had left its mark behind which his companions saw after the lamp was alight again.

Many people have subsequently tried to solve the mystery but never succeeded.

The house remained untenanted for a long time and finally it was rented by an Australian horse dealer who however did not venture to occupy the building itself, and contented himself with erecting his stables and offices in the compound where he is not molested by the unearthly visitors.

There is another ghostly house and it is in the United Provinces. The name of the town has been intentionally omitted. Various people saw numerous things in that house but a correct report never came. Once a friend of mine passed a night in that house. He told me what he had seen. Most wonderful! And I have no reason to disbelieve him.

"I went to pass a night in that house and I had only a comfortable chair, a small table and a few magazines besides a loaded revolver. I had taken care to load that revolver myself so that there might be no trick and I had given everybody to understand that.

"I began well. The night was cool and pleasant. The lamp bright – the chair comfortable and the magazine which I took up – interesting.

"But at about midnight I began to feel rather uneasy.

"At one in the morning I should probably have left the place if I had not been afraid of friends whose servants I knew were watching the house and its front door.

"At half past one I heard a peculiar sigh of pain in the next room. 'This is rather interesting,' I thought. To face something tangible is comparatively easy; to wait for the unknown is much more difficult. I took out the revolver from my pocket and examined it. It looked quite all right – this small piece of metal which could have killed six men in half a minute. Then I waited – for what – well.

"A couple of minutes of suspense and the sigh was repeated. I went to the door dividing the two rooms and pushed it open. A long thick ray of light at once penetrated the darkness, and I walked into the other room. It was only partially light. But after a minute I could see all the corners. There was nothing in that room.

"I waited for a minute or two. Then I heard the sigh in the room which I had left. I came back, – stopped – rubbed my eyes—

"Sitting in the chair which I had vacated not two minutes ago was a young girl calm, fair, beautiful with that painful expression on her face which could be more easily imagined than described. I had heard of her. So many others who had came to pass a night in that house had seen her and described her (and I had disbelieved).

"Well – there she sat, calm, sad, beautiful, in my chair. If I had come in five minutes later I might have found her reading the magazine which I had left open, face downwards. When I was well within the room she stood up facing me and I stopped. The revolver fell from my hand. She smiled a sad sweet smile. How beautiful she was!

"Then she spoke. A modern ghost speaking like Hamlet's father, just think of that!

"'You will probably wonder why I am here – I shall tell you, I was murdered – by my own father…. I was a young widow living in this house which belonged to my father I became unchaste and to save his own name he poisoned me when I was *enceinte* – another week and I should have become a mother; but he poisoned me and my innocent child died too – it would have been such a beautiful baby – and you would probably want to kiss it'

"And horror of horrors, she took out the child from her womb and showed it to me. She began to move in my direction with the child in her arms saying – 'You will like to kiss it.'

"I don't know whether I shouted – but I fainted.

"When I recovered consciousness it was broad day-light, and I was lying on the floor, with the revolver by my side. I picked it up and slowly walked out of the house with as much dignity as I could command. At the door I met one of my friends to whom I told a lie that I had seen nothing. – It is the first time that I have told you what I saw at the place.

"The ghostly woman spoke the language of the part of the country in which the ghostly house is situate."

The friend who told me this story is a responsible Government official and will not make a wrong statement. What has been written above has been confirmed by others – who had passed nights in that ghostly house; but they had generally shouted for help and fainted at the sight of the ghost, and so they had not heard her story from her lips as reproduced here.

The house still exists, but it is now a dilapidated old affair, and the roof and the doors and windows are so bad that people don't care to go and pass a night there.

There is also a haunted house in Assam. In this house a certain gentleman committed suicide by cutting his own throat with a razor.

You often see him sitting on a cot in the verandah heaving deep sighs.

Mention of this house has been made in a book called *Tales from the Tiger Land* published in England. The Author says he has passed a night in the house in question and testifies to the accuracy of all the rumours that are current.

* * *

Talking about haunted houses reminds me of a haunted tank. I was visiting a friend of mine in the interior of Bengal during our annual summer holidays when I was yet a student. This friend of mine was the son of a rich man and in the village had a large ancestral house where his people usually resided. It was the first week of June when I reached my friend's house. I was informed that among other things of interest, which were, however, very few in that particular part of the country, there was a large Pukka tank belonging to my friend's people which was haunted.

What kind of ghost lived in the tank or near it nobody could say, but what everybody knew was this, that on *Jaistha Shukla Ekadashi* (that is on the eleventh day after the new moon in the month of Jaistha) that occurs about the middle of June, the ghost comes to bathe in the tank at about midnight.

Of course, *Jaistha Shukla Ekadashi* was only three days off, and I decided to prolong my stay at my friend's place, so that I too might have a look at the ghost's bath.

On the eventful day I resolved to pass the night with my friend and two other intrepid souls, near the tank.

After a rather late dinner, we started with a bedding and a hookah and a pack of cards and a big lamp. We made the bed (a mattress and a sheet) on a platform on the bank. There were six steps, with risers about nine inches each, leading from the platform to the water. Thus we were about four and a half feet from the water level; and from this coign of vantage we could command a full view of the tank, which covered an area of about four acres. Then we began our game of cards. There was a servant with us who was preparing our hookah.

At midnight we felt we could play no longer.

The strain was too great; the interest too intense.

We sat smoking and chatting and asked the servant to remove the lamp as a lot of insects was coming near attracted by the light. As a matter of fact we did not require any light because there was a brilliant moon. At one o'clock in the morning there was a noise as of rushing wind – we looked round and found that not a leaf was moving but still the whizzing noise as of a strong wind continued. Then we found something advancing towards the tank from the opposite bank. There was a number of cocoanut trees on the bank on the other side, and in the moonlight we could not see clearly what it really was. It looked like a huge white elephant. It approached the tank at a rapid pace – say the pace of a fast trotting horse. From the bank it took a long leap and with a tremendous splash fell into the water. The plunge made the water rise on our side and it rose as high as four and a half feet because we got wet through and through.

The mattress and the sheet and all our clothes were wet. In the confusion we forgot to keep our eyes on the ghost or white elephant or whatever it was and when we again looked in that direction everything was quiet. The apparition had vanished.

The most wonderful thing was the rise in the water level. For the water to rise four and a half feet would have been impossible under ordinary circumstances even if a thousand elephants had got into the water.

We were all wide awake – we went home immediately because we required a change of clothes.

The old man (my friend's father) was waiting for us. "Well you are wet" he said.

"Yes" said we.

"Rightly served" said the old man.

He did not ask what had happened. We were told subsequently that he had got wet like us a number of times when he was a youngster himself.

What the Professor Saw

S. Mukerji

THIS STORY IS NOT SO PAINFUL as the one entitled 'What Uncle Saw'. How we wish that uncle had seen something else, but all the same how glad we are that uncle did not see what the professor saw. The professor is an M.A. of the University of Calcutta, in Chemistry, and is a Lecturer in a big college. This, of course, I only mention to show that this is not the invention of a foolish person.

I shall now tell the story as I heard it from the professor.

"I was a professor of chemistry in a Calcutta college in the year 18—. One morning I received a letter from home informing me that my eldest brother was ill. It was a case of fever due to cold. Of course, a man does sometimes catch cold and get fever too. There was nothing extraordinary about that.

"In the evening I did not receive any further news. This meant that my brother was better, because in any other case they would have written.

"A number of friends came to my diggings in the evening and invited me to join their party then going to a theatre. They had reserved some seat but one of the party for whom a seat had been reserved was unavoidably detained and hence a vacant seat. The news of my brother's illness had made me a little sad, the theatre, I thought, would cheer me up. So I joined.

"We left the theatre at about one in the morning. Coming to my house along the now deserted but well-lighted 'College Street' of Calcutta I saw from a distance a tall man walking to and fro on the pavement in front of the Senate Hall. When I approached nearer I found that it was my brother of whose illness I had heard in the morning. I was surprised.

"'What are you doing here – brother.' I asked.

"'I came to tell you something.'

"'But you were ill – I heard this morning – by what train did you come?' I asked.

"'I did not come by train – never mind – I went to your '*Basa*' (lodgings) and found you were out – gone to the theatre, so I waited for you here as I thought you would prefer walking home instead of taking a hackney carriage—'

"'Very fortunate I did not take one—'

"'In that case I would have seen you at your quarters.'

"'Then come along with me—' I said.

"'No' he said 'I shall stay where I am – what I have come to tell you is this, that after I am gone you will take care of the mother and see that she has everything she wants—'

"'But where are you going—' I asked puzzled.

"'Never mind where I am going – but will you promise—'

"'Promise what—?' I asked.

"'That you will see that the mother has everything she wants.'

"'Certainly – but where on earth are you going—' I asked again.

"'I can depend upon your promise then' he said and vanished.

"He vanished mysteriously. In what direction he went I could not say. There was no bye-lane near. It was a very well-lighted part of the city. He vanished into the thin air. I rubbed my eyes and looked round.

"A policeman was coming along. He was about fifty feet away.

"I inquired him if he had seen the gentleman who was talking to me.

"'Did you see the other gentleman, officer?' I asked.

"'Yes' he said looking around 'there were two of you –where is the other – has he robbed you of all you had – these pickpockets have a mysterious way of disappearing—'

"'He was my brother' I said 'and no pickpocket.'

"The policeman looked puzzled too.

"I shouted aloud calling my brother by name but received no reply. I took out my gold watch. It was half past one. I walked home at a brisk pace.

"At home I was informed by the servant that my brother had come to look for me an hour ago but on being informed that I was out, had gone away.

"Whenever he came to Calcutta from the suburbs he put up with a friend of his instead of with me. So I decided to look him up at his friend's house in the morning. But I was not destined to carry out that plan.

"Early the next morning I received a telegram that my brother was dead. The telegram had been sent at one twenty a.m. He must have died an hour before. Well – there it was.

"I had seen him and so had the policeman. The servant had seen him too. There could be no mistake about that.

"I took an early train and reached my suburban home at ten a.m. I was informed that my brother had died at midnight. But I had seen him at about half past one and the servant had seen him at about twelve thirty. I did not tell anybody anything at that time. But I did so afterwards. I was not dreaming – because the conversation we had was a pretty long one. The servant and the police constable could not have been mistaken either. But the mystery remains."

This was the exact story of the professor.

The Boy Who Was Caught

S. Mukerji

NOTHING IS MORE COMMON in India than seeing a ghost. Every one of us has seen ghost at some period of his existence; and if we have not actually seen one, some other person has, and has given us such a vivid description that we cannot but believe to be true what we hear.

This is, however, my own experience. I am told others have observed the phenomenon before.

When we were boys at school we used, among other things, to discuss ghosts. Most of my fellow students asserted that they did not believe in ghosts, but I was one of those who not only believed in their existence but also in their power to do harm to human beings if they liked. Of course, I was in the minority. As a matter of fact I knew that all those who said that they did not believe in ghosts told a lie. They believed in ghosts as much as I did, only they had not the courage to admit their weakness and differ boldly from the sceptics. Among the lot of unbelievers was one Ram Lal, a student of the Fifth Standard, who swore that he did not believe in ghosts and further that he would do anything to convince us that they did not exist.

It was, therefore, at my suggestion that he decided to go one moon-light night and hammer down a wooden peg into the soft sandy soil of the Hindoo Burning *Ghat*, it being well known that the ghosts generally put in a visible appearance at a burning *ghat* on a moon-light night. (A burning *ghat* is the place where dead bodies of Hindoos are cremated).

It was the warm month of April and the river had shrunk into the size of a *nullah* or drain. The real *pukka ghat* (the bathing place, built of bricks and lime) was about two hundred yards from the water of the main stream, with a stretch of sand between.

The *ghats* are only used in the morning when people come to bathe, and in the evening they are all deserted. After a game of football on the school grounds we sometimes used to come and sit on the *pukka ghat* for an hour and return home after nightfall.

Now, it was the 23rd of April and a bright moon-light night, every one of us (there were about a dozen) had told the people at home that there was a function at the school and he might be late. On this night, it was arranged that the ghost test should take place.

The boy who had challenged the ghost, Ram Lal, was to join us at the *pukka ghat* at eight p.m.; and then while we waited there he would walk across the sand and drive the peg into the ground at the place where a dead body had been cremated that very morning. We were to supply the peg and the hammer. (I had to pay the school gardener two *annas* for the loan of a peg and a hammer).

Well, we procured the peg and the hammer and proceeded to the *pukka ghat*. If the gardener had known what we required the peg and the hammer for, I am sure he would not have lent these to us.

Though I was a firm believer in ghosts yet I did not expect that Ram Lal would be caught. What I hoped for was that he would not turn up at the trysting place. But to my disappointment Ram Lal did turn up and at the appointed hour too. He came boasting as usual, took the peg and the hammer and started across the sand saying that he would break the head of any ghost who might venture within the reach of the hammerhead. Well, he went along and we waited for his return at the *pukka ghat*. It was a glorious night, the whole expanse of sand was shining in the bright moon-light.

On and on went Ram Lal with the peg in his left hand and the hammer in his right. He was dressed in the usual upcountry Indian style, in a long coat or *Achkan* which reached well below his knees and fluttered in the breeze.

As he went on his pace slackened. When he had gone about half the distance he stopped and looked back. We hoped he would return. He put down the hammer and the peg, sat down on the sand facing us, took off his shoes. Only some sand had got in. He took up the peg and hammer and walked on.

But then we felt that his courage was oozing away. Another fifty yards and he again stopped, and looked back at us.

Another fifty yards remained. Will he return? No! he again proceeded, but we could clearly see that his steps were less jaunty than when he had started. We knew that he was trembling, we knew that he would have blessed us to call him back. But we would not yield, neither would he. Looking in our direction at every step he proceeded and reached the burning *ghat*. He reached the identical spot where the pyre had been erected in the morning.

There was very little breeze, – not a mouse stirring. Not a soul was within two hundred yards of him and he could not expect much help from us. How poor Ram Lal's heart must have palpitated! When we see Ram Lal now how we feel that we should burst.

Well, Ram Lal knelt down, fixed the peg in the wet sandy soil and began hammering. After each stroke he looked at us and at the river and in all directions. He struck blow after blow and we counted about thirty. That his hands had become nerveless we would understand, for otherwise a dozen strokes should have been enough to make the peg vanish in the soft sandy soil.

The peg went in and only about a couple of inches remained visible above the surface; and then Ram Lal thought of coming back. He was kneeling still. He tried to stand up, gave out a shrill cry for help and fell down face foremost.

It must have been his cry for help that made us forget our fear of the ghost, and we all ran at top speed towards the *ghat*. It was rather difficult to run fast on the sand but we managed it as well as we could, and stopped only when we were about half a dozen yards from the unconscious form of Ram Lal.

There he lay senseless as if gone to sleep. Our instinct told us that he was not dead. We thanked God, and each one of us sent up a silent prayer. Then we cried for help and a boatman who lived a quarter of a mile away came up. He took up Ram Lal in his arms and as he was doing it *tr – rrrrrrrrr*— went Ram Lal's long coat. The unfortunate lad had hammered the skirt of his long coat along with the peg into the ground.

We took Ram Lal to his house and explained to his mother that he had a bad fall in the football field, and there we left him.

The next morning at school, one student, who was a neighbour of Ram Lal, told us that the whole mischief had become known.

Ram Lal, it appears, got high fever immediately after we had left him and about midnight he became delirious and in that condition he disclosed everything in connection with his adventure at the *ghat*.

In the evening we went to see him. His parents were very angry with us.

The whole story reached the ears of the school authorities and we got, what I thought I richly deserved (for having allowed any mortal being to defy a ghost) but what I need not say.

Ram Lal is now a grown up young man. He holds a responsible government appointment and I meet him sometimes when he comes to tour in our part of the Province.

I always ask him if he has seen a ghost since we met last.

* * *

In this connection it will not be out of place to mention two simple stories one from my own experience and another told by a friend.

I shall tell my friend's story first, in his own words.

"I used to go for a bath in the Ganges early every morning. I used to start from home at four o'clock in the morning and walked down to the Ganges which was about three miles from my house. The bath took about an hour and then I used to come back in my carriage which went for me at about six in the morning.

"On this eventful morning when I awoke it was brilliant moonlight and so I thought it was dawn.

"I started from home without looking at the clock and when I was about a mile and a half from home and about the same distance from the river I realized that I was rather early. The policeman under the railway bridge told me that it was only two o'clock. I knew that I should have to cross the small *maidan* through which the road ran and I remembered that there was a rumour that a ghost had sometimes been seen in the *maidan* and on the road. This however did not make me nervous, because I really did not believe in ghosts; but all the same I wished I could have gone back. But then in going back I should have to pass the policeman and he would think that I was afraid; so I decided to go on.

"When I entered the *maidan* a creepy sensation came over me. My first idea was that I was being followed, but I did not dare look back, all the same I went on with quick steps.

"My next idea was that a gust of wind swept past me, and then I thought that a huge form was passing over the trees which lined the road.

"By this time I was in the middle of the *maidan* about half a mile from the nearest human being.

"And then, horror of horrors, the huge form came down from the trees and stood in the middle of the road about a hundred yards ahead of me, barring my way.

"I instinctively moved to the side – but did not stop. By the time I reached the spot, I had left the metalled portion of the road and was actually passing under the road-side trees allowing their thick trunks to intervene between me and the huge form standing in the middle of the road. I did not look at it, but I was sure it was extending a gigantic arm towards me. It could not, however, catch me and I walked on with vigorous strides. After I had passed the figure I nearly ran under the trees, my heart beating like a sledge hammer within me.

"After a couple of minutes I saw two glaring eyes in front of me. This I thought was the end. The eyes were advancing towards me at a rapid pace and then I heard a shout like that of a cow in distress. I stopped where I was. I hoped the ghost would pass along the road overlooking me. But when the ghost was within say fifty yards of me it gave another howl and I knew that it had seen me. A cry for help escaped my lips and I fainted.

"When I regained consciousness I found myself on the grassy foot-path by the side of the road, about four or five human beings hovering about me and a motor car standing near.

"Then the whole mystery became clear as day-light. The eyes that I had seen were the headlights of the twenty-four h.p. Silent Knight Minerva of Captain ——. He had gone on a pleasure-trip to the next station and was returning home with two friends and his wife in his motor car when in that part of the road he saw something like a man standing in the middle of the road and sounded his horn. As the figure in the middle of the road would not move aside he slowed down and then heard my cry.

"The rest the reader may guess. The figure that had loomed so large with out-stretched arm was only a municipal danger signal erected in the middle of the road. A red lamp had been placed on the top of the erection but it had been blown out."

This was the whole story of my friend. It shows how even our prosaic but overwrought imagination sometimes gives to airy nothings a local habitation and a name. My own personal experience which I shall describe now will also, I am sure, be interesting.

It was on a brilliant moon-light night in the month of June that we were sleeping in the open court-yard of our house.

Of course, the court-yard had a wall all round with a partition in the middle; on one side of the partition slept three girls of the family and on the other were the younger male members, four in number.

It was our custom to have a long chat after dinner and before retiring to bed.

On this particular night the talk had been about ghosts. Of course, the girls are always ready to believe everything and so when we left them we knew that they would not sleep very comfortably that night. We retired to our part of the court-yard, but we could overhear the conversation of the girls. One was trying to convince the other two that ghosts did not exist and if they did exist they never came into contact with human beings.

Then we fell asleep.

How long we had slept we did not know, but a sudden cry from, one of the girls awoke us and within three seconds we were across the low partition wall, and with her. She was sitting up in bed pointing with her fingers. Following the direction we saw in the clear moonlight the figure of a short woman standing in the corner of the court-yard about twenty yards from us pointing her finger at something (not towards us).

We looked in that direction but could see nothing peculiar there.

Our first idea was that it was one of the maid-servants, who had heard our after-dinner conversation, playing the ghost. But this particular ghostly lady was very short, much shorter than any servant in the establishment. After some, hesitation all (four) of us advanced towards the ghost. I remember how my heart throbbed as I advanced with the other three boys.

Then we laughed loud and long.

What do you think it was?

It was only the Lawn Tennis net wrapped round the pole standing against the wall. The handle of the ratchet arrangement looked like an extending finger.

But from a distance in the moon-light it looked exactly like a short woman draped in white.

This story again shows what trick our imagination plays with us at times.

* * *

Talking of ghosts reminds me of a very funny story told by a friend of my grand-father – a famous medical man of Calcutta.

This famous doctor was once sent for to treat a gentleman at Agra. This gentleman was a rich *Marwari* who was suffering from indigestion. When the doctor reached Agra he was lodged in very comfortable quarters and a number of horses and carriages was placed at his disposal.

He was informed that the patient had been treated by all the local and provincial practitioners but without any result.

The doctor who was as clever a man of the world as of medicine, at once saw that there was really nothing the matter with the patient. He was really suffering from a curious malady which could in a phrase be called – 'want of physical exercise'.

Agra, the city after which the Province is named, abounds in old magnificent buildings which it takes the tourist a considerable time to see, and the doctor, of course, was enjoying all the sights in the meantime.

He also prescribed a number of medicines which proved of no avail. The doctor had anticipated it, and so he had decided what medicine he would prescribe next.

During the sight-seeing excursions into the environs of the city the doctor had discovered a large pukka well not far from a main street and at a distance of three miles from his patient's house.

This was a very old disused well and it was generally rumoured that a ghost dwelt in it. So nobody would go near the well at night. Of course, there was a lot of stories as to what the ghost looked like and how he came out at times and stood on the brink and all that, – but the doctor really did not believe any of these. He, however, believed that this ghost, (whether there really was any or not in that well) would cure his patient.

So one morning when he saw his patient he said "Lalla Saheb – I have found out the real cause of your trouble – it is a ghost whom you have got to propitiate and unless you do that you will never get well – and no medicine will help you and your digestion will never improve."

"A ghost?" asked the patient.

"A ghost!" exclaimed the people around.

"A ghost" said the doctor sagely.

"What shall I have to do?" inquired the patient, anxiously –

"You will have to go every morning to that well (indicating the one mentioned above), and throw a basketful of flowers in" said the doctor.

"I shall do that every day" said the patient.

"Then we shall begin from to-morrow" said the doctor.

The next morning everybody had been ready to start long before the doctor was out of bed. He came at last and all got up to start. Then a big landau and pair drew up to take the doctor and the patient to the abode of the ghost in the well. Just as the patient was thinking of getting in the doctor said "We don't require a carriage Lalla Saheb – we shall all have to walk – and bare-footed too, and between you and me we shall have to carry the basket of flowers also."

The patient was really troubled. Never indeed in his life had he walked a mile – not to say of three – and that, bare-footed and carrying a basket of flowers in his hands. However he had to do it. It was a goodly procession. The big millionaire – the big doctor with a large number of followers walking bare-footed – caused amazement and amusement to all who saw them.

It took them a full hour and a half to reach the well – and there the doctor pronounced the *mantra* in Sanskrit and the flowers were thrown in. The *mantra* (charm) was in Sanskrit, the doctor who knew a little of the language had taken great pains to compose it the night before and even then it was not grammatically quite correct.

At last the party returned, but not on foot. The journey back was performed in the carriages that had followed the patient and his doctor. From that day the practice was followed regularly. The patient's health began to improve and he began to regain his power of digestion fast. In a month he was all right; but he never discontinued the practice of going to the well and throwing in a basketful of flowers with his own hands. He had also learnt the *mantra* (the mystic charm) by heart; but the doctor had sworn him to secrecy and he told it to nobody. Shoes with felt sole were soon procured from England (it being forty years before any Indian Rope Sole Shoe Factory came into existence) and thus the inconvenience of walking this distance bare-footed was easily obviated.

After a month's further stay the doctor came away from Agra having earned a fabulous fee, and he always received occasional letters and presents from his patient who never discontinued the practice of visiting the well till his death about seventeen years later.

"The three-mile walk is all that he requires" said the doctor to his friends (among whom evidently my grand-father was one) on his return from Agra, "and since he has got used to it now he won't discontinue even if he comes to know of the deception I have practiced on him – and I have cured his indigestion after all."

The patient, of course, never discovered the fraud. He never gave the matter his serious consideration. His friends, who were as ignorant and prejudiced as he himself was, believed in the *ghost* as much as he did himself. The medical practitioners of Agra who probably were in the Doctor's secret never told him anything – and if they had told him anything they would probably have heard language from Our patient that could not well be described as quite parliamentary, for they had all tried to cure him and failed.

This series of stories will prove how much 'imagination' works upon the external organs of a human being.

If a person goes about with the idea that there is a ghost somewhere about he will probably see the ghost in everything.

But has it ever struck the reader that sometimes horses and dogs do not quite enjoy going to a place which is reputed to be haunted?

In a village in Bengal not far from my home there is a big Jack-fruit tree which is said to be haunted.

I visited this place once – the local *zamindar* had sent me his elephant. The *Gomashta* (estate manager) who knew that I had come to see the haunted tree, told me that I should probably see nothing during the day, but the elephant would not go near the tree.

I passed the tree. It was about three miles from the railway station. There was nothing extraordinary about it. This was about eleven o'clock in the morning. Then I went to the shooting box (usually called the cutchery or court house – where the *zamindars* and their servants put up when they pay a visit to this part of their possessions) to have my bath and breakfast most hospitably provided by my generous host. I ordered the elephant to be put under this tree, and this was done though the people there told me that the elephant would not remain there long.

At about two p.m. I heard an extraordinary noise from the tree.

It was only the elephant. It was wailing and was looking as bad as it possibly could.

We all went there but found nothing. The elephant was not ill.

I ordered it to be taken away from under the tree. As soon as the chain was removed from the animal's foot it rushed away like a race horse and would not stop within two hundred yards of the tree. I was vastly amused. I had never seen an elephant running before. But under the tree we found nothing. What made the elephant so afraid has remained a secret.

The servants told me (what I had heard before) that it was only elephants, horses and dogs that did not stay long under that tree. No human eyes have ever seen anything supernatural or fearful there.

A Strange Incident

S. Mukerji

WHEN I WAS AT COLLEGE there happened what was a most inexplicable incident.

The matter attracted some attention at that time, but has now been forgotten as it was really not so very extraordinary. The police in fact, when called in, explained the matter or at least thought they had done so, to everybody's satisfaction. I was, however, not satisfied with the explanation given by the police. This was what actually happened.

The college was a very big one with a large boarding-house attached to it. The boarding-house was a building separate from the college situated at a distance of about one hundred yards from the college building. It was in the form of a quadrangle with a lawn in the centre. The area of this lawn must have been two and a half thousand square yards. Of course it was surrounded on all sides by buildings, that is, by a row of single rooms on each side.

In the boarding-house there was a common room for the amusement of the students. There were all sorts of indoor games including a miniature billiard table in this common room. I was a regular visitor there. I did not care for any other indoor game than chess. Of course chess meant keeping out of bed, till late at night.

On this particular occasion, I think it was in November, a certain gentleman, who was an ex-student of the college, was paying us a visit. He was staying with us in the boarding-house. He had himself passed four years in that boarding-house and naturally had a love for it. In his time he was very popular with the other boarders and with the superintendent. Dr. M.N., an English gentleman who was also an inmate of the boarding-house. With the permission of the learned doctor, the superintendent, we decided to make a night of it, and so we all assembled in the common room after dinner. I can picture to myself the cheerful faces of all the students present on that occasion in the well lighted hall. So far as I know only one of that group is now dead. He was the most jovial and the best beloved of all. May he rest in peace!

Now to return from this mournful digression. I could see old Mathura sitting next to me with a hookah with a very long stem, directing the moves of the chessmen. There was old Birju at the miniature billiard table poking at everybody with his cue who laughed when he missed an easy shot.

Then came in the superintendent, Dr. M.N. and in a hurry to conceal his hookah (Indians never smoke in the presence of their elders and superiors) old Mathura nearly upset the table on which the chessmen were; and the mirth went on with redoubled vigour as the doctor was one of the loudest and merriest of the whole lot on such occasions.

Thus we went on till nearly one in the morning when the doctor ordered everybody to go to bed. Of course we were glad to retire but we were destined to be soon disturbed.

Earlier the same evening we had been playing a friendly hockey match, and one of the players, let us call him Ram Gholam, had been slightly hurt. As a matter of fact he always got hurt whenever he played.

During the evening the hurt had been forgotten but as soon as he was in bed it was found that he could not sleep. The matter was reported to the superintendent who finding that there was really nothing the matter with him suggested that the affected parts should be washed with hot water and finally wrapped in heated castor leaves and bandaged over with flannel. (This is the best medicine for gouty pain – not for hurt caused by a hockey stick).

There was a castor tree in the compound and a servant was despatched to bring the leaves. In the meantime a few of us went to the kitchen, made a fire and boiled some water. While thus engaged we heard a noise and a cry for help. We rushed out and ran along the verandah (corridor) to the place whence the cry came. It was coming from the room of Prayag, one of the boarders. We pushed the door but found that it was bolted from inside, we shouted to him to open but he would not. The door had four glass panes on the top and we discovered that the upper bolt only had been used; as a matter of fact the lower bolts had all been removed, because on closing the door from outside, once it had been found that a bolt at the bottom had dropped into its socket and the door had to be broken before it could be opened.

Prayag's room was in darkness. There was a curtain inside and so we could see nothing from outside. We could hear Prayag groaning. The superintendent came up. To break the glass pane nearest to the bolt was the work of a minute. The door was opened and we all rushed in. It was a room fourteen feet by twelve feet; many of us could not, therefore, come in. When we went in we took a light with us. It was one of the hurricane lanterns – the one we had taken to the kitchen. The lamp suddenly went out. At the same time a brickbat came rattling down from the roof and fell near my feet, thus I could feel it with my feet and tell what it was. And Prayag groaned again. Dr. M.N. came in, and we helped Prayag out of his bed and took him out on the verandah. Then we saw another brickbat come from the roof of the verandah, and fell in front of Prayag a few inches from his feet. We took him to the central lawn and stood in the middle of it. This time a whole solid brick came from the sky. It fell a few inches from my feet and remained standing on its edge. If it had toppled over it would have fallen on my toes.

By this time all the boarders had come up. Prayag stood in the middle of the group shivering and sweating. A few more brickbats came but not one of us was hurt. Then the trouble ceased. We removed Prayag to the superintendent's room and put him in the doctor's bed. There were a reading lamp on a stool near the head of the bed and a Holy Bible on it. The learned doctor must have been reading it when he was disturbed. Another bed was brought in and the doctor passed the night in it.

In the morning came the police.

They found a goodly heap of brickbats and bones in Prayag's room and on the lawn. There was an investigation, but nothing came out of it. The police however explained the matter as follows:

There were some people living in the two-storied houses in the neighbourhood. The brickbats and the bones must have come from there. As a matter of fact the police discovered that the boarding house students and the people who lived in these houses were not on good terms. Those people had organized a music party and the students had objected to it. The matter had been reported to the magistrate and had ended in a decision in favour of the students. Hence the strained relations. This was the most natural explanation and the only explanation. But this explanation did not satisfy me for several reasons.

The first reason was that the college compound contained another well kept lawn that stood between the hostel buildings and those two-storied houses. There were no brickbats on this lawn. If brickbats had been thrown from those houses some at least would have fallen upon the lawn.

Then as regarded the brickbats that were in the room, they had all dropped from the ceiling; but in the morning we found the tiles of the roof intact. Thirdly, in the middle of the central lawn there was at least one whole brick. The nearest building from which a brick might have been thrown was at a distance of one hundred yards and to throw a whole brick nine inches by four and a half inches by three inches such a distance would require a machine of some kind or other and none was found in the house.

The last thing that created doubts in my mind was this that not one brickbat had hit anybody. There were so many of us there and there was such an abundance of brickbats still not one of us was hit, and it is well known that brickbats hurled by ghostly hands do not hit anybody. In fact the whole brick that came and stood on edge within three inches of my toe would have hurt me if it had only toppled over.

* * *

It is known to most of the readers that *Sutteeism* was the practice of burning the widows on the funeral pyre of their dead husbands. This practice was prevalent in Bengal down to the year 1828 when a law forbidding the aiding and abetting of *Sutteeism* was passed. Before the act, of course, many women were, in a way, forced to become *Suttees*. The public opinion against a widow's surviving was so great that she preferred to die rather than live after her husband's death.

The law has, however, changed the custom and the public opinion too.

Still, every now and then there are found cases of determined *Sutteeism* among all classes in India who profess Hinduism. Frequent instances are found in Bengal; and whenever a case comes to the notice of the public the newspapers report it in a manner which shows that respect for the *Suttee* is not yet dead.

Sometimes a verdict of 'Suicide during temporary insanity' is returned, but, of course, whoever reads the report understands how matters stand.

I know of a recent case in which a gentleman who was in government service died leaving a young widow.

When the husband's dead body was being removed the wife looked so jolly that nobody suspected that anything was wrong with her.

But when all the male members of the family had gone away with the bier the young widow quietly procured a tin of Kerosine oil and a few bed sheets. She soaked the bed sheets well in the oil and then wrapped them securely round her person and further secured them by means of a rope. She then shut all the doors of her room and set the clothes on fire. By the time the doors were forced open (there were only ladies in the house at that time) she was dead.

Of course this was a case of suicide pure and simple and there was the usual verdict of suicide during temporary insanity, but I personally doubt the temporary insanity very much. This case, however, is too painful.

The one that I am now going to relate is more interesting and more mysterious, and probably more instructive.

Babu Bhagwan Prasad, now the late Babu Bhagwan Prasad, was a clerk in the —— office in the United Provinces. He was a grown-up man of forty-five when the incident happened.

He had an attack of cold which subsequently developed into pneumonia and after a lingering illness of eight days he died at about eight o'clock one morning.

He had, of course, a wife and a number of children.

Babu Bhagwan Prasad was a well paid officer and maintained a large family consisting of brothers – their wives and their children.

At the time of his death, in fact, when the doctor went away in the morning giving his opinion that it was a question of minutes, his wife seemed the least affected of all. While all the members of the family were collected round the bed of their dying relative the lady withdrew to her room saying that she was going to dress for the journey. Of course nobody took any notice of her at the time. She retired to her room and dressed herself in the most elaborate style, and marked her forehead with a large quantity of 'Sindur' for the last time.

['Sindur' is red oxide of mercury or lead used by orthodox Hindu women in some parts of India whose husbands are alive; widows do not use it.]

After dressing she came back to the room where her dying husband was and approached the bed. Those who were there made way for her in surprise. She sat down on the bed and finally lay down by her dying husband's side. This demonstration of sentimentalism could not be tolerated in a family where the Purda is strictly observed and one or two elderly ladies tried to remonstrate.

But on touching her they found that she was dead. The husband was dead too. They had both died simultaneously. When the doctor arrived he found the lady dead, but he could not ascertain the cause of her death.

Everybody thought she had taken poison but nothing could be discovered by post mortem examination. There was not a trace of any kind of poison in the body.

The funeral of the husband and the wife took place that afternoon and they were cremated on the same pyre.

The stomach and some portions of the intestines of the deceased lady were sent to the chemical examiner and his report (which arrived a week later) did not disclose anything.

The matter remains a mystery.

It will never be found out what force killed the lady at such a critical moment. Probably it was the strong will of the *Suttee* that would not allow her body to be separated from that of her husband even in death.

* * *

Another very strange incident is reported from a place near Agra in the United Provinces.

There were two respectable residents of the town who were close neighbours. For the convenience of the readers we shall call them Smith and Jones.

Smith and Jones, as has been said already, were close neighbours and the best of friends. Each had his wife and children living with him.

Now Mr. Smith got fever, on a certain very hot day in June. The fever would not leave him and on the tenth day it was discovered that it was typhoid fever of the worst type.

Now typhoid fever is in itself very dangerous, but more so in the case of a person who gets it in June. So poor Smith had no chance of recovery. Of course Jones knew it. Mrs. Smith was a rather uneducated elderly lady and the children were too young. So the medical treatment as well as the general management of Mr. Smith's affairs was left entirely in the hands of Mr. Jones.

Mr. Jones did his best. He procured the best medical advice. He got the best medicines prescribed by the doctors and engaged the best nurse available. But his efforts were of no avail. On a certain Thursday afternoon Smith began to sink fast and at about eight in the evening he died.

Mr. Jones on his return from his office that day at about four in the afternoon had been informed that Mr. Smith's condition was very bad, and he had at once gone over to see what he could do.

He had sent for half a dozen doctors, but they on their arrival had found that the case was hopeless. Three of the doctors had accordingly gone away, but the other three had stayed behind.

When however Smith was dead, and these three doctors had satisfied themselves that life was quite extinct, they too went away with Mr. Jones leaving the dead body in charge of the mourning members of the family of the deceased.

Mr. Jones at once set about making arrangements for the funeral early the next morning; and it was well after eleven at night that he returned to a very late dinner at his own house. It was a particularly hot night and after smoking his last cigar for the day Mr. Jones went to bed, but not to sleep, after midnight. The death of his old friend and neighbour had made him very sad and thoughtful. The bed had been made on the open roof on the top of the house which was a two storied building and Mr. Jones lay watching the stars and thinking.

At about one in the morning there was a loud knock at the front door. Mr. Jones who was wide awake thought it was one of the servants returning home late and so he did not take any notice of it.

After a few moments the knock was repeated at the door which opened on the stairs leading to the roof of the second storey on which Mr. Jones was sleeping. [The visitor had evidently passed through the front door]. This time Mr. Jones knew it was no servant. His first impression was that it was one of the mutual friends who had heard of Smith's death and was coming to make enquiries. So he shouted out "Who is there?"

"It is I, – Smith" was the reply.

"Smith – Smith is dead" stammered Mr. Jones.

"I want to speak to you, Jones – open the door or I shall come and kill you" said the voice of Smith from beyond the door. A cold sweat stood on Mr. Jones's forehead. It was Smith speaking, there was no doubt of that, – Smith, whom he had seen expire before his very eyes five hours ago. Mr. Jones began to look for a weapon to defend himself.

There was nothing available except a rather heavy hammer which had been brought up an hour earlier that very night to fix a nail in the wall for hanging a lamp. Mr. Jones took this up and waited for the spirit of Smith at the head of the stairs.

The spirit passed through this closed door also. Though the staircase was in total darkness still Mr. Jones could see Smith coming up step by step.

Up and up came Smith and breathlessly Jones waited with the hammer in his hand. Now only three steps divided them.

"I shall kill you" hissed Smith. Mr. Jones aimed a blow with the hammer and hit Smith between the eyes. With a groan Smith fell down. Mr. Jones fainted.

A couple of hours later there was a great commotion at the house of Mr. Smith. The dead body had mysteriously disappeared.

The first thing they could think of was to go and inform Mr. Jones.

So one of the young sons of Smith came to Mr. Jones's house. The servant admitted him and told him where to find the master.

Young Smith knocked at the door leading to the staircase but got no reply. "After his watchful nights he is sleeping soundly" thought young Smith.

But then Jones must be awakened.

The whole household woke up but not Mr. Jones. One of the servants then procured a ladder and got upon the roof. Mr. Jones was not upon his bed nor under it either. The servant thought he would open the door leading to the staircase and admit the people who were standing outside beyond the door at the bottom of the stairs. There was a number of persons now at the door including Mrs. Jones, her children, servants and young Smith.

The servant stumbled upon something. It was dark but he knew it was the body of his master. He passed on but then he stumbled again. There was another human being in the way. "Who is this other? – probably a thief" thought the servant.

He opened the door and admitted the people who were outside. They had lights with them. As they came in it was found that the second body on the stairs two or three steps below the landing was the dead body of Smith while the body on the landing was the unconscious form of Mr. Jones.

Restoratives were applied and Jones came to his senses and then related the story that has been recorded above. A doctor was summoned and he found the wound caused by Jones's hammer on Smith's head. There was a deep cut but no blood had come out, therefore, it appeared that the wound must have been caused at least two or three hours after death.

The doctors never investigated whether death could have been caused by the blow given by the hammer. They thought there was no need of an investigation either, because they had left Smith quite dead at eight in the evening.

How Smith's dead body was spirited away and came to Jones's house has been a mystery which will probably never be solved.

* * *

Thinking over the matter recorded above the writer has come to the conclusion that probably a natural explanation might be given of the affair.

Taking however all the facts of the case as given above to be true (and there is no reason to suppose that they are not) the only explanation that could be given and in fact that was given by some of the sceptical minds of Agra at that time was as follows:

"Smith was dead. Jones was a very old friend of his. He was rather seriously affected. He must have, in an unconscious state of mind like a somnambulist, carried the dead body of Smith to his own house without being detected in the act. Then his own fevered imagination endowed Smith with the faculty of speech, dead though the latter was; and in a moment of – well – call it temporary insanity, if you please – he inflicted the wound on the forehead of Smith's dead body."

This was the only plausible explanation that could be given of the affair; but regard being had to the fact that Smith's dead body was lying in an upper storey of the house and that there was a number of servants between the death chamber and the main entrance to the house, the act of removing the dead body without their knowing it was a difficult task, nay utterly impracticable.

Over and above this it was not feasible to carry away even at night, the dead body along the road, which is a well frequented thoroughfare, without being observed by anybody.

Then there is the third fact that Jones was really not such a strong person that he could carry alone Smith's body that distance with ease.

Smith's dead body as recovered in Jones's house had bare feet; whether there was any dust on the feet, had not been observed by anybody; otherwise some light might have been thrown on this apparently miraculous incident.

The Boy Possessed

S. Mukerji

I THINK IT WAS IN 1906 that in one of the principle cities in India the son of a rich man became ill. He had high fever and delirium and in his insensible state he was constantly talking in a language which was some kind of English but which the relatives could not understand.

This boy was reading in one of the lower classes of a school and hardly knew the English language.

When the fever would not abate for twenty-four hours a doctor was sent for.

The doctor arrived, and went in to see the patient in the sick-room.

The boy was lying on the bed with his eyes closed. It was nearly evening.

As soon as the doctor entered the sick-room the boy shouted "Doctor – I am very hungry, order some food for me."

Of course, the doctor thought that the boy was in his senses. He did not know that the boy had not sufficient knowledge of the English language to express his ideas in that tongue. So the doctor asked his relations when he had taken food last. He was informed that the patient had had nothing to eat for the last eight or ten hours.

"What will you like to have?" asked the doctor.

"Roast mutton and plenty of vegetables" said the boy.

By this time the doctor had approached the bed-side, but it was too dark to see whether the eyes of the patient were open or not.

"But you are ill – roast mutton will do you harm" said the doctor.

"No it won't – I know what is good for me" said the patient. At this stage the doctor was informed that the patient did not really know much English and that he was probably in delirium. A suggestion was also made that probably he was possessed by a ghost.

The doctor who had been educated at the Calcutta Medical College did not quite believe the ghost theory. He, however, asked the patient who he was.

In India, I do not know whether this is so in European countries too, lots of people are possessed by ghosts and the ghost speaks through his victim. So generally a question like this is asked by the exorcist "Who are you and why are you troubling the poor patient?" The answer, I am told, is at once given and the ghost says what he wants. Of course, I personally, have never heard a ghost talk. I know a case in which a report was made to me that the wife of a groom of mine had become possessed by a ghost. On being asked what ghost it was the woman was reported to have said "the big ghost of the house across the drain." I ran to the out-houses to find out how much was true but when I reached the stables the woman I was told was not talking. I found her in convulsions.

To return to our story; the doctor asked the patient who he was.

"I am General ——" said the boy.

"Why are you here" asked the doctor.

"I shall tell you that after I have had my roast mutton and the vegetables—" said the boy or rather the ghost.

"But how can we be convinced that you are General ——" asked the doctor.

"Call Captain X—— of the XI Brahmans and he will know," said the ghost, "in the meantime get me the food or I shall kill the patient."

The father of the patient at once began to shout that he would get the mutton and the vegetables. The doctor in the meantime rushed out to procure some more medical assistance as well as to fetch Captain X of the XI Brahmans.

The few big European officers of the station were also informed and within a couple of hours the sick-room was full of sensible educated gentle men. The mutton was in the meantime ready.

"The mutton is ready" said the doctor.

"Lower it into the well in the compound" said the ghost.

A basket was procured and the mutton and the vegetables were lowered into the well.

But scarcely had the basket gone down five yards (the well was forty feet deep) when somebody from inside the well shouted.

"Take it away – take it away – there is no salt in it."

Those that were responsible for the preparation had to admit their mistake.

The basket was pulled out, some salt was put in, and the basket was lowered down again.

But as the basket went in about five or six yards somebody from inside the well pulled it down with such force that the man who was lowering it narrowly escaped being dragged in; fortunately he let the rope slip through his hands with the result that though he did not fall into the well his hands were bleeding profusely.

Nothing happened after that and everybody returned to the patient.

After a few minutes silence the patient said:

"Take away the rope and the basket, why did you not tie the end of the rope to the post."

"Why did you pull it so hard" said one of the persons present.

"I was hungry and in a hurry" said the ghost.

They asked several persons to go down into the well but nobody would. At last a fishing hook was lowered down. The basket, which had at first completely disappeared, was now floating on the surface of the water. It was brought up, quite empty.

Captain X in the meantime had arrived and was taken to the patient. Two high officials of government (both Europeans) had also arrived.

As soon as the captain stepped into the sick room the patient (we shall now call him the ghost) said. "Good evening Captain X, these people will not believe that I am General — and I want to convince them."

The captain was as surprised as the others had been before.

"You may ask me anything you like Captain X, and I shall try to convince you" said the ghost.

The captain stood staring.

"Speak, Captain X, – are you dumb?" said the ghost.

"I don't understand anything" stammered the captain.

He was told everything by those present. After hearing it the captain formulated a question from one of the military books.

A correct reply was immediately given. Then followed a number of questions by the captain, the replies to all of which were promptly given by the ghost.

After this the ghost said, "If you are all convinced, you may go now, and see me again to-morrow morning."

Everybody quietly withdrew.

The next morning there was a large gathering in the sick room. A number of European officers who had heard the story at the club on the previous evening dropped in. "Introduce each of these new comers to me" said the ghost.

Captain X introduced each person in solemn form.

"If anybody is curious to know anything I shall tell him" said the ghost.

A few questions about England – position of buildings, – shops, – streets in London, were asked and correctly answered.

After all the questions the Indian doctor who had been in attendance asked "Now, general, that we are convinced you are so and so why are you troubling this poor boy?"

"His father is rich" said the ghost.

"Not very," said the doctor "but what do you want him to do?"

"My tomb at ——pur has been destroyed by a branch of a tree falling upon it, I want that to be properly repaired" said the ghost.

"I shall get that done immediately" said the father of the patient.

"If you do that within a week I shall trouble your boy no longer" said the ghost.

The monument was repaired and the boy has been never ill since.

This is the whole story; a portion of it appeared in the papers; and there were several respectable witnesses, though the whole thing is too wonderful.

Inexplicable as it is – it appears that dead persons are a bit jealous of the sanctity of their tombs.

I have heard a story of a boy troubled by a ghost who had inscribed his name on the tomb of a Mahommedan fakir.

His father had to repair the tomb and had to put an ornamental iron railing round it.

Somehow or other the thing looks like a fairy tale. The readers may have heard stories like this themselves and thought them as mere idle gossip.

I, therefore, reproduce here the whole of a letter as it appeared in *The Leader* of Allahabad, India – on the 15th July, 1913.

The letter is written by a man, who, I think, understands quite well what he is saying.

A SUPERNATURAL PHENOMENON

Sir, It may probably interest your readers to read the account of a supernatural phenomenon that occurred, a few days ago, in the house of B. Rasiklal Mitra, B.A., district surveyor, Hamirpur. He has been living with his family in a bungalow for about a year. It is a good small bungalow, with two central and several side rooms. There is a verandah on the south and an enclosure, which serves the purpose of a court-yard for the ladies, on the north. On the eastern side of this enclosure is the kitchen and on the western, the privy. It has a big compound all round, on the south-west corner of which there is a tomb of some Shahid, known as the tomb of Phulan Shahid.

At about five o'clock in the evening on 26th June, 1913, when Mr. Mitra was out in office, it was suddenly noticed that the southern portion of the privy was on fire. People ran for rescue and by their timely assistance it was possible to completely extinguish the fire by means of water which they managed to get at the moment, before the fire could do any real damage. On learning of the fire, the ladies and children, all bewildered, collected in a room, ready to quit the building in case the fire was not checked or took a serious turn. About a square foot of the thatch was burnt. Shortly after this another corner of the house was seen burning. This was in the kitchen. It was not a continuation of the former fire as the latter had been completely extinguished. Not even smoke or a spark was left to kindle. The two places are completely separated from each other being divided by an open court-yard of thirty yards in length and there is no connection between them at all.

There was no fire at the time in the kitchen even, and there were no outsiders besides the ladies and children who were shut up in a room. This too was extinguished without any damage having been done. By this time Mr. Mitra and his several friends turned up on getting the news of the fire in his house. I was one of them. In short the fire broke out in the house at seven different places within an hour or an hour and a half, all these places situated so apart from one another that one was astonished to find how it broke out one after the other without any visible sign of the possibility of a fire from outside. We were all at a loss to account for the breaking out of the fire. To all appearance it broke out each time spontaneously and mysteriously. The fact that fire broke out so often as seven times within the short space of about an hour and a half, each time at a different place without doing any perceptible damage to the thatching of the bungalow or to any other article of the occupant of the house, is a mystery which remains to be solved. After the last breaking out, it was decided that the house must be vacated at once. Mr. Mitra and his family consequently removed to another house of Padri Ahmad Shah about two hundred yards distant therefrom. To the great astonishment of all nothing happened after the 'vacation' of the house for the whole night. Next morning Mr. Mitra came with his sister to have his morning meals prepared there, thinking that there was no fire during the night. To his great curiosity he found that the house was ablaze within ten or fifteen minutes of his arrival. They removed at once and everything was again all right. A day or two after he removed to a pucca house within the town, not easy to catch fire. After settling his family in the new house Mr. Mitra went to a town (Moudha) some twenty-one miles from the head quarters. During the night following his departure, a daughter of Mr. Mitra aged about ten years saw in dream a boy who called himself Shahid Baba. The girl enquired of him about the reason of the fire breaking in her last residence and was told by him that she would witness curious scenes next morning, after which she would be told the remedy. Morning came and it was not long before fire broke out in the second storey of the new house. This was extinguished as easily as the previous ones and it did not cause any damage. Next came the turn of a dhoti of the girl mentioned above which was hanging in the house. Half of it was completely burnt down before the fire could be extinguished. In succession, the pillow wrapped in a bedding, a sheet of another bedding and lastly the dhoti which the girl was wearing caught fire and were extinguished after they were nearly half destroyed. Mr. Mitra's son aged about four months was lying on a cot: as soon as he was lifted up – a portion of the bed on which he was lying was seen burning. Although the pillow was burnt down there was no mark of fire on the bedding. Neither the girl nor the boy received any injury. Most curious of all, the papers enclosed in a box were burnt although the box remained closed. B. Ganesh Prasad, munsif, and the post master hearing of this, went to the house and in their presence a mirzai of the girl which was spread over a cot in the court-yard caught fire spontaneously and was seen burning.

Now the girl went to sleep again. It was now about noon. She again saw the same boy in the dream. She was told this time that if the tomb was whitewashed and a promise to repair it within three months made, the trouble would cease. They were also ordained to return to the house which they had left. This command was soon obeyed by the troubled family which removed immediately after the tomb was whitewashed to the bungalow in which they are now peacefully living without the least disturbance or annoyance of any sort. I leave to your readers to draw their own conclusions according to their own experience of life and to form such opinion as they like.

Permeshwar Dayal Amist, B.A.,
July 9.
Vakil, High Court

The Barber and the Ghost

Ram Satya Mukharji

IN THE DISTRICT OF BURDWAN, there lived a barber who was very idle. He would do no work, and devote all his time to his toilet which consisted only of an old looking-glass and a broken comb. His old mother constantly rebuked him for this, but with no effect. At last one day she got extremely annoyed and in a fit of anger struck him with a broom she was sweeping with, at the time. The young barber took this chastisement to heart and left home, determined not to return, unless he amassed wealth. He repaired to a distant forest, in order by prayer, in its deep silence, to move the gods to his help. But no sooner had he entered it than he met a Brahma-Daitya dancing before him. He became extremely frightened and knew not what to do. However, he soon took courage and devised a plan to discomfit the aerial being. With this purpose he too began to dance, and asked the ghost: "Pray, why are you dancing, sir?"

The ghost laughed and replied in a deep sonorous voice. "You seem to be an arrant fool not to understand the reason. It is simply because I wish to make a sumptuous feast upon your delicate flesh, but, tell me what made you dance?"

"I have," retorted the barber, "far better reasons: our king's son is dangerously ill, the physicians have prescribed for his cure the heart's blood of one hundred and one Brahma-Daityas and His Majesty has proclaimed by beat of drum to give away half of his kingdom and one of his beautiful daughters to any one who would be able to get the medicine. I have, with much difficulty, captured one hundred ghosts and in you I make up the full number. I have seized you already and you are in my pocket." So saying he took out his pocket-mirror and held it before the Brahma-Daitya's eyes. The terrified ghost found his image reflected in the glass by the clear moon light and thought himself actually captured. He trembled and prayed for his release. The barber did not agree at first, but on the ghost's promising wealth worth seven kings' ransom he subsequently yielded and said: "Where is the wealth, and who is to carry it and me home at this dead hour of night?"

"The wealth", replied the Brahma-Daitya, "is underneath yonder tree, I shall presently show it to you and carry you with it on my shoulders to your house in an instant, as you know we spirits have superhuman powers."

Saying this, he uprooted the tree and brought out seven golden jars full of precious stones from under it. The poor barber was quite amazed at the sight of the enormous wealth, but as he was cunning he concealed his emotions and boldly ordered the ghost to carry the jars and himself forthwith to his house. The ghost obeyed, and in an instant the barber was safely carried home, with the wealth. The ghost then prayed for his release, but the wily *Narasundar* not wishing to part with his services so soon, asked him to cut the paddy of his field and bring the crop home. The ghost believing himself still under the clutches of the barber had no other means left but to agree, so he went out to reap the corn.

As he was cutting the paddy, a brother ghost happened to pass that way, and finding him thus employed, asked for the reason. The Brahma-Daitya replied that he had accidently fallen into the hands of a shrewd man and that there was no means of his escape unless he reaped the paddy. The other ghost laughed and said: "Have you gone mad, my friend! We, ghosts, are beings superior to men and are more powerful. How is it possible that a mortal would have any power over us ? Can you show me the house of your captor?

"I can," replied the Brahma-Daitya, "but from a distance as I do not venture to go near it till I have reaped the paddy." They then both left for the barber's house.

Meanwhile the barber having obtained so much wealth had purchased a big fish to give a treat to his friends, but unfortunately a cat having entered the kitchen through a broken window had eaten up a good portion of it. The barber's wife was awfully angry and wanted to kill the animal, but it escaped. Expecting a return, as the cats generally do on such an occasion, she stood concealed with a fish-knife in hand by the side of the window. Now the Brahma-Daitya having shown the house of the barber to his friend from a distance went back to the field. The other ghost was approaching stealthily towards the house to have a look at his friend's captor. Coming near the kitchen he thrust in his bushy head through the broken window by the side of which stood the irate wife expecting the return of the mischievous cat every moment. No sooner, therefore, was the head of the ghost pushed in than she struck a severe blow to it with her sharp knife causing a clean cut of the tip of his nose. In pain and fright the ghost ran straight away, ashamed of meeting his friend with a disfigured face.

The Brahma-Daitya after having reaped the paddy got his release. The wily barber this time, presented the back of his mirror before the ghost, who, not finding his image in it, was satisfied of his release and went home merrily.

Last Train Onwards

Lena Ng

WE HAVE A LEGEND from where I come from, back in the old country, where there are no skyscrapers or neon lights. Where rice paddies are planted by hand and soybeans are seeded in the fields. Where over the years, the rural population's youth have drained into the city, lured away by the call of fortune, taken away by trains. The gardens have given way to weeds and the timbers of the traditional thatched-roof houses have rotted, cracked, and fallen. More houses stand abandoned than shelter the living.

Once vibrant with families, our village had a market, school, community centre, and izakaya, our version of a pub, where skewers of chicken or leeks were grilled over a charcoal fire, the food accompanied by sake or beer. There are only a handful of us left, the ones left behind, now elderly or infirm. More ghosts than people occupy the land. The one-room school has closed, the izakaya shuttered, the community hall no longer hosts weddings. I find myself talking to shadows.

Our village is located in the Yano Valley, in an isolated mountainous region, one side bounded by the sea. Our sacred mountain, Mount Kenji, stands guard. There is a winding path through the forest to the summit where we go to pray. A shrine was built from red-painted columns and prayers scrolls fluttered in the breeze. A pair of *komainu* statues, sculpted as wide-eyed lion-dogs, protect the entrance by warding away evil spirits with their open-mouthed snarls. Offerings of bowls of rice, apples from our orchards, and flowers such as blue asagao and yellow sunflowers adorned the wooden altar. The scent of incense, their smoke rising to the heavens, lingered in the air.

After I visited the shrine, my prayers preceded by a ring of a bell and clap of my hands, I moved to a clear spot where I could watch the ocean. Sometimes peaceful, sometimes angry, the great waves tumbled with frothing, white caps against the cliffs. The boats of the fisherman lilted and turned. They looked like toys.

When I was a young man, we still had train service to our village. We were part of the Keibu line, which travelled between Dayo and Odasei, bringing those returning home. It was a joy to see the train coming into the station, and those whom we had not seen in months, their familiar faces. Over the years, the train service was privatized, and due to lack of demand, eventually shuttered.

Although it has been many years since service to our train station has stopped and the village's section of track is no longer in use, occasionally through the thick fog, you can hear the train's whistle. Under the right conditions of wind and pressure, the sound carries from a distance away. When we hear the train's whistle, the few remaining villagers huddle in their houses.

But for some, the train's whistle is a call to the final journey. Legend has it, that on chill evenings, the ghost train appears. The whistle is first heard, a low, grumbling thrum. Then through the dense gray cover, although the air is chill and no fog should form, the dark form of steel and aluminum emerges, rattling the ground. It is said that it looks like a hearse. When it comes to rest at the platform, the doors together as one slide open, but no employees appear. No one knows its destination. For those who wish to travel onwards, they get their chance to board. None have ever returned. I think it goes to a land of shadows, where loved ones have gone before.

It is on these nights that one-by-one the villagers have disappeared. It is rumoured some offered themselves to the mountain, a practice called *ubasute*. When one reaches an age to become a burden, their family carries them to the shrine near to the summit of Mount Kenji. The sons will carry their elderly mothers on their backs. The parents here know sacrifice. They meditate in the lotus position until they die of starvation or exposure.

Others disappear by flinging themselves into the ocean. Those who are fishermen give their lives to the water which had given them life. Their bodies have never been recovered. Some disappear into the forests, the bodies scavenged by wild animals or decayed back into the earth. Or they evaporate into the air in a practice called *jouhatsu* where one escapes life by vanishing. They don't want to be themselves anymore so finding them wouldn't bring them back.

We villagers like to say the train has taken them away. It's our euphemism for death. It also keeps alive the hope that they will someday return and we can anticipate the joy of reuniting.

Not only do we have ghosts of the dead, but we also have ghosts of the living. Mrs. Sato, now in her eighties but hale and energetic, has taken to creating life-size figures to replace the departed, made from cloth stretched over wire frames and stuffed with straw. They stare at you as they sit along the road or propped up as though they were working in the fields, or dressed in their fishing gear. There are more dolls than villagers. Some of them resemble deceased family members while others have no unique characteristics, white-faced and featureless. There are no more children here. Instead, there are child-sized dolls which sit silently in the classroom, picture books propped open before them with illustrations of octopuses or other creatures of the sea, while their soundless teachers watch over them. Some dolls sit at the bus station where no more buses run. Others gather at the abandoned train station where the train no longer travels.

Mrs. Sato had started by making a doll of her father, dressing it in his clothes. Over time, the rest of her family reappeared. This hobby keeps her busy and lifts her loneliness. I find it eerie, reminders of what was lost or what was never had.

Sometimes I see the ghosts of a different life. If I had found a wife and had children, I would have been surrounded by their love. I might have been called Itsuki-chan, my first name with 'chan' added as an endearment, instead of Mr. Tanaka as all the villagers call me out of respect. I might have someone to sit close to me by the fire on long winter nights, to drink tea with on summer mornings, to help climb the stairs, or to pick daikon – white radishes – in the early fall. I might have left this village to live with my daughter in the city to help babysit the grandchildren. The silence might have been replaced with chatter or scoldings, with gossip or stories of our ancestors.

Many years ago, after I had turned six, my father disappeared in the fog. I was playing with my toy cars in the corner. My mother was putting away the dishes. My father, brooding, perked up as though he heard something in the distance. Without a word, he left our home. The whispers were that he killed himself. I like to think the train came and took him away. His straw effigy sits on one of the cliff's edges and overlooks the sea.

All that remains in our village is silence. It has a strange quality – empty and mournful. This strange type of silence starts after the autumn moon festival, stretches out through the winter, and lifts in the spring. It is like the sound of sleeping. The return of cherry blossoms in spring brings a burgeoning joy, along with the melancholy that their lives, as ours, are short, and the petals will eventually fall like tears. The feeling arises that nothing lasts, called *mono no aware*, or the wistfulness of impermanence, the passing of all things like the ghost train in the night. Our village grows smaller and smaller. Though the people are gone, reminders of their presence surround us.

Sometimes I hear laughter rustling in the fields, in the creeping stems of the grasses. Joyous youthful laughter from my friends growing up. They are friends now of the past. They travelled onwards while I remained here. When I turned twenty-three, I tried to kill myself. At the time, I thought of myself as a failure. I didn't go on to study at the university. I had stood on the platform as the train rolled away, taking with it my classmates. I had to stay home to take care of my mother. Because I thought I was valued for what I could achieve, I viewed myself as worthless for being just me.

When my classmates returned for visits and stories, each peal of laughter brought with it a weight to my heart. Their lives were moving forward while mine was standing still. Their visits grew farther in time apart until the train brought no one.

That terrible day, the train thundered in the distance. I had prepared myself to jump. In my hesitation, it sped by, and in a flash, I saw my father as the conductor. He tipped his hat at me as the train raced away.

For how many more years will I see the cherry blossoms? Their petals float in the wind, brush my cheeks as I tend to my garden.

More time passes and more dolls appear. Cracked mirrors in vacant houses reflect no one. The grass grows taller, wilder. I looked for the towel hanging from Mr. Yamamoto's window, my neighbour I've paired with for wellbeing checks. Since we who remain are so old, we have developed a system to check on one another. Every morning, we hang a towel from the window and every evening we remove it. This is to signal that we are alive and everything is all right. On the morning when no towel is hung, we know to say a prayer before we enter their house. The body gets tired and the spirit long to fly upwards. We are sad and happy at the same time.

The evening air was crisp and the moon was a bright white marble we used to play with as children. I heard the train's whistle over the field. A pull of yearning brought me to the station. A doll with my face awaited me. It had my close-set eyes and long, thin chin. It stood on the platform. It looked like my father. It could have looked like my son.

Mrs. Sato straightened its blue sun hat, her softly wrinkled face round like the moon. She smiled at the similarity of my face to that of the doll. "Fine weather, isn't it?" she asked. It was chill and I could hear the wind rustling through the trees, through the grass. I heard the train's whistle, louder. The mist rolled down from the sacred mountain, trundled over the forested slopes, and gathered around our feet.

The wall of fog opened and the train slowed into the station. It was larger than I had imagined with a hulking black engine and the quiet air of a hearse.

The conductor pulled a lever and I swear his profile was that of my father. When he turned to look at me, the moonlight glanced off his beloved expression with a rare look of happiness. "Last train," he said with a gentle, welcoming voice, his conductor's cap crowned with a wreath of new cherry blossoms. "All aboard."

I glanced around the empty platform. Mrs. Sato had disappeared. The doors slid open as one. As I boarded the steps onto the train, my aches and stiffness fell away. My body straightened as I walked down the aisle. I felt joy awakening in my heart. I saw several familiar faces, and I hastened towards the section holding my mother, grandmother and grandfather, and their grandmothers and grandfathers. I settled in the remaining seat, and with a slow, silent roll, the train moved into the night.

The Spirit of the Lantern

Yei Theodora Ozaki

SOME THREE HUNDRED YEARS AGO, in the province of Kai and the town of Aoyagi, there lived a man named Koharu Tomosaburo, of well-known ancestry. His grandfather had been a retainer of Ota Dokan, the founder of Yedo, and had committed suicide when his lord fell in battle.

This brave clansman's grandson was Tomosaburo, who, when this story begins, had been happily married for many years to a woman of the same province and was the proud father of a son some ten years of age.

At this time it happened, one day, that his wife fell suddenly ill and was unable to leave her bed. Physicians were called in but had to acknowledge themselves baffled by the curious symptoms of the patient: to relieve the paroxysms of pain from which she suffered, *Moxa* was applied and burned in certain spots down her back. But half a month passed by and the anxious household realized that there was no change for the better in the mysterious malady that was consuming her: day by day she seemed to lose ground and waste away.

Tomosaburo was a kind husband and scarcely left her bedside: day and night he tenderly ministered to his stricken wife, and did all in his power to alleviate her condition.

One evening, as he was sitting thus, worn out with the strain of nursing and anxiety, he fell into a doze. Suddenly there came a change in the light of the standing-lantern, it flushed a brilliant red, then flared up into the air to the height of at least three feet, and within the crimson pillar of flame there appeared the figure of a woman.

Tomosaburo gazed in astonishment at the apparition, who thus addressed him:

"Your anxiety concerning your wife's illness is well-known to me, therefore I have come to give you some good advice. The affliction with which she is visited is the punishment for some faults in her character. For this reason she is possessed of a devil. If you will worship me as a god, I will cast out the tormenting demon."

Now Tomosaburo was a brave, strong-minded *samurai*, to whom the sensation of fear was totally unknown.

He glared fiercely at the apparition, and then, half unconsciously, turned for the *samurai's* only safeguard, his sword, and drew it from its sheath. The sword is regarded as sacred by the Japanese knight and was supposed to possess the occult power assigned to the sign of the cross in mediæval Europe – that of exorcising evil.

The spirit laughed superciliously when she saw his action.

"No motive but the kindest of intentions brought me here to proffer you my assistance in your trouble, but without the least appreciation of my goodwill you show this enmity towards me. However, your wife's life shall pay the penalty," and with these malicious words the phantom disappeared.

From that hour the unhappy woman's sufferings increased, and to the distress of all about her, she seemed about to draw her last breath.

Her husband was beside himself with grief. He realized at once what a false move he had made in driving away the friendly spirit in such an uncouth and hostile manner, and, now thoroughly alarmed at his wife's desperate plight, he was willing to comply with any demand, however strange. He thereupon prostrated himself before the family shrine and addressed fervent prayers to the Spirit of the Lantern, humbly imploring her pardon for his thoughtless and discourteous behaviour.

From that very hour the invalid began to mend, and steadily improving day by day, her normal health was soon entirely regained, until it seemed to her as though her long and strange illness had been but an evil dream.

One evening after her recovery, when the husband and wife were sitting together and speaking joyfully of her unexpected and almost miraculous restoration to health, the lantern flared up as before and in the column of brilliant light the form of the spirit again appeared.

"Notwithstanding your unkind reception of me the last time I came, I have driven out the devil and saved your wife's life. In return for this service I have come to ask a favour of you, Tomosaburo San," said the spirit. "I have a daughter who is now of a marriageable age. The reason of my visit is to request you to find a suitable husband for her."

"But I am a human being," remonstrated the perplexed man, "and you are a spirit! We belong to different worlds, and a wide and impassable gulf separates us. How would it be possible for me to do as you wish?"

"It is an easier matter than you imagine," replied the spirit. "All you have to do is to take some blocks of *kiri*-wood and to carve out from them several little figures of men; when they are finished I will bestow upon one of them the hand of my daughter."

"If that is all, then it is not so difficult as I thought, and I will undertake to do as you wish," assented Tomosaburo, and no sooner had the spirit vanished than he opened his tool box and set to work upon the appointed task with such alacrity that in a few days he had fashioned out in miniature several very creditable effigies of the desired bridegroom, and when the wooden dolls were completed he laid them out in a row upon his desk.

The next morning, on awaking, he lost no time in ascertaining what had befallen the quaint little figures, but apparently they had found favour with the spirit, for all had disappeared during the night. He now hoped that the strange and supernatural visitant would trouble them no more, but the next night she again appeared:

"Owing to your kind assistance my daughter's future is settled. As a mark of our gratitude for the trouble you have taken, we earnestly desire the presence of both yourself and your wife at the marriage feast. When the time arrives promise to come without fail."

By this time Tomosaburo was thoroughly wearied of these ghostly visitations and considered it highly obnoxious to be in league with such weird and intangible beings, yet fully aware of their powers of working evil, he dared not offend them. He racked his brains for some way of escape from this uncanny invitation, but before he could frame any reply suitable to the emergency, and while he was hesitating, the spirit vanished.

Long did the perplexed man ponder over the strange situation, but the more he thought the more embarrassed he became: and there seemed no solution of his dilemma.

The next night the spirit again returned.

"As I had the honour to inform you, we have prepared an entertainment at which your presence is desired. All is now in readiness. The wedding ceremony has taken place and the assembled company await your arrival with impatience. Kindly follow me at once!" and the wraith made imperious gestures to Tomosaburo and his wife to accompany her. With a sudden movement she darted from the lantern flame and glided out of the room, now and again looking back with furtive glances to see that they were surely following – and thus they passed, the spirit guiding them, along the passage to the outer porch.

The idea of accepting the spirit's hospitality was highly repugnant to the astonished couple, but remembering the dire consequences of his first refusal to comply with the ghostly visitor's request, Tomosaburo thought it wiser to simulate acquiescence. He was well aware that in some strange and incomprehensible manner his wife owed her sudden recovery to the spirit's agency, and for this boon he felt it would be both unseemly and ungrateful – and possibly dangerous – to refuse. In great embarrassment, and at a loss for any plausible excuse, he felt half dazed, and as though all capacity for voluntary action was deserting him.

What was Tomosaburo's surprise on reaching the entrance to find stationed there a procession, like the train of some great personage, awaiting him. On their appearance the liveried bearers hastened to bring forward two magnificent palanquins of lacquer and gold, and at the same moment a tall man garbed in ceremonial robes advanced and with a deep obeisance requested them not to hesitate, saying:

"Honoured sir, these *kago* are for your august conveyance – deign to enter so that we may proceed to your destination."

At the same time the members of the procession and the bearers bowed low, and in curious high-pitched voices all repeated the invitation in a chorus:

"Please deign to enter the *kago*!"

Both Tomosaburo and his wife were not only amazed at the splendour of the escort which had been provided for them, but they realized that what was happening to them was most mysterious, and might have unexpected consequences. However, it was too late to draw back now, and all they could do was to fall in with the arrangement with as bold a front as they could muster. They both stepped valiantly into the elaborately decorated *kago*; thereupon the attendants surrounded the palanquins, the bearers raised the shafts shoulder high, and the procession formed in line and set out on its ghostly expedition.

The night was still and very dark. Thick masses of sable cloud obscured the heavens, with no friendly gleams of moon or stars to illumine their unknown path, and peering through the bamboo blinds nothing met Tomosaburo's anxious gaze but the impenetrable gloom of the inky sky.

Seated in the palanquins the adventurous couple were undergoing a strange experience. To their mystified senses it did not seem as if the *kago* was being borne along over the ground in the ordinary manner, but the sensation was as though they were being swiftly impelled by some mysterious unseen force, which caused them to skim through the air like the flight of birds. After some time had elapsed the sombre blackness of the night somewhat lifted, and they were dimly able to discern the curved outlines of a large mansion which they were now approaching, and which appeared to be situated in a spacious and thickly wooded park.

The bearers entered the large roofed gate and, crossing an intervening space of garden, carefully lowered their burdens before the main entrance of the house, where a body of servants and retainers were already waiting to welcome the expected guests with assiduous attentions. Tomosaburo and his wife alighted from their conveyances and were ushered into a reception room of great size and splendour, where, as soon as they were seated in the place of honour near the alcove, refreshments were served by a bevy of fair waiting-maids in ceremonial costumes. As soon as they were rested from the fatigues of their journey an usher appeared and bowing profoundly to the bewildered new-comers announced that the marriage feast was about to be celebrated and their presence was requested without delay.

Following this guide they proceeded through the various ante-rooms and along the corridors. The whole interior of the mansion, the sumptuousness of its appointments and the delicate beauty of its finishings, were such as to fill their hearts with wonder and admiration.

The floors of the passages shone like mirrors, so fine was the quality of the satiny woods, and the richly inlaid ceilings showed that no expense or trouble had been spared in the selection of all that was ancient and rare, both in materials and workmanship. Certain of the pillars were formed by the trunks of petrified trees, brought from great distances, and on every side perfect taste and limitless wealth were apparent in every detail of the scheme of decoration.

More and more deeply impressed with his surroundings, Tomosaburo obediently followed in the wake of the ushers. As they neared the stately guest-chamber an eerie and numbing sensation seemed to creep through his veins.

Observing more closely the surrounding figures that flitted to and fro, with a shock of horror he suddenly became aware that their faces were well known to him and of many in that shadowy throng he recognized the features and forms of friends and relatives long since dead. Along the corridors leading to the principal hall numerous attendants were gathered: all their features were familiar to Tomosaburo, but none of them betrayed the slightest sign of recognition. Gradually his dazed brain began to understand that he was visiting in the underworld, that everything about him was unreal – in fact, a dream of the past – and he feebly wondered of what hallucination he could be the victim to be thus abruptly bidden to such an illusory carnival, where all the wedding guests seemed to be denizens of the *Meido*, that dusky kingdom of departed spirits! But no time was left him for conjecture, for on reaching the ante-room they were immediately ushered into a magnificent hall where all preparations for the feast had been set out, and where the Elysian Strand and the symbols of marriage were all duly arranged according to time-honoured custom.

Here the bridegroom and his bride were seated in state, both attired in elegant robes as befitting the occasion. Tomosaburo, who had acted such a strange and important part in providing the farcical groom for this unheard-of marriage, gazed searchingly at the newly wedded husband, whose mien was quite dignified and imposing, and whose thick dark locks were crowned with a nobleman's coronet. He wondered what part the wooden figures he had carved according to the spirit's behest had taken in the composition of the bridegroom he now saw before him. Strangely, indeed, his features bore a striking resemblance to the little puppets that Tomosaburo had fashioned from the *kiri*-wood some days before.

The nuptial couple were receiving the congratulations of the assembled guests, and no sooner had Tomosaburo and his wife entered the room than the wedding party all came forward in a body to greet them and to offer thanks for their condescension in gracing that happy occasion with their presence. They were ceremoniously conducted to seats in a place of honour, and invited with great cordiality to participate in the evening's entertainment.

Servants then entered bearing all sorts of tempting dainties piled on lacquer trays in the form of large shells; the feast was spread before the whole assemblage; wine flowed in abundance, and by degrees conversation, laughter, and merriment became universal and the banquet-hall echoed with the carousal of the ghostly throng.

Under the influence of the good cheer Tomosaburo's apprehension and alarm of his weird environment gradually wore off, he partook freely of the refreshments, and associated himself more and more with the gaiety and joviality of the evening's revel.

* * *

The night wore on and when the hour of midnight struck the banquet was at its height.

In the mirth and glamour of that strange marriage feast Tomosaburo had lost all track of time, when suddenly the clear sound of a cock's crow penetrated his clouded brain and, looking up, the transparency of the *shoji* of the room began to slowly whiten in the grey of dawn. Like a flash of lightning Tomosaburo and his wife found themselves transported back, safe and sound, into their own room.

On reflection he found his better nature more and more troubled by such an uncanny experience, and he spent much time pondering over the matter, which seemed to require such delicate handling. He determined that at all costs communications must be broken off with the importunate spirit.

A few days passed and Tomosaburo began to cherish the hope that he had seen the last of the Spirit of the Lantern, but his congratulations on escaping her unwelcome attentions proved premature.

That very night, no sooner had he laid himself down to rest, than lo! and behold, the lantern shot up in the familiar shaft of light, and there in the lurid glow appeared the spirit, looking more than ever bent on mischief. Tomosaburo lost all patience. Glaring savagely at the unwelcome visitant he seized his wooden pillow and, determining to rid himself of her persecutions once and for all, he exerted his whole strength and hurled it straight at the intruder. His aim was true, and the missile struck the goblin squarely on the forehead, overturning the lantern and plunging the room into black darkness. "Wa, Wa!" wailed the spirit in a thin haunting cry, that gradually grew fainter and fainter till she finally disappeared like a luminous trail of vanishing blue smoke.

From that very hour Tomosaburo's wife was again stricken with her former malady, and no remedies being of any avail, within two days it took a turn for the worse and she died.

The sorrow-stricken husband bitterly regretted his impetuous action in giving way to that fatal fit of anger and, moreover, in appearing so forgetful of the past favour he had received from the spirit. He therefore prayed earnestly to the offended apparition, apologizing with humble contrition for his cruelty and ingratitude.

But the Spirit of the Lantern had been too deeply outraged to return, and Tomosaburo's repentance for his rash impulse proved all in vain.

These melancholy events caused the unhappy husband to take a strong aversion to the house, which he felt sure must be haunted, and he decided to leave that neighbourhood with as little delay as possible.

As soon as a suitable dwelling was found and the details of his migration arranged, the carriers were summoned to transport his household goods to the new abode, but to the alarm and consternation of every one, when the servants attempted to move the furniture, the whole contents of the house by some unseen power adhered fast to the floor, and no human power was available to dislodge them.

Then Tomosaburo's little son fell ill and died. Such was the revenge of the Spirit of the Lantern.

The Badger-Haunted Temple

Yei Theodora Ozaki

ONCE LONG AGO, in southern Japan, in the town of Kumamoto, there lived a young *samurai*, who had a great devotion to the sport of fishing. Armed with his large basket and tackle, he would often start out in the early morning and pass the whole day at his favourite pastime, returning home only at nightfall.

One fine day he had more than usual luck. In the late afternoon, when he examined his basket, he found it full to overflowing. Highly delighted at his success, he wended his way homewards with a light heart, singing snatches of merry songs as he went along.

It was already dusk when he happened to pass a deserted Buddhist temple. He noticed that the gate stood half open, and hung loosely on its rusty hinges, and the whole place had a dilapidated and tumbledown appearance.

What was the young man's astonishment to see, in striking contrast to such a forlorn environment, a pretty young girl standing just within the gate.

As he approached she came forward, and looking at him with a meaning glance, smiled, as if inviting him to enter into conversation. The *samurai* thought her manner somewhat strange, and at first was on his guard. Some mysterious influence, however, compelled him to stop, and he stood irresolutely admiring the fair young face, blooming like a flower in its sombre setting.

When she noticed his hesitation she made a sign to him to approach. Her charm was so great and the smile with which she accompanied the gesture so irresistible, that half-unconsciously, he went up the stone steps, passed through the semi-open portal, and entered the courtyard where she stood awaiting him.

The maiden bowed courteously, then turned and led the way up the stone-flagged pathway to the temple. The whole place was in the most woeful condition, and looked as if it had been abandoned for many years.

When they reached what had once been the priest's house, the *samurai* saw that the interior of the building was in a better state of preservation than the outside led one to suppose. Passing along the verandah into the front room, he noticed that the *tatami* were still presentable, and that a sixfold screen adorned the chamber.

The girl gracefully motioned her guest to sit down in the place of honour near the alcove.

"Does the priest of the temple live here?" asked the young man, seating himself.

"No," answered the girl, "there is no priest here now. My mother and I only came here yesterday. She has gone to the next village to buy some things and may not be able to come back to-night. But honourably rest awhile, and let me give you some refreshment."

The girl then went into the kitchen apparently to make the tea, but though the guest waited a long time, she never returned.

By this time the moon had risen, and shone so brightly into the room, that it was as light as day. The *samurai* began to wonder at the strange behaviour of the damsel, who had inveigled him into such a place only to disappear and leave him in solitude.

Suddenly he was startled by some one sneezing loudly behind the screen. He turned his head in the direction from whence the sound came. To his utter amazement, not the pretty girl whom he had expected, but a huge, red-faced, bald-headed priest stalked out. He must have been about seven feet in height, for his head towered nearly to the ceiling, and he carried an iron wand, which he raised in a threatening manner.

"How dare you enter my house without my permission?" shouted the fierce-looking giant. "Unless you go away at once I will beat you into dust."

Frightened out of his wits, the young man took to his heels, and rushed with all speed out of the temple.

As he fled across the courtyard he heard peals of loud laughter behind him. Once outside the gate he stopped to listen, and still the strident laugh continued. Suddenly it occurred to him, that in the alarm of his hasty exit, he had forgotten his basket of fish. It was left behind in the temple. Great was his chagrin, for never before had he caught so much fish in a single day; but lacking the courage to go back and demand it, there was no alternative but to return home empty-handed.

The following day he related his strange experience to several of his friends. They were all highly amused at such an adventure, and some of them plainly intimated that the seductive maiden and the aggressive giant were merely hallucinations that owed their origin to the sake flask.

At last one man, who was a good fencer, said:

"Oh, you must have been deluded by a badger who coveted your fish. No one lives in that temple. It has been deserted ever since I can remember. I will go there this evening and put an end to his mischief."

He then went to a fishmonger, purchased a large basket of fish, and borrowed an angling rod. Thus equipped, he waited impatiently for the sun to set. When the dusk began to fall he buckled on his sword and set out for the temple, carefully shouldering his bait that was to lead to the undoing of the badger. He laughed confidently to himself as he said: "I will teach the old fellow a lesson!"

As he approached the ruin what was his surprise to see, not one, but three girls standing there.

"O, ho! that is the way the wind lies, is it, but the crafty old sinner won't find it such an easy matter to make a fool of me."

No sooner was he observed by the pretty trio than by gestures they invited him to enter. Without any hesitation, he followed them into the building, and boldly seated himself upon the mats. They placed the customary tea and cakes before him, and then brought in a flagon of wine and an extraordinarily large cup.

The swordsman partook neither of the tea nor the sake, and shrewdly watched the demeanour of the three maidens.

Noticing his avoidance of the proffered refreshment, the prettiest of them artlessly inquired:

"Why don't you take some sake?"

"I dislike both tea and sake," replied the valiant guest, "but if you have some accomplishment to entertain me with, if you can dance or sing, I shall be delighted to see you perform."

"Oh, what an old-fashioned man of propriety you are! If you don't drink, you surely know nothing of love either. What a dull existence yours must be! But we can dance a little, so if you will condescend to look, we shall be very pleased to try to amuse you with our performance, poor as it is."

The maidens then opened their fans and began to posture and dance. They exhibited so much skill and grace, however, that the swordsman was astonished, for it was unusual that country girls should be so deft and well-trained. As he watched them he became more and more fascinated, and gradually lost sight of the object of his mission.

Lost in admiration, he followed their every step, their every movement, and as the Japanese storyteller says, he forgot himself entirely, entranced at the beauty of their dancing.

Suddenly he saw that the three performers had become *headless*! Utterly bewildered, he gazed at them intently to make sure that he was not dreaming. Lo! and behold! each was holding her own head in her hands. They then threw them up and caught them as they fell. Like children playing a game of ball, they tossed their heads from one to the other. At last the boldest of the three threw her head at the young fencer. It fell on his knees, looked up in his face, and laughed at him. Angered at the girl's impertinence, he cast the head back at her in disgust, and drawing his sword, made several attempts to cut down the goblin dancer as she glided to and fro playfully tossing up her head and catching it.

But she was too quick for him, and like lightning darted out of the reach of his sword.

"Why don't you catch me?" she jeered mockingly. Mortified at his failure, he made another desperate attempt, but once more she adroitly eluded him, and sprang up to the top of the screen.

"I am here! Can you not reach me this time?" and she laughed at him in derision.

Again he made a thrust at her, but she proved far too nimble for him, and again, for the third time, he was foiled.

Then the three girls tossed their heads on their respective necks, shook them at him, and with shouts of weird laughter they vanished from sight.

As the young man came to his senses he vaguely gazed around. Bright moonlight illumined the whole place, and the stillness of the midnight was unbroken save for the thin tinkling chirping of the insects. He shivered as he realized the lateness of the hour and the wild loneliness of that uncanny spot. His basket of fish was nowhere to be seen. He understood, that he, too, had come under the spell of the wizard-badger, and like his friend, at whom he had laughed so heartily the day before, he had been bewitched by the wily creature.

But, although deeply chagrined at having fallen such an easy dupe, he was powerless to take any sort of revenge. The best he could do was to accept his defeat and return home.

Among his friends there was a doctor, who was not only a brave man, but one full of resource. On hearing of the way the mortified swordsman had been bamboozled, he said:

"Now leave this to me. Within three days I will catch that old badger and punish him well for all his diabolical tricks."

The doctor went home and prepared a savoury dish cooked with meat. Into this he mixed some deadly poison. He then cooked a second portion for himself. Taking these separate dishes and a bottle of sake with him, towards evening he set out for the ruined temple.

When he reached the mossy courtyard of the old building he found it solitary and deserted. Following the example of his friends, he made his way into the priest's room, intensely curious to see what might befall him, but, contrary to his expectation, all was empty and still. He knew that goblin-badgers were such crafty animals that it was almost impossible for anyone, however cautious, to be able to cope successfully with their snares and *Fata Morganas*. But he determined to be particularly wide awake and on his guard, so as not to fall a prey to any hallucination that the badger might raise.

The night was beautiful, and calm as the mouldering tombs in the temple graveyard. The full moon shone brightly over the great black sloping roofs, and cast a flood of light into the room where the doctor was patiently awaiting the mysterious foe. The minutes went slowly by, an hour elapsed, and still no ghostly visitant appeared. At last the baffled intruder placed his flask of wine before him and began to make preparations for his evening meal, thinking that possibly the badger might be unable to resist the tempting savour of the food.

"There is nothing like solitude," he mused aloud. "What a perfect night it is! How lucky I am to have found this deserted temple from which to view the silvery glory of the autumn moon."

For some time he continued to eat and drink, smacking his lips like a country gourmet in enjoyment of the meal. He began to think that the badger, knowing that he had found his match at last, Intended to leave him alone. Then to his delight, he heard the sound of footsteps. He watched the entrance to the room, expecting the old wizard to assume his favourite disguise, and that some pretty maiden would come to cast a spell upon him with her fascinations.

But, to his surprise, who should come into sight but an old priest, who dragged himself into the room with faltering steps and sank down upon the mats with a deep long-drawn sigh of weariness. Apparently between seventy and eighty years of age, his clothes were old and travel-stained, and in his withered hands he carried a rosary. The effort of ascending the steps had evidently been a great trial to him, he breathed heavily and seemed in a state of great exhaustion. His whole appearance was one to arouse pity in the heart of the beholder.

"May I inquire who are you?" asked the doctor.

The old man replied, in a quavering voice, "I am the priest who used to live here many years ago when the temple was in a prosperous condition. As a youth I received my training here under the abbot then in charge, having been dedicated from childhood to the service of the most holy Buddha by my parents. At the time of the great Saigo's rebellion I was sent to another parish. When the castle of Kumamoto was besieged, alas! my own temple was burned to the ground. For years I wandered from place to place and fell on very hard times. In my old age and misfortunes my heart at last yearned to come back to this temple, where I spent so many happy years as an acolyte. It is my hope to spend my last days here. You can imagine my grief when I found it utterly abandoned, sunk in decay, with no priest in charge to offer up the daily prayers to the Lord Buddha, or to keep up the rites for the dead buried here. It is now my sole desire to collect money and to restore the temple. But alas! age and illness and want of food have robbed me of my strength, and I fear that I shall never be able to achieve what I have planned," and here the old man broke down and shed tears – a pitiful sight.

When wiping his eyes with the sleeve of his threadbare robe, he looked hungrily at the food and wine on which the doctor was regaling himself, and added, wistfully:

"Ah, I see you have a delicious meal there and wine withal, which you are enjoying while gazing at the moonlit scenery. I pray you spare me a little, for it is many days since I have had a good meal and I am half-famished."

At first the doctor was persuaded that the story was true, so plausible did it sound, and his heart was filled with compassion for the old bonze. He listened carefully till the melancholy recital was finished.

Then something in the accent of speech struck his ear as being different to that of a human being, and he reflected.

"This may be the badger! I must not allow myself to be deceived! The crafty cunning animal is planning to palm off his customary tricks on me, but he shall see that I am as clever as he is."

The doctor pretended to believe in the old man's story, and answered:

"Indeed, I deeply sympathize with your misfortunes. You are quite welcome to share my meal – nay, I will give you with pleasure all that is left, and, moreover, I promise to bring you some more to-morrow. I will also inform my friends and acquaintances of your pious plan to restore the temple, and will give all the assistance in my power in your work of collecting subscriptions." He then pushed forward the untouched plate of food which contained poison, rose from the mats, and took his leave, promising to return the next evening.

All the friends of the doctor who had heard him boast that he would outwit the badger, arrived early next morning, curious to know what had befallen him. Many of them were very sceptical regarding the tale of the badger trickster, and ascribed the illusions of their friends to the sake bottle.

The doctor would give no answer to their many inquiries, but merely invited them to accompany him.

"Come and see for yourselves," he said, and guided them to the old temple, the scene of so many uncanny experiences.

First of all they searched the room where he had sat the evening before, but nothing was to be found except the empty basket in which he had carried the food for himself and the badger. They investigated the whole place thoroughly, and at last, in one of the dark corners of the temple-chamber, they came upon the dead body of an old, old badger. It was the size of a large dog, and its hair was grey with age. Everyone was convinced that it must be at least several hundred years old.

The doctor carried it home in triumph. For several days the people in the neighbourhood came in large numbers to gloat over the hoary carcase, and to listen in awe and wonder to the marvellous stories of the numbers of people that had been duped and befooled by the magic powers of the old goblin-badger.

The writer adds that he was told another badger story concerning the same temple. Many of the old people in the parish remember the incident, and one of them related the following story.

Years before, when the sacred building was still in a prosperous state, the priest in charge celebrated a great Buddhist festival, which lasted some days. Amongst the numerous devotees who attended the services he noticed a very handsome youth, who listened with profound reverence, unusual in one so young, to the sermons and litanies. When the festival was over and the other worshippers had gone, he lingered around the temple as though loth to leave the sacred spot. The head-priest, who had conceived a liking for the lad, judged from his refined and dignified appearance that he must be the son of a high-class *samurai* family, probably desirous of entering the priesthood.

Gratified by the youth's apparent religious fervour, the holy man invited him to come to his study, and thereupon gave him some instruction in the Buddhist doctrines. He listened with the utmost attention for the whole afternoon to the bonze's learned discourse, and thanked him repeatedly for the condescension and trouble he had taken in instructing one so unworthy as himself.

The afternoon waned and the hour for the evening meal came round. The priest ordered a bowl of macaroni to be brought for the visitor, who proved to be the owner of a phenomenal appetite, and consumed three times as much as a full-grown man.

He then bowed most courteously and asked permission to return home. In bidding him good-bye, the priest, who felt a curious fascination for the youth, presented him with a gold-lacquered medicine-box (*inro*) as a parting souvenir.

The lad prostrated himself in gratitude, and then took his departure.

The next day the temple servant, sweeping the graveyard, came across a badger. He was quite dead, and was dressed in a straw-covering put on in such a way as to resemble the clothes of a human being. To his side was tied a gold-lacquered *inro*, and his paunch was much distended and as round as a large bowl. It was evident that the creature's gluttony had been the cause of his death, and the priest, on seeing the animal, identified the *inro* as the one which he had bestowed upon the good-looking lad the day before, and knew that he had been the victim of a badger's deceiving wiles.

It was thus certain that the temple had been haunted by a pair of goblin-badgers, and that when this one had died, its mate had continued to inhabit the same temple even after it had been abandoned. The creature had evidently taken a fantastic delight in bewitching wayfarers and travellers, or anyone who carried delectable food with them, and while mystifying them with his tricks and illusions, had deftly abstracted their baskets and bundles, and had lived comfortably upon his stolen booty.

The Frightened Yakā

H. Parker

IN A CERTAIN COUNTRY there are a woman and a man, it is said; there is also a boy of those two persons. In front of the house there is also a Murungā tree. A Yakā having come, remained seven years in the Murungā tree in order to 'possess' the woman.

While they were in that manner, one day the man and the boy went on a journey somewhere or other. The woman that day having [previously] put away the bill-hook, brought it to the doorway, and while preparing to cut a vegetable, said, "This bill-hook is indeed good [enough] to cut a Yakā."

The Yakā who stayed in the Murungā tree at the doorway, having heard what the woman said, became afraid, and having waited until the time when the woman goes into the house [after] cutting the vegetable, the Yakā slowly descended from the Murungā tree.

When he was going away, the woman's husband and boy, having gone on the journey, are coming back. The Yakā met them. Then the Yakā asked at the hand of those two, "Where did you go? I stayed seven years in the Murungā tree at the doorway of your house, to 'possess' your wife. To-day your wife, sharpening a bill-hook, came to the doorway, and looking in my direction said, 'This bill-hook is indeed good for cutting a Yakā.' Because of it, I am here, going away. Don't you go; that wicked woman will cut you. Come, and go with me; I will give you a means of subsistence. I, having now gone in front, will 'possess' such and such a woman of such and such a village. You two having said that you are Yaksa Vedarālas, and having come [there], when you have told me to go I will go. Then the men having said that you are [really] Yaksa Vedarālas, will give you many things. When you have driven me from that woman, again I will 'possess' still [another] woman. Thus, in that manner, until the time when the articles are sufficient for you, I will 'possess' women. When they have become sufficient do not come [to drive me out]."

Having said [this], the Yakā went in front and 'possessed' the woman. After that, the man and the boy went and drove out the Yakā. From that day, news spread in the villages that the two persons were Yaksa Vedarālas. From that place the two persons obtained articles.

The Yakā having gone, 'possessed' yet a woman also. Having driven him from there, too, these two persons got articles. The Yakā 'possessed' still [another] woman also. Thus, in that manner, until the very time when the things were sufficient for the two persons, the Yakā 'possessed' women.

After the articles became sufficient for the two persons, one day the Yakā said to the two, "The articles are sufficient for you, are they not?" The two persons said, "They are sufficient."

Then the Yakā said, "If so, I shall 'possess' the queen of such and such a king. From there I shall not go. Don't you come to drive me away." Having said it, the Yakā went to that city, and 'possessed' the queen.

The two Yaksa Vedarālas came to their village, taking the articles they had obtained. Then a message came from the king for the Yaksa Vedarālas to go. The two persons not having gone, remained [at home], because of the Yakā's having said that he would not go.

After that, the king sent a message that if they did not come he would behead the Yaksa Vedarālas. After that, the two persons, being unable to escape, went to drive out the Yakā.

Having gone there, they utter and utter spells for the Yakā to go. The Yakā does not go. Anger came to the Yakā. In anger that, putting [out of consideration] his saying, "Don't," the two persons went and uttered spells, the queen whom the Yakā has 'possessed', taking a rice pestle, came turning round the house after him in three circles to kill the Vedarāla. When she was raising the rice pestle to strike the Vedarāla, the man's boy said, "Look there, Yakā! Our mother!"

Then, because he had been afraid [of her] formerly, when the boy said it, the Yakā, saying, "Where, Bola?" and also rolling the queen over on the path, face upwards, and saying "Hū," went away. The queen came to her senses.

The king gave the two persons many articles. The Yakā did not again come to 'possess' women. That man and boy having come to their village, and become very wealthy, remained without a deficiency of anything.

The Faithless Widow

Pu Songling; translated by Herbert A. Giles

MR. NIU WAS A KIANGSI MAN who traded in piece goods. He married a wife from the Chêng family, by whom he had two children, a boy and a girl. When thirty-three years of age he fell ill and died, his son Chung being then only twelve and his little girl eight or nine. His wife did not remain faithful to his memory, but, selling off all the property, pocketed the proceeds and married another man, leaving her two children almost in a state of destitution with their aunt, Niu's sister-in-law, an old lady of sixty, who had lived with them previously, and had now nowhere to seek a shelter.

A few years later this aunt died, and the family fortunes began to sink even lower than before; Chung, however, was now grown up, and determined to carry on his father's trade, only he had no capital to start with. His sister marrying a rich trader named Mao, she begged her husband to lend Chung ten ounces of silver, which he did, and Chung immediately started for Nanking. On the road he fell in with some bandits, who robbed him of all he had, and consequently he was unable to return; but one day when he was at a pawnshop he noticed that the master of the shop was wonderfully like his late father, and on going out and making inquiries he found that this pawnbroker bore precisely the same names. In great astonishment, he forthwith proceeded to frequent the place with no other object than to watch this man, who, on the other hand, took no notice of Chung; and by the end of three days, having satisfied himself that he really saw his own father, and yet not daring to disclose his own identity, he made application through one of the assistants, on the score of being himself a Kiangsi man, to be employed in the shop. Accordingly, an indenture was drawn up; and when the master noticed Chung's name and place of residence he started, and asked him whence he came. With tears in his eyes Chung addressed him by his father's name, and then the pawnbroker became lost in a deep reverie, by-and-by asking Chung how his mother was.

Now Chung did not like to allude to his father's death, and turned the question by saying, "My father went away on business six years ago, and never came back; my mother married again and left us, and had it not been for my aunt our corpses would long ago have been cast out in the kennel." Then the pawnbroker was much moved, and cried out, "I am your father!" seizing his son's hand and leading him within to see his step-mother. This lady was about twenty-two, and, having no children of her own, was delighted with Chung, and prepared a banquet for him in the inner apartments.

Mr. Niu himself was, however, somewhat melancholy, and wished to return to his old home; but his wife, fearing that there would be no one to manage the business, persuaded him to remain; so he taught his son the trade, and in three months was able to leave it all to him. He then prepared for his journey, whereupon Chung informed his step-mother that his father was really dead, to which she replied in great consternation that she knew him only as a trader to the place, and that six years previously he had married her, which proved conclusively that he couldn't be dead. He then recounted the whole story, which was a perfect mystery to both of them; and twenty-four hours afterwards in walked his father, leading a woman whose hair was all dishevelled. Chung looked at her and saw that she was his own mother; and Niu took her by the ear and began to revile her, saying, "Why did you desert my children?" to which the wretched woman made no reply. He then bit her across the neck, at which she screamed to Chung for assistance, and he, not being able to bear the sight, stepped in between them. His father was more than ever enraged at this, when, lo! Chung's mother had disappeared. While they were still lost in astonishment at this strange scene, Mr. Niu's colour changed; in another moment his empty clothes had dropped upon the ground, and he himself became a black vapour and also vanished from their sight. The step-mother and son were much overcome; they took Niu's clothes and buried them, and after that Chung continued his father's business and soon amassed great wealth. On returning to his native place he found that his mother had actually died on the very day of the above occurrence, and that his father had been seen by the whole family.

The Cloth Merchant

Pu Songling; translated by Herbert A. Giles

A CERTAIN CLOTH MERCHANT went to Ch'ing-chou, where he happened to stroll into an old temple, all tumble-down and in ruins. He was lamenting over this sad state of things, when a priest who stood by observed that a devout believer like himself could hardly do better than put the place into repair, and thus obtain favour in the eyes of Buddha. This the merchant consented to do; whereupon the priest invited him to walk into the private quarters of the temple, and treated him with much courtesy; but he went on to propose that our friend the merchant should also undertake the general ornamentation of the place both inside and out. The latter declared he could not afford the expense, and the priest began to get very angry, and urged him so strongly that at last the merchant, in terror, promised to give all the money he had. After this he was preparing to go away, but the priest detained him, saying, "You haven't given the money of your own free will, and consequently you'll be owing me a grudge: I can't do better than make an end of you at once." Thereupon he seized a knife, and refused to listen to all the cloth merchant's entreaties, until at length the latter asked to be allowed to hang himself, to which the priest consented; and, showing him into a dark room, told him to make haste about it.

At this juncture, a Tartar-General happened to pass by the temple; and from a distance, through a breach in the old wall, he saw a damsel in a red dress pass into the priest's quarters. This roused his suspicions, and dismounting from his horse, he entered the temple and searched high and low, but without discovering anything. The dark room above-mentioned was locked and double-barred, and the priest refused to open it, saying the place was haunted. The general in a rage burst open the door, and there beheld the cloth merchant hanging from a beam. He cut him down at once, and in a short time he was brought round and told the general the whole story. They then searched for the damsel, but she was nowhere to be found, having been nothing more than a divine manifestation. The general cut off the priest's head and restored the cloth merchant's property to him, after which the latter put the temple in thorough repair and kept it well supplied with lights and incense ever afterwards.

The Fisherman and His Friend

Pu Songling; translated by Herbert A. Giles

IN THE NORTHERN PARTS of Tzŭ-chou there lived a man named Hsü, a fisherman by trade. Every night when he went to fish he would carry some wine with him, and drink and fish by turns, always taking care to pour out a libation on the ground, accompanied by the following invocation: "Drink too, ye drowned spirits of the river!" Such was his regular custom; and it was also noticeable that, even on occasions when the other fishermen caught nothing, he always got a full basket. One night, as he was sitting drinking by himself, a young man suddenly appeared and began walking up and down near him. Hsü offered him a cup of wine, which was readily accepted, and they remained chatting together throughout the night, Hsü meanwhile not catching a single fish. However, just as he was giving up all hope of doing anything, the young man rose and said he would go a little way down the stream and beat them up towards Hsü, which he accordingly did, returning in a few minutes and warning him to be on the look-out. Hsü now heard a noise like that of a shoal coming up the stream, and, casting his net, made a splendid haul, – all that he caught being over a foot in length. Greatly delighted, he now prepared to go home, first offering his companion a share of the fish, which the latter declined, saying that he had often received kindnesses from Mr. Hsü, and that he would be only too happy to help him regularly in the same manner if Mr. Hsü would accept his assistance. The latter replied that he did not recollect ever meeting him before, and that he should be much obliged for any aid the young man might choose to afford him; regretting, at the same time, his inability to make him any adequate return. He then asked the young man his name and surname; and the young man said his surname was Wang, adding that Hsü might address him when they met as Wang Liu-lang, he having no other name.

Thereupon they parted, and the next day Hsü sold his fish and bought some more wine, with which he repaired as usual to the river bank. There he found his companion already awaiting him, and they spent the night together in precisely the same way as the preceding one, the young man beating up the fish for him as before. This went on for some months, until at length one evening the young man, with many expressions of his thanks and his regrets, told Hsü that they were about to part for ever. Much alarmed by the melancholy tone in which his friend had communicated this news, Hsü was on the point of asking for an explanation, when the young man stopped him, and himself proceeded as follows: "The friendship that has grown up between us is truly surprising; and, now that we shall meet no more, there is no harm in telling you the whole truth. I am a disembodied spirit – the soul of one who was drowned in this river when tipsy. I have been here many years, and your former success in fishing was due to the fact that I used secretly to beat up the fish towards you, in return for the libations you were accustomed to pour out. To-morrow my time is up: my substitute will arrive, and I shall be born again in the world of mortals. We have but this one evening left, and I therefore take advantage of it to express my feelings to you." On hearing these words, Hsü was at first very much alarmed; however, he had grown so accustomed to his friend's society, that his fears soon passed away; and, filling up a goblet, he said, with a sigh, "Liu-lang, old fellow, drink this up, and away with melancholy. It's hard to lose you; but I'm glad enough for your sake, and won't think of my own sorrow." He then inquired of Liu-lang who was to be his substitute; to which the latter replied, "Come to the river-bank to-morrow afternoon and you'll see a woman drowned: she is the one." Just then the village cocks began to crow, and, with tears in their eyes, the two friends bade each other farewell.

Next day Hsü waited on the river bank to see if anything would happen, and lo! a woman carrying a child in her arms came along. When close to the edge of the river, she stumbled and fell into the water, managing, however, to throw the child safely on to the bank, where it lay kicking and sprawling and crying at the top of its voice. The woman herself sank and rose several times, until at last she succeeded in clutching hold of the bank and pulled herself, dripping, out; and then, after resting awhile, she picked up the child and went on her way. All this time Hsü had been in a great state of excitement, and was on the point of running to help the woman out of the water; but he remembered that she was to be the substitute of his friend, and accordingly restrained himself from doing so. Then when he saw the woman get out by herself, he began to suspect that Liu-lang's words had not been fulfilled. That night he went to fish as usual, and before long the young man arrived and said, "We meet once again: there is no need now to speak of separation." Hsü asked him how it was so; to which he replied, "The woman you saw had already taken my place, but I could not bear to hear the child cry, and I saw that my one life would be purchased at the expense of their two lives, wherefore I let her go, and now I cannot say when I shall have another chance. The union of our destinies may not yet be worked out."

"Alas!" sighed Hsü, "this noble conduct of yours is enough to move God Almighty."

After this the two friends went on much as they had done before, until one day Liu-lang again said he had come to bid Hsü farewell. Hsü thought he had found another substitute, but Liu-lang told him that his former behaviour had so pleased Almighty Heaven, that he had been appointed guardian angel of Wu-chên, in the Chao-yüan district, and that on the following morning he would start for his new post. "And if you do not forget the days of our friendship," added he, "I pray you come and see me, in spite of the long journey."

"Truly," replied Hsü, "you well deserved to be made a god; but the paths of gods and men lie in different directions, and even if the distance were nothing, how should I manage to meet you again?" "Don't be afraid on that score," said Liu-lang, "but come"; and then he went away, and Hsü returned home. The latter immediately began to prepare for the journey, which caused his wife to laugh at him and say, "Supposing you do find such a place at the end of that long journey, you won't be able to hold a conversation with a clay image." Hsü, however, paid no attention to her remarks, and travelled straight to Chao-yüan, where he learned from the inhabitants that there really was a village called Wu-chên, whither he forthwith proceeded and took up his abode at an inn. He then inquired of the landlord where the village temple was; to which the latter replied by asking him somewhat hurriedly if he was speaking to Mr. Hsü. Hsü informed him that his name was Hsü, asking in reply how he came to know it; whereupon the landlord further inquired if his native place was not Tzŭ-chou. Hsü told him it was, and again asked him how he knew all this; to which the landlord made no answer, but rushed out of the room; and in a few moments the place was crowded with old and young, men, women, and children, all come to visit Hsü. They then told him that a few nights before they had seen their guardian deity in a vision, and he had informed them that Mr. Hsü would shortly arrive, and had bidden them to provide him with travelling expenses, &c. Hsü was very much astonished at this, and went off at once to the shrine, where he invoked his friend as follows: "Ever since we parted I have had you daily and nightly in my thoughts; and now that I have fulfilled my promise of coming to see you, I have to thank you for the orders you have issued to the people of the place. As for me, I have nothing to offer you but a cup of wine, which I pray you accept as though we were drinking together on the river-bank." He then burnt a quantity of paper money, when lo! a wind suddenly arose, which, after whirling round and round behind the shrine, soon dropped, and all was still. That night Hsü dreamed that his friend came to him, dressed in his official cap and robes, and very different in appearance from what he used to be, and thanked him, saying, "It is truly kind of you to visit me thus: I only regret that my position makes me unable to meet you face to face, and that though near we are still so far. The people here will give you a trifle, which pray accept for my sake; and when you go away, I will see you a short way on your journey." A few days afterwards Hsü prepared to start, in spite of the numerous invitations to stay which poured in upon him from all sides; and then the inhabitants loaded him with presents of all kinds, and escorted him out of the village. There a whirlwind arose and accompanied him several miles, when he turned round and invoked his friend thus: "Liu-lang, take care of your valued person. Do not trouble yourself to come any farther. Your noble heart will ensure happiness to this district, and there is no occasion for me to give a word of advice to my old friend." By-and-by the whirlwind ceased, and the villagers, who were much astonished, returned to their own homes. Hsü, too, travelled homewards, and being now a man of some means, ceased to work any more as a fisherman. And whenever he met a Chao-yüan man he would ask him about that guardian angel, being always informed in reply that he was a most beneficent God. Some say the place was Shih-k'êng-chuang, in Chang-ch'in: I can't say which it was myself.

The Wei-ch'i Devil

Pu Songling; translated by Herbert A. Giles

A CERTAIN GENERAL, who had resigned his command, and had retired to his own home, was very fond of roaming about and amusing himself with wine and *wei-ch'i*. One day – it was the ninth of the ninth moon, when everybody goes up high – as he was playing with some friends, a stranger walked up, and watched the game intently for some time without going away. He was a miserable-looking creature, with a very ragged coat, but nevertheless possessed of a refined and courteous air. The general begged him to be seated, an offer which he accepted, being all the time extremely deferential in his manner.

"I suppose you are pretty good at this," said the general, pointing to the board; "try a bout with one of my friends here." The stranger made a great many apologies in reply, but finally accepted, and played a game in which, apparently to his great disappointment, he was beaten. He played another with the same result; and now, refusing all offers of wine, he seemed to think of nothing but how to get some one to play with him. Thus he went on until the afternoon was well advanced; when suddenly, just as he was in the middle of a most exciting game, which depended on a single place, he rushed forward, and throwing himself at the feet of the general, loudly implored his protection.

The general did not know what to make of this; however, he raised him up, and said, "It's only a game: why get so excited?" To this the stranger replied by begging the general not to let his gardener seize him; and when the general asked what gardener he meant, he said the man's name was Ma-ch'êng. Now this Ma-ch'êng was often employed as a lictor by the Ruler of Purgatory, and would sometimes remain away as much as ten days, serving the warrants of death; accordingly, the general sent off to inquire about him, and found that he had been in a trance for two days. His master cried out that he had better not behave rudely to his guest, but at that very moment the stranger sunk down to the ground, and was gone. The general was lost in astonishment; however, he now knew that the man was a disembodied spirit, and on the next day, when Ma-ch'êng came round, he asked him for full particulars.

"The gentleman was a native of Hu-hsiang," replied the gardener, "who was passionately addicted to *wei-ch'i*, and had lost a great deal of money by it. His father, being much grieved at his behaviour, confined him to the house; but he was always getting out, and indulging the fatal passion, and at last his father died of a broken heart. In consequence of this, the Ruler of Purgatory curtailed his term of life, and condemned him to become a hungry devil, in which state he has already passed seven years. And now that the Phœnix Tower is completed, an order has been issued for the literati to present themselves, and compose an inscription to be cut on stone, as a memorial thereof, by which means they would secure their own salvation as a reward. Many of the shades failing to arrive at the appointed time, God was very angry with the Ruler of Purgatory, and the latter sent off me, and others who are employed in the same way, to hunt up the defaulters. But as you, Sir, bade me treat the gentleman with respect, I did not venture to bind him." The general inquired what had become of the stranger; to which the gardener replied, "He is now a mere menial in Purgatory, and can never be born again."

"Alas!" cried his master, "thus it is that men are ruined by any inordinate passion."

The Clay Image

Pu Songling; translated by Herbert A. Giles

ON THE RIVER I there lived a man named Ma, who married a wife from the Wang family, with whom he was very happy in his domestic life. Ma, however, died young; and his wife's parents were unwilling that their daughter should remain a widow, but she resisted all their importunities, and declared firmly she would never marry again. "It is a noble resolve of yours, I allow," argued her mother; "but you are still a mere girl, and you have no children. Besides, I notice that people who start with such rigid determinations always end by doing something discreditable, and therefore you had better get married as soon as you can, which is no more than is done every day."

The girl swore she would rather die than consent, and accordingly her mother had no alternative but to let her alone. She then ordered a clay image to be made, exactly resembling her late husband; and whenever she took her own meals, she would set meat and wine before it, precisely as if her husband had been there. One night she was on the point of retiring to rest, when suddenly she saw the clay image stretch itself and step down from the table, increasing all the while in height, until it was as tall as a man, and neither more nor less than her own husband. In great alarm she called out to her mother, but the image stopped her, saying, "Don't do that! I am but shewing my gratitude for your affectionate care of me, and it is chill and uncomfortable in the realms below. Such devotion as yours casts its light back on generations gone by; and now I, who was cut off in my prime because my father did evil, and was condemned to be without an heir, have been permitted, in consequence of your virtuous conduct, to visit you once again, that our ancestral line may yet remain unbroken."

Every morning at cock-crow her husband resumed his usual form and size as the clay image; and after a time he told her that their hour of separation had come, upon which husband and wife bade each other an eternal farewell. By-and-by the widow, to the great astonishment of her mother, bore a son, which caused no small amusement among the neighbours who heard the story; and, as the girl herself had no proof of what she stated to be the case, a certain beadle of the place, who had an old grudge against her husband, went off and informed the magistrate of what had occurred. After some investigation, the magistrate exclaimed, "I have heard that the children of disembodied spirits have no shadow; and that those who have shadows are not genuine." Thereupon they took Ma's child into the sunshine, and lo! there was but a very faint shadow, like a thin vapour. The magistrate then drew blood from the child, and smeared it on the clay image; upon which the blood at once soaked in and left no stain. Another clay image being produced and the same experiment tried, the blood remained on the surface so that it could be wiped away. The girl's story was thus acknowledged to be true; and when the child grew up, and in every feature was the counterpart of Ma, there was no longer any room for suspicion.

Dishonesty Punished

Pu Songling; translated by Herbert A. Giles

AT CHIAO-CHOU there lived a man named Liu Hsi-ch'uan, who was steward to His excellency Mr. Fa. When already over forty a son was born to him, whom he loved very dearly, and quite spoilt by always letting him have his own way. When the boy grew up he led a dissolute, extravagant life, and ran through all his father's property. By-and-by he fell sick, and then he declared that nothing would cure him but a slice off a fat old favourite mule they had; upon which his father had another and more worthless animal killed; but his son found out he was being tricked, and, after abusing his father soundly, his symptoms became more and more alarming.

The mule was accordingly killed, and some of it was served up to the sick man; however, he only just tasted it and sent the rest away. From that time he got gradually worse and worse, and finally died, to the great grief of his father, who would gladly have died too. Three or four years afterwards, as some of the villagers were worshipping on Mount Tai, they saw a man riding on a mule, the very image of Mr. Liu's dead son; and, on approaching more closely, they saw that it was actually he. Jumping from his mule, he made them a salutation, and then they began to chat with him on various subjects, always carefully avoiding that one of his own death. They asked him what he was doing there; to which he replied that he was only roaming about, and inquired of them in his turn at what inn they were staying; "For," added he, "I have an engagement just now, but I will visit you to-morrow."

So they told him the name of the inn, and took their leave, not expecting to see him again. However, the next day he came, and, tying his mule to a post outside, went in to see them. "Your father," observed one of the villagers, "is always thinking about you. Why do you not go and pay him a visit?" The young man asked to whom he was alluding; and, at the mention of his father's name, he changed colour and said, "If he is anxious to see me, kindly tell him that on the seventh of the fourth moon I will await him here." He then went away, and the villagers returned and told Mr. Liu all that had taken place.

At the appointed time the latter was very desirous of going to see his son; but his master dissuaded him, saying that he thought from what he knew of his son that the interview might possibly not turn out as he would desire; "Although," added he, "if you are bent upon going, I should be sorry to stand in your way. Let me, however, counsel you to conceal yourself in a cupboard, and thus, by observing what takes place, you will know better how to act, and avoid running into any danger." This he accordingly did, and, when his son came, Mr. Fa received him at the inn as before.

"Where's Mr. Liu?" cried the son. "Oh, he hasn't come," replied Mr. Fa.

"The old beast! What does he mean by that?" exclaimed his son; whereupon Mr. Fa asked him what he meant by cursing his own father.

"My father!" shrieked the son; "why he's nothing more to me than a former rascally partner in trade, who cheated me out of all my money, and for which I have since avenged myself on him. What sort of a father is that, I should like to know?" He then went out of the door; and his father crept out of the cupboard from which, with the perspiration streaming down him and hardly daring to breathe, he had heard all that had passed, and sorrowfully wended his way home again.

The Picture Horse

Pu Songling; translated by Herbert A. Giles

A CERTAIN MR. TS'UI, of Lin-ch'ing, was too poor to keep his garden walls in repair, and used often to find a strange horse lying down on the grass inside. It was a black horse marked with white, and having a scrubby tail, which looked as if the end had been burnt off; and, though always driven away, would still return to the same spot. Now Mr. Ts'ui had a friend, who was holding an appointment in Shansi; and though he had frequently felt desirous of paying him a visit, he had no means of travelling so far. Accordingly, he one day caught the strange horse and, putting a saddle on its back, rode away, telling his servant that if the owner of the horse should appear, he was to inform him where the animal was to be found. The horse started off at a very rapid pace, and, in a short time, they were thirty or forty miles from home; but at night it did not seem to care for its food, so the next day Mr. Ts'ui, who thought perhaps illness might be the cause, held the horse in, and would not let it gallop so fast. However, the animal did not seem to approve of this, and kicked and foamed until at length Mr. Ts'ui let it go at the same old pace; and by mid-day he had reached his destination. As he rode into the town, the people were astonished to hear of the marvellous journey just accomplished, and the prince sent to say he should like to buy the horse. Mr. Ts'ui, fearing that the real owner might come forward, was compelled to refuse this offer; but when, after six months had elapsed, no inquiries had been made, he agreed to accept eight hundred ounces of silver, and handed over the horse to the prince. He then bought himself a good mule, and returned home.

Subsequently, the prince had occasion to use the horse for some important business at Lin-ch'ing; and when there it took the opportunity to run away. The officer in charge pursued it right up to the house of a Mr. Tsêng, who lived next door to Mr. Ts'ui, and saw it run in and disappear. Thereupon he called upon Mr. Tsêng to restore it to him; and, on the latter declaring he had never even seen the animal, the officer walked into his private apartments, where he found, hanging on the wall, a picture of a horse, by Tzŭ-ang, exactly like the one he was in search of, and with part of the tail burnt away by a joss-stick. It was now clear that the prince's horse was a supernatural creature; but the officer, being afraid to go back without it, would have prosecuted Mr. Tsêng, had not Ts'ui, whose eight hundred ounces of silver had since increased to something like ten thousand, stepped in and paid back the original purchase-money. Mr. Tsêng was exceedingly grateful to him for this act of kindness, ignorant, as he was, of the previous sale of the horse by Ts'ui to the prince.

The Marriage of the Fox's Daughter

Pu Songling; translated by Herbert A. Giles

A PRESIDENT OF THE BOARD OF CIVIL OFFICE, named Yin, and a native of Li-ch'êng, when a young man, was very badly off, but was endowed with considerable physical courage. Now in his part of the country there was a large establishment, covering several acres, with an unbroken succession of pavilions and verandahs, and belonging to one of the old county families; but because ghosts and apparitions were frequently seen there, the place had for a long time remained untenanted, and was overgrown with grass and weeds, no one venturing to enter in even in broad daylight. One evening when Yin was carousing with some fellow-students, one of them jokingly said, "If anybody will pass a night in the haunted house, the rest of us will stand him a dinner." Mr. Yin jumped up at this, and cried out, "What is there difficult in that?" So, taking with him a sleeping-mat, he proceeded thither, escorted by all his companions as far as the door, where they laughed and said, "We will wait here a little while. In case you see anything, shout out to us at once."

"If there are any goblins or foxes," replied Yin, "I'll catch them for you." He then went in, and found the paths obliterated by long grass, which had sprung up, mingled with weeds of various kinds. It was just the time of the new moon, and by its feeble light he was able to make out the door of the house. Feeling his way, he walked on until he reached the back pavilion, and then went up on to the Moon Terrace, which was such a pleasant spot that he determined to stop there. Gazing westwards, he sat for a long time looking at the moon – a single thread of light embracing in its horns the peak of a hill – without hearing anything at all unusual; so, laughing to himself at the nonsense people talked, he spread his mat upon the floor, put a stone under his head for a pillow, and lay down to sleep. He had watched the Cow-herd and the Lady until they were just disappearing, and was on the point of dropping off, when suddenly he heard footsteps down below coming up the stairs. Pretending to be asleep, he saw a servant enter, carrying in his hand a lotus-shaped lantern, who, on observing Mr. Yin, rushed back in a fright, and said to someone behind, "There is a stranger here!" The person spoken to asked who it was, but the servant did not know; and then up came an old gentleman, who, after examining Mr. Yin closely, said, "It's the future president: he's as drunk as can be. We needn't mind him; besides, he's a good fellow, and won't give us any trouble." So they walked in and opened all the doors; and by-and-by there were a great many other people moving about, and quantities of lamps were lighted, till the place was as light as day. About this time Mr. Yin slightly changed his position, and sneezed; upon which the old man, perceiving that he was awake, came forward and fell down on his knees, saying, "Sir, I have a daughter who is to be married this very night. It was not anticipated that Your Honour would be here. I pray, therefore, that we may be excused." Mr. Yin got up and raised the old man, regretting that, in his ignorance of the festive occasion, he had brought with him no present.

"Ah, Sir," replied the old man, "your very presence here will ward off all noxious influences; and that is quite enough for us." He then begged Mr. Yin to assist in doing the honours, and thus double the obligation already conferred. Mr. Yin readily assented, and went inside to look at the gorgeous arrangements they had made. He was here met by a lady, apparently about forty years of age, whom the old gentleman introduced as his wife; and he had hardly made his bow when he heard the sound of flageolets, and someone came hurrying in, saying, "He has come!" The old gentleman flew out to meet this personage, and Mr. Yin also stood up, awaiting his arrival. In no long time, a bevy of people with gauze lanterns ushered in the bridegroom himself, who seemed to be about seventeen or eighteen years old, and of a most refined and prepossessing appearance. The old gentleman bade him pay his respects first to their worthy guest; and upon his looking towards Mr. Yin, that gentleman came forward to welcome him on behalf of the host. Then followed ceremonies between the old man and his son-in-law; and when these were over, they all sat down to supper.

Hosts of waiting-maids brought in profuse quantities of wine and meats, with bowls and cups of jade or gold, till the table glittered again. And when the wine had gone round several times, the old gentleman told one of the maids to summon the bride. This she did, but some time passed and no bride came. So the old man rose and drew aside the curtain, pressing the young lady to come forth; whereupon a number of women escorted out the bride, whose ornaments went *tinkle tinkle* as she walked along, sweet perfumes being all the time diffused around. Her father told her to make the proper salutation, after which she went and sat by her mother. Mr. Yin took a glance at her, and saw that she wore on her head beautiful ornaments made of kingfisher's feathers, her beauty quite surpassing anything he had ever seen. All this time they had been drinking their wine out of golden goblets big enough to hold several pints, when it flashed across him that one of these goblets would be a capital thing to carry back to his companions in evidence of what he had seen. So he secreted it in his sleeve, and, pretending to be tipsy, leaned forward with his head upon the table as if going off to sleep.

"The gentleman is drunk," said the guests; and by-and-by Mr. Yin heard the bridegroom take his leave, and there was a general trooping downstairs to the tune of a wedding march. When they were all gone the old gentleman collected the goblets, one of which was missing, though they hunted high and low to find it. Someone mentioned the sleeping guest; but the old gentleman stopped him at once for fear Mr. Yin should hear, and before long silence reigned throughout. Mr. Yin then arose. It was dark, and he had no light; but he could detect the lingering smell of the food, and the place was filled with the fumes of wine. Faint streaks of light now appearing in the east, he began quietly to make a move, having first satisfied himself that the goblet was still in his sleeve. Arriving at the door, he found his friends already there; for they had been afraid he might come out after they left, and go in again early in the morning. When he produced the goblet they were all lost in astonishment; and on hearing his story, they were fain to believe it, well knowing that a poor student like Yin was not likely to have such a valuable piece of plate in his possession.

Later on Mr. Yin took his doctor's degree, and was appointed magistrate over the district of Fei-ch'iu, where there was an old-established family of the name of Chu. The head of the family asked him to a banquet in honour of his arrival, and ordered the servants to bring in the large goblets. After some delay a slave-girl came and whispered something to her master which seemed to make him very angry. Then the goblets were brought in, and Mr. Yin was invited to drink. He now found that these goblets were of precisely the same shape and pattern as the one he had at home, and at once begged his host to tell him where he had had these made.

"Well," said Mr. Chu, "there should be eight of them. An ancestor of mine had them made, when he was a minister at the capital, by an experienced artificer. They have been handed down in our family from generation to generation, and have now been carefully laid by for some time; but I thought we would have them out to-day as a compliment to your Honour. However, there are only seven to be found. None of the servants can have touched them, for the old seals of ten years ago are still upon the box, unbroken. I don't know what to make of it."

Mr. Yin laughed, and said, "It must have flown away! Still, it is a pity to lose an heir-loom of that kind; and as I have a very similar one at home, I shall take upon myself to send it to you." When the banquet was over, Mr. Yin went home, and taking out his own goblet, sent it off to Mr. Chu. The latter was somewhat surprised to find that it was identical with his own, and hurried away to thank the magistrate for his gift, asking him at the same time how it had come into his possession. Mr. Yin told him the whole story, which proves conclusively that although a fox may obtain possession of a thing, even at a distance of many hundred miles, he will not venture to keep it altogether.

Little Chu

Pu Songling; translated by Herbert A. Giles

A MAN NAMED LI HUA dwelt at Ch'ang-chou. He was very well off, and about fifty years of age, but he had no sons; only one daughter, named Hsiao-hui, a pretty child on whom her parents doted. When she was fourteen she had a severe illness and died, leaving their home desolate and depriving them of their chief pleasure in life. Mr. Li then bought a concubine, and she by-and-by bore him a son, who was perfectly idolized, and called Chu, or the Pearl. This boy grew up to be a fine manly fellow, though so extremely stupid that when five or six years old he didn't know pulse from corn, and could hardly talk plainly. His father, however, loved him dearly, and did not observe his faults.

Now it chanced that a one-eyed priest came to collect alms in the town, and he seemed to know so much about everybody's private affairs that the people all looked upon him as superhuman. He himself declared he had control over life, death, happiness, and misfortune; and consequently no one dared refuse him whatever sum he chose to ask of them. From Li he demanded one hundred ounces of silver, but was offered only ten, which he refused to receive. This sum was increased to thirty ounces, whereupon the priest looked sternly at Li and said, "I must have one hundred; not a fraction less." Li now got angry, and went away without giving him any, the priest, too, rising up in a rage and shouting after him, "I hope you won't repent." Shortly after these events little Chu fell sick, and crawled about the bed scratching the mat, his face being of an ashen paleness. This frightened his father, who hurried off with eighty ounces of silver, and begged the priest to accept them.

"A large sum like this is no trifling matter to earn," said the priest, smiling; "but what can a poor recluse like myself do for you?" So Li went home, to find that little Chu was already dead; and this worked him into such a state that he immediately laid a complaint before the magistrate. The priest was accordingly summoned and interrogated; but the magistrate wouldn't accept his defence, and ordered him to be bambooed. The blows sounded as if falling on leather, upon which the magistrate commanded his lictors to search him; and from about his person they drew forth two wooden men, a small coffin, and five small flags. The magistrate here flew into a passion, and made certain mystic signs with his fingers, which when the priest saw he was frightened, and began to excuse himself; but the magistrate would not listen to him, and had him bambooed to death. Li thanked him for his kindness, and, taking his leave, proceeded home.

In the evening, after dusk, he was sitting alone with his wife, when suddenly in popped a little boy, who said, "Pa! why did you hurry on so fast? I couldn't catch you up." Looking at him more closely, they saw that he was about seven or eight years old, and Mr. Li, in some alarm, was on the point of questioning him, when he disappeared, re-appearing again like smoke, and, curling round and round, got upon the bed. Li pushed him off, and he fell down without making any sound, crying out, "Pa! why do you do this?" and in a moment he was on the bed again. Li was frightened, and ran away with his wife, the boy calling after them, "Pa! Ma! boo-oo-oo." They went into the next room, bolting the door after them; but there was the little boy at their heels again. Li asked him what he wanted, to which he replied, "I belong to Su-chou; my name is Chan; at six years of age I was left an orphan; my brother and his wife couldn't bear me, so they sent me to live at my maternal grandfather's. One day, when playing outside, a wicked priest killed me by his black art underneath a mulberry-tree, and made of me an evil spirit, dooming me to everlasting devildom without hope of transmigration. Happily you exposed him; and I would now remain with you as your son."

"The paths of men and devils," replied Li, "lie in different directions. How can we remain together?"

"Give me only a tiny room," cried the boy, "a bed, a mattress, and a cup of cold gruel every day. I ask for nothing more." So Li agreed, to the great delight of the boy, who slept by himself in another part of the house, coming in the morning and walking in and out like any ordinary person. Hearing Li's concubine crying bitterly, he asked how long little Chu had been dead, and she told him seven days. "It's cold weather now," said he, "and the body can't have decomposed. Have the grave opened, and let me see it; if not too far gone, I can bring him to life again."

Li was only too pleased, and went off with the boy; and when they opened the grave they found the body in perfect preservation; but while Li was controlling his emotions, lo! the boy had vanished from his sight. Wondering very much at this, he took little Chu's body home, and had hardly laid it on the bed when he noticed the eyes move. Little Chu then called for some broth, which put him into a perspiration, and then he got up. They were all overjoyed to see him come to life again; and, what is more, he was much brighter and cleverer than before. At night, however, he lay perfectly stiff and rigid, without shewing any signs of life; and, as he didn't move when they turned him over and over, they were much frightened, and thought he had died again. But towards daybreak he awaked as if from a dream, and in reply to their questions said that when he was with the wicked priest there was another boy named Ko-tzǔ; and that the day before, when he had been unable to catch up his father, it was because he had stayed behind to bid adieu to Ko-tzǔ; that Ko-tzǔ was now the son of an official in Purgatory named Chiang, and very comfortably settled; and that he had invited him (Chan) to go and play with him that evening, and had sent him back on a white-nosed horse. His mother then asked him if he had seen little Chu in Purgatory; to which he replied, "Little Chu has already been born again. He and our father here had not really the destiny of father and son. Little Chu was merely a man named Yen Tzǔ-fang, from Chin-ling, who had come to reclaim an old debt."

Now Mr. Li had formerly traded to Chin-ling, and actually owed money for goods to a Mr. Yen; but he had died, and no one else knew anything about it, so that he was now greatly alarmed when he heard this story. His mother next asked (the quasi) little Chu if he had seen his sister, Hsiao-hui; and he said he had not, promising to go again and inquire about her. A few days afterwards he told his mother that Hsiao-hui was very happy in Purgatory, being married to a son of one of the judges; and that she had any quantity of jewels, and crowds of attendants when she went abroad.

"Why doesn't she come home to see her parents?" asked his mother.

"Well," replied the boy, "dead people, you know, haven't got any flesh or bones; however, if you can only remind them of something that happened in their past lives, their feelings are at once touched. So yesterday I managed, through Mr. Chiang, to get an interview with Hsiao-hui; and we sat together on a coral couch, and I spoke to her of her father and mother at home, all of which she listened to as if she was asleep. I then remarked, 'Sister, when you were alive you were very fond of embroidering double-stemmed flowers; and once you cut your finger with the scissors, and the blood ran over the silk, but you brought it into the picture as a crimson cloud. Your mother has that picture still, hanging at the head of her bed, a perpetual souvenir of you. Sister, have you forgotten this?' Then she burst into tears, and promised to ask her husband to let her come and visit you."

His mother asked when she would arrive; but he said he could not tell. However, one day he ran in and cried out, "Mother, Hsiao-hui has come, with a splendid equipage and a train of servants; we had better get plenty of wine ready." In a few moments he came in again, saying, "Here is my sister," at the same time asking her to take a seat and rest. He then wept; but none of those present saw anything at all. By-and-by he went out and burnt a quantity of paper money and made offerings of wine outside the door, returning shortly and saying he had sent away her attendants for a while. Hsiao-hui then asked if the green coverlet, a small portion of which had been burnt by a candle, was still in existence. "It is," replied her mother, and, going to a box, she at once produced the coverlet. "Hsiao-hui would like a bed made up for her in her old room," said her (quasi) brother; "she wants to rest awhile, and will talk with you again in the morning."

Now their next-door neighbour, named Chao, had a daughter who was formerly a great friend of Hsiao-hui's, and that night she dreamt that Hsiao-hui appeared with a turban on her head and a red mantle over her shoulders, and that they talked and laughed together precisely as in days gone by.

"I am now a spirit," said Hsiao-hui, "and my father and mother can no more see me than if I was far separated from them. Dear sister, I would borrow your body, from which to speak to them. You need fear nothing."

On the morrow when Miss Chao met her mother, she fell on the ground before her and remained some time in a state of unconsciousness, at length saying, "Madam, it is many years since we met; your hair has become very white."

"The girl's mad," said her mother, in alarm; and, thinking something had gone wrong, proceeded to follow her out of the door. Miss Chao went straight to Li's house, and there with tears embraced Mrs. Li, who did not know what to make of it all. "Yesterday," said Miss Chao, "when I came back, I was unhappily unable to speak with you. Unfilial wretch that I was, to die before you, and leave you to mourn my loss. How can I redeem such behaviour?" Her mother thereupon began to understand the scene, and, weeping, said to her, "I have heard that you hold an honourable position, and this is a great comfort to me; but, living as you do in the palace of a judge, how is it you are able to get away?" "My husband," replied she, "is very kind; and his parents treat me with all possible consideration. I experience no harsh treatment at their hands." Here Miss Chao rested her cheek upon her hand, exactly as Hsiao-hui had been wont to do when she was alive; and at that moment in came her brother to say that her attendants were ready to return. "I must go," said she, rising up and weeping bitterly all the time; after which she fell down, and remained some time unconscious as before.

Shortly after these events Mr. Li became dangerously ill, and no medicines were of any avail, so that his son feared they would not be able to save his life. Two devils sat at the head of his bed, one holding an iron staff, the other a nettle-hemp rope four or five feet in length. Day and night his son implored them to go, but they would not move; and Mrs. Li in sorrow began to prepare the funeral clothes. Towards evening her son entered and cried out, "Strangers and women, leave the room! My sister's husband is coming to see his father-in-law." He then clapped his hands, and burst out laughing.

"What is the matter?" asked his mother.

"I am laughing," answered he, "because when the two devils heard my sister's husband was coming, they both ran under the bed, like terrapins, drawing in their heads." By-and-by, looking at nothing, he began to talk about the weather, and ask his sister's husband how he did, and then he clapped his hands, and said, "I begged the two devils to go, but they would not; it's all right now." After this he went out to the door and returned, saying, "My sister's husband has gone. He took away the two devils tied to his horse. My father ought to get better now. Besides, Hsiao-hui's husband said he would speak to the judge, and obtain a hundred years' lease of life both for you and my father."

The whole family rejoiced exceedingly at this, and, when night came, Mr. Li was better, and in a few days quite well again. A tutor was engaged for (the quasi) little Chu, who shewed himself an apt pupil, and at eighteen years of age took his bachelor's degree. He could also see things of the other world; and when anyone in the village was ill, he pointed out where the devils were, and burnt them out with fire, so that everybody got well. However, before long he himself became very ill, and his flesh turned green and purple; whereupon he said, "The devils afflict me thus because I let out their secrets. Henceforth I shall never divulge them again."

Miss Quarta Hu

Pu Songling; translated by Herbert A. Giles

MR. SHANG WAS A NATIVE OF T'AI-SHAN, and lived quietly with his books alone. One autumn night when the Silver River was unusually distinct and the moon shining brightly in the sky, he was walking up and down under the shade, with his thoughts wandering somewhat at random, when lo! a young girl leaped over the wall, and, smiling, asked him, "What are you thinking about, sir, all so deeply?" Shang looked at her, and seeing that she had a pretty face, asked her to walk in. She then told him her name was Hu, and that she was called Tertia; but when he wanted to know where she lived, she laughed and would not say. So he did not inquire any further; and by degrees they struck up a friendship, and Miss Tertia used to come and chat with him every evening. He was so smitten that he could hardly take his eyes off her, and at last she said to him, "What *are* you looking at?"

"At you," cried he, "my lovely rose, my beautiful peach. I could gaze at you all night long."

"If you think so much of poor me," answered she, "I don't know where your wits would be if you saw my sister Quarta."

Mr. Shang said he was sorry he didn't know her, and begged that he might be introduced; so next night Miss Tertia brought her sister, who turned out to be a young damsel of about fifteen, with a face delicately powdered and resembling the lily, or like an apricot-flower seen through mist; and altogether as pretty a girl as he had ever seen. Mr. Shang was charmed with her, and inviting them in, began to laugh and talk with the elder, while Miss Quarta sat playing with her girdle, and keeping her eyes on the ground. By-and-by Miss Tertia got up and said she was going, whereupon her sister rose to take leave also; but Mr. Shang asked her not to be in a hurry, and requested the elder to assist in persuading her.

"You needn't hurry," said she to Miss Quarta; and accordingly the latter remained chatting with Mr. Shang without reserve, and finally told him she was a fox. However, Mr. Shang was so occupied with her beauty, that he didn't pay any heed to that; but she added, "And my sister is very dangerous; she has already killed three people. Any one bewitched by her has no chance of escape. Happily, you have bestowed your affections on me, and I shall not allow you to be destroyed. You must break off your acquaintance with her at once."

Mr. Shang was very frightened, and implored her to help him; to which she replied, "Although a fox, I am skilled in the arts of the Immortals; I will write out a charm for you which you must paste on the door, and thus you will keep her away." So she wrote down the charm, and in the morning when her sister came and saw it, she fell back, crying out, "Ungrateful minx! you've thrown me up for him, have you? You two being destined for each other, what have I done that you should treat me thus?" She then went away; and a few days afterwards Miss Quarta said she too would have to be absent for a day, so Shang went out for a walk by himself, and suddenly beheld a very nice-looking young lady emerge from the shade of an old oak that was growing on the hill-side.

"Why so dreadfully pensive?" said she to him; "those Hu girls can never bring you a single cent." She then presented Shang with some money, and bade him go on ahead and buy some good wine, adding, "I'll bring something to eat with me, and we'll have a jolly time of it." Shang took the money and went home, doing as the young lady had told him; and by-and-by in she herself came, and threw on the table a roast chicken and a shoulder of salt pork, which she at once proceeded to cut up. They now set to work to enjoy themselves, and had hardly finished when they heard some one coming in, and the next minute in walked Miss Tertia and her sister. The strange young lady didn't know where to hide, and managed to lose her shoes; but the other two began to revile her, saying, "Out upon you, base fox; what are you doing here?" They then chased her away after some trouble, and Shang began to excuse himself to them, until at last they all became friends again as before.

One day, however, a Shensi man arrived, riding on a donkey, and coming to the door said, "I have long been in search of these evil spirits: now I have got them." Shang's father thought the man's remark rather strange, and asked him whence he had come.

"Across much land and sea," replied he; "for eight or nine months out of every year I am absent from my native place. These devils killed my brother with their poison, alas! alas! and I have sworn to exterminate them; but I have travelled many miles without being able to find them. They are now in your house, and if you do not cut them off, you will die even as my brother."

Now Shang and the young ladies had kept their acquaintanceship very dark; but his father and mother had guessed that something was up, and, much alarmed, bade the Shensi man walk in and perform his exorcisms. The latter then produced two bottles which he placed upon the ground, and proceeded to mutter a number of charms and cabalistic formulæ; whereupon four wreaths of smoke passed two by two into each bottle.

"I have the whole family," cried he, in an ecstasy of delight; as he proceeded to tie down the mouths of the bottles with pig's bladder, sealing them with the utmost care. Shang's father was likewise very pleased, and kept his guest to dinner; but the young man himself was sadly dejected, and approaching the bottles unperceived, bent his ear to listen.

"Ungrateful man," said Miss Quarta from within, "to sit there and make no effort to save me." This was more than Shang could stand, and he immediately broke the seal, but found that he couldn't untie the knot. "Not so," cried Miss Quarta; "merely lay down the flag that now stands on the altar, and with a pin prick the bladder, and I can get out." Shang did as she bade him, and in a moment a thin streak of white smoke issued forth from the hole and disappeared in the clouds. When the Shensi man came out, and saw the flag lying on the ground, he started violently, and cried out, "Escaped! This must be your doing, young sir." He then shook the bottle and listened, finally exclaiming, "Luckily only one has got away. She was fated not to die, and may therefore be pardoned." Thereupon he took the bottles and went his way.

Some years afterwards Shang was one day superintending his reapers cutting the corn, when he descried Miss Quarta at a distance, sitting under a tree. He approached, and she took his hand, saying, "Ten years have rolled away since last we met. Since then I have gained the prize of immortality; but I thought that perhaps you had not quite forgotten me, and so I came to see you once more." Shang wished her to return home with him; to which she replied, "I am no longer what I was that I should mingle in the affairs of mortals. We shall meet again." And as she said this, she disappeared; but twenty years later, when Shang was one day alone, Miss Quarta walked in. Shang was overjoyed, and began to address her; but she answered him, saying, "My name is already enrolled in the Register of the Immortals, and I have no right to return to earth. However, out of gratitude to you I determined to announce to you the date of your dissolution that you might put your affairs in order. Fear nothing; I will see you safely through to the happy land." She then departed, and on the day named Shang actually died. A relative of a friend of mine, Mr. Li Wên-yü, frequently met the above-mentioned Mr. Shang.

Miss Lien-hsiang

Pu Songling; translated by Herbert A. Giles

THERE WAS A YOUNG MAN named Sang Tzŭ-ming, a native of I-chou, who had been left an orphan when quite young. He lived near the Saffron market, and kept himself very much to himself, only going out twice a day for his meals to a neighbour's close by, and sitting quietly at home all the rest of his time. One day the said neighbour called, and asked him in joke if he wasn't afraid of devil-foxes, so much alone as he was. "Oh," replied Sang, laughing, "what has the superior man to fear from devil-foxes. If they come as men, I have here a sharp sword for them; and if as women, why, I shall open the door and ask them to walk in."

The neighbour went away, and having arranged with a friend of his, they got a young lady of their acquaintance to climb over Sang's wall with the help of a ladder, and knock at the door. Sang peeped through, and called out, "Who's there?" to which the girl answered, "A devil!" and frightened Sang so dreadfully that his teeth chattered in his head. The girl then ran away, and next morning when his neighbour came to see him, Sang told him what had happened, and said he meant to go back to his native place. The neighbour then clapped his hands, and said to Sang, "Why didn't you ask her in?" Whereupon Sang perceived that he had been tricked, and went on quietly again as before.

Some six months afterwards, a young lady knocked at his door; and Sang, thinking his friends were at their old tricks, opened it at once, and asked her to walk in. She did so; and he beheld to his astonishment a perfect Helen for beauty. Asking her whence she came, she replied that her name was Lien-hsiang, and that she lived not very far off, adding that she had long been anxious to make his acquaintance. After that she used to drop in every now and again for a chat; but one evening when Sang was sitting alone expecting her, another young lady suddenly walked in. Thinking it was Lien-hsiang, Sang got up to meet her, but found that the new-comer was somebody else. She was about fifteen or sixteen years of age, wore very full sleeves, and dressed her hair after the fashion of unmarried girls, being otherwise very stylish-looking and refined, and apparently hesitating whether to go on or go back. Sang, in a great state of alarm, took her for a fox; but the young lady said, "My name is Li, and I am of a respectable family. Hearing of your virtue and talent, I hope to be accorded the honour of your acquaintance." Sang laughed, and took her by the hand, which he found was as cold as ice; and when he asked the reason, she told him that she had always been delicate, and that it was very chilly outside. She then remarked that she intended to visit him pretty frequently, and hoped it would not inconvenience him; so he explained that no one came to see him except another young lady, and that not very often.

"When she comes, I'll go," replied the young lady, "and only drop in when she's not here." She then gave him an embroidered slipper, saying that she had worn it, and that whenever he shook it she would know that he wanted to see her, cautioning him at the same time never to shake it before strangers. Taking it in his hand he beheld a very tiny little shoe almost as fine pointed as an awl, with which he was much pleased; and next evening, when nobody was present, he produced the shoe and shook it, whereupon the young lady immediately walked in. Henceforth, whenever he brought it out, the young lady responded to his wishes and appeared before him. This seemed so strange that at last he asked her to give him some explanation; but she only laughed, and said it was mere coincidence.

One evening after this Lien-hsiang came, and said in alarm to Sang, "Whatever has made you look so melancholy?" Sang replied that he did not know, and by-and-by she took her leave, saying, they would not meet again for some ten days. During this period Miss Li visited Sang every day, and on one occasion asked him where his other friend was. Sang told her; and then she laughed and said, "What is your opinion of me as compared with Lien-hsiang?" "You are both of you perfection," replied he, "but you are a little *colder* of the two." Miss Li didn't much like this, and cried out, "*Both of us perfection* is what you say to *me*. Then she must be a downright Cynthia, and I am no match for her." Somewhat out of temper, she reckoned that Lien-hsiang's ten days had expired, and said she would have a peep at her, making Sang promise to keep it all secret. The next evening Lien-hsiang came, and while they were talking she suddenly exclaimed, "Oh, dear! how much worse you seem to have become in the last ten days. You must have encountered something bad." Sang asked her why so; to which she answered, "First of all your appearance; and then your pulse is very thready. You've got the devil-disease."

The following evening when Miss Li came, Sang asked her what she thought of Lien-hsiang. "Oh," said she, "there's no question about her beauty; but she's a fox. When she went away I followed her to her hole on the hill side." Sang, however, attributed this remark to jealousy, and took no notice of it; but the next evening when Lien-hsiang came, he observed, "I don't believe it myself, but some one has told me you are a fox." Lien-hsiang asked who had said so, to which Sang replied that he was only joking; and then she begged him to explain what difference there was between a fox and an ordinary person.

"Well," answered Sang, "foxes frighten people to death, and, therefore, they are very much dreaded."

"Don't you believe that!" cried Lien-hsiang; "and now tell me who has been saying this of me."

Sang declared at first that it was only a joke of his, but by-and-by yielded to her instances, and let out the whole story.

"Of course I saw how changed you were," said Lien-hsiang; "she is surely not a human being to be able to cause such a rapid alteration in you. Say nothing, to-morrow I'll watch her as she watched me."

The following evening Miss Li came in; and they had hardly interchanged half-a-dozen sentences when a cough was heard outside the window, and Miss Li ran away. Lien-hsiang then entered and said to Sang, "You are lost! She is a devil, and if you do not at once forbid her coming here, you will soon be on the road to the other world."

"All jealousy," thought Sang, saying nothing, as Lien-hsiang continued, "I know that you don't like to be rude to her; but I, for my part, cannot see you sacrificed, and to-morrow I will bring you some medicine to expel the poison from your system. Happily, the disease has not yet taken firm hold of you, and in ten days you will be well again." The next evening she produced a knife and chopped up some medicine for Sang, which made him feel much better; but, although he was very grateful to her, he still persisted in disbelieving that he had the devil-disease. After some days he recovered and Lien-hsiang left him, warning him to have no more to do with Miss Li. Sang pretended that he would follow her advice, and closed the door and trimmed his lamp. He then took out the slipper, and on shaking it Miss Li appeared, somewhat cross at having been kept away for several days.

"She merely attended on me these few nights while I was ill," said Sang; "don't be angry."

At this Miss Li brightened up a little; but by-and-by Sang told her that people said she was a devil. "It's that nasty fox," cried Miss Li, after a pause, "putting these things into your head. If you don't break with her, I won't come here again." She then began to sob and cry, and Sang had some trouble in pacifying her. Next evening Lien-hsiang came and found out that Miss Li had been there again; whereupon she was very angry with Sang, and told him he would certainly die. "Why need you be so jealous?" said Sang, laughing; at which she only got more enraged, and replied, "When you were nearly dying the other day and I saved you, if I had not been jealous, where would you have been now?" Sang pretended he was only joking, and said that Miss Li had told him his recent illness was entirely owing to the machinations of a fox; to which she replied, "It's true enough what you say, only you don't see *whose* machinations.

However, if any thing happens to you, I should never clear myself even had I a hundred mouths; we will, therefore, part. A hundred days hence I shall see you on your bed." Sang could not persuade her to stay, and away she went; and from that time Miss Li became a regular visitor.

Two months passed away, and Sang began to experience a feeling of great lassitude, which he tried at first to shake off, but by-and-by he became very thin, and could only take thick gruel. He then thought about going back to his native place; however, he could not bear to leave Miss Li, and in a few more days he was so weak that he was unable to get up. His friend next door, seeing how ill he was, daily sent in his boy with food and drink; and now Sang began for the first time to suspect Miss Li. So he said to her, "I am sorry I didn't listen to Lien-hsiang before I got as bad as this." He then closed his eyes and kept them shut for some time; and when he opened them again Miss Li had disappeared. Their acquaintanceship was thus at an end, and Sang lay all emaciated as he was upon his bed in his solitary room longing for the return of Lien-hsiang.

One day, while he was still thinking about her, some one drew aside the screen and walked in. It was Lien-hsiang; and approaching the bed she said with a smile, "Was I then talking such nonsense?" Sang struggled a long time to speak; and, at length, confessing he had been wrong, implored her to save him. "When the disease has reached such a pitch as this," replied Lien-hsiang, "there is very little to be done. I merely came to bid you farewell, and to clear up your doubts about my jealousy." In great tribulation, Sang asked her to take something she would find under his pillow and destroy it; and she accordingly drew forth the slipper, which she proceeded to examine by the light of the lamp, turning it over and over. All at once Miss Li walked in, but when she saw Lien-hsiang she turned back as though she would run away, which Lien-hsiang instantly prevented by placing herself in the doorway. Sang then began to reproach her, and Miss Li could make no reply; whereupon Lien-hsiang said, "At last we meet. Formerly you attributed this gentleman's illness to me; what have you to say now?"

Miss Li bent her head in acknowledgment of her guilt, and Lien-hsiang continued, "How is it that a nice girl like you can thus turn love into hate?" Here Miss Li threw herself on the ground in a flood of tears and begged for mercy; and Lien-hsiang, raising her up, inquired of her as to her past life.

"I am a daughter of a petty official named Li, and I died young, leaving the web of my destiny incomplete, like the silkworm that perishes in the spring. To be the partner of this gentleman was my ardent wish; but I had never any intention of causing his death."

"I have heard," remarked Lien-hsiang, "that the advantage devils obtain by killing people is that their victims are ever with them after death. Is this so?"

"It is not," replied Miss Li; "the companionship of two devils gives no pleasure to either. Were it otherwise, I should not have wanted for friends in the realms below. But tell me, how do foxes manage not to kill people?"

"You allude to such foxes as suck the breath out of people?" replied Lien-hsiang; "I am not of that class. Some foxes are harmless; no devils are, because of the dominance of the *yin* in their compositions." Sang now knew that these two girls were really a fox and a devil; however, from being long accustomed to their society, he was not in the least alarmed. His breathing had dwindled to a mere thread, and at length he uttered a cry of pain. Lien-hsiang looked round and said, "How shall we cure him?" upon which Miss Li blushed deeply and drew back; and then Lien-hsiang added, "If he does get well, I'm afraid you will be dreadfully jealous." Miss Li drew herself up, and replied, "Could a physician be found to wipe away the wrong I have done to this gentleman, I would bury my head in the ground. How should I look the world in the face?"

Lien-hsiang here opened a bag and drew forth some drugs, saying, "I have been looking forward to this day. When I left this gentleman I proceeded to gather my simples, as it would take three months for the medicine to be got ready; but then, should the poison have brought anyone even to death's door, this medicine is able to call him back. The only condition is that it be administered by the very hand which wrought the ill." Miss Li did as she was told and put the pills Lien-hsiang gave her one after another into Sang's mouth. They burnt his inside like fire; but soon vitality began to return, and Lien-hsiang cried out, "He is cured!" Just at this moment Miss Li heard the cock crow and vanished, Lien-hsiang remaining behind in attendance on the invalid, who was unable to feed himself. She bolted the outside door and pretended that Sang had returned to his native place, so as to prevent visitors from calling. Day and night she took care of him, and every evening Miss Li came in to render assistance, regarding Lien-hsiang as an elder sister, and being treated by her with great consideration and kindness.

Three months afterwards Sang was as strong and well as ever he had been, and then for several evenings Miss Li ceased to visit them, only staying a few moments when she did come, and seeming very uneasy in her mind. One evening Sang ran after her and carried her back in his arms, finding her no heavier than so much straw; and then, being obliged to stay, she curled herself up and lay down, to all appearance in a state of unconsciousness, and by-and-by she was gone. For many days they heard nothing of her, and Sang was so anxious that she should come back that he often took out her slipper and shook it.

"I don't wonder at your missing her," said Lien-hsiang, "I do myself very much indeed."

"Formerly," observed Sang, "when I shook the slipper she invariably came. I thought it very strange, but I never suspected her of being a devil. And now, alas! all I can do is to sit and think about her with this slipper in my hand." He then burst into a flood of tears.

Now a young lady named Yen-êrh, belonging to the wealthy Chang family, and about fifteen years of age, had died suddenly, without any apparent cause, and had come to life again in the night, when she got up and wished to go out. They barred the door and would not hear of her doing so; upon which she said, "I am the spirit daughter of a petty magistrate. A Mr. Sang has been very kind to me, and I have left my slipper at his house. I am really a spirit; what is the use of keeping me in?"

There being some reason for what she said, they asked her why she had come there; but she only looked up and down without being able to give any explanation. Some one here observed, that Mr. Sang had already gone home, but the young lady utterly refused to believe them. The family was much disturbed at all this; and when Sang's neighbour heard the story, he jumped over the wall, and peeping through beheld Sang sitting there chatting with a pretty-looking girl. As he went in, there was some commotion, during which Sang's visitor had disappeared, and when his neighbour asked the meaning of it all, Sang replied, laughing, "Why, I told you if any ladies came I should ask them in." His friend then repeated what Miss Yen-êrh had said; and Sang, unbolting his door, was about to go and have a peep at her, but unfortunately had no means of so doing. Meanwhile Mrs. Chang, hearing that he had not gone away, was more lost in astonishment than ever, and sent an old woman-servant to get back the slipper. Sang immediately gave it to her, and Miss Yen-êrh was delighted to recover it, though when she came to try it on it was too small for her by a good inch. In considerable alarm, she seized a mirror to look at herself; and suddenly became aware that she had come to life again in some one else's body. She therefore told all to her mother, and finally succeeded in convincing her, crying all the time because she was so changed for the worse as regarded personal appearance from what she had been before. And whenever she happened to see Lien-hsiang, she was very much disconcerted, declaring that she had been much better off as a devil than now as a human being. She would sit and weep over the slipper, no one being able to comfort her; and finally, covering herself up with bed-clothes, she lay all stark and stiff, positively refusing to take any nourishment. Her body swelled up, and for seven days she refused all food, but did not die; and then the swelling began to subside, and an intense hunger to come upon her which made her once more think about eating. Then she was troubled with a severe irritation, and her skin peeled entirely away; and when she got up in the morning, she found that the shoes had fallen off. On trying to put them on again, she discovered that they did not fit her any longer; and then she went back to her former pair which were now exactly of the right size and shape. In an ecstasy of joy, she grasped her mirror, and saw that her features had also changed back to what they had formerly been; so she washed and dressed herself and went in to visit her mother. Every one who met her was much astonished; and when Lien-hsiang heard the strange story, she tried to persuade Mr. Sang to make her an offer of marriage. But the young lady was rich and Sang was poor, and he did not see his way clearly. However, on Mrs. Chang's birthday, when she completed her cycle of sixty-one years, Sang went along with the others to wish her many happy returns of the day; and when the old lady knew who was coming, she bade Yen-êrh take a peep at him from behind the curtain. Sang arrived last of all; and immediately out rushed Miss Yen-êrh and seized his sleeve, and said she would go back with him. Her mother scolded her well for this, and she ran in abashed; but Sang, who had looked at her closely, began to weep, and threw himself at the feet of Mrs. Chang who raised him up without saying anything unkind. Sang then took his leave, and got his uncle to act as medium between them; the result being that an auspicious day was fixed upon for the wedding.

At the appointed time Sang proceeded to the house to fetch her; and when he returned he found that, instead of his former poor-looking furniture, beautiful carpets were laid down from the very door, and thousands of coloured lanterns were hung about in elegant designs. Lien-hsiang assisted the bride to enter, and took off her veil, finding her the same bright girl as ever. She also joined them while drinking the wedding cup, and inquired of her friend as to her recent transmigration; and Yen-êrh related as follows:

"Overwhelmed with grief, I began to shrink from myself as some unclean thing; and, after separating from you that day, I would not return any more to my grave. So I wandered about at random, and whenever I saw a living being, I envied its happy state. By day I remained among trees and shrubs, but at night I used to roam about anywhere. And once I came to the house of the Chang family, where, seeing a young girl lying upon the bed, I took possession of her mortal coil, unknowing that she would be restored to life again."

When Lien-hsiang heard this she was for some time lost in thought; and a month or two afterwards became very ill. She refused all medical aid and gradually got worse and worse, to the great grief of Mr. Sang and his wife, who stood weeping at her bedside. Suddenly she opened her eyes, and said, "You wish to live; I am willing to die. If fate so ordains it, we shall meet again ten years hence." As she uttered these words, her spirit passed away, and all that remained was the dead body of a fox. Sang, however, insisted on burying it with all the proper ceremonies.

Now his wife had no children; but one day a servant came in and said, "There is an old woman outside who has got a little girl for sale." Sang's wife gave orders that she should be shown in; and no sooner had she set eyes on the girl than she cried out, "Why, she's the image of Lien-hsiang!" Sang then looked at her, and found to his astonishment that she was really very like his old friend. The old woman said she was fourteen years old; and when asked what her price was, declared that her only wish was to get the girl comfortably settled, and enough to keep herself alive, and ensure not being thrown out into the kennel at death. So Sang gave a good price for her; and his wife, taking the girl's hand, led her into a room by themselves. Then, chucking her under the chin, she asked her, smiling, "Do you know me?" The girl said she did not; after which she told Mrs. Sang that her name was Wei, and that her father, who had been a pickle-merchant at Hsü-ch'êng, had died three years before. Mrs. Sang then calculated that Lien-hsiang had been dead just ten years; and, looking at the girl, who resembled her so exactly in every trait, at length patted her on the head, saying, "Ah, my sister, you promised to visit us again in ten years, and you have not played us false."

The girl here seemed to wake up as if from a dream, and, uttering an exclamation of surprise, fixed a steady gaze upon Sang's wife. Sang himself laughed, and said, "Just like the return of an old familiar swallow."

"Now I understand," cried the girl, in tears; "I recollect my mother saying that when I was born I was able to speak; and that, thinking it an inauspicious manifestation, they gave me dog's blood to drink, so that I should forget all about my previous state of existence. Is it all a dream, or are you not the Miss Li who was so ashamed of being a devil?" Thus they chatted of their existence in a former life, with alternate tears and smiles; but when it came to the day for worshipping at the tombs, Yen-êrh explained that she and her husband were in the habit of annually visiting and mourning over her grave. The girl replied that she would accompany them; and when they got there they found the whole place in disorder, and the coffin wood all warped.

"Lien-hsiang and I," said Yen-êrh to her husband, "have been attached to each other in two states of existence. Let us not be separated, but bury my bones here with hers." Sang consented, and opening Miss Li's tomb, took out the bones and buried them with those of Lien-hsiang, while friends and relatives, who had heard the strange story, gathered round the grave in gala dress to the number of many hundreds.

I learnt the above when travelling through I-chou, where I was detained at an inn by rain, and read a biography of Mr. Sang written by a comrade of his named Wang Tzǔ-chang. It was lent me by a Mr. Liu Tzǔ-ching, a relative of Sang's, and was quite a long account. This is merely an outline of it.

The Young Gentleman Who Couldn't Spell

Pu Songling; translated by Herbert A. Giles

AT CHIA-P'ING THERE LIVED a certain young gentleman of considerable talent and very prepossessing appearance. When seventeen years of age he went up for his bachelor's degree; and as he was passing the door of a house, he saw within a pretty-looking girl, who not only riveted his gaze, but also smiled and nodded her head at him. Quite pleased at this, he approached the young lady and began to talk, she, meanwhile, inquiring of him where he lived, and if alone or otherwise. He assured her he was quite by himself; and then she said, "Well, I will come and see you, but you mustn't let any one know." The young gentleman agreed, and when he got home he sent all the servants to another part of the house, and by-and-by the young lady arrived. She said her name was Wên-chi, and that her admiration for her host's noble bearing had made her visit him, unknown to her mistress. "And gladly," added she, "would I be your handmaid for life."

Our hero was delighted, and proposed to purchase her from the mistress she mentioned; and from this time she was in the habit of coming in every other day or so. On one occasion it was raining hard, and, after hanging up her wet cloak upon a peg, she took off her shoes, and bade the young gentleman clean them for her. He noticed that they were newly embroidered with all the colours of the rainbow, but utterly spoilt by the soaking rain; and was just saying what a pity it was, when the young lady cried out, "I should never have asked you to do such menial work except to show my love for you." All this time the rain was falling fast outside, and Wên-chi now repeated the following line:

> *"A nipping wind and chilly rain fill the river and the city."*

"There," said she, "cap that." The young gentleman replied that he could not, as he did not even understand what it meant. "Oh, really," retorted the young lady, "if you're not more of a scholar than that, I shall begin to think very little of you." She then told him he had better practice making verses, and he promised he would do so.

By degrees Miss Wên-chi's frequent visits attracted the notice of the servants, as also of a brother-in-law named Sung, who was likewise a gentleman of position; and the latter begged our hero to be allowed to have a peep at her. He was told in reply that the young lady had strictly forbidden that any one should see her; however, he concealed himself in the servants' quarters, and when she arrived he looked at her through the window. Almost beside himself, he now opened the door; whereupon Wên-chi jumping up, vaulted over the wall and disappeared. Sung was really smitten with her, and went off to her mistress to try and arrange for her purchase; but when he mentioned Wên-chi's name, he was informed that they had once had such a girl, who had died several years previously. In great amazement Sung went back and told his brother-in-law, and he now knew that his beloved Wên-chi was a disembodied spirit. So when she came again he asked her if it was so; to which she replied, "It is; but as you wanted a nice wife and I a handsome husband, I thought we should be a suitable pair. What matters it that one is a mortal and the other a spirit?" The young gentleman thoroughly coincided in her view of the case; and when his examination was over, and he was homeward bound, Wên-chi accompanied him, invisible to others and visible to him alone. Arriving at his parents' house, he installed her in the library; and the day she went to pay the customary bride's visit to her father and mother, he told his own mother the whole story. She and his father were greatly alarmed, and ordered him to have no more to do with her; but he would not listen to this, and then his parents tried by all kinds of devices to get rid of the girl, none of which met with any success.

One day our hero had left upon the table some written instructions for one of the servants, wherein he had made a number of mistakes in spelling, such as *paper* for *pepper, jinjer* for *ginger,* and so on; and when Wên-chi saw this, she wrote at the foot:

> *"Paper for pepper do I see?*
> *Jinjer for ginger can it be?*
> *Of such a husband I'm afraid;*
> *I'd rather be a servant-maid."*

She then said to the young gentleman, "Imagining you to be a man of culture, I hid my blushes and sought you out the first. Alas, your qualifications are on the outside; should I not thus be a laughing-stock to all?" She then disappeared, at which the young gentleman was much hurt; but not knowing to what she alluded, he gave the instructions to his servant, and so made himself the butt of all who heard the story.

The Man Who Was Thrown Down a Well

Pu Songling; translated by Herbert A. Giles

MR. TAI, OF AN-CH'ING, was a wild fellow when young. One day as he was returning home tipsy, he met by the way a dead cousin of his named Chi; and having, in his drunken state, quite forgotten that his cousin was dead, he asked him where he was going. "I am already a disembodied spirit," replied Chi; "don't you remember?" Tai was a little disturbed at this; but, being under the influence of liquor, he was not frightened, and inquired of his cousin what he was doing in the realms below. "I am employed as scribe," said Chi, "in the court of the Great King."

"Then you must know all about our happiness and misfortunes to come," cried Tai.

"It is my business," answered his cousin, "so of course I know. But I see such an enormous mass that, unless of special reference to myself or family, I take no notice of any of it. Three days ago, by the way, I saw your name in the register." Tai immediately asked what there was about himself, and his cousin replied, "I will not deceive you; your name was put down for a dark and dismal hell."

Tai was dreadfully alarmed, and at the same time sobered, and entreated his cousin to assist him in some way. "You may try," said Chi, "what merit will do for you as a means of mitigating your punishment; but the register of your sins is as thick as my finger, and nothing short of the most deserving acts will be of any avail. What can a poor fellow like myself do for you? Were you to perform one good act every day, you would not complete the necessary total under a year and more, and it is now too late for that. But henceforth amend your ways, and there may still be a chance of escape for you."

When Tai heard these words he prostrated himself on the ground, imploring his cousin to help him; but, on raising his head, Chi had disappeared; he therefore returned sorrowfully home, and set to work to cleanse his heart and order his behaviour.

Now Tai's next door neighbour had long suspected him of paying too much attention to his wife; and one day meeting Tai in the fields shortly after the events narrated above, he inveigled him into inspecting a dry well, and then pushed him down. The well was many feet deep, and the man felt certain that Tai was killed; however, in the middle of the night he came round, and sitting up at the bottom, he began to shout for assistance, but could not make any one hear him. On the following day, the neighbour, fearing that Tai might possibly have recovered consciousness, went to listen at the mouth of the well; and hearing him cry out for help, began to throw down a quantity of stones. Tai took refuge in a cave at the side, and did not dare utter another sound; but his enemy knew he was not dead, and forthwith filled the well almost up to the top with earth. In the cave it was as dark as pitch, exactly like the Infernal Regions; and not being able to get anything to eat or drink, Tai gave up all hopes of life. He crawled on his hands and knees further into the cave, but was prevented by water from going further than a few paces, and returned to take up his position at the old spot.

At first he felt hungry; by-and-by, however, this sensation passed away; and then reflecting that there, at the bottom of a well, he could hardly perform any good action, he passed his time in calling loudly on the name of Buddha. Before long he saw a number of Will-o'-the-Wisps flitting over the water and illuminating the gloom of the cave; and immediately prayed to them, saying, "O Will-o'-the-Wisps, I have heard that ye are the shades of wronged and injured people. I have not long to live, and am without hope of escape; still I would gladly relieve the monotony of my situation by exchanging a few words with you." Thereupon, all the Wills came flitting across the water to him; and among them was a man of about half the ordinary size. Tai asked him whence he came; to which he replied, "This is an old coal-mine. The proprietor, in working the coal, disturbed the position of some graves; and Mr. Lung-fei flooded the mine and drowned forty-three workmen. We are the shades of those men." He further said he did not know who Mr. Lung-fei was, except that he was secretary to the City God, and that in compassion for the misfortunes of the innocent workmen, he was in the habit of sending them a quantity of gruel every three or four days. "But the cold water," added he, "soaks into our bones, and there is but small chance of ever getting them removed. If, Sir, you some day return to the world above, I pray you fish up our decaying bones and bury them in some public burying-ground. You will thus earn for yourself boundless gratitude in the realms below."

Tai promised that if he had the luck to escape he would do as they wished; "but how," cried he, "situated as I am, can I ever hope to look again upon the light of day?" He then began to teach the Wills to say their prayers, making for them beads out of bits of mud, and repeating to them the liturgies of Buddha. He could not tell night from morning; he slept when he felt tired, and when he waked he sat up. Suddenly, he perceived in the distance the light of lamps, at which the shades all rejoiced, and said, "It is Mr. Lung-fei with our food." They then invited Tai to go with them; and when he said he couldn't because of the water, they bore him along over it so that he hardly seemed to walk. After twisting and turning about for nearly a quarter of a mile, he reached a place at which the Wills bade him walk by himself; and then he appeared to mount a flight of steps, at the top of which he found himself in an apartment lighted by a candle as thick round as one's arm. Not having seen the light of fire for some time, he was overjoyed and walked in; but observing an old man in a scholar's dress and cap seated in the post of honour, he stopped, not liking to advance further. But the old man had already caught sight of him, and asked him how he, a living man, had come there.

Tai threw himself on the ground at his feet, and told him all; whereupon the old man cried out, "My great-grandson!" He then bade him get up; and offering him a seat, explained that his own name was Tai Ch'ien, and that he was otherwise known as Lung-fei. He said, moreover, that in days gone by a worthless grandson of his named T'ang, had associated himself with a lot of scoundrels and sunk a well near his grave, disturbing the peace of his everlasting night; and that therefore he had flooded the place with salt water and drowned them. He then inquired as to the general condition of the family at that time.

Now Tai was a descendant of one of five brothers, from the eldest of whom T'ang himself was also descended; and an influential man of the place had bribed T'ang to open a mine alongside the family grave. His brothers were afraid to interfere; and by-and-by the water rose and drowned all the workmen; whereupon actions for damages were commenced by the relatives of the deceased, and T'ang and his friend were reduced to poverty, and T'ang's descendants to absolute destitution. Tai was a son of one of T'ang's brothers, and having heard this story from his seniors, now repeated it to the old man.

"How could they be otherwise than unfortunate," cried the latter, "with such an unfilial progenitor? But since you have come hither, you must on no account neglect your studies." The old man then provided him with food and wine, and spreading a volume of essays according to the old style before him, bade him study it most carefully. He also gave him themes for composition, and corrected his essays as if he had been his tutor. The candle remained always burning in the room, never needing to be snuffed and never decreasing. When he was tired he went to sleep, but he never knew day from night. The old man occasionally went out, leaving a boy to attend to his great-grandson's wants. It seemed that several years passed away thus, but Tai had no troubles of any kind to annoy him. He had no other book except the volume of essays, one hundred in all, which he read through more than four thousand times.

One day the old man said to him, "Your term of expiation is nearly completed, and you will be able to return to the world above. My grave is near the coal-mine, and the grosser breeze plays upon my bones. Remember to remove them to Tung-yüan." Tai promised he would see to this; and then the old man summoned all the shades together and instructed them to escort Tai back to the place where they had found him. The shades now bowed one after the other, and begged Tai to think of them as well, while Tai himself was quite at a loss to guess how he was going to get out.

Meanwhile, Tai's family had searched for him everywhere, and his mother had brought his case to the notice of the officials, thereby implicating a large number of persons, but without getting any trace of the missing man. Three or four years passed away and there was a change of magistrate; in consequence of which the search was relaxed, and Tai's wife, not being happy where she was, married another husband. Just then an inhabitant of the place set about repairing the old well and found Tai's body in the cave at the bottom. Touching it, he found it was not dead, and at once gave information to the family. Tai was promptly conveyed home, and within a day he could tell his own story.

Since he had been down the well, the neighbour who pushed him in had beaten his own wife to death; and his father-in-law having brought an action against him, he had been in confinement for more than a year while the case was being investigated. When released he was a mere bag of bones; and then hearing that Tai had come back to life, he was terribly alarmed and fled away. The family tried to persuade Tai to take proceedings against him, but this he would not do, alleging that what had befallen him was a proper punishment for his own bad behaviour, and had nothing to do with the neighbour. Upon this, the said neighbour ventured to return; and when the water in the well had dried up, Tai hired men to go down and collect the bones, which he put in coffins and buried all together in one place. He next hunted up Mr. Lung-fei's name in the family tables of genealogy, and proceeded to sacrifice all kinds of nice things at his tomb. By-and-by the Literary Chancellor heard this strange story, and was also very pleased with Tai's compositions; accordingly, Tai passed successfully through his examinations, and, having taken his master's degree, returned home and reburied Mr. Lung-fei at Tung-yüan, repairing thither regularly every spring without fail.

Chou K'o-ch'ang and His Ghost

Pu Songling; translated by Herbert A. Giles

AT HUAI-SHANG there lived a graduate named Chou T'ien-i, who, though fifty years of age, had but one son, called K'o-ch'ang, whom he loved very dearly. This boy, when about thirteen or fourteen, was a handsome, well-favoured fellow, strangely averse to study, and often playing truant from school, sometimes for the whole day, without any remonstrance on the part of his father. One day he went away and did not come back in the evening; neither, after a diligent search, could any traces of him be discovered. His father and mother were in despair, and hardly cared to live; but after a year and more had passed away, lo and behold! K'o-ch'ang returned, saying that he had been beguiled away by a Taoist priest, who, however, had not done him any harm, and that he had seized a moment while the priest was absent to escape and find his way home again. His father was delighted, and asked him no more questions, but set to work to give him an education; and K'o-ch'ang was so much cleverer and more intelligent than he had been before, that by the following year he had taken his bachelor's degree and had made quite a name for himself. Immediately all the good families of the neighbourhood wanted to secure him as a son-in-law. Among others proposed there was an extremely nice girl, the daughter of a gentleman named Chao, who had taken his doctor's degree, and K'o-ch'ang's father was very anxious that he should marry the young lady. The youth himself would not hear of it, but stuck to his books and took his master's degree, quite refusing to entertain any thought of marriage; and this so exasperated his mother that one day the good lady began to rate him soundly.

K'o-ch'ang got up in a great rage and cried out, "I have long been wanting to get away, and have only remained for your sakes. I shall now say farewell, and leave Miss Chao for any one that likes to marry her." At this his mother tried to detain him, but in a moment he had fallen forwards on the ground, and there was nothing left of him but his hat and clothes. They were all dreadfully frightened, thinking that it must have been K'o-ch'ang's ghost who had been with them, and gave themselves up to weeping and lamentation; however, the very next day K'o-ch'ang arrived, accompanied by a retinue of horses and servants, his story being that he had formerly been kidnapped and sold to a wealthy trader, who, being then childless, had adopted him, but who, when he subsequently had a son born to him by his own wife, sent K'o-ch'ang back to his old home. And as soon as his father began to question him as to his studies, his utter dulness and want of knowledge soon made it clear that he was the real K'o-ch'ang of old; but he was already known as a man who had got his master's degree, (that is, the ghost of him had got it) so it was determined in the family to keep the whole affair secret. This K'o-ch'ang was only too ready to espouse Miss Chao; and before a year had passed over their heads his wife had presented the old people with the much longed-for grandson.

Courage Tested

Pu Songling; translated by Herbert A. Giles

MR. TUNG WAS A HSÜ-CHOU MAN, very fond of playing broad-sword, and a light-hearted, devil-may-care fellow, who was often involving himself in trouble. One day he fell in with a traveller who was riding on a mule and going the same way as himself; whereupon they entered into conversation, and began to talk to each other about feats of strength and so on. The traveller said his name was T'ung, and that he belonged to Liao-yang; that he had been twenty years away from home, and had just returned from beyond the sea. "And I venture to say," cried Tung, "that in your wanderings on the Four Seas you have seen a great many people; but have you seen any supernaturally clever ones?" T'ung asked him to what he alluded; and then Tung explained what his own particular hobby was, adding how much he would like to learn from them any tricks in the art of broad-sword.

"Supernatural," replied the traveller, "are to be found everywhere. It needs but that a man should be a loyal subject and a filial son for him to know all that the supernaturals know."

"Right you are, indeed!" cried Tung, as he drew a short sword from his belt, and, tapping the blade with his fingers, began to accompany it with a song. He then cut down a tree that was by the wayside, to shew T'ung how sharp it was; at which T'ung smoothed his beard and smiled, begging to be allowed to have a look at the weapon. Tung handed it to him, and, when he had turned it over two or three times, he said, "This is a very inferior piece of steel; now, though I know nothing about broad-sword myself, I have a weapon which is really of some use." He then drew from beneath his coat a sword of a foot or so in length, and with it he began to pare pieces off Tung's sword, which seemed as soft as a melon, and which he cut quite away like a horse's hoof. Tung was greatly astonished, and borrowed the other's sword to examine it, returning it after carefully wiping the blade. He then invited T'ung to his house, and made him stay the night; and, after begging him to explain the mystery of his sword, began to nurse his leg and sit listening respectfully without saying a word.

It was already pretty late, when suddenly there was a sound of scuffling next door, where Tung's father lived; and, on putting his ear to the wall, he heard an angry voice saying, "Tell your son to come here at once, and then I will spare you." This was followed by other sounds of beating and a continued groaning, in a voice which Tung knew to be his father's. He therefore seized a spear, and was about to rush forth, but T'ung held him back, saying, "You'll be killed for a certainty if you go. Let us think of some other plan." Tung asked what plan he could suggest; to which the other replied, "The robbers are killing your father: there is no help for you; but as you have no brothers, just go and tell your wife and children what your last wishes are, while I try and rouse the servants." Tung agreed to this, and ran in to tell his wife, who clung to him and implored him not to go, until at length all his courage had ebbed away, and he went upstairs with her to get his bow and arrows ready to resist the robbers' attack. At that juncture he heard the voice of his friend T'ung, outside on the eaves of the house, saying, with a laugh, "All right; the robbers have gone;" but on lighting a candle, he could see nothing of him. He then stole out to the front door, where he met his father with a lantern in his hand, coming in from a party at a neighbour's house; and the whole court-yard was covered with the ashes of burnt grass, whereby he knew that T'ung the traveller was himself a supernatural.

The Shui-mang Plant

Pu Songling; translated by Herbert A. Giles

THE SHUI-MANG is a poisonous herb. It is a creeper, like the bean, and has a similar red flower. Those who eat of it die, and become *shui-mang* devils, tradition asserting that such devils are unable to be born again unless they can find some one else who has also eaten of this poison to take their place. These *shui-mang* devils abound in the province of Hunan, where, by the way, the phrase 'same-year man' is applied to those born in the same year, who exchange visits and call each other brother, their children addressing the father's 'brother' as uncle. This has now become a regular custom there.

A young man named Chu was on his way to visit a same-year friend of his, when he was overtaken by a violent thirst. Suddenly he came upon an old woman sitting by the roadside under a shed and distributing tea gratis, and immediately walked up to her to get a drink. She invited him into the shed, and presented him with a bowl of tea in a very cordial spirit; but the smell of it did not seem like the smell of ordinary tea, and he would not drink it, rising up to go away. The old woman stopped him, and called out, "San-niang! bring some good tea." Immediately a young girl came from behind the shed, carrying in her hands a pot of tea. She was about fourteen or fifteen years old, and of very fascinating appearance, with glittering rings and bracelets on her fingers and arms. As Chu received the cup from her his reason fled; and drinking down the tea she gave him, the flavour of which was unlike any other kind, he proceeded to ask for more. Then, watching for a moment when the old woman's back was turned, he seized her wrist and drew a ring from her finger. The girl blushed and smiled; and Chu, more and more inflamed, asked her where she lived.

"Come again this evening," replied she, "and you'll find me here."

Chu begged for a handful of her tea, which she stowed away with the ring, and took his leave. Arriving at his destination, he felt a pain in his heart, which he at once attributed to the tea, telling his friend what had occurred. "Alas! you are undone," cried the other; "they were *shui-mang* devils. My father died in the same way, and we were unable to save him. There is no help for you." Chu was terribly frightened, and produced the handful of tea, which his friend at once pronounced to be leaves of the *shui-mang* plant. He then shewed him the ring, and told him what the girl had said; whereupon his friend, after some reflection, said, "She must be San-niang, of the K'ou family."

"How could you know her name?" asked Chu, hearing his friend use the same words as the old woman.

"Oh," replied he, "there was a nice-looking girl of that name who died some years ago from eating of the same herb. She is doubtless the girl you saw." Here some one observed that if the person so entrapped by a devil only knew its name, and could procure an old pair of its shoes, he might save himself by boiling them in water and drinking the liquor as medicine. Chu's friend thereupon rushed off at once to the K'ou family, and implored them to give him an old pair of their daughter's shoes; but they, not wishing to prevent their daughter from finding a substitute in Chu, flatly refused his request. So he went back in anger and told Chu, who ground his teeth with rage, saying, "If I die, she shall not obtain her transmigration thereby." His friend then sent him home; and just as he reached the door he fell down dead. Chu's mother wept bitterly over his corpse, which was in due course interred; and he left behind one little boy barely a year old. His wife did not remain a widow, but in six months married again and went away, putting Chu's son under the care of his grandmother, who was quite unequal to any toil, and did nothing but weep morning and night. One day she was carrying her grandson about in her arms, crying bitterly all the time, when suddenly in walked Chu. His mother, much alarmed, brushed away her tears, and asked him what it meant. "Mother," replied he, "down in the realms below I heard you weeping. I am therefore come to tend you. Although a departed spirit, I have a wife, who has likewise come to share your toil. Therefore do not grieve."

His mother inquired who his wife was, to which he replied, "When the K'ou family sat still and left me to my fate I was greatly incensed against them; and after death I sought for San-niang, not knowing where she was. I have recently seen my old same-year friend, and he told me where she was. She had come to life again in the person of the baby-daughter of a high official named Jen; but I went thither and dragged her spirit back. She is now my wife, and we get on extremely well together." A very pretty and well-dressed young lady here entered, and made obeisance to Chu's mother, Chu saying, "This is San-niang, of the K'ou family;" and although not a living being, Mrs. Chu at once took a great fancy to her. Chu sent her off to help in the work of the house, and, in spite of not being accustomed to this sort of thing, she was so obedient to her mother-in-law as to excite the compassion of all. The two then took up their quarters in Chu's old apartments, and there they continued to remain.

Meanwhile San-niang asked Chu's mother to let the K'ou family know; and this she did, notwithstanding some objections raised by her son. Mr. and Mrs. K'ou were much astonished at the news, and, ordering their carriage, proceeded at once to Chu's house. There they found their daughter, and parents and child fell into each other's arms. San-niang entreated them to dry their tears; but her mother, noticing the poverty of Chu's household, was unable to restrain her feelings.

"We are already spirits," cried San-niang; "what matters poverty to us? Besides, I am very well treated here, and am altogether as happy as I can be." They then asked her who the old woman was; to which she replied, "Her name was Ni. She was mortified at being too ugly to entrap people herself, and got me to assist her. She has now been born again at a soy-shop in the city." Then, looking at her husband, she added, "Come, since you are the son-in-law, pay the proper respect to my father and mother, or what shall I think of you?" Chu made his obeisance, and San-niang went into the kitchen to get food ready for them, at which her mother became very melancholy, and went away home, whence she sent a couple of maid-servants, a hundred ounces of silver, and rolls of cloth and silk, besides making occasional presents of food and wine, so that Chu's mother lived in comparative comfort. San-niang also went from time to time to see her parents, but would never stay very long, pleading that she was wanted at home, and such excuses; and if the old people attempted to keep her, she simply went off by herself. Her father built a nice house for Chu with all kinds of luxuries in it; but Chu never once entered his father-in-law's door.

Subsequently a man of the village who had eaten *shui-mang*, and had died in consequence, came back to life, to the great astonishment of everybody. However, Chu explained it, saying, "I brought him back to life. He was the victim of a man named Li Chiu; but I drove off Li's spirit when it came to make the other take his place." Chu's mother then asked her son why he did not get a substitute for himself; to which he replied, "I do not like to do this. I am anxious to put an end to, rather than take advantage of, such a system. Besides, I am very happy waiting on you, and have no wish to be born again." From that time all persons who had poisoned themselves with *shui-mang* were in the habit of feasting Chu and obtaining his assistance in their trouble. But in ten years' time his mother died, and he and his wife gave themselves up to sorrow, and would see no one, bidding their little boy put on mourning, beat his breast, and perform the proper ceremonies. Two years after Chu had buried his mother, his son married the granddaughter of a high official named Jen. This gentleman had had a daughter by a concubine, who had died when only a few months old; and now, hearing the strange story of Chu's wife, came to call on her and arrange the marriage. He then gave his granddaughter to Chu's son, and a free intercourse was maintained between the two families. However, one day Chu said to his son, "Because I have been of service to my generation, God has appointed me Keeper of the Dragons; and I am now about to proceed to my post." Thereupon four horses appeared in the court-yard, drawing a carriage with yellow hangings, the flanks of the horses being covered with scale-like trappings. Husband and wife came forth in full dress, and took their seats, and, while son and daughter-in-law were weeping their adieus, disappeared from view. That very day the K'ou family saw their daughter arrive, and, bidding them farewell, she told them the same story. The old people would have kept her, but she said, "My husband is already on his way," and, leaving the house, parted from them for ever. Chu's son was named Ngo, and his literary name was Li-ch'ên. He begged San-niang's bones from the K'ou family, and buried them by the side of his father's.

The Painted Skin

Pu Songling; translated by Herbert A. Giles

AT T'AI-YÜAN THERE LIVED a man named Wang. One morning he was out walking when he met a young lady carrying a bundle and hurrying along by herself. As she moved along with some difficulty, Wang quickened his pace and caught her up, and found she was a pretty girl of about sixteen. Much smitten he inquired whither she was going so early, and no one with her.

"A traveller like you," replied the girl, "cannot alleviate my distress; why trouble yourself to ask?"

"What distress is it?" said Wang; "I'm sure I'll do anything I can for you."

"My parents," answered she, "loved money, and they sold me as concubine into a rich family, where the wife was very jealous, and beat and abused me morning and night. It was more than I could stand, so I have run away." Wang asked her where she was going; to which she replied that a runaway had no fixed place of abode. "My house," said Wang, "is at no great distance; what do you say to coming there?" She joyfully acquiesced; and Wang, taking up her bundle, led the way to his house. Finding no one there, she asked Wang where his family were; to which he replied that that was only the library. "And a very nice place, too," said she; "but if you are kind enough to wish to save my life, you mustn't let it be known that I am here." Wang promised he would not divulge her secret, and so she remained there for some days without anyone knowing anything about it. He then told his wife, and she, fearing the girl might belong to some influential family, advised him to send her away. This, however, he would not consent to do; when one day, going into the town, he met a Taoist priest, who looked at him in astonishment, and asked him what he had met.

"I have met nothing," replied Wang.

"Why," said the priest, "you are bewitched; what do you mean by not having met anything?" But Wang insisted that it was so, and the priest walked away, saying, "The fool! Some people don't seem to know when death is at hand." This startled Wang, who at first thought of the girl; but then he reflected that a pretty young thing as she was couldn't well be a witch, and began to suspect that the priest merely wanted to do a stroke of business.

When he returned, the library door was shut, and he couldn't get in, which made him suspect that something was wrong; and so he climbed over the wall, where he found the door of the inner room shut too. Softly creeping up, he looked through the window and saw a hideous devil, with a green face and jagged teeth like a saw, spreading a human skin upon the bed and painting it with a paint-brush. The devil then threw aside the brush, and giving the skin a shake out, just as you would a coat, threw it over its shoulders, when, lo! it was the girl. Terrified at this, Wang hurried away with his head down in search of the priest who had gone he knew not whither; subsequently finding him in the fields, where he threw himself on his knees and begged the priest to save him.

"As to driving her away," said the priest, "the creature must be in great distress to be seeking a substitute for herself; besides, I could hardly endure to injure a living thing." However, he gave Wang a fly-brush, and bade him hang it at the door of the bedroom, agreeing to meet again at the Ch'ing-ti temple. Wang went home, but did not dare enter the library; so he hung up the brush at the bedroom door, and before long heard a sound of footsteps outside. Not daring to move, he made his wife peep out; and she saw the girl standing looking at the brush, afraid to pass it. She then ground her teeth and went away; but in a little while came back, and began cursing, saying, "You priest, you won't frighten me. Do you think I am going to give up what is already in my grasp?" Thereupon, she tore the brush to pieces, and bursting open the door, walked straight up to the bed, where she ripped open Wang and tore out his heart, with which she went away.

Wang's wife screamed out, and the servant came in with a light; but Wang was already dead and presented a most miserable spectacle. His wife, who was in an agony of fright, hardly dared cry for fear of making a noise; and next day she sent Wang's brother to see the priest. The latter got into a great rage, and cried out, "Was it for this that I had compassion on you, devil that you are?" proceeding at once with Wang's brother to the house, from which the girl had disappeared without anyone knowing whither she had gone. But the priest, raising his head, looked all round, and said, "Luckily she's not far off." He then asked who lived in the apartments on the south side, to which Wang's brother replied that he did; whereupon the priest declared that there she would be found. Wang's brother was horribly frightened and said he did not think so; and then the priest asked him if any stranger had been to the house. To this he answered that he had been out to the Ch'ing-ti temple and couldn't possibly say; but he went off to inquire, and in a little while came back and reported that an old woman had sought service with them as a maid-of-all-work, and had been engaged by his wife.

"That is she," said the priest, as Wang's brother added she was still there; and they all set out to go to the house together. Then the priest took his wooden sword, and standing in the middle of the court-yard, shouted out, "Base-born fiend, give me back my fly-brush!" Meanwhile the new maid-of-all-work was in a great state of alarm, and tried to get away by the door; but the priest struck her and down she fell flat, the human skin dropped off, and she became a hideous devil. There she lay grunting like a pig, until the priest grasped his wooden sword and struck off her head. She then became a dense column of smoke curling up from the ground, when the priest took an uncorked gourd and threw it right into the midst of the smoke. A sucking noise was heard, and the whole column was drawn into the gourd; after which the priest corked it up closely and put it in his pouch. The skin, too, which was complete even to the eyebrows, eyes, hands, and feet, he also rolled up as if it had been a scroll, and was on the point of leaving with it, when Wang's wife stopped him, and with tears entreated him to bring her husband to life. The priest said he was unable to do that; but Wang's wife flung herself at his feet, and with loud lamentations implored his assistance. For some time he remained immersed in thought, and then replied, "My power is not equal to what you ask. I myself cannot raise the dead; but I will direct you to some one who can, and if you apply to him properly you will succeed." Wang's wife asked the priest who it was; to which he replied, "There is a maniac in the town who passes his time grovelling in the dirt. Go, prostrate yourself before him, and beg him to help you. If he insults you, shew no sign of anger." Wang's brother knew the man to whom he alluded, and accordingly bade the priest adieu, and proceeded thither with his sister-in-law.

They found the destitute creature raving away by the road side, so filthy that it was all they could do to go near him. Wang's wife approached him on her knees; at which the maniac leered at her, and cried out, "Do you love me, my beauty?" Wang's wife told him what she had come for, but he only laughed and said, "You can get plenty of other husbands. Why raise the dead one to life?" But Wang's wife entreated him to help her; whereupon he observed, "It's very strange: people apply to me to raise their dead as if I was king of the infernal regions." He then gave Wang's wife a thrashing with his staff, which she bore without a murmur, and before a gradually increasing crowd of spectators. After this he produced a loathsome pill which he told her she must swallow, but here she broke down and was quite unable to do so. However, she did manage it at last, and then the maniac crying out, "How you do love me!" got up and went away without taking any more notice of her. They followed him into a temple with loud supplications, but he had disappeared, and every effort to find him was unsuccessful. Overcome with rage and shame, Wang's wife went home, where she mourned bitterly over her dead husband, grievously repenting the steps she had taken, and wishing only to die. She then bethought herself of preparing the corpse, near which none of the servants would venture; and set to work to close up the frightful wound of which he died.

While thus employed, interrupted from time to time by her sobs, she felt a rising lump in her throat, which by-and-by came out with a pop and fell straight into the dead man's wound. Looking closely at it, she saw it was a human heart; and then it began as it were to throb, emitting a warm vapour like smoke. Much excited, she at once closed the flesh over it, and held the sides of the wound together with all her might. Very soon, however, she got tired, and finding the vapour escaping from the crevices, she tore up a piece of silk and bound it round, at the same time bringing back circulation by rubbing the body and covering it up with clothes. In the night, she removed the coverings, and found that breath was coming from the nose; and by next morning her husband was alive again, though disturbed in mind as if awaking from a dream and feeling a pain in his heart. Where he had been wounded, there was a cicatrix about as big as a cash, which soon after disappeared.

The Magic Sword

Pu Songling; translated by Herbert A. Giles

NING LAI-CH'ÊN WAS A CHEKIANG MAN, and a good-natured, honourable fellow, fond of telling people that he had only loved once. Happening to go to Chinhua, he took shelter in a temple to the north of the city; very nice as far as ornamentation went, but overgrown with grass taller than a man's head, and evidently not much frequented. On either side were the priest's apartments, the doors of which were ajar, with the exception of a small room on the south side, where the lock had a new appearance. In the east corner he espied a group of bamboos, growing over a large pool of water-lilies in flower; and, being much pleased with the quiet of the place, determined to remain; more especially as, the Grand Examiner being in the town, all lodgings had gone up in price. So he roamed about waiting till the priests should return; and in the evening, a gentleman came and opened the door on the south side. Ning quickly made up to him, and with a bow informed him of his design.

"There is no one here whose permission you need ask," replied the stranger; "I am only lodging here, and if you don't object to the loneliness, I shall be very pleased to have the benefit of your society." Ning was delighted, and made himself a straw bed, and put up a board for a table, as if he intended to remain some time; and that night, by the beams of the clear bright moon, they sat together in the verandah and talked. The stranger's name was Yen Ch'ih-hsia, and Ning thought he was a student up for the provincial examination, only his dialect was not that of a Chekiang man. On being asked, he said he came from Shensi; and there was an air of straightforwardness about all his remarks. By-and-by, when their conversation was exhausted, they bade each other good night and went to bed; but Ning, being in a strange place, was quite unable to sleep; and soon he heard sounds of voices from the room on the north side. Getting up, he peeped through a window, and saw, in a small court-yard the other side of a low wall, a woman of about forty with an old maid-servant in a long faded gown, humped-backed and feeble-looking. They were chatting by the light of the moon; and the mistress said, "Why doesn't Hsiao-ch'ien come?"

"She ought to be here by now," replied the other. "She isn't offended with you; is she?" asked the lady.

"Not that I know of," answered the old servant; "but she seems to want to give trouble."

"Such people don't deserve to be treated well," said the other; and she had hardly uttered these words when up came a young girl of seventeen or eighteen, and very nice looking. The old servant laughed, and said, "Don't talk of people behind their backs. We were just mentioning you as you came without our hearing you; but fortunately we were saying nothing bad about you. And, as far as that goes," added she, "if I were a young fellow why I should certainly fall in love with you."

"If *you* don't praise me," replied the girl, "I'm sure I don't know who will;" and then the lady and the girl said something together, and Mr. Ning, thinking they were the family next door, turned round to sleep without paying further attention to them In a little while no sound was to be heard; but, as he was dropping off to sleep, he perceived that somebody was in the room. Jumping up in great haste, he found it was the young lady he had just seen; and detecting at once that she was going to attempt to bewitch him, sternly bade her begone. She then produced a lump of gold which he threw away, and told her to go after it or he would call his friend. So she had no alternative but to go, muttering something about his heart being like iron or stone. Next day, a young candidate for the examination came and lodged in the east room with his servant. He, however, was killed that very night, and his servant the night after; the corpses of both shewing a small hole in the sole of the foot as if bored by an awl, and from which a little blood came. No one knew who had committed these murders, and when Mr. Yen came home, Ning asked him what he thought about it. Yen replied that it was the work of devils, but Ning was a brave fellow, and that didn't frighten him much.

In the middle of the night Hsiao-ch'ien appeared to him again, and said, "I have seen many men, but none with a steel cold heart like yours. You are an upright man, and I will not attempt to deceive you. I, Hsiao-ch'ien, whose family name is Nieh, died when only eighteen, and was buried alongside of this temple. A devil then took possession of me, and employed me to bewitch people by my beauty, contrary to my inclination. There is now nothing left in this temple to slay, and I fear that imps will be employed to kill you." Ning was very frightened at this, and asked her what he should do. "Sleep in the same room with Mr. Yen," replied she.

"What!" asked he, "cannot the spirits trouble Yen?"

"He is a strange man," she answered, "and they don't like going near him." Ning then inquired how the spirits worked. "I bewitch people," said Hsiao-ch'ien, "and then they bore a hole in the foot which renders the victim senseless, and proceed to draw off the blood, which the devils drink. Another method is to tempt people by false gold, the bones of some horrid demon; and if they receive it, their hearts and livers will be torn out. Either method is used according to circumstances." Ning thanked her, and asked when he ought to be prepared; to which she replied, "To-morrow night." At parting she wept, and said, "I am about to sink into the great sea, with no friendly shore at hand. But your sense of duty is boundless, and you can save me. If you will collect my bones and bury them in some quiet spot, I shall not again be subject to these misfortunes."

Ning said he would do so, and asked where she lay buried. "At the foot of the aspen-tree on which there is a bird's nest," replied she; and passing out of the door, disappeared. The next day Ning was afraid that Yen might be going away somewhere, and went over early to invite him across. Wine and food were produced towards noon; and Ning, who took care not to lose sight of Yen, then asked him to remain there for the night. Yen declined, on the ground that he liked being by himself; but Ning wouldn't hear any excuses, and carried all Yen's things to his own room, so that he had no alternative but to consent. However, he warned Ning, saying, "I know you are a gentleman and a man of honour. If you see anything you don't quite understand, I pray you not to be too inquisitive; don't pry into my boxes, or it may be the worse for both of us." Ning promised to attend to what he said, and by-and-by they both lay down to sleep; and Yen, having placed his boxes on the window-sill, was soon snoring loudly.

Ning himself could not sleep; and after some time he saw a figure moving stealthily outside, at length approaching the window to peep through. It's eyes flashed like lightning, and Ning in a terrible fright was just upon the point of calling Yen, when something flew out of one of the boxes like a strip of white silk, and dashing against the window-sill returned at once to the box, disappearing very much like lightning. Yen heard the noise and got up, Ning all the time pretending to be asleep in order to watch what happened. The former then opened the box, and took out something which he smelt and examined by the light of the moon. It was dazzlingly white like crystal, and about two inches in length by the width of an onion leaf in breadth. He then wrapped it up carefully and put it back in the broken box, saying, "A bold-faced devil that, to come so near my box;" upon which he went back to bed; but Ning, who was lost in astonishment, arose and asked him what it all meant, telling at the same time what he himself had seen.

"As you and I are good friends," replied Yen, "I won't make any secret of it. The fact is I am a Taoist priest. But for the window-sill the devil would have been killed; as it is, he is badly wounded." Ning asked him what it was he had there wrapped up, and he told him it was his sword, on which he had smelt the presence of the devil. At Ning's request he produced the weapon, a bright little miniature of a sword; and from that time Ning held his friend in higher esteem than ever.

Next day he found traces of blood outside the window which led round to the north of the temple; and there among a number of graves he discovered the aspen-tree with the bird's nest at its summit. He then fulfilled his promise and prepared to go home, Yen giving him a farewell banquet, and presenting him with an old leather case which he said contained a sword, and would keep at a distance from him all devils and bogies. Ning then wished to learn a little of Yen's art; but the latter replied that although he might accomplish this easily enough, being as he was an upright man, yet he was well off in life, and not in a condition where it would be of any advantage to him. Ning then pretending he had to go and bury his sister, collected Hsiao-ch'ien's bones, and, having wrapped them up in grave-clothes, hired a boat, and set off on his way home.

On his arrival, as his library looked towards the open country, he made a grave hard by and buried the bones there, sacrificing, and invoking Hsiao-ch'ien as follows: "In pity for your lonely ghost, I have placed your remains near my humble cottage, where we shall be near each other, and no devil will dare annoy you. I pray you reject not my sacrifice, poor though it be." After this, he was proceeding home when he suddenly heard himself addressed from behind, the voice asking him not to hurry; and turning round he beheld Hsiao-ch'ien, who thanked him, saying, "Were I to die ten times for you I could not discharge my debt. Let me go home with you and wait upon your father and mother; you will not repent it." Looking closely at her, he observed that she had a beautiful complexion, and feet as small as bamboo shoots, being altogether much prettier now that he came to see her by daylight. So they went together to his home, and bidding her wait awhile, Ning ran in to tell his mother, to the very great surprise of the old lady.

Now Ning's wife had been ill for a long time, and his mother advised him not to say a word about it to her for fear of frightening her; in the middle of which in rushed Hsiao-ch'ien, and threw herself on the ground before them. "This is the young lady," said Ning; whereupon his mother in some alarm turned her attention to Hsiao-ch'ien, who cried out, "A lonely orphan, without brother or sister, the object of your son's kindness and compassion, begs to be allowed to give her poor services as some return for favours shewn."

Ning's mother, seeing that she was a nice pleasant-looking girl, began to lose fear of her, and replied, "Madam, the preference you shew for my son is highly pleasing to an old body like myself; but this is the only hope of our family, and I hardly dare agree to his taking a devil-wife."

"I have but one motive in what I ask," answered Hsiao-ch'ien, "and if you have no faith in disembodied people, then let me regard him as my brother, and live under your protection, serving you like a daughter." Ning's mother could not resist her straightforward manner, and Hsiao-ch'ien asked to be allowed to see Ning's wife, but this was denied on the plea that the lady was ill. Hsiao-ch'ien then went into the kitchen and got ready the dinner, running about the place as if she had lived there all her life. Ning's mother was, however, much afraid of her, and would not let her sleep in the house; so Hsiao-ch'ien went to the library, and was just entering when suddenly she fell back a few steps, and began walking hurriedly backwards and forwards in front of the door. Ning seeing this, called out and asked her what it meant; to which she replied, "The presence of that sword frightens me, and that is why I could not accompany you on your way home."

Ning at once understood her, and hung up the sword-case in another place; whereupon she entered, lighted a candle, and sat down. For some time she did not speak: at length asking Ning if he studied at night or not – "For," said she, "when I was little I used to repeat the Lêng-yen sutra; but now I have forgotten more than half, and, therefore, I should like to borrow a copy, and when you are at leisure in the evening you might hear me."

Ning said he would, and they sat silently there for some time, after which Hsiao-ch'ien went away and took up her quarters elsewhere. Morning and night she waited on Ning's mother, bringing water for her to wash in, occupying herself with household matters, and endeavouring to please her in every way. In the evening before she went to bed, she would always go in and repeat a little of the sutra, and leave as soon as she thought Ning was getting sleepy.

Now the illness of Ning's wife had given his mother a great deal of extra trouble – more, in fact, than she was equal to; but ever since Hsiao-ch'ien's arrival all this was changed, and Ning's mother felt kindly disposed to the girl in consequence, gradually growing to regard her almost as her own child, and forgetting quite that she was a spirit. Accordingly, she didn't make her leave the house at night; and Hsiao-ch'ien, who being a devil had not tasted meat or drink since her arrival, now began at the end of six months to take a little thin gruel. Mother and son alike became very fond of her, and henceforth never mentioned what she really was; neither were strangers able to detect the fact. By-and-by, Ning's wife died, and his mother secretly wished him to espouse Hsiao-ch'ien, though she rather dreaded any unfortunate consequences that might arise. This Hsiao-ch'ien perceived, and seizing an opportunity said to Ning's mother, "I have been with you now more than a year, and you ought to know something of my disposition. Because I was unwilling to injure travellers I followed your son hither. There was no other motive; and, as your son has shewn himself one of the best of men, I would now remain with him for three years in order that he may obtain for me some mark of Imperial approbation which will do me honour in the realms below."

Ning's mother knew that she meant no evil, but hesitated to put the family hopes of a posterity into jeopardy. Hsiao-ch'ien, however, reassured her by saying that Ning would have three sons, and that the line would not be interrupted by his marrying her. On the strength of this the marriage was arranged to the great joy of Ning, a feast prepared, and friends and relatives invited; and when in response to a call the bride herself came forth in her gay wedding-dress, the beholders took her rather for a fairy than for a devil. After this, numbers of congratulatory presents were given by the various female members of the family, who vied with one another in making her acquaintance; and these Hsiao-ch'ien returned by gifts of paintings of flowers, done by herself, in which she was very skilful, the receivers being extremely proud of such marks of her friendship.

One day she was leaning at the window in a despondent mood, when suddenly she asked where the sword-case was. "Oh," replied Ning, "as you seemed afraid of it, I moved it elsewhere."

"I have now been so long under the influence of surrounding life," said Hsiao-ch'ien, "that I shan't be afraid of it any more. Let us hang it on the bed."

"Why so?" asked Ning.

"For the last three days," explained she, "I have been much agitated in mind; and I fear that the devil at the temple, angry at my escape, may come suddenly and carry me off." So Ning brought the sword-case, and Hsiao-ch'ien, after examining it closely, remarked, "This is where the magician puts people. I wonder how many were slain before it got old and worn out as it is now. Even now when I look at it my flesh creeps." The case was then hung up, and next day removed to over the door. At night they sat up and watched, Hsiao-ch'ien warning Ning not to go to sleep; and suddenly something fell down flop like a bird. Hsiao-ch'ien in a fright got behind the curtain; but Ning looked at the thing, and found it was an imp of darkness, with glaring eyes and a bloody mouth, coming straight to the door. Stealthily creeping up it made a grab at the sword-case, and seemed about to tear it in pieces, when bang! – the sword-case became as big as a wardrobe, and from it a devil protruded part of his body and dragged the imp in. Nothing more was heard, and the sword-case resumed its original size. Ning was greatly alarmed, but Hsiao-ch'ien came out rejoicing, and said, "There's an end of my troubles." In the sword-case they found only a few quarts of clear water; nothing else.

After these events Ning took his doctor's degree and Hsiao-ch'ien bore him a son. He then took a concubine, and had one more son by each, all of whom became in time distinguished men.

The Magnanimous Girl

Pu Songling; translated by Herbert A. Giles

AT CHIN-LING THERE LIVED a young man named Ku, who had considerable ability but was very poor; and having an old mother, he was very loth to leave home. So he employed himself in writing or painting for people, and gave his mother the proceeds, going on thus till he was twenty-five years of age without taking a wife. Opposite to their house was another building, which had long been untenanted; and one day an old woman and a young girl came to occupy it, but there being no gentleman with them young Ku did not make any inquiries as to who they were or whence they hailed.

Shortly afterwards it chanced that just as Ku was entering the house he observed a young lady come out of his mother's door. She was about eighteen or nineteen, very clever and refined looking, and altogether such a girl as one rarely sets eyes on; and when she noticed Mr. Ku, she did not run away, but seemed quite self-possessed. "It was the young lady over the way; she came to borrow my scissors and measure," said his mother, "and she told me that there was only her mother and herself. They don't seem to belong to the lower classes. I asked her why she didn't get married, to which she replied that her mother was old. I must go and call on her to-morrow, and find out how the land lies. If she doesn't expect too much, you could take care of her mother for her."

So next day Ku's mother went, and found that the girl's mother was deaf, and that they were evidently poor, apparently not having a day's food in the house. Ku's mother asked what their employment was, and the old lady said they trusted for food to her daughter's ten fingers. She then threw out some hints about uniting the two families, to which the old lady seemed to agree; but, on consultation with her daughter, the latter would not consent. Mrs. Ku returned home and told her son, saying, "Perhaps she thinks we are too poor. She doesn't speak or laugh, is very nice-looking, and as pure as snow; truly no ordinary girl." There ended that; until one day, as Ku was sitting in his study, up came a very agreeable young fellow, who said he was from a neighbouring village, and engaged Ku to draw a picture for him. The two youths soon struck up a firm friendship and met constantly, when it happened that the stranger chanced to see the young lady of over the way.

"Who is that?" said he, following her with his eyes. Ku told him, and then he said, "She is certainly pretty, but rather stern in her appearance."

By-and-by Ku went in, and his mother told him the girl had come to beg a little rice, as they had had nothing to eat all day. "She's a good daughter," said his mother, "and I'm very sorry for her. We must try and help them a little." Ku thereupon shouldered a peck of rice, and, knocking at their door, presented it with his mother's compliments. The young lady received the rice but said nothing; and then she got into the habit of coming over and helping Ku's mother with her work and household affairs, almost as if she had been her daughter-in-law, for which Ku was very grateful to her, and whenever he had anything nice he always sent some of it in to her mother, though the young lady herself never once took the trouble to thank him.

So things went on until Ku's mother got an abscess on her leg, and lay writhing in agony day and night. Then the young lady devoted herself to the invalid, waiting on her and giving her medicine with such care and attention that at last the sick woman cried out, "Oh, that I could secure such a daughter-in-law as you, to see this old body into its grave!"

The young lady soothed her, and replied, "Your son is a hundred times more filial than I, a poor widow's only daughter."

"But even a filial son makes a bad nurse," answered the patient; "besides, I am now drawing towards the evening of my life, when my body will be exposed to the mists and the dews, and I am vexed in spirit about our ancestral worship and the continuance of our line." As she was speaking Ku walked in; and his mother, weeping, said, "I am deeply indebted to this young lady; do not forget to repay her goodness." Ku made a low bow, but the young lady said, "Sir, when you were kind to my mother, I did not thank you; why, then, thank me?" Ku thereupon became more than ever attached to her; but could never get her to depart in the slightest degree from her cold demeanour towards himself. One day, however, he managed to squeeze her hand, upon which she told him never to do so again; and then for some time he neither saw nor heard anything of her.

She had conceived a violent dislike to the young stranger above-mentioned; and one evening when he was sitting talking with Ku, the young lady reappeared. After a while she got angry at something he said, and drew from her robe a glittering knife about a foot long. The young man, seeing her do this, ran out in a fright and she after him, only to find that he had vanished. She then threw her dagger up into the air, and whish! a streak of light like a rainbow, and something came tumbling down with a flop. Ku got a light, and ran to see what it was; and lo! there lay a white fox, head in one place and body in another. "There is your *friend*," cried the girl; "I knew he would cause me to destroy him sooner or later." Ku dragged it into the house, and said, "Let us wait till to-morrow to talk it over; we shall then be more calm."

Next day the young lady arrived, and Ku inquired about her knowledge of the black art; but she told Ku not to trouble himself about such affairs, and to keep it secret or it might be prejudicial to his happiness. Ku then entreated her to consent to their union, to which she replied that she had already been as it were a daughter-in-law to his mother, and there was no need to push the thing further.

"Is it because I am poor?" asked Ku.

"Well, I am not rich," answered she, "but the fact is I had rather not." She then took her leave, and the next evening when Ku went across to their house to try once more to persuade her, the young lady had disappeared, and was never seen again.

Miss Chiao-no

Pu Songling; translated by Herbert A. Giles

K'UNG HSÜEH-LI was a descendant of Confucius. He was a man of considerable ability, and an excellent poet. A fellow-student, to whom he was much attached, became magistrate at T'ien-t'ai, and sent for K'ung to join him. Unfortunately, just before K'ung arrived his friend died, and he found himself without the means of returning home; so he took up his abode in a Buddhist monastery, where he was employed in transcribing for the priests. Several hundred paces to the west of this monastery there was a house belonging to a Mr. Shan, a gentleman who had known better days, but who had spent all his money in a heavy law-suit; and then, as his family was a small one, had gone away to live in the country and left his house vacant.

One day there was a heavy fall of snow which kept visitors away from the monastery; and K'ung, finding it dull, went out. As he was passing by the door of the house above-mentioned, a young man of very elegant appearance came forth, who, the moment he saw K'ung, ran up to him, and with a bow, entered into conversation, asking him to be pleased to walk in. K'ung was much taken with the young man, and followed him inside. The rooms were not particularly large, but adorned throughout with embroidered curtains, and from the walls hung scrolls and drawings by celebrated masters. On the table lay a book, the title of which was, *Jottings from Paradise*; and turning over its leaves, K'ung found therein many strange things. He did not ask the young man his name, presuming that as he lived in the Shan family mansion, he was necessarily the owner of the place. The young man, however, inquired what he was doing in that part of the country, and expressed great sympathy with his misfortunes, recommending him to set about taking pupils.

"Alas!" said K'ung, "who will play the Mæcenas to a distressed wayfarer like myself?"

"If," replied the young man, "you would condescend so far, I for my part would gladly seek instruction at your hands." K'ung was much gratified at this, but said he dared not arrogate to himself the position of teacher, and begged merely to be considered as the young man's friend. He then asked him why the house had been shut up for so long; to which the young man replied, "This is the Shan family mansion. It has been closed all this time because of the owner's removal into the country. My surname is Huang-fu, and my home is in Shen-si; but as our house has been burnt down in a great fire, we have put up here for a while." Thus Mr. K'ung found out that his name was not Shan.

That evening they spent in laughing and talking together, and K'ung remained there for the night. In the morning a lad came in to light the fire; and the young man, rising first, went into the private part of the house. Mr. K'ung was sitting up with the bed-clothes still huddled round him, when the lad looked in and said, "Master's coming!" So he jumped up with a start, and in came an old man with a silvery beard, who began to thank him, saying, "I am very much obliged to you for your condescension in becoming my son's tutor. At present he writes a villainous hand; and I can only hope you will not allow the ties of friendship to interfere with discipline." Thereupon, he presented Mr. K'ung with an embroidered suit of clothes, a sable hat, and a set of shoes and stockings; and when the latter had washed and dressed himself he called for wine and food.

K'ung could not make out what the valances of the chairs and tables were made of: they were so very bright-coloured and dazzling. By-and-by, when the wine had circulated several times, the old gentleman picked up his walking-stick and took his leave. After breakfast, the young man handed in his theme, which turned out to be written in an archaic style, and not at all after the modern fashion of essay-writing. K'ung asked him why he had done this, to which the young man replied that he did not contemplate competing at the public examinations. In the evening they had another drinking-bout, but it was agreed that there should be no more of it after that night. The young man then called the boy and told him to see if his father was asleep or not; adding, that if he was, he might quietly summon Miss Perfume. The boy went off, first taking a guitar out of a very pretty case; and in a few minutes in came a very nice-looking young girl. The young man bade her play the *Death of Shun*; and seizing an ivory plectrum she swept the chords, pouring forth a vocal melody of exquisite sweetness and pathos. He then gave her a goblet of wine to drink, and it was midnight before they parted.

Next morning they got up early and settled down to work. The young man proved an apt scholar; he could remember what he had once read, and at the end of two or three months had made astonishing progress. Then they agreed that every five days they would indulge in a symposium, and that Miss Perfume should always be of the party. One night when the wine had gone into K'ung's head, he seemed to be lost in a reverie; whereupon his young friend, who knew what was the matter with him, said, "This girl was brought up by my father. I know you find it lonely, and I have long been looking out for a nice wife for you."

"Let her only resemble Miss Perfume," said K'ung, "and she will do."

"Your experience," said the young man, laughing, "is but limited, and, consequently, anything is a surprise to you. If Miss Perfume is your *beau ideal*, why it will not be difficult to satisfy you."

Some six months had passed away, when one day Mr. K'ung took it into his head that he would like to go out for a stroll in the country. The entrance, however, was carefully closed; and on asking the reason, the young man told him that his father wished to receive no guests for fear of causing interruption to his studies. So K'ung thought no more about it; and by-and-by, when the heat of summer came on, they moved their study to a pavilion in the garden. At this time Mr. K'ung had a swelling on the chest about as big as a peach, which, in a single night, increased to the size of a bowl. There he lay groaning with the pain, while his pupil waited upon him day and night. He slept badly and took hardly any food; and in a few days the place got so much worse that he could neither eat nor drink. The old gentleman also came in, and he and his son lamented over him together. Then the young man said, "I was thinking last night that my sister, Chiao-no, would be able to cure Mr. K'ung, and accordingly I sent over to my grandmother's asking her to come. She ought to be here by now."

At that moment a servant entered and announced Miss Chiao-no, who had come with her cousin, having been at her aunt's house. Her father and brother ran out to meet her, and then brought her in to see Mr. K'ung. She was between thirteen and fourteen years old, and had beautiful eyes with a very intelligent expression in them, and a most graceful figure besides. No sooner had Mr. K'ung beheld this lovely creature than he quite forgot to groan, and began to brighten up. Meanwhile the young man was saying, "This respected friend of mine is the same to me as a brother. Try, sister, to cure him." Miss Chiao-no immediately dismissed her blushes, and rolling up her long sleeves approached the bed to feel his pulse. As she was grasping his wrist, K'ung became conscious of a perfume more delicate than that of the epidendrum; and then she laughed, saying, "This illness was to be expected; for the heart is touched. Though it is severe, a cure can be effected; but, as there is already a swelling, not without using the knife." Then she drew from her arm a gold bracelet which she pressed down upon the suffering spot, until by degrees the swelling rose within the bracelet and overtopped it by an inch and more, the outlying parts that were inflamed also passing under, and thus very considerably reducing the extent of the tumour. With one hand she opened her robe and took out a knife with an edge as keen as paper, and pressing the bracelet down all the time with the other, proceeded to cut lightly round near the root of the swelling.

The dark blood gushed forth, and stained the bed and the mat; but Mr. K'ung was delighted to be near such a beauty, – not only felt no pain, but would willingly have continued the operation that she might sit by him a little longer. In a few moments the whole thing was removed, and the place looked like the knot on a tree where a branch has been cut away. Here Miss Chiao-no called for water to wash the wound, and from between her lips she took a red pill as big as a bullet, which she laid upon the flesh, and, after drawing the skin together, passed round and round the place. The first turn felt like the searing of a hot iron; the second like a gentle itching; and at the third he experienced a sensation of lightness and coolness which penetrated into his very bones and marrow. The young lady then returned the pill to her mouth, and said, "He is cured," hurrying away as fast as she could.

Mr. K'ung jumped up to thank her, and found that his complaint had quite disappeared. Her beauty, however, had made such an impression on him that his troubles were hardly at an end. From this moment he gave up his books, and took no interest in anything. This state of things was soon noticed by the young man, who said to him, "My brother, I have found a fine match for you."

"Who is it to be?" asked K'ung.

"Oh, one of the family," replied his friend. Thereupon Mr. K'ung remained some time lost in thought, and at length said, "Please don't!" Then turning his face to the wall, he repeated these lines:

> "Speak not of lakes and streams to him who once has seen the sea;
> The clouds that circle Wu's peak are the only clouds for me."

The young man guessed to whom he was alluding, and replied, "My father has a very high opinion of your talents, and would gladly receive you into the family, but that he has only one daughter, and she is much too young. My cousin, Ah-sung, however, is seventeen years old, and not at all a bad-looking girl. If you doubt my word, you can wait in the verandah until she takes her daily walk in the garden, and thus judge for yourself." This Mr. K'ung acceded to, and accordingly saw Miss Chiao-no come out with a lovely girl – her black eyebrows beautifully arched, and her tiny feet encased in phœnix-shaped shoes – as like one another as they well could be. He was of course delighted, and begged the young man to arrange all preliminaries; and the very next day his friend came to tell him that the affair was finally settled. A portion of the house was given up to the bride and bridegroom, and the marriage was celebrated with plenty of music and hosts of guests, more like a fairy wedding than anything else.

Mr. K'ung was very happy, and began to think that the position of Paradise had been wrongly laid down, until one day the young man came to him and said, "For the trouble you have been at in teaching me, I shall ever remain your debtor. At the present moment, the Shan family law-suit has been brought to a termination, and they wish to resume possession of their house immediately. We therefore propose returning to Shen-si, and as it is unlikely that you and I will ever meet again, I feel very sorrowful at the prospect of parting." Mr. K'ung replied that he would go too, but the young man advised him to return to his old home. This, he observed, was no easy matter; upon which the young man said, "Don't let that trouble you: I will see you safe there."

By-and-by his father came in with Mr. K'ung's wife, and presented Mr. K'ung with one hundred ounces of gold; and then the young man gave the husband and wife each one of his hands to grasp, bidding them shut their eyes. The next instant they were floating away in the air, with the wind whizzing in their ears. In a little while he said, "You have arrived," and opening his eyes, K'ung beheld his former home. Then he knew that the young man was not a human being. Joyfully he knocked at the old door, and his mother was astonished to see him arrive with such a nice wife. They were all rejoicing together, when he turned round and found that his friend had disappeared. His wife attended on her mother-in-law with great devotion, and acquired a reputation both for virtue and beauty, which was spread round far and near.

Some time passed away, and then Mr. K'ung took his doctor's degree, and was appointed governor of the gaol in Yen-ngan. He proceeded to his post with his wife only, the journey being too long for his mother, and by-and-by a son was born. Then he got into trouble by being too honest an official, and threw up his appointment; but had not the wherewithal to get home again.

One day when out hunting he met a handsome young man riding on a nice horse, and seeing that he was staring very hard looked closely at him. It was young Huang-fu. So they drew bridle, and fell to laughing and crying by turns, – the young man then inviting K'ung to go along with him. They rode on together until they had reached a village thickly shaded with trees, so that the sun and sky were invisible overhead, and entered into a most elaborately-decorated mansion, such as might belong to an old-established family. K'ung asked after Miss Chiao-no, and heard that she was married; also that his own mother-in-law was dead, at which tidings he was greatly moved. Next day he went back and returned again with his wife. Chiao-no also joined them, and taking up K'ung's child played with it, saying, "Your mother played us truant."

Mr. K'ung did not forget to thank her for her former kindness to him, to which she replied, "You're a great man now. Though the wound has healed, haven't you forgotten the pain yet?" Her husband, too, came to pay his respects, returning with her on the following morning. One day the young Huang-fu seemed troubled in spirit, and said to Mr. K'ung, "A great calamity is impending. Can you help us?" Mr. K'ung did not know what he was alluding to, but readily promised his assistance. The young man then ran out and summoned the whole family to worship in the ancestral hall, at which Mr. K'ung was alarmed, and asked what it all meant.

"You know," answered the young man, "I am not a man but a fox. To-day we shall be attacked by thunder; and if only you will aid us in our trouble, we may still hope to escape. If you are unwilling, take your child and go, that you may not be involved with us." Mr. K'ung protested he would live or die with them, and so the young man placed him with a sword at the door, bidding him remain quiet there in spite of all the thunder. He did as he was told, and soon saw black clouds obscuring the light until it was all as dark as pitch. Looking round, he could see that the house had disappeared, and that its place was occupied by a huge mound and a bottomless pit. In the midst of his terror, a fearful peal was heard which shook the very hills, accompanied by a violent wind and driving rain. Old trees were torn up, and Mr. K'ung became both dazed and deaf. Yet he stood firm until he saw in a dense black column of smoke a horrid thing with a sharp beak and long claws, with which it snatched some one from the hole, and was disappearing up with the smoke.

In an instant K'ung knew by her clothes and shoes that the victim was no other than Chiao-no, and instantly jumping up he struck the devil violently with his sword, and cut it down. Immediately the mountains were riven, and a sharp peal of thunder laid K'ung dead upon the ground. Then the clouds cleared away, and Chiao-no gradually came round, to find K'ung dead at her feet. She burst out crying at the sight, and declared that she would not live since K'ung had died for her. K'ung's wife also came out, and they bore the body inside. Chiao-no then made Ah-sung hold her husband's head, while her brother prised open his teeth with a hair-pin, and she herself arranged his jaw. She next put a red pill into his mouth, and bending down breathed into him. The pill went along with the current of air, and presently there was a gurgle in his throat, and he came round. Seeing all the family about him, he was disturbed as if waking from a dream. However they were all united together, and fear gave place to joy; but Mr. K'ung objected to live in that out-of-the-way place, and proposed that they should return with him to his native village. To this they were only too pleased to assent – all except Chiao-no; and when Mr. K'ung invited her husband, Mr. Wu, as well, she said she feared her father and mother-in-law would not like to lose the children. They had tried all day to persuade her, but without success, when suddenly in rushed one of the Wu family's servants, dripping with perspiration and quite out of breath. They asked what was the matter, and the servant replied that the Wu family had been visited by a calamity on the very same day, and had every one perished. Chiao-no cried very bitterly at this, and could not be comforted; but now there was nothing to prevent them from all returning together. Mr. K'ung went into the city for a few days on business, and then they set to work packing-up night and day. On arriving at their destination, separate apartments were allotted to young Mr. Huang-fu, and these he kept carefully shut up, only opening the door to Mr. K'ung and his wife.

Mr. K'ung amused himself with the young man and his sister Chiao-no, filling up the time with chess, wine, conversation, and good cheer, as if they had been one family. His little boy, Huan, grew up to be a handsome young man, with a fox-like penchant for roaming about; and it was generally known that he was actually the son of a fox.

The Ghost in Love

Pu Songling; translated by George Soulié

ON THE FIFTEENTH DAY of the First Moon, in the second year of the period of 'Renewed Principles', the streets of the town of the Eastern Lake were thronged with people who were strolling about.

At the setting of the sun every shop was brightly lit up; processions of people moved hither and thither; strings of boys were carrying lanterns of every form and colour; whole families passed, every member of whom, young or old, small or big, was holding at the end of a thin bamboo the lighted image of a bird, an animal, or a flower.

Richer ones, several together, were carrying enormous dragons whose luminous wings waved at every motion and whose glaring eyes rolled from right to left. It was the Fête of the Lanterns.

A young man, clothed in a long pale green dress, allowed himself to be pushed about by the crowd; the passers-by bowed to him:

"How is my Lord Li The-peaceful?"

"The humble student thanks you; and you, how are you?"

"Very well, thanks to your happy influence."

"Does the precious student soon pass his second literary examination?"

"In two months; ignorant that I am. I am idling instead of working."

The fête was drawing to a close when The-peaceful quitted the main street, and went towards the East Gate, where the house was to be found in which he lived alone.

He went farther and farther: the moving lights were rarer; ere long he only saw before him the fire of a white lantern decorated with two red peonies. The paper globe was swinging to the steps of a tiny girl clothed in the blue linen that only slaves wore. The light, behind, showed the elegant silhouette of another woman, this one covered with a long jacket made in a rich pink silk edged with purple.

As the student drew nearer, the belated walker turned round, showing an oval face and big long eyes, wherein shone a bright speck, cruel and mysterious.

Li The-peaceful slackened his pace, following the two strangers, whose small feet glided silently on the shining flagstones of the street.

He was asking himself how he could begin a conversation, when the mistress turned round again, softly smiled, and in a low, rich voice, said to him:

"Is it not strange that in the advancing night we are following the same road?"

"I owe it to the favour of Heaven," he at once replied; "for I am returning to the East Gate; otherwise I should never have dared to follow you."

The conversation, once begun, continued as they walked side by side. The student learned that the pretty walker was called 'Double-peony', that she was the daughter of Judge Siu, that she lived out of the city in a garden planted with big trees, on the road to the lake.

On arriving at his house The-peaceful insisted that his new friend should enter and take a cup of tea. She hesitated; then the two young people pushed the door, crossed the small yard bordered right and left with walls covered with tiles, and disappeared in the house....

The servant remained under the portal.

Daylight was breaking when the young girl came out again, calling the servant, who was asleep. The next evening she came again, always accompanied by the slave bearing the white lantern with two red peonies. It was the same each day following.

A neighbour who had watched these nocturnal visits was inquisitive enough to climb the wall which separated his yard from that of the lovers, and to wait, hidden in the shade of the house.

At the accustomed hour the street-door, left ajar, opened to let in the visitors.

Once in the courtyard, they were suddenly transformed, their eyes became flaming and red; their faces grew pale; their teeth seemed to lengthen; an icy mist escaped from their lips.

The neighbour did not see any more: terrified, he let himself slide to the ground and ran to his inner room.

The next morning he went to the student and told him what he had seen. The lover was paralyzed with fear: in order to reassure himself he resolved to find out everything he could about his mistress.

He at once went outside the ramparts, on the road to the lake, hoping to find the house of Judge Siu. But at the place he had been told of there was no habitation; on the left, a fallow plain, sown with tombs, went up to the hills; on the right, cultivated fields extended as far as the lake.

However, a small temple was hidden there under big trees. The student had given up all hope; he entered, notwithstanding, into the sacred enclosure, knowing that travellers stayed there sometimes for several weeks.

In the first yard a bonze was passing in his red dress and shaven head; he stopped him.

"Do you know Judge Siu? He has a daughter—"

"Judge Siu's daughter?" asked the priest, astonished. "Well – yes – but wait, I will show her to you."

The-peaceful felt his heart overflowing with joy; his beloved one was living; he was going to see her by the light of day. He quickly followed his companion.

Passing the first court, they crossed a threshold and found themselves in a yard planted with high pine-trees and bordered by a low pavilion. The bonze, passing in first, pushed a door, and, turning round, said:

"Here is Judge Siu's daughter!"

The other stopped, terrified; on a trestle a heavy black lacquered coffin bore this inscription in golden letters: 'Coffin of Double-peony, Judge Siu's daughter'.

On the wall was an unfolded painting representing the little maid; a white lantern decorated with two red peonies was hung over it.

"Yes, she has been there for the last two years; her parents, according to the rite, are waiting for a favourable day to bury her."

The student silently turned on his heel and went back, not deigning to reply to the mocking bow of the priest.

Evening arrived; he locked himself in, and, covering his head with his blankets, he waited; sleep came to him only at daybreak.

But he could not cease to think of her whom he no longer saw; his heart beat as if to burst, when in the street he perceived the silhouette of a woman which reminded him of his friend.

At last he was incapable of containing himself any longer; one evening he stationed himself behind the door. After a few minutes there was a knock; he opened the door; it was only the little maid:

"My mistress is in tears; why do you never open the door? I come every evening. If you will follow me, perhaps she will forgive you."

The-peaceful, blinded by love, started at once, walking by the light of the white lantern.

* * *

The next day the neighbours, seeing that the student's door was open, and that his house was empty, made a declaration to the governor of the town.

The police made an inquest; they collected the evidence of several people who had been watching the nightly visitors the student had received. The bonze of the temple outside the city walls came to say what he knew. The chief of the police went to the road leading to the lake; he crossed the threshold of the little edifice, passed the first yard and at last opened the door of the pavilion.

Everything was in order, but under the lid of the heavy coffin one could see the corner of the long green dress of the student.

In order to do away with evil influences there was a solemn funeral.

* * *

Ever since this time, on light clear nights, the passers-by often meet the two lovers entwined together, slowly walking on the road which leads to the lake.

Love's-slave

Pu Songling; translated by George Soulié

IN THE CITY-BETWEEN-THE-RIVERS lived a young student named Lan. He had just passed successfully his second literary examination, and, walking in the Street-of-the-precious-stones, asked himself what he would now do in life.

While he was going, looking vacantly at the passers-by, he saw an old friend of his father, and hastened to join his closed fists and to salute him very low, as politeness orders.

"My best congratulations!" answered the old man. "What are you doing in this busy street?"

"Nothing at all; I was asking myself what profession I am now to pursue."

"What profession? Which one would be more honourable than that of teacher? It is the only one an 'elevated man' *Kiu-jen* of the second degree, can pursue. By the by, would you honour my house with your presence? My son is nearly eighteen. He is not half as learned as he should be, and, besides, he has a very bad temper. I feel very old; if I knew you would consent to give him the right direction and be a second father to him, I would not dread so much to die and leave him alone."

Lan bowed and said:

"I am much honoured by your proposition, and I accept it readily. I will go to-morrow to your palace."

Two hours after, a messenger brought to the young man a packet containing one hundred ounces of silver, with a note stating that this comparatively great sum represented his first year's salary.

In the evening he knocked at his pupil's door and was ushered into the sitting-room. The old man introduced him to the whole family: first his son, a lad with a decided look boding no good; then a young and beautiful girl of seventeen, his daughter, called Love's-slave. Lan was struck by the sweet and refined appearance of his pupil's sister.

"The sight of her will greatly help me to stay here," thought he.

The next morning, when his first lesson was ended, he strolled out into the garden, admiring here a flower and there an artificial little waterfall among diminutive mountain-rocks. Behind a bamboo-bush he suddenly saw Love's-slave and was discreetly turning back, when she stopped him by a few words of greeting.

Every day they thus met in the solitude of the flowers and trees and grew to love each other. Lan's task with his pupil was greater and harder than he had supposed; but for Love's-slave's sake, he would never have remained in the house.

After three months the old man fell ill; the doctors were unable to cure him; he died, and was buried in the family ground, behind the house.

When Lan, after the funeral, told his pupil to resume his lessons, he met with such a reception that he went immediately to his room and packed his belongings. Love's-slave, hearing from a servant what had happened, went straight to her lover's room and tried to induce him to stay.

"How can you ask that from me?" said he. "After such an insult, I would consider myself as the basest of men if I stayed. I have 'lost face'; I must go."

The girl, seeing that nothing could prevail upon his resolution, went out of the room, but silently closed and locked the outer gate.

Lan left on a table what remained of the silver given him by the old man, and wrote a note to inform his pupil of his departure.

When he tried the gate and found it locked, he did not know at first what to do. Then he remembered a place where he could easily climb over the enclosure, went there, threw his luggage over the wall, and let himself out in this somewhat undignified way.

Before going back to his house, he went round to the tomb of the old man and burnt some sticks of perfume. Kneeling down, he explained respectfully to the dead what had happened and excused himself for having left unfinished the task he had undertaken. Rising at last, he went away.

The next morning Love's-slave, pleased with her little trick, came to the student's room and looked for him; he was nowhere to be found. She saw the silver on the table, and, reading the note he had left, she understood that he would never come back.

Her grief stifled her; heavy tears at last began running down her rosy cheeks. She took the silver, went straight to her father's tomb, fastened the heavy metal to her feet, and unrolled a sash from her waist. Then, making a knot with the sash round her neck, she climbed up the lower branches of a big fir-tree, fastened the other end of the coloured silk as high as she could and threw herself down. A few minutes afterwards she was dead. She was discovered by a member of the family, and quietly buried in the same enclosure.

Lan, who did not know anything, came back two or three days after to see her. The servants told him the truth. Silently and sullenly, he went to the tomb, and long remained absorbed in his thoughts; dusk was gathering; the first star shone in the sky. All of a sudden, hearing a sound as of somebody laughing, he turned round. Love's-slave was before his eyes.

"I was waiting for you, my love," she said in a strange and muffled voice. "Why are you coming so late?"

As he wanted to kiss her, she stopped him:

"Oh dear! I am dead. But it is decreed that I will come again to life if a magician performs the ceremony prescribed in the *Book-of-Transmutations*."

Immaterial like an evening fog, she disappeared in the growing darkness.

Lan returned immediately to the town, and, entering the first Taoist temple he saw, he explained to the priest what he wanted.

"If she has said it is decreed she should come back to life, we have only to go and open her tomb, while here my disciples will sing the proper chapters of the Book. Let us go now."

Giving some directions to his companions, he took a spade and started with Lan. The moon was shining, so that without any lantern they were able to perform their gloomy task.

Once the heavy lid of the coffin was unscrewed and taken off, the body of the young girl appeared as fresh as if she had been sleeping.

When the cold night-air bathed her face, she raised her head, sneezed, and sat up; looking at Lan, she said in a low voice:

"At last, you have come! I am recalled to life by your love. But now I am feeble; don't speak harshly to me; I could not bear it."

Lan, kissing her lovingly, took her in his arms and brought her to his house. After some days she was able to walk and live like ordinary people do.

They married and lived happily together for a year. Then, one day, Lan, having come back half-drunk from a friend's house, was rebuked by her, and, incensed, pushed her back. She did not say a word but, fainting, she fell down. Blood ran from her nostrils and mouth; nothing could recall her departing spirit.

The Man and the Ghost

A.L. Shelton

As you desire the sun, so you desire your friend's return.
– Tibetan Proverb.

ONCE UPON A TIME a man was walking along a narrow mountain path, when he met a ghost. The ghost turned around at once and walked along beside him. The man was very much frightened, but didn't care to let the ghost know it. Pretty soon they came to a river which had to be crossed, and as there was no bridge or boat both had to swim it. The man, of course, made a good deal of noise, splashing and paddling the water, while the ghost made none at all.

Said the ghost to the man: "How does it happen that you make so much noise in the water?"

The man answered, "Oh, I am a ghost and have a right to make all the noise I want to."

"Well," the ghost replied, "suppose we two become good friends, and if I can help you I will, and if you can ever aid me you will do so."

The man agreed, and as they walked along the ghost asked him what he feared more than anything else in the world. The man said he wasn't afraid of anything he saw, though inwardly quaking all the while. Then he asked the ghost what he was afraid of. "Of nothing at all," said the ghost, "but the wind as it blows through the tall-headed barley fields."

By and by they came near a city, and the ghost said he was going in to town. But the man said he was tired and that he would lie down and sleep a while in the barley field at the edge of the city. The ghost went on into town and played havoc, as ghosts generally do. He proceeded to steal the soul of the king's son and tying it up in a yak hair sack carried it out to the edge of the barley field where the man lay asleep, and called out to him, "Here is the soul of the king's son in this bag. I'll leave it here for a while and you can take care of it for me, as I have a little business elsewhere."

So saying, he put the sack down and went away. The man now disguised himself as a holy lama, begging *tsamba*, and, carrying his prayer wheel and the sack, started for the city. When he arrived he heard at once that the king's son was about to die and he knew what was the matter with him. So he went to the palace begging and the king's chamberlain said to him, "You are a very holy man, perhaps you can do something to help the king's son get well." The man said he would try if they would let him in to see the king.

When the king saw him he said, "If you will heal my son, I'll give you half of all I have, lands, gold, cattle and everything." So the man said he would. He took his yak hair sack, sat down on the ground, cross-legged, as all Buddhists sit, made a little idol of *tsamba* meal, opened the sack and thrust it in, allowing the soul to escape. Then he tied the mouth of the bag with nine knots, blew his breath upon it, said many charms and prayers over it, and while he talked, lo, they brought the king word that the boy was recovering. The father was so pleased and happy, he kept his word and gave the man half of all he possessed. The ghost never, so the story goes, came back or claimed the sack he had left with the man, and the man thought, "Perhaps that is the customary etiquette between a man and a ghost."

Stories Our Parents Told Us

Ayida Shonibar

I ALWAYS LIKED RED, even back when I was still alive. It was one of the things I looked forward to most about my wedding, the rich hue of the bridal shari my mother had picked out for me. The colour of life. Of love. Of blood.

There were other things I anticipated on my wedding day, too, of course. The idea of joining with a life partner, of our bodies and souls coming together for seven lifetimes as we circled the marriage fire, thrilled me. As soon as we were nestled in the privacy of our chambers, my skin prickled with the desire to be touched. Kissed. Revered.

My parents had fawned over my husband's good looks, raved over his charming manners. I can't recall his name anymore. He hadn't appealed to me at first, but I was assured my fondness for him would grow with time. My mother had insisted it would, the same way she'd fallen for my father over the years they'd built our home together.

I had grown up watching my mother find any excuse to work beside my father when he was home, or him going out of his way on trading travels to collect pretty things to gift her upon his return. That was what I wanted for myself, the yearning for another person that engulfed all else.

In the sweet fragrance of the flower garlands draping our marriage bed, I couldn't wait for the happy ending my mother had promised. My shell and coral bangles rattled invitingly as I drew my husband to me.

But everything happened too fast. There was no poetry, no dance. He flipped my petticoats up, finished his part, and turned to put out the candles for the night. I caught his face to stall him, my gesture urging him to attend to me, demanding he take more time with me.

He stared in confusion. Muttered, "Sweet dreams." A moment later, darkness suffused the room, and soon his snores shook the empty space between us.

* * *

On our anniversary, my bridal shari spilled from the closet I was tidying. I tried it on, a desperate attempt to revive the ghost of the excitement I had once felt.

As I dressed, my husband called from outside that he was going fishing. On a whim, I announced I would join him. Rather than stewing in the misery of my loneliness, I would have him suffer the awkward discomfort of my company on this auspicious day.

The lake was deserted that hot, stifling evening. My mood sparked dangerously, volatile like kindling under the sizzling sun.

"Let's go swimming," I said, seeking to disrupt his mundane task.

He gazed at me with his usual disconcertion, not commenting on my peculiar choice of attire. Perhaps he didn't recognise it from our wedding.

I snatched his hand, my coral and shell bangles clacking against each other, and guided him into the murky water. It stirred as if greeting us, egging us on. Our feet ventured deeper until the ground beneath them fell away.

I didn't intend to kill him. I hadn't known then what lived beneath the surface.

Something gripped our ankles, winding like possessed pondweed. My legs slipped free, but my husband gasped as the waves took him.

I tried to swim back to the shore, but his thrashing hands caught me in desperation. His nails dug into my wrist, breaking skin. My own head sank into the whirlpool.

The last thing I saw before the water filled my lungs was my husband's panicked face. My crimson aanchol came undone and drifted in the current, bright like the blood leaking from his tight grasp on me. As the lake dragged our bodies down, I remembered this was the man I would be tied to for the next six reincarnations.

My mouth opened in a wretched scream.

* * *

My mother had told me that after I died, I would pass into the next life.

Instead, released from having to hold breath I no longer needed, I slipped away from my husband's sinking body, which tempted me as little in death as it had in life. Out of habit, I adjusted the scarlet shari over my rotting, waterlogged shoulder, finally noticing the busy underworld of the lake.

All around me, vengeful spirits searched for victims to yank below – as they had claimed us. A gathering of ghosts whose unfulfilled appetites had turned voracious after death.

This is where the monsters who didn't fit my mother's stories came to dwell.

* * *

By the time I clawed my way back to the surface, the sun had risen and set countless times. The moon watched as I hauled myself onto the banks, shell and coral bangles dragging against the uneven ground. My red shari descended into the water behind me, stretching in a long, angry train.

A soft murmuring soothed my inflamed temper. I inched toward the trees from which the noise came. When I peered over a gnarled branch, I discovered a young couple caught in a heated embrace.

The man whispered into the woman's ear, and she blushed prettily. He twirled a strand of her hair around his finger. She turned her head to catch his lips with hers.

My own lip curled as I watched them sharing the sort of affection I had never been granted.

But if this was something I was denied in life, now I could take it for myself.

* * *

I lurked by the trees until the lovers parted. Then I followed her home, increasing my pace until I came close enough to catch the enticing coconut scent drifting from her loose hair.

I reached out my withered hand and latched on, twisting her silky black locks around my bangles covetously. Her head jerked back, beautiful brown eyes widening with terror when she caught sight of me. And when she opened her delicate mouth to scream, I stepped into her inhale before she could utter a sound. She sucked me into herself, and before she could fathom what I had done, the battle was already lost.

My will subdued hers quickly. Her body fell to my command.

* * *

Her sweetheart waited by the same trees the following night. My heart swelled in her chest when I saw him, pounding with anticipation.

I approached him shyly, unsure how to initiate this romantic tryst. It was an experience I didn't have much familiarity with.

Yet.

When he kissed me, I searched for fireworks against my eyelids. As his hand trailed through my hair, I waited for goosebumps to erupt over my skin. He called me his lovely flower, and I wanted a melody to ring through my ears.

I peered at him through my lashes and thought perhaps we weren't close enough for a genuine connection to take root. My parents had held themselves together like palms pressed in a greeting gesture when they hadn't known I was looking. I wrapped my fingers around the lover's neck and pulled him flush to me.

He spluttered, his face turning the deep shade of my wedding shari – a promising sign, surely. I tightened my caress.

When he collapsed in my arms, dead as my husband, I shrieked in rage and relinquished the woman whose love had failed me as bitterly as my own.

* * *

I returned to the lake to cool my fury. Simmering beneath the surface, I watched people dipping their toes and casting out fishing lines and floating in boats far above me. Their voices drifted to the depths below, carrying news from across the region.

They talked of the young raja who had ascended the throne. He was known to seduce many women but refused to choose one for his rani. Years passed, conflict with a neighbouring state worsened, and he agreed to a marriage that would broker peace. His bride was to arrive by royal caravan the following month, for a union so powerful it would shape history.

Night fell that spring, and I climbed out of the lake again. The path I followed expanded gradually into broader roads. In the distance, a cloud of dust heralded the arrival of a large crowd. As I waited, I fixed the pleats in my red shari, a most suitable outfit for this upcoming occasion.

The procession stopped for the evening, setting up tents to camp near a waterfall. Guards surrounded the river's edge to protect the rani's privacy as she bathed gracefully and submerged her head to wash her alluring long hair.

They did not think to shield her from creatures skulking underneath.

* * *

The raja scrutinised me. "You aren't like other people I've met. And I've known plenty." His gaze raked down my shapely form and lingered at my feet. "Your shoes are … the wrong way around. Is this common where you're from?"

I stooped to swap the rani's left sandal with the right, worrying about customs I may have forgotten during my time below water.

"I picked these from my gardens to welcome you." He lifted a bunch of wildflowers, and I distantly recalled my father doting on my mother with presents in another era.

My arms stretched to accept the bouquet, and I brought it to my face to inhale their fragrance. Warmth filled the hollow inside me. "Thank you."

His mouth dropped open. "Is that another norm in your homeland?"

I set the flowers aside, flustered. "Should we retire to bed?"

He sat beside me and brought his lips to my cheek. In our glorious regalia, we were poised as if for a painting. Picture perfect. Royal spouses destined for a great future, to be remembered by the world.

His pulse thrummed beneath his gold-embroidered sherwani, a living clock ticking out the increments of human feelings. If only I could hear it better, gain closer access, I would immerse myself in the intimacy I had craved for over a lifetime.

I reached for the core of his sentiment. His heart.

He cried out as a vivid liquid spilled through his tunic and onto my manicured nails. An indication of his love bursting for me. I dug deeper and waited for the emotion to sweep me off my feet.

A strangled gurgle tore from his throat. Ignoring my needs completely, he collapsed onto the bed, unconscious. Just like my husband had done all those years ago.

Indignantly, I shook him by the shoulders to revive him.

Alerted by his earlier shout, guards threw open the door to the chamber. They took one look at the scene before them and pointed their spears in my direction, obsidian tips quivering in their shaking grips.

My hands flew across the room again, arms extending like fishing line in the sleeves of my wedding blouse, to knock aside the weapons. The guards yelled in horror and shrank away. Stumbling over my toes that protruded from the back of the rani's ungainly feet, I released her body and slithered out of the open window.

As I fled from another spoiled ending, I wept disconsolate tears for the curse of unfulfilled longing my mother's promises had instilled in me, bound to haunt me for the rest of eternity.

* * *

I've lost count of the number of failures. It became an almost mindless routine, discovering a love that defined an era, clambering from the water in my soaked shari like a moth drawn to a flame, only to burn up in disappointment when one man after another betrayed my ardent embrace.

Each time I returned to the lake with a tear-streaked face and broken heart, vowing to never make myself vulnerable again. But years would pass. I would hear of another couple like no other. A handsome man and a stunning woman. And I could not resist claiming what she possessed, the thing I desired with every fibre of my being.

Every time I emerged from the lake, the land above had undergone a transformation from my previous visit. Below the surface, the water suspended us forlorn spirits like a jar of pickled achaar, preserving our essence and wants while the world moved on without us.

For some reason, fate withheld the romance my mother had told me I deserved. Refusing to let me take root. Allowing me to fade into oblivion even as my physical presence refused to let go.

But there were parts of myself I had left to fester out there without realising it. For when an entire garrison of guards witnessed the events of their monarch's death, they recounted my inhuman abilities to anybody who would listen. Tales of my scarlet shari and backward feet, of the sound of my wedding bangles and my unnaturally stretching arms, passed from one generation to the next.

Though I rotted underwater like a piece of discarded debris, I also lived on in humankind through the stories they told of me.

Not residing amongst them, I didn't know this.

* * *

One warm autumn, a cow came to drink from my lake.

People no longer frequented the body of water, which hummed audibly with the growing population of disgruntled ghosts in its depths. But a young woman chased after the errant animal, disturbing our brooding silence.

"Goru!" she huffed, looking dishevelled. Her damp hair tumbled over her shoulder as if she had rushed from bathing to catch the escapee. "There's so much to prepare before my husband returns from his trip, why did you choose today to wreak havoc?"

My ears pricked.

"It's mine," one of the other spirits hissed at my side. "I want the four-legged beast."

"Take it," I replied, "but leave me the wife."

We raced to the surface, fixated on our own goals. The vermilion shari dripped from my advancing legs like a fresh wound, as if an artery had been sliced open and gushed rivulets onto the ground. I curled my fingers into that marvellous hair, revelling in the way its cascade emphasised the lovely figure beneath it. The woman gasped when I held her, horror etched into her contorted features.

But it lasted only a moment. I sank into her with practiced ease, smoothing her modern outfit, settling her distressed composure. Behind me, the cow descended mechanically into the murky water until its body disappeared.

I surveyed the mostly unblemished earth and followed the footprints back to the woman's house.

* * *

"You haven't cooked the rice yet?" the father-in-law asked as soon as I entered the building. "I didn't take down the dry clothes from the line, either. We're very late!"

"No problem. I'll have everything ready before my husband gets here," I said. My arms stretched to retrieve the cooking pot and ingredients from all corners of the kitchen, elongating to rapidly gather the things I needed to put together a nice meal.

The father-in-law's eyes boggled. When I stepped carefully over the threshold to collect the clean laundry from the yard, his stare fell to my feet and narrowed.

"Bouma, you've been rushing around since the crack of dawn," he said. "Why don't you rest and save your energy while I walk to the train station and meet my son?"

I frowned, wanting to be with the husband as soon as possible. I had waited many decades since my last contact with a paramour. In any case, we wouldn't have privacy until he arrived at home, so I didn't argue.

But when the father-in-law came back, it wasn't with his son.

A woman wearing a tunic cropped to the waist – the contemporary fashion – appraised me through the gate that stood ajar. When I reached across the long entryway to open the door, a smirk tilted her mouth, which was painted as deep a red as my wedding shari.

"Shakchunni," she whispered, and held up a rectangular device that emitted a flash of light at me. "It's an honour to meet you at last."

Then she stepped inside and locked the door behind her.

"Who are you?" I demanded. "Where is my husband?"

She watched my approach with a calculated gaze. "No need to keep up the pretence, I know what you are. I'm an exorcist of your kind, a scholar who studies lost spirits and monsters. I've seen them all – the lurking bhoot and roaming pret, the ravenous pishach and violent rakkhosh. All except you, with your backwards feet and elongated arms." Her thick-framed spectacles glinted in the dim light. "I've only heard glorious tales of you, memorised the hypothetical diagrams circulated through online forums. The accounts I read describe you possessing women and murdering their lovers."

"Murder?" I shook my head. "The only thing I've done is search for the affection I'm starved of. I'm a plant in need of watering, not a weapon."

The scholar raised her eyebrows. "The Shakchunni craves love?" She laughed quietly to herself. "Don't we all. After your fruitless attempts, you must know there won't be any lasting romance between you and this husband. You should let him go before you destroy another family."

"I cannot let go of my hope for love. It's the only thing that sustains me."

She stared at me with her inscrutable brown eyes. I considered stepping close to her and wrapping my hands around her sharp cheekbones, leaning in and yanking until she drew me into herself on a shocked inhale. But her dark hair, streaked with scarlet to match her lip colour – perhaps red was her favourite, too – was twisted firmly into a bun and tucked out of my reach.

As if guessing the direction of my thoughts, the scholar retreated. Just when I thought she would unlock the door and leave me in peace, she drew something from her pocket and set it aflame.

I recoiled, covering my face. "What is that awful smell?"

"Turmeric." She grinned. "You might be something of a legend in my course of study, but at the end of the day, you're still one more ghost with a ghostly weakness."

Choking on the acrid air, I backed into a wall. "Stop!"

"You won't need to breathe once you release her."

Sobbing with desperation, I climbed out of the woman's body the way I had hoisted myself out of the lake. Her form thudded against the floor as she regained her consciousness and bearings.

The scholar moved toward me, but I shoved past her and broke down the door in my haste to escape the toxic fumes and my shattered dreams.

* * *

Her voice roused me from my morose weeping at the bottom of the lake.

"Shakchunni," she wheedled. "I know you're in there. The lady you possessed told me where you appeared from. Won't you come up and say hello?"

With the sharp bite of the scholar's turmeric still burning in my throat, I pressed my mouth resolutely shut.

She returned the next day, skipping stones across the water as if to provoke a reaction. "Will you linger here forever, snuffing out the lives of men who don't provide the happy ending you feel owed? You know I can't let you do that."

One of the bhoots glared at me. "Can I take her, if you won't?"

I shrugged petulantly.

The spirit cackled in glee and soared to the surface. Through the fractured evening light, something glowed hot and menacing against the dark sky.

A scream pierced the night. Before I could wonder whether the ghost had gotten the scholar after all, it plummeted back into the depths with smoke emanating from the general vicinity of its head.

"That one's a vicious monster," it snarled, "that even we demons must shun."

* * *

She stopped by the lake every day, taunting and coaxing me to reveal myself. She teased me with stories of my failed dalliance with the raja, of my first lover, of the dozens who had come after. Her details were skewed in places, some of the tales incomplete, but she did indeed know who I was.

I ventured toward her voice, hovering just beneath the surface to steal glances at her. She peered into the darkness, unable to see me but searching with a fervour I recognised. Once or twice, her attention almost tempted me to breach the surface.

As I watched her one evening, a strange chirping interrupted her cajoling. She held her light-emitting rectangular device to her ear. "Ma's in hospital? I'll be right there."

She hasn't come back since.

* * *

After days of silence, I grow frustrated. Wondering if this is a trap to lure me out, I raise myself warily onto the bank.

It's deserted.

A panic claws at my chest like a vacuum created from a space newly emptied. I weave through the trees, red shari dragging behind me, until I stumble upon a woman napping in the grass. Her open hair fans around her face in a halo.

I grab it.

Her eyes shoot open, mouth soon following, and I hurl myself into her without pausing to care about her romantic circumstances.

I retrace my steps to the house with the family that has – *had* – the cow. When I knock, the father-in-law answers.

"I'm looking for the scholar who studies monsters and spirits," I say. "It's urgent, and I heard you know where to find her."

He gives me her address. When I arrive there, the neighbour explains she's scattering her mother's ashes at the local beach.

The skies tip down their last monsoon showers of the year. A lone figure braves the downpour, the red highlights in her loose hair calling to me like a beacon.

"I never got to bid my family farewell." I gesture at her urn.

The scholar wipes wet hair and more from her eyes. "It can be bittersweet if you do."

"Why?"

"My mother didn't like my interests. She worried. Said I should live life to the fullest instead of withering into darkness with creatures who don't know how to be properly alive."

"It sounds like you discovered your true passion and pursued it. I'm sure your mother would have been happy for you if she understood," I offer. "Mine told me where to seek joy, but I never succeeded."

The scholar looks at me. "You've still got time."

The rain pulls her bangs into her eyes again. Instinctively, I reach out to brush them away, breaching the distance between us with my extending arm. My fingers linger in her drenched hair, gently feeling the soft texture against my skin.

"It's you," she breathes, and I realise my mistake.

I propel the vessel body at her. In her moment of distraction, I throw myself into the sea and disappear into its depths.

* * *

"Show yourself, Shakchunni," the scholar says. "You already revealed something to me that nobody else knows. Is it true? Your mother taught you the love you can't let go?"

I touch a finger to the surface. She notices the ripple.

"I won't hurt you if you remain in your own form," she says. "What are you afraid of?"

Her bronze skin is taut, eyes alight in a way mine haven't been since the day I died. I'm the kind of monster her mother wanted to keep her from.

"I want to see you," she says. "The real you."

Her words pull me from the water like an angler reeling in their catch. Her lips part when I emerge, her smouldering gaze drinking in my shari and matching bangles.

I sift corroded fingers through her streaked hair, marvelling at her beauty. She stands so close that my arms don't elongate.

"You're majestic." Her words whisper against my face.

Then she leans into me, hesitating to ask permission, and when I nod, her lips are on mine and exploding the world. She opens her mouth, makes me a part of her. I don't have to thwart her consciousness or take over her body – she's part of me, too.

Her kiss sears through me, the rush of red intense behind my closed eyelids.

And finally, I can let go.

The Procession of Ghosts

Richard Gordon Smith

SOME FOUR OR FIVE HUNDRED YEARS AGO there was an old temple not far from Fushimi, near Kyoto. It was called the Shozenji temple, and had been deserted for many years, priests fearing to live there, on account of the ghosts which were said to haunt it. Still, no one had ever seen the ghosts. No doubt the story came into the people's minds from the fact that the whole of the priests had been killed by a large band of robbers many years beyond the memory of men – for the sake of loot, of course.

So great a horror did this strike into the minds of all, that the temple was allowed to rot and run to ruin.

One year a priest, a pilgrim and a stranger, passed by the temple, and, not knowing its history, went in and sought refuge from the weather, instead of continuing his journey to Fushimi. Having cold rice in his wallet, he felt that he could not do better than pass the night there; for, though the weather might be cold, he would at all events save drenching the only clothes which he had, and be well off in the morning.

The good man took up his quarters in one of the smaller rooms, which was in less bad repair than the rest of the place; and, after eating his meal, said his prayers and lay down to sleep, while the rain fell in torrents on the roof and the wind howled through the creaky buildings. Try as he might, the priest could not sleep, for the cold draughts chilled him to the marrow. Somewhere about midnight the old man heard weird and unnatural noises. They seemed to proceed from the main building.

Prompted by curiosity, he arose; and when he got to the main building he found *Hiyakki Yakô* (meaning a procession of one hundred ghosts) – a term, I believe, which had been generally applied to a company of ghosts. The ghosts fought, wrestled, danced, and made merry. Though greatly alarmed at first, our priest became interested. After a few moments, however, more awful spirit-like ghosts came on the scene. The priest ran back to the small room, into which he barred himself; and he spent the rest of the night saying masses for the souls of the dead.

At daybreak, though the weather continued wet, the priest departed. He told the villagers what he had seen, and they spread the news so widely that within three or four days the temple was known as the worst-haunted temple in the neighbourhood.

It was at this time that the celebrated painter Tosa Mitsunobu heard of it. Having ever been anxious to paint a picture of *Hiyakki Yakô*, he thought that a sight of the ghosts in Shozenji temple might give him the necessary material: so off to Fushimi and Shozenji he started.

Mitsunobu went straight to the temple at dusk, and sat up all night in no very happy state of mind; but he saw no ghosts, and heard no noise.

Next morning he opened all the windows and doors and flooded the main temple with light. No sooner had he done this than he found the walls of the place covered, as it were, with the figures or drawings of ghosts of indescribable complexity. There were far more than two hundred, and all different.

Could he but remember them! That was what Tosa Mitsunobu thought. Drawing his notebook and brush from his pocket, he proceeded to take them down minutely. This occupied the best part of the day.

During his examination of the outlines of the various ghosts and goblins which he had drawn, Mitsunobu saw that the fantastic shapes had come from cracks in the damp deserted walls; these cracks were filled with fungi and mildew, which in their turn produced the toning, colouring, and eventually the figures from which he compiled his celebrated picture *Hiyakki Yakô*. Grateful was he to the imaginative priest whose stories had led him to the place. Without him never would the picture have been drawn; never could the horrible aspects of so many ghosts and goblins have entered the mind of one man, no matter how imaginative.

Ghost Story of the Flute's Tomb

Richard Gordon Smith

LONG AGO, at a small and out-of-the-way village called Kumedamura, about eight miles to the south-east of Sakai city, in Idsumo Province, there was made a tomb, the *Fuezuka* or Flute's Tomb, and to this day many people go thither to offer up prayer and to worship, bringing with them flowers and incense-sticks, which are deposited as offerings to the spirit of the man who was buried there. All the year round people flock to it. There is no season at which they pray more particularly than at another.

The *Fuezuka* tomb is situated on a large pond called Kumeda, some five miles in circumference, and all the places around this pond are known as of Kumeda Pond, from which the village of Kumeda took its name.

Whose tomb can it be that attracts such sympathy? The tomb itself is a simple stone pillar, with nothing artistic to recommend it. Neither is the surrounding scenery interesting; it is flat and ugly until the mountains of Kiushu are reached. I must tell, as well as I can, the story of whose tomb it is.

Between seventy and eighty years ago there lived near the pond in the village of Kumedamura a blind *amma* called Yoichi. Yoichi was extremely popular in the neighbourhood, being very honest and kind, besides being quite a professor in the art of massage – a treatment necessary to almost every Japanese. It would be difficult indeed to find a village that had not its *amma*.

Yoichi was blind, and, like all men of his calling, carried an iron wand or stick, also a flute or '*fuezuka*' – the stick to feel his way about with, and the flute to let people know he was ready for employment. So good an *amma* was Yoichi, he was nearly always employed, and, consequently, fairly well off, having a little house of his own and one servant, who cooked his food.

A little way from Yoichi's house was a small teahouse, placed upon the banks of the pond. One evening (April 5th; cherry-blossom season), just at dusk, Yoichi was on his way home, having been at work all day. His road led him by the pond. There he heard a girl crying piteously. He stopped and listened for a few moments, and gathered from what he heard that the girl was about to drown herself. Just as she entered the lake Yoichi caught her by the dress and dragged her out.

"Who are you, and why in such trouble as to wish to die?" he asked.

"I am Asayo, the teahouse girl," she answered. "You know me quite well. You must know, also, that it is not possible for me to support myself out of the small pittance which is paid by my master. I have eaten nothing for two days now, and am tired of my life."

"Come, come!" said the blind man. "Dry your tears. I will take you to my house, and do what I can to help you. You are only twenty-five years of age, and I am told still a fair-looking girl. Perhaps you will marry! In any case, I will take care of you, and you must not think of killing yourself. Come with me now; and I will see that you are well fed, and that dry clothes are given you."

So Yoichi led Asayo to his home.

A few months found them wedded to each other. Were they happy? Well, they should have been, for Yoichi treated his wife with the greatest kindness; but she was unlike her husband. She was selfish, bad-tempered, and unfaithful. In the eyes of Japanese infidelity is the worst of sins. How much more, then, is it against the country's spirit when advantage is taken of a husband who is blind?

Some three months after they had been married, and in the heat of August, there came to the village a company of actors. Among them was Sawamura Tamataro, of some repute in Asakusa.

Asayo, who was very fond of a play, spent much of her time and her husband's money in going to the theatre. In less than two days she had fallen violently in love with Tamataro. She sent him money, hardly earned by her blind husband. She wrote to him love-letters, begged him to allow her to come and visit him, and generally disgraced her sex.

Things went from bad to worse. The secret meetings of Asayo and the actor scandalized the neighbourhood. As in most such cases, the husband knew nothing about them. Frequently, when he went home, the actor was in his house, but kept quiet, and Asayo let him out secretly, even going with him sometimes.

Every one felt sorry for Yoichi; but none liked to tell him of his wife's infidelity.

One day Yoichi went to shampoo a customer, who told him of Asayo's conduct. Yoichi was incredulous.

"But yes: it is true," said the son of his customer. "Even now the actor Tamataro is with your wife. So soon as you left your house he slipped in. This he does every day, and many of us see it. We all feel sorry for you in your blindness, and should be glad to help you to punish her."

Yoichi was deeply grieved, for he knew that his friends were in earnest; but, though blind, he would accept no assistance to convict his wife. He trudged home as fast as his blindness would permit, making as little noise as possible with his staff.

On reaching home Yoichi found the front door fastened from the inside. He went to the back, and found the same thing there. There was no way of getting in without breaking a door and making a noise. Yoichi was much excited now; for he knew that his guilty wife and her lover were inside, and he would have liked to kill them both. Great strength came to him, and he raised himself bit by bit until he reached the top of the roof. He intended to enter the house by letting himself down through the '*tem-mado*'. Unfortunately, the straw rope he used in doing this was rotten, and gave way, precipitating him below, where he fell on the *kinuta*. He fractured his skull, and died instantly.

Asayo and the actor, hearing the noise, went to see what had happened, and were rather pleased to find poor Yoichi dead. They did not report the death until next day, when they said that Yoichi had fallen downstairs and thus killed himself.

They buried him with indecent haste, and hardly with proper respect.

Yoichi having no children, his property, according to the Japanese law, went to his bad wife, and only a few months passed before Asayo and the actor were married. Apparently they were happy, though none in the village of Kumeda had any sympathy for them, all being disgusted at their behaviour to the poor blind shampooer Yoichi.

Months passed by without event of any interest in the village. No one bothered about Asayo and her husband; and they bothered about no one else, being sufficiently interested in themselves. The scandal-mongers had become tired, and, like all nine-day wonders, the history of the blind *amma*, Asayo, and Tamataro had passed into silence.

However, it does not do to be assured while the spirit of the injured dead goes unavenged.

Up in one of the western provinces, at a small village called Minato, lived one of Yoichi's friends, who was closely connected with him. This was Okuda Ichibei. He and Yoichi had been to school together. They had promised when Ichibei went up to the north-west always to remember each other, and to help each other in time of need, and when Yoichi had become blind Ichibei came down to Kumeda and helped to start Yoichi in his business of *amma*, which he did by giving him a house to live in – a house which had been bequeathed to Ichibei. Again fate decreed that it should be in Ichibei's power to help his friend. At that time news travelled very slowly, and Ichibei had not immediately heard of Yoichi's death or even of his marriage. Judge, then, of his surprise, one night on awaking, to find, standing near his pillow, the figure of a man whom by and by he recognized as Yoichi!

"Why, Yoichi! I am glad to see you," he said; "but how late at night you have arrived! Why did you not let me know you were coming? I should have been up to receive you, and there would have been a hot meal ready. But never mind. I will call a servant, and everything shall be ready as soon as possible. In the meantime be seated, and tell me about yourself, and how you travelled so far. To have come through the mountains and other wild country from Kumeda is hard enough at best; but for one who is blind it is wonderful."

"I am no longer a living man," answered the ghost of Yoichi (for such it was). "I am indeed your friend Yoichi's spirit, and I shall wander about until I can be avenged for a great ill which has been done me. I have come to beg of you to help me, that my spirit may go to rest. If you listen I will tell my story, and you can then do as you think best."

Ichibei was very much astonished (not to say a little nervous) to know that he was in the presence of a ghost; but he was a brave man, and Yoichi had been his friend. He was deeply grieved to hear of Yoichi's death, and realized that the restlessness of his spirit showed him to have been injured. Ichibei decided not only to listen to the story but also to revenge Yoichi, and said so.

The ghost then told all that had happened since he had been set up in the house at Kumedamura. He told of his success as a masseur; of how he had saved the life of Asayo, how he had taken her to his house and subsequently married her; of the arrival of the accursed acting company which contained the man who had ruined his life; of his own death and hasty burial; and of the marriage of Asayo and the actor. "I must be avenged. Will you help me to rest in peace?" he said in conclusion.

Ichibei promised. Then the spirit of Yoichi disappeared, and Ichibei slept again.

Next morning Ichibei thought he must have been dreaming; but he remembered the vision and the narrative so clearly that he perceived them to have been actual. Suddenly turning with the intention to get up, he caught sight of the shine of a metal flute close to his pillow. It was the flute of a blind *amma*. It was marked with Yoichi's name.

Ichibei resolved to start for Kumedamura and ascertain locally all about Yoichi.

In those times, when there was no railway and a rickshaw only here and there, travel was slow. Ichibei took ten days to reach Kumedamura. He immediately went to the house of his friend Yoichi, and was there told the whole history again, but naturally in another way. Asayo said:

"Yes: he saved my life. We were married, and I helped my blind husband in everything. One day, alas, he mistook the staircase for a door, falling down and killing himself. Now I am married to his great friend, an actor called Tamataro, whom you see here."

Ichibei knew that the ghost of Yoichi was not likely to tell him lies, and to ask for vengeance unjustly. Therefore he continued talking to Asayo and her husband, listening to their lies, and wondering what would be the fitting procedure.

Ten o'clock passed thus, and eleven. At twelve o'clock, when Asayo for the sixth or seventh time was assuring Ichibei that everything possible had been done for her blind husband, a wind storm suddenly arose, and in the midst of it was heard the sound of the *amma*'s flute, just as Yoichi played it; it was so unmistakably his that Asayo screamed with fear.

At first distant, nearer and nearer approached the sound, until at last it seemed to be in the room itself. At that moment a cold puff of air came down the *tem-mado*, and the ghost of Yoichi was seen standing beneath it, a cold, white, glimmering and sad-faced wraith.

Tamataro and his wife tried to get up and run out of the house; but they found that their legs would not support them, so full were they of fear.

Tamataro seized a lamp and flung it at the ghost; but the ghost was not to be moved. The lamp passed through him, and broke, setting fire to the house, which burned instantly, the wind fanning the flames.

Ichibei made his escape; but neither Asayo nor her husband could move, and the flames consumed them in the presence of Yoichi's ghost. Their cries were loud and piercing.

Ichibei had all the ashes swept up and placed in a tomb. He had buried in another grave the flute of the blind *amma*, and erected on the ground where the house had been a monument sacred to the memory of Yoichi.

It is known as FUEZUKA NO KWAIDAN ('The Flute Ghost Tomb').

The Spirit of Yenoki

Richard Gordon Smith

THERE IS A MOUNTAIN in the province of Idsumi called Oki-yama (or Oji Yam a); it is connected with the Mumaru-Yama mountains. I will not vouch that I am accurate in spelling either. Suffice it to say that the story was told to me by Fukuga Sei, and translated by Mr. Ando, the Japanese translator of our Consulate at Kobe. Both of these give the mountain's name as Okiyama, and say that on the top of it from time immemorial there has been a shrine dedicated to Fudo-myo-o (*Achala*, in Sanskrit, which means 'immovable', and is the god always represented as surrounded by fire and sitting uncomplainingly on as an example to others; he carries a sword in one hand, and a rope in the other, as a warning that punishment awaits those who are unable to overcome with honour the painful struggles of life).

Well, at the top of Oki-yama (high or big mountain) is this very old temple to Fudo, and many are the pilgrimages which are made there annually. The mountain itself is covered with forest, and there are some remarkable cryptomerias, camphor and pine trees.

Many years ago, in the days of which I speak, there were only a few priests living up at this temple. Among them was a middle-aged man, half-priest, half-caretaker, called Yenoki. For twenty years had Yenoki lived at the temple; yet during that time he had never cast eyes on the figure of Fudo, over which he was partly set to guard; it was kept shut in a shrine and never seen by any one but the head priest. One day Yenoki's curiosity got the better of him. Early in the morning the door of the shrine was not quite closed. Yenoki looked in, but saw nothing. On turning to the light again, he found that he had lost the use of the eye that had looked: he was stone-blind in the right eye.

Feeling that the divine punishment served him well, and that the gods must be angry, he set about purifying himself, and fasted for one hundred days. Yenoki was mistaken in his way of devotion and repentance, and did not pacify the gods; on the contrary, they turned him into a *tengu* (long-nosed devil who dwells in mountains, and is the great teacher of *jujitsu*).

But Yenoki continued to call himself a priest – 'Ichigan Hoshi', meaning the one-eyed priest – for a year, and then died; and it is said that his spirit passed into an enormous cryptomeria tree on the east side of the mountain. After that, when sailors passed the Chinu Sea (Osaka Bay), if there was a storm they used to pray to the one-eyed priest for help, and if a light was seen on the top of Oki-yama they had a sure sign that, no matter how rough the sea, their ship would not be lost.

It may be said, in fact, that after the death of the one-eyed priest more importance was attached to his spirit and to the tree into which it had taken refuge than to the temple itself. The tree was called the Lodging of the One-eyed Priest, and no one dared approach It – not even the woodcutters who were familiar with the mountains. It was a source of awe and an object of reverence.

At the foot of Oki-yama was a lonely village, separated from others by fully two *ri* (five miles), and there were only one hundred and thirty houses in it.

Every year the villagers used to celebrate the 'Bon' by engaging, after it was over, in the dance called 'Bon Odori'. Like most other things in Japan, the 'Bon' and the 'Bon Odori' were in extreme contrast. The Bon' was a ceremony arranged for the spirits of the dead, who are supposed to return to earth for three days annually, to visit their family shrines – something like our All Saints' Day, and in any case quite a serious religious performance. The 'Bon Odori' is a dance which varies considerably in different provinces. It is confined mostly to villages – for one cannot count the pretty *geisha* dances in Kyoto which are practically copies of it. It is a dance of boys and girls, one may say, and continues nearly all night on the village green. For the three or four nights that it lasts, opportunities for flirtations of the most violent kind are plentiful. There are no chaperons (so to speak), and (to put it vulgarly) every one 'goes on the bust'! Hitherto-virtuous maidens spend the night out as impromptu sweethearts; and, in the village of which this story is told, not only is it they who let themselves go, but even young brides also.

So it came to pass that the village at the foot of Oki-yama mountain – away so far from other villages – was a bad one morally. There was no restriction to what a girl might do or what she might not do during the nights of the 'Bon Odori'. Things went from bad to worse until, at the time of which I write, anarchy reigned during the festive days. At last it came to pass that after a particularly festive 'Bon', on a beautiful moonlight night in August, the well-beloved and charming daughter of Kurahashi Yozaemon, O Kimi, aged eighteen years, who had promised her lover Kurosuke that she would meet him secretly that evening, was on her way to do so. After passing the last house in her mountain village she came to a thick copse, and standing at the edge of it was a man whom O Kimi at first took to be her lover. On approaching she found that it was not Kurosuke, but a very handsome youth of twenty-three years. He did not speak to her; in fact, he kept a little away. If she advanced, he receded. So handsome was the youth, O Kimi felt that she loved him. "Oh how my heart beats for him!" said she. "After all, why should I not give up Kurosuke? He is not good-looking like this man, whom I love already before I have even spoken to him. I hate Kurosuke, now that I see this man."

As she said this she saw the figure smiling and beckoning, and, being a wicked girl, loose in her morals, she followed him and was seen no more. Her family were much exercised in their minds. A week passed, and O Kimi San did not return.

A few days later Tamae, the sixteen-year-old daughter of Kinsaku, who was secretly in love with the son of the village Headman, was awaiting him in the temple grounds, standing the while by the stone figure of Jizodo (Sanskrit, *Kshitigarbha*, Patron of Women and Children). Suddenly there stood near Tamae a handsome youth of twenty-three years, as in the case of O Kimi; she was greatly struck by the youth's beauty, so much so that when he took her by the hand and led her off she made no effort to resist, and she also disappeared.

And thus it was that nine girls of amorous nature disappeared from this small village. Everywhere for thirty miles round people talked and wondered, and said unkind things.

In Oki-yama village itself the elder people said:

"Yes: it must be that our children's immodesty since the 'Bon Odori' has angered Yenoki San: perhaps it is he himself who appears in the form of this handsome youth and carries off our daughters."

Nearly all agreed in a few days that they owed their losses to the Spirit of the Yenoki Tree; and as soon as this notion had taken root the whole of the villagers locked and barred themselves in their houses both day and night. Their farms became neglected; wood was not being cut on the mountain; business was at a standstill. The rumour of this state of affairs spread, and the Lord of Kishiwada, becoming uneasy, summoned Sonobé Hayama, the most celebrated swordsman in that part of Japan.

"Sonobé, you are the bravest man I know of, and the best fighter. It is for you to go and inspect the tree where lodges the spirit of Yenoki. You must use your own discretion. I cannot advise as to what it is best that you should do. I leave it to you to dispose of the mystery of the disappearances of the nine girls."

"My lord," said Sonobé, "my life is at your lordship's call. I shall either clear the mystery or die."

After this interview with his master Sonobé went home. He put himself through a course of cleansing. He fasted and bathed for a week, and then repaired to Oki-yama.

This was in the month of October, when to me things always look their best. Sonobé ascended the mountain, and went first to the temple, which he reached at three o'clock in the afternoon, after a hard climb. Here he said prayers before the god Fudo for fully half an hour. Then he set out to cross the short valley which led up to the Oki-yama mountain, and to the tree which held the spirit of the one-eyed priest, Yenoki.

It was a long and steep climb, with no paths, for the mountain was avoided as much as possible by even the most adventurous of woodcutters, none of whom ever dreamed of going up as far as the Yenoki tree. Sonobé was in good training and a bold warrior. The woods were dense; there was a chilling damp, which came from the spray of a high waterfall. The solitude was intense, and once or twice Sonobé put his hand on the hilt of his sword, thinking that he heard some one following in the gloom; but there was no one, and by five o'clock Sonobé had reached the tree and addressed it thus:

"Oh, honourable and aged tree, that has braved centuries of storm, thou hast become the home of Yenoki's spirit. In truth there is much honour in having so stately a lodging, and therefore he cannot have been so bad a man. I have come from the Lord of Kishiwada to upbraid him, however, and to ask what means it that Yenoki's spirit should appear as a handsome youth for the purpose of robbing poor people of their daughters. This must not continue; else you, as the lodging of Yenoki's spirit, will be cut down, so that it may escape to another part of the country."

At that moment a warm wind blew on the face of Sonobé, and dark clouds appeared overhead, rendering the forest dark; rain began to fall, and the rumblings of earthquake were heard.

Suddenly the figure of an old priest appeared in ghostly form, wrinkled and thin, transparent and clammy, nerve-shattering; but Sonobé had no fear.

"You have been sent by the Lord of Kishiwada," said the ghost. "I admire your courage for coming. So cowardly and sinful are most men, they fear to come near where my spirit has taken refuge. I can assure you that I do no evil to the good. So bad had morals become in the village, it was time to give a lesson. The villagers' customs defied the gods. It is true that I, hoping to improve these people and make them godly, assumed the form of a youth, and carried away nine of the worst of them. They are quite well. They deeply regret their sins, and will reform their village. Every day I have given them lectures. You will find them on the 'Mino toge', or second summit of this mountain, tied to trees. Go there and release them, and afterwards tell the Lord of Kishiwada what the spirit of Yenoki, the one-eyed priest, has done, and that it is always ready to help him to improve his people. Farewell!"

No sooner had the last word been spoken than the spirit vanished. Sonobé, who felt somewhat dazed by what the spirit had said, started off nevertheless to the 'Mino toge'; and there, sure enough, were the nine girls, tied each to a tree, as the spirit had said. He cut their bonds, gave them a lecture, took them back to the village, and reported to the Lord of Kishiwada.

Since then the people have feared more than ever the spirit of the one-eyed priest. They have become completely reformed, an example to the surrounding villages. The nine houses or families whose daughters behaved so badly contribute annually the rice eaten by the priests of Fudo-myo-o Temple. It is spoken of as 'the nine-families rice of Oki'.

The Spirit of the Lotus Lily

Richard Gordon Smith

FOR SOME TIME I have been hunting for a tale about the lotus lily. My friend Fukuga has at last found one which is said to date back some two hundred years. It applies to a castle that was then situated in what was known as Kinai, now incorporated into what may be known as the Kyoto district. Probably it refers to one of the castles in that neighbourhood, though I myself know of only one, which is now called Nijo Castle.

Fukuga (who does not speak English) and my interpreter made it very difficult for me to say that the story does not really belong to a castle in the province of Idzumi, for after starting it in Kyoto they suddenly brought me to Idzumi, making the hero of it the Lord of Koriyama. In any case, I was first told that disease and sickness broke out in Kinai (Kyoto). Thousands of people died of it. It spread to Idzumi, where the feudal Lord of Koriyama lived, and attacked him also. Doctors were called from all parts; but it was no use. The disease spread, and, to the dismay of all, not only the Lord of Koriyama but also his wife and child were stricken.

There was a panic terror in the country – not that the people feared for themselves, but because they were in dread that they might lose their lord and his wife and child. The Lord Koriyama was much beloved. People flocked to the castle. They camped round its high walls, and in its empty moats, which were dry, there having been no war for some time.

One day, during the illness of this great family, Tada Samon, the highest official in the castle (next to the Lord Koriyama himself), was sitting in his room, thinking what was best to be done on the various questions that were awaiting the *Daimio*'s recovery. While he was thus engaged, a servant announced that there was a visitor at the outer gate who requested an interview, saying that he thought he could cure the three sufferers.

Tada Samon would see the caller, whom the servant shortly after fetched.

The visitor turned out to be a *yamabushi* (mountain recluse) in appearance, and on entering the room bowed low to Samon, saying:

"Sir, it is an evil business – this illness of our lord and master – and it has been brought about by an evil spirit, who has entered the castle because you have put up no defence against impure and evil spirits. This castle is the centre of administration for the whole of the surrounding country, and it was unwise to allow it to remain un-fortified against impure and evil spirits. The saints of old have always told us to plant the lotus lily, not only in the one inner ditch surrounding a castle, but also in both ditches or in as many as there be, and, moreover, to plant them all around the ditches. Surely, sir, you know that the lotus, being the most emblematic flower in our religion, must be the most pure and sacred; for this reason it drives away uncleanness, which cannot cross it. Be assured, sir, that if your lord had not neglected the northern ditches of his castle, but had kept them filled with water, clean, and had planted the sacred lotus, no such evil spirit would have come as the present sent by Heaven to warn him. If I am allowed to do so, I shall enter the castle to-day and pray that the evil spirit of sickness leave; and I ask that I may be allowed to plant lotuses in the northern moats. Thus only can the Lord of Koriyama and his family be saved."

Samon nodded in answer, for he now remembered that the northern moats had neither lotus nor water, and that this was partly his fault – a matter of economy in connection with the estates. He interviewed his master, who was more sick than ever. He called all the court officials. It was decided that the *yamabushi* should have his way. He was told to carry out his ideas as he thought best. There was plenty of money, and there were hundreds of hands ready to help him – anything to save the master.

The *yamabushi* washed his body, and prayed that the evil spirit of sickness should leave the castle. Subsequently he superintended the cleansing and repairing of the northern moats, directing the people to fill them with water and plant lotuses. Then he disappeared mysteriously – vanished almost before the men's eyes. Wonderingly, but with more energy than ever, the men worked to carry out the orders. In less than twenty-four hours the moats had been cleaned, repaired, filled, and planted.

As was to be expected, the Lord Koriyama, his wife, and son became rapidly better. In a week all were able to be up, and in a fortnight they were as well as ever they had been.

Thanksgivings were held, and there were great rejoicings all over Idzumi. Later, people flocked to see the splendidly-kept moats of lotuses, and the villagers went so far as to rename among themselves the castle, calling it the Lotus Castle.

Some years passed before anything strange happened. The Lord Koriyama had died from natural causes, and had been succeeded by his son, who had neglected the lotus roots. A young *samurai* was passing along one of the moats. This was at the end of August, when the flowers of the lotus are strong and high. The *samurai* suddenly saw two beautiful boys, about six or seven years of age, playing at the edge of the moat.

"Boys," said he, "it is not safe to play so near the edge of this moat. Come along with me."

He was about to take them by the hand and lead them off to a safer place, when they sprang into the air a little way, smiling at him the while, and fell into the water, where they disappeared with a great splash that covered him with spray.

So astonished was the *samurai*, he hardly knew what to think, for they did not reappear. He made sure they must be two kappas (mythical animals), and with this idea in his mind he ran to the castle and gave information.

The high officials held a meeting, and arranged to have the moats dragged and cleaned; they felt that this should have been done when the young lord had succeeded his father.

The moats were dragged accordingly from end to end; but no kappa was found. They came to the conclusion that the *samurai* had been indulging in fancies, and he was chaffed in consequence.

Some few weeks later another *samurai*, Murata Ippai, was returning in the evening from visiting his sweetheart, and his road led along the outer moat. The lotus blossoms were luxuriant; and Ippai sauntered slowly on, admiring them and thinking of his lady-love, when suddenly he espied a dozen or more of the beautiful little boys playing near the water's edge. They had no clothing on, and were splashing one another with water.

"Ah!" reflected the *samurai*, "these, surely, are the kappas, of which we were told before. Having taken the form of human beings, they think to deceive me! A *samurai* is not frightened by such as they, and they will find it difficult to escape the keen edge of my sword."

Ippai cast off his clogs, and, drawing his sword, proceeded stealthily to approach the supposed kappas. He approached until he was within some twenty yards, then he remained hidden behind a bush, and stood for a minute to observe.

The children continued their play. They seemed to be perfectly natural children, except that they were all extremely beautiful, and from them was wafted a peculiar scent, almost powerful, but sweet, and resembling that of the lotus lily. Ippai was puzzled, and was almost inclined to sheathe his sword on seeing how innocent and unsuspecting the children looked; but he thought that he would not be acting up to the determination of a *samurai* if he changed his mind. Gripping his sword with renewed vigour, therefore, he dashed out from his hiding-place and slashed right and left among the supposed kappas.

Ippai was convinced that he had done much slaughter, for he had felt his sword strike over and over again, and had heard the dull thuds of things falling; but when he looked about to see what he had killed there arose a peculiar vapour of all colours which almost blinded him by its brilliance. It fell in a watery spray all round him.

Ippai determined to wait until the morning, for he could not, as a *samurai*, leave such an adventure unfinished; nor, indeed, would he have liked to recount it to his friends unless he had seen the thing clean through.

It was a long and dreary wait; but Ippai was equal to it and never closed his eyes during the night.

When morning dawned he found nothing but the stalks of lotus lilies sticking up out of the water in his vicinity.

"But my sword struck more than lotus stalks," thought he. "If I have not killed the kappas which I saw myself in human form, they must have been the spirits of the lotus. What terrible sin have I committed? It was by the spirits of the lotus that our Lord of Koriyama and his family were saved from death! Alas, what have I done – I, a *samurai*, whose every drop of blood belongs to his master? I have drawn my sword on my master's most faithful friends! I must appease the spirits by disembowelling myself."

Ippai said a prayer, and then, sitting on a stone by the side of the fallen lotus flowers, did *harakiri*.

The flowers continued to bloom; but after this no more lotus spirits were seen.

The Spirit of the Willow Tree Saves Family Honour

Richard Gordon Smith

LONG AGO THERE LIVED in Yamada village, Sarashina Gun, Shinano Province, one of the richest men in the northern part of Japan. For many generations the family had been rich, and at last the fortune descended in the eighty-third generation to Gobei Yuasa. The family had no title; but the people treated them almost with the respect due to a princely house. Even the boys in the street, who are not given to bestowing either compliments or titles of respect, bowed ceremoniously when they met Gobei Yuasa. Gobei was the soul of good-nature, sympathetic to all in trouble.

The riches which Gobei had inherited were mainly money and land, about which he worried himself very little; it would have been difficult to find a man who knew less and cared less about his affairs than Gobei. He spent his money freely, and when he came to think of accounts his easy nature let them all slide. His great pleasures were painting *kakemono* pictures, talking to his friends, and eating good things. He ordered his steward not to worry him with unsatisfactory accounts of crops or any other disagreeable subjects. "The destiny of man and his fate is arranged in Heaven," said he. Gobei was quite celebrated as a painter, and could have made a considerable amount of money by selling his *kakemonos*; but no – that would not be doing credit to his ancestors and his name.

One day, while things were going from bad to worse, and Gobei was seated in his room painting, a friend came to gossip. He told Gobei that the village people were beginning to talk seriously about a spirit that had been seen by no fewer than three of them. At first they had laughed at the man who saw the ghost; the second man who saw it they were inclined not to take quite seriously; but now it had been seen by one of the village elders, and so there could be no doubt about it.

"Where do they see it?" asked Gobei.

"They say that it appears under your old willow tree between eleven and twelve o'clock at night – the tree that hangs some of its boughs out of your garden into the street."

"That is odd," remarked Gobei. "I can remember hearing of no murder under that tree, nor even spirit connection with any of my ancestors; but there must be something if three of our villagers have seen it. Yet, again, where there is an old willow tree some one is sure to say, sooner or later, that he has seen a ghost. If there is a spirit there, I wonder whose it is? I should like to paint the ghost if I could see it, so as to leave it to my descendants as the last ominous sign on the road which has led to the family's ruin. That I shall make an effort to do. This very evening I will sit up to watch for the thing."

Never had Gobei been seized with such energy before. He dismissed his friend, and went to bed at four o'clock in the afternoon, so as to allow himself to be up at ten o'clock. At that hour his servant awoke him; but even then he could not be got up before eleven. By twelve o'clock, midnight, Gobei was at last out in his garden, hidden in bushes facing the willow. It was a bright night, and there was no sign of any ghost until after one o'clock, when clouds passed over the moon. Just when Gobei was thinking of going back to bed, he beheld, arising from the ground under the willow, a thin column of white smoke, which gradually assumed the form of a charming girl.

Gobei stared in astonishment and admiration. He had never thought that a ghost could be such a vision of beauty. Rather had he expected to see a white, wild-eyed, dishevelled old woman with protruding bones, the spectacle of whom would freeze his marrow and make his teeth clatter.

Gradually the beautiful figure approached Gobei, and hung its head, as if it wished to address him.

"Who and what are you?" cried Gobei. "You seem too beautiful, to my mind, to be the spirit of one who is dead. If you are indeed spectral, do tell me, if you may, whose spirit you are and why you appear under this willow tree!"

"I am not the spirit or ghost of man, as you say," answered the spirit, "but the spirit of this willow tree."

"Then why do you leave the tree now, as they tell me you have done several times within the last ten days?"

"I am, as I say, the spirit of this willow, which was planted here in the twenty-first generation of your family. That is now about six centuries ago. I was planted to mark the place where your wise ancestor buried a treasure – twenty feet below the ground, and fifteen from my stem, facing east. There is a vast sum of gold in a strong iron chest hidden there. The money was buried to save your house when it was about to fall. Never hitherto has there been danger; but now, in your time, ruin has come, and it is for me to step forth and tell you how by the foresight of your ancestor you have been saved from disgracing the family name by bankruptcy. Pray dig the strong box up and save the name of your house. Begin as soon as you can, and be careful in future."

Then she vanished.

Gobei returned to his house, scarcely believing it possible that such good luck had come to him as the spirit of the willow tree planted by his wise ancestor had said. He did not go to bed, however. He summoned a few of his most faithful servants, and at daybreak began digging. What excitement there was when at nineteen feet they struck the top of an iron chest! Gobei jumped with delight; and it may almost be said that his servants did the same, for to see their honoured master's name fall into the disgrace of bankruptcy would have caused many of them to disembowel themselves.

They tore and dug with all their might, until they had the huge and weighty case out of the hole. They broke off the top with pickaxes, and then Gobei saw a collection of old sacks. He seized one of these; but the age of it was too great. It burst, and sent rolling out over a hundred immense old-fashioned oblong gold coins of ancient times, which must have been worth thirty pounds each. Gobei Yuasa's hand shook. He could hardly realize as true the good fortune which had come to him. Bag after bag was pulled out, each containing a small fortune, until finally the bottom of the box was reached. Here was found a letter some six hundred years of age, saying:

"He of my descendants who is obliged to make use of the treasure to save our family reputation will read aloud and make known that this treasure has been buried by me, Fuji Yuasa, in the twenty-first generation of our family, so that in time of need or danger a future generation will be able to fall back upon it and save the family name. He whose great misfortune necessitates the use of the treasure must say: 'Greatly do I repent the folly that has brought the affairs of our family so low, and necessitated the assistance of an early ancestor. I can only repay such by diligent attention to my household affairs, and also show high appreciation and give kindness to the willow tree which has so long been watching and guarding my ancestor's treasure. These things I vow to do. I shall reform entirely.'"

Gobei Yuasa read this out to his servants and to his friends. He became a man of energy. His lands and farms were properly taken care of, and the Yuasa family regained its influential position.

Gobei painted a *kakemono* of the spirit of the willow tree as he had seen her, and this he kept in his own room during the rest of his life. It is the famous painting, in the Yuasa Gardens to-day, which is called 'The Willow Ghost', and perhaps it is the model from which most of the willow-tree-ghost paintings have sprung.

Gobei fenced in the famous willow tree, and attended to it himself; as did those who followed him.

The Dragon-Shaped Plum Tree

Richard Gordon Smith

IN THE YEAR 1716 of the *Kyoho* Era – 191 years ago – there lived at Momoyama Fushimi, an old gardener, Hambei, who was loved and respected for his kindliness of nature and his great honesty. Though a poor man, Hambei had saved enough to live on; and he had inherited a house and garden from his father. Consequently, he was happy. His favourite pastime was tending the garden and an extraordinarily fine plum tree known in Japan as of the *furyo* kind (which means 'lying dragon'). Such trees are of great value, and much sought after for the arrangement of gardens. Curiously enough, though one may see many beautiful ones, trees growing on mountains or on wild islands, they are very rarely touched except near the larger commercial centres. Indeed, the Japanese have almost a veneration for some of these fantastic *furyo*-shaped trees, and leave them alone, whether they be pines or plums.

The tree in question Hambei loved so much that no offer people could make would induce him to part with it. So notoriously beautiful were the tints and curves of this old stunted tree, large sums had many times been offered for it. Hambei loved it not only for its beauty but also because it had belonged to his father and grandfather. Now in his old age, with his wife in her dotage and his children gone, it was his chief companion. In the autumn he tended it in its untidiness of dead and dying leaves. He felt sorry and sympathetic for it in its cold and bare state in November and December; but in January he was happily employed in watching the buds which would blossom in February. When they did bloom it was his custom to let the people come at certain hours daily to see the tree and listen to stories of historical facts, and also to stories of romance, regarding the plum tree, of which the Japanese mind is ever full. When this again was over Hambei pruned and tied the tree. In the hot season he lingered under it smoking his pipe, and was often rewarded for his care by two or three dozen delicious plums, which he valued and loved as much almost as if they had been his own offspring.

Thus, year after year, the tree had become so much Hambei's companion that a king's ransom would not have bought it from him.

Alas! no man is destined to be let alone in this world. Some one is sure, sooner or later, to covet his property. It came to pass that a high official at the emperor's court heard of Hambei's *furyo* tree and wanted it for his own garden. This dainagon sent his steward, Kotaro Naruse, to see Hambei with a view to purchase, never for a moment doubting that the old gardener would readily sell if the sum offered were sufficient.

Kotaro Naruse arrived at Momoyama Fushimi, and was received with due ceremony. After drinking a cup of tea, he announced that he had been sent to inspect and make arrangements to take the *furyo* plum tree for the dainagon.

Hambei was perplexed. What excuse for refusal should he make to so high a personage? He made a fumbling and rather stupid remark, of which the clever steward soon took advantage.

"On no account," said Hambei, "can I sell the old tree. I have refused many offers for it already."

"I never said that I was sent to buy the tree for money," said Kotaro. "I said that I had come to make arrangements by which the dainagon could have it conveyed carefully to his palace, where he proposes to welcome it with ceremony and treat it with the greatest kindness. It is like taking a bride to the palace for the dainagon. Oh, what an honour for the plum tree, to be united by marriage with one of such illustrious lineage! You should indeed be proud of such a union for your tree! Please be counselled by me and grant the dainagon's wish!"

What was Hambei now to say? Such a lowly-born person, asked by a gallant *samurai* to grant a favour to no less a person than the dainagon!

"Sir," he answered, "your request in behalf of the dainagon has been so courteously made that I am completely prevented from refusing. You must, however, tell the dainagon that the tree is a present, for I cannot sell it."

Kotaro was greatly pleased with the success of his manœuvres, and, drawing from his clothes a bag, said:

"Please, as is customary on making a gift, accept this small one in return."

To the gardener's great astonishment, the bag contained gold. He returned it to Kotaro, saying that it was impossible to accept the gift; but on again being pressed by the smooth-tongued *samurai* he retracted.

The moment Kotaro had left, Hambei regretted this. He felt as if he had sold his own flesh and blood – as if he had sold his daughter – to the dainagon.

That evening he could not sleep. Towards midnight his wife rushed into his room, and, pulling him by the sleeve, shouted:

"You wicked old man! You villainous old rascal! At your age too! Where did you get that girl? I have caught you! Don't tell me lies! You are going to beat me now – I see by your eyes. I am not surprised if you avenge yourself in this way – you must feel an old fool!"

Hambei thought his wife had gone off her head for good this time. He had seen no girl.

"What is the matter with you, obaa San?" he asked. I have seen no girl, and do not know what you are talking about."

"Don't tell me lies! I saw her! I saw her myself when I went down to get a cup of water!"

"Saw, saw – what do you mean?" said Hambei. "I think you have gone mad, talking of seeing girls!"

"I did see her! I saw her weeping outside the door. And a beautiful girl she was, you old sinner, – only seventeen or eighteen years of age."

Hambei got out of bed, to see for himself whether his wife had spoken the truth or had gone truly mad.

On reaching the door he heard sobbing, and, on opening, beheld a beautiful girl.

"Who are you, and why here?" asked Hambei.

"I am the Spirit of the Plum Tree, which for so many years you have tended and loved, as did your father before you. I have heard – and grieve greatly at it – that an arrangement has been made whereby I am to be removed to the dainagon's gardens. It may seem good fortune to belong to a noble family, and an honour to be taken into it. I cannot complain; yet I grieve at being moved from where I have been so long, and from you, who have so carefully tended to my wants. Can you not let me remain here a little longer – as long as I live? I pray you, do!"

"I have made a promise to send you off on Saturday to the dainagon in Kyoto; but I cannot refuse your plea, for I love to have you here. Be easy in your mind, and I will see what can be done," said Hambei.

The spirit dried its tears, smiled at Hambei, and disappeared as it were into the stem of the tree, while Hambei's wife stood looking on in wonder, not at all reassured that there was not some trick on her husband's part.

At last the fatal Saturday on which the tree was to be removed arrived, and Kotaro came with many men and a cart. Hambei told him what had happened – of the tree's spirit and of what it had implored of him.

"Here! take the money, please," said the old man. Tell the story to the dainagon as I tell it to you, and surely he will have mercy."

Kotaro was angry, and said:

"How has this change come about? Have you been drinking too much sake, or are you trying to fool me? You must be careful, I warn you; else you shall find yourself headless. Even supposing the spirit of the tree did appear to you in the form of a girl, did it say that it would be sorry to leave your poor garden for a place of honour in that of the dainagon? You are a fool, and an insulting fool – how dare you return the dainagon's present? How could I explain such an insult to him, and what would he think of me? As you are not keeping your word, I will take the tree by force, or kill you in place of it."

Kotaro was greatly enraged. He kicked Hambei down the steps, and, drawing his sword, was about to cut off his head, when suddenly there was a little puff of wind scented with plum blossom, and then there stood in front of Kotaro the beautiful girl, the Spirit of the Plum Tree!

"Get out of my way, or you will get hurt," shouted Kotaro.

"No: I will not go away. You had better kill me, the spirit that has brought such trouble, instead of killing a poor innocent old man," said the spirit.

"I don't believe in the spirits of plum trees," said Kotaro. "That you are a spirit is evident; but you are only that of an old fox. So I will comply with your request, and at all events kill you first.'

No sooner had he said this than he made a cut with his sword, and he distinctly felt that he cut through a body. The girl disappeared, and all that fell was a branch of the plum tree and most of the flowers that were blooming.

Kotaro now realized that what the gardener had told him was true, and made apologies accordingly.

"I will carry this branch to the dainagon," said he, "and see if he will listen to the story."

Thus was Hambei's life saved by the spirit of the tree.

The dainagon heard the story, and was so moved that he sent the old gardener a kind message, and told him to keep the tree and the money, as an expression of his sorrow for the trouble which he had brought about.

Alas, however, the tree withered and died soon after Kotaro's cruel blow and in spite of Hambei's care. The dead stump was venerated for many years.

The Chessboard Cherry Tree

Richard Gordon Smith

IN OLDEN TIMES, long before the misfortunes of Europeanization came to Japan, there lived at Kasamatsu, in Nakasatani, near Shichikwai mura Shinji gun, Hitachi Province, a hotheaded old *Daimio*, Oda Sayemon. His castle stood on the top of a pine-clad hill about three miles from what is now known as Kamitachi station on the Nippon Railway. Sayemon was noted for his bravery as a soldier, for his abominable play at go (or *goban*), and for his bad temper and violence when he lost, which was invariably.

His most intimate friends among his retainers had tried hard to reform his manners after losing at go; but it was hopeless. All those who won from him he struck in the face with a heavy iron fan, such as was carried by warriors in those days; and he would just as readily have drawn his sword and cut his best friend's head off as be interfered with on those occasions. To be invited to play go with their lord was what all his bold *samurai* dreaded most. At last it was agreed among them that sooner than suffer the gross indignity of being struck by him when they won they would let him win. After all, it did not much matter, there being no money on the game. Thus Sayemon's game grew worse and worse, for he never learned anything; yet in his conceit he thought he was better than everybody.

On the 3rd of March, in honour of his little daughter O Chio, he gave a dinner-party to his retainers. The 3rd of March is the Dolls' Day (*Hina-no-sekku*) – the day upon which girls bring out their dolls. People go from house to house to see them, and the little owners offer you sweet white sake in a doll's cup with much ceremony. Sayemon, no doubt, chose this day of feasting as a compliment to his daughter – for he gave sweet white sake after their food, to be drunk to the health of the dolls, instead of men's sake, which the guests would have liked much better. Sayemon himself absolutely disliked sweet sake. So as soon as the feast was over he called Saito Ukon, one of his oldest and most faithful warriors, to come and play go with him, leaving the others to drink. Ukon, curiously enough, had not played with his lord before, and he was delighted that he had been chosen. He had made up his mind to die that evening after giving his master a proper lesson.

In a luxuriously decorated room there was placed a *goban* (chessboard) with two go-cases containing the men, which are made of white and black stones. The white stones are usually taken by the superior player and the black by the inferior. Without any apology or explanation, Ukon took the case containing the white stones, and began to place them as if he were without question the superior player.

Sayemon's temper began to work up; but he did not show it. So many games of go had his retainers allowed him to win lately, he was fully confident that he should win again, and that Ukon would have in addition to apologize for presuming to take the white stones.

The game ended in a win for Ukon.

"I must have another game," said Sayemon. "I was careless in that one. I will soon show you how I can beat you when I try."

Again Sayemon was beaten – this time not without losing his temper, for his face turned red, his eyes looked devilish, and with a bullying voice full of passion he roared for a third game.

This also Ukon won. Sayemon's wrath knew no bounds. Seizing his iron fan, he was about to smite Ukon a violent blow in the face. His opponent caught him by the wrist, and said:

"My Lord, what ideas have you about games? Your Lordship seems to think curiously about them! It is the better player who wins; while the inferior must fail. If you fail to beat me at go, it is because you are the inferior player. Is this manner of your Lordship's in taking defeat from a superior up to the form of bushido in a *samurai*, as we are taught it? Be counselled by me, your faithful retainer, and be not so hasty with your anger – it ill befits one in your Lordship's high position." And, with a look full of reproof at Sayemon, Ukon bowed almost to the ground.

"You insolent rascal!" roared Sayemon. "How dare you speak to me like that? Don't move! Stand as you are, with your head bowed, so that I may take it off."

"Your sword is to kill your enemies, not your retainers and friends," said Ukon. "Sheathe your sword, my Lord. You need not trouble yourself to kill me, for I have already done *seppuku* in order to offer you the advice which I have given, and to save all others. See here, my Lord!" Ukon opened his clothes and exhibited an immense cut across his stomach.

Sayemon stood for a minute taken aback, and while he thus stood Ukon spoke to him once more, telling him how he must control his temper and treat his subjects better.

On hearing this advice again Sayemon's passion returned. Seizing his sword, he rushed upon Ukon, and, crying, "Not even by your dying spirit will I allow myself to be advised," made a furious cut at Ukon's head. He missed, and cut the go-board in two instead. Then, seeing that Ukon was dying rapidly, Sayemon dropped beside him, crying bitterly and saying:

"Much do I regret to see you thus die, oh faithful Ukon! In losing you I lose my oldest and most faithful retainer. You have served me faithfully and fought most gallantly in all my battles. Pardon me, I beg of you! I will take your advice. It was surely a sign by the gods that they were displeased at my conduct when they made me miss your head with my sword and cut the go-board."

Ukon was pleased to find his lord at last repentant. He said:

"I shall not even in death forget the relation between master and servant, and my spirit shall be with you and watch over your welfare as long as you live."

Then Ukon breathed his last.

Sayemon was so much moved by the faithfulness of Ukon that he caused him to be buried in his own garden, and he buried the broken go-board with him. From that time on the Lord Sayemon's conduct was completely reformed. He was good and kind to all his subjects, and all his people were happy.

A few months after Ukon's death, a cherry tree sprang out of his grave. In three years the tree grew to be a fine one and bloomed luxuriantly.

On the 3rd of March in the third year, the anniversary of Ukon's death, Sayemon was surprised to find it suddenly in bloom. He was looking at it, and thinking of watering it himself, as usual on that day, when he suddenly saw a faint figure standing by the stem of the tree. Just as he said, "You are, I know, the spirit of faithful Saito Ukon," the figure disappeared. Sayemon ran to the tree, to pour water over the roots, when he noticed that the bark of some feet of the stem had all cracked up to the size and shape of the squares of a go-board! He was much impressed. For years afterwards – until, in fact, Sayemon's death – the ghost of Ukon appeared on each 3rd of March.

A fence was built round the tree, which was held sacred; and even to the present, they say, the tree is to be seen.

The Memorial Cherry Tree

Richard Gordon Smith

IN THE COMPOUND or enclosure of the temple called Bukoji, at Takatsuji (high cross street), formerly called Yabugashita, which means 'under the bush', in Kyoto, a curio-dealer had his little shop. His name was Kihachi.

Kihachi had not much to sell; but what little he had was usually good. Consequently, his was a place that the better people looked into when they came to pray – to see, if not to buy; – for they knew full well if there was a good thing to be bought, Kihachi bought it. It was a small and ancient kind of Christie's, in fact, except that things were not sold by auction. One day, the day on which this story starts, Kihachi was sitting in his shop ready either to gossip or to sell, when in walked a young knight or court noble – '*Kuge*', the Japanese called him in those days; and very different was such an one from a knight of a feudal lord or of a *Daimio*, who was usually a blusterer. This particular knight had been to the temple to pray.

"You have many pretty and interesting things here," said he. "May I come in and look at them until this shower of rain has passed? My name is Sakata, and I belong to the court."

"Come in, come in," said Kihachi, "by all means. Some of my things are pretty, and all are undoubtedly good; but the gentry part with little at present. One wants to live two lives of a hundred years each in my trade – one hundred of distress, revolution, and trouble, wherein one may collect the things cheap; and the next hundred of peace, wherein one may sell them and enjoy the proceeds. My business is rotten and unprofitable; yet, in spite of that, I love the things I buy, and often look at them long before I put them up for sale. Where, sir, are you bound for? I see that you are going to travel – by the clothes you wear and carry."

"That's true," answered Sakata: "you are very shrewd. I am going to travel as far as Toba, in Yamato, to see my dearest friend, who has been taken suddenly and mysteriously ill. It is feared he may not live until I get there!"

"At Toba!" answered the old curio-dealer. "Pardon me if I ask the name of your friend?"

"Certainly," said Sakata. "My friend's name is Matsui."

"Then," said the curio-dealer, "he is the gentleman who is said to have killed the ghost or spirit of the old cherry tree near Toba, growing in the grounds of the temple in which he lives at present with the priests. The people say that this cherry tree is so old that the spirit left it. It appeared in the form of a beautiful woman, and Matsui, either fearing or not liking it, killed it, with the result, they say, that from that very evening, which was about ten days ago, your friend Matsui has been sick; and I may add that when the spirit was killed the tree withered and died."

Sakata, thanking Kihachi for this information, went on his way, and eventually found his friend Matsui being carefully nursed by the priest of the Shonen Temple, Toba, with whom he was closely connected.

Soon after the young knight had left the old curio-dealer Kihachi in his shop it began to snow, and so it continued, and appeared likely to continue for some time. Kihachi, therefore, put up his shutters and retired to bed, as is often very sensibly done in Japan; and he no doubt retired with many old wood-carvings to rub and give an ancient appearance to during the period of darkness.

Not very late in the evening there was a knock at the shutters. Kihachi, not wishing to get out of his warm bed, shouted: "Who are you? Come back in the morning. I do not feel well enough to get up to-night."

"But you must – you must get up! I am sent to sell you a good *kakemono*," called the voice of a young girl, so sweetly and entreatingly that the old curio-dealer got up, and after much fumbling with his numbed fingers opened the door.

Snow had fallen thickly; but now it was clear moonlight, and Kihachi saw standing before him a beautiful girl of fifteen, barefooted, and holding in her hands a *kakemono* half-unfolded.

"See," said she, "I have been sent to sell you this!" She was the daughter of Matsui of Toba, she said.

The old man called her in, and saw that the picture was that of a beautiful woman, standing up. It was well done, and the old man took a fancy to it.

"I will give you one *rio* for it," said he; and to his astonishment the young girl accepted his offer eagerly – so much so that he thought that perhaps she had stolen it. Being a curio-dealer, he said nothing on that point, but paid her the money. She ran away with haste.

"Yes: she has stolen it – stolen it, undoubtedly," muttered the old man. "But what am I supposed to know about that? The *kakemono* is worth fully fifty *rio* if it is worth a cent, and not often do such chances come to me.'

So delighted was Kihachi with his purchase, he lit his lamp, hung the picture in his *kakemono* corner, arid sat watching it. It was indeed a beautiful woman well painted, and worth more even than the fifty *rio* he at first thought. But, by all the saints, it seems to change! Yes: it is no longer a beautiful woman. The face has changed to that of a fearful and horrible figure. The face of the woman has become haggard. It is covered with blood. The eyes open and shut, and the mouth gasps. Kihachi feels blood dropping on his head; it comes from a wound in the woman's shoulder. To shut out so horrid a sight, he put his head under the bed-clothes and remained thus, sleeplessly, until dawn.

When he opened his eyes, the *kakemono* was the same as when he had bought it: a beautiful woman. He supposed that his delight in having made a good bargain must have made him dream so he thought nothing more about the horror.

Kihachi, however, was mistaken. The *kakemono* again kept him awake all night, showing the same bloody face, and occasionally even shrieking. Kihachi got no sleep, and perceived that instead of a cheap bargain he had got a very expensive one; for he felt that he must go to Toba and return it to Matsui, and he knew that he could claim no expenses.

After fully two days of travel, Kihachi reached the Shoncn Temple, near Toba, where he asked to see Matsui. He was ushered ceremoniously into his room. The invalid was better; but on being handed the *kakemono* with the figure of a lady painted on it he turned pale, tore it to fragments, and threw it into the temple fire ('*irori*'); after which he jumped in with his daughter himself, and both were burned to death.

Kihachi was sick for many days after this sight. The story soon spread over the whole surrounding country.

Prince Nijo, Governor of Kyoto, had a thorough inquiry made into the circumstances of the case; and it was found beyond doubt that the trouble to Matsui and his family came through his having killed the spirit of the old cherry tree. The spirit, to punish him and show that there was invisible life in old and dead things and often of the best, appeared to Matsui as a beautiful woman being killed; the spirit went into his beautiful picture and haunted him.

Prince Nijo had a fine young cherry tree planted on the spot of the old to commemorate the event, and it is called the 'Memorial Cherry Tree' to this day.

A Haunted Temple in Inaba Province

Richard Gordon Smith

ABOUT THE YEAR 1680 there stood an old temple on a wild pine-clad mountain near the village of Kisaichi, in the Province of Inaba. The temple was far up in a rocky ravine. So high and thick were the trees, they kept out nearly all daylight, even when the sun was at its highest. As long as the old men of the village could remember the temple had been haunted by a shito dama and the skeleton ghost (they thought) of some former priestly occupant. Many priests had tried to live in the temple and make it their home but all had died. No one could spend a night there and live.

At last, in the winter of 1701, there arrived at the village of Kisaichi a priest who was on a pilgrimage. His name was Jogen, and he was a native of the Province of Kai.

Jogen had come to see the haunted temple. He was fond of studying such things. Though he believed in the shito dama form of spiritual return to earth, he did not believe in ghosts. As a matter of fact, he was anxious to see a shito dama, and, moreover, wished to have a temple of his own. In this wild mountain temple, with a history which fear and death prevented people from visiting or priests inhabiting, he thought that he had (to put it in vulgar English) 'a real good thing'. Thus he had found his way to the village on the evening of a cold December night, and had gone to the inn to eat his rice and to hear all he could about the temple.

Jogen was no coward; on the contrary, he was a brave man, and made all inquiries in the calmest manner.

"Sir," said the landlord, "your holiness must not think of going to this temple, for it means death. Many good priests have tried to stay the night there, and every one has been found next morning dead, or has died shortly after daybreak without coming to his senses. It is no use, sir, trying to defy such an evil spirit as comes to this temple. I beg you, sir, to give up the idea. Badly as we want a temple here, we wish for no more deaths, and often think of burning down this old haunted one and building a new."

Jogen, however, was firm in his resolve to find and see the ghost.

"Kind sir," he answered, "your wishes are for my preservation; but it is my ambition to see a shito dama, and, if prayers can quiet it, to reopen the temple, to read its legends from the old books that must lie hidden therein, and to be the head priest of it generally."

The innkeeper, seeing that the priest was not to be dissuaded, gave up the attempt, and promised that his son should accompany him as guide in the morning, and carry sufficient provisions for a day.

Next morning was one of brilliant sunshine, and Jogen was out of bed early, making preparations. Kosa, the innkeeper's twenty-year-old son, was tying up the priest's bedding and enough boiled rice to last him nearly two full days. It was decided that Kosa, after leaving the priest at the temple, should return to the village, for he as well as every other villager refused to spend a night at the weird place; but he and his father agreed to go and see Jogen on the morrow, or (as some one grimly put it) "to carry him down and give him an honourable funeral and decent burial."

Jogen entered fully into this joke, and shortly after left the village, with Kosa carrying his things and guiding the way.

The gorge in which the temple was situated was very steep and wild. Great moss-clad rocks lay strewn everywhere. When Jogen and his companion had got half-way up they sat down to rest and eat. Soon they heard voices of persons ascending, and ere long the innkeeper and some eight or nine of the village elders presented themselves.

"We have followed you," said the innkeeper, "to try once more to dissuade you from running to a sure death. True, we want the temple opened and the ghosts appeased; but we do not wish it at the cost of another life. Please consider!"

"I cannot change my mind," answered the priest. "Besides, this is the one chance of my life. Your village elders have promised me that if I am able to appease the spirit and reopen the temple I shall be the head priest of the temple, which must hereafter become celebrated."

Again Jogen refused to listen to advice, and laughed at the villagers' fears. Shouldering the packages that had been carried by Kosa, he said:

"Go back with the rest. I can find my own way now easily enough. I shall be glad if you return to-morrow with carpenters, for no doubt the temple is in sad want of repairs, both inside and out. Now, my friends, until to-morrow, farewell. Have no fear for me: I have none for myself."

The villagers made deep bows. They were greatly impressed by the bravery of Jogen, and hoped that he might be spared to become their priest. Jogen in his turn bowed, and then began to continue his ascent. The others watched him as long as he remained in view, and then retraced their steps to the village; Kosa thanking the good fortune that had not necessitated his having to go to the temple with the priest and return in the evening alone. With two or three people he felt brave enough; but to be here in the gloom of this wild forest and near the haunted temple alone – no: that was not in his line.

As Jogen climbed he came suddenly in sight of the temple, which seemed to be almost over his head, so precipitous were the sides of the mountain and the path. Filled with curiosity, the priest pressed on in spite of his heavy load, and some fifteen minutes later arrived panting on the temple platform, or terrace, which, like the temple itself, had been built on driven piles and scaffolding.

At first glance Jogen recognized that the temple was large; but lack of attention had caused it to fall into great dilapidation. Rank grasses grew high about its sides; fungi and creepers abounded upon the damp, sodden posts and supports; so rotten, in fact, did these appear, the priest mentioned in his written notes that evening that he feared the spirits less than the state of the posts which supported the building.

Cautiously Jogen entered the temple, and saw that there was a remarkably large and fine gilded figure of Buddha, besides figures of many saints. There were also fine bronzes and vases, drums from which the parchment had rotted off, incense-burners, or *koros*, and other valuable or holy things.

Behind the temple were the priests' living quarters; evidently, before the ghost's time, the temple must have had some five or six priests ever present to attend to it and to the people who came to pray.

The gloom was oppressive, and as the evening was already approaching Jogen bethought himself of light. Unpacking his bundle, he filled a lamp with oil, and found temple-sticks for the candles which he had brought with him. Having placed one of these on either side of the figure of Buddha, he prayed earnestly for two hours, by which time it was quite dark. Then he took his simple meal of rice, and settled himself to watch and listen. In order that he might see inside and outside the temple at the same time, he had chosen the gallery. Concealed behind an old column, he waited, in his heart disbelieving in ghosts, but anxious, as his notes said, to see a shito dama.

For some two hours he heard nothing. The wind – such little as there was – sighed round the temple and through the stems of the tall trees. An owl hooted from time to time. Bats flew in and out. A fungusy smell pervaded the air.

Suddenly, near midnight, Jogen heard a rustling in the bushes below him, as if somebody were pushing through. He thought it was a deer, or perhaps one of the large red-faced apes so fond of the neighbourhood of high and deserted temples; perhaps, even, it might be a fox or a badger.

The priest was soon undeceived. At the place whence the sound of the rustling leaves had come, he saw the clear and distinct shape of the well-known shito dama. It moved first one way and then another, in a hovering and jerky manner, and from it a voice as of distant buzzing proceeded; but – horror of horrors! – what was that standing among the bushes?

The priest's blood ran cold. There stood the luminous skeleton of a man in loose priest's clothes, with glaring eyes and a parchment skin! At first it remained still; but as the shito dama rose higher and higher the ghost moved after it – sometimes visible, sometimes not.

Higher and higher came the shito dama, until finally the ghost stood at the base of the great figure of Buddha, and was facing Jogen.

Cold beads of sweat stood out on the priest's forehead; the marrow seemed to have frozen in his bones; he shook so that he could hardly stand. Biting his tongue to prevent screaming, he dashed for the small room in which he had left his bedding, and, having bolted himself in, proceeded to look through a crack between the boards. Yes! there was the figure of the ghost, still seated near the Buddha; but the shito dama had disappeared.

None of Jogen's senses left him; but fear was paralysing his body, and he felt himself no longer capable of moving – no matter what should happen. He continued, in a lying position, to look through the hole.

The ghost sat on, turning only its head, sometimes to the right, sometimes to the left, and sometimes looking upwards.

For full an hour this went on. Then the buzzing sound began again, and the shito dama reappeared, circling and circling round the ghost's body, until the ghost vanished, apparently having turned into the shito dama; and after circling round the holy figures three or four times it suddenly shot out of sight.

Next morning Kosa and five men came up to the temple. They found the priest alive but paralysed. He could neither move nor speak. He was carried to the village, dying before he got there.

Much use was made of the priest's notes. No one else ever volunteered to live at the temple, which, two years later, was struck by lightning and burned to the ground. In digging among the remains, searching for bronzes and metal Buddhas, villagers came upon a skeleton buried, only a foot deep, near the bushes whence Jogen had first heard the sounds of rustling.

Undoubtedly the ghost and shito dama were those of a priest who had suffered a violent death and could not rest.

The bones were properly buried and masses said, and nothing has since been seen of the ghost.

All that remains of the temple are the moss-grown pedestals which formed the foundations.

Great Fire Caused by a Lady's Dress

Richard Gordon Smith

SOME ONE HUNDRED AND TWENTY years ago, in the year of *Temmei*, a most terrible fire broke out in the western corner of Yedo, – the worst fire, probably, that is known to the world's history, for it is said to have destroyed no fewer than one hundred and eighty-eight thousand persons.

At that time there lived in Yedo, now Tokio, a very rich pawnbroker, Enshu Hikoyemon, the proud possessor of a beautiful daughter aged sixteen, whose name was O Same, which in this instance is probably derived from the word '*sameru*' (to fade away), for in truth O Same San did fade away.

Enshu Hikoyemon loved his daughter dearly, and, he being a widower with no other child, his thoughts and affections were concentrated on her alone. He had long been rich enough to cast aside the mean thoughts and characteristics which had enabled him to reach his present position. From being a hard-hearted relentless money-grubber, Enshu Hikoyemon had become softhearted and generous – as far, at all events, as his daughter was concerned.

Once day the beautiful O Same went to pray at her ancestors' graves. She was accompanied by her maid, and, after saying her prayers, passed the Temple of Hommyoji, which is in the same grounds at Hongo Maru Yama, and there, as she repeated her prayers before the image of Buddha, she saw a young priest, with whom she fell instantly in love. Thitherto she had had no love-affair; nor, indeed, did she fully realize what had happened, beyond the fact that the youth's face pleased her to gaze upon. It was a solemn and noble face. As O Same lit a joss-stick and handed it to the priest, to be placed before Buddha, their hands met, and she felt pass through her body a thrill the like of which she had never experienced. Poor O Same was what is known as madly in love at first sight, – in love so much that as she arose and left the temple all she could see was the face of the young priest; wherever she looked she saw nothing else. She spoke not a word to her maid on the way home, but went straight to her room.

Next morning she announced to the maid that she was indisposed. "Go," she said, "and tell my dear father that I shall remain in bed. I do not feel well this day."

Next day was much the same, and so were the next and the next.

Hikoyemon, disconsolate, tried every means to enliven his daughter. He sought to get her away to the seaside. He offered to take her to the Holy Temple of Ise or to Kompira. She would not go. Doctors were called, and could find nothing wrong with O Same San. "She has something on her mind, and when you can get it off she will be well," was all that they could say.

At last O Same confessed to her father that she had lost her heart to a young priest in the Hommyoji Temple. "Nay," she said: "be not angry with me, father, for I do not know him, and have seen him only once. In that once I loved him, for he has a noble face, which haunts me night and day; and so it is that my heart is heavy, and my body sickens for the want of him. Oh, father, if you love me and wish to save my life, go and find him and tell him that I love him, and that without him I must die!"

Poor Hikoyemon! Here was a nice business – his daughter in love – dying of love for an unknown priest! What was he to do? First he humoured his daughter, and at last, after several days, persuaded her to accompany him to the temple. Unfortunately, they did not see the priest in question; nor did they on a second visit; and after this O Same became more disconsolate than ever, absolutely refusing to leave her room. Night and day her sobs were heard all over the house, and her father was utterly wretched, especially as he had now found out secretly that the priest with whom his daughter had fallen in love was one of the most strict of Buddha's followers, and not likely to err from the disciplinarian rules of religion.

In spite of this, Hikoyemon determined to make an effort in behalf of his daughter. He ventured to the temple alone, saw the priest, told him of his daughter's love, and asked if a union would be possible.

The priest spurned the idea, saying, "Is it not evident to you by my robes that I have devoted my love to Buddha? It is an insult that you should make such a proposition to me!"

Hikoyemon returned to his home deeply mortified at the rebuff; but felt it his duty to be candid with his daughter.

O Same wept herself into hysterics. She grew worse day by day. Hoping to distract her mind, her father had got made for her a magnificent dress which cost nearly four thousand *yen*. He thought that O Same would be vain enough to wish to put it on, and to go out and show it.

This was no use. O Same was not like other women. She cared not for fine raiment or for creating sensations. She put the costume on in her room, to please her father; but then she took it off again, and went back to her bed, where, two days later, she died of a broken heart.

Hikoyemon felt the loss of his pretty daughter very much. At the funeral there must have been half a mile of flower-bearers.

The superb dress was presented to the temple. Such dresses are carefully kept; they remind the priests to say prayers for their late owners as, every two or three months, they are being dusted and cleaned.

The vicar or head priest of this temple, however, was not a good man. He stole this particular dress of O Same's, knowing the value, and sold it secretly to a second-hand dealer in such things.

Some twelve months later the dress was again donated to the same temple by another father whose daughter had died of a love-affair, he having bought the dress at the second-hand clothes-shop. (This girl died and was buried on the same day of the same month as O Same.)

The priest of the temple was not sorry to see the valuable garment return as a gift to his church, and, being mercenary, he sold it again. It seemed, indeed, a sort of gold-mine to himself and his church. Imagine, therefore, the feeling among the priests when, in the following year, in the same month and on exactly the same day as that on which O Same and the other girl had died, another girl of exactly the same age was buried in their cemetery, having died also of a love-affair, and having also worn the splendid dress that O Same was given, which was duly presented to the temple, at the conclusion of her burial service, for the third time.

To say that the chief priest was astonished would be to say little. He and the rest of them were sorely perplexed and troubled.

There were the honest priests, who had had nothing to do with the selling of the garment, and the dishonest head priest or vicar. The honest men were puzzled. The vicar was frightened into thinking honesty the best policy amid the circumstances. Accordingly, he assembled all the priests of the temple, made a hasty confession, and asked for advice.

The priests came to one conclusion, and that was that the spirit of O Same San was in the dress, and that it must be burned, and burned with some ceremony, so as to appease her spirit. Accordingly a time was fixed. When the day arrived many people came to the temple. A great ceremony was held, and finally the valuable garment was placed upon a stone cut in the shape of a lotus flower and lighted.

The weather was calm at the time; but as the garment took fire a sudden gust of wind came, instantly fanning the whole into flame. The gust increased into a storm, which carried one of the sleeves of the dress up to the ceiling of the temple, where it caught between two rafters and burned viciously. In less than two or three minutes the whole temple was on fire. The fire went on for seven days and seven nights, at the expiration of which time nearly the whole of the south and western portions of Yedo were gone; and gone also were one hundred and eighty-eight thousand people.

The charred remains (as far as possible) were collected and buried, and a temple (which now exists), called 'Eko In', was built at the spot, to invoke the blessing of Buddha on their souls.

Cape of the Woman's Sword

Richard Gordon Smith

DOWN IN THE PROVINCE OF HIGO are a group of large islands, framing with the mainland veritable little inland seas, deep bays, and narrow channels. The whole of this is called Amakusa. There are a village called Amakusa mura, a sea known as Amakusa umi, an island known as Amakusa shima, and the Cape known as Joken Zaki, which is the most prominent feature of them all, projecting into the Amakusa sea.

History relates that in the year 1577 the *Daimio* of the province issued an order that every one under him was to become a Christian or be banished.

During the next century this decree was reversed; only, it was ordered that the Christians should be executed. Tens of thousands of Christianized heads were collected and sent for burial to Nagasaki, Shimabara and Amakusa.

This – repeated from *Murray* – has not much to do with my story. After all, it is possible that at the time the Amakusa people became Christian the sword in question, being in some temple, was with the gods cast into the sea, and recovered later by a coral or pearl diver in the *Bunroku* period, which lasted from 1592 to 1596. A history would naturally spring from a sword so recovered. But to the story.

The Cape of Joken Zaki (the Woman's Sword Cape) was not always so called. In former years, before the *Bunroku* period, it had been called Fudozaki (Fudo is the God of Fierceness, always represented as surrounded by fire and holding a sword) or Fudo's Cape. The reason of the change of names was this.

The inhabitants of Amakusa lived almost entirely on what they got out of the sea, so that when it came to pass that for two years of the *Bunroku* period no fish came into their seas or bay and they were sorely distressed, many actually starved, and their country was in a state of desolation. Their largest and longest nets were shot and hauled in vain. Not a single fish so large as a sardine could they catch. At last things got so bad that they could not even see fish schooling outside their bay. Peculiar rumbling sounds were occasionally heard coming from under the sea off Cape Fudo; but of these they thought little, being Japanese and used to earthquakes.

All the people knew was that the fish had completely gone – where they could not tell, or why, until one day an old and much-respected fisherman said:

"I fear, my friends, that the noise we so often hear off Cape Fudo has nothing to do with earthquakes, but that the God of the Sea has been displeased."

One evening a few days after this a sailing junk, the *Tsukushi-maru*, owned by one Tarada, who commanded her, anchored for the night to the lee of Fudozaki.

After having stowed their sails and made everything snug, the crew pulled their beds up from below (for the weather was hot) and rolled them out on deck. Towards the middle of the night the captain was awakened by a peculiar rumbling sound seeming to come from the bottom of the sea. Apparently it came from the direction in which their anchor lay; the rope which held it trembled visibly. Tarada said the sound reminded him of the roaring of the falling tide in the Naruto Channel between Awa and Awaji Island. Suddenly he saw towards the bows of the junk a beautiful maid clothed in the finest of white silks (he thought). She seemed, however, hardly real, being surrounded by a glittering haze.

Tarada was not a coward; nevertheless, he aroused his men, for he did not quite like this. As soon as he had shaken the men to their senses, he moved towards the figure, which, when but ten or twelve feet away, addressed him in the most melodious of voices, thus:

"Ah! could I but be back in the world! That is my only wish."

Tarada, astonished and affrighted, fell on his knees, and was about to pray, when a sound of roaring waters was heard again, and the white-clad maiden disappeared into the sea.

Next morning Tarada went on shore to ask the people of Amakusa if they had ever heard of such a thing before, and to tell them of his experiences.

"No," said the village elder. "Two years ago we never heard the noises which we hear now off Fudo Cape almost daily, and we had much fish here before then; but we have even now never seen the figure of the girl whom (you say) you saw last night. Surely this must be the ghost of some poor girl that has been drowned, and the noise we hear must be made by the God of the Sea, who is in anger that her bones and body are not taken out of this bay, where the fish so much liked to come before her body fouled the bottom."

A consultation was held by the fishermen. They concluded that the village elder was right – that some one must have been drowned in the bay, and that the body was polluting the bottom. It was her ghost that had appeared on Tarada's ship, and the noise was naturally caused by the angry God of the Sea, offended that his fish were prevented from entering the bay by its uncleanness.

What was to be done was quite clear. Some one must dive to the bottom in spite of the depth of water, and bring the body or bones to the surface. It was a dangerous job, and not a pleasant one either, – the bringing up of a corpse that had lain at the bottom for well over a year.

As no one volunteered for the dive, the villagers suggested a man who was a great swimmer – a man who had all his life been dumb and consequently was a person of no value, as no one would marry him and no one cared for him. His name was Sankichi or (as they called him) Oshi-no-Sankichi, Dumb Sankichi. He was twenty-six years of age; he had always been honest; he was very religious, attending at the temples and shrines constantly; but he kept to himself, as his infirmity did not appeal to the community. As soon as this poor fellow heard that in the opinion of most of them there was a dead body at the bottom of the bay which had to be brought to the surface, he came forward and made signs that he would do the work or die in the attempt. What was his poor life worth in comparison with the hundreds of fishermen who lived about the bay, their lives depending upon the presence of fish? The fishermen consulted among themselves, and agreed that they would let Oshi-no-Sankichi make the attempt on the morrow; and until that time he was the popular hero.

Next day, when the tide was low, all the villagers assembled on the beach to give Dumb Sankichi a parting cheer. He was rowed out to Tarada's junk, and, after bidding farewell to his few relations, dived into the sea off her bows.

Sankichi swam until he reached the bottom, passing through hot and cold currents the whole way. Hastily he looked, and swam about; but no corpse or bones did he come across. At last he came to a projecting rock, and on the top of that he espied something like a sword wrapped in old brocade. On grasping it he felt that it really was a sword. On his untying the string and drawing the blade, it proved to be one of dazzling brightness, with not a speck of rust.

"It is said," thought Sankichi, "that Japan is the country of the sword, in which its spirit dwells. It must be the Goddess of the Sword that makes the roaring sound which frightens away the fishes – when she comes to the surface."

Feeling that he had secured a rare treasure, Sankichi lost no time in returning to the surface. He was promptly hauled on board the *Tsukushi-maru* amid the cheers of the villagers and his relations. So long had he been under water, and so benumbed was his body, he promptly fainted. Fires were lit, and his body was rubbed until he came to, and gave by signs an account of his dive. The head official of the neighbourhood, Naruse Tsushimanokami, examined the sword; but, in spite of its beauty and excellence, no name could be found on the blade, and the official expressed it as his opinion that the sword was a holy treasure. He recommended the erection of a shrine dedicated to Fudo, wherein the sword should be kept in order to guard the village against further trouble. Money was collected. The shrine was built. Oshi-no-Sankichi was made the caretaker, and lived a long and happy life.

The fish returned to the bay, for the spirit of the sword was no longer dissatisfied by being at the bottom of the sea.

Sagami Bay

Richard Gordon Smith

HATSUSHIMA ISLAND is probably unknown to all foreigners, and to nine thousand, nine hundred and ninety-nine out of every ten thousand Japanese; consequently, it is of not much importance. Nevertheless, it has produced quite a romantic little story, which was told to me by a friend who had visited there some six years before.

The island is about seven miles south-east of Atami, in Sagami Bay (Izu Province). It is so far isolated from the mainland that very little intercourse goes on with the outer world. Indeed, it is said that the inhabitants of Hatsushima Island are a queer people, and prefer keeping to themselves. Even to-day there are only some two hundred houses, and the population cannot exceed a thousand. The principal production of the island is, of course, fish; but it is celebrated also for its jonquil flowers (*suisenn*). Thus it will be seen that there is hardly any trade. What little the people buy from or sell to the mainland they carry in their own fishing-boats. In matrimony also they keep to themselves, and are generally conservative and all the better for it.

There is a well-known fisherman's song of Hatsushima Island. It means something like the following, and it is of the origin of that queer verse that the story is:

> *To-day is the tenth of June. May the rain fall in torrents!*
> *For I long to see my dearest O Cho San.*
> *Hi, Hi, Ya-re-ko-no-sa! Ya-re-ko-no-sa!*

Many years ago there lived on the island the daughter of a fisherman whose beauty even as a child was extraordinary. As she grew, Cho – for such was her name – improved in looks, and, in spite of her lowly birth, she had the manners and refinement of a lady. At the age of eighteen there was not a young man on the island who was not in love with her. All were eager to seek her hand in marriage; but hardly any dared to ask, even through the medium of a third party, as was usual.

Amongst them was a handsome fisherman of about twenty years whose name was Shinsaku. Being less simple than the rest, and a little more bold, he one day approached Gisuke, O Cho's brother, on the subject. Gisuke could see nothing against his sister marrying Shinsaku; indeed, he rather liked Shinsaku; and their families had always been friends. So he called his sister O Cho down to the beach, where they were sitting, and told her that Shinsaku had proposed for her hand in marriage, and that he thought it an excellent match, of which her mother would have approved had she been alive. He added: "You must marry soon, you know. You are eighteen, and we want no spinsters on Hatsushima, or girls brought here from the mainland to marry our bachelors."

"Stay, stay, my dear brother! I do not want all this sermon on spinsterhood," cried O Cho. "I have no intention of remaining single, I can tell you; and as for Shinsaku I would rather marry him than any one else – so do not worry yourself further on that account. Settle the day of the happy event."

Needless to say, young Gisuke was delighted, and so was Shinsaku; and they settled that the marriage should be three days thence.

Soon, when all the fishing-boats had returned to the village, the news spread; and it would be difficult to describe the state of the younger men's feelings. Hitherto every one had hoped to win the pretty O Cho San; all had lived in that happy hope, and rejoiced in the uncertain state of love, which causes such happiness in its early stages. Shinsaku had hitherto been a general favourite. Now the whole of their hopes were dashed to the ground. O Cho was not for any of them. As for Shinsaku, how they suddenly hated him! What was to be done? they asked one another, little thinking of the comical side, or that in any case O Cho could marry only one of them.

No attention was paid to the fish they had caught; their boats were scarcely pulled high enough on the beach for safety; their minds were wholly given to the question how each and every one of them could marry O Cho San. First of all, it was decided to tell Shinsaku that they would prevent his marriage if possible. There were several fights on the quiet beach, which had never before been disturbed by a display of ill-feeling. At last Gisuke, O Cho's brother, consulted with his sister and Shinsaku; and they decided, for the peace of the island, to break off the marriage, O Cho and her lover determining that at all events they would marry no one else.

However, even this great sacrifice had no effect. There were fully thirty men; in fact, the whole of the bachelors wanted to marry O Cho; they fought daily; the whole island was thrown into a discontent. Poor O Cho San! What could she do? Had not she and Shinsaku done enough already in sacrificing happiness for the peace of the island? There was only one more thing she could do, and, being a Japanese girl, she did it. She wrote two letters, one to her brother Gisuke, another to Shinsaku, bidding them farewell. "The island of Hatsushima has never had trouble until I was born," she said. "For three hundred years or more our people, though poor, have lived happily and in peace. Alas! now it is no longer so, on account of me. Farewell! I shall be dead. Tell our people that I have died to bring them back their senses, for they have been foolish about me. Farewell!"

After leaving the two letters where Gisuke slept, O Cho slipped stealthily out of the house (it was a pouring-wet and stormy night and the 10th of June), and cast herself into the sea from some rocks near her cottage, after well loading her sleeves with stones, so that she might rise no more.

Next morning, when Gisuke found the letters, instinctively he knew what must have happened, and rushed from the house to find Shinsaku. Brother and lover read their letters together, and were stricken with grief, as, indeed, was every one else. A search was made, and soon O Cho's straw slippers were found on the point of rocks near her house. Gisuke knew she must have jumped into the sea here, and he and Shinsaku dived down and found her body lying at the bottom. They brought it to the surface, and it was buried just beyond the rocks on which she had last stood.

From that day Shinsaku was unable to sleep at night. The poor fellow was quite distracted. O Cho's letter and straw slippers he placed beside his bed and surrounded them with flowers. His days he spent decorating and weeping over her tomb.

At last one evening Shinsaku resolved to make away with his own body, hoping that his spirit might find O Cho; and he wandered towards her tomb to take a last farewell. As he did so he thought he saw O Cho, and called her aloud three or four times, and then with outstretched arms he rushed delightedly at her. The noise awoke Gisuke, whose house was close to the grave. He came out, and found Shinsaku clasping the stone pillar which was placed at its head.

Shinsaku explained that he had seen the spirit of O Cho, and that he was about to follow her by taking his life; but from this he was dissuaded.

"Do not do that; devote your life, rather, and I will help with you in building a shrine dedicated to Cho. You will join her when you die by nature; but please her spirit here by never marrying another."

Shinsaku promised. The young men of the place now began to be deeply sorry for Shinsaku. What selfish beasts they had been! they thought. However, they would mend their ways, and spend all their spare time in building a shrine to O Cho San; and this they did. The shrine is called 'The Shrine of O Cho San of Hatsushima', and a ceremony is held there every 10th of June. Curious to relate, it invariably rains on that day, and the fishermen say that the spirit of O Cho comes in the rain. Hence the song:

To-day is the tenth of June. May the rain fall in torrents!
For I long to see my dearest O Cho San.
Hi, Hi, Ya-re-ko-no-sa! Ya-re-ko-no-sa!

The shrine still stands, I am told.

The Secret of Iidamachi Pond

Richard Gordon Smith

IN THE FIRST YEAR OF BUNKIU, 1861-1864, there lived a man called Yehara Keisuke in Kasumigaseki, in the district of Kojimachi. He was a *hatomoto* – that is, a feudatory vassal of the Shogun – and a man to whom some respect was due; but apart from that, Yehara was much liked for his kindness of heart and general fairness in dealing with people. In Iidamachi lived another *hatomoto*, Hayashi Hayato. He had been married to Yehara's sister for five years. They were exceedingly happy; their daughter, four years old now, was the delight of their hearts. Their cottage was rather dilapidated; but it was Hayashi's own, with the pond in front of it, and two farms, the whole property comprising some two hundred acres, of which nearly half was under cultivation. Thus Hayashi was able to live without working much. In the summer he fished for carp; in the winter he wrote much, and was considered a bit of a poet.

At the time of this story, Hayashi, having planted his rice and sweet potatoes (*sato-imo*), had but little to do, and spent most of his time with his wife, fishing in his ponds, one of which contained large *suppon* (terrapin turtles) as well as *koi* (carp). Suddenly things went wrong.

Yehara was surprised one morning to receive a visit from his sister O Komé.

"I have come, dear brother," she said, "to beg you to help me to obtain a divorce or separation from my husband."

"Divorce! Why should you want a divorce? Have you not always said you were happy with your husband, my dear friend Hayashi? For what sudden reason do you ask for a divorce? Remember you have been married for five years now, and that is sufficient to prove that your life has been happy, and that Hayashi has treated you well."

At first O Komé would not give any reason why she wished to be separated from her husband; but at last she said:

"Brother, think not that Hayashi has been unkind. He is all that can be called kind, and we deeply love each other; but, as you know, Hayashi's family have owned the land, the farms on one of which latter we live, for some three hundred years. Nothing would induce him to change his place of abode, and I should never have wished him to do so until some twelve days ago."

"What has happened within these twelve wonderful days?" asked Yehara.

"Dear brother, I can stand it no longer," was his sister's answer. "Up to twelve days ago all went well; but then a terrible thing happened. It was very dark and warm, and I was sitting outside our house looking at the clouds passing over the moon, and talking to my daughter. Suddenly there appeared, as if walking on the lilies of the pond, a white figure. Oh, so white, so wet, and so miserable to look at! It appeared to arise from the pond and float in the air, and then approached me slowly until it was within ten feet. As it came my child cried: "Why, mother, there comes O Sumi – do you know O Sumi?" I answered her that I did not, I think; but in truth I was so frightened I hardly know what I said. The figure was horrible to look at. It was that of a girl of eighteen or nineteen years, with hair dishevelled and hanging loose, over white and wet shoulders. 'Help me! help me!' cried the figure, and I was so frightened that I covered my eyes and screamed for my husband, who was inside. He came out and found me in a dead faint, with my child by my side, also in a state of terror. Hayashi had seen nothing. He carried us both in, shut the doors, and told me I must have been dreaming. 'Perhaps,' he sarcastically added, 'you saw the kappa which is said to dwell in the pond, but which none of my family have seen for over one hundred years.' That is all that my husband said on the subject. Next night, however, when in bed, my child seized me suddenly, crying in terror-stricken tones, 'O Sumi – here is O Sumi – how horrible she looks! Mother, mother, do you see her?' I did see her. She stood dripping wet within three feet of my bed, the whiteness and the wetness and the dishevelled hair being what gave her the awful look which she bore. 'Help me! Help me!' cried the figure, and then disappeared. After that I could not sleep; nor could I get my child to do so. On every night until now the ghost has come – O Sumi, as my child calls her. I should kill myself if I had to remain longer in that house, which has become a terror to myself and my child. My husband does not see the ghost, and only laughs at me; and that is why I see no way out of the difficulty but a separation."

Yehara told his sister that on the following day he would call on Hayashi, and sent his sister back to her husband that night.

Next day, when Yehara called, Hayashi, after hearing what the visitor had to say, answered:

"It is very strange. I was born in this house over twenty years ago; but I have never seen the ghost which my wife refers to, and have never heard about it. Not the slightest allusion to it was ever made by my father or mother. I will make inquiries of all my neighbours and servants, and ascertain if they ever heard of the ghost, or even of any one coming to a sudden and untimely end. There must be something: it is impossible that my little child should know the name 'Sumi', she never having known any one bearing it."

Inquiries were made; but nothing could be learned from the servants or from the neighbours. Hayashi reasoned that, the ghost being always wet, the mystery might be solved by drying up the pond – perhaps to find the remains of some murdered person, whose bones required decent burial and prayers said over them.

The pond was old and deep, covered with water plants, and had never been emptied within his memory. It was said to contain a kappa (mythical beast, half-turtle, half-man). In any case, there were many terrapin turtle, the capture of which would well repay the cost of the emptying. The bank of the pond was cut, and next day there remained only a pool in the deepest part; Hayashi decided to clear even this and dig into the mud below.

At this moment the grandmother of Hayashi arrived, an old woman of some eighty years, and said:

"You need go no farther. I can tell you all about the ghost. O Sumi does not rest, and it is quite true that her ghost appears. I am very sorry about it, now in my old age; for it is my fault – the sin is mine. Listen and I will tell you all."

Every one stood astonished at these words, feeling that some secret was about to be revealed.

The old woman continued:

"When Hayashi Hayato, your grandfather, was alive, we had a beautiful servant girl, seventeen years of age, called O Sumi. Your grandfather became enamoured of this girl, and she of him. I was about thirty at that time, and was jealous, for my better looks had passed away. One day when your grandfather was out I took Sumi to the pond and gave her a severe beating. During the struggle she fell into the water and got entangled in the weeds; and there I left her, fully believing the water to be shallow and that she could get out. She did not succeed, and was drowned. Your grandfather found her dead on his return. In those days the police were not very particular with their inquiries. The girl was buried; but nothing was said to me, and the matter soon blew over. Fourteen days ago was the fiftieth anniversary of this tragedy. Perhaps that is the reason of Sumi's ghost appearing; for appear she must, or your child could not have known of her name. It must be as your child says, and that the first time she appeared Sumi communicated her name."

The old woman was shaking with fear, and advised them all to say prayers at O Sumi's tomb. This was done, and the ghost has been seen no more. Hayashi said:

"Though I am a *samurai*, and have read many books, I never believed in ghosts; but now I do."

The Temple of the Awabi

Richard Gordon Smith

IN NOTO PROVINCE there is a small fishing-village called Nanao. It is at the extreme northern end of the mainland. There is nothing opposite until one reaches either Korea or the Siberian coast – except the small rocky islands which are everywhere in Japan, surrounding as it were by an outer fringe the land proper of Japan itself.

Nanao contains not more than five hundred souls. Many years ago the place was devastated by an earthquake and a terrific storm, which between them destroyed nearly the whole village and killed half of the people.

On the morning after this terrible visitation, it was seen that the geographical situation had changed. Opposite Nanao, some two miles from the land, had arisen a rocky island about a mile in circumference. The sea was muddy and yellow. The people surviving were so overcome and awed that none ventured into a boat for nearly a month afterwards; indeed, most of the boats had been destroyed. Being Japanese, they took things philosophically. Every one helped some other, and within a month the village looked much as it had looked before; smaller, and less populated, perhaps, but managing itself unassisted by the outside world. Indeed, all the neighbouring villages had suffered much in the same way, and after the manner of ants had put things right again.

The fishermen of Nanao arranged that their first fishing expedition should be taken together, two days before the 'Bon'. They would first go and inspect the new island, and then continue out to sea for a few miles, to find if there were still as many *tai* fish on their favourite ground as there used to be.

It would be a day of intense interest, and the villages of some fifty miles of coast had all decided to make their ventures simultaneously, each village trying its own grounds, of course, but all starting at the same time, with a view to eventually reporting to each other the condition of things with regard to fish, for mutual assistance is a strong characteristic in the Japanese when trouble overcomes them.

At the appointed time two days before the festival the fishermen started from Nanao. There were thirteen boats. They visited first the new island, which proved to be simply a large rock. There were many rock fish, such as wrasse and sea-perch, about it, but beyond that there was nothing remarkable. It had not had time to gather many shell-fish on its surface, and there was but little edible seaweed as yet. So the thirteen boats went farther to sea, to discover what had occurred to their old and excellent *tai* grounds.

These were found to produce just about what they used to produce in the days before the earthquake; but the fishermen were not able to stay long enough to make a thorough test. They had meant to be away all night; but at dusk the sky gave every appearance of a storm: so they pulled up their anchors and made for home.

As they came close to the new island they were surprised to see, on one side of it, the water for the space of two hundred and forty feet square lit up with a strange light. The light seemed to come from the bottom of the sea, and in spite of the darkness the water was transparent. The fishermen, very much astonished, stopped to gaze down into the blue waters. They could see fish swimming about in thousands; but the depth was too great for them to see the bottom, and so they gave rein to all kinds of superstitious ideas as to the cause of the light, and talked from one boat to the other about it. A few minutes afterwards they had shipped their immense paddling oars and all was quiet. Then they heard rumbling noises at the bottom of the sea, and this filled them with consternation – they feared another eruption. The oars were put out again, and to say that they went fast would in no way convey an idea of the pace that the men made their boats travel over the two miles between the mainland and the island.

Their homes were reached well before the storm came on; but the storm lasted for fully two days, and the fishermen were unable to leave the shore.

As the sea calmed down and the villagers were looking out, on the third day cause for astonishment came. Shooting out of the sea near the island rock were rays that seemed to come from a sun in the bottom of the sea. All the village congregated on the beach to see this extraordinary spectacle, which was discussed far into the night. Not even the old priest could throw any light on the subject. Consequently, the fishermen became more and more scared, and few of them were ready to venture to sea next day; though it was the time for the magnificent *sawara* (king mackerel), only one boat left the shore, and that belonged to Master Kansuke, a fisherman of some fifty years of age, who, with his son Matakichi, a youth of eighteen and a most faithful son, was always to the fore when anything out of the common had to be done.

Kansuke had been the acknowledged bold fisherman of Nanao, the leader in all things since most could remember, and his faithful and devoted son had followed him from the age of twelve through many perils; so that no one was astonished to see their boat leave alone.

They went first to the *tai* grounds and fished there during the night, catching some thirty odd *tai* between them, the average weight of which would be four pounds. Towards break of day another storm showed on the horizon. Kansuke pulled up his anchor and started for home, hoping to take in a hobo line which he had dropped overboard near the rocky island on his way out – a line holding some two hundred hooks. They had reached the island and hauled in nearly the whole line when the rising sea caused Kansuke to lose his balance and fall overboard.

Usually the old man would soon have found it an easy matter to scramble back into the boat. On this occasion, however, his head did not appear above water; and so his son jumped in to rescue his father. He dived into water which almost dazzled him, for bright rays were shooting through it. He could see nothing of his father, but felt that he could not leave him. As the mysterious rays rising from the bottom might have something to do with the accident, he made up his mind to follow them: they must, he thought, be reflections from the eye of some monster.

It was a deep dive, and for many minutes Matakichi was under water. At last he reached the bottom, and here he found an enormous colony of the *awabi* (ear-shells). The space covered by them was fully two hundred square feet, and in the middle of all was one of gigantic size, the like of which he had never heard of. From the holes at the top through which the feelers pass shot the bright rays which illuminated the sea, – rays which are said by the Japanese divers to show the presence of a pearl. The pearl in this shell, thought Matakichi, must be one of enormous size – as large as a baby's head. From all the *awabi* shells on the patch he could see that lights were coming, which denoted that they contained pearls; but wherever he looked Matakichi could see nothing of his father. He thought his father must have been drowned, and if so, that the best thing for him to do would be to regain the surface and repair to the village to report his father's death, and also his wonderful discovery, which would be of such value to the people of Nanao. Having after much difficulty reached the surface, he, to his dismay, found the boat broken by the sea, which was now high. Matakichi was lucky, however. He saw a bit of floating wreckage, which he seized; and as sea, wind, and current helped him, strong swimmer as he was, it was not more than half an hour before he was ashore, relating to the villagers the adventures of the day, his discoveries, and the loss of his dear father.

The fishermen could hardly credit the news that what they had taken to be supernatural lights were caused by ear-shells, for the much-valued ear-shell was extremely rare about their district; but Matakichi was a youth of such trustworthiness that even the most sceptical believed him in the end, and had it not been for the loss of Kansuke there would have been great rejoicing in the village that evening.

Having told the villagers the news, Matakichi repaired to the old priest's house at the end of the village, and told him also.

"And now that my beloved father is dead," said he, "I myself beg that you will make me one of your disciples, so that I may pray daily for my father's spirit."

The old priest followed Matakichi's wish and said, "Not only shall I be glad to have so brave and filial a youth as yourself as a disciple, but also I myself will pray with you for your father's spirit, and on the twenty-first day from his death we will take boats and pray over the spot at which he was drowned."

Accordingly, on the morning of the twenty-first day after the drowning of poor Kansuke, his son and the priest were anchored over the place where he had been lost, and prayers for the spirit of the dead were said.

That same night the priest awoke at midnight; he felt ill at ease, and thought much of the spiritual affairs of his flock.

Suddenly he saw an old man standing near the head of his couch, who, bowing courteously, said:

"I am the spirit of the great ear-shell lying on the bottom of the sea near Rocky Island. My age is over one thousand years. Some days ago a fisherman fell from his boat into the sea, and I killed and ate him. This morning I heard your reverence praying over the place where I lay, with the son of the man I ate. Your sacred prayers have taught me shame, and I sorrow for the thing I have done. By way of atonement I have ordered my followers to scatter themselves, while I have determined to kill myself, so that the pearls that are in my shell may be given to Matakichi, the son of the man I ate. All I ask is that you should pray for my spirit's welfare. Farewell!"

Saying which, the ghost of the ear-shell vanished. Early next morning, when Matakichi opened his shutters to dust the front of his door, he found thereat what he took at first to be a large rock covered with seaweed, and even with pink coral. On closer examination Matakichi found it to be the immense ear-shell which he had seen at the bottom of the sea off Rocky Island. He rushed off to the temple to tell the priest, who told Matakichi of his visitation during the night.

The shell and the body contained therein were carried to the temple with every respect and much ceremony. Prayers were said over it, and, though the shell and the immense pearl were kept in the temple, the body was buried in a tomb next to Kansuke's, with a monument erected over it, and another over Kansuke's grave. Matakichi changed his name to that of Nichige, and lived happily.

There have been no ear-shells seen near Nanao since, but on the rocky island is erected a shrine to the spirit of the ear-shell.

The 'Jirohei' Cherry Tree, Kyoto

Richard Gordon Smith

THE JAPANESE SAY that ghosts in inanimate nature generally have more liveliness than ghosts of the dead. There is an old proverb which says something to the effect that 'the ghosts of trees love not the willow'; by which, I suppose, is meant that they do not assimilate. In Japanese pictures of ghosts there is nearly always a willow tree. Whether Hokusai, the ancient painter, or Okyo Maruyama, a famous painter of Kyoto of more recent date, was responsible for the pictures with ghosts and willow trees, I do not know; but certainly Maruyama painted many ghosts under willow trees – the first from his wife, who lay sick.

Exactly what this has to do with the following story I cannot see; but my story-teller began with it.

In the northern part of Kyoto is a Shinto temple called Hirano. It is celebrated for the fine cherry trees that grow there. Among them is an old dead tree which is called 'Jirohei', and is much cared for; but the story attached to it is little known, and has not been told, I believe, to a European before.

During the cherry blossom season many people go to view the trees, especially at night.

Close to the Jirohei cherry tree, many years ago, was a large and prosperous tea-house, once owned by Jirohei, who had started in quite a small way. So rapidly did he make money, he attributed his success to the virtue of the old cherry tree, which he accordingly venerated. Jirohei paid the greatest respect to the tree, attending to its wants. He prevented boys from climbing it and breaking its branches. The tree prospered, and so did he.

One morning a *samurai* (of the blood-and-thunder kind) walked up to the Hirano Temple, and sat down at Jirohei's tea-house, to take a long look at the cherry blossom. He was a powerful, dark-skinned, evil-faced man about five feet eight in height.

"Are you the landlord of this tea-house?" asked he.

"Yes, sir," Jirohei answered meekly: "I am. What can I bring you, sir?"

"Nothing: I thank you," said the *samurai*. "What a fine tree you have here opposite your tea-house!"

"Yes, sir: it is to the fineness of the tree that I owe my prosperity. Thank you, sir, for expressing your appreciation of it."

"I want a branch off the tree," quoth the *samurai*, "for a *geisha*."

"Deeply as I regret it, I am obliged to refuse your request. I must refuse everybody. The temple priests gave orders to this effect before they let me erect this place. No matter who it may be that asks, I must refuse. Flowers may not even be picked off the tree, though they may be gathered when they fall. Please, sir, remember that there is an old proverb which tells us to cut the plum tree for our vases, but not the cherry!"

"You seem to be an unpleasantly argumentative person for your station in life," said the *samurai*. "When I say that I want a thing I mean to have it: so you had better go and cut it."

"However much you may be determined, I must refuse," said Jirohei, quietly and politely.

"And, however much you may refuse, the more determined am I to have it. I as a *samurai* said I should have it. Do you think that you can turn me from my purpose? If you have not the politeness to get it, I will take it by force." Suiting his action to his words, the *samurai* drew a sword about three feet long, and was about to cut off the best branch of all. Jirohei clung to the sleeve of his sword arm, crying:

"I have asked you to leave the tree alone; but you would not. Please take my life instead."

"You are an insolent and annoying fool: I gladly follow your request"; and saying this the *samurai* stabbed Jirohei slightly, to make him let go the sleeve. Jirohei did let go; but he ran to the tree, where in a further struggle over the branch, which was cut in spite of Jirohei's defence, he was stabbed again, this time fatally. The *samurai*, seeing that the man must die, got away as quickly as possible, leaving the cut branch in full bloom on the ground.

Hearing the noise, the servants came out of the house, followed by Jirohei's poor old wife.

It was seen that Jirohei himself was dead; but he clung to the tree as firmly as in life, and it was fully an hour before they were able to get him away.

From this time things went badly with the tea-house. Very few people came, and such as did come were poor and spent but little money. Besides, from the day of the murder of Jirohei the tree had begun to fade and die; in less than a year it was absolutely dead. The tea-house had to be closed for want of funds to keep it open. The old wife of Jirohei had hanged herself on the dead tree a few days after her husband had been killed.

People said that ghosts had been seen about the tree, and were afraid to go there at night. Even neighbouring tea-houses suffered, and so did the temple, which for a time became unpopular.

The *samurai* who had been the cause of all this kept his secret, telling no one but his own father what he had done; and he expressed to his father his intention of going to the temple to verify the statements about the ghosts. Thus on the third day of March in the third year of *Keio* (that is, forty-two years ago) he started one night alone and well armed, in spite of his father's attempts to stop him. He went straight to the old dead tree, and hid himself behind a stone lantern.

To his astonishment, at midnight the dead tree suddenly came out into full bloom, and looked just as it had been when he cut the branch and killed Jirohei.

On seeing this he fiercely attacked the tree with his keen-edged sword. He attacked it with mad fury, cutting and slashing; and he heard a fearful scream which seemed to him to come from inside the tree.

After half an hour he became exhausted, but resolved to wait until daybreak, to see what damage he had wrought. When day dawned, the *samurai* found his father lying on the ground, hacked to pieces, and of course dead. Doubtless the father had followed to try and see that no harm came to the son.

The *samurai* was stricken with grief and shame. Nothing was left but to go and pray to the gods for forgiveness, and to offer his life to them, which he did by disembowelling himself.

From that day the ghost appeared no more, and people came as before to view the cherry-bloom by night as well as by day; so they do even now. No one has ever been able to say whether the ghost which appeared was the ghost of Jirohei, or that of his wife, or that of the cherry tree which had died when its limb had been severed.

The Snow Tomb

Richard Gordon Smith

MANY YEARS AGO there lived a young man of the *samurai* class who was much famed for his skill in fencing in what was called the style of *Yagyu*. So adept was he, he earned by teaching, under his master, no less than thirty barrels of rice and two 'rations' – which, I am told, vary from one to five *sho* – a month. As one *sho* is 0.666 feet square, our young *samurai*, Rokugo Yakeiji, was well off.

The seat of his success was at Minami-wari-gesui, Hongo Yedo. His teacher was Sudo Jirozaemon, and the school was at Ishiwaraku.

Rokugo was in no way proud of his skill. It was the modesty of the youth, coupled with cleverness, that had prompted the teacher to make his pupil an assistant-master. The school was one of the best in Tokio, and there were over one hundred pupils.

One January the pupils were assembled to celebrate the New Year, and on this the seventh day of it were drinking *nanakusa* – a kind of sloppy rice in which seven grasses and green vegetables are mixed, said to keep off all diseases for the year. The pupils were engaged in ghost stories, each trying to tell a more alarming one than his neighbour, until the hair of many was practically on end, and it was late in the evening. It was the custom to keep the 7th of January in this way, and they took their turns by drawing numbers. One hundred candles were placed in a shed at the end of the garden, and each teller of a story took his turn at bringing one away, until they had all told a story; this was to upset, if possible, the bragging of the pupil who said he did not believe in ghosts and feared nothing.

At last it came to the turn of Rokugo. After fetching his candle from the end of the garden, he spoke as follows:

"My friends, listen to my story. It is not very dreadful; but it is true. Some three years ago, when I was seventeen, my father sent me to Gifu, in Mino Province. I reached on the way a place called Nakimura about ten o'clock in the evening. Outside the village, on some wild uncultivated land, I saw a curious fireball. It moved here and there without noise, came quite close to me and then went away again, moving generally as if looking for something; it went round and round over the same ground time after time. It was generally five feet off the ground; but sometimes it went lower. I will not say that I was frightened, because subsequently I went to the Miyoshiya inn, and to bed, without mentioning what I had seen to any one; but I can assure you all that I was very glad to be in the house. Next morning my curiosity got the better of me. I told the landlord what I had seen, and he recounted to me a story. He said: "About two hundred years ago a great battle was fought here, and the general who was defeated was himself killed. When his body was recovered, early in the action, it was found to be headless. The soldiers thought that the head must have been stolen by the enemy. One, more anxious than the rest to find his master's head, continued to search while the action went on. While searching he himself was killed. Since that evening, two hundred years ago, the fireball has been burning after ten o'clock. The people from that time till now have called it *'Kubi sagashi no hi'*. As the master of the inn finished relating this story, my friends, I felt an unpleasant sensation in the heart. It was the first thing of a ghostly kind that I had seen."

The pupils agreed that the story was strange. Rokugo pushed his toes into his *'geta'* (clogs), and started to fetch his candle from the end of the garden. He had not proceeded far into the garden before he heard the voice of a woman. It was not very dark, as there was snow on the ground; but Rokugo could see no woman. He had got as far as the candles when he heard the voice again, and, turning suddenly, saw a beautiful woman of some eighteen summers. Her clothes were fine. The *obi* (belt) was tied in the *tateyanojiri* (shape of the arrow standing erect, as an arrow in a quiver). The dress was all of the pine-and-bamboo pattern, and her hair was done in the *shimada* style. Rokugo stood looking at her with wonder and admiration. A minute's reflection showed him that it could be no girl, and that her beauty had almost made him forget that he was a *samurai*.

"No: it is no real woman: it is a ghost. What an opportunity for me to distinguish myself before all my friends!"

Saying which, he drew his sword, tempered by the famous Moriye Shinkai, and with one downward cut severed head, body, and all, into halves.

He ran, seized a candle, and took it back to the room where the pupils were awaiting him; there he told the story, and begged them to come and see the ghost. All the young men looked at one another, none of them being partial to ghosts in what you may call real life. None cared to venture; but by and by Yamamoto Jonosuke, with better courage than the rest, said, "I will go," and dashed off. As soon as the other pupils saw this, they also, gathering pluck, went forth into the garden.

When they came to the spot where the dead ghost was supposed to lie, they found only the remains of a snow man which they themselves had made during the day; and this was cut in half from head to foot, just as Rokugo had described. They all laughed. Several of the young *samurai* were angry, for they thought that Rokugo had been making fools of them; but when they returned to the house they soon saw that Rokugo had not been trifling. They found him sitting with an air of great haughtiness, and thinking that his pupils would now indeed see how able a swordsman he was.

However, they looked at Rokugo scornfully, and addressed him thus:

"Indeed, we have received remarkable evidence of your ability. Even the small boy who throws a stone at a dog would have had the courage to do what you did!"

Rokugo became angry, and called them insolent. He lost his temper to such an extent that for a moment his hand flew to his sword hilt, and he even threatened to kill one or two of them.

The *samurai* apologized for their rudeness, but added: "Your ghost was only the snow man we made ourselves this morning. That is why we tell you that a child need not fear to attack it."

At this information Rokugo was confounded, and he in his turn apologized for his temper; nevertheless, he said he could not understand how it was possible for him to mistake a snow man for a female ghost. Puzzled and ashamed, he begged his friends not to say any more about the matter, but keep it to themselves; thereupon he bade them farewell and left the house.

It was no longer snowing; but the snow lay thick upon the ground. Rokugo had had a good deal of sake, and his gait was not over-steady as he made his way home to Warigesui.

When he passed near the gates of the Korinji Temple he noticed a woman coming faster than he could understand through the temple grounds. He leaned against the fence to watch her. Her hair was dishevelled, and she was all out of order. Soon a man came running behind her with a butcher's knife in his hand, and shouted as he caught her:

"You wicked woman! You have been unfaithful to your poor husband, and I will kill you for it, for I am his friend."

Stabbing her five or six times, he did so, and then moved away. Rokugo, resuming his way homewards, thought what a good friend must be the man who had killed the unfaithful wife. A bad woman justly rewarded with death, thought he.

Rokugo had not gone very far, however, when, to his utter astonishment, he met face to face the woman whom he had just seen killed. She was looking at him with angry eyes, and she said:

"How can a brave *samurai* watch so cruel a murder as you have just seen, enjoying the sight?"

Rokugo was much astonished.

"Do not talk to me as if I were your husband," said he, "for I am not. I was pleased to see you killed for being unfaithful. Indeed, if you are the ghost of the woman I shall kill you myself!" Before he could draw his sword the ghost had vanished.

Rokugo continued his way, and on nearing his house he met a woman, who came up to him with horrible face and clenched teeth, as if in agony.

He had had enough troubles with women that evening. They must be foxes who had assumed the forms of women, thought he, as he continued to gaze at this last one.

At that moment he recollected that he had heard of a fact about fox-women. It was that fire coming from the bodies of foxes and badgers is always so bright that even on the darkest night you can tell the colour of their hair, or even the figures woven in the stuffs they wear, when assuming the forms of men or women; it is clearly visible at one *ken* (six feet). Remembering this, Rokugo approached a little closer to the woman; and, sure enough, he could see the pattern of her dress, shown up as if fire were underneath. The hair, too, seemed to have fire under it.

Knowing now that it was a fox he had to do with, Rokugo drew his best sword, the famous one made by Moriye, and proceeded to attack carefully, for he knew he should have to hit the fox and not the spirit of the fox in the woman's form. (It is said that whenever a fox or a badger transforms itself into human shape the real presence stands beside the apparition. If the apparition appears on the left side, the presence of the animal himself is on the right.)

Rokugo made his attack accordingly, killing the fox and consequently the apparition.

He ran to his house, and called up his relations, who came flocking out with lanterns. Near a myrtle tree which was almost two hundred years old, they found the body – not of fox or badger, but – of an otter. The animal was carried home. Next day invitations were issued to all the pupils at the fencing-school to come and see it, and a great feast was given. Rokugo had wiped away a great disgrace. The pupils erected a tomb for the beast; it is known as '*Yukidzuka*' (The Snow Tomb), and is still to be seen in the Korinji Temple at Warigesui Honjo, in Tokio.

The Skeleton

Rabindranath Tagore

IN THE ROOM next to the one in which we boys used to sleep, there hung a human skeleton. In the night it would rattle in the breeze which played about its bones. In the day these bones were rattled by us. We were taking lessons in osteology from a student in the Campbell Medical School, for our guardians were determined to make us masters of all the sciences. How far they succeeded we need not tell those who know us; and it is better hidden from those who do not.

Many years have passed since then. In the meantime the skeleton has vanished from the room, and the science of osteology from our brains, leaving no trace behind.

The other day, our house was crowded with guests, and I had to pass the night in the same old room. In these now unfamiliar surroundings, sleep refused to come, and, as I tossed from side to side, I heard all the hours of the night chimed, one after another, by the church clock near by. At length the lamp in the corner of the room, after some minutes of choking and spluttering, went out altogether. One or two bereavements had recently happened in the family, so the going out of the lamp naturally led me to thoughts of death. In the great arena of nature, I thought, the light of a lamp losing itself in eternal darkness, and the going out of the light of our little human lives, by day or by night, were much the same thing.

My train of thought recalled to my mind the skeleton. While I was trying to imagine what the body which had clothed it could have been like, it suddenly seemed to me that something was walking round and round my bed, groping along the walls of the room. I could hear its rapid breathing. It seemed as if it was searching for something which it could not find, and pacing round the room with ever-hastier steps. I felt quite sure that this was a mere fancy of my sleepless, excited brain; and that the throbbing of the veins in my temples was really the sound which seemed like running footsteps. Nevertheless, a cold shiver ran all over me. To help to get rid of this hallucination, I called out aloud: "Who is there?" The footsteps seemed to stop at my bedside, and the reply came: "It is I. I have come to look for that skeleton of mine."

It seemed absurd to show any fear before the creature of my own imagination; so, clutching my pillow a little more tightly, I said in a casual sort of way: "A nice business for this time of night! Of what use will that skeleton be to you now?"

The reply seemed to come almost from my mosquito-curtain itself. "What a question! In that skeleton were the bones that encircled my heart; the youthful charm of my six-and-twenty years bloomed about it. Should I not desire to see it once more?"

"Of course," said I, "a perfectly reasonable desire. Well, go on with your search, while I try to get a little sleep."

Said the voice: "But I fancy you are lonely. All right; I'll sit down a while, and we will have a little chat Years ago I used to sit by men and talk to them. But during the last thirty-five years I have only moaned in the wind in the burning-places of the dead. I would talk once more with a man as in the old times."

I felt that some one sat down just near my curtain. Resigning myself to the situation, I replied with as much cordiality as I could summon: "That will be very nice indeed. Let us talk of something cheerful."

"The funniest thing I can think of is my own life-story. Let me tell you that."

The church clock chimed the hour of two.

"When I was in the land of the living, and young, I feared one thing like death itself, and that was my husband. My feelings can be likened only to those of a fish caught with a hook. For it was as if a stranger had snatched me away with the sharpest of hooks from the peaceful calm of my childhood's home – and from him I had no means of escape. My husband died two months after my marriage, and my friends and relations moaned pathetically on my behalf. My husband's father, after scrutinizing my face with great care, said to my mother-in-law: 'Do you not see, she has the evil eye?' – Well, are you listening? I hope you are enjoying the story?"

"Very much indeed!" said I. "The beginning is extremely humorous."

"Let me proceed then. I came back to my father's house in great glee. People tried to conceal it from me, but I knew well that I was endowed with a rare and radiant beauty. What is your opinion?"

"Very likely," I murmured. "But you must remember that I never saw you."

"What! Not seen me? What about that skeleton of mine? Ha! ha! ha! Never mind. I was only joking. How can I ever make you believe that those two cavernous hollows contained the brightest of dark, languishing eyes? And that the smile which was revealed by those ruby lips had no resemblance whatever to the grinning teeth which you used to see? The mere attempt to convey to you some idea of the grace, the charm, the soft, firm, dimpled curves, which in the fulness of youth were growing and blossoming over those dry old bones makes me smile; it also makes me angry. The most eminent doctors of my time could not have dreamed of the bones of that body of mine as materials for teaching osteology. Do you know, one young doctor that I knew of, actually compared me to a golden *champak* blossom. It meant that to him the rest of humankind was fit only to illustrate the science of physiology, that I was a flower of beauty. Does any one think of the skeleton of a *champak* flower?

"When I walked, I felt that, like a diamond scattering splendour, my every movement set waves of beauty radiating on every side. I used to spend hours gazing on my hands – hands which could gracefully have reined the liveliest of male creatures.

"But that stark and staring old skeleton of mine has borne false-witness to you against me, while I was unable to refute the shameless libel. That is why of all men I hate you most! I feel I would like once for all to banish sleep from your eyes with a vision of that warm rosy loveliness of mine, to sweep out with it all the wretched osteological stuff of which your brain is full."

"I could have sworn by your body," cried I, "if you had it still, that no vestige of osteology has remained in my head, and that the only thing that it is now full of is a radiant vision of perfect loveliness, glowing against the black background of night. I cannot say more than that."

"I had no girl-companions," went on the voice. "My only brother had made up his mind not to marry. In the *zenana* I was alone. Alone I used to sit in the garden under the shade of the trees, and dream that the whole world was in love with me; that the stars with sleepless gaze were drinking in my beauty; that the wind was languishing in sighs as on some pretext or other it brushed past me; and that the lawn on which my feet rested, had it been conscious, would have lost consciousness again at their touch. It seemed to me that all the young men in the world were as blades of grass at my feet; and my heart, I know not why, used to grow sad.

"When my brother's friend, Shekhar, had passed out of the Medical College, he became our family doctor. I had already often seen him from behind a curtain. My brother was a strange man, and did not care to look on the world with open eyes. It was not empty enough for his taste; so he gradually moved away from it, until he was quite lost in an obscure corner. Shekhar was his one friend, so he was the only young man I could ever get to see. And when I held my evening court in my garden, then the host of imaginary young men whom I had at my feet were each one a Shekhar. – Are you listening? What are you thinking of?"

I sighed as I replied: "I was wishing I was Shekhar!"

"Wait a bit. Hear the whole story first. One day, in the rains, I was feverish. The doctor came to see me. That was our first meeting. I was reclining opposite the window, so that the blush of the evening sky might temper the pallor of my complexion. When the doctor, coming in, looked up into my face, I put myself into his place, and gazed at myself in imagination. I saw in the glorious evening light that delicate wan face laid like a drooping flower against the soft white pillow, with the unrestrained curls playing over the forehead, and the bashfully lowered eyelids casting a pathetic shade over the whole countenance.

"The doctor, in a tone bashfully low, asked my brother: 'Might I feel her pulse?'

"I put out a tired, well-rounded wrist from beneath the coverlet. 'Ah!' thought I, as I looked on it, 'if only there had been a sapphire bracelet.' I have never before seen a doctor so awkward about feeling a patient's pulse. His fingers trembled as they felt my wrist. He measured the heat of my fever, I gauged the pulse of his heart. – Don't you believe me?"

"Very easily," said I; "the human heart-beat tells its tale."

"After I had been taken ill and restored to health several times, I found that the number of the courtiers who attended my imaginary evening reception began to dwindle till they were reduced to only one! And at last in my little world there remained only one doctor and one patient.

"In these evenings I used to dress myself secretly in a canary-coloured *sari*; twine about the braided knot into which I did my hair a garland of white jasmine blossoms; and with a little mirror in my hand betake myself to my usual seat under the trees.

"Well! Are you perhaps thinking that the sight of one's own beauty would soon grow wearisome? Ah no! for I did not see myself with my own eyes. I was then one and also two. I used to see myself as though I were the doctor; I gazed, I was charmed, I fell madly in love. But, in spite of all the caresses I lavished on myself, a sigh would wander about my heart, moaning like the evening breeze.

"Anyhow, from that time I was never alone. When I walked I watched with downcast eyes the play of my dainty little toes on the earth, and wondered what the doctor would have felt had he been there to see. At mid-day the sky would be filled with the glare of the sun, without a sound, save now and then the distant cry of a passing kite. Outside our garden-walls the hawker would pass with his musical cry of 'Bangles for sale, crystal bangles.' And I, spreading a snow-white sheet on the lawn, would lie on it with my head on my arm. With studied carelessness the other arm would rest lightly on the soft sheet, and I would imagine to myself that some one had caught sight of the wonderful pose of my hand, that some one had clasped it in both of his and imprinted a kiss on its rosy palm, and was slowly walking away. – What if I ended the story here? How would it do?"

"Not half a bad ending," I replied thoughtfully. "It would no doubt remain a little incomplete, but I could easily spend the rest of the night putting in the finishing touches."

"But that would make the story too serious. Where would the laugh come in? Where would be the skeleton with its grinning teeth?

"So let me go on. As soon as the doctor had got a little practice, he took a room on the ground-floor of our house for a consulting-chamber. I used then sometimes to ask him jokingly about medicines and poisons, and how much of this drug or that would kill a man. The subject was congenial and he would wax eloquent. These talks familiarized me with the idea of death; and so love and death were the only two things that filled my little world. My story is now nearly ended – there is not much left."

"Not much of the night is left either," I muttered.

"After a time I noticed that the doctor had grown strangely absent-minded, and it seemed as if he were ashamed of something which he was trying to keep from me. One day he came in, somewhat smartly dressed, and borrowed my brother's carriage for the evening.

"My curiosity became too much for me, and I went up to my brother for information. After some talk beside the point, I at last asked him: 'By the way, Dada, where is the doctor going this evening in your carriage?'

"My brother briefly replied: 'To his death.'

"'Oh, do tell me,' I importuned. 'Where is he really going?'

"'To be married,' he said, a little more explicitly.

"'Oh, indeed!' said I, as I laughed long and loudly.

"I gradually learnt that the bride was an heiress, who would bring the doctor a large sum of money. But why did he insult me by hiding all this from me? Had I ever begged and prayed him not to marry, because it would break my heart? Men are not to be trusted. I have known only one man in all my life, and in a moment I made this discovery.

"When the doctor came in after his work and was ready to start, I said to him, rippling with laughter the while: 'Well, doctor, so you are to be married to-night?'

"My gaiety not only made the doctor lose countenance; it thoroughly irritated him.

"'How is it,' I went on, 'that there is no illumination, no band of music?'

"With a sigh he replied: 'Is marriage then such a joyful occasion?'

"I burst out into renewed laughter. 'No, no,' said I, 'this will never do. Who ever heard of a wedding without lights and music?'

"I bothered my brother about it so much that he at once ordered all the trappings of a gay wedding.

"All the time I kept on gaily talking of the bride, of what would happen, of what I would do when the bride came home. 'And, doctor,' I asked, 'will you still go on feeling pulses?' Ha! ha! ha! Though the inner workings of people's, especially men's, minds are not visible, still I can take my oath that these words were piercing the doctor's bosom like deadly darts.

"The marriage was to be celebrated late at night. Before starting, the doctor and my brother were having a glass of wine together on the terrace, as was their daily habit. The moon had just risen.

"I went up smiling, and said: 'Have you forgotten your wedding, doctor? It is time to start.'

"I must here tell you one little thing. I had meanwhile gone down to the dispensary and got a little powder, which at a convenient opportunity I had dropped unobserved into the doctor's glass.

"The doctor, draining his glass at a gulp, in a voice thick with emotion, and with a look that pierced me to the heart, said: 'Then I must go.'

"The music struck up. I went into my room and dressed myself in my bridal-robes of silk and gold. I took out my jewellery and ornaments from the safe and put them all on; I put the red mark of wifehood on the parting in my hair. And then under the tree in the garden I prepared my bed.

"It was a beautiful night. The gentle south wind was kissing away the weariness of the world. The scent of jasmine and *bela* filled the garden with rejoicing.

"When the sound of the music began to grow fainter and fainter; the light of the moon to get dimmer and dimmer; the world with its lifelong associations of home and kin to fade away from my perceptions like some illusion; – then I closed my eyes, and smiled.

"I fancied that when people came and found me they would see that smile of mine lingering on my lips like a trace of rose-coloured wine, that when I thus slowly entered my eternal bridal-chamber I should carry with me this smile, illuminating my face. But alas for the bridal-chamber! Alas for the bridal-robes of silk and gold! When I woke at the sound of a rattling within me, I found three urchins learning osteology from my skeleton. Where in my bosom my joys and griefs used to throb, and the petals of youth to open one by one, there the master with his pointer was busy naming my bones. And as to that last smile, which I had so carefully rehearsed, did you see any sign of that?

"Well, well, how did you like the story?"

"It has been delightful," said I.

At this point the first crow began to caw. "Are you there?" I asked. There was no reply.

The morning light entered the room.

The Lost Jewels

Rabindranath Tagore; translated by W.W. Pearson

MY BOAT WAS MOORED beside an old bathing *ghat* of the river, almost in ruins. The sun had set.

On the roof of the boat the boatmen were at their evening prayer. Against the bright background of the Western sky their silent worship stood out like a picture. The waning light was reflected on the still surface of the river, in every delicate shade of colour from gold to steel blue.

A huge house with broken windows, tumble-down verandahs and all the appearance of old age was in front of me. I sat alone on the steps of the *ghat* which were cracked by the far-reaching roots of a banyan tree. A feeling of sadness began to come over me, when suddenly I was startled to hear a voice asking:

"Sir, where have you come from?"

I looked up and saw a man who seemed half-starved and out of fortune. His face had a dilapidated look such as is common among my countrymen who take up service away from home. His dirty coat of Assam silk was greasy and open at the front. He appeared to be just returning from his day's work and to be taking a walk by the side of the river at a time when he should have been taking his evening meal.

The new-comer took his seat beside me on the steps. I said in answer to his question:

"I come from Ranchi."

"What occupation?"

"I am a merchant."

"What sort?"

"A dealer in cocoons and timber."

"What name?"

After a moment's hesitation I gave a name, but it was not my own.

Still the stranger's curiosity was not satisfied. Again he questioned me:

"What have you come here for?"

I replied:

"For a change of air."

My cross-examiner seemed a little astonished. He said:

"Well, sir, I have been enjoying the air of this place for nearly six years, and with it I have taken a daily average of fifteen grains of quinine, but I have not noticed that I have benefited much."

I replied:

"Still you must acknowledge that, after Ranchi, I shall find the air of this place sufficient of a change."

"Yes, indeed," said he. "More than you bargain for. But where will you stay here?"

Pointing to the tumble-down house above the *ghat*, I said:

"There."

I think my friend had a suspicion that I had come in search of hidden treasure. However he did not pursue the subject. He only began to describe to me what had happened in this ruined building some fifteen years before.

I found that he was the schoolmaster of the place. From beneath an enormous bald head his two eyes shone out from their sockets with an unnatural brightness in a face that was thin with hunger and illness.

The boatmen, having finished their evening prayer, turned their attention to their cooking. As the last light of the day faded the dark and empty house stood silent and ghostly above the deserted *ghat*.

The schoolmaster said:

"Nearly ten years ago, when I came to this place, Bhusan Saha used to live in this house. He was the heir to the large property and business of his uncle Durga Saha, who was childless.

"But he was modernized. He had been educated, and not only spoke faultless English but actually entered sahibs' offices with his shoes on. In addition to that he grew a beard; thus he had not the least chance of bettering himself so far as the sahibs were concerned. You had only to look at him to see that he was a modernized Bengali.

"In his own home too he had another drawback. His wife was beautiful. With his college education on the one hand, and on the other his beautiful wife, what chance was there of his preserving our good old traditions in his home?

"Sir, you are certainly a married man, so that it is hardly necessary to tell you that the ordinary female is fond of sour green mangoes, hot chillies, and a stern husband. A man need not necessarily be ugly or poor to be cheated of his wife's love, but he is sure to be too gentle.

"If you ask me why this is so, I have much to say on this subject, for I have thought a good deal about it. A stag chooses a hardwood tree on which to sharpen its horns, and would get no pleasure in rubbing them against a banana tree. From the very moment that man and woman became separate sexes woman has been exercising all her faculties in trying by various devices to fascinate and bring man under her control. The wife of a man who is, of his own accord, submissive is altogether out of employment. All those weapons which she has inherited from her grand-mothers of the untold centuries, are useless in her hands: the force of her tears, the fire of her anger, and the snare of her glances lie idle.

"Under the spell of modern civilization man has lost the God-given power of his barbaric nature and this has loosened the conjugal ties. The unfortunate Bhusan had been turned out of the machine of modern civilization an absolutely faultless man. He was therefore neither successful in business, nor in his own home.

"Mani was Bhusan's wife. She used to get her caresses without asking, her Dacca muslin *saris* without tears, and her bangles without being able to pride herself on a victory. In this way her woman's nature became atrophied and with it her love for her husband. She simply accepted things without giving anything in return. Her harmless and foolish husband used to imagine that to give is the way to get. The fact was just the contrary.

"The result of this was that Mani looked upon her husband as a mere machine for turning out her Dacca muslins and her bangles – so perfect a machine indeed that never for a single day did she need to oil its wheels.

"Bhusan's wife did not talk very much, nor did she mix much with her neighbours. To feed Brahmans in obedience to a sacred vow, or to give a few pice to a religious mendicant was not her way. In her hands nothing was ever lost: whatever she got she saved up most carefully, with the one exception of the memory of her husband's caresses. The extraordinary thing was that she did not seem to lose the least atom of her youthful beauty. People said that whatever her age was she never looked older than sixteen. I suppose youth is best preserved with the aid of the heart that is an ice chest.

"But as far as work was concerned Manimalika was very efficient. She never kept more servants than were absolutely necessary. She thought that to pay wages to anyone to do work which she herself could do was like playing the pickpocket with her own money.

"Not being anxious about anyone, never being distracted by love, always working and saving, she was never sick nor sorry.

"For the majority of husbands this is quite sufficient, not only sufficient, but fortunate. For the loving wife is a wife who make it difficult for her husband to forget her and the fatigue of perpetual remembrance wears out life's bloom. It is only when a man has lumbago that he becomes conscious of his waist. And lumbago, in domestic affairs, is to be made conscious, by the constant imposition of love, that you have such a thing as a wife. Excessive devotion to her husband may be a merit for the wife, but not comfortable for the husband, – that is my candid opinion.

I hope I am not tiring you, sir? I live alone, you see; I am banished from the company of my wife and there are many important social questions which I have leisure to think about, but cannot discuss with my pupils. In course of conversation you will see how deeply I have thought of them."

Just as he was speaking, some jackals began to howl from a neighbouring thicket. The schoolmaster stopped for a moment the torrent of his talk. When the sound had ceased and the earth and the water relapsed into a deeper silence, he opened his glowing eyes wide in the darkness of the night and resumed the thread of his story.

"Suddenly a tangle occurred in Bhusan's complicated business. What exactly happened it is not possible for a layman like myself either to understand or to explain. Suffice it to say that, for some sudden reason, he found it difficult to get credit in the market. If only he could, by hook or by crook, raise a *lakh* and a half of *rupees*, and only for a few days rapidly flash it before the market, then his credit would be restored and he would be able to sail fair again.

"So he began to cast about to see whether he could not raise a loan. But, in that case, he would be bound to give some satisfactory security, and the best security of all is jewelry.

"So Bhusan went to his wife. But unfortunately he was not able to face his wife as easily as most men are. His love for her was of that kind which has to tread very carefully, and cannot speak out plainly what is in the mind; it is like the attraction of the sun for the earth, which is strong, yet which leaves immense space between them.

"Still even the hero of a high class romance does sometimes, when hard pressed, have to mention to his beloved such things as mortgage deeds and promissory notes. But words stick, and the tune does not seem right, and shrinking of reluctance makes itself felt. The unfortunate Bhusan was totally powerless to say, 'Look here, I am in need of money, bring out your jewels.'

"He did broach the subject to his wife at last, but with such extreme delicacy, that it only titilated her opposition without bending it to his own purpose. When Mani set her face hard and said nothing, he was deeply hurt, yet he was incapable of returning the hurt back to her. The reason was that he had not even a trace of that barbarity, which is the gift of the male. If any one had upbraided him for this, then most probably he would have expressed some such subtle sentiment as the following:

'If my wife, of her own free choice, is unwilling to trust me with my jewelry, then I have no right to take them from her by force.'

"What I say is, has God given to man such ferocity and strength only for him to spend his time in delicate measurement of fine-spun ideals?

"However that may be, Bhusan, being too proud to touch his wife's jewels, went to Calcutta to try some other way of raising the money.

"As a general rule in this world the wife knows the husband far better than the husband ever knows the wife; but extremely modern men in their subtlety of nature are altogether beyond the range of those unsophisticated instincts which womankind has acquired through ages. These men are a new race, and have become as mysterious as women themselves. Ordinary men can be divided roughly into three main classes, some of them are barbarians, some are fools, and some are blind; but these modern men do not fit into any of them.

"So Mani called her counsellor for consultation. Some cousin of hers was engaged as assistant-steward on Bhusan's estate. He was not the kind of man to profit himself by dint of hard work; but by help of his position in the family he was able to save his salary, and even a little more.

"Mani called him and told him what had happened. She ended up by asking him: 'Now what is your advice?'

"He shook his head wisely and said: 'I don't like the look of things at all.' The fact is that wise men never like the look of things.

"Then he added: 'Babu will never be able to raise the money, and in the end he will have to fall back upon that jewelry of yours.'

"From what she knew of human nature she thought that this was not only possible, but likely. Her anxiety became keener than ever. She had no child to love, and though she had a husband, she was scarcely able to realize his very existence. So her blood froze at the very thought that her only object of love, – the wealth which like a child had grown from year to year, – was to be in a moment thrown into the bottomless abyss of trade. She gasped: 'What then is to be done?'

"Modhu said: 'Why not take your jewels and go to your father's house?' In his heart of hearts he entertained the hope that a portion, and possibly the larger portion, of that jewelry would fall to his lot.

"Mani at once agreed. It was a rainy night towards the end of summer. At this very *ghat* a boat was moored. Mani wrapped from head to foot in a thick shawl, stepped into the boat. The frogs croaked in the thick darkness of the cloudy dawn. Modhu, waking up from sleep, roused himself from the boat and said: 'Give me the box of jewels.'

"Mani replied: 'Not now, afterwards. Now let us start.'

"The boat started, and floated swiftly down the current. Mani had spent the whole night in covering every part of her body with her ornaments. She was afraid that if she put her jewels into a box they might be snatched away from her hands. But if she wore them on her person then no-one could take them away without murdering her. Manimalika did not understand Bhusan, it is true; but there was no doubt about her understanding of Modhu.

"Modhu had written a letter to the chief steward to the effect that he had started to take his mistress to her father's house. The steward was an ancient retainer of Bhusan's father. He was furiously angry, and wrote a lengthy epistle full of misspellings to his master. Although the letter was weak in its grammar, yet it was forcible in its language and clearly expressed the writer's disapproval of giving too much indulgence to womankind. Bhusan on receiving it understood what was the motive of Mani's secret departure. What hurt him most was the fact that, in spite of his having given way to the unwillingness of his wife to part with her jewels, in this time of his desperate straits, his wife should still suspect him.

"When he ought to have been angry, Bhusan was only distressed. God has so arranged it, that man, for the most trifling reason, will burst forth in anger like a forest fire, and woman will burst into tears like a rain cloud for no reason at all. But the weather cycle seems to have changed, and this appears no longer to hold good.

"The husband bent his head and said to himself: 'Well, if this is your judgment, let it be so, I will simply do my own duty.' Bhusan, who ought to have been born five or six centuries hence, when the world will be moved by psychic forces, was unfortunate enough not only to be born in the nineteenth century, but also to marry a woman who belonged to that eternal primitive age which persists through all time. He did not write a word on the subject to his wife, and determined in his mind that he would never mention it to her again. What an awful penalty!

"Ten or twelve days later, having secured the necessary loan, Bhusan returned to his home. He imagined that Mani, after completing her mission, had by this time come back from her father's house. And so he approached the door of the inner apartments, wondering whether his wife would show any signs of shame or penitence for her undeserved suspicion.

"He found the door shut. Breaking the lock, he entered the room and saw that it was empty.

"At first Bhusan did not trouble about his wife's absence. He thought that if she wanted to come back she would do so. His old steward however came to him and said: 'What good will come of taking no notice of it? You ought to get some news of the mistress.' Acting on this suggestion messengers were sent to Mani's father's house. The news was brought that up to that time neither Mani nor Modhu had turned up there.

"Then a search began in every direction. Men went along both banks of the river making enquiries. The police were given a description of Modhu, but all in vain. They were unable to find out what boat they had taken, what boatman they had hired, or by what way they had gone.

"One evening, when all hope had been abandoned of ever finding his wife, Bhusan entered his deserted bed-room. It was the festival of Krishna's birth, and it had been raining incessantly from early morning. In celebration of the festival there was a fair going on in the village, and in a temporary building a theatrical performance was being held. The sound of distant singing could be heard mingling with the sound of pouring rain. Bhusan was sitting alone in the darkness at the window there which hangs loose upon its hinges. He took no notice of the damp wind, the spray of the rain, and the sound of the singing. On the wall of the room were hanging a couple of pictures of the goddesses Lakshmi and Saraswati, painted at the Art Studio; on the clothes' rank a towel and a bodice, and a pair of *saris* were laid out ready for use. On a table in one corner of the room there was a box containing betel leaves, prepared by Mani's own hand, but now quite dry and uneatable. In a cupboard, with a glass door, all sorts of things were arranged with evident care, – her China dolls of childhood's days, scent bottles, decanters of coloured glass, a sumptuous pack of cards, large brightly polished shells, and even empty soapboxes. In a niche there was a favourite little lamp with its round globe. Mani had been in the habit of lighting it with her own hands every evening. One who goes away leaving everything empty, leaves the imprint of a living heart even on lifeless objects.

"In the dead of night when the heavy rain had ceased and the songs of the village opera troupe had become silent, Bhusan was sitting in the same position as before. Outside the window there was such an impenetrable darkness that it seemed to him as if the very gates of oblivion were before him reaching to the sky, – as if he had only to cry out to be able to recover sight of those things which seemed to have been lost for ever.

"Just as he was thinking thus, the jingling sound as of ornaments was heard. It seemed to be advancing up the steps of the *ghat*. The water of the river and the darkness of the night were indistinguishable. Thrilling with excitement, Bhusan tried to pierce and push through the darkness with his eager eyes, – till they ached, but he could see nothing. The more anxious he was to see, the denser the darkness became and the more shadowy the outer world.

"The sound reached the top step of the bathing *ghat* and now began to come towards the house. It stopped in front of the door, which had been locked by the porter before he went to the fair. Then upon that closed door there fell a rain of jingling blows, as if with some ornaments. Bhusan was not able to sit still another moment, but making his way through the unlighted rooms and down the dark staircase he stood before the closed door. It was padlocked from the outside so he began to shake it with all his might. The force with which he shook the door and the sound which he made woke him suddenly. He found he had been asleep and in his sleep he had made his way down to the door of the house. His whole body was wet with perspiration, his hands and feet were icy cold, and his heart was fluttering like a lamp just about to go out. His dream, broken, he realized that there was no sound outside except the pattering of the rain which had commenced again.

"Although the whole thing was a dream, Bhusan felt as if for some very small obstacle he had been cheated of the wonderful realization of his impossible hope. The incessant patter of the rain seemed to say to him: 'This awakening is a dream. This world is vain.'

"The festival was continued on the following day, and the doorkeeper again had leave. Bhusan gave orders that the hall door was to be left open all night.

"That night, having extinguished the light, Bhusan took his seat at the open window of his bedroom as before. The sky was dark with rain clouds and there was a silence as of something indefinite and impending. The monotonous croaking of the frogs and the sound of the distant songs were not able to break that silence, but only seemed to add an incongruity to it.

"Late at night, the frogs and the crickets and the boys of the opera party became silent, and a still deeper darkness fell upon the night. It seemed that now the time had come.

"Just as on the night before, a clattering and jingling sound came from the *ghat* by the river. But this time Bhusan did not look in that direction, lest by his over-anxiety and restlessness, his power of sight and hearing should become overwhelmed. He made a supreme effort to control himself, and sat still.

"The sound of the ornaments gradually advanced from the *ghat* and entered the open door. Then it came winding up the spiral staircase which led to the inner apartments. It became difficult for Bhusan to control himself, his heart began to thump wildly and his throat was choking with suppressed excitement. Having reached the head of the spiral stairs the sound came slowly along the verandah towards the door of the room, where it stopped just outside with a clanking sound. It was now only just on the other side of the threshold.

"Bhusan could contain himself no longer, and his pent-up excitement burst forth in one wild cry of, 'Mani', and he sprang up from his chair with lightning rapidity. Thus startled out of his sleep he found that the very window-panes were rattling with the vibration of his cry. And outside he could hear the croaking of the frogs and patter of rain.

"Bhusan struck his forehead in despair.

"Next day the fair broke up, and the stallkeepers and the players' party went away. Bhusan gave orders that no-one should sleep in the house that night except himself.

"In the evening he took his seat at the window of the empty house. That night there were breaks in the clouds, showing the stars twinkling through the rain-washed air. The moon was late in rising, and as the fair was over there was not a single boat on the flooded river. The villagers, tired out by two nights' dissipation, were sound asleep.

"Bhusan, sitting with his head resting on the back of his chair, was gazing up at the stars.

"As he watched them they one by one disappeared. From the sky above and from the earth beneath screens of darkness met like tired eyelids upon weary eyes. To-night Bhusan's mind was full of peace. He felt certain that the moment had come when his heart's desire would be fulfilled, and that Death would reveal his mysteries to his devotee.

"The sound came from the river *ghat* just as on the previous nights, and advanced up the steps. Bhusan closed his eyes and sat in deep meditation. The sound reached the empty hall. It came winding up the spiral stairs. Then it crossed the long verandah, and paused for a long while at the bedroom door.

"Bhusan's heart beat fast; his whole body trembled. But this time he did not open his eyes. The sound crossed the threshold. It entered the room. Then it went slowly round the room stopping before the rack where the clothes were hanging, the niche with its little lamp, the table where the dried betel leaves were lying, the *almirah* with its various nicknacks, and, last of all it came and stood close to Bhusan himself.

"Bhusan opened his eyes. He saw by the faint light of the crescent moon that there was a skeleton standing right in front of his chair. It had rings on all its fingers, bracelets on its wrists and armlets on its arms, necklaces on its neck, and a golden tiara on its head, – its whole body glittered and sparkled with gold and diamonds. The ornaments hung loosely on the limbs, but did not fall off. Most dreadful of all was the fact that the two eyes, which shone out from the bony face, were living, – two dark moist eyeballs looking out with a fixed and steady stare from between the long thick eyelashes. As he looked his blood froze in his veins. He tried hard to close his eyes, but could not; they remained open staring like those of a dead man.

"Then the skeleton, fixing its gaze upon the face of the motionless Bhusan, silently beckoned with its outstretched hand, the diamond rings on its bony fingers glittering in the pale moonlight.

"Bhusan stood up as one who had lost his senses, and followed the skeleton which left the room, its bones and ornaments rattling with a hollow sound. The verandah was crossed. Winding down the pitch-dark spiral staircase, the bottom of the stairs was reached. Crossing the lower verandah, they entered the empty lampless hall. Passing through it, they came out on to the brick paved path of the garden. The bricks crunched under the tread of the bony feet. The faint moonlight struggled through the thick network of branches and the path was difficult to discern. Making their way through the flitting fireflies, which haunted the dark shadowy path, they reached the river *ghat*.

"By those very steps, up which the sound had come, the jewelled skeleton went down, step by step, with a stiff gait and hard sound. On the swift current of the river, flooded by the heavy rain, a faint streak of moon-light was visible.

"The skeleton descended to the river, and Bhusan, following it, placed one foot in the water. The moment he touched the water, he woke with a start. His guide was no longer to be seen. Only the trees, on the opposite bank of the river, were standing still and silent; and overhead the half-moon was staring as if astonished. Starting from head to foot Bhusan slipped and fell headlong into the river. From the midst of dreams he had stepped, for a moment only, into the borderland of waking life, – the next moment to be plunged into eternal sleep."

Having finished his story the schoolmaster was silent for a little. Suddenly, the moment he stopped, I realized that except for him the whole world had become silent and still. For a long time I also remained speechless, and in the darkness he was unable to see from my face what was its expression.

At last he asked me, "Don't you believe this story?"

I asked, "Do you?"

He said, "No, – and I can give you one or two reasons why. In the first place Dame Nature does not write novels, she has enough to do without all that."

I interrupted him and said, "And, in the second place, my name happens to be Bhusan Shaha."

The schoolmaster, without the least sign of shame, said, "I guessed as much. And what was your wife's name?"

I answered, "Nritya-Kali."

The Hungry Stones

Rabindranath Tagore; translated by C.F. Andrews

MY KINSMAN AND MYSELF were returning to Calcutta from our Puja trip when we met the man in a train. From his dress and bearing we took him at first for an up-country Mahomedan, but we were puzzled as we heard him talk. He discoursed upon all subjects so confidently that you might think the Disposer of All Things consulted him at all times in all that He did. Hitherto we had been perfectly happy, as we did not know that secret and unheard-of forces were at work, that the Russians had advanced close to us, that the English had deep and secret policies, that confusion among the native chiefs had come to a head. But our newly-acquired friend said with a sly smile: "There happen more things in heaven and earth, Horatio, than are reported in your newspapers." As we had never stirred out of our homes before, the demeanour of the man struck us dumb with wonder. Be the topic ever so trivial, he would quote science, or comment on the *Vedas*, or repeat quatrains from some Persian poet; and as we had no pretence to a knowledge of science or the *Vedas* or Persian, our admiration for him went on increasing, and my kinsman, a theosophist, was firmly convinced that our fellow-passenger must have been supernaturally inspired by some strange 'magnetism' or 'occult power', by an 'astral body' or something of that kind. He listened to the tritest saying that fell from the lips of our extraordinary companion with devotional rapture, and secretly took down notes of his conversation. I fancy that the extraordinary man saw this, and was a little pleased with it.

When the train reached the junction, we assembled in the waiting room for the connection. It was then ten p.m., and as the train, we heard, was likely to be very late, owing to something wrong in the lines, I spread my bed on the table and was about to lie down for a comfortable doze, when the extraordinary person deliberately set about spinning the following yarn. Of course, I could get no sleep that night.

When, owing to a disagreement about some questions of administrative policy, I threw up my post at Junagarh, and entered the service of the Nizam of Hydria, they appointed me at once, as a strong young man, collector of cotton duties at Barich.

Barich is a lovely place. The Susta 'chatters over stony ways and babbles on the pebbles', tripping, like a skilful dancing girl, in through the woods below the lonely hills. A flight of one hundred and fifty steps rises from the river, and above that flight, on the river's brim and at the foot of the hills, there stands a solitary marble palace. Around it there is no habitation of man – the village and the cotton mart of Barich being far off.

About two hundred and fifty years ago the Emperor Mahmud Shah II had built this lonely palace for his pleasure and luxury. In his days jets of rose-water spurted from its fountains, and on the cold marble floors of its spray-cooled rooms young Persian damsels would sit, their hair dishevelled before bathing, and, splashing their soft naked feet in the clear water of the reservoirs, would sing, to the tune of the guitar, the *ghazals* of their vineyards.

The fountains play no longer; the songs have ceased; no longer do snow-white feet step gracefully on the snowy marble. It is but the vast and solitary quarters of cess-collectors like us, men oppressed with solitude and deprived of the society of women. Now, Karim Khan, the old clerk of my office, warned me repeatedly not to take up my abode there. "Pass the day there, if you like," said he, "but never stay the night." I passed it off with a light laugh. The servants said that they would work till dark and go away at night. I gave my ready assent. The house had such a bad name that even thieves would not venture near it after dark.

At first the solitude of the deserted palace weighed upon me like a nightmare. I would stay out, and work hard as long as possible, then return home at night jaded and tired, go to bed and fall asleep.

Before a week had passed, the place began to exert a weird fascination upon me. It is difficult to describe or to induce people to believe; but I felt as if the whole house was like a living organism slowly and imperceptibly digesting me by the action of some stupefying gastric juice.

Perhaps the process had begun as soon as I set my foot in the house, but I distinctly remember the day on which I first was conscious of it.

It was the beginning of summer, and the market being dull I had no work to do. A little before sunset I was sitting in an arm-chair near the water's edge below the steps. The Susta had shrunk and sunk low; a broad patch of sand on the other side glowed with the hues of evening; on this side the pebbles at the bottom of the clear shallow waters were glistening. There was not a breath of wind anywhere, and the still air was laden with an oppressive scent from the spicy shrubs growing on the hills close by.

As the sun sank behind the hill-tops a long dark curtain fell upon the stage of day, and the intervening hills cut short the time in which light and shade mingle at sunset. I thought of going out for a ride, and was about to get up when I heard a footfall on the steps behind. I looked back, but there was no one.

As I sat down again, thinking it to be an illusion, I heard many footfalls, as if a large number of persons were rushing down the steps. A strange thrill of delight, slightly tinged with fear, passed through my frame, and though there was not a figure before my eyes, methought I saw a bevy of joyous maidens coming down the steps to bathe in the Susta in that summer evening. Not a sound was in the valley, in the river, or in the palace, to break the silence, but I distinctly heard the maidens' gay and mirthful laugh, like the gurgle of a spring gushing forth in a hundred cascades, as they ran past me, in quick playful pursuit of each other, towards the river, without noticing me at all. As they were invisible to me, so I was, as it were, invisible to them. The river was perfectly calm, but I felt that its still, shallow, and clear waters were stirred suddenly by the splash of many an arm jingling with bracelets, that the girls laughed and dashed and spattered water at one another, that the feet of the fair swimmers tossed the tiny waves up in showers of pearl.

I felt a thrill at my heart – I cannot say whether the excitement was due to fear or delight or curiosity. I had a strong desire to see them more clearly, but naught was visible before me; I thought I could catch all that they said if I only strained my ears; but however hard I strained them, I heard nothing but the chirping of the cicadas in the woods. It seemed as if a dark curtain of two hundred and fifty years was hanging before me, and I would fain lift a corner of it tremblingly and peer through, though the assembly on the other side was completely enveloped in darkness.

The oppressive closeness of the evening was broken by a sudden gust of wind, and the still surface of the Susta rippled and curled like the hair of a nymph, and from the woods wrapt in the evening gloom there came forth a simultaneous murmur, as though they were awakening from a black dream. Call it reality or dream, the momentary glimpse of that invisible mirage reflected from a far-off world, two hundred and fifty years old, vanished in a flash. The mystic forms that brushed past me with their quick unbodied steps, and loud, voiceless laughter, and threw themselves into the river, did not go back wringing their dripping robes as they went. Like fragrance wafted away by the wind they were dispersed by a single breath of the spring.

Then I was filled with a lively fear that it was the Muse that had taken advantage of my solitude and possessed me – the witch had evidently come to ruin a poor devil like myself making a living by collecting cotton duties. I decided to have a good dinner – it is the empty stomach that all sorts of incurable diseases find an easy prey. I sent for my cook and gave orders for a rich, sumptuous *moghlai* dinner, redolent of spices and *ghi*.

Next morning the whole affair appeared a queer fantasy. With a light heart I put on a *sola* hat like the *sahebs*, and drove out to my work. I was to have written my quarterly report that day, and expected to return late; but before it was dark I was strangely drawn to my house – by what I could not say – I felt they were all waiting, and that I should delay no longer. Leaving my report unfinished I rose, put on my *sola* hat, and startling the dark, shady, desolate path with the rattle of my carriage, I reached the vast silent palace standing on the gloomy skirts of the hills.

On the first floor the stairs led to a very spacious hall, its roof stretching wide over ornamental arches resting on three rows of massive pillars, and groaning day and night under the weight of its own intense solitude. The day had just closed, and the lamps had not yet been lighted. As I pushed the door open a great bustle seemed to follow within, as if a throng of people had broken up in confusion, and rushed out through the doors and windows and corridors and verandahs and rooms, to make its hurried escape.

As I saw no one I stood bewildered, my hair on end in a kind of ecstatic delight, and a faint scent of *attar* and unguents almost effected by age lingered in my nostrils. Standing in the darkness of that vast desolate hall between the rows of those ancient pillars, I could hear the gurgle of fountains plashing on the marble floor, a strange tune on the guitar, the jingle of ornaments and the tinkle of anklets, the clang of bells tolling the hours, the distant note of *nahabat*, the din of the crystal pendants of chandeliers shaken by the breeze, the song of *bulbuls* from the cages in the corridors, the cackle of storks in the gardens, all creating round me a strange unearthly music.

Then I came under such a spell that this intangible, inaccessible, unearthly vision appeared to be the only reality in the world – and all else a mere dream. That I, that is to say, Srijut So-and-so, the eldest son of So-and-so of blessed memory, should be drawing a monthly salary of four hundred and fifty *rupees* by the discharge of my duties as collector of cotton duties, and driving in my dog-cart to my office every day in a short coat and *sola* hat, appeared to me to be such an astonishingly ludicrous illusion that I burst into a horse-laugh, as I stood in the gloom of that vast silent hall.

At that moment my servant entered with a lighted kerosene lamp in his hand. I do not know whether he thought me mad, but it came back to me at once that I was in very deed Srijut So-and-so, son of So-and-so of blessed memory, and that, while our poets, great and small, alone could say whether inside of or outside the earth there was a region where unseen fountains perpetually played and fairy guitars, struck by invisible fingers, sent forth an eternal harmony, this at any rate was certain, that I collected duties at the cotton market at Banch, and earned thereby four hundred and fifty *rupees* per *mensem* as my salary. I laughed in great glee at my curious illusion, as I sat over the newspaper at my camp-table, lighted by the kerosene lamp.

After I had finished my paper and eaten my *moghlai* dinner, I put out the lamp, and lay down on my bed in a small side-room. Through the open window a radiant star, high above the Avalli hills skirted by the darkness of their woods, was gazing intently from millions and millions of miles away in the sky at Mr. Collector lying on a humble camp-bedstead. I wondered and felt amused at the idea, and do not knew when I fell asleep or how long I slept; but I suddenly awoke with a start, though I heard no sound and saw no intruder – only the steady bright star on the hilltop had set, and the dim light of the new moon was stealthily entering the room through the open window, as if ashamed of its intrusion.

I saw nobody, but felt as if some one was gently pushing me. As I awoke she said not a word, but beckoned me with her five fingers bedecked with rings to follow her cautiously. I got up noiselessly, and, though not a soul save myself was there in the countless apartments of that deserted palace with its slumbering sounds and waiting echoes, I feared at every step lest any one should wake up. Most of the rooms of the palace were always kept closed, and I had never entered them.

I followed breathless and with silent steps my invisible guide – I cannot now say where. What endless dark and narrow passages, what long corridors, what silent and solemn audience-chambers and close secret cells I crossed!

Though I could not see my fair guide, her form was not invisible to my mind's eye, – an Arab girl, her arms, hard and smooth as marble, visible through her loose sleeves, a thin veil falling on her face from the fringe of her cap, and a curved dagger at her waist! Methought that one of the thousand and one Arabian Nights had been wafted to me from the world of romance, and that at the dead of night I was wending my way through the dark narrow alleys of slumbering Baghdad to a trysting-place fraught with peril.

At last my fair guide stopped abruptly before a deep blue screen, and seemed to point to something below. There was nothing there, but a sudden dread froze the blood in my heart-methought I saw there on the floor at the foot of the screen a terrible negro eunuch dressed in rich brocade, sitting and dozing with outstretched legs, with a naked sword on his lap. My fair guide lightly tripped over his legs and held up a fringe of the screen. I could catch a glimpse of a part of the room spread with a Persian carpet – some one was sitting inside on a bed – I could not see her, but only caught a glimpse of two exquisite feet in gold-embroidered slippers, hanging out from loose saffron-coloured *paijamas* and placed idly on the orange-coloured velvet carpet. On one side there was a bluish crystal tray on which a few apples, pears, oranges, and bunches of grapes in plenty, two small cups and a gold-tinted decanter were evidently waiting the guest. A fragrant intoxicating vapour, issuing from a strange sort of incense that burned within, almost overpowered my senses.

As with trembling heart I made an attempt to step across the outstretched legs of the eunuch, he woke up suddenly with a start, and the sword fell from his lap with a sharp clang on the marble floor. A terrific scream made me jump, and I saw I was sitting on that camp-bedstead of mine sweating heavily; and the crescent moon looked pale in the morning light like a weary sleepless patient at dawn; and our crazy Meher Ali was crying out, as is his daily custom, "Stand back! Stand back!!" while he went along the lonely road.

Such was the abrupt close of one of my Arabian Nights; but there were yet a thousand nights left.

Then followed a great discord between my days and nights. During the day I would go to my work worn and tired, cursing the bewitching night and her empty dreams, but as night came my daily life with its bonds and shackles of work would appear a petty, false, ludicrous vanity.

After nightfall I was caught and overwhelmed in the snare of a strange intoxication, I would then be transformed into some unknown personage of a bygone age, playing my part in unwritten history; and my short English coat and tight breeches did not suit me in the least. With a red velvet cap on my head, loose *paijamas*, an embroidered vest, a long flowing silk gown, and coloured handkerchiefs scented with *attar*, I would complete my elaborate toilet, sit on a high-cushioned chair, and replace my cigarette with a many-coiled *narghileh* filled with rose-water, as if in eager expectation of a strange meeting with the beloved one.

I have no power to describe the marvellous incidents that unfolded themselves, as the gloom of the night deepened. I felt as if in the curious apartments of that vast edifice the fragments of a beautiful story, which I could follow for some distance, but of which I could never see the end, flew about in a sudden gust of the vernal breeze. And all the same I would wander from room to room in pursuit of them the whole night long.

Amid the eddy of these dream-fragments, amid the smell of henna and the twanging of the guitar, amid the waves of air charged with fragrant spray, I would catch like a flash of lightning the momentary glimpse of a fair damsel. She it was who had saffron-coloured *paijamas*, white ruddy soft feet in gold-embroidered slippers with curved toes, a close-fitting bodice wrought with gold, a red cap, from which a golden frill fell on her snowy brow and cheeks.

She had maddened me. In pursuit of her I wandered from room to room, from path to path among the bewildering maze of alleys in the enchanted dreamland of the nether world of sleep.

Sometimes in the evening, while arraying myself carefully as a prince of the blood-royal before a large mirror, with a candle burning on either side, I would see a sudden reflection of the Persian beauty by the side of my own. A swift turn of her neck, a quick eager glance of intense passion and pain glowing in her large dark eyes, just a suspicion of speech on her dainty red lips, her figure, fair and slim crowned with youth like a blossoming creeper, quickly uplifted in her graceful tilting gait, a dazzling flash of pain and craving and ecstasy, a smile and a glance and a blaze of jewels and silk, and she melted away. A wild glist of wind, laden with all the fragrance of hills and woods, would put out my light, and I would fling aside my dress and lie down on my bed, my eyes closed and my body thrilling with delight, and there around me in the breeze, amid all the perfume of the woods and hills, floated through the silent gloom many a caress and many a kiss and many a tender touch of hands, and gentle murmurs in my ears, and fragrant breaths on my brow; or a sweetly-perfumed kerchief was wafted again and again on my cheeks. Then slowly a mysterious serpent would twist her stupefying coils about me; and heaving a heavy sigh, I would lapse into insensibility, and then into a profound slumber.

One evening I decided to go out on my horse – I do not know who implored me to stay – but I would listen to no entreaties that day. My English hat and coat were resting on a rack, and I was about to take them down when a sudden whirlwind, crested with the sands of the Susta and the dead leaves of the Avalli hills, caught them up, and whirled them round and round, while a loud peal of merry laughter rose higher and higher, striking all the chords of mirth till it died away in the land of sunset.

I could not go out for my ride, and the next day I gave up my queer English coat and hat for good.

That day again at dead of night I heard the stifled heart-breaking sobs of some one – as if below the bed, below the floor, below the stony foundation of that gigantic palace, from the depths of a dark damp grave, a voice piteously cried and implored me: "Oh, rescue me! Break through these doors of hard illusion, deathlike slumber and fruitless dreams, place by your side on the saddle, press me to your heart, and, riding through hills and woods and across the river, take me to the warm radiance of your sunny rooms above!"

Who am I? Oh, how can I rescue thee? What drowning beauty, what incarnate passion shall I drag to the shore from this wild eddy of dreams? O lovely ethereal apparition! Where didst thou flourish and when? By what cool spring, under the shade of what date-groves, wast thou born – in the lap of what homeless wanderer in the desert? What Bedouin snatched thee from thy mother's arms, an opening bud plucked from a wild creeper, placed thee on a horse swift as lightning, crossed the burning sands, and took thee to the slave-market of what royal city? And there, what officer of the Badshah, seeing the glory of thy bashful blossoming youth, paid for thee in gold, placed thee in a golden palanquin, and offered thee as a present for the seraglio of his master? And O, the history of that place! The music of the *sareng*, the jingle of anklets, the occasional flash of daggers and the glowing wine of Shiraz poison, and the piercing flashing glance! What infinite grandeur, what endless servitude!

The slave-girls to thy right and left waved the chamar as diamonds flashed from their bracelets; the Badshah, the king of kings, fell on his knees at thy snowy feet in bejewelled shoes, and outside the terrible Abyssinian eunuch, looking like a messenger of death, but clothed like an angel, stood with a naked sword in his hand! Then, O, thou flower of the desert, swept away by the blood-stained dazzling ocean of grandeur, with its foam of jealousy, its rocks and shoals of intrigue, on what shore of cruel death wast thou cast, or in what other land more splendid and more cruel?

Suddenly at this moment that crazy Meher Ali screamed out: "Stand back! Stand back!! All is false! All is false!!" I opened my eyes and saw that it was already light. My *chaprasi* came and handed me my letters, and the cook waited with a *salam* for my orders.

I said; "No, I can stay here no longer." That very day I packed up, and moved to my office. Old Karim Khan smiled a little as he saw me. I felt nettled, but said nothing, and fell to my work.

As evening approached I grew absent-minded; I felt as if I had an appointment to keep; and the work of examining the cotton accounts seemed wholly useless; even the *Nizamat* of the Nizam did not appear to be of much worth. Whatever belonged to the present, whatever was moving and acting and working for bread seemed trivial, meaningless, and contemptible.

I threw my pen down, closed my ledgers, got into my dog-cart, and drove away. I noticed that it stopped of itself at the gate of the marble palace just at the hour of twilight. With quick steps I climbed the stairs, and entered the room.

A heavy silence was reigning within. The dark rooms were looking sullen as if they had taken offence. My heart was full of contrition, but there was no one to whom I could lay it bare, or of whom I could ask forgiveness. I wandered about the dark rooms with a vacant mind. I wished I had a guitar to which I could sing to the unknown: "O fire, the poor moth that made a vain effort to fly away has come back to thee! Forgive it but this once, burn its wings and consume it in thy flame!"

Suddenly two tear-drops fell from overhead on my brow. Dark masses of clouds overcast the top of the Avalli hills that day. The gloomy woods and the sooty waters of the Susta were waiting in terrible suspense and in an ominous calm. Suddenly land, water, and sky shivered, and a wild tempest-blast rushed howling through the distant pathless woods, showing its lightning-teeth like a raving maniac who had broken his chains. The desolate halls of the palace banged their doors, and moaned in the bitterness of anguish.

The servants were all in the office, and there was no one to light the lamps. The night was cloudy and moonless. In the dense gloom within I could distinctly feel that a woman was lying on her face on the carpet below the bed – clasping and tearing her long dishevelled hair with desperate fingers. Blood was tricking down her fair brow, and she was now laughing a hard, harsh, mirthless laugh, now bursting into violent wringing sobs, now rending her bodice and striking at her bare bosom, as the wind roared in through the open window, and the rain poured in torrents and soaked her through and through.

All night there was no cessation of the storm or of the passionate cry. I wandered from room to room in the dark, with unavailing sorrow. Whom could I console when no one was by? Whose was this intense agony of sorrow? Whence arose this inconsolable grief?

And the mad man cried out: "Stand back! Stand back!! All is false! All is false!!"

I saw that the day had dawned, and Meher Ali was going round and round the palace with his usual cry in that dreadful weather. Suddenly it came to me that perhaps he also had once lived in that house, and that, though he had gone mad, he came there every day, and went round and round, fascinated by the weird spell cast by the marble demon.

Despite the storm and rain I ran to him and asked: "Ho, Meher Ali, what is false?"

The man answered nothing, but pushing me aside went round and round with his frantic cry, like a bird flying fascinated about the jaws of a snake, and made a desperate effort to warn himself by repeating: "Stand back! Stand back!! All is false! All is false!!"

I ran like a mad man through the pelting rain to my office, and asked Karim Khan: "Tell me the meaning of all this!"

What I gathered from that old man was this: That at one time countless unrequited passions and unsatisfied longings and lurid flames of wild blazing pleasure raged within that palace, and that the curse of all the heart-aches and blasted hopes had made its every stone thirsty and hungry, eager to swallow up like a famished ogress any living man who might chance to approach. Not one of those who lived there for three consecutive nights could escape these cruel jaws, save Meher Ali, who had escaped at the cost of his reason.

I asked: "Is there no means whatever of my release?" The old man said: "There is only one means, and that is very difficult. I will tell you what it is, but first you must hear the history of a young Persian girl who once lived in that pleasure-dome. A stranger or a more bitterly heart-rending tragedy was never enacted on this earth."

Just at this moment the coolies announced that the train was coming. So soon? We hurriedly packed up our luggage, as the tram steamed in. An English gentleman, apparently just aroused from slumber, was looking out of a first-class carriage endeavouring to read the name of the station. As soon as he caught sight of our fellow-passenger, he cried, "Hallo," and took him into his own compartment. As we got into a second-class carriage, we had no chance of finding out who the man was nor what was the end of his story.

I said; "The man evidently took us for fools and imposed upon us out of fun. The story is pure fabrication from start to finish." The discussion that followed ended in a lifelong rupture between my theosophist kinsman and myself.

Ghost

Karen Tay

THE GHOST OF THANH'S SISTER came to stay on the second day of Tet.

She took up residence again in the little-girl bedroom that had been locked up since last spring, and could be seen floating down the hallway past the witching hour, small naked feet dripping ghost water on the pristine beige carpet.

Thanh had not seen his sister since the day her spirit succumbed to the waves at Piha.

He slipped into a feverish twilight world on the evening a fisherman hooked out her body, swollen with salt water, the folds of flesh white and gelatinous from her long soak. The corners of her eyelids, her fingertips and toes were nibbled raw.

She had been in the ocean for three sleeps.

By the time Thanh recovered enough to sit up and eat some plain hot congee, spooned into his reluctant mouth by one of Ma's church friends, Phuong was already dressed and buried, with her new next-world name of Sophia.

* * *

The dead Phuong-Sophia spoke much less now that she was a ghost than she had in life.

In fact, she said nothing at all in the first few days, content to just hover in doorways and thresholds. While the adults peeled open banana leaf parcels and dug into square sticky banh chu'ng stuffed with fatty pork and lotus seeds, Thanh and his friends played with sparklers in the backyard. Phuong-Sophia would peek over shoulders or sit cross-legged in silence.

In the second week of her stay, Thanh screwed up enough courage to take the rusty iron key from his mother's dresser drawer and unlock the door to her bedroom. He found her sleeping sideways on the narrow single bed with its lucky red sheets, thumb in mouth.

"Phuong," he hissed at her.

Then when she didn't move: "Sophia."

His sister didn't blink or yawn. She took her thumb out of her mouth and sat up.

"Em trai – little brother" she said in her soft voice.

"What time is it? I'm hungry."

* * *

Thanh's Ma slapped him when he tried to tell her about Phuong-Sophia. She thought he was being disrespectful

"Don't tell me your stupid stories. If you have so much time to waste, you should be opening your books more."

Her round arms went up into the air, whapping down on a lump of white dough. A little bowl of sultanas sat nearby, for the scones.

Ma was perpetually tired. She was at the bakery from sunup to sundown, causing some of her customers to joke that they must be open twenty-four hours.

The shop closed at around five pm, but she would surreptitiously sell steamed pork buns and greasy fried ban xeo through the back door to late night drunkards.

Thanh's Ba, who left the raising of children and other household matters to Hung, referred to his wife as 'the boss'.

Besides, he was perennially exhausted himself – working six-day, twelve-hour shifts at the plastics factory.

All he wanted when he arrived home was a cup of strong, dark Vietnamese coffee, sweetened with condensed milk and accompanied by a few Tim Tams, before washing his feet and hopping into bed.

"Mind your mother, son," he said tiredly to Thanh whenever he tried to complain about her strictness.

"She's a little hard on you, but it's for your own good."

* * *

So Sophia stayed Thanh's secret.

He found that it was easy enough to feed her. Hung would cook dinner the night before and leave instructions on what to heat up to her husband and son in the morning.

Thanh's father usually worked late and would bring his share of dinner to the factory in old cookie tins.

Thanh would take his own meal – something simple like fried egg vermicelli (his favourite), or more typically, stir-fried greens and garlic, caramelised pork stew (his least favourite), a small fried fish and always some kind of soup, up to his sister's room.

He'd set the plate down before Sophia and she would put her face next to the food and sniff like a cat, ingesting aroma.

When she was done, Thanh would pick up his chopsticks and dig into the meat or fish, drowning his rice in a sea of soup and leaving the leafy yucky greens till last.

They played together too. Most of the time it was Monopoly – Sophia had been obsessed with the game before the accident.

She always chose the little scottie dog, and Thanh would be the top hat.

Or they would pretend to be camping, something Ma never let them do because of the dirt and disease. They would make a fort out of sheets, pitching them up like a tent, hollow and white in the glow of the torch.

* * *

"What was it like? When you died?"

Sophia was in her second year of intermediate when she died.

Ma gathered the flowers and teddy bears left by her friends and teacher, secretly burning them so she could scatter the ashes at sea. In the spot where she guessed her daughter might have drowned.

Popular. It was a word that applied to pretty, sassy Sophia, who had been her school's best goalkeep at netball and was so brainy she didn't need to brown nose anybody.

Thanh wished popularity could be inherited, then maybe his sister could pass on hers, like jewellery or toys or something.

"I don't really remember."

Her face scrunched up.

"It was real cold in the water and I swam for a long time, but my legs got tired and then heavier and heavier."

Thanh waited, but Sophia didn't finish her story. Instead, she rattled the dice in the palm of her hand and released.

"Sixes. I get to roll again."

* * *

A new girl started at Thanh's school.

She was half-Samoan, half-Chinese, with long, dark curly hair, eyes that tipped up at the corners and thin, strong brown legs. Jeanna Ting was a little beauty, but she was also more than that. Within the first week, she had also stood up to the class bully when she was cornered in the girls' toilet.

The bully, a little shit with a stomach as wide as she was tall, had demanded that Jeanna hand over her schoolbag for a sticky-fingered inspection.

She refused.

When the bully howled with rage and reached for her, Jeanna reacted fast. She ducked low, pinched the bully's knees together with one wiry arm, reached up under her skirt and dug her fingers into the girl's pubic bone

"Touch me again and I'll break your pelvis," she said fiercely.

Nobody quite knew what a pelvis was, but the bully ran away howling and Jeanna's star soared.

Girls fought to sit next to her. Boys left fake tattoos, chocolate bars and cheap two dollar shop trinkets outside her locker.

Thanh worshipped Jeanna, whose father was a solicitor and mother owned an art gallery on K'Rd. She always kept a piece of grape Hubba Bubba inside her cheek to chew on when the teacher's back was turned.

Her wild curls, smooth and oiled and kept in a perfectly brushed ponytail with rainbow coloured elastics, smelled like spring rain.

And though she had any number of grazed knees, cuts, small bumps and bruises like anyone else, she also had the coolest plasters of superheroes like Wonder Woman, Batman and Iron Man.

Her cousins sent them to her all the way from America.

* * *

"You got a new friend at school, eh?"

Thanh was picking at his meal. Fried chicken pieces, julienned green beans fried in egg and rice. Chicken and ginger soup today, thick yellow slices floating on top with the fat and skin. He looked up from his food.

Sophia was toying with a hunk of hair, sliding it between her small white teeth like floss. The wet, pointed tip looked like a watercolour brush.

"Yeah, I guess. Her name's Jeanna."

"Ooooo Thanh's got a g-i-r-l-f-r-i-e-n-d!"

"Shut up!"

He could feel his cheeks grow hot, redden like Ba's face after he'd had a glass of wine.

"Ooooo you l-i-k-e her!"

"Not even."

Sophia's cat-like eyes narrowed, she pursed her lips as if about to blow a bubble.

"Well, you better not forget me, em trai."

Thanh looked at her then, really looked at her. He realised something that had been bothering him lately: Sophia was growing more diaphanous.

He could see the cream coloured curtains with their little blue flowers straight through her hips. Her face and neck looked normal, solid, but she was definitely dissipating from the feet up.

"I won't," he mumbled, prodding the top hat forward on the board.

"Cause you know what Ma would say, if she found out you were friends with someone like that."

"Who's gonna tell her then? You're dead."

Sophia wasn't upset though. She just stuck her tongue out at him. He could see through the pink to the back of her throat.

* * *

The students of Room Five were having a Cultural Exchange Evening. They were paired up – with each couple instructed to write a song, a poem or a story about their culture.

"We would love to hear more about Vietnam, Thanh," said Mrs Harrison. She always pronounced his name as 'tan-h', as if she had run out of breath at the end.

Most of the kids in class said his name the same way, and he had never bothered correcting them. Ma always said there was no point making a fuss if it wasn't going to change anything.

Mrs Harrison was always careful around Thanh. There were no other Asian children in Room Five apart from Jeanna, who was only half and Mohammad, but he was Muslim and his parents were from Malaysia.

Thanh was polite to her, mainly because he knew he'd have his ears twisted and his legs smacked with a ruler when he got home if he was rude. But he hated her.

Once, when he'd been sent to the staff rooom to deliver a note during interval, he overheard her talking to some other teachers.

Mrs Harrison was wearing a purple velvet top and matching skirt, looking like a large stuffed grape.

"... the boy's name was Dick Shih! I just about killed myself keeping a straight face. Bloody hell! Of course, he was picked on from day one by the other kids. Poor thing. But I can't say I blame the children. His parents should have checked first before they named him, but they were you know, fresh off the boat. Oh, hello Thanh."

She had taken the note and read it while waving one hand dismissively at him.

It did not come as a surprise to Thanh that when it came to pairing up the students, she put him with Jeanna.

There was a slightly nervous moment when it seemed that she would choose Mohammad instead. In the end though, Mohammad went with Cindy Ropati and Thanh got Jeanna all to himself.

* * *

The night before the cultural performance – they were going to sing a mash-up of the Chinese and Vietnamese national anthems, Thanh came down with the flu.

It was the real thing, complete with aching body parts, a high temperature, blocked nose, headache and swollen lymph nodes. If he had been even slightly better, Thanh would have insisted on going to school.

But he felt so sick that he didn't even fuss when Ma dosed him with the strong bitter tea that relatives had brought in especially from Vietnam.

He just quietly sipped the scalding brew, brought to him in Ba's special green Milo mug (free with purchase), grateful that the flu had tamped down his taste buds, then lay back in bed and slept.

* * *

He dreamed. Oh how he dreamed.

He was a baby again, in his mother's womb. Floating in a warm soothing ocean of amniotic fluid. Then he was a goldfish, his fishy mouth opening and closing in gasps as he swam down the birth canal, gushing out into the world in a flood of red salt.

Ba tiptoed into the room at one point. He must have come home early from the factory to check on Thanh. Ba touched his forehead and his hand felt like an icy imprint.

There was Ma's voice, less shrill than usual. She was speaking in Vietnamese, but so fast that Thanh couldn't follow except for the occasional phrase.

All he knew was that he wanted water. Big long gulps of it, so cold that the glass frosted over. He was so thirsty.

He was a thirsty bear. Yogi Bear in the desert. How he loved Yogi Bear, with his pert green tie and jaunty little hat.

An auntie had dropped off a bundle of her daughter's old things a couple of years ago. Among the well-worn possessions was a video player and tapes of the hungry bear. Thanh was addicted for a time, watching and rewinding the tapes over and over again.

A voice dropped out of the blue sky and boomed at him.

"I'm smarter than the average bear!"

His tongue darted out again, tasting moisture from an ice cube someone was slowly rubbing between his lips.

* * *

"My children's mother."

Ba gently touched Ma's shoulder. She had been sitting on the hospital bed for far too long. Days. Her body gave off an unwashed smell.

He did not like hospitals.

Their scent of futility reminded him too much of the crowded Cho Ray Hospital in Saigon, where his mother had been taken after she was run over by a train while crossing the tracks on her motorbike.

The train was carrying a load of white tourists to Nha Trang, where they would ride a river boat down the Song Cai and clap their hands as they watched amusing water puppet shows put on by illiterate children who had dropped out of school to earn American dollars.

Ba's mother had died in that place that stunk of disease long before you entered the doorway.

They had amputated both her legs, first below the knees, then higher and higher as gangrene set in until the doctors finally admitted defeat. There was too much poison to excise. Her body was nothing but blackness.

His wife did not respond. She was too busy telling beads on the rosary. Hail Mary. Our Father. Glory Be.

Ba did not know if he believed in the western god – he had been raised Buddhist by his grandmother, who was a practising vegetarian, so devout she would step over an ant on the ground rather than crush it.

He knew something about women though. So Ba stayed by his wife's side, without touching her again, as they both stared at their son's inert body.

As if they could raise him up by the power of love alone.

* * *

"Em trai."

What a sorrowful little voice! All the cheer leached out of it.

"Chi gai – big sister."

He was calling out into a yawning dark cave.

Thanh's eyes were unseeing as a bat's. His hands and his body curved into a fetal position. He was hanging upside down from the roof.

"Where are you, chi gai? I can't see."

It was a physical impossibility to move his limbs. They were rock-heavy.

He had been dreaming of running through the desert again with his friend, Yogi Bear. The bear had called out:

"Hey there, Boo Boo!"

They leaped over sand dunes, feeling the scorching grains give beneath bare brown feet. But then Yogi had disappeared and a dark and frightening fog spread over the land, blackening everything.

"I'm here, over here."

A sliver of light floating through the nightscape like a wedge of silver cake, then Sophia's face loomed oval and shinypale.

"Oh. Thanh."

She gummed a hand to her face and sobbed. Tears leaked out noiselessly from between her fingers like small gems and sploshed to the cave floor, leaving a trail of light.

"Help me get down."

He was hollering, he realised, but his ears were buzzing so it was hard to tell how loud he was being. Why was she just standing there? Sophia took one step toward him, stopped and shook her head.

"I'm so sorry, em trai, I can't."

"Why not? Don't be a dick!"

If Ma was here, she would have pinched his mouth for that, but Thanh felt he was justified, under the circumstances.

"You're too far gone, my brother," she said.

Her still-liquid eyes were caressing beacons in the black.

"I can't follow you now."

* * *

Thanh drew his last breath as the clock stopped at quarter past midnight. His parents and Sophia were there by the bedside when the doctor turned off his life support. Ba and Ma were grey, faded. They had aged twenty years in the three seconds it took for their son to exhale his last breath.

* * *

He was dead, but not gone.

Thanh floated on the ceiling of the hospital, looking down at his body. So small and skinny. Bushy black hair spilling onto the antiseptic pillow.

Ba had gone to get cheap filter coffee from the cafeteria. Ma was on the phone outside to her prayer group, informing them that their daily supplications hadn't worked and Jesus wouldn't save her son after all.

Only Sophia was in the room. She sat silently by his body, holding his steadily cooling hand tenderly in her own.

"Thanh."

He wanted to go down to her, but wasn't sure how to navigate his new body. It was like a cloud, with his head stuck in the middle.

"Thanh."

He concentrated hard, again.

Then just like that, he figured it out. By squeezing his thoughts into one, he could pull himself together, sparkle down to his sister in her slightly too-big pink sneakers. The toes stuffed with newspaper. Ma always bought shoes a size too big. She said they'd grow into them.

"Am I really dead?"

Sophia answered by sniffing and wiping her nose on her sleeve, leaving a sticky snot residue.

"Cooooool." He let out a long whistle.

It was pretty neat, if you thought about it. There was a twinge of regret about Jeanna Ting. He would have liked to see her grow up, pictured the wild fierce beauty she would become.

Thanh thought, no, was sure that he would have liked to go on a date with Jeanna. Steal a kiss at the end of the night.

"You think it's cool, right?"

Sophia didn't seem to be as excited as he was. Perhaps she was jealous. It would be just like his sister to think that she had some kind of first dibs on being dead. Like how she always thought she was smarter because she was older.

She took a deep breath, bent her head down and kissed him with trembling lips. On the forehead.

Ba walked in at that moment, carrying a half-empty cup. He regarded the scene in the room, and fumbled with the zip of his blue and white polyester parka.

"Phuong."

The name sounded crabby in his mouth, washed-out. Phuong looked up just as Thanh realised he'd lost his train of thought and was weightless, back on the ceiling. His father and sister looked like miniature dolls.

"Let's go home, daughter. We have a funeral to prepare."

* * *

My little brother Thanh died just after Tet. The doctors said it was bacterial meningitis, the worst kind, or so I heard. My parents don't talk about it much. I guess it's not the Asian thing to do, to share your feelings non-stop.

I know Ma blamed herself for thinking it was the flu at first, and making Thanh drink that stupid herbal mix. Death by bitter tea.

The night before he slipped away from us, I had the craziest dream. I was swimming in the ocean at Piha, where we had gone for our last family holiday together the previous spring.

My arms cut through the water in long, even strokes. When I looked down at my body, I saw that I was wearing a long white ao dai.

The colour of mourning.

Little fish were swimming around me in a circle, in all shades of the rainbow. There was light shining on the water. I felt safe and protected, as if nothing could hurt me.

I stayed in the sea a long time, my feet treading water, the skin of my fingers and toes pruning like the sour lips of an old woman.

In our culture, we choose a new name for those entering the next world. Ma might have converted to Catholicism, but she was traditional at heart. She wouldn't send her son to the afterlife without a way to go on.

Come what may.

We thought about it a long time, debating over whether to give him a Vietnamese or western death-name. In the end, I was the one who spoke up. The name itself was crystal clear in my head, as if Thanh himself had whispered it in my ear.

"Yogi," I said.

Ghost Fire

Emily Teng

I WAS TEN YEARS OLD when my parents stitched my grandmother's ghost to me.

Until she died, I hadn't known that my grandmother was still alive. My father had run away from his parents at the age of sixteen and hadn't once, in twenty years, returned home. When the nightmares and misfortunes began, he'd thought he was simply plagued by a string of back luck. It wasn't until a traveling priest happened by that we learned the root of the troubles was the ghost of his mother, my grandmother, who had died earlier that year and had hunted down her only son to exact vengeance for having abandoned her parents.

Father had always been a cunning bargainer. It was what made him so successful in business. In exchange for her promise to leave the rest of the family alone, he offered her his firstborn child, hoping she would assume that it was my brother. We had been born barely a year apart, and I had always been small for my age. When we walked down the street together, people often thought him the eldest child. It was a tempting offer: unrestricted access to the firstborn son, the one to carry on the family line.

Grandmother accepted.

My memories of the ritual are torn, gilt-bright scraps of the senses: the painfully hard floor against my knees, father's hand clutched on my shoulder, the priest's droning chant, the incense smoke making me want to sneeze. Before the ritual started, white thread had been looped around my fingers – fate-threads, meant to bind two souls together for all eternity.

Afterwards, when it was done, mother put me in bed, and brought me hot ginger soup. The steam rising from the soup bowl twisted the room into strange new mirages. Mother fed me the entire bowl, her eyes welled up with tears the whole time.

She cried again when, three days later, grandmother discovered how she had been tricked, and vented her anger on me until I was screaming in pain, but this time from relief.

By the time I was sixteen, all memory of what my life had been like before my grandmother's ghost had faded to a smoke haze on the horizon. She accompanied me everywhere I went, critical and dissatisfied, her voice a poisonous hiss in my ear. She loathed being bound to me, worthless girl-child that I was, not enough to satisfy her hunger. She would have killed me, but she still needed me. I was all she had, and she was all I had.

I never was able to figure out who the hatred first came from, my grandmother or me.

* * *

Men walked through town: a dozen or so of them, all hard-eyed and weathered as ancient statues, but with a pinched, hungry look to them of too few meals and too little sleep indoors. I wasn't the only one who stared, looking up to watch them pass. If mother had been there, she would have scolded me, telling me how unseemly it was for an unmarried maiden to stare brazenly at men. Never mind that no man in town would so much as look at me, which she well knew.

I found myself watching the man in front. He wasn't handsome, and yet I couldn't look away. He didn't so much walk as swagger, carrying himself with the easy confidence of someone who knows their place in the world. If I were to guess, I would have said he was their leader.

His gaze fell on me, and I braced myself. But nothing happened: no pause, no narrowing of the eyes. I was just another townsperson in the marketplace; I meant nothing to him.

Something in my belly twisted and shivered.

I turned to the vendor whose stall I had stopped in front of. "Who are those men?"

The seller startled at being directly addressed by me. He appeared to be debating whether to answer me or not, and finally he said, "Soldiers."

"On which side?"

He avoided my eyes. "Does it matter?"

I wanted to ask him more, but he was looking so unsettled already that I merely thanked him and walked off, pretending not to notice how he shuddered at my smile.

That night at dinner, father talked about the day's business. I paid only half-attention until I heard the mention of a band of bandits who had come to town and were staying at an inn on the other side of the river.

I looked up from my bowl. "Bandits?"

"A whole band of them. Walking through town in the middle of the day, the arrogance."

"You mean the soldiers."

"Maybe they were once, but not any longer. Did you see what direction they came from? East. Away from the war, not towards it. I bet they're deserters, only looking out for their own fortunes." He lifted a slice of pork and smacked his lips.

He's one to talk, grandmother sneered from the corner.

"Grandmother says they aren't bandits. She knows what bandits are like, and they aren't them," I blurted out in the middle of his rant, interrupting him.

Father's cup froze halfway to his lips. We never spoke about grandmother out loud, smothering what had been done to me in silence as if by not speaking of it, we could pretend it hadn't happened, that she didn't exist. Fear flickered through his eyes before he made it go away. "If grandmother says so."

Brother continued to eat as if nothing had happened, shoveling food into his mouth with the single-minded intensity of a growing boy, without so much as a flicker of a glance in my direction. Mother looked down, the way she always did at times like this, to keep me from seeing the expression of relief on her face.

I finished my dinner in silence.

* * *

I waited until night had fallen before I slipped out. A full moon hung in the sky like a pearl earring, and the familiar streets were doused with a silvered darkness like a sheen of gilt over rotting wood. I had bound my hair up and tucked it under a hat, but still I kept my head down in case anyone I knew saw me.

The inn was easy enough to find. It was also dark and silent, gloomy and apparently uninhabited. Right across the street, though, was a teahouse. Light and laughter spilled from the doorway and from behind the oiled-paper windows. The soldiers might lay their heads at the inn, but I had no doubt where they spent their waking hours. I walked over to the teahouse door, then hesitated.

Grandmother, who had been drifting silently alongside until now, suddenly said, *What are you planning?*

"I just want to talk to them," I said, avoiding the question.

I know what you're thinking. You think they'll help you, why? Because that man caught your eye in the market? Because you like the way he looks? She let out a derisive snort. *I know his type. He won't help you. If you want help you need to look elsewhere for it.*

"He will," I said.

And you know this how?

"Because I know hunger when I see it," I said, and pushed the door open.

Inside, the teahouse looked surprisingly similar to home: rich wood furniture, silk tapestries, and patterned tiles. But our house had never been so choked on scented smoke, or been so filled with voices and the plunked strings of zithers. Sheer silk screens veiled off rooms, transforming people on the other side into shadow-puppet characters, flattened into cryptic outlines.

I walked down the hall, pulling back curtains a finger's width to peer into the rooms as I passed. In the second room from the end I finally found the soldiers, all crammed into a room that would have been snug at half the number. The men were younger than I'd first realized, seeing them walk through town. My brother's age.

I was trying to figure out which one of them was the man I was looking for when a hand fell on my shoulder. "Little sister," a hard voice said, "what are you doing spying on us, eh?"

It was him.

I stepped away from the curtain, letting it swing shut, and faced him. "I was looking for you."

One eyebrow lifted. Up close, his looks were even more plain and ordinary than before. "For me, eh? What for?"

"Business."

"Business," he repeated. He lifted a lock of hair from my shoulder, coiling the black strands around his finger. "Your face is white from staying indoors, your hands are soft and uncalloused, and your hair smells of jasmine oil. You're wearing a man's coat, but it's made of silk and the weave is fine. You're a rich man's daughter, or I'm an idiot, and I don't do business with rich men's daughters."

"Not even when you can have all that rich man's wealth?"

A roar of laughter washed out of the room. He glanced over briefly, then back to me. "This house is a place for fun. If you want to talk business, we'll do it in my room."

It was a challenge; a dare to place my honor in his hands and go unchaperoned to his room. Did he think I would refuse?

His room was little more than a bare space with a padded bench for a bed and a stand with a wash basin in one corner. I moved over to the wash stand as he lit a candle and seated himself on the bed. "So, what is it that you want with me?"

Grandmother's hand was an icy claw on my shoulder, chilling me all the way to the bone. *Careful,* her grip warned. "My father is one of the wealthiest merchants in town. Last year he made a profit of over two thousand marks of silver. The year before that, three thousand. We have chests of silver buried beneath the larch tree in the back courtyard. My mother has jewels: pearls and jade and amber. She hides her jewelry in a compartment in her bedroom that she thinks no one knows about, but I do."

He frowned. "And you're telling me all this, why?"

"Isn't it obvious? So you can rob them."

"Is that what people think we are? Robbers?"

"Are you not?" The look he gave me was hard and bitter and cold. I pressed on. "You're hungry, are you not? Why not fill that hunger?"

"Wanting something doesn't give you the right to take it."

Yes it does, grandmother said.

I was starting to get impatient. "It's a simple prospect: rob my family. What more are you looking for?"

He crossed his arms over his chest. "I'm curious, I suppose. It's not every day a rich man's daughter comes up and asks me and my men to rob her family blind. Why are you doing this?"

A lifetime's worth of bitterness and hatred surged in me, all the anger that I kept smothered flaring up with such sudden fury that I half-expected flames to start licking up my wrists. Because, I wanted to say, I remembered the way father's hand heavy on my shoulder, anchoring me in place as incense smoke tickled my nose, keeping me from running away. The way mother wept afterwards, feeding me, the relief rolling off of her in painfully clear cold waves that her only son wouldn't have to be sacrificed to appease my grandmother's appetite. The way my brother had accepted this as his rightful due, since he was male and the family heir, and I was just a girl, my life worth less than his. The way all our neighbors moved out of my way whenever I walked through town and not a single marriage proposal had ever been made, because who would want to welcome a ghost into their house? The way I had been sacrificed, and my sacrifice buried or washed away in the course of years.

But it wasn't just my own hatred that drove me. It was grandmother's as well. Her hatred of father for leaving home in the first place so that she'd been forced to bury her husband, and then when she died, gone unmourned so that her spirit had warped in anger and hatred. Hatred for my family, for saddling her onto this worthless girl-child, denying her the full sating of her hunger. I, who was not good enough, who was not the one she wanted.

But he didn't need to know all of that. Instead, I simply said, "Because I hate them."

He was silent a long while. "Come closer. Let me see you."

I stepped forward, cupped myself in candlelight so he could see me. I met his gaze squarely: there was no hiding, he might as well see it all at once. And I saw the sudden widening of his own eyes, the dawning realization as he met my gaze and saw in their pale, unnatural shine what it was that lived with me, bound to me. It was a look I knew far too well. I felt a sudden flash of contempt that I was having to rely on such a weak man to achieve my goals. But he was the tool I had been given, and I wouldn't have another chance like this.

You frighten him, grandmother said. *We frighten him. He won't do it.*

For a long while all he did was stare, and I was afraid that grandmother was right. Then he took a deep, steadying breath. "How do I know this isn't a trap?"

"You want assurance?"

"What can you give?"

There was only one thing I had to give, and we both knew it. I kept my gaze level so he could see the clear burn of them like a night lake ablaze with moonlight, as I reached up and slipped my brother's jacket from my shoulders.

* * *

It hurt to walk home, though not as much as I'd been afraid it would. Grandmother kept pace with me, ranting in contempt and revulsion, eyes gleaming with the pleasure of moral disgust. *Ruined,* she whispered. *You're a ruined woman. You've ruined yourself. No one will ever marry you now.*

"No one would have married me anyways."

So you think just because of that you can do whatever you please? You think you can act so shameless, sell yourself so cheap?

"It wasn't selling. It was making a promise."

Two ways of saying one thing.

"We'll see what you think tomorrow night."

The house was silent and still when I snuck back in and crawled into bed. I closed my eyes, trying to ignore both the throbbing between my legs and my grandmother's continued stream of invectives, and the next time I opened them, the sun had risen to burn the fog of night away.

The plan we'd agreed on the night before had been simple. He would wait until the third hour of night, then bring his men with him, circling around town to approach from the rear of the house. I would open the back door for them. They would take everything of value, destroy what they couldn't, and burn my father's contracts. They would smash the larch tree to kindling and rip every scrap of silk apart. I had wanted them to kill or disfigure my family, but I knew that would be too much to ask. Grandmother and I would have to be satisfied with destroying any hope of a good future for my family, that was all. And when the men left, they would take me with them.

The last point he had been reluctant to agree to, but I had insisted. With our vengeance exacted, I would be free to leave for the first time in my life. I could go anywhere I wanted.

"And where would that be?" he had wanted to know.

His eyes had jittered as he asked it, darting to my face and away again. How long do I have to put up with you, was what he was really asking. "Just until the next town," I'd said, "and then I'll go on my own way." The flash of relief in his eyes had been unmistakable.

All day long, I vibrated with anticipation. Grandmother, for all her disapproval, couldn't help but feel the end approaching too and she trembled and pulled at her hair in agonies of incipient ecstasy.

This lasted all the way up through dinner, when father returned from town with news that the bandits had left town.

"Left?"

Father mistook the spike of emotion in my voice for relief. "Some of the magistrate's men spotted them leaving by the west gate a little after dawn. Some of them still looked hung over from the night before. They spent the whole night drinking and carousing, and then they're gone. Good riddance."

I was trembling so hard that my tea was threatening to spill over. I set my cup down. "Maybe it's a trick. Maybe they're planning to sneak back later tonight when everyone's asleep."

"The magistrate thought the same. He had his men follow them all the way to the river. Trust me when I say they're long gone."

I sat there, unable to speak, unable even to move. Eventually dinner ended. Somehow I stood. I followed mother to her antechamber, where she put my embroidery into my hands and picked up her own. I watched my hand rise and fall, the needle plunging in and out, in and out of the silk, dragging tendrils of carmine in its wake. I worked until the candle began to gutter low and finally it was time to go to bed. I went to my own room, where, instead of undressing, I simply stood there in the dark with my back pressed against the door and at last, at last, allowed myself to feel the emotions that had been coursing through me, bottled up, since dinner.

He had lied. I should have realized, I understood, that however tempting the promise of all those riches were, they weren't enough to overcome his fear of a vengeful ghost. He had promised me, had taken the only thing I had of value, knowing full well that he never intended to deliver on his promises, and then he and his men had fled. I had seen the fear in his eyes, but I had gambled on his greed outweighing his fear; I had thought he would have understood hunger enough to want what I was offering. I was wrong.

I felt humiliated. Used. *Soiled.*

The air was hot and suffocating. I moved to the windows, threw the shutters open to tempt in a breeze. From here I could see into the back courtyard where the larch tree grew, interrupting the view to the master residence where mother and father had their rooms. Candlelight guttered in a single window, but even as I watched it was snuffed out, and then there was nothing left to illuminate the scene except the hard, bitten moon above.

"Grandmother," I whispered, "what do I do?"

But for once, she was silent. Waiting. Frustrated, just as I was.

Except I wasn't just frustrated. I was furious.

So what are you going to do about it? a voice murmured in my ear. Not grandmother's voice. My own.

From beyond the walls I heard the sound of a cart rolling by, horses whickering and wheels clattering along the paving stone. Lives in motion, while I remained tied to this place until death by the threads of my grandmother's fate.

I slipped out into the courtyard. The whisper of my slippers against stone sounded far too loud to my ears. I kicked them off and padded barefoot down the walkway to the kitchen, which was quiet and cold at this time of night, all except for the smoldering bank of embers in the stove. I felt disjointed, disconnected, as if all the knots about me had come undone.

In one corner stood the huge vats where we stored soy sauce, vinegar, and cooking oil. It was this last one that I wanted. I unsealed the jar.

It took I don't know how many trips to spill a trail of oil from the kitchen all the way to my parents' rooms and my brother's. I inscribed glistening circles on the grounds around them, and around the larch tree, making sure to generously splash it around the paving stones and soak the tree itself.

Back in the kitchen again, I picked up a coal and clutched it tight in my hand. I imagined the skin scorching away, transmuting into smoke and ash: an offering to the dead, to those who craved the taste of meat and in whose hunger would notice.

"Grandmother," I whispered, "answer me."

And at last, my grandmother responded. *What do you want?*

I opened my mouth. The voice that came out, raw and gleeful with hungry need, could just as well have been my grandmother's as it could have been mine.

"I want my family to burn."

The coal burst into flames. With a cry, I dropped it. It landed on a splash of oil, which lit ablaze at once. The flames raced down the trail of oil, gobbling it up, streaking along faster than an ordinary fire should have been able to move. But this wasn't ordinary fire. This was my grandmother's fire. A ghost fire, fueled by a hunger that no living thing could match. Fire enough to devour the night whole.

I didn't stay to watch. As I slipped out the side door, I heard a scream, high and thin, rising above the crackle of burning wood.

More shouts sounded from the surrounding houses, and doors slammed open. The neighbors were waking up. I slipped down a back alley and ran, the night air slapping against my cheeks. Only once did I glance behind me, to see flames howling skyward: a funeral pyre, an offering to those who hadn't been given their due in life.

I didn't stop until I had left town, then I collapsed to the ground, the breath shuddered in and out of me like hysterical laughter. I had to roll over onto my back otherwise I felt I would have choked.

At last my breathing calmed, and I got to my feet. I had nothing on me but the clothes on my back and the hair on my head. I didn't even have shoes: I had run out barefoot, and my feet were cut and bleeding. I had nothing with me.

No, that wasn't quite true. I had grandmother.

She stood next to me, the moonlight gilding her edges silver. From the tilt of her head and the way her eyes narrowed, I could see she was pleased. Proud of me, for the first time since she'd been bound to me, and I felt a flush of warmth at her approval. "Satisfied?"

She licked her lips, her tongue long and sinuous over her teeth. *For now,* she said. *And you, dear girl. What now?*

I stared down the road, an unwept river unspooling across the landscape. An image rose to mind: a man's face, nondescript and ordinary, hovering above mine in the darkness. The face of a man I had trusted. The face of a betrayer.

The words hissed out of me, venomous as anything that had ever dripped out of my grandmother's mouth. "We're not done yet."

I set my feet on the road and began to walk.

The Silence of Farewells

Yilin Wang

For my waipo, Yang Xuhua

CAN YOU SEE THE PURPLE JELLYFISH drifting slowly alongside me in the Yangtze? They look like giant mushrooms, their translucent domed heads each holding a neon pink flower with four outstretched petals. Their long wispy tentacles flow like silvery gusts of incense smoke, gentle unspoken prayers from my world to yours.

Come home, I said with a trembling voice when I called you three months ago, on the final day I was alive. *Granny will wait around for you, for as long as possible.*

You must have been asleep then, with your phone turned off or on silent, our days and nights reversed on opposite sides of the world. *You have reached my voicemail and I'm currently not available*, a recording of your voice answered. *Please leave me a message and I'll return your call as soon as I can.*

Even if you picked up the phone then and jumped onto a flight immediately, you would have never made it back in time, and besides, you couldn't have returned that night anyways, burdened by final exams for the last semester of your undergraduate degree in English Literature and interviews for your first full-time job. But I kept calling you anyways, over and over again, desperately beckoning you homewards as the clock in my living room made its slow momentous countdown to an end date that I couldn't predict but could feel drawing near.

You have finally made it back, at last.

The shuttered windows of our living room swing open with an ancient groan, and you lean out to glance at the riverbank below. I swim closer towards the shore, carried by the waves of the muddy river. The wind stirs, filling the air with the scent of your favorite perfume, the sharp notes of musty paper and fresh lemongrass.

Please scatter my ashes into the Yangtze, I wrote in the will I left for your great-aunt. She followed every word of my instructions with care, as unconventional as they were. I didn't want to be tied down to land or stone, had no need for paper money or grave sweeping on the Day of Qingming. All I want is to remain, watching over the shoreline as tides rise and fall, as houses are torn down and rebuilt, as the skylines shift with the coming of tomorrow and the days after.

You take out a small bag of fish feed, open it, and scatter it into the waves. The feed drifts and disappears among chunks of floating grass and seaweed. Faint shadows swim past me, as if summoned by your return. It's as if we're feeding fish together again, and although you don't speak, I can almost hear the question at the tip of your tongue. You were always a curious kid who begged me to tell you yet another story. *What are the shadows and where are they from?*

These jellyfish haven't surfaced since you were a baby. Legend says that they were once the tears of Wang Zhaojun. A servant girl from the Han dynasty who was not much older than you are now, she was said to have volunteered to marry a prince in a distant land as a part of a peace treaty, although how much choice did one really have in that situation? Before she left, she returned to this same place, her hometown, on a wooden boat, visiting it one last time to say goodbye.

She strummed the chords of her pipa as she glanced at the village where she was born. A few drops of her tears fell into the river, transforming into jellyfish, which became known as taohuayu, peach blossom fish, because they resembled fallen petals blooming again in a second life.

Zhaojun never made it back home to her birthplace, but you have returned, although not for long. The jellyfish glow through the murky surface, abloom once more. Who knew that ghosts are still able to cry?

* * *

On the next morning, your footsteps are slow, gentle, and tentative as you make your way across creaky floorboards, tiptoeing towards a small pile of paper boxes at the center of the living room, all that remains of my belongings. Your great-aunt's sons have already cleared out most of the house in accordance to my will, leaving only these final boxes I left specifically for you.

You approach the boxes one step at a time, as if you were a teenager again, sneaking home after a long night out with friends, as if you fear that your movement will wake me from my eternal sleep even though I have long become a part of the river. Don't fret, your footsteps are nothing but soothing in this place where the only music has become silence.

You begin to sift through the piles of notebooks, paper, and books that I left behind for you. Thick folders hold stacks of folded articles torn from newspapers, with titles like 'Five Ways to Protect Your Health for a Long Life' and 'Top Tips for Teaching Reading to Elementary School Students'. You grin with excitement as you discover a notebook. The thin white journals have yellowing covers stained by a few splatters of tea. The last time I wrote in it, its pages were so fragile, the wrinkled wings of a newborn butterfly emerging from its chrysalis, unfurling its wings as it prepares to take flight.

You open the pages and sift through them. The pages inside contain quotes I have copied, maxims about life. None of the words are mine.

"Granny, I remember you were writing a collection of folktales. Is it here somewhere?" Your whispers echo against the walls. "Did you leave any final messages for me?" You step away from the boxes with a sigh of exasperation.

I wish I could sit down beside you and tell you all the stories that I carry, but I don't know if you can even hear me, although we're so close by. Let me tell you another tale, one about the girl Xiuyun, who lived centuries ago and longed to read all the books inside Tianyi Ge, the oldest private library in all of China. The name Tianyi alludes to 'tianyi shengshui'. The first to emerge in the universe was water. The name was chosen as a protective charm against fire, the most feared enemy of any book collector. Water is where we all come from and where I have chosen to return.

Xiuyun must have sighed and cried out in exasperation just like you, when she found out that she couldn't access the library of her dreams. She had pleaded with her parents and matchmakers to let her marry into the family that owned it, in an age where girls couldn't freely choose whom to marry. But the family's ancestors had set an unbreakable rule that women couldn't enter the library, and so, the library's doors remained shut to her.

Xiuyun stared at the locked gates for endless days, embroidering one rue plant after another until her fingers began to blister and bleed. Every night she dreamed of transforming into a rue plant that was used to protect books from insects, until one day, she passed away without ever setting foot inside the library.

In her next life, Xiuyun became a rue plant near the grounds of Tianyi Ge, and eventually, the rue plant was picked and finally, she was taken inside the locked gates that had been shut to her for so many years.

If you open the front door of our house now and peer out, you will find a solitary rue plant growing slowly by the entrance, its leaves shriveled as it stands tall against ruthless winds. Yes, bend down, lean in, and take a closer look. Break off a leaf. Take it away with you, wherever you go, and place it between the pages of a book that I have yet to know, just like Xiuyun was carried into Tianyi Ge.

* * *

The house is the emptiest I have ever seen.

No furniture. No boxes. You have arranged for everything that I left you to be shipped away to your great-aunt's home for storage, although you still have my notebook with the tea-stained cover in your hands. Tomorrow, you'll jump onto a plane once more and return overseas. In the coming days and weeks, this little house will be sold to another family and become their home. Our ties to this place will be severed like a broken bowl, the cracks irreparable no matter how hard we try to piece the fragments back together.

If you scrutinize the wall to the right of the window facing the riverbank, you'll find a column of Nüshu characters, the last message my spirit wrote as my heartbeat fell to a stop. All I could manage were five characters:

When are you coming back? The characters ask.

You approach the wall and lean in to study the marks. Nüshu script, 'women's writing', is long and slender, graceful and fluid like the willow branches that sway beside creeks. Willows may appear to bend to the whims of the ever-changing breeze, but they're merely adapting to the wind without letting themselves be broken. The script was invented by women in Jiangyong many decades ago, an act of rebellion in the days when women couldn't attend school. Although the script was born in a faraway town, its home is another place where rivers intertwine, a spot that feels like a second home.

I never told you that I started learning Nüshu after you went overseas, because I didn't want to distract you from your overwhelming schoolwork. Nor did I ever share that I was the first woman from my village to attend school, the first in my generation of our family to break through the cursed rules that kept women from making choices about their lives and education. It's this history that made me want to learn Nüshu. The language is always taught by the old to the young, used by women to write letters to each other when far apart. Although I won't be able to pass it along to you now, let me tell you one more tale, my favorite story of how Nüshu originated.

Panqiao, a young woman, was once unjustly arrested by an official who lusted after her beauty and her hands that could embroider the most elegant tapestries. He wanted to keep her trapped. The world is a dangerous place for girls like you.

Panqiao searched desperately for a way to escape from prison, but she couldn't write a message to seek help because she had no knowledge of Hanzi characters. She knew embroidery patterns, however, and with those symbols, she invented Nüshu. She sewed a message calling for help and found a way to pass it along to her puppy, who sneaked away and delivered the message to her friends. They also understood embroidery and decoded her message, and with their aid, she finally managed to escape.

Your brows furl with questions again as you lean close to the wall. To you, the script must look like random scratches. Mysterious symbols. Indecipherable codes. No, don't let confusion stop you from delving into this more. You pull out your phone to snap a photo, and at that moment, I can tell that you'll never stop searching for answers, not until you discover and learn Nüshu. May the script protect you one day if you ever need it, just as it helped Panqiao.

The threads of another realm tug at me, reminding me that I have stayed in the mortal world for far too long, long past my allotted time for saying goodbye, and if I remain, I'll become a lost soul wandering this earth, never to be reborn. *You shouldn't measure the time that we transient souls spend between the world of the mortals and ghosts in terms of human days,* I reply to the nagging messenger from the underworld. *You must measure time based on the hours we get to spend with our kin.*

The departed always has three days to see their loved ones before they leave and drink Madame Meng's Soup of Forgetting, and if we measure it that way, the time I have spent with you is just right. You must not blame your granny for leaving first this time. On the day we last said goodbye, I watched your silhouette disappear as I leaned back on a rocking chair, and we never got to speak in person again. No, wipe those tears, and don't weep in front of me. Take care of yourself. We shall meet again. We most certainly will.

Faithful Mo

Yi Ryuk; translated by James S. Gale

PRINCE HA HAD A SLAVE who was a landed proprieter and lived in Yang-ju county. He had a daughter, fairest of the fair, whom he called *Mo* (Nobody), beautiful beyond expression. An Yun was a noted scholar, a man of distinction in letters. He saw Mo, fell in love with her and took her for his wife. Prince Ha heard of this and was furiously angry. Said he, "How is it that you, a slave, dare to marry with a man of the aristocracy?" He had her arrested and brought home, intending to marry her to one of his bondsmen. Mo learned of this with tears and sorrow, but knew not what to do. At last she made her escape over the wall and went back to An. An was delighted beyond expression to see her; but, in view of the old prince, he knew not what to do. Together they took an oath to die rather than to be parted.

Later Prince Ha, on learning of this, sent his underlings to arrest her again and carry her off. After this all trace of her was lost till Mo was discovered one day in a room hanging by the neck dead.

Months of sorrow passed over An till once, under cover of the night, he was returning from the Confucian Temple to his house over the ridge of Camel Mountain. It was early autumn and the wooded tops were shimmering in the moonlight. All the world had sunk softly to rest and no passers were on the way. An was just then musing longingly of Mo, and in heartbroken accents repeating love verses to her memory, when suddenly a soft footfall was heard as though coming from among the pines. He took careful notice and there was Mo. An knew that she was long dead, and so must have known that it was her spirit, but because he was so buried in thought of her, doubting nothing, he ran to her and caught her by the hand, saying, "How did you come here?" but she disappeared. An gave a great cry and broke into tears. On account of this he fell ill. He ate, but his grief was so great he could not swallow, and a little later he died of a broken heart.

Kim Champan, who was of the same age as I, and my special friend, was also a cousin of An, and he frequently spoke of this. Yu Hyo-jang, also, An's nephew by marriage, told the story many times. Said he, "Faithful unto death was she. For even a woman of the literati, who has been born and brought up at the gates of ceremonial form, it is a difficult matter enough to die, but for a slave, the lowest of the low, who knew not the first thing of Ceremony, Righteousness, Truth or Devotion, what about her? To the end, out of love for her husband, she held fast to her purity and yielded up her life without a blemish. Even of the faithful among the ancients was there ever a better than Mo?"

Strangely Stricken Dead

Yi Ryuk; translated by James S. Gale

THERE WAS ONCE A MAN called Kim Tok-saing, a soldier of fortune, who had been specially honoured at the Court of Tai-jong. He had several times been generalissimo of the army, and on his various campaigns had had an intimate friend accompany him, a friend whom he greatly loved. But Kim had been dead now for some ten years and more, when one night this friend of his was awakened with a start and gave a great outcry. He slept again, but a little later was disturbed once more by a fright, at which he called out. His wife, not liking this, inquired as to what he meant. The friend said, "I have just seen General Kim riding on a white horse, with bow and arrows at his belt. He called to me and said, 'A thief has just entered my home, and I have come to shoot him dead.' He went and again returned, and as he drew an arrow from his quiver, I saw that there were blood marks on it. He said, 'I have just shot him, he is dead.'" The husband and wife in fear and wonder talked over it together.

When morning came the friend went to General Kim's former home to make inquiry. He learned that that very night Kim's young widow had decided to remarry, but as soon as the chosen *fiancé* had entered her home, a terrible pain shot him through, and before morning came he died in great agony.

The Mysterious Hoi Tree

Yi Ryuk; translated by James S. Gale

PRINCE PA-SONG'S HOUSE was situated just inside of the great East Gate, and before it was a large Hoi tree. On a certain night the prince's son-in-law was passing by the roadway that led in front of the archers' pavilion. There he saw a great company of bowmen, more than he could number, all shooting together at the target. A moment later he saw them practicing riding, some throwing spears, some hurling bowls, some shooting from horseback, so that the road in front of the pavilion was blocked against all comers. Some shouted as he came by, "Look at that impudent rascal! He attempts to ride by without dismounting." They caught him and beat him, paying no attention to his cries for mercy, and having no pity for the pain he suffered, till one tall fellow came out of their serried ranks and said in an angry voice to the crowd, "He is my master; why do you treat him so?" He undid his bonds, took him by the arm and led him home. When the son-in-law reached the gate he looked back and saw the man walk under the Hoi tree and disappear. He then learned, too, that all the crowd of archers were spirits and not men, and that the tall one who had befriended him was a spirit too, and that he had come forth from their particular Hoi tree.

Purple Wildflowers

Alda Yuan

NOT YET, said the voice in her head.

Nell frowned and reached up to adjust her low brim hat to better shield her face from the hot California sun. *We've been out here half the day.*

Do you trust me or not?

With a sigh, Nell settled back on her haunches and let the cart rattle past her and down the road, cloud of dust rising into the clear sky and wafting to where she sat, out of sight in the long grass. For all of Whinny's faults, and they were many, he had always been an unerring judge of character. Perhaps there were still some benefits to godhood, even for a god who had been lost and drifting above the ocean swells for centuries before she came to intercept him as a somewhat unwilling host.

Whinny rewarded her patience almost immediately. The next time Nell heard the rumble of carriage wheels, he indicated that she could stand up, walk to the side of the road and hold her hand up high to hail it. Upon seeing the two young men, one drowsy and slowly masticating a wad of chewing tobacco, the other with his sleeves rolled all the way up to his pale shoulders, Nell nearly blanched. But Whinny had never led her wrong before and she didn't let her winning smile falter.

The sleeveless man noticed her first and blinked even as he instinctively tugged gently on the reins to halt the pair of horses hitched to the front of the wagon. He elbowed his friend, who startled and put a hand to his six shooter before concluding there was no danger.

"Gentlemen," Nell greeted as she walked up and doffed her hat. "You look to be headed up to Stockton. Might I trouble you for a ride?"

The two young Americans were obviously baffled by her mannerisms, her lack of accent, and her clothes. The man with the chewing tobacco shrugged at his companion and waved toward the bed of the cart. "You don't look like you weigh much."

Nell dipped her head in a bow and went around to hop on the back of the cart, positioning herself on one of the barrels. "Thank you for the hospitality. I won't be a bit of trouble."

"Don't mention it. It wouldn't do to let a lady walk, especially as you're not from these parts. I'm Roscoe. Muscles here is Morris. He doesn't talk much." As if to confirm this, Morris flicked the reins to urge the horses onward without a word.

Nell didn't need Whinny to tell her the other man was going to be talkative. She smiled at him when he turned around in the seat and said, "I'm Nell."

Roscoe tipped his head to the side. "That your original name?"

"Ah no," she admitted. "Saion is what the folks back home called me, but I reckon it might not roll off your tongue." She ignored Whinny's titter at the way she let some drawl creep into her voice.

In any case, it worked because Roscoe chuckled. "You'd be right about that. My old man changed his name too when he came over."

A talker, Whinny remarked.

Let him, Nell responded. And Roscoe did talk, about how his father died fighting in the war, how he took his sister out west with him since they had no one else but each other. Eventually though, talking about his own life made him curious about her. She was prepared when he finally asked, "What brings you all the way out here? I thought your people stuck mighty close to San Francisco."

"Some of the mining towns use foreign labor too. I'm headed to a small depot that does processing for a mine in the mountains."

Even Morris half turned to look at her skeptically. And well, Nell had certainly seen scrawnier miners, but she could understand. Roscoe said, "You're not thinking about joining up."

"You ever hear of folks who can talk to the dead?" Nell asked.

Roscoe thought about this. "Seances with all the thumping tables? Or shamans who dance around fires?"

Nell had some friends who might object to the latter characterization, but it was close enough for her purposes. "I'm one of those, but for my people. There aren't many of us so I have to travel around."

"Is there much call for speaking with the dead amongst your people?" Roscoe asked with the sort of genuine curiosity that forced Nell to admit Whinny had been right about waiting to hail this carriage. Not that she planned to say as much.

And because of his genuine curiosity, Nell didn't say what she really thought, that this entire country was haunted land. Instead, she smiled, "Sometimes people just miss the old country. Familiar rituals can be a help." So, of course, Roscoe had questions about those.

Eventually, they rumbled close to the depot, visible in the distance as a collection of rickety buildings. The depot had no name, just a wooden sign hammered into the ground warning travelers this was private property.

Roscoe spit over the side as he looked at the shacks in the distance. "You're alright getting off here?"

"Right as rain," Nell said as she hopped off the back and bowed once more at the two men. "Thanks for the ride, my friends."

"We'll be coming back up this way in a couple days' time," Morris said as he flicked the reins. Nell waved as they rumbled away and started to amble toward the buildings.

Someone spotted her approach because two of the miners came out to meet her, one limping but steady, the other tall and stately but whose gaze darted in every direction. As she approached, Nell clasped her hands and bowed over them and tried the language of her native Canton as even those who hadn't come from the province usually spoke it. "I hear you have a ghost problem."

The two men exchanged a glance and Nell didn't need Whinny to tell her they had no confidence in her. She encountered this often. Even those who heard of the female spirit medium who dressed in an amalgamation of western and traditional clothing were often surprised by her youth. They must have been truly desperate however because the man with the limp introduced himself as Yu Yick and his taller companion as Wei Jeong.

"Your letter spoke of possessions," Nell said as she strode past the two men and headed into town, leaving them to follow her.

Jeong twitched as if she struck him and whispered. "It's gotten worse. All of us fear to be next."

Nell pulled a notebook out of one of the many pouches hanging from her belt as well as a charcoal pencil. "Symptoms? You described the usual moaning and wailing but is there anything else?"

Again, the two men looked at each other. And it was Yick who said, "All the men possessed, they have gorged themselves on dried dates."

That gave Nell some pause and she lowered her notebook to raise an eyebrow. "Interesting."

"Is that useful?" Jeong wanted to know as she continued on.

"It certainly means something," Nell said as she jotted down some notes, mostly for show. "And after the possession is over? Do the victims remember anything?"

Yick walked past her and approached the door of one of the shacks. He pushed it open and said, "There isn't an after."

The scent of human stink hit Nell as she strode closer and saw half a dozen men lying catatonic on woven mats. Most of them had the same thin, malnourished look of most mining adjacent workers she encountered. Now though, they were also wan and pallid, sweat pasting hair to their foreheads, hunched in on themselves.

This is not good, Whinny said.

Don't know what I would do without your wisdom, Nell told him as she tried not to hint at how serious the situation was. Upon further questioning, Yick told her the first man fell sick ten days ago and it wasn't until the second followed that they thought there might be something more at work than illness and homesickness. Nell sent Jeong off for a brazier and started to assemble a bundle of herbs. Most of them had neither any medicinal effect, nor any effect on spirits. But they smelled like medicine and she found it had a calming effect on the humans, even if it did little for the ghosts and ghouls.

This wasn't the only thing she did for show. Her methods were different in kind, but she witnessed some seances by the white women who called themselves witches or mediums and it seemed prudent to adopt some of their tricks. She sat down at a table, made herself comfortable as the bitter aroma of the herbs burning slowly above the coals begun to fill the room. Nell held her hands out over the table, palms up as if ready to receive something. Whinny indicated his readiness before she asked. At first, Nell initiated the transition without fanfare, but once she learned that observers were comforted by some physical signal, she taught herself to roll her eyes back into her head. She did it now, letting her arms go limp so her hands would thump into the table. Then she reached out to Whinny and like twirling dancers, they laced their mental fingers together and switched places.

Nell peeled out of her body and became incorporeal, interstitial, intransient. She saw the world with Whinny's eyes, not objects defined by their physical form but bleeding into each other as auras of the energy that flowed between all things. *Don't overdo it on the possession, will you? I nearly fell over the last time because you moved my feet around too much.*

Worry about your end of things.

Nell grunted at him and then turned her attention to the rest of the room. Immediately, she saw the spirit, an emaciated figure with a bulging stomach, hunched in the corner, head down in his hands, glowing tears leaking from his eyes.

Never seen one of these, have you? Whinny asked.

No, but I've heard about them. This is an egui, an extremely powerful one at that.

Be careful then.

Nell floated closer to the egui, moving slowly and deliberately so as to not appear a threat. As she approached, she noticed how haggard his face was, the permanent stains left on his cheeks, the defeated bent of his shoulders. Little wonder those he possessed ended up laid out on their beds. She wouldn't want to be in this spirit's head either.

Still, she cleared her throat and said, "Sir?"

The spirit started, scrambling away from her, flailing his limbs and crying out in a mournful, wordless sound that made her heart ache. He recovered himself after a bit when he caught sight of her. "Who are you?"

"You can call me Nell. I'm here to help. What's your name?"

Nell struggled not to flinch away when the question led the egui to scream so forcefully that her entire incorporeal body shook in response. In fact, the scream vibrated through the room and Nell was not surprised to hear Whinny report all half dozen men in the room moaning.

"Not the right question," Nell muttered as the egui continued to scream. After the initial explosion of passion and sound however, the screams became more and more desolate. As they tapered off, Nell focused on the palm of her hand, bringing a small wrinkled fruit into ghostly existence. She held it up and knew she did something right when the scream choked off.

The egui stared at the ethereal date first and then looked up at Nell. This time his eyes were more human, a bit of brown leaching back into the white planes. "I don't know who I am. All I know is that this dirt is not of my home. I don't recognize the roughness of the stones against my palm or the glitter of this sun."

"Maybe I can help you with that. First, though, why the dates?"

"My daughter's favorite," the egui said with a whistling sigh.

"I can work with that. But you know, it's impolite to force other people to eat them for you." Immediately, Nell could tell he had no idea what she meant. And that decided her course of action. The lore and legend on egui was not flattering. She saw some wisdom in this for the most powerful of them could bring misery on innocent bystanders as this egui had. Still, if she might be able to bring him a measure of peace, she ought to try. "Anything else you can tell me? Do the names Yick and Jeong mean anything to you?"

Nell nodded at the spark of recognition in his eyes and reached back out for Whinny. They linked up, swung each other around and Nell jerked upright. She blinked as if truly coming out of a trance and got to her feet. The men, who leaned closer while Whinny occupied her body, sprang back.

Nell picked her hat up, set it on her head and strode for the door. Jeong and Jim, this depot's closest equivalent to a doctor, scrambled to make room for her. Whinny once accused her of enjoying the power this role gave her and Nell hadn't bothered to deny it.

Outside, Nell let herself bask in the sun for a moment before turning to face the men who spilled out of the shack after her. As she turned, she noticed a small audience, a handful of people who stood in the doorways of their own shacks but came no closer. She ignored them, addressing mainly Yick. "Have any men died recently?"

"Is that important?" Jeong wanted to know.

Rather than answer the question, Nell waited, to let them decide. Yick didn't take too long with it. "It's not uncommon in this line of work. Jung Hang was the last to pass. Is this his doing?"

"It's complicated," Nell said, leaving it at that. "Did he have a daughter back home?"

Yick frowned, clearly not certain. But then someone else spoke up and Nell turned as a burly young man with unshaven scruff, unusual amongst the miners she came across, gestured at the shack behind him. "Hang and I were bunk mates. He didn't know his characters, but he would sometimes narrate letters he would have written his daughter."

Long practice meant it didn't take too long for Nell to wrestle down the flash of pain. Instead, she nodded firmly and said, "In that case, I have some work to do." She started with Hang's bunkmate, but she didn't stop there. Over the next couple of days, she talked to nearly every one of the five dozen men who worked at this depot.

Most were confused by her questions. Almost everyone looked at Yick for confirmation before answering her. Each time he answered with a sharp nod, they relaxed marginally and told her what they knew. At the end, when their stories were exhausted, their knowledge tapped, Nell had a full notebook and the beginnings of an understanding of who Hang had been. It would have to be enough. Once more, she sat down in the shack where the sick convalesced and once more, she and Whinny exchanged places.

The gut-wrenching, face peeling scream that filled her disembodied ears nearly sent her reeling back into her own body. The scream carried the agony of a man who could never go home, who lost everything, who wanted so desperately to claw back the feeling of belonging to something.

Nell often found herself sympathizing with the spirits she encountered through her work. Happy and contented people rarely turned into vengeful ghosts. Yet something about the raw desperation and hunger in Hang's scream almost broke her. In flashes, she saw herself as a young girl on the deck of the ship that brought her to this dusty land, papers clutched to her chest, saw herself writhing in a cot as the room tilted in the waves, other passengers looking on in horror and fascination, saw herself stumbling through her first attempts to ply this trade she never wanted.

I'm sorry, Whinny said, subdued.

We've made the best of it, Nell told him. And then she was screaming back at the ghost, at first unable to compete with his sheer volume and power but forging ahead regardless. "Your name is Jung Hang. You loved purple wildflowers and the shift in the atmosphere before rain. You named your daughter for them and nothing made you happier than putting her on your shoulders and walking up the mountain by your home. You had two older brothers and a younger sister who died before adulthood. You buried her in the village cemetery, but you also built a shrine for her in the space behind her favorite waterfall. Before you left your home, you went there for the last time, to visit with her and to sit in the heavy silence of her absence. You told your bunkmate she said not to go and you regretted not listening to her."

As Nell talked, the egui's scream petered out. It slid closer to her, eyes fixed on her face, ears twitching with interest.

"You snored during naps but never at night. You chewed loudly and sometimes tried to sneak an extra spoonful of food when you thought no one else was looking. You always stretched with the morning sun and sang off key. When the immigration officer at the port leered at a young boy, you pretended to be his father and took him to his family, though it cost you. You've never seen him again, but you think about him all the time. You nearly lost your right ring finger as a child, fell out of countless trees, once bit your own mother when she needed your help with a chore. You always wanted a pet fox and used to sneak outside after dark to count the stars when you couldn't sleep. You never sneezed so much as you did working at this depot and sometimes wished you paid better attention to your grandparents advice. You never prayed, but every now and then, you cried. You were not afraid of showing your sorrow or your fear and that helped others to show it too." On it went, Nell trying to trace the shape of a life not yet lived to its fullest and the egui drinking it in, letting it help him remember who he used to be. Words could not describe a person and the impressions of five dozen other men could not form a complete picture of another. But as Nell spoke what she knew of a more complex truth, remembering Hang to himself, his form shifted.

By the time she finished, a man with a despondent face and bushy eyebrows stood in front of her. "I never meant to hurt anyone."

"I know, but you don't belong here anymore."

"I'm not sure I ever belonged here."

Nell smiled sadly at him. "I know the feeling."

"Do you know anything of my family?"

"I'm sorry, I asked, but no one has heard anything."

"Do they even know I'm dead?"

"Not yet. I don't know if that's a comfort to you."

"I'm not sure. Where will I go?"

"I don't know."

"I appreciate the honesty," Hang said.

"I think I owe you that."

"You freed me. I owe you."

Nell shook her head. "This wasn't your fault. Now, are you ready?"

"No. But I doubt anyone ever is. Thank you."

She didn't tell him she didn't need the thanks. She simply borrowed Whinny's power to send him on his way. As his energy left the room, leaving behind only wisps of evidence that he had ever been, Nell dropped back into her body. From the stiffness in her joints, the chill at her fingertips, she knew she had been gone a long time. Unlike the last time, Nell did not spring to her feet. She let some of her exhaustion show as she opened her eyes, worked her fingers to get the blood flowing. Slowly, she massaged her own arms and worked at the knot at the back of her neck as the men looked on.

"Is it done?" Yick finally asked.

"It's done," Nell told him. "The spirit has been banished and the men should begin to recover soon. They might not remember much of what happened."

Yick looked at the victims and sighed. "Perhaps that's for the best. We held a ceremony for Hang when he passed. Should we hold another?"

"It can't hurt," Nell said as she got to her feet, still feeling stiff but knowing it would not go away until she walked it off. "I'll leave behind some herbs."

"You're going now?" Yick asked, surprised.

"If I don't miss my guess, I have a ride to catch," Nell said, looking out the window at the position of the sun.

Sure enough, not long after Nell posted up by the road, she saw a familiar cart rumbling in her direction, flatbed filled with lumpy packages instead of barrels. Roscoe noticed her too and waved with more enthusiasm than Nell expected, but she raised a hand in greeting anyway. As they approached, she looked behind her shoulder at the depot, which ground Hang down until it killed him.

Do you think we did something good here? Nell asked, thinking that though she helped Hang's spirit, she also ensured the depot could continue to operate.

Something necessary, Whinny said. *Maybe that's enough.*

Biographies & Sources

C.F. Andrews

The Hungry Stones

(Originally published in *The Hungry Stones and Other Stories*, 1916)

C.F. Andrews (1871–1940) was an Anglican missionary, educator, and social reformer. Born in Newcastle Upon Tyne, Andrews joined the Cambridge Mission in 1904 and travelled to Delhi, where he taught philosophy. Becoming a friend of Mahatma Gandhi and Rabindranath Tagore, Andrews played a significant role in the struggle for Indian independence. Andrews would translate a number of stories into English for Tagore's collection *The Hungry Stones and Other Stories* (1916).

Im Bang and Yi Ryuk

Im Bang: *The Story of Chang To-Ryong* to *Haunted Houses*

Yi Ryuk: *Faithful Mo* to *The Mysterious Hoi Tree*

(Originally published in *Korean Folk Tales,* 1913)

Im Bang (1640–1724) was a Korean author who wrote traditional stories capturing Korea's folklore and culture. He is best known for his stories that appear in *Korean Folk Tales: Imps, Ghosts, and Fairies* (1913), a classical collection which also features works by fellow Korean author Yi Ryuk (1438–98).

Joshua Bartolome

Juramentado

(First publication)

Joshua Bartolome is a Filipino-Canadian writer living in Calgary, Alberta. His prose poem 'The Cadaver' was shortlisted for the Montreal Poetry Prize, while in 2017, his screenplay *The Red Death* won the Silver Screamfest award for best horror script. 'Aswang', a tale of poverty, misery and violence, was published in the anthology *Tales of Blood and Squalor*. Another short story, 'The Last Confession of Dottore Gepetto', was published in the We Shall Be Monsters anthology, and his cosmic horror story 'Barker, Alberta' was included in *Postcards from the Void*, an anthology by the Darkwater Syndicate. In late 2019, his horror screenplay *The Crossing* became a semifinalist in the Academy Nicholl Competition.

Cecil Henry Bompas

The Pious Woman

(Originally published in *Folklore of the Santal Parganas*, 1909)

Cecil Henry Bompas was born in London in 1868. In addition to working in the Indian Civil Service, Bompas was also a translator of Asian myths and tales. His best-known work is *Folklore of the Santal Parganas* (1909), an extensive collection of folk tales belonging to a South Asian ethnic group called the Santals.

John Yu Branscum

On the Jiangshi and Other Returns, One Extra at a Wedding (both co-translated with Yi Izzy Yu)

(Both originally published in *The Shadow Book of Ji Yun: The Chinese Classic of Weird True Tales, Horror Stories, and Occult Knowledge*, 2021)

John Yu Branscum teaches comparative literature and creative writing at Indiana University of

Pennsylvania. His books include *Skinwalkers* (Argus House Press; Affrilachian Poetry Award winner); *Red Holler* (Sarabande Books: Bruckheimer Award Winner) and, with his wife Yi Izzy Yu, *The Shadow Book of Ji Yun* and *Zhiguai: Chinese True Tales of the Paranormal and Glitches in the Matrix*. In his spare time, he likes to get lost on purpose, stare hard at strange things, and bust moves with his daughter Frankie.

Eliza Chan

Kikinasai

(Originally published in *Thirty Years of Rain*, 2016)

Eliza Chan writes about East Asian mythology, British folklore and madwomen in the attic, but preferably all three at once. She likes to collect folk tales and modernize them with a drizzle of sesame oil, a pinch of pepper and a kilo of weird. Her work has been published in *The Dark*, *Podcastle*, *Fantasy Magazine* and *The Best of British Fantasy 2019*. She is currently working on a contemporary Asian-inspired fantasy novel about seafolk in a flooded world. You can find her on Twitter @elizawchan or elizachan.co.uk.

F. Hadland Davis

Kyuzaemon's Ghostly Visitor

(Originally published in *Myths and Legends of Japan*, 1912)

Frederick Hadland Davis was a writer and a historian – author of *The Land of the Yellow Spring and Other Japanese Stories* (1910) and *The Persian Mystics* (1908 and 1920). His books describe these cultures to the western world and tell stories of ghosts, creation, mystical creatures and more. He is best known for his book *Myths and Legends of Japan* (1912).

Lal Behari Dey

The Ghost-Brahman to *The Story of Brahmadaitya*

(Originally published in *Folk-Tales of Bengal*, 1912)

Lal Behari Dey (1824–92) was born in the Bengal Presidency but spent much of his life in Calcutta. Converting to Christianity in 1843, Dey became a missionary and minister, as well as a journalist. He later worked as a professor of English at various government-administered colleges in Berhampore and Hooghly. He is known for his short story collection *Folk-Tales of Bengal* (1912) and *Govinda Samanta, or The History of Bengal Ráiyat* (1874).

Alice Elizabeth Dracott

The Bunniah's Ghost, A Legend of Sardana

(Originally published in *Simla Village Tales: Or, Folk Tales From the Himalayas* (1906)

Alice Elizabeth Dracott was the author of *Simla Village Tales: Or, Folk Tales From the Himalayas* (1906), the source of the story 'The Magician and the Merchant'.

Dean S. Fansler

The Manglalabas, Mabait and the Duende, The Wicked Woman's Reward

(Originally published in *Filipino Popular Tales*, 1921)

Dean S. Fansler (b. 1885) was a folklorist of Filipino culture. After earning degrees at Northwestern University and Columbia University, Fansler moved from the United States to the Philippines, where he worked at the University of the Philippines and endeavoured to collect and preserve Filipino folk tales. His book *Filipino Popular Tales*, published in 1921, remains one of the best-known collections of stories from the Philippines.

Eugie Foster

Returning My Sister's Face

(Originally published in *Realms of Fantasy, Sovereign Media*, February 2005. Original Copyright 2004 by Eugie Foster – now the Eugie & Matthew Foster Foundation.)

Eugie Foster lived in a mildly haunted, fey-infested home in metro Atlanta. After receiving her master's degree in Psychology, she retired from academia to pen flights of fancy. She also became an editor for the Georgia General Assembly, which she considered another venture into flights of fancy. She won the 2010 Nebula Award for her novelette *Sinner, Baker, Fabulist, Priest; Red Mask, Black Mask, Gentleman, Beast* and has been nominated for multiple other Nebula, BSFA, and Hugo Awards. The Eugie Foster Memorial Award for Short Fiction is given in her honour.

James S. Gale

Im Bang: *The Story of Chang To-Ryong* to *Haunted Houses*

Yi Ryuk: *Faithful Mo* to *The Mysterious Hoi Tree*

(Originally published in *Korean Folk Tales,* 1913)

James S. Gale (1863–1937) was a translator and Presbyterian missionary. Born in Ontario, Canada, he studied arts at the University of Toronto. Following his studies, he became a missionary for the university's YMCA and moved to Korea in 1888, where he taught English at the Christian School in Pusan. He is known for his translation of the collection *Korean Folk Tales: Imps, Ghosts, and Fairies* (1913) by Im Bang and Yi Ryuk. He was also a member of a board that worked to translate the Bible into Korean.

Herbert A. Giles

The Faithless Widow to *Miss Chiao-no*

(Originally published in *Strange Stories from a Chinese Studio*, 1880)

Herbert Allen Giles (1845–1935) was a British diplomat and sinologist, working in Mawei, Shanghai, Tamsui and finally as British Consul at Ningpo. In 1897 he became professor of Chinese language at Cambridge University, a post that lasted for 35 years. He published many writings on Chinese language, as well as on literature and religion, such as his *Chinese-English Dictionary* (1891), and several translations of classic Chinese tales, including Pu Songling's *Strange Stories from a Chinese Studio* (1880).

Lafcadio Hearn

Furisodé to *Nightmare-Touch*

(Originally published in *Glimpses of Unfamiliar Japan*, 1894, *In Ghostly Japan*, 1899, *Shadowings*, 1900, *Kottō: Being Japanese Curios, with Sundry Cobwebs*, 1902, *Kwaidan: Stories and Studies of Strange Things*, 1903)

After being abandoned by both of his parents, Lafcadio Hearn (1850–1904) was sent from Greece to Ireland and later to the United States where he became a newspaper reporter in Cincinnati and later New Orleans where he contributed translations of French authors to the *Times Democrat*. His wandering life led him eventually to Japan where he spent the rest of his life finding inspiration from the country and, especially, its legends and ghost stories. Hearn published many books in his lifetime, informative on aspects of Japanese custom, culture and religion and which influenced future folklorists and writers whose writings feature in this collection – standout examples of Hearn's output include *Glimpses of Unfamiliar Japan* (1894), *Kokoro: Hints and Echoes of Japanese Inner Life* (1896), *Japanese Fairy Tales* (1898, and sequels), *Shadowings* (1900), *Kottō: Being Japanese Curios, with Sundry Cobwebs* (1902) and *Kwaidan: Stories and Studies of Strange Things* (1903). In 1891 Hearn married and had four children but later died of heart failure in Tokyo in 1904.

T.M. Hurree
Notes on a Haunted Patient
(First publication)
T.M. Hurree is an Indian-Australian writer, currently studying medicine at the University of Queensland. His short fiction has previously won the Queensland Young Writers Award, and appeared in *Dark Matter Magazine*, *The Griffith Review*, and *Overland*. Hurree writes whenever he finds a spare minute, and loves to explore the liminal spaces between people and places. 'Notes on a Haunted Patient' was heavily inspired by his own family's twisting history, and by all those who have struggled and fought to provide a better life for their children.

Nur Nasreen Ibrahim
Picture of a Dying World
(First publication)
Nur Nasreen Ibrahim is a journalist, writer, and producer based in New York City. Originally from Lahore, Pakistan, she writes speculative and literary fiction, as well as personal essays. Her fiction and nonfiction has been included in anthologies and collections from Harper Perennial, Catapult, Hachette India, Platypus Press, The Aleph Review, Salmagundi magazine, Barrelhouse, and more. She is a two-time finalist for The Salam Award for Imaginative Fiction. She is a 2021–23 recipient of the Lighthouse Writers Book Project Teaching Fellowship.

Frances Lu-Pai Ippolito
Qian Xian
(Originally published in an Earlier Form in The Red Penguin Collection *Stand Out*, 2021)
Frances Lu-Pai Ippolito is an emerging Chinese American writer based in Portland, Oregon. When she's not spending time with her husband and children outdoors, she's crafting short stories in horror, sci-fi, fantasy, or whatever genre-bending she can get away with. Her writing has appeared in *Nailed Magazine*, *HauntedMTL*, Red Penguin's Collections, and *Buckman Journal's Issue 006*. Her work has also been featured in the Ooligan Press Writers of Color Showcase 2020 in Portland, Oregon.

Grace James
The Strange Story of the Golden Comb
(Originally published in *Japanese Fairy Tales*, 1910)
Grace James (1882–1965) was born in Tokyo to English parents. Growing up in Japan until the age of twelve when her family moved back to England, James was fascinated with Japanese culture and became a Japanese folklorist. She published retellings of traditional stories in her collection *Japanese Fairy Tales* (1910) and wrote about her experiences of Japan in her memoir *Japan: Recollections and Impressions* (1936). James was also an author of children's fiction including the *John and Mary* series.

Rudyard Kipling
The Phantom 'Rickshaw, My Own True Ghost Story
(Originally published in *The Phantom 'Rickshaw and Other Tales*, 1888)
English writer and poet Rudyard Kipling (1865–1936) was born in Bombay, India. He was educated in England but returned to India in his youth, which inspired many of his later writings, most famously seen in The Jungle Book. He later returned to England, and after travelling the United States settled in Vermont, America. He was awarded the Nobel Prize for Literature in 1907, which made him the first English-language writer to receive the accolade. His narrative style is inventive and provides an engaging commentary on imperialism, making it no surprise that his works of fiction and poetry have become classics.

K.P. Kulski

The Pavilion of Far-Reaching Fragrance

(First publication)

K.P. Kulski is the author of the novel *Fairest Flesh*, a gothic horror from Strangehouse Books. Her short fiction and poetry have appeared in various publications including *Fantasy Magazine*, *Unnerving Magazine*, the HWA's *Poetry Showcase*, and *Not All Monsters*. Born in Honolulu, Hawaii to a Korean mother and American-military father, she spent her youth wandering and living in many places. So far, her life has been quite a journey, from serving in the U.S. military to teaching college history. Now she resides in the woods of Northeast Ohio. Check out her website, garnetonwinter.com, or follow her on Twitter @garnetonwinter.

K. Hari Kumar

Foreword

K. Hari Kumar, a.k.a. 'Horror Kumar', is an Indian screenwriter and bestselling author of horror novels. Hari is the first Indian writer to be listed on Amazon.com's top 50 bestsellers in the horror category. He has also written 50 horror short stories that were published in his 2019 book *India's Most Haunted* (HarperCollins India), which *The Times of India* deemed a must-read horror book and which was listed among HarperCollins India's 100 best books written by Indian writers. His 2018 psychological thriller, *The Other Side of Her*, spawned the acclaimed Hindi language web series *Bhram* (2019). Currently, he is producing a series of Hindi-language short horror films based on Indian myths and folktales.

Monte Lin

Little Bone Collector

(First publication)

While being rained on adjacent to Portland, Oregon, Monte Lin edits and plays tabletop roleplaying games and writes short stories. Clarion West got him to write about dying universes, edible sins, dreaming mountains, and singularities made of anxieties. His stories have been published at *Cossmass Infinities*, *Cast of Wonders*, *Lamplight*, *The Buckman Journal*, *Nightmare*, and Flame Tree Publishing. His nonfiction has been published at *Strange Horizons*. He can be found tweeting *Doctor Who* news, Asian American diaspora discourse, and his board game losses at @Monte_Lin.

Luo Hui

Introduction

Dr. Luo Hui is a senior lecturer in the School of Languages & Cultures at Victoria University of Wellington. His PhD thesis from the University of Toronto delved into the strange and slippery realm of Pu Songling's ghost stories, and it has been a topic of personal and academic fascination ever since. He recorded an episode on Chinese ghost tales for the BBC Radio 4 series, *A History of Ghosts*, in 2020. His creative nonfiction, 'Ghost Records', appeared in *A Clear Dawn: New Asian Voices from Aotearoa New Zealand* in 2021.

Usman T. Malik

The Fortune of Sparrows

(Originally published in *Black Feathers*, 2017)

Usman T. Malik's fiction has been reprinted in several year's best anthologies including *The Best American Science Fiction & Fantasy* series. He has been nominated for the World Fantasy Award and the Nebula Award, and has won the Bram Stoker Award and the British Fantasy Award. Usman's debut collection *Midnight Doorways: Fables from Pakistan* was listed on The Washington Post's Best SFF collections list for 2021 and can be ordered at usmanmalik.org. See more at Twitter @usmantm and Instagram @usmantanveermalik.

Samuel Marzioli

Devil on the Night Train

(Originally published in *Fantastic Trains: An Anthology of Phantasmagorical Engines and Rail Riders*, 2019)

Samuel Marzioli is a Filipino-American author of dark fiction. His work has appeared in numerous publications and podcasts, including the *Best of Apex Magazine, Shock Totem, InterGalactic Medicine Show, The NoSleep Podcast*, and *LeVar Burton Reads*. 'Devil on the Night Train' is one of seven in a series of short stories he's written inspired by Filipino folklore and urban legends. Two others ('Multo' and 'Pagpag') appear in his debut collection *Hollow Skulls and Other Stories*, released by JournalStone Publishing. You can follow him on Twitter @marzioli.

Rena Mason

Jaded Winds

(Originally published in the Bram Stoker Award-winning anthology *The Library of the Dead*)

Rena Mason is an American author of Thai-Chinese descent and a multiple Bram Stoker Award recipient for *The Evolutionist* and 'The Devil's Throat', as well as a 2014 Stage 32/The Blood List Search for New Blood Screenwriting Contest Quarter-Finalist. She has published fiction and nonfiction in various anthologies, magazines, and books on writing, and she writes a monthly column. She is a member of the Horror Writers Association, Mystery Writers of America, International Thriller Writers, The International Screenwriters' Association, and the Public Safety Writers Association. Please visit her website for more information: www.RenaMason.Ink.

Major J.F.A. McNair and Thomas Lambert Barlow

How an Evil Spirit Was Exorcised

(Originally published in *Oral Tradition from the Indus*, 1908)

Major J.F.A. McNair (1828–1910) was born in Bath, England. After studying at King's College London and the School of Mines, he moved to Southeast Asia and became a civil servant in the Straits Settlements. His best-known work, written with Thomas Lambert Barlow, is *Oral Tradition from the Indus* (1908).

S. Mukerji

His Dead Wife's Photograph to *The Boy Possessed*

(Originally published in *Indian Ghost Stories*, 1917)

S. Mukerji was an Indian writer. His collection *Indian Ghost Stories* was published in 1917, presenting supernatural tales from India for an English audience. The collection includes such works as 'The Boy Possessed', 'The Messenger of Death', and 'His Dead Wife's Photograph'.

Ram Satya Mukharji

The Barber and the Ghost

(Originally published in *Indian Folkore*, 1904)

Ram Satya Mukharji was an Indian author whose collection *Indian Folkore* (1904) preserved some of the nation's traditional folk tales. These include 'How Darraf Khan Became a Hindu', 'The Brahman and His Idols', and supernatural stories such as 'The Barber and the Ghost'.

Lee Murray

Associate Editor

Lee Murray is a multi-award-winning author-editor from Aotearoa-New Zealand (Sir Julius Vogel, Australian Shadows awards), and double Bram Stoker Award-winner. Author of the Taine McKenna Adventures, The

Path of Ra trilogy (with Dan Rabarts) and *Grotesque: Monster Stories*, she has edited seventeen volumes of speculative fiction, including *Black Cranes: Tales of Unquiet Women*. She is co-founder of Young NZ Writers and of the Wright-Murray Residency for Speculative Fiction Writers, HWA Mentor of the Year for 2019, NZSA Honorary Literary Fellow, and the Grimshaw Sargeson Fellow for 2021. Read more at leemurray.info

Lena Ng
Last Train Onwards
(First publication)
Lena Ng lives in Toronto, Canada, and is of Chinese-Mauritian descent. She has short stories in over sixty publications including *Amazing Stories* and the anthology *We Shall Be Monsters*, which was a finalist for the 2019 Prix Aurora Award. Her story was inspired by the Nagoro Doll Village in Tokushima Prefecture on the island of Shikoku, Japan. She spends much of her free time deconstructing short stories and movies, and trying to reconstruct them again in her own story writing. *Under an Autumn Moon* is her short story collection. She is currently seeking a publisher for her novel *Darkness Beckons*, a Gothic romance.

Yei Theodora Ozaki
The Spirit of the Lantern, The Badger-Haunted Temple
(Originally published in *Romances of Old Japan*, 1920)
The translations of Japanese stories and fairy tales by Yei Theodora Ozaki (1871–1932) were, by her own admission, fairly liberal ('I have followed my fancy in adding such touches of local colour or description as they seemed to need or as pleased me'), and yet proved popular. They include *Japanese Fairy Tales* (1908), 'translated from the modern version written by Sadanami Sanjin', and *Warriors of Old Japan, and Other Stories* (1909).

H. Parker
The Frightened Yakā
(Originally published in *Village Folk Tales of Ceylon, Vol. II*, 1904)
H. Parker was a British engineer in the former colony of Ceylon, which was later to become Sri Lanka. Working in the Irrigation Department between 1873 and 1904, Parker also collected and translated numerous tales and myths from Sri Lankan culture. He published these works in three volumes entitled *Village Folk Tales of Ceylon* (1910–14). His other work includes *Ancient Ceylon* (1909).

W.W. Pearson
The Lost Jewels
(Originally published in *The Modern Review*, 1917)
W.W. Pearson (1881–1923) was born in Manchester, England. After graduating from Cambridge University, he moved to Calcutta in 1907 to teach botany at the London Missionary College in Bhavanipur. Pearson translated a number of Indian writings including Rabindranath Tagore's story 'The Lost Jewels' (1917) along with some of his other works. Pearson also became Tagore's secretary in 1916, travelling with him to Japan and the United States. His other translated works include *For India* (1917) and *The Dawn of the New Age, and Other Essays* (1922).

A.L. Shelton
The Man and the Ghost
(Originally published in *Tibetan Folk Tales*, 1925)
A.L. Shelton (1875–1922) was an American missionary, born in Indianapolis, Indiana. Following his studies at Emporia State University in Kansas and the University of Kentucky, Shelton became a Protestant missionary

and travelled to China. He established a mission in Batang, Tibet, where he amassed cultural artifacts to sell to museums and learned about traditional Tibetan stories. Shelton was killed in 1922 by brigands while on his way to Markam Gatok, and his collection *Tibetan Folk Tales* (1925) was published posthumously.

Ayida Shonibar
Stories Our Parents Told Us
(First publication)
Ayida Shonibar (she/they) grew up as an Indian-Bengali immigrant in Europe and now works in North America. Her creative writing received national recognition in the Scholastic Art and Writing Awards, and she was selected for the 2021 We Need Diverse Books mentorship programme. An enthusiastic reader of diverse stories, she also likes writing about subversive characters in complicated relationships. 'Stories Our Parents Told Us' is a sapphic reinterpretation of the Bengali folk tale of the Shakchunni.

Richard Gordon Smith
The Procession of Ghosts to *The Snow Tomb*
(Originally published in *Ancient Tales and Folklore of Japan*, 1908)
Richard Gordon Smith (1858–1918) was a British naturalist and sportsman. He travelled widely throughout East and Southeast Asia, spending considerable time in Japan. Living in Kyoto for many years, Smith recorded Japanese folk tales and detailed observations of nature and life in Japan. His collection *Ancient Tales and Folklore of Japan* was published in 1908. Smith also collected animal and plant species, many of which had been previously unknown to science. His diaries were posthumously published as *Travels in the Land of the Gods: The Japan Diaries of Richard Gordon Smith* (1986).

Pu Songling
The Faithless Widow to *Love's-slave*
(Originally published in *Strange Stories from a Chinese Studio*, 1740, and *Strange Stories From the Lodge of Leisure*, 1913)
Pu Songling (1640–1715) was a Chinese writer who lived during the Qing dynasty. Earning the Xiucai degree in the Imperial examination at the age of eighteen, Songling later became a private tutor. He spent his life collecting Chinese folk stories, and, aged seventy-one, he was awarded the Gongsheng, or 'tribute student', degree for his accomplishments in literature. His collected stories were posthumously published as *Strange Stories from a Chinese Studio* in 1740.

George Soulié
The Ghost in Love, Love's-slave
(Originally published in *Strange Stories From the Lodge of Leisure*, 1913)
George Soulié (1878–1955) was born in Paris, France. Working at a bank for several years, in 1899 his employer sent him to China, where he gained a mastery of the Chinese language. Soulié later joined the French consular service in China, where he worked as a diplomat. He also became a scholar and translator of Chinese literature. His translated works include the collection *Strange Stories from the Lodge of Leisures* (1913) by Pu Songling. He is also credited for helping introduce Chinese acupuncture to the West.

Rabindranath Tagore
The Skeleton, The Lost Jewels, The Hungry Stones
(Originally published in *The Hungry Stones and Other Stories*, 1916, *The Modern Review*, 1917, *Mashi and Other Stories*, 1918)

Rabindranath Tagore (1861–1941) was a Bengali polymath who created poetry, literature, plays, musical compositions, paintings, and other artworks at a prolific level. Born in Calcutta, Tagore began writing poetry at the age of eight and went on to have a significant impact on Bengali literature, music, and art. He was the first non-European to win the Nobel Prize in Literature in 1913. One of his most well-known works is his collection of tales entitled *Mashi and Other Stories* (1918).

Karen Tay
Ghost
(Originally published in *A Clear Dawn*, 2021)
Karen Tay is a writer, former journalist and avid reader living in Aotearoa New Zealand. She previously worked as a journalist for national newspapers the *Sunday Star Times* and the *New Zealand Herald*. For several years, she also wrote a book blog for Stuff.co.nz, the country's biggest news website. Karen holds a BA in English and History from the University of Auckland, and a Master of Creative Writing. She is a great fan of dystopian and speculative fiction but loves beautiful writing in all forms, with her favourite authors being Margaret Atwood, David Mitchell and Toni Morrison.

Emily Teng
Ghost Fire
(First publication)
Emily Teng was born and raised in Texas. She studied creative writing at Texas A&M University and won the Gordone Award for Undergraduate Fiction for her short story 'Skin Deep'. She now lives in Seattle, where she works as a narrative designer, inventing fantasy worlds for games. 'Ghost Fire' is her first publication. Emily is fascinated by fairy tales, and particularly enjoys dark, twisted takes on stories that really should never have been sanitized to begin with.

Yilin Wang
The Silence of Farewells
(First publication)
Yilin Wang (she/they) is a writer, poet, and Chinese-English translator based in Canada. Her writing has appeared in *Clarkesworld, Fantasy Magazine, The Malahat Review, The Toronto Star, The Tyee, Words Without Borders*, and elsewhere. She has been a two-time finalist for the Far Horizons Award for Short Fiction, a finalist for the David TK Wong Fellowship, and longlisted for the CBC Poetry Prize. Her translations have appeared or are forthcoming in *Asymptote, Samovar, Pathlight*, and the anthology *The Way Spring Arrives and Other Stories* (Tor.com). She is a graduate of the Clarion West Writers Workshop 2021.

Yi Izzy Yu
On the Jiangshi and Other Returns, One Extra at a Wedding (both co-translated with John Yu Branscum)
(Both originally published in *The Shadow Book of Ji Yun: The Chinese Classic of Weird True Tales, Horror Stories, and Occult Knowledge*, 2021)
Yi Izzy Yu's creative work has appeared in magazines ranging from *Strange Horizons – Samovar* to *New England Review*. Currently, she lives outside of Pittsburgh, where she teaches and translates Chinese and investigates shadows. She loves so many things. Her collaborative literary translations are collected in *The Shadow Book of Ji Yun* and *Zhiguai: Chinese True Tales of the Paranormal and Glitches in the Matrix*.

Alda Yuan
Purple Wildflowers
(First publication)
Alda Yuan is an attorney, indie game designer, and cartographer. In addition to fiction, she writes on healthcare policy, space law, and open science. She runs the Integral States Project, which reimagines the US states and territories as fantasy maps as a catalyst for thinking about the pre-colonial history of those lands. Alda has contributed to the *in*die zine*, a quarterly publication of games and game supplements, as well as served as an editor for Unbreakable RPG, tabletop adventures written by Asian game designers.

Ji Yun
On the Jiangshi and Other Returns, One Extra at a Wedding
(Originally published in *The Shadow Book of Ji Yun: The Chinese Classic of Weird True Tales, Horror Stories, and Occult Knowledge*, 2021)
A philosopher, writer, politician and scholar, Ji Yun (1724–1805) held many roles over his remarkable lifetime, from unofficial poet laureate to the Qianlong Emperor to chief editor of the *Siku Quanshu*, the largest collection of books in Chinese history, as well as government posts including Minister of War and Minister of Personnel. It is for his writing that he is perhaps best remembered, however; over the course of ten years from 1789–98 Ji Yun produced five volumes of supernatural tales, and along with Pu Songling and Yuan Mei he was one of three great writers of strange tales during the Qing Dynasty.

FLAME TREE PUBLISHING
Epic, Dark, Thrilling & Gothic
New & Classic Writing

Flame Tree's Gothic Fantasy books offer a carefully curated series of new titles, each with combinations of original and classic writing:

*Chilling Horror • Chilling Ghost • Asian Ghost • Science Fiction • Murder Mayhem
Crime & Mystery • Swords & Steam • Dystopia Utopia • Supernatural Horror
Lost Worlds • Time Travel • Heroic Fantasy • Pirates & Ghosts • Agents & Spies
Endless Apocalypse • Alien Invasion • Robots & AI • Lost Souls • Haunted House
Cosy Crime • American Gothic • Urban Crime • Epic Fantasy • Detective Mysteries
Detective Thrillers • A Dying Planet • Footsteps in the Dark
Bodies in the Library • Strange Lands • Weird Horror • Lost Atlantis
Lovecraft Mythos • Terrifying Ghosts • Black Sci-Fi • Chilling Crime
Compelling Science Fiction • Christmas Gothic • First Peoples Shared Stories
Alternate History • Hidden Realms • Immigrant Sci-Fi • Spirits & Ghouls*

Also, new companion titles offer rich collections of classic fiction, myths and tales in the gothic fantasy tradition:

*Charles Dickens Supernatural • George Orwell Visions of Dystopia • H.G. Wells
Sherlock Holmes • Edgar Allan Poe • Bram Stoker Horror • Mary Shelley Horror
Lovecraft • M.R. James Ghost Stories • The Divine Comedy • The Age of Queen Victoria
Brothers Grimm Fairy Tales • Hans Christian Andersen Fairy Tales • Moby Dick
Alice's Adventures in Wonderland • King Arthur & The Knights of the Round Table
The Wonderful Wizard of Oz • Ramayana • The Odyssey and the Iliad • The Aeneid
Paradise Lost • The Decameron • One Thousand and One Arabian Nights
Persian Myths & Tales • African Myths & Tales • Celtic Myths & Tales
Greek Myths & Tales • Norse Myths & Tales • Chinese Myths & Tales
Japanese Myths & Tales • Native American Myths & Tales • Irish Fairy Tales
Heroes & Heroines Myths & Tales • Gods & Monsters Myths & Tales
Beasts & Creatures Myths & Tales • Witches, Wizards, Seers & Healers Myths & Tales*

Available from all good bookstores, worldwide, and online at
flametreepublishing.com

See our new fiction imprint
FLAME TREE PRESS | FICTION WITHOUT FRONTIERS
New and original writing in Horror, Crime, SF and Fantasy

And join our monthly newsletter with offers and more stories:
FLAME TREE FICTION NEWSLETTER
flametreepress.com

GOTHIC FANTASY

For our books, calendars, blog
and latest special offers please see:
flametreepublishing.com